LORD OF ALL THINGS

LORD OF ALL THINGS

ANDREAS ESCHBACH

Translated by Samuel Willcocks

amazoncrossing

Text copyright © 2011 by Andreas Eschbach and Bastei Lübbe GmbH & Co. KG
English translation copyright © 2014 by Samuel Willcocks

Lord of All Things was first published in 2011 by Bastei Lübbe GmbH & Co. KG as Herr aller Dinge. Translated from German by Samuel Willcocks.

Published in English in 2014 by AmazonCrossing, Seattle.

www.apub.com

ISBN-13: 9781477849811
ISBN-10: 1477849815
Cover design by Edward Bettison
Library of Congress Control Number: 2013913063

PROLOGUE

"I know what you'd have to do so that everyone could be rich," said Hiroshi.

"That's rubbish," said Charlotte. "Can't be done."

"No, it can be," he insisted.

"Hurry up and swing," she said. She was annoyed by the way Hiroshi just sat there, rattling the chain. She pushed off the ground with her feet and began to swing. "Come on! Let's see who can go highest."

The evening sky was like dark blue glass, infinitely wide and mysterious. There was not a cloud to be seen, just a first tiny star, winking and twinkling away. As if sending an invitation: *Come and visit.* What would it be like to fly up there? And the grass smelled warm, of summer and strange herbs and fresh-cut grass.

"Come on, swing!" she called out. "I don't believe you anyway."

"You'll see."

"I know what you're thinking," Charlotte yelled as the swing took her higher and higher, and the wind tugged deliciously at her dress. "You think that if we just printed enough banknotes, everybody would be rich. But it doesn't work that way. My papa explained it all to me. All that would happen is that everything would get more expensive—just because you have more banknotes, doesn't mean you'd have more things to buy."

Hiroshi looked up at her scornfully. "I know that much," he called.

"Well then. Come on and swing! Jump if you dare."

Charlotte whooped. Today she would dare. She would swing as high as she could and then let go. And she would fly!

"You'll see," Hiroshi called again. Then he began to swing, too, shoving off from the ground and flinging himself full-length on the seat to catch up with her. "That's what I'll do when I grow up."

"Do what?"

"Make everybody rich. Really rich! So that everybody can have whatever they want. And as much as they want."

Charlotte swung and swung for all she was worth, wondering what Hiroshi had dreamed up. The swing creaked dreadfully and shook a little from side to side, since one of the poles had begun to come loose from the concrete that was supposed to keep it steady. "How are you going to do that?"

"I'm not telling you."

"Because you don't know. You're just showing off."

Hiroshi didn't care that she'd called him a show-off. She knew he wouldn't care; he never did. He was always so completely sure of himself.

"Just wait," he shouted, flinging his legs up high. Now he was swinging higher than her.

Charlotte was panting from the effort to keep up. "If it's true, then you have to jump!"

"Okay!" Hiroshi was swooping up and down, back and forward, plunging and soaring as though he wanted to loop the loop and wrap the chain around the top of the swing. "But do you know what I don't understand?"

"What?"

"Why nobody had the idea of how to do it before me," Hiroshi yelled. "It's so incredibly simple."

Then he let go and flew through the air like a shot from a cannon. For a moment he seemed to float, as though he would fly up and ever up, right up to the sky and out into space. But then he landed on the lawn, rolling, whooping, and laughing out loud. Charlotte looked at him enviously. She had stopped pumping her legs and instead just held on to the chains and waited until the swing came to a halt. When the moment had come to let go, she couldn't do it. Why not? She had wanted to so badly.

Charlotte Malroux knew more about the past than anyone else ever could, but she didn't know the future. She was only ten years old, and she didn't know yet what a blessing that was.

The Island
of the Saints

1

Hiroshi and his mother lived on the third floor of an apartment building across from the French embassy, where she worked in the laundry room. They had two rooms and a bath. Mother slept in the smaller room, while the other served as kitchen, dining room, and living room. Hiroshi's bed was behind a folding screen, along with a shelf where he kept his things. Over his bed was a narrow window with three panes of glass that he could slant open to let in the fresh air. When there was any. Here in the middle of Tokyo, the air wasn't fresh all year round. In summer the nights were often so sticky and warm that Hiroshi couldn't sleep, and sometimes not even the rain helped him nod off.

It was on just such a night that he saw the girl for the first time.

A light, silver rain fell, shimmering in the moonlight and the streetlamps like a magic curtain. The flat smelled of the miso soup they'd had for dinner and of the laundry strung across the room on a line, which was taking its time to dry. Hiroshi stood up and put his hand out the window to test whether it was beginning to cool down outside. It wasn't. He stood there for a while, looking down at the vast, dark embassy garden, unsure whether he was sleepy or not. Eventually, since there was nothing else to do, he lay back down on his bed.

The third time he got up to look outside, there was a girl standing in the garden. She just stood there, her arms spread wide, looking up into the sky. Her long, dark hair cascaded down her back. She was wearing nothing but a nightgown, which clung to her body, soaked through. Hiroshi shut his eyes, counted to ten, and then opened them again. The girl was still standing there in the middle of the lawn. She swayed back and forth, slowly, dreamily, as the warm rain poured down onto her. Had he made some noise in his surprise? Hiroshi didn't know, but he heard the door slide open behind him and his mother enter the room.

"What is it?" she asked. "You should be asleep."

"There's a girl in the garden," Hiroshi said.

Mother shuffled across to the bigger window. After watching the scene down below for a while in silence, she said thoughtfully, "So that's how it starts. How rich people go mad, sooner or later."

"Why is she doing that?" Hiroshi asked.

"There's a new ambassador. That might be his daughter. I heard somewhere that he has a daughter."

"She's all wet."

"Go to sleep," said his mother.

"I can't. It's too warm."

"You have to get some sleep, or you won't be able to keep your eyes open in school tomorrow. At least lie down and try to rest a bit."

Hiroshi didn't move from where he was any more than the girl did. It looked as though she were praying to the moon. Or waiting for something to fall from the sky so that she could hug it.

"What about her? She has to go to school as well."

"What business of yours is it what she does?" Now his mother sounded indignant. "They're rich folk. We have nothing to do with the likes of them."

"Why are they rich?"

"They just are. Now go to sleep," said Mother and left.

That seemed to be the biggest problem in the world: that some people were rich and others weren't. Mother often talked about it.

At that moment the girl let her arms fall. She looked back at the house, and it seemed somebody was calling her from there. Hiroshi couldn't hear anything over the sound of the rain, but he saw her reluctantly move away, saw her walking barefoot through the grass toward an open door. Hiroshi waited till she had vanished from sight, then lay down. When he finally did fall asleep, he dreamed about her, of course.

From then on he lay in wait. Every afternoon he hurried home from school and took up his post at the window. He fell into the habit of doing his schoolwork there and would have liked to eat by the window as well, but his mother wouldn't hear of it.

"What's this all about? she grumbled. "What are you doing there?"

"Nothing," Hiroshi said, and in a way he was right: most of the time all he did was stare down into the embassy garden, waiting for something—he couldn't say what. Waiting for the girl, of course. But why? What did he hope would happen if he saw her again? He didn't know. He only knew he couldn't help standing by the window for hours at a time, even though all he ever saw was an occasional pale dot behind a window—which might or might not have been a face—and from time to time a shadow, a movement.

The problem was that, from his apartment, he could only see a small section of the garden. Hiroshi knew the garden was very big, but the buildings all around and the many plants that grew there blocked his view. For instance, he knew there was a swimming pool there, but he couldn't catch so much as a glimpse of it through the trees. He often saw the gardener, Mr. Takagi; Hiroshi only knew him from afar. He mowed the lawns and trimmed the bushes in a special way—the way they did it in France, he had told Mother once.

Other than that, not much happened. Hiroshi watched the birds hopping from branch to branch. He watched the shadows move across the lawn and tried to work out the time without looking at the clock. It was hot and uncomfortable by the window, but now that he had started he couldn't give up.

When Hiroshi brought home his report card just before the summer holidays, Mother grumbled about his grades. "You could do so much better if you only made an effort. The way you remember everything, school should be easy for you. But you just don't seem to care. You think, school, grades—so what? But it matters. For later. If you want to get a good job, one where they'll look after you, with a good company, then you have to go to a good college. And they'll only take you if you have good grades."

"All I need to do is pass the entrance exam," Hiroshi protested.

"If your grades aren't good enough, they won't even let you take it," Mother shot back. "You know that very well."

"Yes, I do," he admitted.

It was always the same speech over and over again. She was right, though: Hiroshi really didn't care about school. But was that his fault? Why didn't they ever learn anything interesting, like how robots worked? Instead, it was just boring old mathematics, boring old Japanese, boring old geography . . . It would be years before they got to something even halfway interesting, like physics. But at least the summer holidays had arrived. That meant he could spend all day waiting by the window.

Of course, his mother didn't like that at all. "Why don't you do something useful with your time, the way other children do?" she shouted every day when she came home from work. "Why did I bother buying you that tool kit you wanted so much? It's just standing in the corner, gathering dust!"

"I'll use it soon enough," Hiroshi answered.

It would be a long while before he got another expensive present like that; he would have to parcel out the time he spent with it. And it wasn't as though the toolbox was going to run away in the meantime.

"Other children go to their school clubs. They do sports, they play football."

"I don't want to," said Hiroshi.

Play football? Somehow his mother didn't seem to see he was smaller and weaker than everyone else in the class—in other words, he had no chance. In gym class he was always the last to be picked for a team, the one who scored least points, the useless one. And that was if you ignored the fact that the other boys called him a bastard because his father was American. *Daken* they called him when the teachers were out of earshot: mongrel. And there was nothing he could do about it.

"Or go swimming. All you need to do is go to the school office and you can get yourself a cheap holiday pass for the pool. That would be better than sitting around here in the heat all day."

"It's not all that hot," Hiroshi answered. But it was, of course. In the evenings he sometimes felt sick from the heat.

"Fine," his mother said at last. "You'll have to tear yourself away from your window when we go to Minamata."

Hiroshi slumped. Minamata again.

"When are we going?" he asked.

"For the Bon festival, of course. That's when we always go."

He ran through the calendar in his head. The Bon festival began on August 13.

"There's still time."

"I'm just telling you."

A few days later he had to try on his "good" pants to see whether they still fit. Of course, they were too short by now. Even if he was the smallest in his class, he was still growing.

"I can let these down," his mother said thoughtfully as she knelt in front of him and tugged at his pants leg, "but this is too narrow here. We'll go and buy you a new pair before we fly out."

"We're flying?"

"Yes. Mrs. Nozomi got me the tickets; she knows someone. We'll have to get up early, because the airplane leaves at ten to six. But ever since they raised the prices on the Shinkansen, it's cheaper than taking the train." She looked at Hiroshi. "Aren't you pleased? You like flying."

"Yes," said Hiroshi.

That had been two years ago, the first time he had ever flown in his life. But in fact Hiroshi feared the trips to visit family in Minamata. Not because of his grandparents, who were kind enough to him but always held back a little, but because in the end he was half *gaijin* and he didn't really belong. Most of all, he was afraid of Aunt Kumiko, his mother's older sister. When she was younger, she had fallen ill with mercury poisoning, like so many people in that area, and now she just lay in bed, cramped and motionless, her arms clamped to her chest, her eyes turned inward. The doctors said it was astonishing she was still alive; most patients with her illness had died by now. At least she no longer screamed the way she used to. And she had stopped those dreadful convulsions.

The Bon festival was always the same in Minamata. Everyone would pretend they were one big happy family who all loved one another and that everything was fine and dandy. And then, after he and Mother had returned home, she would spend weeks complaining about the pollution and the car fumes and the noise. She would work herself into a state about poisons in the water and buy gallons upon gallons of bottled water, which Hiroshi would have to carry upstairs into the apartment.

He decided not to think about it. And he stayed sitting where he was at the window. Until at last something happened to reward his patience.

The curtains were all drawn again, and the rooms were as gloomy as if somebody had just died. Charlotte tried not to make any noise as she crept through the apartment looking for her mother. She finally found her in the living room, lying on the couch, one arm across her face and apparently asleep. Half-asleep at least.

"Maman?" Charlotte knew what the matter was already without even having to ask: Mother had a headache again. She was always having headaches.

A martyred groan from the sofa. "My child! What is it?" Moaning. "I have a headache."

"Today we were going to . . ." Charlotte began, and then she stopped midsentence. It was hopeless, she knew, but she had to ask.

"Ah yes." A long, loud indrawn breath. Then, after a while, "Some other time."

"Why am I never allowed to go out?"

"You are allowed out."

"I don't mean out in the garden. Out on the street."

Maman groaned reluctantly. "Get that idea out of your head. It's much too dangerous."

Charlotte felt herself growing angry—angry and disappointed. As the dark feelings brewed inside her, she found it harder and harder to keep them bottled up. "I liked it better in Delhi," she proclaimed. "Why can't I go to an international school here as well?"

"I don't want you spending all your time at schools where they only ever speak English," Mother replied in a feeble voice.

"What's so bad about that?"

A sigh heaved up from the bottom of a grave. "A child should not contradict her mother. Go and find something to do, and leave me alone. I have a headache."

So Charlotte crept away. She was so bored. She went out onto the terrace, sat down in the shadow of the wall, and watched the gardener watering the flowers by the pool. She could take a swim. But she had done that so many times recently that she no longer cared to. After a while she crept back to her mother, who was still lying motionless in the dark.

"Yumiko could take me to the museum," she suggested warily.

Mother sat up, startled. "What? *Mon Dieu*! You and your museums all the time! What kind of child are you? No normal child volunteers to go to a museum."

She hadn't actually said no, Charlotte realized. If there was any chance at all of making the day worthwhile, this was it. "But Yumiko could take me, couldn't she? She knows Tokyo. She can look after me."

Silence. Sour, suffering silence.

"It was a mistake to employ a Japanese nanny," Mother murmured bitterly.

"Yumiko is very nice," Charlotte retorted. That wasn't completely true, but most of the time she was easy to get along with.

"She's a silly cow!" Mother screamed all of a sudden and threw a cushion across the room, then another right behind it. "Can't you see I'm not well? Can't you just leave me alone? Don't you have homework to do? Don't you have lessons, damn it all?"

No, there was no saving the day now. Charlotte fled without another word.

After one more walk through the vast, dark apartment, she crept off to her room. Homework? She didn't have any homework. It was the holidays, even for children like her who had a private tutor. That was the whole problem. She picked up a doll from the end of her bed, where she kept all the things she didn't have a proper place for. It was a doll Papa had given her as a present when they had to move from Delhi to Tokyo. Charlotte didn't even know what to call it. When she got the doll, it had been wearing its long blond hair in a hair band with the name Denise written across it, but Charlotte thought that was a stupid name for a doll.

"Well then, what do you want to do?" asked Charlotte, looking curiously at the doll. She pressed the button on its back that made it talk.

"I want to go dancing," the blond doll declared.

"Dancing? We're not even allowed out of the house, so put that idea out of your head."

"Come on, let's have a party," the doll demanded.

"A party?" Charlotte shook the doll, frustrated. What a stupid squeaky voice it had. "Are you crazy? We have to be quiet, because Mother's got a headache. We can't even go to the museum."

"Isn't life wonderful?"

That was the moment when all of Charlotte's anger and disappointment popped inside her like a bubble. Screaming with rage, she hurled the doll across the room. "You're a silly cow!" she yelled after it. "You don't understand a thing!"

The very next moment she was sorry, but the harm was done: its head hung down, snapped off, with a tangle of wires sticking out. The hair had come off, along with one arm.

"It serves you right," Charlotte declared. "A child should not contradict her mother."

There was nothing she could do about it; the doll with no name was a wreck. Charlotte looked around, helpless. What should she do with the broken bits? It would be a bad idea to leave them lying around; her mother would see the damage this evening when she kissed her good-night and tell her off. But if the doll wasn't even there, then she wouldn't even notice, what with all the other dolls Charlotte had. She fetched a plastic bag, stuffed the bits into it, and hurried out of the room and down the stairs to the side door where she knew the housekeepers put out the trash.

There was the girl. Hiroshi held his breath.

She emerged from the same door she had vanished into that night. She was holding something in her hand, an orange plastic bag from the Daiei supermarket. And she seemed to be feeling guilty about something, the way she peered around to all sides, listening, lurking. She didn't look in his direction. Hiroshi stared at her. How pale her skin was. And how her long black hair shone! She looked like an angel by daylight as well. What was her name, he wondered? And what did she do inside all day long?

She started to move. She scampered over to the bins that stood in a corner between the house and a sliding gate, lifted one of the lids, and flung the plastic bag inside. A moment later she was back inside the house.

Hiroshi slumped back, disappointed. That had all been too quick. He hadn't even seen her face properly, since she had been glancing in all directions. What was in the bag that she had thrown away so furtively? He could find that out, if he was brave enough. And having waited this long, he would be stupid not to be brave.

Hiroshi jumped up, slipped his shoes on, and ran out of the apartment. He knew every nook and cranny of his neighborhood, of course. And he had walked all the way around the embassy countless times. There was a huge, green sliding gate at the main entrance with spikes on top, behind which the French flag was visible on a pole. Beyond the gate to the right was a street that led to the Meguro toll road, so narrow that a car could only just go down it. It was a lane really, flanked by houses and their little front gardens on one side and the embassy wall on the other. It was an old wall, with a great fringe of spikes on the top. No point trying to climb that.

But there was one spot where the wall curved slightly inward to leave room for a huge, old tree. It was easy enough to climb up between the trunk and the wall, and he was hidden from sight, too. Up at the top, the frame that held the spikes in place had rusted away a bit because it was always damp from the tree, and a piece of the framework had snapped. Someone small enough, like Hiroshi, could wriggle through.

Of course, it wasn't allowed. He knew that. You needed special permission to enter the embassy compound, and you had to carry a pass with you when you did. Mother had a pass, written in Japanese and French, saying exactly where she was allowed to go inside the building, which in her case was limited to the laundry room and housekeeping areas. But he didn't actually plan to enter the compound. Just a little bit. Right on the edge. He would just have a look to see what the girl had thrown away, and then he'd slip away.

Well, if he were honest, he had to admit he'd been here often enough. He couldn't resist the challenge—over time he had explored the whole compound. It wasn't difficult, given that there were trees and bushes everywhere where a child could hide easily enough. The only tricky bit was keeping out of the way of all the cameras. His mother would be dreadfully angry if she ever found out. The hardest part was getting down to the ground on the other side of the wall. It needed a rope, which had to be left hanging from the spikes so that he could climb back up again later.

The embassy garden was like an enchanted otherworld. It was strange to think only a wall divided it from the everyday world. But Hiroshi didn't have time today to revel in the enchantment. He had to hurry—for all he knew, the garbage was just about to be collected. He slipped between the compound wall and a little, low, windowless building that must have had something to do with the heating, since a tangle of white metal pipes led out from it in all directions. From there he scrambled through the bushes until he reached the edge of the patch of lawn where he had seen the girl standing in the rain. He peered up at the windows. Was there somebody there? He couldn't see anyone. He scurried across the lawn and the narrow strip of fine, white gravel in front of the building, lifted the lid of the second garbage bin from the right, and fished out the orange supermarket bag. Then he scuttled back to the safety of the bushes with his prize. The whole operation had lasted less than twenty seconds.

Full of curiosity, he opened the bag. A doll? The remains of a doll, rather. Odd. He had always thought girls loved their dolls. It was news to him that they smashed them to pieces. He inspected the bits, pondering the matter as he fitted them back together. The head was broken off, but perhaps he could stick it back on again. The doll was obviously supposed to talk, but the speech unit no longer worked. Hiroshi thought of his new toolbox, the kit that he had wanted so much. Perhaps he could use it to make some repairs. He would take the broken doll back with him.

It took him three days to repair the doll. He did it in secret, of course, during the day while his mother was at work. When she came home, she was happy to see him no longer sitting by the window but busy with his tool kit, though she never saw what had him so absorbed— he always hid the doll away in good time.

Hiroshi finished the job at about ten o'clock on the third day, a Friday. It was a neat bit of repair work, he decided; you could hardly spot it. The doll looked as good as new. And it was working again. When he pressed the big button between the shoulders, it spoke various phrases in a melodious language he didn't recognize.

What should he do with it now? He would have to give it back to the girl, but it only dawned on him then that this would be a much greater challenge than actually repairing the damage. He would have to leave his apartment block carrying the doll. If someone from his class saw him with it, he'd never get over the embarrassment. He felt sick even thinking about it. Maybe it would be better just to throw it away—after all, that's what the girl had done; she may not even want it back. She clearly didn't like it.

Hiroshi went back to the window, looked down at the embassy garden, and thought of all the time he had spent standing here waiting, of the night she had stood down there in the rain. No. No, he wouldn't throw the doll away; he would just bring it back in the same bag in which he had found it. And he could hand it in at the main gate. It wasn't far, and the security guards would take care of the rest.

He broke into a sweat as soon as he stepped out the front door with the bag in his hand, but surely that was just because it was so baking hot outside. There was nobody in sight. He didn't really need to hurry, but then again he wanted to get the thing off his hands as soon as possible. Maybe there was a mailbox and he could just drop it in? Of course, there wasn't. He knew that; he'd been past the embassy often enough. He had no choice but to ring the bell at the sentry box.

A man appeared at the thick glass window. Not a Japanese. He opened his mouth and said something, and it took Hiroshi a while to understand he was trying to ask him what he wanted in Japanese. Hiroshi bowed politely, as he had been taught to do with grown-ups he didn't know.

"Hello, sir," he said. He held up the bag. "I found something that belongs to the ambassador's daughter. I would like to give it to you so that she gets it back, if that is not too much trouble."

The man stared at him stonily. It was obvious he hadn't understood a word.

"*Nan desu ka?*" he asked, or at least something that sounded like it. "What do you want?"

As Hiroshi began to repeat what he had said, the man raised his hand and cut him off midsentence, then turned around to call for someone. A moment later another guard appeared, Japanese this time, who took over behind the pane of glass.

"Well? What do you want?" the man asked rudely. "This isn't a playground. Move along."

Hiroshi paid no attention to his glowering expression. He was used to being glowered at; he had had plenty of practice ignoring it at school. "It's about the ambassador's daughter," he said.

The glower turned into a glare of suspicion. "What are you talking about?"

"She lost a doll and I found it." He had no choice but to open the bag and take the doll out for a moment so the man could see what he was talking about. Then Hiroshi dropped it quickly back into the bag. "I thought she would like to have it back."

The man made a face. His cheeks were pitted with old acne scars. "What's this all about? Where did you get the doll?"

"I found it." Hiroshi waved his hand vaguely in the direction of his block. "Over there."

"And how do you know whose it is?"

"I was looking out of my window when I saw a girl lose it. She lives in this house." Hiroshi pointed toward the ambassadorial villa, though he could only see part of the roof from where he was standing at the main entrance.

"That is impossible. The daughter of the honorable ambassador only very rarely leaves the house, and when she does, she certainly does not take her . . . *dolls* with her." He spat the word out with audible disdain.

Hiroshi realized the guard felt embarrassed as well. He almost laughed out loud.

"It was a girl about my age," he said. "A European with long black hair. I've seen the same girl on the lawn in front of the house."

The guard considered all this. "Good," he said at last and pressed a button that opened the iron door in front of Hiroshi. "Come inside."

Hiroshi swallowed hard as he stepped across the threshold. A barrier divided the sentry post inside in two, and the only way from one side of the room to the other was through a metal detector. There was also an X-ray belt for luggage, just like at the airport.

The guard stepped in front of Hiroshi and put out his hand. "Show me."

Hiroshi handed him the bag. The man opened it and lifted up the doll to see whether there was anything underneath it, but he didn't take it out. It was clear he didn't like touching it; he handled the bag as though it held some noisome substance.

"I'll have to X-ray this," the man said, looking sternly at Hiroshi. "You really just found it? Are you quite sure nobody gave it to you and told it to bring it here?"

"Quite sure," Hiroshi said. "I found it." That was even true, sort of.

"What's your name?"

Crap. He hadn't thought that they would ask him that. There was nothing he could do but to answer the question.

"Kato Hiroshi," he answered. "My mother works here in the embassy. In the laundry." They would have found out anyway.

"And what's your mother's name?"

"Kato Miyu."

The man consulted his computer. "I see," he said at last. "Mrs. Kato from the laundry. I know her." All the same he wrote the name down before putting the bag with the doll through the X-ray machine.

Hiroshi watched with curiosity and wondered, not for the first time, how a machine like that worked. There was no clear explanation of it in any of the books he had read. It had something to do with electromagnetic radiation, he knew that much—but how could radiation show whether explosives were hidden in something? It was high time they started studying physics in school.

The guard didn't find explosives in the doll or anything else suspicious. He came through the metal detector, picked up the bag from the belt, and put it down on a table. "I'll pass it along," he promised.

By the sound of it, he was more likely to just throw it in the trash as soon as Hiroshi was through the door, but he no longer cared what they did with it.

"Charlotte!"

Her mother's voice. With an ominous undertone to it. Charlotte switched off the television and stayed sitting for a moment. Could she get away with pretending she hadn't heard? Probably not. She got up quietly and went to her mother, albeit slowly and on tiptoe.

"Charlotte Malroux," her mother called again. "Please come here immediately."

"I'm coming," Charlotte called as she entered the room they called the Yellow Salon. But her mother wasn't there. She finally found her standing in the front hallway.

She gave a start. Mother was holding her doll in her hand—the blond doll with no name. Except that it no longer looked broken.

"I never gave you permission to go out in the street," Mother said sharply.

Charlotte blinked in astonishment. "What? I've never gone out in the street!"

Mother held up the doll. "A boy saw you lose this. He handed it in at the gate."

"What?" What was going on here? Charlotte shook her head. "But I never went out!"

"Don't lie. I can't abide that."

"I'm not lying."

Mother came toward her, looked down at her sternly, and held the doll up in front of her eyes. "This is your doll, isn't it? I remember quite well that your father brought it back for you from Paris." *Paris.* The way she said it made it sound as though the dratted doll was special for that reason alone.

Charlotte put out her hand to take it, but her mother held it up out of reach. "How did he get ahold of it if you didn't go outside?"

"I don't know." Hesitantly, she added, "The doll was broken."

"Broken? What do you mean, broken?"

"I dropped it." Now she was lying. No. She just wasn't telling the whole truth: that was different. "Part of the head broke off. After that it couldn't talk anymore. I left it out in the garden." That wasn't completely untrue, at least—after all, the trash bins were out in the garden, sort of.

Mother examined the doll. She was probably thinking the gardener had found the doll and put it out with the trash, and that

that was how the doll had gotten out into the street, where the boy found it.

"Hmm," Mother mused, running her finger around the doll's neck. "Someone must have repaired it. I can see the break here, and it's been glued back in place." She pressed the button at the back and the doll said, "Aren't I pretty?"

Charlotte stretched out her hand, and this time she got the doll back. She hugged it tight and shut her eyes for a moment. "It was the boy," she declared. "He repaired the doll. He's been watching me from his window the whole time."

"I beg your pardon?" said Mother, baffled. "Why didn't you tell me that before?"

Hiroshi and his mother were just sitting down to dinner when the doorbell rang. Hiroshi went to open it. It was Mr. Inamoto, the head of the company Mother worked for, a cleaning business that had had the French embassy contract for a long time.

"Hello, Hiroshi," he said. "I must speak with your mother."

Hiroshi didn't much like Mr. Inamoto, with his spidery fingers and fat face. Especially the way he always looked at Hiroshi as though he suspected him of some mischief. It was clear Mr. Inamoto didn't like children.

Mother came over. Hiroshi returned to the table and waited. He listened to the voices out in the corridor. Mr. Inamoto sounded flustered but spoke so softly that Hiroshi could hardly understand a word.

". . . says that she left the doll lying in the garden. And the gardener never saw it. So how did it get out in the street, where . . . ?"

Mother mumbled something.

"I've told you in no uncertain terms that the boy is not allowed into the embassy compound," Mr. Inamoto scolded her. "I've told you not to take him with you, and to keep your keys and your access card in a safe place."

"Yes," Hiroshi heard his mother say. "You've told me that. And I've told him, too. He knows it perfectly well."

"You must realize this is not meant unkindly. It's the normal security routine for an embassy. It's just the way these things are done."

"Yes, of course."

Hiroshi felt angry whenever he heard Mother speaking in such a submissive manner. He was angry that people like Inamoto existed, people who only ever thought about money and always had their way just because they were rich.

"You know he pays you far too little," Hiroshi said when the conversation was over and his mother had bowed to her boss several times and then returned to the table. "He must charge the embassy twice what he pays you."

Mother wasn't even listening, which is how she reacted whenever he broached the topic. Instead she cross-examined him about the doll.

"I just found it," Hiroshi said sulkily. "And then I brought it back. What's the problem with that?"

"Where did you find it?"

Hiroshi had already come up with an answer to this question while she was talking to Inamoto. Since there was no way he could admit to having been in the garden, he said, "Over by the little gate."

Though his answer didn't say which side of the gate he had been on when he found the doll, it wasn't completely untrue. Who was going to prove otherwise? Mother knew which gate he meant: the narrow, gray iron door in the alleyway across the road, where the embassy trash cans stood, usually collected every Tuesday afternoon. Something could have fallen out when they were picking up the trash.

"There was a doll lying in front of the little gate?" She looked at him skeptically. "I didn't see it. When was this?"

"On Tuesday. And the doll was in a plastic shopping bag from Daiei."

"And why didn't you give it back to the embassy until today?"

Hiroshi shrugged. "I just didn't."

"Why were you even out there? You spend your whole time looking out the window."

"I was just outside, that's all. You're always saying that I should get out more."

Mother considered all this, her chopsticks motionless in her hand. The whole meal was getting cold just because of that silly doll. He should have just thrown it away.

"Inamoto-san said somebody had repaired the doll," Mother said, not letting the topic drop. "Was that you?"

Hiroshi hesitated, then shrugged. "The head was broken off. I just stuck it back together so they wouldn't say I had broken it."

"And you knew that it belonged to the girl?"

"I've seen her playing with it." *Playing* wasn't exactly the right word, since all he had seen was her throwing it away, but that was just a detail in the end, wasn't it?

Mother shook her head, concerned. "Why do you do that? Sit at the window all day, just to see this girl. It's not good. You're still much too young for that."

Hiroshi was silent. What could he say? Because he had to, that's why. If she didn't understand that, there was nothing he could do about it.

Mother fished a bit of radish out of the pickle dish and said, "I don't want to lose my job because of some mischief you get into. It's a good job. We have enough money to get by. We have a nice apartment in a good neighborhood. We would lose all that."

Hiroshi had no answer to that either. That mustn't be allowed to happen, that much was clear. If only because if the worst came to the worst, they would have to move to Minamata to live with his grandparents and Aunt Kumiko. But why should Mother lose her job just because he had repaired a doll and given it back?

"In any case," Mother went on, chewing, "you'll have to come with me tomorrow morning. The honorable ambassador's wife wants to meet you."

2

You would have thought that they were going to an audience with the emperor himself the way everybody carried on. Mother had to produce her access card time after time and answer questions from every security guard they met along the way. Yes, that's right: they were on their way to see the honorable lady ambassador. Today. Now. At that, every guard they met furrowed his brow and telephoned through for confirmation. Every time, he listened to what whoever it was on the other end of the line had to say, bowed stiffly, hung up, and waved them through.

"The honorable ambassador is giving a reception this evening," one of the men deigned to tell them. "It's unusual that you should be called for like this."

They passed through one metal detector, then another, and all the while Hiroshi's mother was warning him to be on his best behavior. *Speak only when spoken to; bow like a good boy.* "Imagine you're standing in front of the emperor," she said.

What had he done? Hiroshi felt the sweat gathering on the palms of his hands with every step they took. He probably wouldn't be able to say a word whether anyone addressed him or not. Why did the ambassador's wife want to see him anyway? He had worried about it all night long. It could be anything. Did she want to give him a medal for having rescued her daughter's precious doll? Or would she have him arrested for having stolen it?

The bare, gray corridors eventually came to an end, and they were led into a vast and splendid hall. There was a sudden intense smell of flowers and perfume. Huge draped curtains hung down to the floor at every window, just like in old American films. Gigantic oil paintings in massive golden frames were displayed all over the walls. All of a sudden Hiroshi wasn't sure whether he was awake or dreaming. What had he gotten himself into?

And then a tall, slender woman was walking toward him. Her pale blond hair was piled up on top of her head, and she was dressed in a golden, shimmering gown. She was a fantastically beautiful woman with porcelain skin and dark eyes, but she clearly hadn't been expecting them. Wasn't she the ambassador's wife, though? The lady who had asked to see them? Hiroshi didn't think she seemed angry at him—or pleased either. She looked confused—that was it. She seemed startled, as though she had only just at that moment remembered they were supposed to be there.

"Bow!" Hiroshi heard his mother whisper, and it was a good thing she did, for otherwise he would have forgotten all her warnings.

Well then, now! Bow like a good boy! Show that he had been well brought up, even if just to please Mother. Hiroshi bowed down low, his back straight, his hands neatly by his thighs, and waited like that until he was spoken to, just as he should. The woman said something. It took Hiroshi some time to realize she had said "*Konnichiwa*," "hello," or at least she had been trying to. Actually, it had sounded more like *goninshiki*, which meant "making a mistake," which he actually found funny.

He straightened up but kept his head bowed. He replied to her greeting with polite reserve and then waited to see what would happen next. The woman seemed unhappy about something. She kept calling out to the back of the room in her own melodious language, and he heard one word over and over again, something like *tara doko-têr*, a word that could have meant anything.

"Do you speak English?" the woman finally asked.

Hiroshi bowed his head lower. "Yes, madam," he replied, though as he said the words aloud he felt that was probably stretching the truth. His mother had always insisted he work especially hard in English class because it was his father's language. She spoke very good English herself, gave him little tests all the time, and never let him get bad grades. In reality, however, though Hiroshi could read English—which was very useful for the Internet—and understood quite a lot, he strongly suspected his pronunciation would make most foreigners burst out laughing.

But when he heard the next words the ambassador's wife spoke, he realized she spoke even worse English than Shigeru, the boy in his class who drove Mr. Matsuba, his English teacher, to distraction; Hiroshi couldn't understand a word. Helplessly, he glanced at his mother, who simply looked back at him in shock. So she couldn't understand her either. What in the world did this lady want? She seemed to be expecting an answer, but what should he say? He couldn't possibly tell her he hadn't understood—that would be the height of rudeness.

The woman called again for the mysterious *tara doko-têr*. She seemed to be gradually losing patience. Since Hiroshi couldn't help her, he kept his gaze fixed on the floor. He felt that any moment fat beads of sweat would start dripping down from his hands onto the carpet. Then he noticed a movement out of the corner of his eye. Somebody was coming into the room. Hiroshi turned his head to get a better look. It was the girl. Although he knew that he shouldn't, he couldn't help but lift his head and look at her.

And then the girl said in impeccable Japanese, "My mother would like to thank you for finding my doll and bringing it back, and she would like to know where you found it."

Charlotte couldn't resist eavesdropping when she heard her mother had summoned the boy who had repaired her doll and brought it back. More than anything, she wanted to see what he looked like, what kind of boy would do something like that.

Maman was in a good mood today; she always was when they were giving a reception. She never had headaches on those days. But of course she had got herself into trouble again. She had forgotten to tell the interpreter when to come and only remembered when the main gate called up to say the boy and his mother were on their way. She had raced through the house and torn the secretary, Madame Chadal, away from her desk, ordering her to fetch the interpreter immediately and ignoring every protestation that he would never be able to make it in Tokyo's Saturday morning traffic.

When she'd heard the door open, Maman had shuddered. "They're already here," she muttered. "*Quelle horreur!*"

Then she'd straightened her shoulders, put on her best smile, and strode out into the hall.

Charlotte had scurried through the Yellow Salon and hidden behind the display cabinets by the other door to get a look at their visitor. She had often seen the woman carrying baskets of laundry through the courtyard. She didn't look as though she had done this sort of work all her life but, rather, gave the strange impression she was hiding here from someone. She must have been beautiful once. She probably still could be beautiful if she ever wore anything but those baggy gray overalls and tidied herself up a bit.

Maman greeted the two of them with the few snatches of Japanese she had managed to learn. Not only did they obviously not understand a word, it wouldn't have helped anyway, since Maman would never have been able to continue the conversation in Japanese.

"*Où est le traducteur?*" she called again, but Madame Chadal was the only person on the other side of the door. She was holding the phone in her hand and shrugging helplessly, because the interpreter wasn't even answering his phone, nor was his backup.

Charlotte had never seen the boy before. He couldn't be much older than she, and he was quite small, but the way he stood—even though he held that deep bow for such a long time—she felt there was something unyielding in him, a core of tempered steel. Maman then tried in English. Though she certainly spoke the language, her French accent was so strong that the guests were just as lost as before.

Charlotte was torn. If she rushed in to help, Maman would know she had been eavesdropping, which was strictly forbidden. On the other hand, she couldn't stand here and watch her mother making a fool of herself just because she was so awful at foreign languages. So she came out of her hiding place and into the hall.

"How do you know Japanese?" her mother asked in surprise once Charlotte had translated the boy's answer—that he had found the doll on the street by the gate where the trash was taken away.

"Yumiko taught me," Charlotte declared, though that was an exaggeration. Yumiko had her good points, but the ability to actually teach anyone anything would never be one of them. It would do for now, though.

Her mother could hardly stop shaking her head. "Well how about that . . . incredible." She cleared her throat. "Well then. Tell them that I . . . no, that you . . . no, that we were very pleased by his, hmm, his good deed and . . . uh, yes, we must show our appreciation somehow. I just don't know how at the moment. Try to find out from the boy how we can thank him."

"Okay," said Charlotte. She turned and asked the boy, "Why did you do it?"

He blinked. "Do what?"

"Repair my doll."

He shrugged. "I don't know. Shouldn't I have?"

Charlotte gnawed her lower lip. She didn't know what to say to that. "It just broke," she explained at last.

He nodded as though that were the most natural thing in the world. "I see."

"Do you want to see my room?"

"Yes."

"Good. Come with me." She turned to her mother and said, "Ça va. We've decided to go play together. I'm going to show him my room and all my toys."

"*Mais non!*" Maman opened her eyes wide. "I meant a little present or something like that."

"That's not what he wants," Charlotte claimed, shocking herself just a little with her own daring. The boy was nice, though, in a way. Maybe they would become friends.

"But not now! We have the reception today . . ."

"That's not until this evening. It's hours away." She couldn't allow any lengthy debate, she knew that much. So, shooing the boy out with Charlotte, she left.

The farther they went, the harder Hiroshi found it to believe they were really in someone's home. Who had an apartment as big as this? What could anybody do with so many enormous rooms? The way all the rooms were filled with what looked like costly antiques, it looked more like an art museum than a home.

"What's your name?" asked the girl.

"Hiroshi," he said, wondering whether he should tell her when he had first seen her. He would have loved to know why she'd gone out in her nightgown to stand in the rain.

"I'm Charlotte," she said. "With an *r* and an *l*. Can you say that?"

He tried it as they went up a wide staircase. "Cha . . . rotte," he managed. She laughed, and he tried again. "Cha-re-rotte?"

She stopped, opened her mouth, and showed him how to do the *l*. "Put the tip of your tongue behind your teeth up at the top. Do you see?" Her mouth looked just like in a picture book, neat and tidy with thin lips and spotless, pearly-white teeth.

"I know," he said. They had practiced in English class. His mother could do it, and she had made him practice, too. "Char . . . lotte."

It felt strange in his mouth, but he seemed to have gotten it right, because she nodded, smiling, and carried on up the stairs.

"Yumiko explained it to me," she said. "How *l* and *r* sound the same to Japanese."

"Who's Yumiko?" he asked.

"My nanny," she answered. "She's very nice. She sometimes takes me out, shows me things, and so on."

"What kind of things?"

"Well, the city. Tokyo. I'm not allowed out on my own. To tell you the truth, I can't even read Japanese."

They had reached the top of the stairs. A long hallway stretched out in both directions with still more framed paintings and thick, patterned carpets. It really did look like a museum.

"My mother doesn't like it," she said. "Me going out, I mean. If it were up to her, I would have to stay inside all the time, or in the garden."

"That must be boring," Hiroshi said.

"It is." Charlotte opened a door. "Well, here's my room."

It was vast and crammed full of toys, all neatly lined up on the shelves and in cupboards—dolls and plush animals, but also crayons, paintbrushes, books, and model cars. An enormous four-poster bed stood in one corner, and there was a desk by the window with exercise books and pens and pencils on it. Hiroshi saw at once that he had guessed right: this was the room where he occasionally saw movement at the window. He had guessed as much when he realized they were walking this way as they crossed through the house.

"And that's the playground." Charlotte led him over to the window. Beneath the trees was a swing and a climbing frame. "There used to be a sandbox as well, but my mother had them clear it away, because I'm too big for it."

Hiroshi knew about the playground, but he didn't let on. Though he couldn't see it from the apartment, he had discovered it on his secret scouting trips through the embassy compound. "You've got a big garden."

"In Delhi we had an even bigger garden," she said. "Not as well kept as this one, but there were monkeys, just imagine that! One of them came in through my window once and stole a schoolbook."

"Monkeys?" Hiroshi was amazed. He didn't actually know where Delhi was—in India, maybe?—but this girl had obviously traveled the world. He was almost envious. "That won't happen to you here."

"Oh, it was funny actually. Besides, it was my math book, so it didn't matter." She chuckled. He liked it when she laughed.

"Where do you go to school?" he asked. If she couldn't read Japanese, then she could hardly go to a normal school.

She stopped laughing abruptly and sighed. "I don't. I have a tutor from Paris who teaches me. My mother says that's so I'll learn the same things as I would at home. But I'd rather have classmates."

Hiroshi knew that she came from a country called France, in Europe. He had looked it up in an atlas, but he found it hard to imagine what it looked like and what it would be like to live there. He thought of the other children in his class and how they liked to tease him for being the smallest. "Classmates aren't always so great," he said.

"I went to an international school in Delhi," Charlotte declared. "I had a best friend there, Brenda." She paused. Hiroshi realized she found it painful to think about it. "We said we would write to each other, but she's never replied to my letters."

"That's too bad," he said.

She nodded. "Yes. It's because my father's an ambassador. So he has to go to a new country every few years, and of course we have to go with him. I've already been to India, and before that it was Congo, and when I was very little we lived in San Francisco." Charlotte looked him up and down. "What does your father do?"

Hiroshi shrugged. "No idea. I don't know him. All I know is that he's American."

"You've never seen him?"

"No."

"Do you have a photo of him at least?"

Hiroshi nodded. "At home."

"You must show me one day." She took a framed picture of herself with her family from her desk. Her father had light brown, slightly wavy hair and a rather sardonic smile. "This is in front of the house where we lived in Delhi." She pointed at the background, which consisted of a few palm trees and some gray trees with curiously intertwined branches. "That was the garden. You can't see any monkeys in the picture, though."

"It sounds as though you liked it better in Delhi than here," Hiroshi suggested.

"I just don't like being alone all the time, that's all." She scooted over to her shelf with all the dolls and took down the one Hiroshi had repaired. "How ever did you do it? It was completely busted."

Hiroshi shrugged. "I have a lot of tools. I just tried things out."

"Real tools?"

"Yes. I always ask for tools for my birthday. Christmas, too. I prefer building things to buying things." For some reason, he didn't want to admit that most of the time he never even had money to buy things.

Charlotte looked thoughtfully at the doll. "Funny. I never really liked this doll before, but she's something special now. I think from now on I'll call her Valérie." She repeated the name as though letting a drop of some delicate flavor melt onto her tongue. "Valérie. Yes, that's her name." She went back to the shelf and carefully put the doll back where it had been sitting. "I'm afraid we can't really play today, because my parents are giving a reception this evening," she said. "I always have to be there as well. I still have to shower and let them do my hair and get me ready. It always takes much too long."

"Ah," said Hiroshi. He didn't quite know what a reception was supposed to be. That must be something that rich people did. "That's too bad."

"But you can come visit me," she suggested. "If you like. We could play when nobody will interrupt us. Out in the garden, too."

Hiroshi nodded. "Yes, okay."

"Tomorrow afternoon maybe? Three o'clock?"

"Okay," said Hiroshi.

Charlotte told herself that evening that all in all it had been a good day. Even the reception was fun, she decided. Not the getting ready, of course. All those interminable hours of washing, drying, and styling her hair and trying on clothes really got on her nerves. But the reception itself was always fantastic; everybody was dressed in their best, making pleasant conversation, and she got to sit at a beautifully decorated table and eat wonderful things.

The guests were always charmed when they saw a ten-year-old girl behaving like a fine lady. Charlotte always gave a little secret smile when she heard them say that. As if it were so difficult. All you had to do was behave nicely and say "Please" and "Thank you" and "Really? How interesting" a lot, know which cutlery to use when (which was easy—it always went from outside to inside), and not spill anything; that was all there was to it. Oh, and of course you had to stay sitting still for as long as the grown-ups did. Actually, that was the hardest part.

Charlotte was particularly well behaved that evening, since she knew it would make her mother happy. And she wanted her mother to be happy, since she was happy as well, happy to have made a friend thanks to Maman; if she hadn't invited Hiroshi and his mother, it would never have happened. She was sitting next to a dear old Japanese gentleman, who was delighted he could speak to her in Japanese. It turned out he was the minister of education for the entire country. Charlotte told him she would much rather go to a real school and have classmates than take private lessons, but that unfortunately she had no choice.

On the other side of her sat a young Russian lady who looked, Charlotte realized with a jolt, astonishingly like the doll that was now called Valérie. However, her name wasn't Valérie but Oksana, and she didn't speak Japanese, just English, and even that not particularly well. Charlotte asked her to teach her a few words and phrases in Russian and then decided she liked the language.

"Perhaps my papa will be transferred to Russia one day. Then I'll learn Russian," Charlotte said.

Oksana smiled. "I'm sure you'll find it easy." The minister of education nodded vigorously in agreement.

After dinner they retired to the Yellow Salon, where the men gathered on one side of the room, smoking and drinking whiskey or pastis. The women took over the other half, where the seats were, and drank liqueurs and chatted.

Charlotte didn't have to go to bed yet; that was part of the arrangement. If she behaved like a fine lady, she was allowed to stay up as long as she liked on evenings like this. She'd had lots of practice staying up late by now. The only thing that bothered her was they expected her to stay over on the ladies' side of the salon. But she was interested in what the men had to say much more so than in the ladies' conversation. The ladies mostly liked to talk about "social trends." Charlotte didn't know what they were; they seemed to be of great concern. Or they chatted about painters and their sensational exhibitions and that sort of thing. That evening they were talking about an American writer called Michael Crichton and his latest novel, which apparently said bad things about Japan. Everybody agreed it was not nice to write novels like that. What Charlotte couldn't understand was why they had to go on and on about it.

She wandered over to the bar that had been set up in the middle of the salon and took another soda. She had noticed that if you drank a lot of soda, it was easier to stay up late. Papa was standing near the bar with the Russian ambassador, who was the guest of honor that evening, and they were talking excitedly. Mikhail Andreievitch Yegorov spoke French fluently with a wonderful Russian accent that sounded like music. He was telling Papa a strange story about an island he called the Devil's Island. It sounded fascinating. Charlotte decided to let good manners go take a flying leap and went over to join them.

His mother hadn't said a word all day, but nevertheless Hiroshi had noticed something was wrong. It wasn't hard to guess it had something to do with what had happened that morning at the embassy. She finally came out with it at suppertime. She said he should leave that girl alone; nothing good could come of it. Said they were rich folk, and he'd best keep his distance from rich folk.

"But why?" asked Hiroshi.

His mother didn't look at him. She gazed into empty space, seeming to see something else, something he knew nothing about. Nothing good, that was for sure.

"We're nothing to them," she said bitterly at last. "People like us aren't important to them. They don't have to care how we feel, so they don't."

Hiroshi thought about this and then about what it had been like to spend time with the girl today. Charlotte. Without making a sound, he practiced the *r* and *l* with his mouth.

"I thought she was nice," was all he said.

His mother looked at him, stared at him for a long time as though he were a stranger, and finally said, "You'll see soon enough what that can lead to. Believe you me."

The Russian ambassador broke off his story when Charlotte approached, bowed to her with a broad, cheerful grin, and said, "Ah, the young lady is doing us quite an honor. Mademoiselle Charlotte!"

She liked how he said Charlotte, rolling his r's in that Russian way. "I hope I'm not intruding," she said politely, the way her mother had told her a lady should.

Yegorov straightened up and laughed out loud. "No," he said. "No, you are not intruding. Quite the opposite. Now tell me, how do you like Japan?"

"Very much," Charlotte said. Of course, she could have complained that apart from a few streets around the embassy and some shopping malls, she had hardly seen any of Japan and so she couldn't really say much about it, but that wasn't the sort of thing you said at a reception, where everybody was on their best behavior and just said nice things to one another. That was the art of diplomacy. So she continued, "We're going to a museum soon; it's called the Island of the Saints. I'm looking forward to it a great deal. It's bound to be interesting."

The Russian raised his bushy eyebrows. "Really? How nice. Although I must confess I've never heard of that museum."

"It's not actually a museum as such," Papa explained offhandedly. "It's a Shinto shrine to the north of Tokyo that is open to visitors once a month. The island itself is just a tiny little place in the middle of an artificial lake, not much bigger than a tabletop. But it's said to be very pretty. Typically Japanese."

"You learn something new every day," Yegorov declared. "And I thought that I'd read my city guide quite thoroughly."

Papa smiled indulgently. "You really mustn't blame yourself, Mikhail Andreievitch. I would imagine most Japanese have never heard of it either. Charlotte's nanny is from that area, which is how we learned of it. It's called Seito-Jinjiya."

"The word *jinjiya* means shrine, and *seito* means Holy Island or Island of the Saints," Charlotte explained.

"Well, well." Yegorov nodded in approval. "And what is there to see?"

"Old things!" squealed Charlotte. The next moment, she held her breath, shocked at her own enthusiasm. She mustn't get carried away. That wasn't how a lady behaved.

"Old things? You like those?"

"Oh yes, very much."

"The shrine," Papa added, "is said to hold some relics that are supposedly among the oldest in Japan, including a sword that belonged to the first emperor." He smiled. "One always wonders whether those sorts of claims are true. I don't know how many swords the first emperor owned, but there must have been an awful lot of them for there to be so many left over."

The Russian ambassador laughed heartily, his belly wobbling under his smoking jacket. "Ah yes, we have the same trouble with relics in Russia. Some of our saints seem to have had twenty fingers and a hundred teeth." He looked down at Charlotte. "And you want to see these things?"

Charlotte nodded. "Yes. I'm hoping my new friend will say he'll come."

The Russian winked at her. "Oh ho, you already have a new friend. And what's his name?"

"Hiroshi," Charlotte told him cheerfully. "His mother works in our laundry, and he, um, found my doll."

Help! She really had gotten carried away, so much so that she had nearly let the cat out of the bag. She had only just kept her cool. It was important to be able to do that if you were going to be a fine lady. Maman had taught her that. You had to keep your cool, and above all you had to think carefully about what to say and what not to say.

Later that evening, when the reception was over and they were standing next to one another in the bathroom, Jean-Arnaud Malroux, ambassador of the French Republic, officer of the Légion d'honneur, and author of several books about France's role in the world, said to his wife, Cécile Malroux, née the countess of Vaniteuil, "I'm always amazed how quickly our daughter learns foreign languages, how easily they come to her. Did you hear her speaking to the Japanese minister of education? He could hardly stop talking about it as he was saying good-bye."

His wife was wiping her makeup from her forehead with a cotton pad. "Charlotte doesn't *learn* languages," she said, "she just *breathes* them in. I don't know who she gets it from; certainly not from me."

The ambassador was brushing his hair—one of the most sublimely useless things one could do at bedtime, but it had become a habit. "Come now. I don't believe that it has any mystical significance. Children are simply better at learning languages; it's only natural. But it nonetheless always surprises me to hear it for myself." He looked at the brush, plucked a few hairs from it, and put them into the bin beneath the washbasin. "But did you also hear what she told Yegorov? That she's made a friend here?"

"I was even there to see it happen, so to speak."

"Really? How did it come about?"

His wife put aside her cotton pad and pulled a tissue from the box. "It was this morning. The boy who brought her doll back. He's the son of someone on the domestic staff."

"You mustn't let Charlotte get too close to her friends here." The ambassador picked up his toothbrush and toothpaste. "I could be recalled from this post any day now, quite literally, and then what would happen? You know how she's still mooning after that girl she spent all her time with in Delhi—what was her name? The little English girl with the strawberry-blond curls."

"Brenda," his wife said. "Brenda Gilliam, and in fact she's Scottish."

"Her father was the professor of medicine?"

"That's right."

"We mustn't put her through another separation like that," the ambassador warned, holding his toothbrush under the warm water that gushed from the tap.

His wife looked at him in the mirror. "Do you know where we'll be going next?"

"Probably South America. They're assigning some new posts out there at the moment—Chile, Argentina, Guatemala . . ."

"Argentina!" his wife repeated enthusiastically. "Argentina would be wonderful." As a young woman, she had lived in Buenos Aires for a year and a half, dancing the tango, partying through the night, and falling in love with a new, fiery young man every month. It had been the one wild time in her life, and she lived off those memories to this day.

"It all depends on when Bernard gets better," her husband said, anxious not to feed any false hopes. "Or at least when he'll be able to work again. I dare say he's never going to get better."

Bernard Beaucour was the actual ambassador for France here in Japan, and Jean-Arnaud Malroux was simply his senior diplomat, representing Bernard in his absence. Beaucour had cancer, but before returning to Paris for treatment he had let it be known he fully intended to serve out his time in Japan even if he died there.

"The sooner the better," Madame Malroux said, taking another cotton pad and soaking it in that chemical goop whose secrets no man could ever fathom even if he spent a lifetime trying. "I don't know immediately . . . It must have something to do with the climate here. Or the city. Or the thought that there may be an earthquake at any moment. An earthquake! It hardly bears thinking about."

3

The next day Hiroshi was standing in front of the embassy gates at three o'clock, but the guard refused to let him through.

"But I have an appointment!" Hiroshi protested.

"Canceled." The guard tapped at a few characters scribbled on his messy notepad. "Says so here."

"But why?"

"I don't know. They don't tell the likes of us such things." He looked regretfully at Hiroshi. "I'm sorry, too, but the best thing for you to do is just go back home."

Hiroshi looked at the man, the iron gate, the flag hanging limp and motionless on its pole. It was a hot, windless day. He wasn't going to get anywhere standing there, that much was certain. He said his thank-yous in a flat voice and walked away.

People like us aren't important to them. They don't have to care how we feel, so they don't.

It had to be a misunderstanding. That was the only possibility. Charlotte had invited him for three o'clock, and no matter what the man at the gate said, that was the plan.

You'll see soon enough what that can lead to.

He had an appointment. And he wasn't going to let anything stop him from keeping it. Hiroshi went around the compound wall and slipped behind the tree with the gap in the spikes. He fetched the rope from its hiding place in the knotted hole where a branch had died, wriggled though the gap, and let himself down as quietly as he could. Then he went the same way he had gone on Tuesday. He didn't run into anyone, and there wasn't a single car parked on the stretch of tarmac he had to cross. That was probably because it was Sunday.

The door into the house next to the trash cans wasn't locked. Hiroshi slipped inside. The room behind the door was bare and ugly, but another door led into the hallway where he had been with Charlotte the day before—the opulent hallway with all the framed oil paintings and thick carpets. He scurried up the stairs and knocked on her door.

She flung it open. "Finally," she said. "I thought you weren't coming."

"They didn't let me in," Hiroshi replied. "Down at the gate."

"Why not? I specifically told them to."

"The man claimed my appointment was canceled and tried to send me home."

She blinked in astonishment. "How did you get in?"

Hiroshi paused. "I have a secret entrance. Otherwise, I would never have been able to get your doll from the trash."

"Ah." Her eyes lit up with curiosity, fascination. "You'll have to show me!"

They went down to the garden together, and Hiroshi showed her the spot. She pulled herself up the rope to the top of the wall. All you could see from up there was the tree and a little bit of the pavement behind it, but Charlotte was delighted. "We could just climb down here and go and see the city, couldn't we?"

"Of course," said Hiroshi and wondered where they could go. There wasn't anything very interesting to see nearby. He could show her his school if she wanted to do that.

Then she hesitated. "Oh well," she said at last, "maybe some other time." She lowered herself to the ground on the inside of the wall.

Hiroshi was relieved. He liked the garden much better than the city all around it. They went back upstairs.

On the way Charlotte pointed at the house where Hiroshi lived with his mother. "That's your place, isn't it?"

"Yes," Hiroshi said.

She moved her slender white arm slightly to one side so that she was pointing directly to the window above Hiroshi's bed. "And that's where you were watching me from when I was standing out in the rain."

He looked at her in amazement. "How do you know that?"

"I just know," Charlotte replied coquettishly. Then she hugged herself tight, as though she were suddenly cold. "Sometimes I do crazy things like that. Just because I want to. I can't help it. And then sometimes I don't even dare to do perfectly ordinary things."

"What sort of ordinary things?"

She shrugged. Somehow, right at that moment Hiroshi thought she looked like a little bird with injured wings. When he was small, he had found a bird like that and wanted to bring it home, but his mother hadn't let him.

"Ordinary things," she said. "Make a phone call. Leave the house. Or wear a particular dress."

"But what might happen just because you wear a particular dress?" Hiroshi asked in surprise.

"Nothing," said Charlotte.

He wondered whether he understood what she was telling him. Not really, but somehow that wasn't important.

"Are there things you don't dare to do?" Charlotte asked him.

Hiroshi thought about it. "At school I steer clear of the big boys who are always starting fights. I'm not strong enough, that's the trouble. I can't fight back when they hit me. I've got no chance against them. And the teachers never believe you when you say you've been bullied."

It was good to be able to say that to somebody even if it didn't change anything. His mother never wanted to hear about that sort of thing. And she absolutely refused to let him take a karate course so that he could learn self-defense. They couldn't afford it, she had decided.

Charlotte said, "That's okay. I'd do the same."

The next moment she seemed to have forgotten the topic entirely. "Come on," she called, setting off at a run. "Let's go on the swings!"

Hiroshi ran after her, and they reached the swings at the same time. She had a whole playground all to herself! He had never seen such a thing, never even dreamed about luxury on such a scale. In kindergarten he had always had to share the playgrounds with loads of other kids. Truth be told, he'd never had enough time on the swings, because he could hardly get started before somebody was shooing him away—either the big boys, the bullies, when he was little, or, once he was a big boy himself, the grown-ups, the teachers, telling him he had to let the little ones have a go.

It was great being rich!

He swung back and forth, flung himself along the arc, climbing higher each time and feeling that moment of weightlessness at the topmost point and then the way gravity snatched him back in the very next breath, pressing him into the seat. Then he let go as he reached the top of the upswing, simply slipped from the seat, and flew through the air—the best feeling he could ever imagine.

"That's great!" Charlotte shrieked.

But when Hiroshi got up from where he had tumbled onto the grass, he saw Charlotte's mother was crossing the lawn toward him. Everything about her threatened anger—the way she walked, the look on her face, her posture. Hiroshi stood where he was and waited. The ambassador's wife didn't even look at him. She marched over to her daughter, who was already ducking her head, and spoke to her in a sharp voice. Hiroshi couldn't understand a word, of course, but he could tell Charlotte's mother was very angry.

Once her mother had stopped scolding her, Charlotte got off the swing and walked over to him, her shoulders drooping. "She says you have to go."

"Oh," Hiroshi said, disappointed but hardly surprised. "Why?"

"I don't know either."

She accompanied him a little ways until a guard turned up and grabbed Hiroshi by the arm to lead him away, asking again and again how Hiroshi had gotten into the compound. He didn't answer, just let himself be led away, his lips clamped tight. As they passed a gate that had opened to let a delivery truck through, Hiroshi tore free. The guard was taken by surprise, and the boy ran.

That evening his mother scolded him roundly. She had heard what had happened, of course. She, too, wanted to know how he had gotten into the garden, telling him he knew perfectly well he wasn't allowed there. He didn't tell her either.

She snorted in disgust. "It'll be your fault if I lose my job and we have to move away," she said accusingly.

Hiroshi ducked his head and hunched his shoulders even further. Any more of this and his neck would vanish entirely. "Why would you lose your job?"

"Those are rich folk, and we're poor. Do you understand that? The best thing is to steer clear of them."

"Why is it like that?"

"Like what?"

"Why are there rich people and poor people?"

Mother flung up her hands. "The questions you ask! It's just the way things are, that's all. It's always been like that. The ones who can grab the most for themselves are rich, and everybody else is poor."

"That's not fair."

"It does no good to rail against it."

Of course, Hiroshi didn't come the next day.

Charlotte was so angry with her mother that she didn't know what to do. And she mustn't even say anything about it, since her mother was lying down somewhere with her usual headache. Charlotte eventually couldn't help but go into her room and fling everything off her shelves—everything—in a blind rage, until the floor was littered with toys.

After that she felt a bit better. A little later she went to work tidying everything up. She put every doll and every plush animal back in its place and gathered up all the games, the dice and cards and little wooden tokens that had fallen from their boxes and scattered across the carpet. She couldn't bear it when her things were in a mess; it was bad luck not to put everything neatly back where it belonged.

Once she was done she sat at the window, looked out, and decided she would never be a fine lady again, never again be polite at the receptions for her parents. It would serve her mother right. Why did she have to spoil everything? No, in future she just wouldn't join in. She wouldn't even let the hairdresser near her. She would shut herself away in her room, her hair in a mess, and she wouldn't wash, and she wouldn't move from the spot no matter how much her mother pleaded or threatened. Eventually, the guests would start arriving downstairs and Mother would have to go greet them . . .

Charlotte sighed. If she were honest with herself, the prospect of sitting all alone in her room while everybody was eating and having fun in the salons downstairs didn't seem like such a good idea. Maybe it wasn't such a good idea. Maybe it would be better to find some other way to get back at her mother. Then she heard a noise and pricked up her ears. It sounded as though someone had knocked at the door, but when she went to open it there was nobody there. And, of course, no Hiroshi.

Hiroshi. That gave her an idea, the kind of idea that stopped her in her tracks and made her hold her breath. She had to think about it very carefully, about whether she really wanted to do it. But by the time she let her breath out again, she had made up her mind.

She hurried into the garden to where Hiroshi had shown her the gap in the spikes. The rope was still hanging there. She hauled herself up, wriggled through, and climbed down the other side between the tree and the wall. That part was easy. She was outside! It was fantastic. She wanted to whoop with pleasure but knew she'd better keep quiet.

There was nobody in the alley. She walked over to the apartment block where Hiroshi lived and then stopped in front of the intercom panel, baffled: of course, all the doorbells were labeled in Japanese. What was she supposed to do now? She wondered whether she should just press all the buttons at once and then say sorry if she had to. After all, most people might not even be at home. Just then she heard a sound behind the door and it opened—and there stood Hiroshi.

"I saw you come," he said instead of hello.

Charlotte looked at him. He was bigger than she remembered him. "I thought I could come visit you. If you like."

"Yes, of course," Hiroshi said, opening the door further. "Come in."

They went upstairs. The staircase was dark and stiflingly narrow—so this was what real life was like for the Japanese. The apartment they went into was just as small—not much bigger than her bedroom. Through the gap in an open sliding door, Charlotte caught sight of a tiny room with a mattress on the floor and a wardrobe piled high with various things: suitcases, blankets, and so on. The front half of the main room was taken up by a low table, where you would have to kneel to eat, a TV, and a kitchen counter. Then there was a folding screen of white paper stretched over a frame of black wood, and behind that was Hiroshi's realm: film posters on the wall, a narrow bookcase, and a couple of boxes. One of them was open, and she could see his tools and spare parts. On the windowsill were the pieces of what might once have been a radio.

"I'm trying to repair that," Hiroshi explained. "But it's not easy. I haven't got the right parts."

Charlotte looked around. There was a set of shelves on the wall across from the window; a rolled-up mattress and, above that, a folded set of bedclothes were tucked onto the lowest shelf.

"Do you have to clear your bed away every morning?" she asked.

"Yes," he said as though it were the most natural thing in the world. "That way I have more room during the day. I don't always do it during the school year, but certainly during the holidays."

"How long are your holidays?"

"Till the end of August. I think school starts again on the twenty-fourth. It's a Tuesday at any rate."

Charlotte ran her hand softly over some of the furniture. So many feelings . . . "And what do you do during the holidays?"

"Nothing. Build stuff. Read. Think about things." Hiroshi sighed. "My mother sometimes scolds me for not joining any of the school clubs like the others do, but I just don't feel like it."

"School clubs? What are those?"

"Oh, they're for sports. Football, basketball, karate, that sort of thing. Or extra tutoring."

"Are you good at school?"

He shrugged. "I get by."

"What do you like to read?"

"Technical books most of the time. How things work and so on. I can borrow them from the library."

It was only then that Charlotte realized what all the film posters on Hiroshi's wall had in common. Every single one of them featured a robot. One was the golden robot from *Star Wars*; another showed a little machine standing on a high cliff being struck by lightning from the dark and stormy sky above.

"You like that sort of thing, don't you?" Charlotte asked. "How things work."

"Yes," said Hiroshi, pointing at the *Star Wars* robot. "Do you know that one?"

"Of course. That's C-3PO." She knew about him from Brenda, who had seen the film on video and told her all about it.

"That's right. Protocol droid, third class. He's really just an actor in a costume, though." Hiroshi pointed at the other robot, the one with the storm cloud. "That's Number 5. He's much more interesting. A real robot. He's supposed to be a military robot, but after he gets struck by lightning, he turns pacifist, and they come after him. He can do really amazing things; for instance, he can read a book in less than a minute. He just goes through it like this"—Hiroshi mimed riffling through pages—"and he can store everything that's in the book."

"I'm not allowed to see films like that," Charlotte admitted. "My mother says I'm too young."

"I even saw it in the theater," Hiroshi said. "When I get good grades in English, my mother sometimes takes me to the movies over in Shinagawa. They show American films there in English. That's where I saw this one. It was pretty funny." He squatted down in front of his shelves, shuffled through a stack of papers, and then showed her a gaudy leaflet with colorful Japanese writing and a picture of a chunky toy robot with a dome-shaped head and sturdy pincer arms.

"I'd like one of these. It's an Omnibot. It can carry things around, pour you a drink, and other stuff. It costs fifty thousand yen, though, so I'd never be able to afford it."

"What would you do with it?" Charlotte asked.

"I'd modify it, of course, so that it can do more things. I'd make it a real mechanical servant."

The idea clearly fascinated him. Charlotte thought it was strange. But then again she'd always found boys a bit strange. "You could pour me a drink, you know," she said. "That's what you do when a lady visits."

"Ah," Hiroshi grunted. He hurried to the fridge and took out a can of soda, which he passed to her. "Here you are."

Charlotte wasn't actually thirsty, and she didn't much like soda, but there was no refusing it now. She took a sip and looked around again. How tiny everything was here. There was one more sliding door. Charlotte wondered where it led. Probably to the bathroom.

"We could arrange a signal," she suggested.

"What kind of signal?"

"For when my mother's not home. Sometimes she goes out in the afternoons."

"And your father?"

"He's always at work. Anyway, I don't think he cares very much if you come." Charlotte went to the window. "Do you see the window of my room? The one with the yellow curtain? When the coast is clear, I'll put the doll you repaired behind the glass there."

"Okay," said Hiroshi.

She handed him the can, only half-drunk. "I think I'd better go back now before anybody notices that I'm gone."

Two days later Charlotte's mother asked her whether she wanted to go downtown to go shopping and maybe get an ice cream. "You need another dress for summer, after all."

"Can we go to a museum as well?" Charlotte asked.

Mother rolled her eyes. "No, most definitely *not*. We're going to a *nice, new* shopping mall."

"I won't join you, then, thank you."

Later, Charlotte watched from the window as her mother got into the car with Madame Chadal and an interpreter and drove out through the main gate. As soon as they were out of sight, she ran to her room and put Valérie in the window.

Hiroshi was there in less than fifteen minutes. "I've had an idea," he said, taking a piece of dark metal from his pocket. The way he held it, it had to be heavy. It turned out to be a magnet—strong enough to send the paper clips skittering around on top of Charlotte's desk when he held it underneath.

"I was reading today that human blood contains iron. Did you know that? There's this stuff called hemoglobin. It's what makes the blood look red, and it has iron in it."

"Really?" Charlotte asked, surprised, and looked at her hands. "Iron?"

"Yes. Not much, of course, or the magnet would just stick to you. But I thought that it had to be possible to stop the hemoglobin from going round if you held a magnet to a vein." He put his left forearm on the desk, his palm facing up so that the veins were visible, and then held the magnet just below his wrist. "It should get darker soon."

Charlotte found it a strange idea but somehow fascinating, too. She waited, not taking her eyes off his arm for an instant. From time to time Hiroshi lifted up the magnet so they could see underneath.

"Maybe my skin's too dark," he said thoughtfully after a while.

Charlotte didn't think his skin was dark at all—not like that of her classmates back in Delhi. But hers was lighter, that was true. She put her forearm next to his. "Try mine."

It was a funny feeling to have the magnet at the vein on her wrist where the doctor usually took her pulse and imagine the hemoglobin gathering beneath it. There was nothing to show it was happening, though, on her skin either.

"Could this be dangerous?" Charlotte asked. "Could I faint or something like that?"

"I'll catch you if you faint," Hiroshi declared.

They waited a bit longer. It was beginning to get boring.

"Maybe there's not enough blood there," Charlotte ventured. She thought. Where was the skin thinner and the blood flow greater?

She jumped up, flung open her wardrobe, and stood in front of the mirror inside the door. "The neck! There's a big vein here, do you see?" She cocked her head to be able to see the side of her own neck. "Here. Hold the magnet right there."

Hiroshi came up behind her and held the magnet to the thick artery pulsing at her neck. The two of them stood there motionless, waiting to see what would happen. They stood that way for hours— or so it seemed to her.

"It's not working," Charlotte declared at last.

He nodded and lowered the magnet. "You're right." He put it back in his pocket. "You can't believe everything you read in books."

"Come on," said Charlotte. "Let's go play on the swings."

It was three days before he saw the doll in the window again. Hiroshi put down the radio—still not fixed—and ran out the door.

When he arrived, Charlotte was holding two big flashlights, one in each hand. She had come up with the idea of exploring the cellar. She wouldn't have dared to do it on her own, but she was dreadfully curious about what might be down there. So curious that Hiroshi, too, got swept up in the fever of discovery. The two of them crept down the stairs to an iron door that led to the cellar.

It was cold down there, especially after the baking summer heat outside. The first thing they found was the heating plant. A steel door opened into a room with an enormous oil tank that occupied almost the entire space. In the next few rooms they came upon old typewriters and shredders and bulky calculating machines, and box after box of forms. Then they reached a bigger room, its metal shelves full of files.

"Ugh!" Charlotte said, shivering. "Old documents. I hate those. Come on, let's get going."

Hiroshi didn't know what was so awful about old documents, but since he didn't think they were especially interesting either, he followed her. At last they came across a lumber room with all sorts of treasures: weird lamps; dusty furniture; garden gnomes; hot plates with thick cloth sleeves around the power cords; framed photos of castles, icebergs, and ships; flowerpots full of shriveled bulbs; a rusty saw; a tricycle with a missing wheel . . .

"Look at this," said Charlotte, holding up a sealed flask full of some yellow fluid with a dead snake rolled up inside.

Hiroshi had found something even better: a big metal tool chest. "Unbelievable," he breathed as he lifted the lid and studied all the racks and pinions, the axles, cogwheels, and baseplates. One compartment held hundreds of nuts and bolts, another three electric motors with their cables. "I could practically build a robot with all this."

He put the chest down on the floor and began to build—something, anything, just to see how the cogwheels fitted together and how the axles turned. Charlotte squatted down next to him, picked up a large cog, and furrowed her brow. She put it back down. She picked up another part, a baseplate dotted with screw holes, and dropped it straightaway.

"You shouldn't play with these," she declared.

Hiroshi looked up. "Why not?"

"They belonged to a boy who killed himself."

"Really?"

"He was in love with a girl who wasn't interested in him. He threatened her, said that he'd kill himself if she didn't go out with him, but she still didn't want to. So he decided to throw himself off the roof of the building where she lived so he would hit the ground right in front of her window." Charlotte was telling the story in a flat, toneless voice. "That's how he planned it, and that's what he did."

Hiroshi looked down at the tool chest in fascination, at all its beautifully made parts. He didn't know whether to feel scared or sad that he had to stop playing with them.

"If I were in love, I wouldn't kill myself," he pronounced.

"What if she didn't want you?" Charlotte asked.

Hiroshi shook his head. "I'd keep trying until she changed her mind."

At supper Hiroshi asked his mother whether she knew anything about a boy who had lived in the embassy and killed himself by jumping off the roof of a girl's house. Though he didn't mention the tool chest, he included the part about the boy jumping right in front of the girl's window.

His mother looked at him, perplexed. "Where did you hear that?"

"Someone told me," Hiroshi said.

She reached out and began clearing away the dishes of rice and pickles. "Something of the sort happened, yes. But it was a long time ago. I wasn't working there yet; one of the old cooks told me about it. It was a gardener's son . . ." She stopped tidying the dishes. "He wanted to play a trick on a girl in his class, dangle something in front of her window to give her a fright, and he fell." She looked sternly at Hiroshi. "Let that be a lesson to you. Don't go playing tricks on people."

Next time Hiroshi saw Charlotte, he called her out. Just because she lived in a big house with a garden, that didn't give her the right to make up stories and pull the wool over his eyes. He was really angry with her.

She listened to his accusations in silence, and once he was done, she said, "It wasn't a lie. Your mother just doesn't know the full story."

"But you do, eh? Am I supposed to believe that?" he shot back at her. "You've only been here a couple of months. My mother's lived here for as long as I've been alive."

Charlotte didn't answer. She just looked at the ground. They were standing on the lawn where he had seen her that night. She had been waiting for him there after she put the doll in the window. The hose that the gardener had watered the plants with that morning was neatly coiled up nearby. Birds were rustling through the bushes in search of food, and they could hear the distant rumble of traffic. A telephone rang through an open window somewhere.

"If I tell you a secret," Charlotte asked, "will you keep it?"

Hiroshi looked at her standing there. She had put her hair up in a ponytail today. He realized he couldn't stay angry at her for long. "Okay," he said.

She sat down on the grass and waited for him to join her. "I have this sort of talent," she explained seriously. "I used to think everyone could do it, but I've realized by now that I might be the only one anywhere who can."

Hiroshi frowned. Was this going to be another lie? "A talent? What kind of talent?"

"When I touch something, I know what happened to it before. I know how old things are; I know whom they belonged to and what kind of people they were. I know what the people felt, what they were afraid of, everything." She ran her hand over the lawn. "This grass is all new. It doesn't belong to anyone, hasn't got any memory. But if I touch the hosepipe for instance"—she stretched out her hand and ran it across the pipe—"then I can feel the gardener. I can feel that he's worried about his wife being ill, that the doctors don't know what's wrong with her."

Hiroshi thought about it. He thought about everything he had read in the books the librarian always said were too difficult for someone his age. He tried to understand how a talent like that would even work. As far as he knew, it wasn't possible. He had never heard of human thoughts being stored inside things.

"I don't believe you," he said.

"When I touched the pieces from the tool chest, I felt the boy's thoughts, how he was going to kill himself. The thoughts are all around the whole box—it practically glows with them—because he always played with it. When I got back the doll you'd repaired, I saw how you had been watching me in the rain, and how you kept a lookout for me all the time after that. That's how I knew where you lived."

"I think it's more likely you just saw me sitting at the window."

"No, I didn't." She shook her head sadly. "I've never told anyone else about this. My mother always wonders why I like going to museums so much. I only like the ones where you can pick things up and touch them, though." She looked up, and now her eyes lit up. "When I touch something that's old—really old—it's like reading a thousand books at once, all in a second. Sometimes I feel hundreds of people at once. I know how they used to live in the old days, what they were afraid of, what they dreamed of . . ."

Hiroshi looked at her skeptically. "I don't understand how something like that could work. I can't believe it."

The two of them sat in silence for a while. Hiroshi wondered what might happen next. Charlotte was probably offended. But what could he do? He couldn't say he believed her when he didn't at all. That would have been a complicated sort of lie.

"I've got an idea," Charlotte said suddenly. She looked right at him. "Next time, bring me something that belonged to your father."

4

Something that had belonged to his father? Easier said than done.

Before he left, Charlotte had explained to him exactly what she would need—something his father had handled, had held. "Glasses are best," she'd said.

"My father didn't wear glasses," Hiroshi had told her.

"A watch, then. Clothes. A chair he used to sit on every day."

They didn't even have any chairs in the apartment. Chairs were a Western invention; in Japan you sat on the floor. His mother no longer had any clothes that had belonged to his father, not anymore—why would she? As for watches, she did have a watch she'd set aside somewhere. She said it was a present from his father, which Hiroshi would be allowed to have once he had finished school. But that, of course, meant his father had never actually worn the watch himself. Hiroshi had a couple of photographs. They were probably no good either; though his father was in the pictures, that didn't mean he had ever held them in his hands.

Hiroshi looked at one of the photos, perplexed. It showed his father as a young man, and the street sign behind him showed it had been taken in Japan. His father had a narrow, fine-featured, good-looking face. Most of all, Hiroshi was fascinated by his hair, a dark gold, tousled mane. Nobody he knew had hair like that. Nor did he; nothing even remotely like it, alas. And then there was his father's smile . . . it was an extraordinary smile, one that drew Hiroshi back to this photo again and again. Some days he thought his father must have been very happy indeed that day; others, he thought that it was a sad smile. It was strange.

Mother seldom spoke of his father. She had told him a few details when he was much younger but had considered the topic closed ever since. His father had come from the US to Tokyo to study, which was when the two of them had met, he knew that much. He also knew she had gone to America with him but that she hadn't liked it there. Then his father had suddenly fallen gravely ill, and his family had told her she had to leave. That was when she went back to Japan with Hiroshi in her womb. She never saw or heard from his father again.

He always felt sad thinking about it. He remembered how, when he was little, he had sometimes made up stories that his father was an important man, an adviser to the US president, or a great scientist, or very busy doing other important things for the world. But one day, he had told himself, his father would come back, put his hand on his shoulder, and say, "This is my son." And then everything would be wonderful.

He had an idea. Hiroshi put the photo away and scooted over to the shelves by the window, where he kept his most private possessions in a tin box on the lower shelf. Actually, it was mostly junk: The movie tickets from the robot films he had been telling Charlotte about. A white glove he had found lying on a park bench when he was a kid, as though the person who had been wearing it had gone up in a puff of smoke the moment before; Hiroshi had been so fascinated that he couldn't help but take the glove home. A notebook with the *Masters of the Universe* characters He-Man and Skeletor on the cover. That had been the first thing he had ever bought with his own pocket money, though he could no longer remember why and didn't know what he should write in it. It had been lying in the box ever since. A little, blue plastic dog. A seashell from a beach he had gone to visit with his mother he had no idea where.

And a penknife that had belonged to his father.

It was a thick penknife, red with a white shield with a cross in it, and opened out into eleven different tools, including a knife, corkscrew, bottle opener, and scissors. When he was little, one of the blades had suddenly snapped shut when he was playing with it and cut his finger badly. He hadn't touched the knife since, had forgotten all about it. But it had belonged to his father, who had carried it every day for years. At least that's what Mother had said.

Hiroshi hesitated. All at once he wasn't so sure he even wanted Charlotte to tell him something about his father. Not even if she was just making up stories. Maybe she would say something horrible about his father, and he didn't know whether he wanted to hear that.

He would have to think about it.

The days passed, and the doll never appeared. When he finally spotted it on the windowsill, Hiroshi hesitated for a moment, then put the penknife in his pocket and ran out of the door.

"Do you have something?" Charlotte asked straightaway, and when he nodded, she said, "Come on, then."

She went out into the garden with him. "I thought my mother would never leave the house again," she remarked as they strode across the lawn. "She's got a friend she usually goes to see, the Italian ambassador's wife I think, but she's not in town at the moment. At least she went to the hairdresser's today—that will take three hours, maybe longer."

"Why are we going out in the garden?" Hiroshi asked.

"It works better outside," Charlotte said, crossing the lawn to a little copse of trees.

In between the trees was a regular thicket; they could hardly see the house from here, and they scratched their skin on the branches, and their clothes were snagged. Charlotte seemed to know the way, though. She marched ahead until they reached a small clearing, then she sat on the ground and put out her hand. "Okay. Hand it over."

Hiroshi took his father's penknife from his pocket and put it reluctantly into her outstretched hand. She closed her fingers around it, shut her eyes—and smiled.

"That gave you a right old shock," she said, without opening her eyes.

"What?" asked Hiroshi.

"When the knife snapped shut."

Hiroshi caught his breath, surprised. How did she know about that? He'd never told anyone, not even his mother.

Charlotte was quiet for a while, keeping her eyes closed and the knife held tight in her hand. "Your father's from Texas," she said at last. "From a rich family. Very rich. His parents wanted him to get a job in the company, but he wasn't interested. He was crazy about Japan, collected everything he could about it. One day he came to Japan to study here even though his family was against it."

Hiroshi looked at her, stunned. He didn't know what to think.

"At first he lived in dormitories," she went on. "He didn't like it, though, because he was living with other foreigners, mostly Americans. So he looked for a room in the city, people who rented out to students. He went to see a family, who showed him a room he didn't really like, because it was dark and didn't have nice furniture, but just as he was about to say so a girl walked in. He fell in love on the spot and took the room."

"And who was that?" Hiroshi asked.

"Your mother."

"Oh."

"He was so deeply in love that he stopped paying attention to his studies. He went into the travel agency where your mother worked and then acted surprised to see her there. He'd really followed her in secret, though."

Hiroshi had to grin. He thought of the photo of his father and tried to imagine him keeping a low profile in the streets of Tokyo. Everybody must have noticed him.

"He was always thinking of ways to talk to your mother more often. She was very shy, but she spoke good English. He finally thought of asking her to help him with his Japanese lessons and improve his pronunciation. It was difficult, because she had to ask for her parents' permission. They sat in the living room with them for the first few lessons and watched very closely." She stopped and giggled suddenly.

"What is it?"

"Your father had a trick up his sleeve. After a few weeks your grandparents left the two of them alone. Your father made up a lesson that was full of sentences like 'I love you' and 'You're so beautiful' and that sort of thing." She giggled again, louder this time. "He had somebody at the university write them down, and then he mocked them up as a set of teaching materials that looked just like the real course. Then he deliberately mispronounced the sentences so that your mother had to correct him all the time. She blushed like crazy, but she went along with it . . ." Charlotte stopped again but didn't giggle. This time she just smiled. "After the lesson they kissed."

Hiroshi looked at her, feeling flustered and uncomfortable. Girls liked that sort of thing—he knew that from school—but he hated kissing. It was quite enough that he would be seeing his grandparents soon and that they would kiss him. However, he knew that one day he would have no choice but to kiss a girl. Otherwise he'd never be able to get married.

"He wanted to marry your mother, but he didn't dare without asking for his parents' permission. That's why he wanted your mother to come with him to America. The third time he asked her, she finally agreed. He wasn't happy when she did, though, because he was so worried about what his family would think. Charlotte opened her eyes and handed the knife back to Hiroshi.

"What else?"

"Nothing else. After that he didn't have the knife on him."

Hiroshi put it in his pocket. "I don't know much about my father," he admitted. "I didn't know that he was from a rich family. I don't even know if he's still alive."

"Of course he's still alive," Charlotte said firmly.

"Do you think so?"

"Yes," she said, getting up and brushing the soil from her dress. "If he had died, you'd have inherited something."

That evening, when Hiroshi's mother came home from work, her back ached so much that she had to lie down. "We washed the curtains from both grand salons today and then hung them up again. That always leaves me feeling half-dead."

"Should I go get some painkillers?" Hiroshi offered.

"Oh no." She patted the futon beside her. "Sit down and tell me something. What have you been up to all day?"

Hiroshi came closer, feeling awkward. "You wouldn't be interested if I was to tell you all the technical stuff."

She made a face that was not quite a smile. "I just want you to take my mind off my aches and pains."

He stood there in thought, feeling the penknife still in his pants pocket, then sat down, took it out, and showed it to her. "Is it true this belonged to my father?"

Mother raised her head with difficulty and looked at the knife. "So you've got it."

"You gave it to me."

"Ah yes. So I did." She sank back down with a groan. "Yes, that belonged to your father."

"And how come you had it?"

"When we flew to America, it was in the pocket of some pants he forgot to pack. Your grandpa and grandma kept all of his things, and I found it when I came back." She smiled a bittersweet smile at the ceiling. "John was so upset about that. He thought he had left it in a taxi."

"Tell me about him," Hiroshi said, putting the knife back in his pocket. It was a handy little tool, with its multiple screwdrivers, the tweezers, and so on. He could find a use for it.

"Oh my. What is there to tell? You already know everything. And anyway, didn't we say that *you* would tell *me* something?"

"No," said Hiroshi. "Just that I would take your mind off it."

His mother shrugged and moaned, turning her head from side to side a little. "This always happens. Every time I feel poorly, Dr. Uchiyama is on holiday."

"Did you love him?"

She sighed and looked at Hiroshi. "Your father? Of course. Very much. I was young and foolish, and he was a handsome man . . ." She stopped for a moment and blinked rapidly. Her eyes were shining now.

She began to tell the story. How one day he was standing there in her parents' living room just as she came home. How she would watch him secretly from her window, see him coming and going but not dare talk to him, because she was afraid her English might not be good enough, or that perhaps she wouldn't understand his Japanese. How, a little while later, he had turned up, of all places, at the travel agency where she worked, an agency that specialized in trips to Australia.

She didn't tell the story of how they first kissed.

"He insisted that I come to America to meet his parents," she continued after a long pause, a silence that somehow sounded like a sigh. "I didn't want to, but he persuaded me in the end. He was the kind of man you couldn't refuse for long. I couldn't anyway. So off we went."

It was as though she were talking about a death sentence.

"It was all very strange for me. America, the endless roads, the land stretching away in all directions. And then the Leak family house—no, not a house, a ranch. They were terribly rich, had a hundred rooms, servants, a swimming pool, dozens of cars, horses, a bowling alley. They even had their own movie theater down in the basement . . . I was quite overwhelmed at first."

Hiroshi tried to imagine it. The way she described it, even the French embassy would look small by comparison.

"His family was very kind when we arrived—or, at least, so I thought. At the time I didn't know any other Americans apart from your father; I didn't know they always smile and act friendly. In reality, though, they were totally against our being together, and not only his parents but his brothers and sisters, too. John's grandfather had fought in the war against Japan. When I happened to run into him on his own one day, he told me he hated the Japanese and that I mustn't imagine for a moment that anyone in that house would ever agree to John marrying me. If John went ahead and married me anyway, the old man said, he would lose his inheritance, and since he'd never learned any way to make a living, we would starve."

"What a horrible thing to say," said Hiroshi.

"They were horrible. After running into the grandfather, I realized a lot of the kind things they said were actually insults dressed up in nice words. In a funny way I was relieved, since I understood why I felt so unwelcome."

"Why didn't you just run away with him?"

"We wanted to. But first John wanted to talk to a lawyer and find out whether his family really could disinherit him, under Texas law. We were just figuring out where to go and what we would do if we did have to fend for ourselves when we both fell ill—first me, and then John the next day. They wouldn't call a doctor for my sake, but when John got sick, they got one to come out, of course." She began to rub her sides as though trying to stretch herself out on the futon. "I can still remember. The doctor looked like that American actor John Wayne. He was wearing thick leather boots and a cowboy hat on his head and had a stethoscope around his neck. He wouldn't let the Leaks order him around, so he went ahead and examined me first. 'Congratulations, ma'am,' he said, 'you're pregnant.' Then he examined John and stood right up and said, 'Get him to the hospital.' Then they found out that John had a brain tumor, a very aggressive one."

Hiroshi swallowed. She had never breathed a word about any of this. It probably meant his father was no longer alive.

"They operated the same day. It was a very long operation, very complicated, and it didn't turn out as well as they'd hoped. We sat there in the clinic until at last, long after midnight, one of the doctors came out and gave us the news. He said the tumor was in a particularly sensitive place, that John was in critical condition, and that even if he lived, he would never be the same. Even in the best case, John would need years of care, maybe for the rest of his life." Hiroshi's mother covered her face with her hands. "The next day, while his son was lying in a coma in the hospital and the doctors were fighting for his life and nobody knew whether he would be alive the next day or even the next hour, John's father was talking to me all that time, urging me to have an abortion. He had it all arranged—can you believe it?—the doctor, the clinic, everything. All I had to do was walk out the door and into the car and that would have been it. You would never have been born."

Hiroshi rubbed his throat, disquieted. It was a strange thought: never to have been born.

"At first, I didn't understand why he wanted me to go through with it or why he was in such a hurry. It was only later that I understood his thinking: if John should die, he didn't want an extra heir making trouble for his other children. It was all about the money for him, all about the family fortune." She drew in a long breath, almost choked. "That was the most terrible day of my life. I'll never forget that fat man sitting there, sweating, trying to persuade me to let them kill my baby. And they were all going along with it—the doctor, the chauffeur, everyone. And all because this man had the money to make them. Because he was rich. He didn't care about you in the least, didn't care about me. All he cared about was his money."

"And what did you do then?" Hiroshi asked, his heart in his mouth.

"I escaped." Her breath was ragged now, and she put her hand on her chest and had to take a few breaths before she could carry on. "John had given me some American money—quite a lot, several hundred dollars—and I still had my plane ticket. When John's father was called away to the phone—something to do with the business—I ran to my room. I shoved whatever I needed into a bag as though the devil himself were after me, and then I ran down the back stairs and out of the house. I had a great stroke of luck just then, because I ran straight into the arms of a man from Japan. I told him they were trying to make me kill my baby and that I had to get away. He simply took me with him. He was a delivery driver for a supermarket, and he was bringing groceries to the Leak ranch like every week. I hid in his van, and nobody stopped us. He helped me change my flight, and most importantly, he made sure my name was spelled differently so that it wouldn't be easy for them to find me if they were after me. And that's how I came back to Tokyo. When I got off the plane, I had just enough money left to get into the city."

"Wow," Hiroshi whispered. That was some story. He would never have guessed his mother had had such adventures.

She seemed to have forgotten all about him. Her voice was just a whisper by now. "I went and hid with my parents. Then you were born, and I went back into hiding again. For years I was afraid John's father might send someone to track me down, to do something to you. That's why I took the job with Inamoto-san; I figured that any-body looking for me would start their investigations in offices, jobs where you have to speak English. I hoped they would never find me in a lowly place like a laundry. Not find me, and not find you."

Hiroshi thought about this. "But he would have been able to find Grandpa and Grandma. And they would have known where you were."

"That's why I persuaded them to move away. I figured Minamata was a good long way away."

Hiroshi sat there, stunned. No wonder she used to make such a dreadful fuss if he was ten minutes late coming home from kinder-garten. She must have been terrified he had been kidnapped.

"Do you think they're still after us?" he asked.

"Oh, they were probably never looking for us at all," his mother said. "But I was so scared for you."

Hiroshi nodded. He could understand that. "And you've never liked rich people since."

"Yes. That's right." She put out her hand and stroked his hair. "Back when I was young, I used to admire rich people. The way they would come into the travel agency, all elegantly dressed with beauti-ful manners, and I could tell they simply didn't care how much a trip might cost . . . I thought life ought to be like that: just doing what you like, collecting possessions and experiences, never mind the cost. And to be honest, I still think that in the back of my mind. I think that life ought to be beautiful. Not about working from morning till night at a job that's no fun most of the time. But if a life like that means you have to be rich . . . if a life like that means being so ruth-less, so hard-hearted that you're willing to take whatever you want from anyone else—that you would even kill for it—then the cost is too high. A life that you pay that price for is not life as it ought to be. Do you understand?"

Hiroshi nodded. "I think I do." He hesitated. "Did you ever find out what happened to my father?"

"No," she said.

"What do you think happened?"

"Sometimes I think he's alive. But if he is, he's forgotten all about me." Her eyes were moist, glistening. "You've seen Aunt Kumiko; you know what can happen. Someone can be full of life, clever as can be, and then lie in bed for the rest of her days and barely know her own name."

Hiroshi looked at the floor and tried to imagine the man he only knew from photographs as a bedridden invalid, helpless and in need of care day and night like Aunt Kumiko. He couldn't imagine it, didn't want to imagine it. He thought the whole story was about the saddest thing he'd ever heard.

For some reason he asked her, "The man who helped you—do you know what his name was?"

His mother hesitated. "His name was the same as yours," she said at last. "Hiroshi."

"You named me after him?"

"He saved your life. It was the least I could do."

Hiroshi had a great deal to think about over the next few days. He had plenty of time to do so, as there was nothing in Charlotte's window. The Bon festival was getting ever closer, though, when they would go to Minamata. Just like every year, Mother grew increasingly nervous as the day approached. The suitcases were brought down from the top of the wardrobe, packed, rearranged, then emptied and packed anew. She called her parents every day, talking for hours about when they would arrive, who would meet them, and other such details. And just as she had threatened, she dragged him downtown to buy a new pair of pants, which he hated—all the more so because he was afraid he might miss a chance to see Charlotte.

"If it were up to you, you'd wear all your clothes until they were rags," his mother chided as he moped and dragged his feet toward the changing room.

"If it were up to me," Hiroshi replied, "clothes would never wear out. And they would grow along with you."

"Well, why don't you invent something like that? But until you do, you're just going to have to try on a pair or two of pants, like it or not," she said, holding out another three pairs that looked identical to the ones he'd just tried on.

But when he had time, when there was nothing else that had to be done, Hiroshi was deep in thought. About his father. About rich and poor, and about whether the world would really be a better place if there were no rich people. Was that what he should wish for? That everybody should be poor? Somehow, that didn't seem right either.

"We're not really poor at all," he told his mother over breakfast one morning. "I mean, we have everything we want, don't we?" Just then he recalled the Omnibot that he would have liked to have, the one that cost far too much. "At least, everything we need."

Mother nodded. "Yes, but only because I work. If I didn't work, then next month we would have nothing to eat and the month after that, nowhere to live."

"And rich people? Don't they work?"

"No. They just boss other people around. They can do that because they're rich and everyone else needs their money. And the rich have the others work for them so they can stay rich."

Hiroshi saw how it all worked. At last he understood what it was all about. "Rich people need poor people to do the work for them!"

"That's exactly it," said his mother and looked at the clock. "And that's why I have to go now."

After she'd gone, Hiroshi sat at the table for a while, feeling as though the sudden insight had almost blinded him. Being rich or poor wasn't about money the way everybody thought, it was about who did the work. But understanding it that way was depressing, too, because it meant there could never be a world where everyone was rich. In a world like that, nobody would be left to do the work, and the work had to be done.

After he had cleared away the dishes—another job somebody had to do—he stood at the window for a long time, looking down at the embassy villa and the big garden. He thought about all the magnificent furniture and artwork inside. Even if he didn't care to live like that himself, he would certainly like to have such a garden one day and all that extra room. But it was a great deal of work to run a house like that. He knew that from what his mother had told him. The embassy employed a gardener, who did nothing but look after the garden all day long. There were cooks and waiters, housekeepers, chauffeurs, security guards, and so on—all so the ambassador's family didn't have to lift a finger. For those three people to be rich, a whole lot of other people had to work—people who didn't have anybody working for them in turn, because they weren't rich. They were the ones who did all the jobs.

Hiroshi let his head droop until his forehead was pressing against the cool glass. If he were honest with himself, he didn't like to work. Not when working meant doing things he didn't want to do. And most of the time that's exactly what work meant; he knew that from his mother as well. Washing laundry was not in fact her favorite way of passing the time.

When it came down to it, he didn't much like going to school either. All right, every now and then he learned something interesting, but was it worth all the time and effort? If he had just been allowed to spend the same amount of time in a library, he would have learned more and discovered far more interesting things.

And later on in life? You had to work hard at school to get good grades to go to a good university and then get a good degree so that you could get a good job in a good company. That's what everybody always told him—even his mother. But when he tried to imagine it, really think about what it would be like, he couldn't. Or at least he couldn't imagine anything that would persuade him it would be much fun. Being rich, though—rich and free—he could imagine that quite easily, and it would be much better.

But he didn't want to have to harden his heart to do it, didn't want a wicked life like his grandfather in Texas, who had been so worried about the money that he had wanted to kill his own grandson. And he didn't want other people to have to do without all the good things in life just so he could live well. That was a hard-hearted way to see the world. Whichever way he looked at it, the problem seemed insoluble. Nevertheless, Hiroshi couldn't stop thinking about it. He could feel his brain almost literally buzzing, as though he might blow a fuse any minute.

He couldn't let it go. He ate and drank and thought. When he went to bed, he thought until he fell asleep. When he woke up in the morning, he had the feeling his brain had been thinking away without him all night long. He thought while he was brushing his teeth and when he was going to the bathroom; he thought as he got dressed and while he watched television, and the whole time he felt as though these thoughts of his were turning and turning around like huge millstones grinding one another to a powder.

He eventually tried to forget the whole thing. He sat down with his toys and his tool kit, leafed through the Omnibot advertising booklet for the thousandth time, and had another go at the broken radio even though he knew he would never be able to fix it as long as he had no replacement parts. He would have to buy them. In the meantime, though, it would do no harm to test the wiring one more time.

And then that evening, just before he fell asleep, he had the idea all of a sudden. The idea of how it could be done.

Thunderstruck, he sat up in bed, switched his reading lamp back on, thought it through once more, and then one more time after that and then one more time again, and he couldn't find a flaw. There was no reason why it shouldn't work. It was wrong to think there had to be poor people so that there could be rich people! It was a fallacy! Totally misguided! Everybody could be as rich as they wanted. Everybody could have whatever they wanted, and nobody would have to harden their hearts or live a wicked life. And best of all, it was such a simple idea. Child's play! The most astonishing thing about it was nobody had stumbled across the idea before him.

There was no way he could sleep now. Hiroshi grabbed a note-pad and pen from the shelf and began to write it all down. This was an important idea. He mustn't forget it, whatever happened. But he wouldn't forget. Quite the opposite. The more he wrote and the longer he thought about it, the more certain he became he had found the answer, the answer to all the problems of rich and poor, money and work, and all the rest.

It took quite some time to write it all down. When he was done, he put the notepad down and turned the light off. His last thought before he fell asleep was that he would tell Charlotte all about it the next time they met.

The next morning it was raining, which was unusual for that time of year. It was a gentle summer rain that seemed to melt away into the air before ever hitting the ground, a rain that felt good. Afterward, the air was wonderfully fresh, and everybody seemed to be in a good mood. And later that afternoon there were five dolls in Charlotte's window.

"I'm just going out for a bit," Hiroshi told his mother as she came through the door.

"Where?" she asked.

He already had his shoes on and was halfway out of the door. "I'm going to meet Charlotte," he called out, making sure he was well out of range before she could protest.

Charlotte was jumping up and down with delight when he arrived. "I thought they'd never leave! Honestly, I could hardly stand the waiting. Come on in," she said, taking his sleeve and pulling him into her room. She dragged him over to the desk, where there was a tray with all sorts of things to eat—tiny little schnitzels, colorful salads, strips of ham rolled up around some pale filling, and plenty of things Hiroshi had never even seen before. "I wheedled some food out of the cook, leftovers from dinner. That way, you don't have to rush home. Come on, dig in! I'll eat a bit as well, but just to be polite, because I'm already full."

"Where are your parents?" Hiroshi asked as he sat down, unsure about this.

"They're at a reception at some other embassy. Argentina, or Chile, or I don't know where. Here, start with these." She pushed a plate toward him that held some salad with finely sliced oranges in it, and a slice of dark ham, and some sort of pink sauce.

It tasted unfamiliar but incredibly good. While he ate and ate—he couldn't get over how good the food tasted—he felt a nasty feeling creep up inside him that almost choked him, a feeling he'd never experienced before. Envy. Plain and simple envy that Charlotte got good things like this to eat every evening, while he didn't. He wanted so badly to be able to eat delicious food like this every day. And then he remembered that now he knew—he knew what to do so that everyone could be rich, including him. The thought calmed him down, and he began to feel happy and confident instead. He looked forward to seeing Charlotte's face when he explained it all to her.

"When you've had enough, we can head out to the swings," she broke in just as he was considering how he would tell her. "It's a beautiful day outside."

"Okay," said Hiroshi, pushing aside the empty plate and pulling the next one toward him, "but not until I've had enough."

He ate every bit of food. He couldn't help himself; it was that good. Afterward, he slumped in his swing and watched her swinging higher and higher. He tried to tell her his idea, but she was hardly listening, just kept on at him to join in and swing. She didn't even want to know how he thought it would work; she just said straightaway that it wouldn't, that not everybody could be rich.

He understood what she was thinking; until the day before he had thought the same way. But it didn't have to be that way. There was an answer, and he was just about to tell her what it was when he suddenly realized something that hadn't occurred to him until that very moment. His idea was simple. It was child's play. If he told her now, then she would tell someone else, maybe her father. And he would certainly tell someone else in turn, and then what? An ambassador can make his voice heard much more easily than some ten-year-old Japanese kid, and people would be more likely to believe the ambassador had thought it up. The idea would get out into the world, and nobody would ever know—or believe it if they found out—that it had been his idea first, that he had been the one to find the answer.

Hiroshi felt as though he had been struck by lightning. He knew now he would have to be the one to make his idea a reality. And that until he did, he would have to keep it quiet.

And it was strange . . . at the very moment he realized this, Charlotte suddenly seemed to become more interested. "How are you going to do that?" she asked as she swung back and forth ever faster, ever higher.

"I'm not telling you," Hiroshi shot back.

"Because you don't know. You're just showing off."

Hiroshi leaned back and flung his legs out in front of him to swing higher. She didn't have a clue. Nobody had a clue. He was the only one. "Just wait," he said and got ready to jump. Jumping from the swing—just letting go and flying through the air—was the best feeling there was.

And so he didn't mention his idea again, not that whole evening, particularly since Charlotte didn't ask again. But when it got dark and he went home, he let his mother scold him till she fell quiet and then he fetched his *Masters of the Universe* notebook from the tin. He finally knew what he would write in it.

5

The first thing Charlotte did when she found out was run to her room and put Valérie in the window. Then she ran straight down to the garden to the spot where Hiroshi would climb over the fence. The quarter hour until his head popped up over the wall lasted an eternity for her.

"Oh, here you are," he said, surprised to see her.

"We're going to the museum tomorrow," she told him excitedly. "And you absolutely have to come along!"

He frowned. "Which museum?"

"Seito-Jinjiya, the Island of the Saints. Tomorrow is the last day it's open this year, and Yumiko's taking me. My mother doesn't want to go. That means that you can come along."

Hiroshi hesitated. "I don't know. We're flying out to see my grandparents in two days. I don't know whether I can get away before then."

"That's in two days," Charlotte thought that Hiroshi was always much too cautious about things. He wanted to make everybody rich, but he couldn't go out to a museum. "Just be at the main gate at nine o'clock tomorrow morning."

Of course, he was standing there the next morning when she came through the gate with Yumiko. Charlotte had managed to persuade her mother to let them take the metro rather than a boring old limousine. Papa had taken her side and explained that Tokyo was really a very safe city, that nobody was going to kidnap Charlotte and Yumiko. He also said that because they were diplomats, they had an obligation to show they trusted the Japanese police to keep order.

How thrilling! Charlotte had never been on Tokyo public transit, nor had she ever been so far from home. All she knew of subway systems was the Paris metro. There had been talk of building a metro in Delhi as well, but the only form of public transit there had been some crummy-looking buses, and Charlotte had never wanted to take those. And now here was the subway station. It was called Hiroo Station, and it was much cleaner than the Paris metro. All along the platform there were yellow lines with textured bumps set into them where you had to stand and wait for the train—Yumiko was very strict about that.

A boxy, silver-gray train with red stripes pulled in and came to a stop. The doors opened by themselves, not like in Paris. Masses of people got off and on, and by the time they boarded there were no seats left.

"Hold on tight," Yumiko told them.

Some of the people who had seats were asleep, many of them slumped almost across their neighbors. When the train pulled into the next station, some of them sat up with a start, leapt to their feet, and left the carriage as though they did this every day of the week.

They had to transfer a couple of times before they resurfaced at ground level. They continued their journey on a green bus, whose seats were upholstered in some weird comic book–figure pattern. They had to get on at the back and take a ticket from a machine, then hold on to it carefully, because they would only pay when they got off at the other end. They rode the bus for a long time. At first it threaded its way through narrow little streets not so different from the ones around the embassy. Then they drove along a main road for a while. Eventually, gardens began to appear along the side of the road, then trees and even meadows.

At last they got off. They passed through a wooden gate guarded by two snarling lions carved from weathered gray stone. A set of very shallow steps led up the hill between bushes and trees to an open space, where lots of people were standing about as though at a festival. Then came the actual entrance, another gate, where they had to bow down deeply and go to a basin to wash with water: first the left hand, then the right, then rinse their mouths.

Charlotte was surprised to see the Island of the Saints itself was only a tiny part of the temple grounds. Beneath a sturdy roof held up by two rows of thick, wooden, almost-black pillars was a rectangular pond hardly bigger than her room at home. In the middle of the pond was an island covered entirely with fine, white gravel. From where they were standing, they could look out across the island to a part of the temple gardens that was not open to visitors, a landscape of mossy rocks, pale green bamboo, and tiny little trees bowed down as though before an unrelenting wind. It was an enchanted landscape, meticulously planned. If you squinted just a little, you could imagine you were a giant looking down onto a world empty of people.

The gravel on the island was raked into smooth curving lines, like waves of stone, rippling outward from a little altar that stood on this side of the island. It was made of some brown wood that looked worn and tired, maybe bamboo, perhaps hundreds of years old. Several objects lay on the altar, including a knife, notched, night black, gleaming dangerously. The sight of the knife took Charlotte's breath away.

"What's that?" she asked Yumiko.

Yumiko smiled indulgently. "It's the Island of the Saints. They say that it is the grave of two holy men who worked miracles here a thousand years ago—"

"No, I mean the knife!" Charlotte grabbed Yumiko's sleeve and dragged her over to a bulletin board that might explain what they were looking at—but it was only in Japanese. "Read it for me. What does it say about the knife?"

Yumiko studied the text. "Hmm. It's a dagger made of *kokuyoseki*. It belonged to the first emperor, Jimmu, and it was probably made three thousand years ago in Honshu."

Charlotte stared at the knife. "What's *kokuyoseki*?" She didn't know the Japanese word for obsidian, and she wouldn't have known the French word either.

"A special sort of stone, I think," Yumiko said hesitantly. "Like marble but black."

Charlotte looked at the knife and felt disappointed by the explanation. It was far too . . . small a story for this thing that held her gaze so hypnotically. From the moment she had seen the knife on the altar, she hadn't been able to take her eyes off it, hadn't been interested in anything else, had found herself coming back again and again to the only place in the whole temple that was really worth seeing.

She let the crowd carry her along but kept glancing back, thinking all the time about the stretch of water between the paved yard and the altar, about how wide the gap was, how deep it might be, whether she could perhaps wade across.

"What's the matter with you?" Hiroshi asked. She didn't reply. She didn't know how to explain it to him. Every time she looked back, it was as though the black knife were looking in turn at her—as though that gleaming knife on the other side of the water were a wild animal in a zoo.

At last she found her chance. Yumiko said she was going to the restrooms back by the gate and told Hiroshi and Charlotte to wait for her.

"Or we could wait by the island?" Charlotte suggested straightaway. "It's very pretty over there."

"Good, then; by the island," Yumiko said, agreeable as always, and hurried away.

Charlotte turned straight to Hiroshi. "Quick," she whispered. "Help me. I want to touch that knife!"

Hiroshi looked at her in astonishment. "What knife?"

"Come on!" Charlotte grabbed his hand and dragged him back to the front of the pond, where only a narrow strip of water separated them from the altar. Though there were plenty of visitors at the shrine that day, by some miracle there was nobody around right at that moment.

"Hold on tight," she ordered, reaching out her left hand to Hiroshi as she stepped up to the edge of the water. "Then I can lean forward and stretch."

Hiroshi did as he was told, holding fast to her left hand and bracing his feet against the lip of the paving stones by the pond. It was barely half an inch high. Charlotte inched her feet down the slope until the tips of her shoes were touching the water. Then she leaned forward, with Hiroshi anchoring her, and stretched out her right hand as far as she could. Her heart was pounding like a drum. She didn't know why she had to touch this knife, but she did. The temptation was incredible, hypnotic, and she leaned out toward the altar on Island of the Saints. But no matter how she strained, willing her arm to grow, no matter how far she stretched her fingers, she couldn't get close enough.

"Come on!" she groaned. "Let me farther down!"

Hiroshi was breathing hard as well, and his hold on her began to slip. "I don't know if it'll work. I can barely hold on to you."

Charlotte stared at the knife and at the inch or so between it and her fingers. "Come on!" she yelled. "Just a little more!"

Of course, Hiroshi's mother had begun to splutter and choke when he had told her he was going to the museum with Charlotte. "You see?" she said reproachfully. "She's already bossing you around."

Though Hiroshi had the feeling that was exactly what Charlotte had done, he answered, "No, she's not. She just wants me to come along. Because we're friends. She doesn't have anyone else in Tokyo."

His mother kept quiet, radiating disapproval.

"Anyway," said Hiroshi, "when I'm grown up, it will all be different. I know what I'm going to do when I'm big. I'll put an end to this difference between rich and poor. Everybody will be rich, and nobody will be able to boss anybody else around or look down on them."

His mother shook her head and sighed. "The things you say!"

"You'll see," said Hiroshi. More than ever, he was sure he was going to change the world, so it made no difference if he let Charlotte boss him around a little bit now.

Which is how he met Yumiko, the nanny Charlotte had been telling him about, for the first time the next day. Yumiko had sturdy, thick legs and waddled rather than walked, but she was the very embodiment of good cheer. She carried a black handbag with every imaginable necessity for a trip like this, and she could conjure up drinks, snacks, tissues, a city map, and all sorts of other things from its depths.

Charlotte was so excited that you would have thought they were going on a jungle expedition. Even the simple trip on the metro filled her with such delight that it was as though she had never been in a train in her life. When they had transferred to the bus in Akabane and could see the city all around—the endless blocks and buildings, the houses, streets, and roofs—she clung to the windowpane, pointing at everything and asking what such and such a building was.

At the shrine she put her hands on absolutely everything she could touch. Hiroshi watched, fascinated, as she ran her fingers over handrails, stone statues, and lanterns, her eyes half-closed, or traced the patterns in the wood carvings. Now and then she would lift her eyebrows in amazement as though she were watching a film play out in her mind's eye, a film only she could see.

"So?" he asked. "What can you see?"

She stopped where she was and looked into empty space for a long while, blinking in confusion. "I don't know," she admitted at last. "I don't understand everything. But it's . . . awesome!"

And then all of a sudden she had a bee in her bonnet about the black dagger lying on the altar with all the other bric-a-brac. She wanted to touch that knife and only the knife; not the carved horn combs, not the polished silver mirror or any of the amulets but the old stone knife.

Hiroshi had thought it would be easier than it actually turned out to be to hold her so she could lean over and touch it. Her fingers were almost touching the knife, but he could hardly keep hold of her other hand. He feared he might lose his balance at any moment and splash down into the pond along with her. But of course she wanted him to let her down just a little bit farther.

"All right then," Hiroshi said. He planted his right foot further down on the bank and tried to imagine he was He-Man or Clamp Champ or some other strongman from *Masters of the Universe*. He wouldn't let go, and he wouldn't lose his balance. No. He would hold on to Charlotte for as long as she wanted him to. But nobody must spot them, not any of the other visitors, and certainly not a Shinto priest.

As Hiroshi watched Charlotte's fingertips close the last half inch, he was sorry her face was turned away from him. He would have liked to see that thoughtful smile again when she finally managed to touch the knife.

But this time Charlotte didn't smile. Charlotte screamed.

The moment her fingers touched the dagger, she let out such a bone-chilling shriek that Hiroshi almost let go. He didn't, but since she went limp the next instant and tumbled forward, he couldn't stop her from slipping and falling into the water.

He didn't let go of her for even a second. He was seized by the terrible thought that the dagger might have been wired up to a current to protect it from being stolen. He yanked Charlotte out of the water, back onto the paving stones. She was shivering all over and her rib cage was heaving up and down like a bellows. But if the knife had been wired—and would that even work, Hiroshi wondered, since it was made of stone?—then he would have felt it, too, wouldn't he? He would have felt the shock as well, since he was holding on to her.

"Charlotte," he whispered. Scared, he shook her. "Say something! What is it?"

People were beginning to appear, startled by Charlotte's scream. They formed a circle around the children, bent down, and asked what had happened, why she had screamed like that.

"She fell in the water," Hiroshi answered helplessly. Then he added, "She slipped."

At last Yumiko turned up, and since she was practically immune to panic, things settled down very quickly.

"We can't leave you alone for five minutes, can we?" she said in a cheerful tone, and, producing a small towel from her bag, she dried Charlotte off as best she could.

Charlotte came round enough to be able to speak. "I want to go home," she whispered.

"We wouldn't do anything else," Yumiko said briskly. "You can't run around town like that, wet as you are."

It was an abrupt end to the day's trip. Luckily, a bus came along straightaway, since Charlotte was shivering violently and her teeth were chattering. There were plenty of free seats, but Yumiko had to spread out the towel before Charlotte could sit down. Yumiko didn't let the incident spoil her enjoyment of the day. She chattered away merrily about her childhood in this part of the city and all the times she and the neighborhood children had soaked one another with water from fountains, boating lakes, and rainwater barrels. She seemed not even to notice Hiroshi wasn't in the least bit interested, or that Charlotte was just staring blankly into space.

Then a woman boarded the bus who must have been an old acquaintance, since Yumiko called out a loud "Hello!" Maybe they had dunked one another in water as children. In any case, they started chatting away quite literally like long-lost friends and simply tuned Hiroshi and Charlotte out. At last. Hiroshi had hardly been able to contain his impatience.

He leaned over to Charlotte and asked softly, "What's wrong?"

It was a moment he would remember for the rest of his life. How she turned to face him; how she looked at him with eyes like windows to infinity, like the mouths of bottomless wells, like black holes. How, when she spoke, her voice sent goose bumps up and down his spine. She said, "It was so unbelievably old!"

What? Hiroshi wanted to ask. The knife? But he couldn't say a word. The sound of her voice had frozen every muscle in his body.

Charlotte didn't say another word all the rest of the way home. She just stared blankly ahead, letting them lead her by the hand. When they got back home, Hiroshi told her, "We're flying to Minamata tomorrow. For a week."

Charlotte nodded, but it didn't look as though she had really understood. Hiroshi watched as she and Yumiko walked through the main gate, then he went home himself. He had the nagging feeling he had done something wrong, though he couldn't for the life of him think what it might have been.

The next day they had to get up hideously early to catch their flight to Minamata. They were flying to see his grandparents, which Hiroshi wasn't looking forward to, and to celebrate the Bon festival, which he didn't really care about. What he liked was the flight itself.

But he didn't like getting up and getting dressed when he still fuzzy with sleep, or leaving the apartment block in the dead silence of the night as the streetlamps shone yellow above them. He could hardly believe there were cars driving around at that hour, even if there were only a few. Perhaps they were going to the airport as well. And he had never seen the metro so empty.

When at last they had boarded their flight, Hiroshi noticed for the first time that there was a section of the plane with larger seats than the rest, wider seats with more space around them, and that it was curtained off from the other passengers before takeoff.

"What's that?" he asked.

"First class," said his mother.

Their seats were quite close to the front, so Hiroshi could peer through a gap in the curtains and see the passengers up there being served larger trays with better food.

"That's how rich people travel," his mother explained. "First class is much, much more expensive than what we pay. For the same flight—just think about it—and it's not as if they arrive any quicker than the rest of us. It's sheer stupidity!" She shook her head in disapproval. "It's just because they're snobs. They can't bear the idea of sitting next to normal people for two hours."

At ten o'clock they landed in Kagoshima. From there they took the train to Minamata, where his grandparents were waiting for them at the station. Hiroshi was still so elated by the flight—by the sight of the huge clouds piled up around them and the tiny landscape down below—that he hardly noticed the obligatory greeting ritual, the kisses, and the talk of how much he had grown. Maybe it wouldn't be so bad this time around.

Dr. Suzuki joined them for dinner. He had been treating Aunt Kumiko for years and was practically one of the family by now. He drank a great deal of sake and never tired of telling anyone who would listen how wonderful it was that Aunt Kumiko had lasted so long, especially given how serious her poisoning was. Hiroshi huddled in his chair and concentrated on his food as the doctor talked and talked. He didn't want to hear any of it. He couldn't see anything wonderful about being sick for a whole lifetime, lying in bed incontinent, and screaming as though tormented by a thousand demons.

He shuddered at the thought that such a thing could even happen, that the smallest particles of matter in existence could do that to a human being. That Aunt Kumiko was the way she was because she had liked to eat fish so much, and there had been just a few more atoms of mercury in the fish than was good for her. Just a few of the wrong atoms in the wrong place could cause convulsions and make a person forget everything she had ever known. Could there be anything more dreadful? And there was nothing anyone could do about it. Atoms were too small even to see. He had read a great deal about it. You could inhale mercury without even noticing. And that wasn't the only atom that could be dangerous; there was a whole zoo of them—cadmium, plutonium, arsenic, sodium, chlorine, and many more.

The next day he swallowed his fears and went to Aunt Kumiko's room. She wasn't screaming any longer; she was just lying there, and as he stepped closer to her bed she did something she hadn't done for a very long time. She turned her head as though she wanted to look at him. But her gaze wandered away; perhaps it had just been a chance movement. Hiroshi stayed until the feeling of revulsion had passed, and he began to feel sorry for her.

Afterward, he crept out of the house and roamed the neighborhood, looking for the places where he had played on holiday as a little boy. The town had changed so much that he couldn't find most of the spots, and the ones he did find were no longer any good for games. A little stream where he and another boy had built a dam with mud from the bank had been filled in, and a supermarket stood right where it had been. It was a sad sight.

He thought of Charlotte and how she had screamed at the shrine. At that moment she had sounded the way Aunt Kumiko used to, just as terrified. Hiroshi used to feel his aunt was looking into a pit full of demons. That was how she had screamed, too. Hiroshi would have liked to have known what it meant. What Charlotte had seen when she had touched the obsidian dagger. Perhaps it wasn't even possible to explain something like that to another human being. Perhaps that was why she hadn't said anything. He was momentarily gripped with fear that Charlotte might end up like Aunt Kumiko. But he quickly thought of something else.

Over the next few days they were all very busy with the festival of the dead. As always, Hiroshi got the job of writing signs displaying the names of all the ancestors, the dead forebears they would remember. Plates were set out on every free surface in the house, and the women stood in the kitchen making dish after dish of all the treats the dead family members had liked best when they were alive—as far as anyone really remembered such things. Then they set the food out on the plates to welcome the spirits when they came. The whole house smelled of good things to eat, and they told a lot of stories, including quite a few Hiroshi had never heard before.

Then they went out to the street festival and watched the dances, which were meant to put the ancestor spirits in a good mood. On the last evening they went down to the river with everyone else and set little paper boats on the water with lanterns in them, then watched as the glimmering lights twirled and swirled together into one vast, twinkling pattern. It drifted slowly away and eventually vanished in the distance; tradition had it that this would help the wandering souls find their way back to the underworld.

Hiroshi tried to come up with a rough estimate of just how densely populated the underworld must be if it really did contain all the souls of all the human beings who had ever lived. The numbers he arrived at made him feel quite dizzy. Had anyone ever considered what might happen if those souls decided not to stay in the underworld any longer? What if one day the underworld were to fill up? But as far as he could see, nobody truly believed anymore that the souls of the dead were really there with them at the Bon festival. It was just a tradition, a chance for the family to get together.

"It's good that you're staying on a few days longer this time," Grandpa said the next morning.

Mother explained that there hadn't really been any choice.

"Oh, yes," Grandma chimed in. "Everything's always booked solid right around the Bon festival. "All of Japan is traveling.""

Everybody agreed it had been a good idea to stay on a few extra days. Hiroshi was the only one who couldn't wait to get back home, and he bit his lip rather than say anything of the kind.

By the time they got home, Charlotte was no longer there. Ambassador Malroux had been called away quite suddenly, they learned, and the whole family had simply packed their bags from one day to the next and left.

One day before. They had missed one another by the narrowest of margins.

Hiroshi stood there thunderstruck as his mother told him the news from the embassy. The previous ambassador, Bernard Beaucour, would be back next week. Jean-Arnaud Malroux had simply been standing in for him while he was ill. Charlotte was gone. And she hadn't even written him a good-bye letter.

"Now you see," Hiroshi's mother said with bitter satisfaction. "You were only ever a toy for her. That's what rich people are like."

Hiroshi told himself Charlotte wouldn't even have been able to write him a letter, since she didn't know how to write Japanese. He told himself that was the only reason, that it had just been a matter of bad luck. But it eventually dawned on him that Charlotte could have written him a letter in English. She had lived in India; of course she knew English. And she knew Hiroshi studied English in school, that he watched films in English, that even if he couldn't speak English very well, he could certainly read it.

In the end he had to admit that if Charlotte had really wanted to, she would have been able to leave him some message. But no message came. He would have to live with that.

"Who knows what all that was about," his mother said one evening when she was in a philosophical mood.

All the same, Hiroshi told himself, Charlotte had helped him toward his great idea. If it had been about anything, perhaps it had been about that. He would forget about Charlotte and concentrate completely on his idea so that one day, when he was grown up, he could make it reality. And since in order to do that he would have to have good grades, from that day onward he became a model student.

TRAVELS

One day when he was fourteen years old, Hiroshi came home from his after-school cybernetics study group to find a man sitting at the kitchen table. He was a Westerner, a big beefy man, somehow bloated, even ugly. He sat at the table with his legs crossed clumsily, and it looked as though he had been sitting there for some time talking with Mother all the while. And for some reason, Mother's eyes were damp.

"Hiroshi," she said quietly, "this is your father."

"For real?" Hiroshi replied, but in fact he knew the moment she said it that it was the truth. In that instant he remembered everything Charlotte had told him about his father—as well as how she had told him, how she had read the feelings from his penknife. In some way he couldn't explain to himself, he felt as though he had known this man forever even though he had never seen him before in his life.

All the same, it was a most peculiar situation. How do you behave around a father who you have always thought was dead? What do you do when all of a sudden he's sitting at the kitchen table, looking like a failed medical experiment?

Hiroshi shook his hand tentatively and said, "Hello, nice to meet you." For the first time he wished he had paid even half as much attention in English class as he always did in computer studies, physics, and all the other sciences.

His father explained in awkward, almost incomprehensible Japanese that he used to speak the language much better, but that unfortunately . . .

Then Mother broke in and said, "John, you can speak English to him. So that he finally understands why I always wanted him to learn it well."

So to everyone's relief, John Maynard Leak switched to his native language and told them what had happened in his life.

Turning to face Hiroshi, he explained that he had eventually recovered from the brain operation, though the doctors had not expected such a thing to be possible. For several years he had been completely helpless and required round-the-clock care. But then a committed physiotherapist had helped him regain enough independence that he could live on his own, well away from the family mansion, and he had hardly anything to do with his family these days. His father had died, and his brothers and sisters had insisted on buying him out so they could carry on the business on their own.

"I never wanted to have anything to do with the business anyway," he said, waving his hand dismissively and very nearly knocking a glass of water from the table. "They can worry about all that if they want and play at being billionaires, but I couldn't care less about any of it. They think they got a good deal, but I have everything I'll ever need, and if you ask me the deal was all in my favor."

He went on to tell them he was still undergoing treatment and on various medications, that he still had to do exercises with his therapist and so on, but despite all that he had been fit enough to travel to Japan. He was visibly proud of this, and when Hiroshi could see how happy his father was to have made it there to be with them, he felt the first spark of affection, felt how this big, clumsy man loved them. Hiroshi realized that the puffy features must be a side effect of the medication he was taking, knew the scars on his scalp were left over from that delicate brain operation. If he looked past all that, though, and made the effort, Hiroshi could recognize the man he knew from the old photographs.

"And so here I am," his father continued. He looked at Hiroshi's mother as though he were about to say something she hadn't heard yet either. "And I came to ask Hiroshi whether he wants to come to the US to get the best possible education."

Mother's face fell. "What's wrong with the school he's at here?"

Father shook his head gently. "I'm talking about what comes after that. He could go to MIT, to Stanford, to Yale, Caltech. . . . They're the best universities in the world."

Hiroshi was gasping for air and couldn't say a word. He felt as though he were standing in front of a door that was swinging wide open to show unimaginable vistas.

"Why?" his mother asked sharply. "There are some excellent universities in Japan as well, and Hiroshi could certainly get a spot at one of them if he took the trouble."

"He certainly could," his father said soothingly and folded his hands to show he meant no offense. "But look at it this way: I was never able to be there for my son. If I can at least help him go study, then all my money will finally have been good for something." He leaned forward. "And as I've said, I'd like it best of all if you could both join me."

Clearly they had already discussed this before Hiroshi came home, because his mother shot straight back, "No! How many times do I have to tell you? Once was quite enough for me."

"It won't be like it was back then. Nothing like it."

"I belong here. I didn't know it then, but I do now."

Only then did Hiroshi realize the curious thing about his father's sudden appearance. "Mother," he butted in, "how did he find us?"

Then Hiroshi learned that his father had hired a big international detective agency, and that it hadn't been hard to track them down. He also learned that the first thing his father had done with the address the agency gave him was to write a long letter. One of the things he had said in the letter was that his father—the man who had wanted to kill Hiroshi before he was even born—was dead. Mother had written a reply, sent him photos of Hiroshi, and told John all about him, about his hobbies and the grades he had been getting in school in the last few years.

"Why did you never tell me about this?" Hiroshi asked.

Mother sighed. "I didn't want you getting your hopes up. Let's see if he answers first, I thought, see if he's interested in you at all. I wanted to spare you the disappointment." She lifted her hands in a helpless gesture and let them fall. "Whoever would have thought he would just turn up here?"

There was a pause, a breathless, significant silence.

Then Hiroshi's father said, "Just think about it." He looked at his watch. "Time for me to go." He got up painfully, took a sheet of note-paper from his pocket, and gave it to Hiroshi's mother. "That's my telephone number at the hotel. Or I could come back again tomorrow."

Mother took the note but didn't say anything. Father stood there for a moment, undecided—a big man who made the apartment look even smaller than it really was—then left. They could hear his shuffling, cumbersome footsteps out on the stairs long after he had closed the door behind him.

It was a good thing the new school year began in April in Japan, but only after the summer holidays in the US, since it meant Hiroshi would have almost five months to get used to his new life.

Mother didn't cry as they said good-bye at the airport. All she said was, "It's a new time in your life now." In the end she had accepted the money Hiroshi's father had offered her and given up the job at the embassy. The first thing she wanted to do was go on a long trip to see the cherry blossoms in Hokkaido, then take a ship to Okinawa.

After that she might work for Mr. Inamoto in his office, where there would finally be a use for her knowledge of English. Time would tell.

"Inamoto's taking advantage of you," Hiroshi scolded her.

"I can't just sit around the house," his mother protested. "Especially not now that I'm all on my own."

Hiroshi's flight left at a little after three in the afternoon. It was by far the longest journey he had ever made in his life. For the first time he got to feel what people meant when they talked about jet lag. When they landed in Atlanta, he was woken from a deep slumber and felt it must be the middle of the night. He had to wait there four hours, battling his lack of sleep, before he continued on a tiny little plane to Alexandria, Louisiana, a short-hop flight of barely two hours. When they landed there, it seemed to him that it must be morning, but instead night was just falling.

His father was waiting for him beyond the customs gate and was visibly overjoyed. He talked on and on at Hiroshi, asking how the flight had been, whether there had been any trouble (well of course not; here he was, after all), how his mother would get on without him (he called her Miyu, which sounded strange to Hiroshi), and so on and so forth. When they left the terminal building, he nodded up at the huge neon sign on the roof and said, "I reckon they're just boasting when they call it Alexandria International Airport. There's not a single international flight starts from here. They don't even fly anywhere near the country's borders."

They climbed into a gigantic sedan, a Chevrolet about the size of a small boat. Hiroshi's father drove very slowly and carefully. Hiroshi found this reassuring at first, but then he noticed his father flinch as another car cut in front of them. Then he understood that his father wasn't actually a very good driver, no doubt because of the brain surgery. After that he didn't find it quite so reassuring.

They went to what looked like a really fancy restaurant, where Hiroshi was surprised to see the whole menu was nothing but hamburgers, absolutely enormous ones that were served on big plates, the top bun lifted off and set to one side. They helped themselves to ketchup, mayonnaise, and all kinds of other sauces he had never seen before, and then the idea was to put the whole thing together and eat it.

"High school doesn't start until fall," his father explained. "You'll have to have got used to all this by then."

"I know," Hiroshi said, staring at his glass. He had ordered a medium cola, which turned out to mean more than half a liter. There was certainly a great deal to get used to here.

His father lived in an unassuming but very roomy house in a quiet side street. The room he had gotten ready for Hiroshi was larger than the whole apartment in Tokyo; it was also the only room in the house that didn't have a single piece of Japanese furniture, not a single silk painting or rice-paper screen. Instead, the walls were covered with photos of cowboys breaking in wild broncos, of urban skylines, and a night launch of the space shuttle. One of the shelves held a blue-green baseball, a mitt, a bat, and a few more things that must have had something to do with sport, but what exactly Hiroshi couldn't begin to fathom.

"This is all to help you settle in," his father commented.

What took the most getting used to was the unusually soft bed. Hiroshi had slept on a futon his entire life and felt like he was going to sink into this wallowing mattress. When midnight had come and gone and he still hadn't got a wink of sleep, he climbed down onto the carpet with the bedcovers. There, he finally fell asleep, exhausted from the long flight.

Over the next few days, whenever they were out and about, Hiroshi tried to work out just what it was that was so new and strange about the town. It wasn't only the streets, which were so much wider than Tokyo's narrow alleyways, and it wasn't only that the people looked different. No, there was something else.

Hiroshi took a while to figure it out. He knew that Alexandria, Louisiana, was a big American city, but as he went around town, he had the sense he was in an oversized campsite. It wasn't that the buildings were on wheels (though he found out later there were some of those as well), but that they all looked terribly temporary, as though they had just been dropped down any which way in the landscape. As though nobody wanted to take the trouble to figure out where exactly the buildings should stand. As though a storm might come along at any moment that could sweep all the houses away and leave only the tarmacked streets behind so that the townsfolk could just build more houses.

He was also baffled to see that most of the time there was nothing to show where one property ended and another began, that the lawns simply flowed into one another from neighbor to neighbor. It was an astonishing sight for someone who had grown up in the middle of Tokyo, where it wasn't unusual to find that even if an apartment had a balcony, it would be easy to lean over the railing and touch the wall of the next building. Hiroshi also saw well-tended gardens with neat picket fences, but in the neighborhood where he and his father lived there was no such thing. Where he lived, people thought you had a garden if you had ploughed over the wild meadow grass and put down a lawn instead.

"This is a good neighborhood," his dad declared when Hiroshi told him one day about everything he had noticed. "Okay, so land is cheap. But our neighbors are fine people. I'd rather not spend my money on a house in some trendy district."

Dad didn't have a job. He still spent a great deal of time with doctors, and he was allowed to park in the handicapped parking spots. Other than that, he mostly collected books about ancient Japan. He occasionally got called in to advise a museum or a gallery somewhere in Louisiana or even farther afield when they were preparing an exhibition about Japan, maybe of the famous "floating world" woodcuts or the picture scrolls from the Heian period, or paintings from the Muromachi period. He kept the posters and catalogs for all the exhibitions he had been involved in and was always proud to point out when he was thanked by name.

He asked Hiroshi to help him work on his rudimentary knowledge of Japanese script. Many evenings they would sit together late into the night, hard at work with expensive brushes and vast sheets of paper. Hiroshi had never written with a brush before in his life, just with ballpoint pens like everybody else. When they worked together like this, Hiroshi noticed his father had trouble retaining new information, recognizing patterns, and learning unfamiliar movements. There was no other way to say it: Dad was clumsy. Awkward. But he was very involved with Hiroshi. He was interested in him in a way no Japanese father Hiroshi had ever seen or heard of was interested in his son. It was so unusual and such a good feeling that Hiroshi never tired of their evenings together.

All the same Hiroshi realized he was hardly a good teacher. He himself didn't understand many of the things his father wanted to know. When should they use kanji script, and when hiragana, and when katakana? Why write this word this way but not that one? He didn't know either; that was just the way it was. Force of habit. As soon as you tried to make a rule to explain it, you were guaranteed to run across an exception the next moment.

Hiroshi found the Roman alphabet to be much more logical. Asian writing was all about simplifying pictures down to their barest lines to stand for words, so that one picture might have nothing at all to do with the next, and they were so abstract that there was no hope of recognizing what they were supposed to be. By comparison, the Western method of building a word up from simple individual parts seemed a much better way of going about things.

He liked the way computers represented information even more. They could get by with just two states, which didn't even require any particular symbols. It could be 1 and 0, or on and off, or high and low—it made no difference. Not only was it the most basic system imaginable, but it had also proven itself to be the most powerful, since it could be used to represent absolutely everything—not just words, but sounds, images, films, and so on.

Hiroshi gradually got to know the neighbors on their street. Dad practically burst with joy every time he got to introduce him, saying, "This is my son." The funniest part was how hard he tried not to look as though he was bursting with joy—and how badly he failed.

One evening, as they were sitting there with their brushes, Hiroshi asked him why he had chosen this town in particular. What did Alexandria, Louisiana, have that other cities didn't?

Dad nodded thoughtfully and set the brush carefully aside. He had to think for a while before he answered. "After my operation," he began at last, "I wasn't good for much of anything. My dad called me 'the cauliflower' and the doctors had pretty much given up on me." He folded his hands in his lap and stared at a spot in the middle of the tabletop. "But there was one therapist who never gave up on me. She kept on coming. Day in, day out for a long, long time, until finally I began to show one or two signs of progress."

Hiroshi looked at him, his brush hanging motionless in his hand. "What kind of progress?"

"Progress like being able to say a word so that people could understand it, like closing my fingers around an object if she put it into the palm of my hand. That kind of progress."

"Oh," Hiroshi said, shocked.

Dad gave a crooked grin. "Actually, I only know that because she told me later. It took a while for my memory to come back, but bit by bit I put my life back together, thanks to her help. And just when I thought maybe I could get back on my feet, she came along and told me she was getting married and moving away and that she was all kinds of sorry."

"Oh," Hiroshi said again. "And then what?"

"I said, 'So where are you moving to?' 'Alexandria,' she said. 'That's where my fiancé works.' 'Good,' I said, 'then I'm moving to

Alexandria, too.'" He looked at Hiroshi and shrugged. "And that's why I'm here."

"But you must have been in pretty good shape if you could move to a new city like that," Hiroshi said.

"Oh no. I still needed nursing during my first two years here, and then a housekeeper for the next two years after that before I could live like this." He sighed, and it was a sound of deep contentment. "But it was the best thing I could have done. I'm so glad I got away from my family."

Hiroshi nodded and shuddered at the same time. "My mother told me what happened back then. The way your father . . ." And then he stopped speaking. For the first time he realized that old man had been his other grandfather.

He really didn't have much luck with grandparents.

"They're still dreadful people, the ones who are left," his father said. "I see them as little as I can. They think my brains aren't right, but let me tell you: they're the ones with no brains. My brothers and sisters have more money than they could ever spend in a lifetime, but whenever I'm visiting they spend the whole darn time complaining. There's always some company trying to pull a fast one on them, taking away their market, chipping away at their share price or I don't know what. The way they yell and holler and carry on, you'd think they were at war. But they're billionaires, all of them. Even if they've never had a happy day in their lives."

At that moment Hiroshi remembered his great idea. It was difficult to think of the people his dad was describing as his uncles and aunts—he'd never met them in his life—but from what he heard, his family sounded terribly afraid of losing their money someday.

Hiroshi spent a long time thinking about this. He finally came to the conclusion that they were afraid because there were so many poor people in the world. If everybody was rich, and if being rich was just the way things were, nobody would have any reason to worry about losing their wealth—they wouldn't even be able to imagine what that might mean. Being rich would be like breathing. There's enough air in the world for everybody to be able to breathe for a lifetime. Which is why most people never worry that there might not be enough air one day. If he managed to make everybody in the world rich, then all the fear and worry over money would vanish, along with all the unpleasant things that happened because of those fears.

Hiroshi understood English pretty well, in no small part because of all the time he had spent at the English-language movie theater and watching DVDs of American films. But his pronunciation was still awful. When his dad noticed Hiroshi hadn't made any improvements after a month, he declared, "We've gotta do something about this."

"I'll learn," Hiroshi objected. "Just give it time."

"If we give it time," his dad replied, "then your bad habits will just take root. I'm not going to let you go through life mangling every word you speak."

And so he dragged Hiroshi along to see the therapist who had brought him back to the land of the living. Her name was Sylvie, and she didn't look like half the miracle worker that his father had said she was. In fact, she was a fat little woman with washed-out brown hair and a great big hook nose. At first, she was just as flat-out against his father's idea as Hiroshi was himself. That wasn't her field of work, she said.

"Well, why don't you just go for a change of pace, Sylvie?" his father said, suddenly charming in a way Hiroshi wasn't used to.

So Hiroshi began to visit her four times a week and spent three-quarters of an hour—although it always seemed much, much longer than that—repeating nonsense syllables, letting her correct even the tiniest mispronunciation, singing English sentences out loud, coughing and gargling words in his throat, and shouting them at the top of his voice. It was astonishingly hard work, but he found the progress he made was just as astonishing. One day that summer he was at the city library and a librarian there said, "I bet you're from Seattle or somewhere near there. I've got an ear for that kind of thing."

"I'm from Seattle," Sylvie declared with a grin when he told her about it. "I guess that means we can stop now."

Dad wanted to know what he had told the librarian in reply.

"I almost said yes," he admitted, "but then I couldn't bring myself to say it."

"That's good," said Dad. "You don't need to deny your roots."

When Hiroshi finally started high school, he saw his father had been right to insist on a clear accent. Americans seemed to be a colorful mix of every nation in the world—although nearly half of the kids at his school were white, there were just as many who were black or Asian so that Hiroshi didn't stand out a bit. Because pretty nearly everybody looked different, the teasing and name-calling was instead based on the way they spoke. The ones who suffered most were the children from those Mexican immigrant families whose English was rudimentary.

The classes themselves weren't particularly hard, and that was putting it mildly. In fact, Hiroshi would have had to make a conscious effort to get a *bad* grade. So, from the very start he ranked among the best students. The only subject where he was below average was sports. First, because he had never enjoyed sports, and second, because he was still smaller and weaker than most of the other boys. Sure, he was tough, but he wasn't strong. He ran slower than the others, he was always the first to knock the bar off on the high jump, and he never even bothered to wonder whether he would be picked for the football team. None of that mattered, however, since Hiroshi Kato turned out to be the best baseball catcher Alexandria High School had ever had. He caught every single ball thrown by every single pitcher during the whole four years he was there, and he never dropped a catch.

Hiroshi had always had good reflexes, and of course his father had spent hours on end throwing him balls that summer. American dads did that sort of thing with their sons. But the balls his dad threw were really no challenge, and they certainly didn't count as training. No, what nobody at school ever found out was that Hiroshi had cobbled together a computer-guided pitching machine that could throw him two hundred balls in a row at every conceivable curve and speed. He practiced and practiced with the machine until he could tell instantly how any ball would fly. By the end of the summer, he could run through the stock of balls five times in an evening and not let a single one through to the net behind him.

However, he never got to be any good at the moments of direct physical confrontation, such as when he had to block home plate. And he was always too slow to react when there was a rundown to tag. And when it was his turn to run, he couldn't even make first base. So although the coach was full of praise for Hiroshi, he always tagged on a stern warning that it was no good harboring dreams of going professional. Hiroshi earnestly reassured him there was nothing he wanted to do less.

Though Hiroshi wasn't unpopular at school—despite his outstandingly good grades—he didn't make any close friends either and was only rarely invited to weekend parties. As for girlfriends, Hiroshi may well have been the one boy in school who was less interested in the girls than they were in him. He hardly looked at them.

Even before high school had begun, Hiroshi had felt less and less happy about his room at home. In the end, he asked his father's permission to take a few things out.

"Do what you like," Dad said right away. "It's your room."

So Hiroshi took down all the photos, put the sports gear, complete with the shelf, down into the cellar, and got to work scraping away the floral wallpaper. His father helped him, and then they repapered the whole room with a simple design and painted it over in white. His father asked him why he liked it better that way.

"I don't know," Hiroshi admitted, thinking it over. "I think I'm just not as American as the room was before."

His father needed no further encouragement to teach him everything he knew about Japanese culture. Hiroshi was amazed to learn more about Japan from his American father than he ever had in all his years at school in Tokyo.

One day Hiroshi mentioned to his father that another student had teased him he would likely commit hara-kiri if he ever flunked a test, and his father replied that hara-kiri wasn't even a word the Japanese traditionally used. It had been invented by the British, he explained, who had just translated the term "belly cut" and meant it as an insult. It was a way of disparaging the ritual suicide of a samurai.

"The correct word is seppuku," he said. "A samurai who had lost face by neglecting his duties could restore his family honor by committing seppuku correctly."

He fetched down some books and catalogs from the shelves and showed Hiroshi what the *tantō* looked like, a slightly curved dagger with one sharp edge, about a foot long, and showed him how it was different from the *wakizashi*, a short sword about twice that length. That was the dagger that would have been used for the seppuku ritual, he told his son. "The warrior would wear a white kimono as a sign of purity and would write a death poem before he carried out the ritual. They called a poem like that *jisei no ku*."

Hiroshi was simultaneously fascinated and horrified as he listened to his father's explanation. It was strange that his dad was the one to explain all this to him. Sure, he had heard something about it at school in Tokyo, but only ever as a subject for dumb jokes.

"Then he sits *seiza*—you know what that means, right?"

Hiroshi nodded. "Sure. It's just the normal way of sitting on the floor."

"Well yes. Normal in Japan. We Westerners think that sitting on a chair is normal." They both sat down on the floor, the soles of their feet tucked underneath them, toes touching. "Then the man bares his torso. He takes up the knife and stabs it into what they called the scarlet field, the *tanden*. It's about two inches under the navel and it's supposed to be the center of the human body, the place where the soul resides. He cuts his belly left to right, with one final cut upward so that the organs tumble out. What generally happens is it cuts through a major blood vessel, the abdominal aorta, which causes his blood pressure to drop right away, and he loses consciousness pretty quick. That's important, because the most important thing for correct seppuku is that the samurai mustn't flinch or groan, not even let the pain show on his face. He mustn't show any fear either, of course. You mustn't be able to see any sign of pain on the dead man or it doesn't count as seppuku."

Hiroshi pondered all this. "Sounds to me like a hell of a mess."

His dad smiled at that. "You could certainly say that. If the seppuku was performed inside a building—which didn't usually happen—they used special tatami mats with white braid. They had to be thrown away afterward, of course."

They had agreed from the start that Hiroshi would fly back to Tokyo once a year to visit his mother, who had by this time taken the job in Inamoto's office. She looked after the Australian side of his business, supplying Japanese groceries to the stores there. Inamoto didn't curse quite so much as he once had—he was getting old, Mother declared—but he still paid her next to nothing. Hiroshi's mother didn't much care about that, since she didn't need the money. By the look of it there was no new man in her life. She had women friends, though, and now and then they would all go on little trips together, and once a week they met to play cards or *renju*.

It was strange for Hiroshi to come back to Tokyo and realize he now felt more at home in Alexandria than he did here. The streets and alleys in the neighborhood seemed to have grown even narrower, and in the tiny apartments he felt like a rooster crammed into a too-small hutch. But it was a son's duty to visit his mother, so he did.

During his senior year at high school, Aunt Kumiko died. Hiroshi flew back to Japan two months earlier than usual, not to Tokyo but directly to Minamata for the funeral. After the ceremony everyone agreed it had been a merciful release for Aunt Kumiko. Even Dr. Suzuki said as much.

"You don't have to visit me just out of a sense of duty," his mother said before he flew back. "Children leave sooner or later; that's just the way it is. It's enough if you call from time to time or write me a letter so that I know how you are. Come back when you feel you really need to."

"Okay," said Hiroshi.

It was to be his last visit for many years.

When he got back to Alexandria, an envelope bearing the crest of the Massachusetts Institute of Technology was waiting for him. The typewritten letter inside said the admissions office had considered his application and granted him a spot.

THE ISLE
OF THE BLESSED

1

"What am I supposed to do there?" Hiroshi asked.

Rodney flung up his hands. "What you do at a party! Have fun. Meet people. Have a good time."

"I meet people every day. And I have fun, too." Hiroshi peered at the computer screen. "Most of the time." Except, for instance, when boring stuff got in the way, like this totally lame assignment paper on a totally dumb topic.

"It's the party of parties. It's the event of the year. It's the inauguration of the new Phi Beta Kappa frat house. You just gotta be there."

"Who says I gotta?" Hiroshi muttered, irritated. Outside the window an enormous garbage truck was trying to turn around, but the parking lot was chock-full of cars as always. It had been maneuvering for about ten minutes, a few centimeters this way, and then a few centimeters back again.

Maybe, Hiroshi reflected, he should have been thinking inch by inch. But he didn't want to have anything more to do with those antiquated American units than he needed to for everyday life.

"They say there's gonna be a whole load of VIPs there, famous Phi Beta Kappa brothers," Rodney said, resuming his argument. "President Bush, President Clinton . . ."

"Wow," said Hiroshi, audibly unimpressed.

"In any case, we've got to get tickets now before they're gone."

"You need tickets? What kind of crazy party is this?"

The garbage truck had backed into a tree, one of the long-suffering birches that stood along the sidewalk. A faint smell of garbage began to drift in through the open window. A man climbed out of the passenger seat to guide the driver.

Rodney sat down on the desk so that Hiroshi had to look at him. "Just listen, man. You're young, I'm young, we're in college, for crying out loud. When we're a pair of old crocks, we'll look back on these days with tears in our eyes. And going to a party now and then is all part of the deal, you get me? Goofing off. Smoking a joint while the girls hold their titties under your nose . . ."

Hiroshi peered past his roommate. The garbage guy down there was beginning to sweat.

All caught up in his talk of the party, Rodney was getting worked up, too. "I'm not saying you've gotta get so drunk you wake up in the gutter the next day," he conceded. "Or next to some girl you've never seen before in your life, or some guy, God forbid . . . you don't have to go smashing things, crashing cars, or whatever. You've just gotta come along and have a good time for once."

Those guys down in the parking lot weren't going to make it. If they had any eye for geometry, they would have realized what they were trying to do was flat-out impossible, since someone had come along after they arrived and parked in the worst possible place.

"Speaking of cars, you should go down there," Hiroshi said, pointing out the window. "Stop them from smashing into yours. You blocked them in."

"Oh shit!" Rodney raced off like greased lightning, and Hiroshi turned back to the totally lame assignment paper and its totally dumb topic.

The assignment was about the effects of robots on automated production processes, with a view to its effect on social systems. Hiroshi knew clear as day what kind of arguments Prof. DeLouche wanted to read: that robots took away people's jobs, and the companies who used them should have to contribute to the social safety net in return. And since he was so sure that was what the prof wanted, Hiroshi set out to argue exactly the opposite. Robots damn well should take away people's jobs. That's what they were invented for, that's what they were built for, and using them for that purpose was socially beneficial in itself. Think, for instance, of a worker who spends eight hours a day feeding sheet metal into a hydraulic press, the same repetitive motion hour after hour, bored beyond words and in constant danger of having his hands crushed. Nobody had the right to tell him his quality of life would be lessened if a robot did the work instead. A robot could repeat the motion twenty-four hours a day and never get bored, never make a mistake. Of course, Hiroshi would raise hackles with that, but he was well accustomed to that.

He watched Rodney talking with the garbage guys, waving his hands, obviously making a joke, since they laughed instead of getting sore at him. Rodney could do that sort of thing, could win people over. Hiroshi would never understand how he managed to do that.

They had met at orientation. As freshmen, the two of them had started off sharing a room in Baker House, where everybody was crazy for architecture and design, and traditions were meticulously observed. One of these was to throw a piano from the roof every year, toward the end of April. They had agreed this was not their kind of thing, and when the chance came up the following year to get neighboring singles in MacGregor House, they had grabbed it. The rooms didn't have breathtaking views over the Charles River the way the brochures always showed; instead, they faced Briggs Field, a rather unprepossessing sports field behind the dorms that lined the riverbank. Hiroshi's room looked onto nothing grander than the parking lot and the access way.

Hiroshi could live with that, though, since when he was occupied with a problem, he shut out the world around him entirely. And he was often occupied.

"Okay, so really," said Rodney, picking up where he had left off just as soon as he came back into the room, "we don't even need to discuss it. I absolutely have to go to this party, and you would be a real buddy if you came with me." He grinned, baring his teeth. "Look at it like an offer you can't refuse."

Hiroshi leaned back, rubbing the bridge of his nose with the palms of both hands. "Which brings me right back to my original question: What am I supposed to do there? You expect me to turn into some sort of party animal? If that's what you expect, you're dreaming."

"I can tell you what you're supposed to do. You're supposed to introduce me to Prof. Bernstein."

Hiroshi blinked. "This is getting weirder. First we have to buy tickets, then there are going to be professors there. Are you sure this is even a party?"

Rodney's expression softened into one of infinite patience and understanding. "That's how these parties work. First, the older brothers sit around all civilized in their jackets and ties, and they have fireside chats on academic topics and all that stuff. Then, when the old guys get up and leave, the fun starts."

"That's when everybody flips out, you mean. And who in the world is Prof. Bernstein?"

Rodney counted off on his fingers. "First, he's professor of mathematics at Harvard, and I happen to know that he was very taken by your paper on automaton theory."

Hiroshi shrugged, unimpressed. "And?"

"Second, he's the brother of Dr. Rachel Warden." Dr. Warden was teaching a requirement course for Rodney's major, and he had to write a term paper for her.

"And third?"

"Third, he's a dyed-in-the-wool *Star Trek* fan."

Hiroshi finally understood. He rolled his eyes and shoved off from the desk with both hands, scooting halfway across the room on his chair. "Rod!" he yelled. "Not again! When are you going to understand that they will never in your life let you—"

"Why not?" Rodney interrupted, stung. "The Drake equation clearly shows there has to be intelligent life out there somewhere, so—"

"The Drake equation!" Hiroshi shook his head. "It doesn't prove a thing. Not one single variable in the whole equation is even close to being defined. You can use that equation to calculate a universe that's empty or bursting at the seams."

"Yes, I know. By the way, it would be great if you could think up some new counterarguments sometime. I might actually get somewhere."

"If I think of something, you'll be the first to know. Honest Injun."

Rodney began to pace up and down the room as though he were in the lecture hall discussing the matter with at least half a dozen Nobel Prize winners. "Nevertheless, if you set the variables for the Drake equation anywhere but at the very lowest limits, then we are forced to conclude a great many alien species out there are about as intelligent as humankind. Which raises the question—"

"Of why we can't even catch an alien TV signal. I know." Hiroshi nodded. This was Rodney's favorite topic—and that was being kind, since it could equally be called his obsession: why, if there was intelligent life out in the universe, nobody on Earth had ever detected it.

"Exactly. And *Star Trek* offers what you might call a popular, accessible literary metaphor here, with that famous Prime Directive that bans interference in the affairs of other species. The argument would be that we're under some kind of quarantine, because we're not yet a fully developed civilization, which is logical enough, since compared with any technological civilization that came to find us via interstellar space travel, we couldn't be. So they're protecting us. They're a more developed civilization, technically and ethically, and they don't want us to be overwhelmed."

"That's not proof, that's tautology. It's pretty near the textbook definition of a fallacy from any seminar in logic."

Rodney made a face. "Hey, I'm not looking to win the Nobel Prize here. I just think it might be fun to write my master's thesis about it, okay?"

Hiroshi crossed his arms. "Right, let me just sum up to make sure that I've understood it right. You want me to introduce you to this Prof. Bernstein—"

"No, no. I want to introduce you to him. Then you talk to him awhile, let the guy tell you how good your paper was, and so on, and then you bring me back into the conversation."

"And I tell him you want to write a thesis in astronomy on the Starfleet Prime Directive. And then you think he'll get so carried away by the idea that he'll threaten never to speak to his sister again if she doesn't let you."

"Something like that."

"You are completely out of your mind."

"You're the one who should know."

Hiroshi folded his hands across his stomach, then sighed and said with resignation, "All right then. What do I care? Let's go to this party."

Rodney's grin spread across his entire face. "You're always a tough nut to crack."

"And a good thing, too," Hiroshi replied, rolling his chair back to the desk.

As he left, Rodney asked, "Should I get a ticket for Dorothy? She called you this morning by the way, something about taking a trip."

"I know." Hiroshi massaged his temples and tried to remember some argument about the totally lame assignment on the totally dumb topic that had flashed through his head while they were talking. "She left me a message on the answering machine just before you came in."

"And? Three tickets?"

Hiroshi turned in his chair. "Is this the kind of party where it's a good idea to take your girlfriend along?"

"To tell you the truth," Rodney said with a grin, "it's not."

"Then get two tickets."

James Michael Bennett III saw the ball go out, throwing up a cloud of red dust on the other side of the white line. Everybody saw it but the umpire, who would brook no discussion. And with that the match was decided. They had lost.

"This is bullshit," Todd said in disgust. He was Bennett's partner, and he was on the verge of smashing his racket on the ground in frustration. "The guy must be going blind!"

"You can say that again," Bennett agreed, "but not until we're off the court."

"JB, that ball was out. If he had seen it and called it, we could have swung the game back."

Bennett wiped the sweat from his forehead. "But he didn't call it. And the umpire's decision is final; that's the rules."

Todd snorted. He was so red in the face it looked like he might burst at any moment. "JB, your dad counts for something in this club. Can't you make them fire the umpire?"

Bennett looked him straight in the eye. "Todd, those are the rules. If you don't want to play by the rules, then don't play. What's winning worth if you don't win by the rules? Nothing."

That gave Todd something to think about. It even seemed to impress him for some reason. He muttered, "Okay, okay," as the two of them walked to the net and shook hands with the winning pair.

"Next time we'll wipe the floor with you," Bennett promised, smiling grimly.

The other two laughed back, as though he was joking. But he wasn't. James Michael Bennett III truly believed that he and Todd would win in the end. After all, one of the other two players was black.

The changing room was full of steam and smelled of cologne and shower gel, like the men's perfume department at an expensive department store. While they stood under the shower, Todd asked if Bennett was planning to attend the Phi Beta Kappa inauguration on Saturday.

"I'm not going to the same party as my girlfriend, man!" Bennett closed his eyes and stood faceup under the warm shower, trying not to think too hard about the party he would go to instead. That one would be in the Epsilon Omega frat house and wouldn't be a big party at all. But it promised to be really wild. Above all, there would be a whole lot of fresh women there. If he came home without having hooked up at least twice, he was doing something wrong. So he'd better not think about it in too much detail, or he'd get a hard-on right then and there under the shower.

He took his time getting dressed. He was in no hurry and spent a while rubbing himself down, stark-naked and well aware he looked great. He knew many of the guys were casting envious sideways glances at him, and he enjoyed that thought.

There was a clash of metal as crazy Lester leapt up from the other side of the lockers, perched up above him, and called down, "Hey, JB, what are these rumors? You're really gonna disappoint all those women?"

Bennett looked up, amused. "What's that?"

Lester hollered out, "They say that the bridges of Boston are lined with desperate women ready to throw themselves in the river." He was suddenly the center of attention, with all eyes upon him. "It must be serious," Lester carried on. "Reliable sources are even using the dreaded word . . ." Loud enough for everyone to hear, he stage-whispered, "Engaged!"

"Hey, not so fast." Bennett leaned over for his towel and tied it around his waist in a leisurely fashion. "You know my motto. You can't fuck every woman in the world . . ."

Lester sat up straight on top of the lockers and drummed with the heels of his hands. "Everybody together now!" he crowed.

And a chorus of male voices chimed in to finish James Michael Bennett's sentence: "But that's no reason not to try!"

It was a hell of a sound. Once again Bennett was the hero of the day.

"Is that true?" Todd asked as they crossed the parking lot. "You're getting engaged?"

Bennett stopped in front of his Jaguar. "Why not?" he said, grinning and throwing his kit bag onto the backseat. "She'll just have to get used to the idea that when kings married, they always kept their mistresses."

Dorothy Golding was relieved when they had finally parked the car and were walking across the meadow filled with the scent of summer flowers, headed for a little wood. She was carrying the picnic basket, and Hiroshi had the blanket. Hiroshi, the city boy, who could hardly ever be persuaded to go anywhere near the great outdoors. But she had managed it.

Dorothy had put a great deal of work into this little trip. It had not been easy to find this romantic little hideaway, nor to make it seem as though they had ended up there quite by chance. Using her best recipes, she had made sandwiches, a noodle salad, and a potato salad, and she had packed Hiroshi's favorite mascarpone dessert in little plastic-lidded pots she had bought just for that purpose.

"Do you like it?" she asked when they were finally sitting in the dappled shade with the vast meadow spread out before them and the branches of the tree sighing above.

"I like it," Hiroshi replied, smacking his lips. "It tastes great."

She looked at him dubiously. He had come along, but as was so often the case, she had the feeling he was not really there, that he was somewhere off in the world of his thoughts. And this was such a beautiful spot. It would have been a beautiful place to say romantic things to one another. Things like "I love you," for instance. It would even be a pretty good place to propose . . . not that she was expecting anything like that. She would have to put a great deal more work into it before Hiroshi was ready for that. But if only he could keep his thoughts here, with her . . .

After the picnic, they lay on the ground, lazy and sated, blinking up into the almost-cloudless sky without speaking. Dorothy waited, thinking of the hours she had spent in the kitchen. She wanted to spend the rest of her life looking after Hiroshi, raising his kids, keeping house. She wanted to be a good wife to him and his lover. Hiroshi would go far, anyone could see that; he would make good money, and they could have such a wonderful life together and all that went with it.

Hiroshi propped himself up on one elbow and looked at her. He smiled. "It's nice here," he said, clearly happy.

Dorothy smiled back but said nothing. Maybe he was getting ready to say something—something important.

Hiroshi turned over onto his stomach and ran his fingers through the grass. "Take a look at this," he said.

She turned over, too, and came closer to him. He was pointing at a single ant that was trying to haul along a pine needle at least five times its own length.

"Hey, look indeed," she said. "Making a real go of it, isn't he?"

"It must have gotten lost." Hiroshi lowered his head for a better view. "It's incredible, don't you think? Tiny little body. Mandible, antennae, legs. And it can shift a load like that."

"How about that," Dorothy said. "Nature is full of wonders, if you only look at what's right in front of you." It could do no harm for him to learn that.

Hiroshi sunk down farther, resting his chin on his folded hands. "One ant like this all on its own can't do a thing," he said thoughtfully. "What counts is working with the others. Swarm intelligence."

Dorothy listened to him on tenterhooks. Was he about to conclude that life was better lived together than all alone?

"Basically, it's a tiny mechanism," Hiroshi went on. "A tiny, simple mechanism. Barely any brain to speak of. You could even build something like it. Not quite so small, but you could do it. What's the difference between an ant and a robot? I can't see any."

Dorothy turned away, disappointed. Robots! That was all Hiroshi ever thought about.

"Hey!" she said, shoving her toes against his leg. "I'm here, too, you know. And I'm no robot!"

He looked at her in surprise, then laughed like a big kid. "True, you're not." He forgot about the ant, turned round, and laid his head on her lap.

"I want to ask you something," he said, a serious tone in his voice.

"Ask away."

"Have you ever had sex outside?"

Dorothy gave a quiet sigh. Was that why he stayed with her? Sex? Probably.

"No," she admitted. "Never."

Hiroshi buried his face between her breasts for a moment, then kissed her, and said, "Wouldn't you like to try it?" He looked around. "I figure nobody could see us. What do you think?"

Dorothy's plans had taken this eventuality into account. When picking the spot, she had made quite sure they couldn't be seen from the road and that there were no hikers' trails nearby, nothing that could cause a hasty interruption. And she had packed condoms just in case.

Even so, she said, "I'm not sure about this."

She was playing coy so that he at least had to make the effort to talk her round. She had to be worth that much to him. If he persisted, she would go along with it—she had made up her mind about that before they had even left the car. It would probably be great. Hiroshi was not a bad lover, and if he was anything, he was persistent. He could practically have invented persistence.

The seminar room where twenty-five students sat waiting for Prof. DeLouche was as white and clean as a laboratory and smelled of disinfectant. It was about as cozy as an operating theater. The only trace of character was the faint rattle from the air-conditioning unit, a constant background irritation.

Hiroshi's cell phone chimed softly. It was a text from Dorothy. "Just thinking about our trip yesterday. WOW!"

Hiroshi smiled. Some kind of bug had bitten him on the backside, and on the way home they had to stop the car so he could pick two dozen ants out of Dorothy's hair. Despite all that, making love under the tree had been sensational.

"Yes," he texted back. "We should do it again soon."

Just as he sent the message, one of his classmates leaned over. Red hair, pimples—Patrick or some name like that.

"Hey," he whispered, "I heard someone say you invented the Wizard's Wand. You know, that doohickey that's on sale in all the DIY stores. Is that true?"

Hiroshi nodded. "Yup." He had invented it right around the end of his first year at MIT. It was nothing special; the whole gadget was nothing more than two digital cameras with fish-eye lenses fixed a certain distance apart. It took 3-D pictures with true perspective that could then be processed and manipulated. The only tricky feature had been the visual-recognition software. That had taken him a couple of weeks of all-night coding sessions. Once he'd cracked that, though, it worked just as he'd planned. All you had to do was hold it up, press the button two or three times, and then hook it up to your computer by USB—then, presto, you had a precision 3-D model of your surroundings, including any furniture, in its exact dimensions and positions. You could then load that model into any CAD program at all.

"That's crazy," said Patrick or whatever his name was. "My pa's company makes furniture and interiors. He has two dozen of those things and he says they're the greatest thing since sliced bread."

"Sliced bread?" Hiroshi had to laugh. "That's the first time I've ever heard that."

The university had helped him patent his invention and sell the license to a manufacturer. Ever since then, he could pay his own tuition fees and other expenses without any help from his father.

"How did you get an idea like that?" asked Patrick-or-whatever.

Hiroshi shrugged. "A simple application of existing robot technology—optical sensors and spatial recognition. Oh yeah, and I'd just done repapering my room, and I hated having to measure all the walls." His phone chimed again. "Uh, excuse me."

"Sure." Patrick-or-whatever ducked out of sight.

It was Dorothy again. "Jane+Boris want us to come over Sat night." Hiroshi made a wry face. Jane was a high school friend of Dorothy's, and Boris, her boyfriend, was a total bore and an investment banker as well. On top of which, Rodney wanted to drag him along to that party on Saturday night.

"No time Saturday," he replied. Then he thought of their trip, and the way the sunlight and shadows had played across her breasts, and he added, "Sorry!"

This time he switched the phone off after he had sent the message. Not a moment too soon, since Prof. DeLouche walked into the room right then and the seminar on "Cybernetics and Society" began. It fulfilled the interdisciplinary requirement for his course load, and Hiroshi had to grant that it had been a good idea to make it a requirement, since otherwise nobody in the room would have wasted their time on it.

DeLouche didn't look like a typical university professor. He was built like a lumberjack, had a gray goatee, and wore thin-rimmed glasses to give him the necessary intellectual flourish. He had long fingers and hair right down his knuckles, which Hiroshi thought was gross.

Today's seminar was going to be devoted to the assignment papers they had mailed in, and judging from the way DeLouche's eyes lit up when he spotted Hiroshi, it was mostly going to be about his paper. DeLouche sat down on the edge of the desk as he always did, weighed the printouts of the assignments in his hand, glanced around the class once, and then said, "Let's start with the really very interesting paper that Mr. Kato turned in. There's a lot to talk about here, like the way he thinks it would be a good thing if robots put us all out of work."

He stared straight at Hiroshi with an acid gaze.

"Sure I do," Hiroshi replied. "It's the declared purpose of all technological development."

There was an audible gasp from the other twenty-four students in the room. Nobody had ever challenged Prof. DeLouche like that.

"That's fascinating," DeLouche said with a dangerous note of sarcasm in his voice. "Would you be so kind as to explain in a little more detail?"

Hiroshi shrugged, unconcerned. "I think it's obvious. Since the Industrial Revolution—at the very latest—the point has been to identify routines in the work we do, isolate these as processes, perfect them, and then hand them over to machines. When a machine can do a certain job as well as a human being or better, it's not worth a human's time. So humans shouldn't have to do it."

"And what would you say to someone who lost his job because of such reasoning?"

"I'd tell him to go find another job," Hiroshi answered dryly.

DeLouche smiled like a shark. "Oh yes? But by your logic, there will be fewer and fewer jobs as time goes on."

"There'll be new jobs. One hundred years ago, one-third of the population was employed in agriculture; today it's only three percent. That doesn't mean we have hordes of unemployed farmers."

"That's a good argument," DeLouche said with a note of triumph in his voice, just like always when he figured he was about to deliver the knockout blow. "But how does it help a worker who has been replaced by a robot and is out on the street looking for work now?"

It was so quiet in the room that they could hear the humming of the clinical white light fittings up on the ceiling. And of course the air-con with its interminable *tak-a-tak-tak-a*.

"To be precise," Hiroshi said thoughtfully, "he doesn't need a job. He needs money. Or speaking more generally, he needs some way to acquire the necessities of living. That's where the real problem lies."

"Which brings us to the social security system," DeLouche responded, peering at Hiroshi over the rim of his glasses. "Can you actually believe that some people like to work? That they see their job as part of who they are? Not just as a way to earn a living?"

"Sure, I would believe that you do," replied Hiroshi, his face impassive, "but my mother was a laundress. She spent years washing, drying, and ironing towels and tablecloths and acres of clothes, day in and day out. She didn't see that work as being any part of who she is. And as soon as she had the chance, she quit."

DeLouche blinked in exasperation. He was losing ground and he knew it. And he clearly disliked it. "Your mother had the choice. A factory worker doesn't have that choice. Don't you think that's a decisive difference?"

Hiroshi took a deep breath. "No, I don't," he replied, not budging one inch. "Here's an example. Before the computer was an invention, it was actually the name of a job that people did. A computer was a kind of clerk, and there were whole halls full of them in the banks and insurance companies, sitting there all day long doing nothing but add up columns of figures by hand. Then after that their sums would be checked all over again by another department to be sure there were no mistakes. By your reasoning, we would actually be better off if those jobs still existed. Which is where I disagree. If we define work as whatever we wouldn't do if we didn't have to, then a work-free society is actually the great goal and vision of all techno-logical development. We're aiming for a world where everybody only has to do what they want."

The others were impressed. Some of them even nodded imper-ceptibly. DeLouche knew he wasn't going to win this one and would do better to bring the discussion to an end.

"An interesting viewpoint," he conceded between gritted teeth, "but I'm afraid we'll have to leave it at that so that we can give all the other papers the time they deserve."

For the rest of the seminar, he didn't once invite Hiroshi to speak. There was no question, however, that when grades were assigned he would make sure Hiroshi remembered this discussion.

The three of them sat in the venerable Loker Reading Room of the venerable Widener Library, leafing listlessly through their books. Not for the first time, Bennett reflected that it may not have been such a great idea to major in anthropology. For some reason he had imagined it would be exciting, but in fact it was dry as dust, and their prof was a dried-up old biddy. Not only was she utterly unresponsive to his charms, she also seemed entirely unimpressed by the fact that his father was one of the richest men in Boston and a major donor to Harvard. In other words, if he wanted good grades he would have to work for them. And "work" was such an ugly word.

Today he just wasn't in the mood. On top of which their third study buddy, Lawrence Kelly, was still new to the group, so he had to be taught an object lesson to give him the right idea.

"You know what?" Bennett whispered to him. "I just picked up this book the other day, *The 100 Most Influential Figures in World History*, and I couldn't believe my eyes. Most of the guys on the list were Brits." He was endlessly fascinated by this, since, with the exception of a couple of aberrations back in the early days, his family was almost entirely of British descent.

"The book must have been written by a Brit," Lawrence whispered back. He didn't seem too absorbed in his reading either.

"That's the thing, though; it was by an American historian. Muhammad was at the top of his list, then Isaac Newton at number two, and Jesus Christ only came after that."

"Muhammad was the most influential figure in the history of the world?" Lawrence said thoughtfully. "I don't know."

"You can argue about that if you like, but if he had never existed, our guys on the ground out there wouldn't be having such a hard time. . . . Hey you, what are you doing?" Bennett asked, turning to Todd.

Todd Walton looked up. He had been busy scribbling notes. "I'm writing a to-do list—topics we should revise for our exam. At least one of us ought to be doing some work."

Bennett was just coming up with a snappy answer when he spotted a skirt slipping between the pillars at the other end of the Reading Room. He thought he recognized the way it moved. He tipped his chair to one side to get a better look. Clinging to the table to stay on his seat, he saw he had been right. That was Terry Miller up there.

"Excuse me, kids," he said, getting up. "I've just seen someone on my own *to-do* list." Then he set off to stalk his prey.

Todd watched him go and then told Lawrence, "He means his to-bang list, of course."

"Really?" said the other. "I heard he's just about to get engaged."

Todd raised his eyebrows. "I think that's why he's in such a hurry."

Bennett caught up with Terry Miller at the checkout desk. She had stuffed three books into her cherry-shaped bag and was just about to leave.

"Hi, Terry," he said, blocking her way.

"Hi." She looked at him skeptically, but at least she had stopped to talk.

"Hey, say there," he burst out, "I saw you, you know, and I wondered if you wanted to come to this really cool party I'm going to

Saturday night. I got an invitation, and I can bring a guest, and I gotta say, this is kind of an insider deal, not the kind of party just anyone could go to."

With his best winning smile and all guns blazing, he cranked up the charm to 100 percent. "So what do you say?"

She smiled noncommittally. "Well, it's sweet of you to have thought of me, but Saturday I'm already going to the Phi Beta Kappa party with someone. You know, the party that just about everyone is going to."

She hoisted her cherry onto her shoulder. "But have fun anyway."

And with that she walked off, leaving him standing in her wake. Him. James Michael Bennett III, quarterback, heir to the Bennett fortune, valedictorian, twice crowned Best-Dressed Man on Campus. A girl had to know her own worth to do something like that.

He watched her go. Her backside was apple-shaped and in that skirt he could see every line and curve. He could just imagine sinking his teeth into it. And she wore her blond hair in a ponytail. Nobody wore a ponytail these days, which was exactly what drove him so wild: the thought of taking her from behind and watching that ponytail swing back and forth in time with his thrusts. . . . He went back to the others.

"So what happened?" Lawrence asked. "She turned you down?"

Bennett looked at him, displeased. The kid didn't have the right idea yet, not by a long way.

"She set me a challenge," he corrected him icily. "And I love a challenge."

Dusk was sinking over the city, casting its warm evening light over the scene as they cruised around Harvard campus looking for somewhere to park. A red glow lit up the roofs, recalling the centuries gone by. Up above the first stars were beginning to appear, and the air smelled intensely of summer.

"Times like this it really does look like the Isle of the Blessed," Rodney said unprompted.

Hiroshi sat up with a start. "What's that?"

"The Isle of the Blessed. That's what they call the Harvard campus around here."

Hiroshi looked out the window, blinking fast. "Really?" The name reminded him of something, but he wasn't quite sure what.

Harvard! Hiroshi still remembered how surprised he had been to learn that two of the world's most famous universities, Harvard and the no-less-famous MIT, were located in the same city just a few miles from each other. Not that this had any practical consequences in his daily life—it was pretty much obligatory for the MIT students to see Harvard people as benighted, old-fashioned, and generally beyond the pale, just as Harvard folk saw MIT as vulgar, brash, and generally beyond the pale. This allowed everyone to get along nicely together. Tonight, however, he was curious about what lay in store. It wasn't that he was looking forward to the party—he thought parties were a waste of time, and he was only going along for Rodney's sake—but he regarded it as an adventure of sorts, like a kind of anthropological field trip. When he looked at it that way, the whole thing had a certain appeal. Besides, he had no objection to drinking beer.

Rodney was still cruising around. By now they were on their third or maybe fourth lap around the green spaces between Old Yard, the Radcliffe Institute, and Harvard Law School, where a crowd had gathered as though for a rock concert. Snatches of music drifted across every so often. Well-dressed people were strolling across the lawns and beneath the trees, all headed for a big, brightly lit house built in the same style as most of the rest of Harvard—red tiles, tall windows, a magnificent facade—where a great throng of people was already gathered on the two rooftop terraces.

Nobody knew for sure who had actually donated the money for the fraternity house, though it was obviously a Harvard alum who was also a Phi Beta Kappa member. Some said it was an Internet billionaire who wanted to remain anonymous. Others added that the Harvard University government had been caught flat-footed by the building work. After all, it was Harvard policy to try to keep the influence of the fraternities to a minimum—studying at Harvard was supposed to be enough of an honor in itself. And now the most influential honor society of all had built this lavish frat house practically slap in the middle of campus.

Finally, they were directed into a parking spot. They got out of the car and joined the flood of people streaming toward the house. They passed groups of professional security guards with bulletproof vests, walkie-talkies, and stern expressions, but when they handed over their invitations at the door, it was to a freshman in a smart suit with a neatly knotted tie. He waved them right in.

Stepping into the house was like stepping into the Tokyo metro at rush hour. The rooms, salons, staircases, and hallways were all packed with people chattering excitedly, holding glasses in their hands, full or no longer so full. There was no way to take even a single step forward without having to let someone else past or detour around them, getting an elbow in the ribs or bumping into someone else in turn. The biggest difference between this and the Tokyo subway was the music playing everywhere: In the main salon someone was tinkling away on the piano—a Gershwin tune. A three-piece blues band was out on the terrace. An old record player in the basement was playing jazz. And rock and pop generated by computer playlists could be heard from the upper floors of the house. Standing on the staircase or in the corridors, where all the different sounds mingled together in a deafening cacophony, was best avoided. Broadly speaking, the party seemed to have split itself in two: down on the first floor the older brothers were crowded into the great front hall, the library, and the dark, paneled committee room, chattering away in black tie and evening gowns; upstairs, the young people ruled the roost.

Once they had fought their way out onto one of the terraces, Hiroshi and Rodney saw some familiar faces, fellow students from MIT who were quite astonished to see Hiroshi there.

"Kato," a pimply blond boy called David shouted out, loud enough to be heard over a thunderous guitar riff by U2. "If someone told you there's a seminar here, I'm afraid they were lying."

"Nobody said it was a seminar," Hiroshi answered dryly. "But I heard there was a study group meeting. Effects of alcohol abuse or something like that."

They looked at one another, grinning. "Oh yeah," another voice called. "You could call it that."

"Are you joining?" David asked.

Hiroshi shrugged. "We'll see. I don't know whether I have all the required credits."

There was a roar of laughter. By the sound of it, he was welcome aboard.

Hiroshi noticed for the first time they had roped off some of the lawn out back and set up white tents serving drinks and food.

"Come on," he told Rodney. "Let's go look for your Prof. Bernstein."

On their way through the different rooms they passed a bar, where they were given a glass of champagne in exchange for the tokens that came with their tickets. They saw a host of celebrities—no US presidents, but famous writers, musicians, astronauts, football players, and so on. The only face that was missing was Prof. Bernstein.

"Bernstein? Not that I know of," was the answer they got from anyone who looked like Harvard faculty. A woman with a mane of silvery-gray hair asked in surprise, "Oh—was he going to come?" And a corpulent man wearing a bolo tie said with a smile, "Bernstein? Here? To be honest, I would be very surprised."

They said their thank-yous and carried on their search.

"I can't understand it," Rodney lamented. "I heard he never misses a party, especially a Phi Beta Kappa event."

"We'll just keep looking," Hiroshi said. "We owe it to the aliens." At least it gave them something to do. And he always felt better when he had something to do.

The terrace rang with the sounds of a wailing harmonica and the song of a weather-beaten bluesman bemoaning how sad and lonely he felt. They did not find Prof. Bernstein there either, but somebody clamped a hand onto Hiroshi's arm as he passed and called out, "Hey! You're Hiroshi Kato, aren't you?"

"I am," Hiroshi admitted and looked at the guy. He was a skinny young man with glasses and an Adam's apple that went up and down like a yo-yo as he talked.

"Bill Adamson," he said, shaking Hiroshi's hand. "I'm at MIT, too. Really, we should have met years ago." He said it in a frosty tone that suggested it was Hiroshi's fault they hadn't.

"Ah well," said Hiroshi. "These things happen."

Of course, he knew Bill Adamson's name; everyone at MIT did. William Hughes Adamson had caused quite a splash a few years earlier when a working group under his direction had developed a robot that could find its way inside buildings with unprecedented accuracy. He had also assiduously promoted his own part in the invention, so that by now the specialist literature simply called it the Adamson robot. It could deliver internal mail in a company or stock medical supplies on shelves in a hospital—at least in theory, since it was still too expensive for such uses.

However, it could also hunt down and shoot terrorists who had barricaded themselves into a building. With that, Bill Adamson had entered a realm where cost was no object, and it was no surprise he was due to take up a post at DARPA, the Defense Advanced Research Projects Agency, after he had finished his doctorate at MIT. Adamson was generally seen as the coming man in robotics, a reputation he took great care to protect. Rodney reported that he felt Hiroshi threatened his position.

"I took apart one of your Wizard's Wands recently," Adamson went on, jabbing Hiroshi in the chest, "and what do I find? You just picked up the spatial-orientation system from our robot and built on it."

A frost seemed to settle around them, there in the warm summer night.

"That's kind of a long way to go about it," Hiroshi said, unruffled. "You could have just read my patent. It's all there in black and white."

What was this about? Surely Adamson wasn't dumb enough to accuse him of IP theft? There was no question that his Wizard's Wand software was sufficiently different from the Adamson robot system to deserve its own separate patent. MIT had its own dedicated legal office to help student inventors scrupulously check this sort of thing before they submitted a patent application.

The finger jabbed again. "We could have invented the thing just as well ourselves."

"True," said Hiroshi, "but you didn't. It was an obvious development, though. I wondered how you could have overlooked it. So I did it myself."

Bill Adamson grinned. The frost was beginning to thaw.

"Okay," he conceded. "Good point." He shook his head. "Man! Those things are everywhere. I have a cousin who's stationed over in Europe; he says they have them over there as well. You must be a millionaire by now, hey?"

"I get by," Hiroshi replied, thinking of the last quarterly statement. It had been just over seven thousand dollars, by far the lowest quarterly return to date. "Could be that the wave has peaked."

"I heard that the manufacturers . . . what are they called? Soho? Solo?"

"Sollo Electronics."

"Uh-huh. I heard they're just buying up their main competitor right now, Cook & Holland. Rumor has it, though, that they've over-extended themselves . . . Yes?" A girl with a prominent overbite had taken his arm and just asked him about someone called Betty. He pointed into the crowd and said something that was drowned out by the wail of the electric guitar.

Hiroshi and Rodney glanced at one another. Rodney didn't say anything, but Hiroshi knew exactly what he was thinking—the same thing he had said with the arrival of every quarterly check so far. "Man, they're ripping you off." They probably were. For the time being, though, Hiroshi didn't much care. He didn't want to get rich; he just wanted to be able to do as he liked.

"Listen, since we're talking business here," Adamson said when the girl with the overbite had vanished again, "I have a project in the works right now. It's kind of a working group, but at the national level. We have people from Caltech, NASA, Carnegie Mellon, all that . . . Anyway, it's called Robot 21, and we're trying to come up with a strategic plan for the future of robot technology. Laying down the ground rules we should follow. Nothing quite as simple as Asimov's laws, but something along those lines. Since that seems to be what you're working on right now, do you want to join the team?"

He was smart, this guy. Though he hadn't come straight out and said that one day their work would be known as Adamson's Laws of Robotics, you could be sure that's what would happen.

"To be honest, no," Hiroshi replied.

"What? Why not?"

"I've heard about your group. And I've read the working papers you posted to the Net." Hiroshi smiled softly. "I'm sorry, but you guys are barking up the wrong tree. What you call the future of robotics is really its past."

Bill Adamson couldn't have looked more stunned if Hiroshi had punched him in the gut. "What do you mean by that?" he asked. The frost was definitely back now.

"Just keep your eyes on me; you'll see what I mean," Hiroshi told him boldly. "It's quite clear to me where things have to go next. I've been wondering for years why nobody else has had the same idea." He raised his empty glass. "I have to go get another drink. Good talking to you."

Hiroshi turned and left. He could feel Adamson's gaze upon him as he walked away. The man was staring daggers at him.

"Man!" Rodney exclaimed. "What was that about? Demonstration class in how to make an enemy for life?"

All Hiroshi said was, "If he's as much of a hotshot as everyone believes, he should prove it."

If you were looking for a place to go slumming, the Epsilon Omega frat house was not a bad choice. Whenever Bennett had had enough of the luxury and unbearable good manners of the world he had been born into, he snuck off here. Epsilon Omega was not a fraternity that instilled lifelong pride in its members—it didn't get donations from former brothers and didn't have its own tie; it was a frat for those who had been turned down everywhere else but still needed a cheap roof over their head and somebody to copy assignments from. And their morals were just as lax as their membership standards. The things that happened at their parties would have been unimaginable anywhere else. This was still the only place where Bennett had slept with three women at once. Another time, a chemistry student had handed round some stuff that had totally blown his mind—Bennett had never tripped like that before.

The frat house was a wreck out on the edge of town, incredibly far from all the faculty buildings and lecture halls, but also a good distance from any neighbors who might complain about the noise. The fraternity brothers were fond of wacky color combinations—most of the rooms were painted in black and purple—but not the least bit fond of repairs. A pane was missing in the fanlight over the front door, and as far as Bennett could remember it had been missing last year as well.

Despite all that, his evening was not going so great. A girl had given him a blow job down in the basement to a soundtrack of Motörhead and Metallica, but she hadn't been particularly good at it. She had taken some kind of pill and was giggling away like crazy but hadn't let him into her panties. He hadn't even been able to get a finger in. She had a pretty good pair of boobs, but she hadn't let him touch those either. Well what the hell? He wasn't going home tonight until he had dipped his wick somewhere. Which was why he was working on a new girl at the moment, although over the course of an evening the drinks they served here made it pretty hard to concentrate.

"Where was I?" he asked, putting his arm around her neck.

"You were just explaining why you're studying anthropology," she said, letting him.

They were lying on a sofa built of sandbags behind the bar. Even when you were sober, it was pretty difficult to get up from it, and the light was suitably low over in this corner. The Epsilon Omega guys called it "the beaver trap."

"Ah yes. Of course. Anthropology. The study of mankind." He looked her over. She had a wild hairdo, a kind of raging lion's mane that was probably meant to distract from the fact she was pretty skinny and barely had any tits to speak of. But he wasn't after tits this evening, not anymore. Whatever else she may or may not have, she had a pussy, and that was what mattered.

"Do you know what the amazing thing is when you study anthropology?" he went on, deciding that a guy wasn't really drunk if he could still say a word like *anthropology*. "How little we really know. Your average Joe just wouldn't believe it. Sure, there are a whole load of theories. But theories is all they are. Stories. When it comes to hard facts, the kind of thing that could convince a jury—pretty near nothing."

"Really?" she said. Was she getting bored? For a moment he thought so, but then he decided he must be mistaken; girls never got bored when James Michael Bennett was around. He looked at her again. What was her name? Ah yes, Belinda. Nice name. Kind of rare.

"Belinda," he cooed, looking deep into her eyes. "That's such a beautiful name, you know that? And so unusual."

"That's the third time you've said that."

He shut up, flabbergasted. Really? He wasn't sure what he'd said by now. Whatever. Didn't matter.

"I could say it all night," he said insistently. "It's such an unusual name. Belinda—a name like that tastes good on the tongue." He flicked his tongue out from his lips for a moment to show her what he meant.

She laughed. "Okay, so you study anthropology because there's not much to study. Did I get you right?"

"No, no." Where on earth did she get that idea? If there was one thing that women shouldn't try, it was logic.

"Because we know so very little," he told her earnestly, "that must mean there's a whole lot of research still to be done, don't you see? Fundamental work. And it means anything is still possible." He shuffled closer and put his mouth close to her face. It smelled good. "And there's something else as well, something I have to whisper in your ear. It's kind of politically incorrect. Extremely."

He was playing her, of course. The music drowned out everything in the room, some British band that sounded like buzz saws on steel; the two of them could have been shouting at the top of their voices and nobody would have overheard them. But women loved it when you whispered in their ear. It got them hot. And flat-chested Belinda was ready to get hot.

She giggled. "That tickles."

"The truth, my dear Belinda, is not democratic. Truth cares only about facts, evidence, solid proof. Truth cares whether the questions we ask can truly be answered." He came still closer to her ear, close enough to lick, and carried on. "The white race is descended from Cro-Magnon man. Everybody agrees on that. However, I suspect there's more to it. It doesn't fit today's orthodoxies, but I strongly suspect that Cro-Magnon man was not descended from *Homo erectus* but represents a much older lineage in its own right. *Homo erectus* was merely the ancestor of the other races." He chuckled. "The white race . . . sounds like Ku Klux Klan stuff, doesn't it? But you mustn't think I'm a racist. I'm a scientist. Let's say the Caucasians then, which means the same thing, but it's a word we're allowed to use. Crazy old world, huh? Taboos everywhere. No wonder we're not making any progress."

It was also proving harder than he had thought to make progress with Belinda. Why was she so tense? He wasn't doing anything to her, wasn't even touching her. Except for his arm around her neck.

"If you look at world history," he went on, "the fact is that all the greatest achievements have been made by Caucasians. Technology. Science. Empires. Landing on the moon . . ."

"Two World Wars," Belinda added. "Environmental havoc. Atom bombs. Global warming."

"I never mentioned morality," Bennett protested. "I said great achievements."

"So what about the Great Wall of China?" she asked. "What about the pyramids? Or Machu Picchu?"

She understood him. At last. It was good when a woman understood what a man was saying. Although there was something a little odd about her examples. He couldn't quite think what at the moment but figured it wasn't important.

"Great achievements," he repeated. "That's it. The Caucasians have some gift for greatness, while the other races—or let's call them ethnic groups . . . okay, other ethnic groups live more in harmony with nature instead, more simply. I'm not saying there's anything wrong with that. I'm just saying it's a difference. And differences are there to be explained. That's what science is for."

He looked at her. There was desire in her glittering eyes, no question. He could see such things.

"And me, dear Belinda. I have a gift for greatness, too," he told her. "And I have a hypothesis that you may have caused it." He took her hand and put it on the fly of his pants. "I think we should subject this to scientific study. Let's go upstairs and see if one of the labs is free. We may achieve great things."

She smiled. Dear Belinda. "I have to go somewhere real quick," she said.

He watched her go and felt a further stirring behind his zipper. Pretty good ass. Almost made up for the small tits. He picked up his drink and tipped it down his throat in one go. Damn good stuff, and crazy-cheap prices. Aimed fair and square at the normal clientele here.

The next thing Bennett knew, someone was shaking him awake, and when he prized his eyelids open, it was unpleasantly bright. And a voice said, "Good morning, champ. Time to go home."

At some point they had just given up looking and gotten on with the party. Partying, it seemed, meant standing around with people they barely knew and talking about stuff that barely mattered. And drinking alcohol at the same time.

Hiroshi decided it was an interesting experience. All the same, he steered clear of the hard stuff and stuck with beer, since he doubted it would remain an interesting experience if he lost his self-control. Besides, he didn't understand how anybody could like whiskey.

A little before midnight he was standing with a group watching from the roof terrace as the alumni left. Some of them were well advanced in years, and they tottered down the front steps, chattering away, laughing fit to burst, and visibly unsteady on their feet. A line of limousines had pulled up. A knot of freshmen was bringing out overcoats and other belongings for the honored guests, opening car doors, and otherwise making sure the dear old souls got away in good order.

Rodney had finally found a girl who was willing to listen to him explain the Fermi paradox. The two of them were sitting on one of the very few comfortable seats in a corner of the terrace, paying no attention to what was going on down below.

"Enrico Fermi," Rodney explained, waving his hands as he spoke, "was an Italian atom physicist who fled the Nazis and came to America. He won the Nobel Prize, so he was generally considered to be a smart guy. And he was thinking about the alien question more than fifty years ago. Imagine that. I mean, that shows it's not just a hobby horse for wackos, right?"

The girl giggled, but in a friendly way. Hiroshi watched the two of them for a moment. He would have been willing to bet good money Rodney had already buttonholed everyone in Boston with his theories. Looked like he was wrong. The girl was kind of plump. She had a mop of messy hair, and she would have looked better in some kind of flowing Indian robe than in the tight jeans and skintight top she had on, but Hiroshi thought she looked nice nevertheless. Cuddly. And she could make a good match for Rodney.

"So, Fermi said all of this back then. Given how large the universe is—with hundreds of billions of galaxies, each containing billions of stars, all of which possibly have planets—it's likely for simply statistical reasons that there are other life-forms out there like us. But then he went on to ask, if that's really the case and aliens exist, then why aren't they here?"

"They live too far away, is that it?" asked the girl, wide-eyed.

There were still five cars downstairs waiting for the last gray-haired passengers standing in front of the open doors, unable to tear themselves away from one another's company. Meanwhile, fraternity brothers were already carrying the parts of a drum kit up the stairs into the great hall, along with loudspeakers, cables, and mic stands.

"Now this party's really gonna get started!" whooped someone standing next to Hiroshi.

Hiroshi wondered what it would look like when the party got started. He had no idea. Was everybody going to strip naked and indulge in pagan orgies? Was this when the drugs showed up? He felt rather like an alien himself, a man who fell to Earth to do an anthropological field survey.

Over in the candlelight, he heard Rodney chuckle. "Yes, well of course they live a long way away. But that's the whole point. Fermi saw it like this: if the aliens are anything like us, then one day they will develop space travel. And if they develop space travel, then we have to think things through and consider what is theoretically possible and what isn't."

"Like in *Star Trek*?" the girl asked. "Warp speed and all that?"

"Well, that's probably going to stay beyond the realm of possibility. You can't travel faster than light. But that doesn't mean that we couldn't fly to another star. It just wouldn't be with starships like we see in the movies. Maybe we could hollow out an asteroid, turn it into a generation ship, and set out on a journey lasting several centuries. Maybe the ones who finally leave the solar system one day will be some religious sect, the Pilgrim Fathers of the future—who knows?"

"I get it. And this Fermi guy figured the aliens would do the same thing?"

"Exactly. Then he calculated how quickly they could get from star to star. The calculations are just fascinating. I'll have to run them by you in detail when we have time. Anyway, he calculated that even if it took centuries to get from one star to the next, the whole of the Milky Way would still be settled within a very short time compared with the age of planet Earth, for instance. He said that if the aliens had reached our stage of development even as recently as one hundred thousand years ago, then they would be everywhere by now. Right at our doorstep." Rod pointed up to the sky, where the stars were just visible despite all the lamps, party lanterns, and spotlights. "Instead of which, silence. Not a peep. We send out all our signals and we're not getting any answer."

Hiroshi looked up, too. It was a clear night. He shivered. "I need another beer," he said to nobody in particular.

He went inside and headed downstairs, carrying his empty glass. The atmosphere had already changed since he'd come up to the roof; it was more febrile, more excited, full of expectation, as though anything might happen at any moment. Though he couldn't have said what he might have wanted to happen, the excitement took hold of him as well.

"Bar's moved," he learned from a guy with a scrubby little beard and striking gray eyes. He waved his hand. "Back there in the gallery. Last room."

Hiroshi wandered off in that direction, shoving his way past kissing couples and groups of people laughing uproariously. He hadn't been in this part of the house before, or at least he didn't think he had. In the hallway through to the bar the crowd got thicker until it was almost like being in the metro again. Everyone here, however, had a drink in their hand.

He'd almost reached it. Between him and the bar were just two more guys—broad shoulders, leather jackets—blocking his way. He tapped them both on the shoulder and asked, "Can I get by?"

He would remember what happened next as though it had taken place in slow motion. The two men stepped aside. Somebody laughed loudly. A white curtain gusted in the wind.

And there was Charlotte standing in front of him.

2

Dorothy liked to sleep in on Sundays. Not only because she was sometimes out late on Saturday night, but for its own sake. It was her way of marking that it was Sunday, so to speak, and if she opened her eyes before ten o'clock, then that counted as early in her book.

And now here she was, awake, even though it was practically still dark. It was little more than twilight outside; she could see outlines and shadows, but no colors. It was early for anyone, not just her.

Her first thought was of Hiroshi and how good it would be to have him lying next to her so that she could snuggle up to him and put ideas in his head. Sex on a Sunday morning, warm and relaxed, then drowsing off to sleep again and finally untangling themselves long enough to have breakfast: it would be the best way to start a Sunday she could imagine.

The doorbell rang. In the same moment, Dorothy realized it was not the first time, that the first ring was what had woken her up. It was horribly loud, especially at that hour, and the dorm had terribly thin walls, as she sometimes had cause to remember. Now, for instance. She jumped out of bed and hurried over to the intercom.

It was Hiroshi. "I have something important to tell you," she heard him say, his voice crackling and buzzing on the line.

"On Sunday morning?" she asked in astonishment, then turned to look at the clock radio on her bedside table. "At twelve minutes past five?"

She was surprised to hear herself say that. Why wasn't she happy that he was here, that he had turned up as if by magic just as she was thinking of him? But she wasn't. Something was wrong.

"It's urgent," Hiroshi said insistently. Once he was in that mood, there was no dissuading him anyway.

"Okay," said Dorothy, pressing the button to let him in.

It was chilly. She looked around. Should she put something on, her robe perhaps—if she could find it? On the other hand, she looked good right now in just her thin nightshirt. Who knew, it might turn into a lovely Sunday morning after all? Outside her door she could hear footsteps echoing on the stairs, and Hiroshi's words echoed in her thoughts: "I have something important to tell you." What could it be? Those three little words, perhaps? She hardly dared think. Suddenly Hiroshi was standing in her doorway. His clothes were awry, he smelled of beer and smoke, his eyes were red, and he looked like he hadn't slept all night.

Dorothy closed the door behind him. "Hey. Um . . . were you at the Phi Beta Kappa party?"

"Yes," Hiroshi answered, his voice rough.

"Without me?"

It hurt, for sure. Why had he gone all of a sudden? She had talked till she was blue in the face about how Hiroshi should go to this or that party with her, as well as all her other invitations. Hiroshi didn't even try to defend himself. He took her hands and drew her over toward the bed. Dorothy hesitated. Sex with a man who stank of beer and smoke was not part of her ideal Sunday. She would send him off to have a shower before she even let him kiss her.

But he didn't even try to kiss her. He just sat down and said, "Something happened to me."

Dorothy felt the hairs stand up on the back of her head. He spoke in the same tone he might use if he had said, "I killed someone."

He began to talk, but he seemed to be speaking some foreign language. Or was there something wrong with her ears? She could barely understand what he was saying—didn't want to understand—as he told her about some woman he had known when he was a child and how he had met her again. He was telling her about a fence he had had to climb, about a doll he had repaired, about taking a flight to see his sick aunt. And he was saying he had to think things through. He said that several times. That something important had happened, that fate had stepped in, that he had to think things through.

And then he uttered the words that pierced her to the heart like a red-hot nail. "I've realized that I don't love you."

Dorothy thought she would fall apart.

"I thought I did," Hiroshi told her earnestly, looking at her with his dark Japanese eyes, which seemed to glow in the half-light of dawn, "but I don't. I realized that tonight. I'm meant to be with Charlotte. Not with you."

"I understand," Dorothy heard herself say. Something inside her took control of the situation—some kind of autopilot, a simple but robust little mechanism that was ready for all emergencies. The rest of her collapsed in uncomprehending misery.

It was one of those moments when she wished everything was just a bad dream but she knew it was no such thing. The worst of it was that, for the very first time since she had met Hiroshi, she felt he was being completely honest with her, opening himself up to her—only to say he didn't love her and never really had.

"Which is why it would be best for us to stop seeing each other."

"Yes," said autopilot Dorothy.

"I'm sorry."

"So am I."

"You don't deserve this," he went on. "You deserve someone who really loves you."

"Yes."

She could never remember afterward whether they had said anything more after that. All she remembered was she had somehow managed to see him out without falling to pieces, and then she had crept into bed, pulled the covers over her head, and screamed—screamed and howled—until she was hoarse.

"You did what?" Rodney stared at him incredulously. The wooden spoon in his hand hung motionless.

Hiroshi pointed to the saucepan. "Hey! That's burning." Rodney was cooking up a batch of his special hangover cure, a combination of all that was sharp and fierce in Mexican cookery. The whole corridor smelled of tomato, garlic, chili, and chocolate. "It wasn't as bad as all that. She took it surprisingly calmly."

"Calmly?" Rodney echoed as the onions turned black in the oil. "You don't really believe that, do you? If I were in your shoes, I would worry she'd do something to herself."

Hiroshi looked at him. He didn't feel well, his eyes were burning, and though he had snatched a couple of hours of restless sleep, it had done nothing to fix the daze he was in. "Don't get such wild ideas," he muttered uncomfortably.

Rodney pushed the pan off the heat, stormed out of the kitchen, and came back with his cell phone. "What's her number?"

Hiroshi took out his own phone and passed it over. "It's on speed dial. Number nine."

"Do you really think she's going to answer if she sees your number?"

Hiroshi told him the number. He dialed it, then went out into the corridor.

"Hi, Dorothy, it's me, Rodney," Hiroshi heard him saying. "My lame-brained roommate has just told me everything, and I wanted to see if you're okay . . . yeah . . . yeah, sure, I understand . . ."

There was a long pause. Hiroshi sighed. He suddenly felt relieved she was all right.

"Yes, quite," he heard Rodney say. "An idiot. I think so, too. A complete idiot. Absolutely. A total, complete and utter . . . no question."

It went on that way for quite some time, until Rodney managed to wrap up the call. When he came back into the kitchen, a dark cloud seemed to be hanging over him. Without a word he went to the stove, put the pan back on the hot plate, and added spices and tomato to the oil. He began to stir like crazy.

"Okay," said Hiroshi. "So she didn't take it quite as calmly as I thought. Maybe I just got that idea because it was so early in the morning. Dorothy's not so great at getting up early, especially not on Sundays."

Rodney carried on stirring. He was clearly furious. "You really are completely crazy, you know that?" he suddenly burst out. "You don't just hang a girl like Dorothy out to dry! On a whim when you're half-drunk."

"It wasn't a whim. It was fate."

"You're talking crap."

"It wouldn't have been honest to carry on the relationship. Simple as that. There was no alternative."

"Now you're talking like an inscrutable Japanese."

"And you're talking like a hot-blooded Chicano."

Rodney slammed the lid onto the pan, turned the heat down, and clattered around, putting the deep-frozen tortillas into the oven. Hiroshi kept quiet. His job was to make strong coffee, and that was already taken care of.

Rodney had vanished with the girl with the tousled hair at some point the night before. Rodney claimed he had gone looking for Hiroshi but hadn't found him, which would have been strange, since he and Charlotte had simply sat on the back terrace and talked until finally someone came to throw them out. Then they had gone to her place to talk some more. In the end, Hiroshi had taken a taxi home, and Rodney had gotten a lift back with the tousled-haired girl, which meant his own car was still at Harvard.

Rodney, skeptical as always, said she had kissed him good-bye. Rodney was strange about women. He had an enviable gift for talking to them and winning them over, but he was very, very careful with his feelings. Any woman who wanted to go to bed with him straightaway had ruled herself right out. But they were planning to go on another date. Last night's girl obviously still had a chance.

"Dorothy really loved you," Rodney grumbled, breaking the silence. "She would have done anything for you. Anything, man!"

"I know," Hiroshi said. "But I didn't love her. I just didn't know it. Until today."

"So who is she, this woman you were meant for?"

Hiroshi cleared his throat. "Her name's Charlotte Malroux—"

"Say what?" Rodney broke in, astonished.

"Charlotte Malroux," Hiroshi repeated. "She's French. Her father is an ambassador, and—"

"Tell me it ain't true!" Rodney collapsed onto the nearest kitchen chair. The look on his face spoke of new heights of surprise and bewilderment, even after everything else he'd heard this morning.

"Why?" Hiroshi asked, perplexed. "Do you know her?"

Rodney squeezed his eyes tight and rubbed his temples. "Oh boy oh boy oh boy! You're even crazier than I thought." He looked up and laughed mirthlessly. "Okay, to be absolutely honest I have no idea how to put this, but have you ever, at any point between last night and this morning, actually given any thought to what your chances might be? Listen, we're talking about Charlotte Malroux here. She's widely recognized to be the hottest ticket Harvard has seen this decade. We're talking about a woman who scores an easy twelve on the scale of one to ten. Charlotte Malroux could be a supermodel without even opening her makeup box. I mean, have you even considered how many men in Boston have the hots for her? All of them, I would say. And that's a conservative estimate."

Hiroshi blinked in astonishment. He hadn't even noticed. Okay, yes, she looked good, but as good as all that? Well, it had been at night, and it was dark.

"On top of which," Rodney went on ruthlessly, "Charlotte Malroux, as everyone but you seems to know, is dating a certain James Michael Bennett III, who, as the name may tell you, is from the very upper crust of Boston society. Do you know the name Bennett Industries? Well, yes, he's the heir. And as if it weren't enough that he's stinking rich, he also looks like a Greek god and is a hotshot at half a dozen different sports. Among other things, he's quarterback for the Harvard football team, he's won the Harvard golf cup several times over, he rides for the polo team, and I don't know what else." Rodney heaved a deep sigh. "I'm really sorry to have to say this, but even with all the luck in the world, I don't see how you can compete."

"I don't think in those terms," Hiroshi declared.

"But those are the terms women think in."

"Not all of them, I hope."

Rodney groaned with despair. "You're a dreamer."

Hiroshi nodded. "I am indeed. And? All great things begin with a dream. That's the way it's always been."

"Kiddo, the woman's got herself a billionaire-to-be for a boyfriend. Maybe a senator-to-be, governor-to-be, could be even a president. And don't you go thinking he's not as good in the sack as mere mortals like us. From what I hear, he's had a lot of practice. Do you think any woman in the world is going to kiss a chance like that good-bye just because she ran into an old flame from her grade-school days?" He shook his head. "No, I gotta tell you you're going to regret what you did to Dorothy."

Hiroshi had been listening with growing resentment. He felt the old rage from his childhood building inside him again as though it had never gone away—his rage at the way the world was.

He snarled, "Ever since I was a kid, people have been telling me I'll regret this or that, that I'll see where it gets me. I'm telling you, I'm fed up with hearing it."

"Let's eat," Rodney said amicably. "What's with the coffee?"

After she woke up, Charlotte lay in bed for a while staring at the ceiling, waiting to be sure she could tell dreaming from waking. Seeing Hiroshi again had not been a dream after all. It hadn't been a dream that they had spent the whole night talking, sometimes even in Japanese, a language she hadn't spoken for half a lifetime. She ran her fingers through her hair. It felt tangled and matted. She had taken a quick shower before she went to bed this morning, but she hadn't dried her hair, not completely; she had been too worn-out.

For a moment she wondered where James was. Then she remembered he had said he'd be visiting his parents today. He hadn't wanted to come to the party last night, claiming that "one of us might get jealous." He had made other plans, and she had instead gone with a couple of her girlfriends but lost sight of them over the course of the evening. Strange to think that if it had happened any other way, she and Hiroshi would never have run into each other. Strange to think, too, that they had both been living in Boston for years and never crossed paths. But strangest of all was how they had recognized one another straightaway even though they had been children back in Tokyo.

Charlotte rolled over in bed and looked at the three dolls lined up on the shelf by her headboard. Hiroshi had been touched when she told him she still had that doll he had fished out of the rubbish and repaired. Valérie. It wasn't here in the States with her, though; these three were from an artists' market in South Boston. Valérie was safely back in Paris in her parents' apartment, where her parents in fact never lived. Her father had recently gotten the Moscow posting he'd long been hoping for and was even trying to learn Russian, to the astonishment and embarrassment of all around him.

Maman had confessed only a couple of years earlier that she had never sent the letters Charlotte had written to Hiroshi after the sudden move to Argentina—long letters in careful English in which she had made an extra effort with her handwriting. Her mother had wanted Charlotte to forget "that boy."

And she had been so disappointed when he had never answered!

After her mother's confession, Charlotte had made one more attempt. But by then Hiroshi's mother was no longer working at the embassy in Tokyo, and there had been no way to find her new address. So her final attempt had run aground, and then she really had forgotten Hiroshi. At least, so she had thought.

She would never have believed they still had so much to say to each other. In fact, she realized, that was what had made it such a very strange encounter. All right, enough pondering. She threw off the covers, jumped out of bed, wriggled out of her pajamas, and got into the shower. After a long, hot shower, she snuggled back into bed in her robe and called Brenda, her best friend. She always told her everything.

Brenda just laughed. "It looks as though you're collecting everyone you've ever met in your life here at Harvard," she commented.

"Yes," Charlotte agreed. "So it seems." She and Brenda Gilliam had first met in Delhi but then lost touch. When Charlotte had been awarded a spot at Harvard, they had reconnected, since by strange coincidence Brenda's father happened to teach at the medical school. Perhaps there were fewer random coincidences in life than people thought.

She found herself looking at a framed photo on the shelf of her and James at a garden party. For the first time she wondered why she had put it there. "The question is, what am I going to do about Hiroshi?"

"That's not hard," Brenda said cheerily. "You two just pick up where you left off. That's what we did, after all, when you turned up here."

"But what if that doesn't work?"

"Then you know that it's over and done with." Brenda was breathtakingly practical about such matters. She could have written for the problem pages. "If you can't think of anything else to do, bring him along next Saturday. I can never have too many strong men around when I'm moving house."

Charlotte realized she was holding the receiver much more tightly than she needed to be. She relaxed her grip and took a deep breath. Every time Brenda's move came up, she couldn't shake the feeling it had something to do with her.

The obligatory first year in a freshman dorm in Old Yard had been a nightmare for Charlotte. She didn't doubt for a moment that living together with others built team spirit or that it was good for developing her study skills, exchanging ideas, and making friends for life. It was just she didn't find that part easy. When she didn't have a moment to herself—and in a shared room, no one had a moment to themselves—she felt on edge, defenseless, vulnerable, not in the least bit prepared to make friendships for life. Even if Al Gore and Tommy Lee Jones had been Harvard roommates. So in her second year she had sought out her own apartment in the city. Ever since then she had lived in Somerville, about two miles from Harvard. She paid significantly more in rent there, but if she ever managed to unpack the last of her boxes and buy some good furniture, she might really feel at home. She enjoyed more peace and quiet there than she ever had in Holworthy Hall. As for friends for life—apart from Brenda, and maybe Hiroshi as well—perhaps she just didn't make friendships the same way everyone else did.

"Well, to tell the truth, Hiroshi is kind of scrawny," Charlotte said.

"Bring him along all the same."

"I'll see what I can do."

She tried to imagine how James and Hiroshi might react to one another. James was always a little condescending about

Brenda—mostly he called her "the plump girl," which was definitely an exaggeration—but he had promised he would come and help. Or almost promised. She could never be quite sure what he would do; James had a marked tendency toward spontaneous decisions.

Well, maybe it wouldn't be a bad idea for the two of them to meet. "If he calls me, I'll ask him," she promised.

"He'll call for sure, won't he?" asked Brenda.

"All right then: when he calls."

Of course he was going to call. After last night, Charlotte told herself, she would have to work hard to make sure Hiroshi didn't fall in love with her.

Waking up was a painful business, and for the first few moments James Michael Bennett didn't know where he was. Then he saw he was in his own bed, which came as something of a relief. Not that he didn't enjoy those times when he woke up somewhere else entirely, next to a woman whose name he didn't know . . . that could be one almighty turn-on. Far out. An adventure. But it had to be the right day for that kind of thing, and today was not that day.

It had something to do with last night. Gradually, he remembered most of what had happened. How he had come home in the early hours of the morning when the night sky was just beginning to pale, the skyline starting to show through the dark blue haze. He hadn't felt too good—in fact, he had felt terrible—and driving his car had probably been one hell of a risk. Those damn drinks they served at Epsilon Omega! Maybe he should find out what on earth they put in them. He'd run into someone in the front hall. Ah yes, George. The butler had helped him upstairs and brought him some kind of tablets with a glass of water. James couldn't actually remember whether he'd taken the things, but if he had they hadn't helped much.

He finally managed to get up and stagger into the shower, after which his head was almost clear. Clear enough at least to be able to think about whether he wanted breakfast—or whatever you might call it at this time of day. What time was it, anyway? Half past one already. Well, great. Breakfast, or a couple of lengths in the pool first, or maybe a jog in the park? No, he'd start with breakfast. He dropped his towel and walked stark-naked through his bedroom, a large room flooded with sunlight at this hour. George had put out fresh clothing and also Saturday's mail on a silver tray, just the way he liked it. Look at that: a big fat letter from England. He picked that up first and checked the sender's address. It was indeed from the genealogist in London, a heraldic expert whom he had hired a while ago to research the Bennett family tree. He tore the envelope open.

He glanced through the letter that came with the report. Thick, creamy paper with an imposing crest, embossed gilt lettering, but also the words "with regret" and the news he had been unable to find any link to the nobility of Great Britain. There were indeed some branches he had not been able to document thoroughly, despite all his efforts, the expert wrote, but in his professional opinion they were unlikely to yield any promising results. The last line of the letter requested that James pay the itemized expenses at his earliest convenience.

James flipped through the pages of the report. Lists of names, lines of descent, collateral and cadet branches. It was no different from all the other expert reports so far—a bunch of ancestors who turned out to have been coopers, sextons, tavern keepers, sailors, and shoemakers. No dukes, no earls, no viscounts—not even a baronet. He yanked open a desk drawer and shoved the pages inside. The London researcher had been recommended to him as the very best in his field, but he was obviously no better at his job than all the rest of them.

He got dressed and went down to the kitchen. Madeleine was there; in fact, it looked like she had been waiting for him. She asked what he wanted for breakfast.

"Ham and scrambled eggs, and a cheese sandwich."

James fished Saturday's newspaper out of the magazine rack; he hadn't had time to read the sports pages yesterday. "Make the coffee as strong as you can. And orange juice, a whole jugful."

"Yes, Mr. Bennett," Madeleine answered. "Right away." Madeleine was from Louisiana, and one of her best qualities was she still knew how servants should behave. It was a shame she was due to retire soon; it would be no easy matter to find a suitable replacement.

She brought in the big glass jug full of fresh-pressed orange juice, and James gulped down the first glass while reading the latest baseball stats. He still had a pounding headache. When at last the coffee appeared on the table, he became aware of the hustle and bustle in the house.

"What's going on today?" he asked as Madeleine put the ham and eggs in front of him.

She cocked her head. "Perihelion meeting. Mercury, on Wednesday."

"Oh yeah." James massaged his temples. "That, too."

The Perihelions were a group of his father's friends who had a thing for astronomy. At some point they had come up with the wacky idea of having Sunday meetings when a planetary perihelion was due—except for the perihelion of Earth. And what was a perihelion? If he remembered right, it was the point in a planet's orbit when it was closest to the sun. James wasn't totally sure about this, but whatever it was, the rule was that everyone had to work out for themselves when it was due. There were no invitations or announcements, and any member who got his calculations wrong had to pay a fixed fine into the "Lost in Space" box, or sing David Bowie's "Space Oddity" to the assembled group.

The whole thing was objectionable for several reasons. The first problem was the perihelion rule was pretty crazy in itself—sometimes they wouldn't see one another for ages, and then they would be meeting one Sunday after another for weeks on end. As far as James understood any of it, Mercury set the pace, since it had a perihelion every eighty-seven days. Other planets didn't matter at all; Uranus, for instance, wasn't due for perihelion until March 2050.

The second problem was his dad was horribly democratic when it came to his friends. James Michael Bennett regarded any random roommate or teammate from Harvard as a lifelong friend, regardless of whether they had made a success of themselves or failed at everything they tried. At these meetings filthy rich lawyers found themselves sitting next to long-haired librarians, successful entrepreneurs rubbed shoulders with blue-collar workers, famous authors alongside spaced-out hippies. Dad welcomed winners and losers alike and loved to behave as though everybody were equal. He even had an expensive facsimile of the Declaration of Independence hanging in his office—"All men are created equal" blah blah blah—and as if that wasn't enough, he also liked having friends of all colors. White, black, yellow—it was all the same to him. Dad had friends who were Mexican, Russian, and Jewish, and if James Michael Bennett III ever breathed a word against any of this, he received a lecture about cosmopolitan values, global citizenship, and the Enlightenment.

"We have to talk."

James sat bolt upright as his mother's voice broke in on his train of thought. The way she spoke made him think her next words would be about some girl who had turned up pregnant claiming he was the father.

"Good morning," he said with studied calm, waiting for what might come next.

"I really don't care when you get up," his mother declared, sitting across the table from him, "but please don't wish me a good morning at two o'clock in the afternoon."

She was tanned an astonishing shade of brown, which made her blond hair look almost unreal, as though she dyed it—which she didn't; indeed, she never even used lipstick.

"I'll try to remember that," James replied. Perhaps it was about something else, then. So far he'd always been lucky. Or had good condoms.

"It's about your engagement party," his mother said, coming to the point at last. "We'll have to arrange it. You can't drag these things out forever. We'll have to set a date, send out invitations. . . . It all needs organizing; it all takes time. The good restaurants with big enough banquet chambers are booked out months in advance." She opened the folder next to her on the table.

"I understand," James said. With an effort he restrained himself from rolling his eyes. Did it have to be today? Given the way he was feeling right now?

He would have his work cut out for him. He knew his mother at least that well.

All day long Hiroshi was wrapped in a strange silence—no, filled with a silence that never left him. It wasn't the silence of the outside world. Rather, it felt as though his ears were blocked, or somebody had rolled him up in yards and yards of cotton wool. He was tired, his throat tickled as though he was catching cold, and his stomach grumbled and cramped from the unaccustomed quantities of alcohol and cheap food, but even so he was overflowing with a warm feeling of contentment. *Overflowing* was the only word that came near describing how he felt. He couldn't get over his surprise at what had happened. He saw his whole life spread out before him, saw the paths that he had taken and how they had finally led him here, to this place, to this moment. All at once everything made sense. Meeting Charlotte so unexpectedly in such an unlikely way seemed a kind of confirmation that fate was at work here. Nothing more, nothing less. A sign he had a task.

They had spent most of the night telling each other their life stories from the day they had been so suddenly separated. Charlotte had gone with her parents to Argentina, to Buenos Aires. After that her father had been posted back to Africa, to Dakar in Senegal. There, Charlotte had learned to speak Wolof, Diola, and Pulaar. She had liked the place even though she had suffered constantly from some kind of stomach trouble and hadn't coped well with the antimalaria tablets.

She told him about a place called the House of Slaves, a museum on an island called Gorée, off the Senegalese coast. Gorée claimed to have been the main transit market for slaves from Africa to America, but Charlotte said she had felt nothing of that in the building. In fact, it had only been set up as a trading post years later and had mostly dealt in ivory and gold; there had never been a single prisoner held in the so-called dungeons down in the cellar. The whole museum was just a replica of other places where the actual slave trade had taken place, but of course they never said as much to visitors.

Hiroshi asked her whether she still had her gift of reading the history of things. Yes, she told him, but it was on the wane. She had to be very deeply in love, or really angry about something—in some state of extreme emotion. Otherwise, things said nothing to her, or she couldn't understand what she felt from them. All the same, she still didn't like going to libraries; old books that had passed through hundreds of hands were sometimes too much to handle. She could hardly bear being near them.

"But don't you have to do a lot of library work?" Hiroshi had asked. "I kind of imagine that's how you study anthropology."

"I mainly want to do excavation work later," she had replied.

"Is that why you picked it as a major? So that you can use your power?"

At that she had given him a strange, secretive look and replied that no, that hadn't been the main reason, but she couldn't tell him now; she would have to show him one day. Hiroshi shook his head, astonished. How long ago it had all been. The girl in the nightgown standing out in the rain late at night; somehow it was like remembering a marvelous dream, but it had really happened. Hard to believe.

He jumped up, looked under the bed for a particular box, and took it out. He blew the dust away and opened the lid. There it was, his old *Masters of the Universe* notebook where he had written down all the secrets of his master plan when he was growing up. He opened the book. It was nearly full, with only the last three pages still blank. Hiroshi leafed through it, looking at the pages he had filled to the very edges with scribbles and cross-section plans. He read his carefully handwritten notes, thoughts and second thoughts, strikethroughs and additions. He had to smile at a lot of what he read, especially in the first pages, his very first naive ideas from when he'd still been a kid. Back then he had thought the world was a whole lot simpler than it actually turned out to be. On the other hand . . . a lot of what he read in this old notebook was amazingly insightful from where he stood today. Bold. Lucid in the true sense. How on earth had he been able to think like that when he had been just thirteen, fourteen years old?

Hiroshi looked up from the pages and out the window, gazing into the sky. Today it was such an intense blue that it seemed to vibrate. He thought back on everything that had happened in his life since then. Thought of his school days. Of all the books he had devoured. Of his scientific work so far. It was a real shock to look back at the Hiroshi of those years, to remember the boundless confidence that had flooded him as a child when he had first had the idea. And what was he doing now? Conducting careful little experiments, proposing tentative theories, studying articles by people who really had no idea, and trying the whole time to be scientifically rigorous in everything he did, making sure there was no angle from which he could be attacked—covering his back.

He leafed through the colorful, rustling pages some more. Here in his hands he had a plan that would change the world from the ground up. He'd had it lying in his desk drawer for years, complete in every detail, and what was he doing? He'd invented a gizmo to save folks the trouble of having to measure a room. He wrote smartass essays for a seminar where the grades were irrelevant. He got into tussles with a professional neurotic over a glass of champagne, risking a black eye for his wisecracks. He was very definitely punching below his weight.

He closed the box, put it back where he'd found it, then sat down at his desk with his old notebook to read it from cover to cover. Every page. To refresh himself on all the thoughts and ideas he had ever had for his grand plan. To remember, remember, remember. It was a trip back in time, almost more than seeing Charlotte again had been. The hours flew by, and he had to laugh, smile indulgently—and raise his eyebrows in wonder. There was so much here that would really work. Maybe not exactly how he had imagined it when he was fourteen, but in principle. At some point he realized he had a pen in his hand and was making more notes. That he was excited.

As he sat there, his initial feeling of having wasted his time all these years changed to a strange certainty he had opened this notebook again at exactly the right moment. That it was good it had spent all those years put aside, almost forgotten. That something had needed time to mature, to age, to ripen in a forgotten corner. That everything that had happened, everything that was happening now, everything that was still to come, was fate.

When he closed the worn, old pages at last, He-Man and Skeletor glared back at him from the cover. He felt a sense of certainty he had not felt for a long time. He picked up his phone and scrolled through the list until he found Charlotte's number, which he had saved last night. He had to see her again. That was the logical next step.

James finally called around four o'clock, all in a flurry. "We're going out! Get yourself ready. I'll pick you up around seven."

Charlotte didn't have a chance to protest. Which was all right by her, she mused as she put the phone down. It meant she didn't have to cook. For some reason she didn't feel like it today.

James always turned up either too early or too late, never right on time. Today he arrived at half past six. Charlotte was just brushing her hair when she saw his Jaguar come roaring up the street and swerve in by her garage. She put the brush down and opened the door, and there was James bounding up the stairs. He flung his arms around her and kissed her passionately as though they hadn't seen each other in weeks.

Charlotte gasped. "For goodness' sake, James!" she said, beginning to worry about her dress.

"I can't help it," he murmured, his mouth nuzzling at her neck. "You look ravishing."

It wasn't as though his compliments were particularly original. But the way he uttered them, she felt he meant every word. On top of which he was so damn good-looking. And strong—the very embodiment of animal masculinity. And so on and so forth. Charlotte closed her eyes and surrendered to his kisses, felt his arousal. Well, she had assumed they would be having sex today anyway, but this felt as though he had forgotten the restaurant entirely and wanted to have her right away. It wouldn't have been the first time.

Just then, however, he let go of her and conjured up a clear plastic box from somewhere with the most marvelous orchid brooch inside. He handed it to Charlotte with a flourish and said, "For the most beautiful woman in the world."

Unoriginal indeed, but it worked. Her fingers trembled as she took the orchid and fixed it to her dress with the pin. It sent up a heavy, intoxicating scent, and for a moment Charlotte felt like an insect queen, wafting out pheromones to lure in males. Perhaps she would eat him whole after sex.

"Is today a special date of some kind?" she had to ask. Normally, she never forgot birthdays or anniversaries.

James gazed adoringly into her eyes. "Every day with you is a special day," he said earnestly. "Also, we're going to Altair."

Charlotte blinked in confusion. She knew the name from some-where. "Altair?"

"*Cuisine française*," James declared grandly.

As always when he mangled her beautiful French language, she shuddered. "And why, all of a sudden?"

"Checking out their menu. Mother thinks we could have the engagement party there."

"Ah." Another of those moments when she thought she must have missed something important. His mother? What did she have to do with anything? It sounded as though preparations were already underway that she knew nothing about—after all, the two of them had never even talked about setting a date. He had simply asked, do you want to? And she had said yes and let him put the ring on her finger. A diamond ring. The diamond had been found by a South African mine worker who couldn't afford to pay a doctor for his sick daughter. James was disappointed she never wore it, but somehow she wasn't ready yet to tell him about her strange gift.

They set out. As Charlotte sank back into the soft, warm leather of the passenger seat, James made some conventional compliment, muffled by the satisfying clunk of the closing door. Some com-ment about envying the upholstery. Charlotte could only summon a crooked smile. It was odd—the idea of going to bed with James tonight didn't excite her as it usually did. She would have liked more than anything else to go home after dinner, tumble into bed, and fall asleep. She already felt as though she might fall asleep on the spot if she kept her eyes closed for more than ten seconds. Last night had been too short.

James drove the way he made love: behind the wheel he was brisk, determined, powerful. That, and the car's solid construction, made her feel safe sitting by his side. The only thing that always annoyed her about the Jaguar was that although she could see the world outside, she couldn't hear a thing. The motor purred away, but even in the densest traffic she could hear herself breathe in this car.

When she looked out the window, she always felt cut off from the world. As though the buildings, the cars, and the pedestrians out there were just a silent film.

"And by the way, Mother has already made us an appointment with a certain Miss Jeffries," James declared. "She looks after the whole organizational side at Altair. We're supposed to talk to her about her ideas, what kind of event she would suggest, all of that. Next Thursday, half past nine. I told her you have Thursday mornings free—isn't that right?"

Charlotte pouted. "This Thursday I'm going to the hairdresser."

James said nothing.

"No problem," she said and sighed. "I can cancel."

He looked across at her for a moment. "Honestly, I have no idea how you can bear to cut off even an inch of your hair. I love it just the way it is."

"When a woman's hair is this long, she has to look after it. If I didn't go to the hairdresser, I would end up looking like I was wearing a mop on my head. I'm sure you wouldn't like that."

He laughed merrily. "You're right," he said.

Charlotte lifted her orchid and inhaled. What was wrong with her? Was it because the topic of the engagement party had come up so suddenly? For some reason she felt ambushed. Was that it? Did she not feel ready yet after all? When she had said something of the kind to her mother recently, Maman had curtly reminded her that when she was her age she was not just married but also practically halfway to the maternity ward.

She remembered what Brenda always said. Her watchword was that you always had to be 100 percent sure. You had to imagine being old as the hills and lying on your deathbed and looking back over your life. And then you had to be able to say yes, I spent it with the right man. Charlotte couldn't really imagine being as old as the hills, and thinking of her deathbed just gave her the shivers. But despite that—yes, she was sure. Fairly sure anyway. And it was perfectly normal at a time like this to be a little fearful of the bold step ahead.

As though he could read her thoughts, James broke in at that very moment to say, "By the way, about giving your friend Brenda a hand moving on Saturday . . ."

"Yes?"

He heaved a great sigh. "I can't come after all. Tennis. My father asked me to play doubles with him against two of his business partners. It's some kind of big deal for the company. Strategic stuff. I couldn't say no."

Charlotte looked at him and wondered whether it was true. It was definitely a pretext of some kind. The plain and simple truth of it was that James just couldn't stand Brenda. In fact, he always found something to criticize in all her friends and acquaintances, male or female. He had told Charlotte once that he wanted to have her all to himself.

"That's too bad," she said.

Altair had valet parking; all they had to do was get out and give the key to a man in a chic gray-blue uniform, who took care of everything.

"That's a good start," James said happily as they walked up the thick, gray-blue carpet to the entrance.

The sun was behind them, low on the horizon, a ball of red fire mirrored in the restaurant windows and drenching the rooms beyond in flame. The sight made Charlotte think of Hiroshi for some reason and how he was bound to call again. Better if he didn't call today of all days. She took her phone from her handbag and switched it off.

The sun was just setting, drenching the sky in blood-red gold. The reflection from the apartment windows across the street almost blinded Hiroshi.

Not that he would have noticed. He sat there with the telephone in his hand, his eyes half-closed, deep in thought. Charlotte's telephone number glowed on the display. His finger hovered over the "Dial" button. All he had to do was press it—so what was holding him back? Was he suddenly shy? Afraid of disappointment? Nothing of the kind, he decided at last as he switched the phone off and put it aside. It just wasn't the right moment, that was all.

3

A wicked rumor had it that Prof. Sheldon Bowers had set his office hours early on Monday mornings so that as few students as possible would ever come to see him. Those who made it anyway were either single-minded or so badly in need of his help that they were even willing to lay off the alcohol over the weekend and get to sleep on time. Hiroshi was one of the single-minded ones. This morning he was already standing waiting at Bowers's door when the prof came in to work.

Bowers was solidly built, his bald head polished to a high shine, and his heavy, black-rimmed glasses perched on an impressive hook nose. Further rumors said he wore only organic cotton, that he was a vegetarian, and he could hold forth at length about what was wrong with the tap water in various states of the union. His academic area was complex-systems research.

"All right, all right," he grumbled once he was near enough he could no longer ignore Hiroshi's presence. "So where's the fire?"

"It's about my term project," Hiroshi said.

"I guessed as much," said Bowers, fishing around in his jacket pocket for his keys. "Let me guess a little more. You're getting bogged down, and you want to focus your topic more tightly."

"Not at all," Hiroshi said. "I want to expand it."

Bowers stopped in his tracks and looked at him, his light gray eyes filled with interest. "You amaze me. Well, this might just turn out to be an interesting week." He turned the key and opened his office door. "Come on in."

The office was a patchwork of furniture, shelves about to collapse under the weight of books, files, and technical equipment, and houseplants parched for lack of watering. In other words, it was a typical MIT prof's office. Bowers gestured curtly toward a chair, dropped his briefcase onto one of the piles of papers heaped up by his desk, and sank into his seat on the other side. Hiroshi handed him the new project proposal, which he had spent last night working on. He had still been writing and revising it at three thirty in the morning and had barely slept afterward, and he felt as though he might fall out of his chair at any moment. But it had to be done this way—there was no time to lose.

Prof. Bowers took the folder without comment, glanced over the text, and then said, "Hmm." He turned back to the beginning and read it closely all the way through. Hiroshi waited patiently.

"So instead of simulating your construction in a computer model, you want to move straight on to building it, is that right?" Bowers asked at last, peering at him over his glasses.

"Exactly," Hiroshi said. "That's the long and the short of it."

"But why? Have you lost your trust in computers?"

"Not at all. But building the apparatus for real would be the next step anyway."

"You want to take two steps at once."

"I want to make real headway, not just take baby steps."

The project was a new kind of robotic position-finding system that would work on the swarm principle—and reading through his old notebook the day before, he had found to his astonishment that he already had the idea when he was thirteen years old. He just hadn't remembered it. The basic idea was to build not a single complex robot that used some sort of signaling system to identify its location, but a whole group of simpler machines that would work together by using one another as reference points. Some robots in the group would take up fixed positions and cling tight to one another; other robots would then use those as a sort of scaffolding to do the actual work. Once the job was done, the workbots would climb back down, the scaffolding elements let go of one another, and then the whole swarm would move on to its next task. For the moment there was no way of knowing what practical applications this technology might have. That, however, was not the point. For MIT to support and finance a research project, the most important consideration was whether it would lead to new insights.

Hiroshi cleared his throat and told the prof what he had just been reading on paper. "A computer simulation would serve to demonstrate the basic working principles of a swarm like this. It could show us how it works, or how the scaffold and the manipulators work together. But it couldn't begin to show us the effects of measurement tolerances, gravity, torque, stress, or any of that. None of those variables would register in a simple computer simulation. If I tell element X to take up position Y, then all that happens is a couple of lines of code do exactly that. But in reality an arm might bend as it reaches out to take hold, or tiny measurement errors might compound as the distances grow, or the cogwheels may not mesh exactly, that sort of thing. None of that would register in a simulation at the level I originally planned to write. If we want to model all these factors, we would have to code it in considerably more detail, describing each and every one of the robots as a finite element model. I estimate that would actually be much more expensive than simply building the machine for a lab test. You can find my figures in Appendix B."

"I see, I see." Prof. Bowers took off his glasses and chewed on one of the ends while he studied a page of formulas in Hiroshi's proposal. "You know, you're probably right. But the problem is a lab test still costs more than the current simulation. I can't just go ahead and approve it, especially since the approval is still pending for your original project."

Hiroshi sat there motionless. "Last time we spoke you said it was just a formality."

"Well sure, but once we increase the budget tenfold, it stops being a formality." Prof. Bowers put his glasses back on, set Hiroshi's proposal down on the desk in front of him, and folded his hands across it. He said, "I'll pass this up the chain. You'll be hearing from me."

"Miss Malroux?" It was Tuesday, after Dr. Thomas Wickersham's seminar. "Could I speak with you for a moment?"

Charlotte stopped. Somehow she managed not to heave a sigh. So it was happening just as she had feared. She waited while the others filed out of the seminar room. Some of them glanced at her knowingly, one or two even mockingly. They knew whatever happened next was bound to be fairly embarrassing.

Dr. Wickersham had a cheerful gaze and a funny little goatee beard. He seemed not the least bit bothered by the fact that even at his early age his hairline was receding rapidly. He had an excellent reputation as a paleoanthropologist and had done a great deal of fieldwork in the Near East, where he spoke several of the local languages. He published in the most prestigious journals, and his seminars were always fascinating, thanks to his gift for presenting the material clearly and memorably without ever cutting corners. But recently the students had all noticed Dr. Wickersham had a soft spot for Charlotte.

"I'd like to ask you something," he began once they had all left. The door to the hallway was still open. "I've realized I could never forgive myself if I didn't ask, so really, best get it over and done with. And of course I hardly need mention that whatever answer you give will have no effect at all on your grade or on any other aspect of this seminar, or on your time here at Harvard."

Charlotte looked at him unhappily. "Yes?"

"Would you do me the great favor of agreeing to a date?" Then he added hastily, as though he had just now realized how rashly he had acted, "I know very little about you, Miss Malroux—far too little. All I know is that your father is a French diplomat and that you have traveled the word a great deal, even as a child . . . I should imagine you must have an unusual life story. I'd like to hear a little more about it. If possible over a good meal."

He was standing on the other side of the lecturer's desk, several yards away, but even so he was taking a considerable risk. Relationships between faculty and students were regarded with deep suspicion at Harvard; indeed, they were basically banned. There were very strict rules against sexual harassment, which Charlotte thought were paranoid. As a result, the male faculty always took great care never to be alone with a female student. If Charlotte chose to run out screaming into the hallway and claim Dr. Wickersham had made a pass at her, there would be no helping him; it would be the end of his career.

"Dr. Wickersham," Charlotte said carefully, "that's a very kind offer, but as it happens I am about to announce my engagement, so I don't know—"

He swallowed and shook his head hastily. "Oh, that makes it all the more urgent, then! Please believe me, I am only proposing a . . . conversation, a pleasant evening between friends . . ." He took a deep breath. "I could book a table at Cloud Eight on Saturday—it's not the haute cuisine you're used to in France, of course, but even so it's the best Boston has to offer. What do you say?"

Charlotte knew the restaurant; James had taken her there a couple of times. At least twenty dollars for an appetizer, and a wine list that would impress even her father.

Now she could sigh. "On Saturday," she said, "I'm helping a friend move. I'm afraid I'll be in no fit state for conversation by the evening. I really don't know. Please don't think that I don't appreciate your invitation, but—"

Dr. Wickersham looked at her attentively. "Would it be shameless of me to invite myself?"

"I'm sorry? Where?"

"To help your friend move house. In my experience another pair of helping hands is always useful."

For a moment Charlotte felt she was dreaming. "Oh, of course," she said without thinking. "That would be wonderful. As it happens, someone's just had to drop out." Was this really happening? Was her paleoanthropology professor actually offering to come and heave crates so that her best friend could move?

"Well then," Wickersham said happily, taking out his appointment book, "you just tell me the time and the address, and I'll be there." He looked up and seemed to notice her astonishment. "I moved nineteen times while I was a student," he explained with a grin. "So many people helped me out back then that I figure I'm still in debt. If nothing else it's a good workout, and you usually meet some interesting people." He raised his eyebrows. "And if we don't sit down afterward to eat a pizza or some such, that would be a first in my experience."

Charlotte couldn't help but laugh. "That's fine," she said. "It seems a little odd, but . . . of course. Happy to have your help." As she gave him Brenda's address and watched him write it down, she suddenly found herself wondering how it would feel to be clasped in those slender hands, what it would be like if he did take hold of her, caress her, full of desire. She felt herself blushing. What on earth was wrong with her?

On Wednesday morning James caught his hand in the car door—not badly, but nonetheless annoying. At lunch he splatted his shirt with ketchup, and then he made a fool of himself in the History of Ceramics class, since he'd forgotten they were supposed to read an article on the Yangshao culture. The Chinese had already been firing ceramics eight thousand years before Christ, for crying out loud, and when Dr. Urban showed them those pots, he, James, had declared that they were Greek. For whatever reason, it didn't seem to be his day.

But then, as he was headed over to the library, resolved to catch up on his reading, things took a turn for the better. He spotted a familiar figure out of the corner of his eye: Terry Miller, standing in front of the bulletin board, jotting something down from a flyer. Terry with her ponytail. What could be absorbing her attention so? James strolled up behind her. The flyer had been put up by someone called Kenny Higgins, who was offering students golf lessons at discount prices.

You've walked right into my trap, little mouse, James thought happily. He stepped up beside her and made sure she noticed him before he spoke. "Hi, Terry. How's it going?"

"Hi, JB," she said, still writing.

"You play golf? Am I going to have to watch my back in the next cup?"

She laughed. "I think you can rest easy for a couple of months yet."

He pointed at the flyer. "I hope you're not thinking of giving your money to that guy."

"It looks like," Terry said, shutting her notebook. She snapped the elastic band around it and stuffed it back into her bag. Today she was carrying a giant sunflower. "He has to make a living."

"Well sure, but he could find some other line of work than teaching beginners how not to play golf." He crossed his arms and looked at her with deep concern in his eyes. "I mean, sure, nothing against Kenny—he's a nice guy and all—but the way he plays golf . . . I just wonder how he thinks he can teach a beginner anything when he never even knows which club to use. That's not to mention his swing. Let's just say it . . . leaves a lot to be desired."

All of which was sheer bluff, of course. He'd never even heard of the guy. Although actually that was a point against him, since James knew most of the really good golfers by name. And it was having the desired effect. Terry was visibly put off. *Little mouse.*

"That's not really true, is it?" she asked, frowning prettily.

Time to spring his trap. He spread his hands, shrugged, and said, "I can't in good faith let Kenny spoil your game before you even get started. I'll make you a friendly offer: let's meet on the course, and I'll teach you some of the basics. Then you can at least think about it—you'll have something to judge him by."

She opened her eyes wide, incredulous. "You'd do that for me?"

"I have to," he answered earnestly. "Golf is far too fine a sport for me to let some half-assed instructor give you the wrong ideas." And, of course, it was an ideal opportunity for them to get to know each other better. Just how much better she would find out soon.

"Okay then, I won't say no." She smiled, little knowing what was to come.

"Okay then. When would you have time? Tomorrow?" Strike while the iron is hot. He heartily approved of the proverb. Chances like this didn't come twice.

"Sure, if you have time."

He gave her a cheerful smile. "You're looking at a free man, my dear. I decide when I have time. So listen: come to the Silverway Golf Course at nine o'clock tomorrow morning, and ask at reception for Charles Hauser. He's a friend of mine, and I'll tell him to fit you out with everything you'll need. And then we'll set out and see whether we can't score a hole in one."

"Do I have to wear anything special?"

Something that comes off quickly, my little mouse, James thought, but he said, "Not really. Short skirt or shorts, a T-shirt, sneakers, and maybe a baseball cap. Something with a brim, for the sun."

"Okay." Now she was grinning as though *she* were the cat who'd got the cream. "Tomorrow then, nine o'clock."

He watched her go, unable to get enough of the way her ponytail swayed back and forth as she walked. Once she was out of sight, he took out his phone and called Charles to put him in the picture. And then, goddamn it all, he remembered he was already booked on Thursday morning. That meeting at Altair to talk about the engagement party. Damn it to hell and back. He'd just have to cancel. It wasn't that urgent, not yet. Although he could already imagine how his mother would cuss him out. Better to call Charlotte first, then. He played with the phone, trying to think up some convincing excuse. Well, in any case, the library clearly wasn't going to happen today.

It turned out to be harder than Hiroshi had thought to reach Charlotte. After talking to Prof. Bowers on Monday morning, he went back home, went back to bed, and slept until evening. Then he tried calling her. "The person you wish to speak to is unavailable," the computerized voice told him and invited him to leave a message. He didn't; instead, he called three more times, always with the same result.

On Tuesday afternoon he gave up and left her a voice mail—nothing special, just saying he'd like to see her again, and could she call him. On Wednesday afternoon, after the last seminar, his voice-mail box showed he had a message. When he called it up, full of anticipation, it turned out not to be Charlotte at all; instead, it was a man's voice, deep and calm, someone called Jens Rasmussen. He was an investor, he said, and a few days ago he had bought out Sollo Electronics. He believed Hiroshi Kato had a contract with them. He'd like to meet and talk.

Sollo Electronics had been bought out? That was news to Hiroshi. On the other hand, he didn't really follow corporate dealings much, so it came as no great surprise. But who in the world was Jens Rasmussen?

Back home Hiroshi sat down at his computer and looked him up. There was indeed a Jens Rasmussen on a list of US billionaires. He had studied forestry and gotten an MBA. He wrote columns, liked to read history books in his spare time, and sponsored studies of the coastal redwoods. And he ran an investment fund. One of the financial magazines had an article that said he was well-known for taking a strong interest in the contracts of firms he had bought up. Okay. It sounded as though it would be worth calling the guy back. A secretary answered, assuring him in a grandmotherly voice his call was expected and she would put him through immediately.

It was about his invention, of course. "You sold yourself way too cheap there," the man told him levelly. "That's not good for business. Now that I've taken over the company, the contract is between you and me, and I'd like to renegotiate."

Hiroshi frowned. "If I sold myself too cheap, surely that's good for you. Or have I misunderstood?"

"Well, that would be the usual way of looking at it, but it's short-sighted. I'm sorry to say that this kind of thinking is far too common in business. I have a different philosophy, and since I've been implementing it quite successfully for the past thirty years, I have to believe that I'm not entirely wrong. The way I see it, business is an exchange of goods and services, and it's just like any biological exchange. Think of it as a kind of circulation. Give and take. You give something so that you get something in return, sure, but you also give to get so that you can go on giving. If all you do is keep on giving, you're acting in accordance with a particular cultural virtue—you're being selfless—but you'll just use yourself up. And where does that lead? Sooner or later you have nothing left to give. And then you're no good to the world at large, and everything else you might have given is lost. Self-sacrifice is a net loss for everybody, at least in this context. Obviously wars and natural disasters are something else entirely."

Hiroshi cleared his throat. It was no mean feat to get a word in edgewise. "Well, I always intended to make money with the Wizard's Wand," he said. "I never thought of it as self-sacrifice, believe me."

"Good, that's certainly a start. But you still weren't paying attention to the right balance of give-and-take."

"I had the MIT intellectual property department look over the contract—"

"The contract is fine. Listen, Mr. Kato, let's keep this simple. I happen to be in Boston on Saturday. If it suits you, I'd like to meet and talk all this over."

Hiroshi thought for a moment. He wasn't doing anything on Saturday he couldn't put off. And it sounded as though what this man had to say was worth listening to. "Saturday would be fine. Where and when?"

"In the afternoon, around four," Rasmussen said straightaway. "I'd really like to come and see you. I don't care for those business meals that are all about pretense. I like to see how and where my business partners live. You're in MacGregor House, aren't you?"

"Yes." Hiroshi looked around his room. For heaven's sake, he would have to clean up—and thoroughly at that.

"Good, I know the place. I will of course return the invitation. Next time you can come to me, and then we'll do the whole food-and-drink thing. On Saturday, though, I don't want you to make any special effort; don't even tidy up. I was a student myself once, and I know how cramped those tiny rooms are." There was a noise like that of a thick leather desk diary closing. "Good then. I'll see you on Saturday at four o'clock. Okay?"

"Okay," Hiroshi said. The man wasted no time, that was for sure. He felt a little as though he had been hustled into it, but there was nothing wrong with that. A person who wasted no time—somehow he had the feeling he could use someone like that.

Charlotte spotted something twinkling out of the corner of her eye. Reflecting the sunlight on the roof across the street, flashing so brightly that she had to draw the curtain across a little. A little gray dog was trotting along the street, sniffing at all the latest doggie news on the trees and looking around as though waiting for someone or expecting a command.

She stared at the cursor blinking on the screen in front of her. She had just sat down to work on her assignment with a cup of tea in hand when James had called to cancel next morning's appointment. Just before he called she had had every line of her paper mapped out in her head, and now she'd forgotten the lot. She sighed. Sometimes it wasn't easy with James and all his spontaneous decisions. Now he "had to" attend some special training session. As though James Michael Bennett III had ever done anything because he had to. He only ever did what he wanted and always got away with it because of his charm. One of his guiding principles was it was easier to ask forgiveness than permission, so he never asked permission in advance. He simply did whatever he felt like, and if you got angry at him he made big puppy eyes until you just had to laugh.

Like the day he had moved his stuff into her wardrobe. One day he had simply turned up with a bag and declared that since things were getting serious between them, he would have to keep a few things at her place. He couldn't spend half his time running around in wrinkled clothes and yesterday's shirt, he told her; he had to think of his reputation. So of course she had made room. She had shoved her own clothes closer together, put some in boxes, and even thrown a few things out. She hadn't protested—quite the opposite. Recently, she had even taken to doing his laundry along with hers and ironing his shirts.

And now he had this training session. Whatever that was. Not that she really cared about meeting with the restaurant people—she hadn't particularly wanted to do that anyway. It was just that . . . James was altogether too fond of causing upset and confusion. She couldn't even get her hair done because of him.

She thought of Hiroshi. He had called several times and finally left a voice mail to ask whether they could get together. She wanted to, but for some reason she hadn't plucked up the nerve. Why not? The truth was it was because she never knew these days what she was doing from one day to the next, or where she would be next week. How was she supposed to make any plans? It was high time she learned to hold her own against James.

She closed her computer and got out her map of the Boston area. Then she rooted through her sewing box and found a spool of white thread. She unwound a good length and got to work. Once she knew what she wanted, she called James back and said, "You have to do me a favor."

"A favor?" he asked, taken by surprise.

"I'll need you to pick me up in the car tomorrow afternoon. Three o'clock."

Oh. That seemed to be a lot to ask. "Hey, listen, I don't know how long the training will last, whether I'll be done by then—"

"You'll manage somehow," she cut him off and picked up her map. "Listen, I'll tell you where I'll be . . ."

When the phone rang again, Hiroshi picked up expecting to hear Rasmussen say there was one more thing. But it was Charlotte.

"Oh," he said. For a heartbeat he felt some nameless fear grip him, felt almost suffocated. A moment during which he looked into the abyss and felt overpowered by the fear of failure, fear of being inadequate, fear of making nothing of his life however hard he tried. Then he got a grip on himself, and the fear vanished as though it had never been. The abyss closed.

"Charlotte. We caught one another at last."

She didn't respond directly. She sounded as though she had just been in a rage about something and was trying to take her mind off it.

"You asked me why I study anthropology of all things," she said.

"Yes," Hiroshi replied.

"And I said I would have to show you if you were to understand at all."

"So you did."

"Do you have time tomorrow?"

Of course he didn't. For years he hadn't had a single day that wasn't all booked up in advance. If he wanted time, he had to make it.

"Of course," he said. He could skip tomorrow's seminar and ask Will Burton from H-5 to fill him in later. He had a meeting scheduled with the technicians who were supposed to work for him once his project was approved, but that could be postponed. And he had an assignment about distributed systems architecture, but he could write that tonight.

"Do you have a backpack?" Charlotte asked.

Where was this leading? "Yes."

"Hiking shoes?"

"I only have sneakers," Hiroshi admitted. "But they're pretty sturdy."

She thought for a moment. "Okay, that should do. Let's meet tomorrow morning, then. Six o'clock at the John Harvard statue."

4

Harvard's campus was still empty at that hour of the morning. Hiroshi found himself walking on tiptoe as though students were not supposed to be up and about so early for some reason.

He had come along a little early just to be sure. He looked around, shivering. He thought he saw a movement behind one of the windows, but it might just have been the reflection of a bird flying past. As far as he knew, all of these redbrick buildings were freshman dormitories, and the freshmen were surely all still asleep at this hour.

A sudden noise made him jump. A man in overalls had opened a metal door in the ground floor of one of the buildings and was rooting through a tangle of gardening tools with no regard for the noise he was making. The statue stood in front of University Hall, a venerable old pile in white granite. The sculpture itself was bronze and showed a man leaning back at ease—almost slumped—in an armchair. An open book lay across his lap, but he wasn't reading; rather, he was gazing into empty space. He looked astonishingly young for somebody who had founded a university. Hiroshi would have expected to see an aged scholar with a long beard, but when he had looked him up the night before, he had learned that John Harvard had died at the age of thirty, just a few months after immigrating to America.

The toe of the left shoe gleamed. Supposedly, it was good luck to give it a polish before you had an exam. Hiroshi took a step back and looked at the inscription on the plinth. "John Harvard—Founder—1638," it said.

"The tour guides call it the Statue of the Three Lies," said Charlotte behind him.

He turned round quickly. There she was, dressed in hiking gear with a backpack slung on her back, as though she had popped up out of nowhere. The noise from the man in overalls had probably masked the sound of her footsteps, he decided.

"Hello," he said.

She gave a wry grin. There was still a trace of yesterday's anger in her eyes. "First lie," she said without returning his greeting, "John Harvard wasn't the founder, just the first benefactor. He left the university his library in his will, all three hundred and twenty books of it, and half his fortune. It was actually founded by a man called Nathaniel Eaton, not in 1638—that's the second lie—but, rather, in 1636. And the third lie: John Harvard looked nothing like the man in the statue. That was just a student who sat for the sculptor as a model."

Hiroshi looked at her. Charlotte was indeed extraordinarily beautiful. Her long black hair fell smoothly over her shoulders, her skin was like porcelain, and her features were regular but too lively to be called doll-like. She was slim, trim, and bursting with energy. But none of that was what attracted him to her; rather, it was the overwhelming feeling that something connected them both, even if Hiroshi couldn't say what. All he knew was that when they had run into each other again on Saturday, he was a restless wanderer who had found his way back home. He had just the same feeling now. The feeling drew him to her—but shocked him as well.

"We didn't meet here to talk about John Harvard?" he asked.

She laughed a marvelous, bubbling laugh. "No. He's just an example of what we tend to think is true when in fact it's just wishful thinking. And of how we so often make a picture of something we know nothing about. There is no surviving portrait of John Harvard. Nevertheless, here we have his statue. And on the campus of a university, mind you, with the motto *Veritas*—truth."

Hiroshi looked at the statue again. There was no question that when he knew all that, he saw it through different eyes. "How curious."

Charlotte put her backpack down and opened it. She took out a bottle of water and a plump plastic bag, and handed them both to him. "Here. These are for you. You have to carry your own."

Hiroshi weighed the bag in his hand. "Supplies. We're going on a hike?"

"Wasn't hard to guess, though, was it?" Charlotte asked. "After all, I asked you if you had hiking shoes."

"No, I was expecting it," Hiroshi admitted. He took off his own backpack and stowed the lunch bag and water bottle. He had also brought along a couple of the energy bars that kept him going when he was coding all night; he always had a supply. He would give her one later. "And where are we going?"

"Into the past," Charlotte declared. She swung the pack onto her back once more and turned toward Johnston Gate, the main entrance to campus. Then she lifted her right foot and took one step forward. "That's a hundred years." She stopped, leaned backward a little, and pointed to a spot just in front of her left boot. "That's when we were born, more or less." She moved her hand to point maybe half a step ahead. "That was the Second World War. And that was the First." She pointed to a spot just behind the heel of her front boot. "Are you with me so far?"

"Yes," said Hiroshi, nodding.

Charlotte took a second step. "The Industrial Revolution. Napoleon. The French Revolution." A third step. "Louis XIV of France, the Sun King." A fourth. "The Thirty Years' War in Germany." A fifth. "The Protestant Reformation." Six. "Copernicus." Seven. "The Black Death." Eight. "Genghis Khan. Marco Polo." Nine.

"The Crusades. Europe is completely Christian by now." Ten. "The Norman conquest of England. One thousand years in the past."

"Okay," Hiroshi said, walking along beside her skeptically. This could be a struggle, given how little he knew about history.

Charlotte took another ten steps and was standing in the middle of the tiny lawn in front of University Hall. "Jesus of Nazareth. Roman Empire." Ten more steps. "One thousand years before Christ. Three thousand years in the past. Iron Age. This is the time of the Pharaohs, Tutankhamun, Ramses."

Twenty steps. They had reached the broad avenue that led into campus. "Three thousand years before Christ. The time of the First Dynasty in Egypt. The pyramids haven't yet been built."

Hiroshi counted along with her. She had already taken fifty steps, and now she took fifty more.

"Eight thousand years before Christ. This is the middle of the Neolithic period. They're already practicing agriculture in China."

Another thirty paces. Now they were standing almost exactly beneath the arch of Johnston Gate, the main entrance to Old Yard. "Eleven thousand BC," Charlotte said, pointing straight down at the ground. "Signs of grain cultivation in Mesopotamia. This is the age of Jerf el Ahmar and Göbekli Tepe, the oldest known temples of humankind."

Hiroshi looked at the distance they had walked from the John Harvard statue to where they stood now and nodded, impressed. "So this is where the story ends."

"Oh no," Charlotte said. "This is just the beginning."

She turned around and walked through the gate out into the street. On the other side of the tarmac strip was a little park, where a curious church tower thrust up into the sky. Charlotte pointed off to her right. "We're going further backward. Now we're in the Würm glaciation."

James swung his 4x4 into the parking place right by the front door Charles had kept free for him, as promised. There was even a sign with his name on it. He hoped Terry had noticed *that*. He bounded out of the car and swung his golf bag out of the trunk. He was fifteen minutes late—just as he had planned. He mustn't look like he needed her. He didn't. He could sleep with Charlotte anytime he liked, or with a dozen other girls from his address book for that matter. No, what he liked was the thrill of the chase. Stalking the prey. Getting the scent. And then the warm body down in the grass. He liked a little resistance.

In a word, he liked a challenge.

"Good morning, Mr. Bennett," said Will the porter as he walked into the clubhouse. Will was a young black guy, not as deferential as his predecessor, but still okay.

"Good morning, Will," he replied. Of course, James had a club membership card, but he liked not needing to use it. His face should be enough to open all doors.

Terry was already there. He spotted her as soon as he walked out onto the fairway—and man oh man did she look hot. She was dressed all in red—to the extent that she was wearing anything at all—and showing a lot of skin. He couldn't have asked for more. She was standing with Charles by a golf cart while he showed her the various clubs. Even from a hundred feet away, James could see how the old fox was holding the clubs so that he had an excellent view of her cleavage as she bent to look.

James put two fingers in his mouth and whistled. That put a stop to their cozy little chat. She all but jumped in the air like a cheer-leader, instantly looking up from the clubs and waving excitedly as he strolled over. She really was excited! Very good. James grinned. The battle was half-won.

She looked even better up close. She was wearing bright red shorts that left little to the imagination. He could see everything, the curve of her buttocks, and then in the front . . . Was she even wearing any panties? It certainly didn't look like it.

She was wearing ankle socks inside her red sneakers, and a baseball cap that topped the whole thing off. Her ponytail poked out through the back of the cap and shone in the sun like pure gold. Her shirt was the only false note in the whole outfit, a cheap-looking thing with sequins and a crazy pattern somebody presumably thought was stylish. Never mind. It gave him a view of her bosom that made his balls as hard as . . . well, as golf balls. And, in his view, that was what shirts were for.

What a day! The sky was deep blue and shining, with barely a cloud; the grass glowed a lusty green; flocks of birds wheeled and sang as they hunted their own small prey. Even at this hour he could feel it would be a hot day, so early in the year. Wasn't life wonderful?

On their way up to the tee he asked her what she knew of the rules and scoring. It looked like she had done her homework. She knew all about handicap, par, score, a hole in one, bogey, and so on.

"What's your major?" he asked.

"Art history," she replied, tossing her head so that her ponytail flew. "I like the finer things in life."

"Well what a coincidence. So do I," said James, grinning. That's the way it always was; the hottest women always studied art history and steered clear of the sciences. Apart from Charlotte, of course, but she was the exception who proved the rule. No point thinking about her now, though.

"And where are you from?" he asked.

"Ohio."

"Ohio's big."

She sighed. "It's a one-horse town, but it has a name. Not that you'll ever have heard of it. Believe me, you've missed nothing."

"Okay," said James. As if he cared where she was from. "How about family?"

"A brother. Though to be honest, I really don't want to talk about my family right now."

"That bad?"

She pouted. Maybe she thought she looked tough, but she just looked cute. "Such narrow-minded people. I can't talk to them. They don't understand that I have what they would call liberal opinions. That I want to enjoy life."

Liberal opinions. Enjoy life. A good plan, Terry my little mouse. Let's start right now.

"So you're the black sheep of the family," James declared, parking his golf cart next to the tee. "Or the red sheep, so to speak." He looked her up and down, letting his appreciation show.

She giggled and gave a little shimmy that made her boobs bounce delightfully. "A sheep? Is that what you see when you look at me?"

He made an *I'm-thinking-hard* face. "A little lamb, then?"

"And that makes you the big bad wolf?"

"You've seen right through me," he declared and got busy finding the right club. "Sure, I just had breakfast, but you look like you could make a pretty little snack. I just have to make you break a sweat. A lamb needs a little sauce, you know."

She tittered again. "I had no idea you were such a joker."

"There's a lot you don't know about me." He decided on the driver. A classic choice. "Okay, now I'll take the first stroke and you just watch what I do." He put the ball on the tee and took up his stance, concentrated. This first shot had to be a good one.

Raise, swing, and—away it flew. He watched the ball happily as it traced its arc, then landed not too far off—in part because he didn't want to discourage her, and also because he was in no hurry.

"Now you. Start off without the ball."

"Just the swing?"

"You swing, I'll correct you, and then you swing again. Come on," he said and pointed to her cart. "I want to see you sweat."

It took her a while to identify the driver. When she got in position at the empty tee, she stood fairly well, but her swing was about as clumsy as could be. If there had been a ball on the tee, it wouldn't even have felt a passing breeze. He told her what she was doing wrong. Let the club hang lower; swing farther back; don't clutch it quite so hard. And again. Swing your hips there, baby. And again.

After the tenth try, she groaned aloud. "Oooh! I'll never get this."

Time to move things along a bit. "Oh, you'll learn. No question about it. You just have to know how to hold the club. Here, allow me," he said, stepping up behind her. He put his arms around her and corrected her grip. "Like that. Now swing back. Easy does it. You can take it slow, yeah?"

He put his hands on her arms and for a moment he forgot all about her, forgot about everything but the task of making sure she held the club correctly, since a bad habit that has taken root is awfully hard to shake off. Then his nose caught a waft of her perfume, a sweet, cheap scent she had washed off last time she took a shower but that still lingered, mingling with the scent of her body, a mixture of musk and violets. And he remembered what he was really here for. The prize in this game.

He looked down at her neck and saw the vein there throbbing. She allowed him to correct her grip, but he could feel as well that she was resisting him on another level. He thought about the kind of hole in one he wanted to score at the end of the course, and could hardly contain himself.

Hiroshi and Charlotte walked along Massachusetts Avenue for a while, then crossed over onto Garden Street, with its comfortably wide, stone-paved sidewalks. The traffic was heavy, and the occasional jogger came panting past. They headed toward another church tower, this one bigger than the one before, left it behind, and continued past the Sheraton Hotel. The trees along the avenue gave way to grand redbrick facades on both sides. An elderly, uniformed hotel porter standing beneath a red canopy looked at them dubiously.

The trees resumed, but the sidewalk had become just concrete slabs, buckled and broken. Dark redbrick town houses took over. The sidewalk became narrower and the trees taller, overshadowing the road itself in places. As they went on, the houses receded from the roadside, sometimes almost out of sight behind the bushes and trees.

Charlotte finally stopped at a side street. "This is the end of the first ice age. Or the last, since we're going backward. And it's not the end, it's the beginning." She looked dubiously at him. "Am I making any sense?"

"No," Hiroshi said and had to laugh. "But I get what you mean." He looked back. They had been walking for about a quarter of an hour and had covered maybe a kilometer, which, going by Charlotte's scale, was around one hundred thousand years into the past. So most of the world had been covered by ice all this time? It was almost unbelievable.

"Okay," said Charlotte. "Remember this point."

Hiroshi looked up and read the street sign. The side street was called Parker Street. The grand old trees on both sides hid what he assumed to be residential buildings. They had been walking along Concord Avenue. Charlotte marched along it for about another 150 meters and then stopped near a bus stop.

"And that," she declared once Hiroshi had caught up with her, "was the interglacial warm period, between the Würm and the Riss glaciations. Anything strike you?"

There was a chicken-wire fence along the sidewalk, behind which rose a slope covered with trees and bushes. Across the street was a school, or maybe a kindergarten, and a little park with a statue of a man raising his hand in blessing. Or was it an angel? Hiroshi didn't know; he wasn't so great on religious stuff.

He looked at the distance they had come from Parker Street. "This period is longer than the whole of recorded history they teach us in school."

"Exactly," Charlotte said. "And it's a period we know next to nothing about."

Hiroshi raised his eyebrows. "That's amazing," he said. "I mean, there were people alive back then as well. They must have fought wars and all that, even then."

"Do you remember the Island of the Saints?" Charlotte asked. "The knife on the altar that I was so keen to touch?"

"Sure," said Hiroshi.

Charlotte pointed ahead. "That was even older."

The first hole took forever. Terry drove her ball off the fairway, into the rough, into a bunker, into the water. . . . She ran into every hazard there was, meaning he had plenty of opportunity to correct her, touch her, breathe in her smell, stroke her bosom, take hold of her hips.

"You have to relax here," James said again as he put his hands on her buttocks and jiggled them about. "Again."

When they finally reached the green, it turned out Terry was no good at putting either. First she hit the ball too hard, sending it past the flag and back onto the fairway, then she tapped it too softly, so that it plopped sullenly back down in the grass. She became quite worked up. Which was hardly a bad thing, since when she was worked up, she shrugged and pouted most appealingly.

"Just relax first," James told her, stepping up behind her and correcting her stance a little. "Legs apart. Yes, that's it. Now look at the ball. Imagine how it's going to land. Just imagine it slipping easily into the hole. Gliding in without the least effort. Think what a great feeling that'll be." He heard her take a deep breath and saw her tremble slightly. So she wasn't just thinking of golf balls. Very good. Not long now and he would have her. "Now swing."

This time she hit the ball just right. It glided across the green as though reeled in on a thread and dropped smoothly into the hole.

"Well hey there," he said admiringly. "You're good at this."

"I have a good teacher," she said and gave him a roguish glance.

"That's true," James said, patting himself on the shoulder. "I'm good at this."

At last they reached the second hole. This had been his objective all along. Not only was there a rough along the edge of the fairway that was only mowed once a year, there was also a copse of trees, an overgrown thicket full of shrubbery probably full of lost balls. It was an unusual feature for a golf course, but city hall had made the wood a condition of the original land purchase, and it was considered a nature reserve. A lot of players complained bitterly about it, but the smarter members of the club recognized the possibilities. He and Terry wouldn't be the first couple to get down in the grass there.

"Can I start this time?" Terry asked.

James nodded magnanimously, while his mind was on his own plans. He would have to drive his ball into the thicket, that much was clear. Then he would act all angry, blame her, tell her she was distracting him with her sexy outfit, and ask how a red-blooded man was supposed to concentrate on the game. She would like that; women liked to be blamed for that sort of thing. And then she wouldn't protest if he shouted at her to come help him look . . . none of which needed planning, he realized as soon as he saw Terry drive.

"Oops," she said.

The two of them watched the ball fly up in a long curving arc toward the wood and vanish between the treetops.

"Am I putting you off your stroke?" James asked, amused.

"It looks like," Terry admitted bashfully.

"I'll come help you look."

"You're a sweetie."

As they made their way into the underbrush, James felt surreptitiously for the condom in his trouser pocket. There it was, within easy reach. Good. Time to spring the trap on this little mouse.

The bushes pushed back against them, clawed at their clothing, and scratched their skin. There was a rustling and scurrying in the undergrowth—wildlife that hadn't been expecting a visit. It was hot, too. They were sweating, and a cloud of hungry midges soon sought them out.

"How am I supposed to be able to drive the ball back out of the wood?" Terry eventually asked. "It's flat-out impossible."

Of course, she wasn't supposed to. That was why they had spare balls in their golf bags. Strictly speaking, the rules gave them five minutes to search for a lost ball, and the only way to find a ball in this wood in that time was to be ridiculously lucky. Right now, though, the rules were the last thing on his mind.

"Stand still a moment," James said.

She stopped, turned around, and looked at him with big eyes. She was gleaming with sweat. This was a good spot, a tiny clearing where the light and shadows chased each other around, and the ground was overgrown with moss and little white flowers, which gave off a heady, sweet scent.

"Little lamb," James said, taking her into his arms. "You shouldn't be alone in the forest with the big bad wolf." She was slack in his grasp, putting up not the least resistance. "Especially not when you're wet through like this." He stooped over her, kissed her neck, and ran his hands down her sides, shoving his fingers into her bright-red shorts.

Now they were picking up the pace. More and more they found themselves hiking along roads that were never meant for pedestrians. Drivers looked at them in surprise from behind the wheel. They passed a lake, great sprawling buildings, filling stations, row homes, and still they were on Concord Avenue. The road seemed never to end.

Hiroshi had asked Charlotte about the knife and what she had read from it, but she didn't want to talk about it. Two kilometers from their last stop, she halted. By now Concorde Avenue had a pleasant strip of green lawn running down the central island, and they had just passed an imposing synagogue. "Oldest known fossils of modern *Homo sapiens*," Charlotte declared. "Excavated at the Omo River site, southwest Ethiopia."

They set off again. "Fossils are very rare indeed," she explained as they went. "Most of the time a dead body decays in its entirety, even the bones. You need very special conditions for a skeleton to survive. Which is why most regions yield no bone finds at all—the soil simply breaks everything down. That's the rule, fossils are the exception."

Hiroshi had never really thought about it, but now it seemed obvious. "If it didn't happen that way, our soil would be full of the bones of dead species, and their calcium would be locked out of the ecosystem."

Charlotte nodded. "Right back at the start of our paleoanthropology seminar, Dr. Wickersham told us that if we gathered up all the human bone fossils that had ever been discovered, we could easily load them into a single truck. That's the underlying problem whenever you want to state anything about human prehistory with any certainty: the evidence is so slim that you'd never get a jury to convict. But there are theories all the same—there have to be—or we'd have nowhere to start from. Generally, they're thought to be incontrovertible. Laymen think so, and even scientists think so if they don't know all the details."

On and on they went. Hiroshi hadn't realized Boston was such a leafy, green city. The sun climbed higher in the sky, the day grew ever hotter, but for long stretches they walked in the pleasant shade of trees. It was hard work and not something he was used to, but he enjoyed it all the same. When they weren't talking, it was a companionable silence, and when they were, they talked about what they had each been doing since the old days. That was companionable, too.

They went through an underpass and then began walking up a slope, sometimes steep, sometimes gentle. The going got a little tougher. They were in an area of huge mansions where single houses stood all on their own in grounds so vast he couldn't see where they ended. Sometimes he could barely see the house. A wealthy neighborhood clearly. And then, sometime after nine o'clock, Concord Avenue ended. For the last couple of miles, they had been walking along grass verges, and they had now reached a junction with Spring Street.

"Anything special here?" asked Hiroshi, out of breath.

"One point three million years in the past," Charlotte answered. "*Homo erectus* is living in Africa. He knows how to use fire, he's lost most of his body hair and has developed dark skin. He can be up to six feet tall, and if we saw him on the street today we could barely tell him apart from modern man." She pointed to the right. "Off we go."

Three kilometers farther on and a good forty minutes later, they were standing by a highway ramp.

"Now we're in the middle of the Olduvai period. We've discovered stone tools, and there are signs we were eating elephants back then. *Homo erectus* has already left Africa, by the way." She pointed ahead. "About another three kilometers and we reach *Homo georgicus*. From Georgia, the Caucasus Mountains, as the name suggests. The oldest hominid find outside Africa."

She didn't want to. My God, he'd never seen this before! She didn't want to. She screamed, struggled, pushed his hands away, and said things like "It's all happening too fast" and "No, JB, no" and "Not here, JB." So what was all that about enjoying life and the finer things? Sure, she said, but not like this. They could go on a date. Get dinner and a movie. Then they could see . . .

At last he let go of her, shaken to the core. This couldn't really be happening, could it? He squatted on his heels, panting, sweaty all over, bitten everywhere by those damned midges. His cock reared upward out of his pants, a monumental hard-on that gleamed golden in the half-light but that seemed to impress her not one bit. She only glanced at it once, damn it all. It was enough to drive a guy mad. There she was, lying before him practically naked on the moss, surrounded by the little white flowers they had trampled down as they tussled. The sweat made her skin gleam like oil. Her red shorts were hanging down around her left ankle, her shirt was pushed up over her breasts, and he could see the nipples standing to attention. My God, he could see she wanted him, could see how wet she was—practically dripping. She wanted him. She was hot for him all right. But she refused. He felt dizzy. What should he do now? It wasn't like he could rape her. That wouldn't count; that wasn't winning the game.

She began to get dressed again, slowly. She pulled the shorts up and could barely get them back over her ass.

"You could at least give me a blow job," James said, his voice cracking. "I can't go play golf like this."

At first, he thought she hadn't heard him, and for a moment he wasn't even sure he'd said it. But after she'd pulled her shirt down, she walked over to him, kneeled down at his side, and put her hand on his penis. She began to stroke it. James sank backward onto his elbows and shut his eyes. Oh, but she was good at this. She was amazingly good. Way better than most girls. Oh goddamn it all, she was good. . . . He felt her shift position and come round in front of him. He opened his eyes. Her face was right in front of his. She looked at him and held his gaze. She wanted him looking at her as she squeezed.

"Is this good?" she whispered huskily.

He nodded, breathing heavily. "Just don't stop."

She didn't stop, but she slowed down, dammit.

"Do you want me?" she breathed.

"You know I do! My God, if you haven't noticed . . ."

"Say it. Say you want me."

A wild hope flared up in him that perhaps he'd get laid after all. She was different from the other girls, got turned on by different things, so maybe if he gave her what she wanted . . . If that was what she wanted to hear him say . . . "Yes, my God," he gasped. "I want you."

She kept stroking, but slowly, too slowly, just enough to keep him trembling on the edge. "You can have me, JB, if you want me," she cooed just loud enough for him to hear. "You can have me, but you have to want me enough. You have to need me. Really, really need me . . . Do you need me?"

"Yes," James yelped helplessly.

"Say it."

"I need you."

"Say my name," she ordered.

What kind of goddamned game was she playing here? What was she up to? Why didn't she just jerk him off and be done with it? He gasped, swallowed, and spluttered her name. "Terry."

She stopped. She just stopped right where she was. Stopped while his balls were bulging. He let out an inarticulate howl.

"Say it again," she demanded. "And look at me. Keep looking at me the whole time."

So he looked at her and said it again. "Terry." Just then she gave a quick tug with her hand, a movement that shot right through him, that brought him right to the edge but not quite over it, not quite . . .

"Say it! Say my name. Say it as fast as you can!"

"Terry." He looked at her. "Terry." Looked into her eyes. "Terry." She had light brown eyes with the strangest green flecks in the iris. Witch eyes. "Terry." Oh God! He was about to burst. "Terry. Terry . . . Terry . . . Terry . . . Terry!"

When he came, he was bawling out her name. He shot his load like a ball from a cannon, and she looked into his eyes the entire time until he was done. It was as though she had some power over him all of a sudden. She gave a thin-lipped smile, then bent over and kissed him quickly on the forehead. Then she got up and left.

James felt like he would never get his breath back. He climbed to his feet with difficulty, pulled his pants back on, and fumbled the button closed. He was trembling all over. That was because he'd been lying awkwardly, sure. He shot a furious glance at where Terry had vanished through the trees. What had all that been about? Whatever else it was, it had been the strangest sexual experience of his life. He swallowed and tasted bugs. Something had flown into his mouth. Shit. This wasn't how winning the game felt.

Around noon Charlotte finally called a halt. They had just passed a little town, no more than a few houses scattered in the woods, and now there was a quiet lake by the roadside, half hidden by trees. It was an inviting spot to rest awhile. They took off their shoes, rolled up their pant legs, and dangled their feet in the water.

It was pleasantly cool here in the shade, and it felt wonderful to soak their feet. Hiroshi couldn't remember ever having walked so far in his life. His clothes were clinging to his body, rubbing and chafing, and he was covered in dust; he yearned for a long, hot shower. Tomorrow he would barely be able to get out of bed, that much was certain. And as he was taking his socks off, he had spotted at least one blister on each foot. Of course, he wouldn't let any of this show. If Charlotte wanted to hike all day, then he would hike all day, and if his feet were bleeding tonight, so be it. He would heal.

They devoured their sandwiches. They were far and away the best sandwiches Hiroshi had ever eaten, and he wasn't sure it was only because he was so hungry. Sandwiches with ham, mayo, and finely chopped salad. Sandwiches with fish paste, which Charlotte told him she made herself from her grandmother's recipe. Delicious. Even the lukewarm water from the bottle tasted wonderful. Little by little Hiroshi got his strength back. He looked up at the treetops and listened to the birds chattering away loudly, and all of a sudden he thought of Dorothy. How he must have hurt her. There was no question he had let her down dreadfully, and he wasn't proud of the way he had broken it off. Sure, he had to end that relationship somehow, but he could have found some other way to do it, some better way. Even if he didn't know how.

At last Charlotte said it was time to get going again.

"How far have we come now?" Hiroshi asked as he carefully dried his feet.

"Two and a half million years," she replied.

"And how far do you want to go? All the way back to the Big Bang?"

Charlotte shrugged her backpack into place. "Not long now. An hour or so."

They hiked off, more slowly now, less talkative. The trees gave way and the sun beat down. Cars sped past, honking their horns in encouragement, some of the drivers waving at them.

And then at last Charlotte stopped and said, "All right, we've gone far enough. Now I can tell you why I study anthropology. Why it has to be anthropology."

Hiroshi would have liked a walking stick to lean on. "Really," he panted, "it was just a question. If I had known the answer would involve all this, I never would have asked."

Charlotte didn't respond. Instead, she pointed to a spot on the roadside where the remains of some poor animal were smeared, maybe a cat or something else about that size. "We've walked just about twenty miles," she said. "That's thirty-two kilometers, or three point two million years. And three point two million years ago a woman was living in Ethiopia—actually, we'd better call her a female specimen of *Australopithecus afarensis*, which was one of the earliest hominid species—and her bones survived after her death. They were excavated in 1974, and she's gone down in the literature as Lucy. The amazing thing about this find was that so much of the skeleton was found, about forty percent. So we could prove that Lucy was already walking upright most of the time."

Charlotte turned around and faced the way they had come. "Now imagine if we were to walk back the same way—don't worry, we're not going to, but just imagine. We start with Lucy, our earliest known female ancestor, and walk back through the whole history of human evolution, through all that time, with millions and millions of people being born, having children, dying. They survive ice ages, plagues, and other natural disasters. They migrate all the way around the earth, from Africa to Europe to Asia, then last of all to America and Australia. Think of how far we walked, think of all that distance—and then think of the last fifty steps up to the John Harvard statue. Only fifty steps. That's the history of every single recorded human culture. Just how likely is it that this was all the civilization there ever was? Thirty kilometers—think of how many times you could take those fifty steps in all that distance. How many other, older civilizations could fit in there, civilizations we know nothing at all about."

Hiroshi had turned around as well and was looking back the way they had come. He was trying to remember the whole distance. From a sheerly geometrical point of view, she was right. Fifty steps was nothing. They must have walked fifty steps while choosing where to sit down for lunch and never even noticed it. But those fifty steps represented all of history ever since the Pharaohs.

"But why do we know nothing about them?" he finally asked. "Wouldn't these civilizations had left some trace?"

Charlotte wiped the sweat from her brow. "Maybe they did, but we don't know what we're looking at. Think of a CD. Just imagine it gets thrown in the trash, and then our civilization collapses. Ten thousand years from now, someone excavates it. What might they think it is? Maybe a mirror. A piece of jewelry. How are they supposed to know it's a data-storage medium? How can they read the data? They can't. It could be they've dug up a piano concerto by Saint-Saëns, or it could be some word-processing software, but nobody will ever be able to listen to that music or run that program."

"I was thinking more of . . . buildings, monuments, something like that. Large-scale finds. Stuff that wouldn't disappear so quickly, that wouldn't be so hard to interpret."

"Buildings survive for centuries. When we're talking thousands of years, it gets more difficult. But if these—hmm, let's call them the first humans—if they lived anytime before the last ice age, if perhaps it was the Ice Age that wiped out their civilization, then none of their buildings would have survived."

Hiroshi thought about that. "So how are you ever going to prove they lived?"

"I don't know yet. First of all, though, you have to believe that such a thing is possible. If you don't, you won't even be able to recognize any traces of them if you come across them." Charlotte put her hands on her hips. "All those countless legends of a vanished golden age—all that stuff about Atlantis, Lemuria, Ys . . . perhaps there's some truth to them after all. Maybe all these legends date back to a time before the civilizations we know about, to another human culture that vanished and was forgotten."

"Or maybe they're just legends."

She tossed her head dismissively. "Heinrich Schliemann was told he was chasing a legend. And he found Troy."

Hiroshi looked at her and felt a warm glow in his heart. He was proud of her—that was it. Proud of her courage, the way she dared to question everything. Dared to face down the whole world if need be. He liked what he saw. He liked it immensely. Then he looked back down the road and thought of how far they had hiked since morning. It was by no means impossible. He could easily believe that she was right. More than that: he found it hard to believe she could be wrong.

Charlotte was exhausted. The long hike tired her out more than she had expected—because of the heat, certainly, but also because every extra kilometer felt like twice that. She had never hiked more than twenty kilometers in a day, and now she'd done thirty-two. She felt half-dead. James would be pretty disappointed that she would be good for nothing the rest of the day. At least she had professional hiking kit. The boots were the best that money could buy, from a Canadian company, and the backpack and breathable clothing were future investments for when she went out on excavations—she was glad she had thought so far ahead.

Hiroshi seemed to be showing no signs of strain. He had just marched along like a robot the whole time. She hadn't wanted to show any signs of weakness, nor did she want to miss meeting James at the pickup point. They were already late; she could only hope he would be waiting for them. If he had come at all.

All the same she felt happy. They didn't have far to go now, and it had all been worthwhile. Hiroshi seemed to have understood why it was so important to her. She thought of all the people she had tried to explain her ideas to before now. Perhaps she should take them on a hike like this. She had first had the idea a long time ago, of how people could be made to feel the vast span of human evolution with their own body, but only Hiroshi had inspired her to really go out and do it. Strange. There was something about him that fired up her scientific spirit. Now Hiroshi was asking again about the knife that had fascinated her so much back at the shrine on the Island of the Saints. He wanted to know what she had seen, how old it was, whether she had ever tried to find out more about it.

"What did I see?" Charlotte thought hard without breaking stride. How could she even explain it? "You can't even call it seeing. It's more like feeling. It feels like when you're standing on top of a street grate and you suddenly realize you're above a tunnel or a pipe, and it's at least a hundred meters straight down. Because you can hear an echo that far down. Maybe that's the best way to describe it."

But it wasn't, of course. There was no way to describe it. Those were just words, not even a pale shadow of how it really felt.

"I touched lots of really old things in the temple that day," she persisted. "I thought the knife wouldn't be any older, but it might be more interesting, because it was a knife after all—maybe people had fought with it, killed with it . . ." She hesitated. Could she trust him? She shot a glance at him. She had never told anybody about this, never in her life, but with Hiroshi she felt that she could. That he would believe it. "When I was a child, I was always fascinated by objects that had killed someone. Halberds, swords, daggers—they always spoke to me. Not because I got a kick out of people dying, but because I thought those objects might open a door to the other side, to the next world. Even if it only opened a crack. I think I hoped it might help me find out what happens to us when we die."

Hiroshi just nodded earnestly. "An interesting thought. I've never looked at it like that." He gazed at her with his dark Japanese eyes. "And? Did the knife ever kill anyone?"

She sighed. "I don't know. Up until that moment, touching very old things was like tripping over the curb. I would drop an inch or so and then find my way back. But touching that knife . . . it was like being pushed off a cliff, falling without end."

"That's what made you scream."

"Yes."

He nodded and thought about it. "Does that mean you don't even know how old it was?"

Charlotte struggled for words. "At some point I just . . . switched off. I didn't want to fall any farther down into the past. But by then I'd already gone back a hundred thousand years at least." All of a sudden she had a vivid memory of that day in the shrine, of the terror she had felt. And she felt vividly, too, the fascination that had driven her on ever since. "An obsidian knife; just think of it! And the workmanship that went into it! If only there were some way of proving that the humans who lived so long ago could produce something like that. It would be a sensation; it would rewrite everything we think we know about human history."

"Did you ever try to get the knife examined?"

"Oh yes. I asked a professor of art history how he would go about it. He called a colleague in Japan who made inquiries with the temple . . . but the knife's gone. The temple said they sold it to an English collector, but they had lost his address. The Japanese professor figured they just didn't want to admit it had been stolen."

"Pity." Hiroshi was thinking hard now. For some reason his footsteps changed pace when he did that. "I've often dreamed of that day," he said at last, and by the sound of it he found it hard to admit as much. "Of the moment you cried out. Sometimes, when I'm dreaming, you scream because I've let go. Sometimes you fall. Sometimes I pull you back at the last moment from between the jaws of a monster that has come out from the lake to eat you." He hesitated. "I remember that moment like I would remember being struck by lightning. It has burnt its way into my heart."

"Yes," said Charlotte before she could stop herself. "Mine, too."

He looked at her. She had never seen such an open, vulnerable look on his face. "I think that ever since then there's been some connection between us," he said. "I never knew it all these years, but I felt it the moment I saw you again. It was no coincidence we met."

Charlotte felt herself shrink inside. She had to stop him from talking this way. She was breathing heavily but said nothing.

Hiroshi gave her a searching look. "Don't you feel it, too? Don't you see that there's some extraordinary connection between us?"

This was the moment she had been afraid of. "Hiroshi," she said with all the tact she could muster. "I'm just about to announce my engagement. You really mustn't get your hopes up."

He didn't reply. In that moment his face showed nothing at all. Inscrutable Japanese.

After another ten steps, he spoke. "That doesn't answer my question."

Charlotte sighed. "There is a connection between us, yes," she said. "A childhood friendship. That's something special. A friendship like that couldn't happen later in life. That's why I want to keep it how it was."

It still didn't answer his question. He was silent in thought for a while, and she was expecting him to say as much when instead he said, "Is that how you feel?"

She stopped and turned to face him, looking straight into his eyes as though they were children again, playing a game. First one to look away loses. Had she and Hiroshi ever actually played that one? She couldn't remember. They had always been so serious. "Yes," she said. "That's how I feel."

But even as she spoke she knew she wasn't telling the truth, that there was something else between them, something she didn't want to admit. And she saw in his eyes that he would never give up trying to find out what it was. Never.

Hiroshi realized he would need all his strength, that he would have to wait a long time for Charlotte, that his resolution would be tested to the limit. But what had he expected? The hand of fate was at work here, nothing more, nothing less. Everything that happened—and everything that didn't—meant something, even if he didn't understand its meaning straightaway. He would need staying power, though. "Stand like a mountain," as they said in the martial arts. Well, there were ways to do that. He breathed in deeply, drawing the breath all the way down, the way his father had taught him. His American father, who felt so at home in the time of the samurai.

They reached a parking lot where a gleaming 4x4 was waiting, the kind of gas-guzzler that did fewer miles to the gallon than a twelve-ton truck. It was painted in a camouflage pattern, as though the driver were about to set out for war, but it was also as clean as a whistle and polished to a high shine. He wondered whether it had gone off-road even once since the day it was built.

The man leaning up against the mudguard, arms crossed, had to be James Michael Bennett III, Charlotte's fiancé. The billionaire's son. Hiroshi had done his homework, of course. If you borrowed a Harvard student's password, you could learn all sorts of things on the Harvard intranet. James Michael Bennett III also studied anthropology, though he was on so many sports teams that it was a wonder he ever had any time left over to study. There was also a great deal about him on the public Internet. He was part of the Boston jet set and was the heir to a company worth billions of dollars. That was all the excuse the newspapers needed to report on all his championship cups and gala dinners and the general social whirl. He was also damnably good-looking in the accompanying photographs. Hiroshi was surprised how unimpressive he was in real life. He seemed abstracted, pale, not quite there. If he had any particular gifts that marked him out as a leader for the business his father had built up, Hiroshi certainly couldn't see them.

James kissed Charlotte absent-mindedly, looking at Hiroshi mistrustfully as he did so. He was clearly wondering what the two of them had been doing all day. He didn't trust her. He was worried about something. Hiroshi would have liked to know what Charlotte saw in this guy, but he couldn't begin to guess. The good looks that served him so well in the newspaper photographs seemed somehow vacant from up close. He looked as though he'd been airbrushed. Hiroshi wondered whether he might have had plastic surgery done to look the way he did. But Bennett was rich. Even if you didn't know that already, you could see it.

Was that it? Did she love him because he was rich? Was she in love with the prospect of a carefree life in the lap of luxury, big houses with swimming pools, an army of servants? Was she in love with the private jet, the costly jewelry, the holidays, and hotels? Hiroshi realized that the very thought unleashed a turmoil of emotions in him he could barely control. He was almost glad to be so exhausted—too tired to get really angry.

James put out a hand for him to shake in the usual hearty American manner. Would he crush Hiroshi's hand in his? He tentatively responded, but it turned out that no, the guy wasn't quite so primitive after all. Almost a pity; it would have been easier to despise someone like that.

"Hi," James said as they shook hands. "I'm JB."

"Hiroshi. As in Nagasaki." A silly joke, but it usually helped people remember. He had said it automatically, and now he was sorry he had. It made him sound eager to be friends. But he didn't want to be friends. James was his rival. His enemy.

The second he had let go of Hiroshi's hand, James paid no more attention to him. "I thought you'd never turn up," he told Charlotte reproachfully.

"I told you it could be a little later," she protested.

He opened the driver's door. "It's no fun standing around in the woods on my own for hours," he said, settling in behind the wheel. "Okay, where are we going?"

"Back to town. We'll run Hiroshi back home, and then . . ." She turned to him, suddenly brisk and attentive. "I'm sorry, I've forgotten which dorm you're in."

"MacGregor House," Hiroshi said. He had the strangest feeling he was standing outside the whole scene, watching it like a theater performance.

"That's one of the new halls down by the river, isn't it?" James asked.

"Yes."

"Okay," he said, nodding curtly.

They got in—Charlotte in the passenger seat, and Hiroshi in the back. For such a military-looking vehicle, it was laughably luxurious. The upholstery was pale creamy leather, every switch and button was gilded. He almost felt guilty about climbing in all covered with sweat and dust.

"How was the training session?" Charlotte asked.

James made a face as he set his GPS. "To tell you the truth, kind of frustrating."

Then he slipped into gear and roared away. The engine was loud enough to be a military model; Hiroshi couldn't catch a word the two of them said to each other in the front. Not that they said a great deal. James seemed to be the type who enjoyed a good sulk. Hiroshi didn't care. It was good just to sit back and enjoy the ride instead of having to make any effort. His feet throbbed and his skin itched. He yearned for a shower, as hot as possible. In an American college dorm that wouldn't be especially hot, alas.

For a moment he felt weak and worn-out. But when he looked at the woman sitting in the seat in front of him he felt strong again, invigorated by the connection he knew they had.

Staying power. That was what he needed now.

5

On Saturday morning Charlotte showed up at Brenda's family home wearing her oldest clothes. The big move was about to get underway. They would start by moving the furniture Brenda had chosen to take with her and get it set up in her new apartment so that she would have somewhere to put the rest of her belongings, which were still in the student dorm. Brenda's room was in Warren Towers B, one of the huge dorms on Commonwealth Avenue, and she had declared flat out she was finally fed up with the commotion of living in the giant tower.

It was cloudy for the first time that week but promised to be a warm day all the same. They were sure to break a sweat. Which would do them good, Charlotte told herself. She had spent all Friday working on an assignment that was due the following week and hadn't managed to write so much as ten lines. She had been utterly unable to concentrate. Her thoughts were all over the place. She wondered whether she might be getting her period, but she wasn't due yet—and she didn't normally feel like this. Most of the time her only symptoms were a slight queasiness and the need to sit and watch a tearjerker on TV with a hot-water bottle on her tummy.

So her thoughts were all over the place because of James. Which was obvious, really. On Thursday night, for the first time since they had started dating, he had failed to get an erection, which had shaken him to the core. It had happened at the worst possible moment, too. After she had showered, the two of them had gone to bed and snuggled for a while, and all of a sudden Charlotte had felt such an urgent need to feel him inside her that she surprised even herself. And that's when it happened. She had to say kind words and reassure him it didn't matter, that that wasn't why they were together—all the usual platitudes—and he must have felt all the while that she didn't mean any of it, that she could have screamed in frustration.

On Friday she was hounded by fantasies of strange men. As she went shopping that morning, she noticed more shapely male buttocks in half an hour than she had all last year. As she stood in line at the checkout, she found herself wondering what would happen if a woman hit on a man. She would have followed any man home who tried to chat her up, but other than the usual timid glances, nothing happened at all.

"Hi, Charlotte," said Brenda's brother Ian. He was backing a rental truck carefully into the driveway. "Hire me!" said the bright red letters on the side.

She returned his greeting. Ian was three years older than Brenda, which had been an enormous age difference back in Delhi. Now he was working toward a degree in church music, though nobody would ever have guessed that from his tumble of carrot-colored curls and muscular build.

He climbed out, shook her hand, and said, "I thought you were bringing James."

"James can't come," Charlotte admitted. "He . . . has to help his father." *That's pretty much a textbook example of making excuses for others*, she thought to herself as she said it.

Ian just raised his eyebrows and said, "Uh-huh." He couldn't stand James, never had been able to. Brenda had once told Charlotte he'd said that a berk with a billion dollars is still a berk.

Brenda came into view and flung her arms around Charlotte, thereby saving her from the unpleasant task of defending James's behavior.

"Oh my goodness, I'm so excited!" she exclaimed. "Just think—when I shut the door behind you guys tonight, I will be all on my own for the very first time in my life! I cannot believe this!"

"Well," Charlotte pointed out, "there's always Susan." Susan was the upstairs tenant.

"She's not here this weekend. That's what makes it so exciting . . . Hi, Gwen. Juanita. How sweet of you to come." Brenda set off to welcome the new arrivals.

Gwen was a plump girl—to put it kindly—with nut-brown corkscrew curls and a breathless laugh. She was from Maine, and the very first thing she ever told a new acquaintance was her parents lived on the same street as Stephen King. She studied design with Brenda. Juanita was something like the anti-Gwen, a wiry, stern-looking woman who could have been typecast as a librarian. She was majoring in American literature and always seemed to be about to pull a checklist out of her bag and start ticking off items.

Brenda's parents appeared next. They shook all the helping hands, and her father said, "This is a big day for us. I can finally order myself a pool table."

It was his British way of trying to crack a joke. In fact, Brenda had told Charlotte, her parents were having a hard time coping with the empty nest now that both their children had left home.

Ian had opened the loading doors on the rental truck and had the gray packing blankets and webbing straps at the ready. He strode over to his sister and said, "Do you realize it's going to be quite a an undertaking to get your wardrobe downstairs? We'll need two strong guys, because there's only room for two people on the staircase."

Brenda looked alarmed. "What if I ask Dad—"

"Forget it," Ian interrupted. "I don't want a repeat of what happened when he slipped a disk last year."

Charlotte was just fumbling for the words to explain that, at least in theory, they might have another man for the team, when he walked up as though on cue. Dr. Thomas Peter Wickersham was strolling across the lawn in shabby overalls, carrying a pair of work gloves in one hand, and wearing a Boston Red Sox cap on his head. He looked good, really good. Why had she turned down his dinner invitation? She could have kicked herself. Charlotte blinked in surprise. What was wrong with her? What was she thinking?

He spoke to Brenda's father first. "Prof. Gilliam?"

"The very same," he said.

"I thought on my way here that it was a campus address." He held out his hand. "Thomas Wickersham. I teach paleoanthropology."

"John Gilliam, medicine. This is my wife, Elizabeth . . ." Brenda's father stopped short. "Excuse me, but are you here because my daughter is moving out?"

Wickersham looked around and pointed to Charlotte. "This young lady lured me here today," he explained. "She told me there was excavation work to be done."

Dr. Gilliam snorted with laughter. "That's very nearly the case. I would be interested to hear your conclusions."

Then Wickersham shook everyone else's hand. When he came to Brenda, he said, "So you're the one who's moving? I'm pleased to meet you."

"I can't believe it," Brenda squealed. "Charley roped her prof in to help?"

"To tell the truth, I insisted," Wickersham corrected her. "For entirely selfish reasons."

"You volunteered for selfish reasons? You'll have to explain."

"I'm still in debt. I have to help out with at least another twelve moves before I'm in the clear—and it seemed best to get it over and done with before I'm too old." He looked around. "I hope there's enough stuff to fetch and carry. Moving a student's gear sometimes only counts as half."

"Don't you worry," Ian broke in. "We'll start with the showstopper."

"Excellent," Wickersham said delightedly. "What's it to be? A piano?"

Brenda broke into fits of giggles.

"It's a wardrobe our grandfather built," Ian explained. "The old man made it practically all of a piece. All we've been able to do is take the doors off the hinges. I have no idea how they ever got it up to the second floor."

"Maybe they built the house around it?" Wickersham suggested.

"I might have thought so, except I remember us moving here."

"So it's a geometry puzzle." Wickersham pulled on his gloves. "Fascinating. Let's get to work!"

The two men heaved the massive heirloom down the stairs, one step at a time, and when they finally got it into the truck, they high-fived with brio. By the looks of it, they had become friends for life. Meanwhile, Charlotte, Gwen, and Brenda were carrying cardboard boxes full of clothes down to the truck, bags full of bed linens, lamps, Brenda's guitar, and every imaginable kind of kitchen appliance. Juanita stood in the back loading it all neatly and efficiently so that not an inch of space went unused. And then an armchair. And then this. And then that. There seemed no end to the furniture and belongings Brenda had stowed away in the house.

"It's all my fault for never be able to resist a bargain," she admitted despairingly.

But somehow they finally got everything stowed and strapped down. Wickersham asked Brenda to ride along with him so that she could show him the way. Charlotte already knew the new address and would give Gwen and Juanita a ride. Ian drove the truck on his own. Brenda hugged and kissed her parents as though she never expected to see them again. Then the convoy set out.

Brenda had spent a long time looking at apartments before choosing. The new house was nothing special at first glance: a blue clapboard house on a quiet street, standing in a large orchard garden. Inside, though, it was a treasure trove, its airy, well-proportioned rooms full of lovingly crafted details. Some days you could smell the Atlantic from here. The upstairs tenant was a woman about ten years older than Brenda who worked as a programmer. She was on a temporary contract in Boston and due to return to Chicago in two years, after which Brenda could decide whether to rent the whole house.

Ian was already there. He had a key and was carrying things inside. Charlotte, Gwen, and Juanita joined in. Wickersham and Brenda turned up much later and were laughing merrily as they climbed out of the car. They seemed to have enjoyed their ride enormously. Charlotte felt a surge of envy, which was absurd, of course. Wickersham had wanted a date with her; what was he doing now having such a good time with her best friend? She had to close her eyes for a moment. What on earth was wrong with her? Was she going mad?

After he'd spent the whole week prevaricating and telling himself that Rasmussen had said there was no need, on Saturday morning Hiroshi got to work tidying up his room after all. Tinny music blared from his old clock radio as he wiped surfaces, straightened things on shelves, and ran the vacuum cleaner over everything, wondering all the while what Rasmussen wanted from him. Why did it have to be a face-to-face meeting? Wasn't that usually the prelude to telling someone they were fired? That would certainly be one way to "renegotiate the contract," as Rasmussen had phrased it over the phone.

But if that wasn't it, then what was it all about? The Wizard's Wand had been simple enough to invent. He had just wanted to know whether he could make money off something like that. And he had, although not vast sums. Even if Rasmussen thought it was good work, Hiroshi didn't plan to spend his life inventing electronic gizmos for some corporation. He had bigger plans. Much bigger. So today's meeting was hardly likely to lead anywhere. It would be interesting, however, to meet one of these legendary investors, who were regarded with reverence and awe at MIT. Half the students he knew dreamed of having a bright idea to pitch to an investor, and making their fortunes that way.

If only he had started cleaning earlier. By late morning his stomach was rumbling, since he had hardly eaten breakfast. He sat there, looking around the room in dismay. It stank of the cleaning fluid's artificial lemon scent. It stank of dust. It stank of the overheating motor on his vacuum cleaner. And it looked worse than ever. He realized glumly there was no way to make up in one morning for what he had spent months—even years—neglecting. The dust bunnies he had chased out from under the bed! And the greasy streaks on every surface—wherever had it all come from? And why on earth did he own so much stuff? Somehow that seemed to be the root of all the other problems, since the dust liked to gather in the cracks and gaps in between, and he could never get the vacuum cleaner in there. Maybe there was some new invention just waiting to be discovered, to fix this problem? Could be worth thinking about.

How odd. Back when he had first flown to America, he had carried all his belongings in a single suitcase and a tote bag. And now? He shuddered at the thought of the day he would have to move out. All the boxes he would have to pack, cart around, and unpack.

He peered into the box of stuff to be thrown away. Not much there. The real trouble was there were so many things he didn't need right at the moment but that he might one day. Until that day came they just lay around taking up space; in a room this small it didn't matter where you tried to stow them, they were always in the way. He'd been hard at work all morning, had picked up practically everything he owned and put it somewhere else, and the room still looked just as it had when he started—like a junk shop. This was embarrassing. Here he was, with plans to change the world, and he couldn't even clean his room.

He had left his door ajar and it suddenly swung open. Rodney stuck his head inside inquisitively. "What kind of unnatural practices are you indulging in here?"

Unnatural? Well, he wasn't far off. Hiroshi felt worn ragged.

He decided to share his latest philosophical insights with Rodney. "The basic problem of cleaning is that cleanliness is an unattainable goal—all we can actually do is reduce the dirt to an acceptable level. On the other hand, that's not so bad. In fact, there's no such thing as dirt. Dirt is merely matter out of place."

"That's an original thought. But not yours." Rodney stepped into the room carefully, picking his way between stacks of old magazines and dustpan sweepings. He shuddered visibly at the sight of all the mess. "Didn't you say you were expecting a visitor today?"

"Why do you think I'm doing all this?" Hiroshi followed Rodney's gaze, and then he shuddered as well. The gaming console he hardly ever used. All the magazines he kept, even though each one had two interesting articles at most, that he never got around to clipping out. The spare parts from various projects, the loose screws, the boxes full of wire . . . and ballpoint pens everywhere, mostly broken.

"Oh wow!" Rodney called. "*Masters of the Universe!* You had that in Japan, too?" He reached for the notebook, but Hiroshi was quicker—he shot out of his chair lightning fast and put his hand on it before Rodney could open the cover.

"Private?" Rodney guessed.

"Very," Hiroshi assured him.

"I see." Rodney nodded and tapped the picture on the cover. "I had one almost like that. Long time ago." He looked around. "On the other hand, what is a Master of the Universe? Master of All the Stuff—now that would be a real superhero."

"Master of All the Stuff?" Hiroshi echoed.

Rodney grinned and turned to the door. "I think I'll let you get on with it." He scooted out.

Hiroshi looked down at his old notebook. That had been a stupid overreaction; Rodney wouldn't have been able to read a word of it anyway, since it was all in Japanese. He opened it up and looked at the columns of hiragana, some hastily scribbled, some written with care. Master of All the Stuff. A silly joke, but for some reason it stuck in his mind. The trick was to be able to master stuff. At the moment his stuff had mastered him, made him clean it, look after it, haul it all over the place. He had bought all these things, but instead of them belonging to him, he belonged to them. And what nonsense it was to feel nostalgic about the days when he had crossed continents with nothing more than a suitcase. Whose fault was it he couldn't do that today? His, and his alone. He could choose to change it anytime. He could become the master, the lord of all things, simply by deciding to be.

His moment had come.

He swept everything from his bed onto the floor. The space he had cleared was roughly enough for two suitcases. More than back then, but it would do. He waded through the sea of possessions cluttering his room and fished out what he would pack into those two cases. It wasn't easy. He had to make some tough decisions, sometimes downright brutal.

At last, a small heap of clothes lay on the bed—just what was really worth wearing, and a few books. A few mementos, his computer of course, and one or two other things. Everything else could go. Without stopping for second thoughts, Hiroshi unrolled all the trash bags he had and shoved everything that still lay on his floor inside. He tied them tight. Since there weren't enough of them, he used the cardboard boxes as well. Then he fetched the cart from the basement, hauled all the bags and boxes downstairs, and threw it all into the trash in the courtyard.

Cleaning his room would be easy now.

Around noon, when everything was in place and tidied up and the house looked almost livable, Brenda conjured up a pot of something she had prepared earlier. As it heated up on the stove, the kitchen began to smell appetizingly of mulligatawny soup. Bowls were hastily unpacked, washed, and put on the table. Spoons clattered. Gwen called out, "Mmm, what's in this?" and Juanita said, "Not bad." Brenda and Dr. Wickersham, it turned out, had stopped for fresh bread on the way over. Charlotte's mouth was watering as well. She hadn't eaten mulligatawny for ages. The soup was thick and yellow, full of vegetables, chicken, rough-chopped cashews, and rice, and it tasted delicious.

Inevitably, conversation turned to their childhood days in Delhi. Wickersham was astonished to learn they had both lived in India when they were young. Charlotte was a diplomat's daughter, of course, so that made sense, but Brenda? Brenda launched into a series of anecdotes, such as the one about the old man who watched the entrance to her parents' compound. He spent his days sitting in a tiny wooden guard hut, like a cage, and at night he would light a fire in there, building it in a rusty old hubcap. Brenda had worried for years that the house would burn down.

Charlotte told the story about the monkey that had come into her bedroom to steal the math book. "I watched him climb back up into the tree to have a closer look at what he'd gotten. The other monkeys found out, though, and did all they could to get the book off him. In the end there was nothing left but confetti." She laughed as she remembered. "I went out to the garden to gather up the scraps so that I could show them to my teacher the next day. I was worried she wouldn't believe me otherwise."

She could see the big villa again in her mind's eye, with its enormous garden. . . . Oh yes, and the dozens of servants always scurrying around. Not that any of them had worked very hard. She remembered groups of women who spent their days sweeping the paths, bent over with simple brooms made of bundles of twigs. All it did was stir up the dust; the flagstones were never actually any cleaner.

"What did you do all day?" Wickersham asked curiously.

Brenda glanced at Charlotte. "Once we'd finished our home-work, we were usually over at your place at the pool, weren't we?"

Charlotte no longer remembered. "Didn't we spend all our time in the courtyard? The one with the broken stone wall?"

"Oh yes! That was where your peacock sometimes attacked us. He was an evil-tempered bird."

"He was indeed. What was his name again? Gerôme. Oh yes, he was one to steer clear of."

She felt lighthearted just thinking of Delhi, telling the old stories. How simple life had been back then.

After lunch it was time for phase two: emptying Brenda's room in Warren Towers. They had let the Office of Parking Services know about the move and had special permission to use the parking garage that took up the first two floors of the enormous dorm complex. The janitor came and freed up an elevator for them so they could go back and forth between Brenda's floor and the truck. It could have been an easy job. Should have been. If Juanita had been able to simply take the books off the shelves and pack them in boxes without stopping to look at every single one. If she didn't know a book, she read its jacket text from start to finish, and if she did, she would give a little lecture on it.

"Ju!" Brenda finally yelled. "The girl who's taking over the room is due next week, already! We have to hurry things along a little."

Juanita was deep in contemplation of a paperback edition of Joseph Conrad's *Heart of Darkness*. "Did you know that Africans hate this book?" she asked.

There was a constant bustle in the hall as neighbors came by to bid Brenda a tearful farewell. They acted as though she were about to emigrate, although in fact they would all see one another on campus on Monday. Charlotte was glad Brenda was finally moving out of

Towers. The concrete hallways had all the charm of a subway station, and it always smelled nasty. Today the omnipresent odor of unwashed socks predominated.

"It's pretty lively here," Wickersham commented to Brenda. "Don't you like that?"

"Oh I do," Brenda replied, piling a cushion on top of the box of books he already held in his arms. "But I have these funny old-fashioned notions of privacy. Up here you can come home beat dead from the day and find there's a party happening in your room and someone's reading aloud from your diary. Not my idea of fun."

Unpacking back at Brenda's new house was much calmer. Charlotte took her time putting towels on the shelves in the bathroom, enjoying the peace and quiet after the chaos of Warren Towers. She had the feeling that peace and quiet was allowed here.

"Charley?" Brenda stuck her head round the door. "Here you are. Hey." She came in and shut the door behind her. "You seem a little down today. Is everything all right with you and James? Did you two have an argument?"

Charlotte took a deep breath. "No," she said and shook her head. "No, we didn't argue."

James hadn't been able to get over that bout of impotence. On Friday he had turned up unexpectedly and thrown himself at her. This time the sex worked. It had been a little quick—too quick for her—but at least it had happened.

"But?" Brenda looked at her in concern.

"Everything's all right with me and James," Charlotte declared with the strangest feeling she was an oyster just starting to cover some inner hurt with mother-of-pearl. "Really, it couldn't be better. I'm happy. Yes. We've been talking about setting dates, you know? We'll announce the engagement in the fall and then get married the following summer." She had to take a deep breath; there was a tightness in her chest. "Then I'll be Mrs. James Bennett. That bothers me a little. I'll get used to it, but . . . it's a lot to take in."

Right at that moment she even believed what she was saying.

Rasmussen wasn't in the least like how Hiroshi expected an investor to look. The word suggested a guy like Gordon Gecko from *Wall Street*—somebody in an expensive suit smelling of expensive cologne. Gelled hair and an arrogant attitude. Rasmussen, however, was wearing linen pants, a polo shirt, and a summer-weight jacket. He had brought along chocolate doughnuts and coffee.

"Just in case," he announced. "I happen to really like doughnuts in the afternoon." Then he looked around and added, "Wow. This is the neatest student room I've ever seen. It's practically Zen. I'm impressed."

Hiroshi offered him a seat, which was much easier to do now with all his stuff gone, and said, "I have some cold drinks, too, if you'd like."

Rasmussen declined. "Let's get to work on these doughnuts, then we'll see."

As they ate, he began to talk. He told Hiroshi how he had watched Sollo Electronics try to take over its rival Cook & Holland, a company at least ten times its size. "They used the old trick—take out a bank loan to buy the shares and then pay off the loan afterward with Cook & Holland assets. Unfortunately, there was some competition, and the share price shot up. The sensible thing would have been to forget the whole thing, unload the shares they had, and cash in the profit, but no, the management at Sollo just said 'full steam ahead.' They took out loans all over the place and bought up more and more Cook & Holland shares, ran up these crazy debts—and then it all blew up in their faces. First, they couldn't pay their suppliers—that's when my alarm bells really started ringing, since two of my companies happen to be among the suppliers—then they couldn't make payroll. After that the cat was out of the bag, and Sollo's share price nose-dived."

Hiroshi had listened attentively, albeit without really understanding what the man was talking about. It was hard to say how old Rasmussen was. He had a weather-beaten look, as though he spent most of his time outside, and his hair was cut so short there was no telling what color it was. Probably gray. He had ice-blue eyes and a steady gaze.

"So what does all that mean?" Hiroshi asked. "Won't there be any more Wizard's Wands?" The idea that his invention might go off the market even before he got his degree depressed him.

Rasmussen raised his hands. "Slow down. That's just the point in the story where I took a closer look at the company. I made a guess at its true value, not the market value; stock prices have nothing to do with reality. I saw a company with amazing prospects but completely incompetent management. Megalomaniac idiots. So I bought Sollo Electronics—for a bargain price, if you disregard their outstanding debts—and I fired the lot of them. Now that I've paid off the debt, I have to turn those prospects I saw into reality." He pointed at Hiroshi. "You, Mr. Kato, are one of those prospects."

Hiroshi shrugged. "I just invented one little gizmo."

"I have a nose for these things," Rasmussen said. "It tells me you'll invent more."

Hiroshi hesitated. "I don't know. Could be."

"I've been talking to tradesmen. Lots of them. I haven't met one who owns a Wizard's Wand and doesn't think it's the bee's knees."

"Well, that's nice." But what good did it do him?

Rasmussen wiped a few crumbs of chocolate from his fingers with a napkin. "I looked at the numbers. Am I right that you weren't particularly pleased with the money you earned from your invention?"

Hiroshi shrugged again. "Well, pleased . . . it covered my tuition, so that was okay. I really just did it because I wanted to learn how that whole thing works. Patents, licensing, all of that."

"Did you know the Wizard's Wand is on sale practically world-wide?"

"I heard something of the kind."

"And weren't you bothered that so little of that money was reaching you?"

"Thirty, forty thousand dollars a year—is that really so little?" Hiroshi asked, though even as he uttered the words, he thought for a man like Rasmussen it probably was.

The investor leaned forward and folded his hands. "Listen, this brings us back to the matter I mentioned on the phone: it has to be an exchange. A tree can't just pump out oxygen; it has to take in its own nutrients. There has to be a proper balance of give and take if these things are to work. You never paid attention to this. You just put your invention out there in the world and let it look after itself. Pardon me for saying so, but that was irresponsible. It harmed you, and I believe that it harmed everyone else."

"But what should I have—"

"What actually happened," Rasmussen went on, with a curious gleam in his eye, "was the bosses at Sollo ripped off their patent holders first when they needed money for the takeover bid. The forty thousand dollars they paid you in the first year was all well and good, but please remember the Wizard's Wand only came on the market in September, that the customers had to get to know it, and so forth. Your take should have been greater the following year. Instead, it was less. At least, in the balance sheet they showed you." He reached into the breast pocket of his jacket and took out a piece of paper, which he handed to Hiroshi. "This is the amount you are actually due. Including the interest for late payment."

Hiroshi stared at the sheet of paper in his hands and felt his heart suddenly start hammering. It was a check for more than three million dollars.

"I did wonder," he heard a voice say, at first not even realizing it was his own, "whether we could integrate a laser pointer into the

Wand to shoot out a coded light pulse. The cameras would pick it up and calculate the coordinates, then you could draw in partition walls or whatever directly in real space. Then, if we added a set of data goggles, the operator could see the new additions in the room right then and there in a virtual image. He could even move new elements around in 3-D."

"You see?" Rasmussen beamed. "No sooner do we get the balance right than your ideas begin to flow. That's how it's supposed to work."

Hiroshi raised the check in his hand. "Three million? That's really something."

He felt dizzy. He had been expecting almost anything, but not this. Three million. That meant he was rich. Not filthy rich, not stinking rich, but rich all the same.

But despite that . . . he felt there was more at stake now than just money. His future was at stake, what he wanted from life, where he wished to go.

"I'm pretty confused," he confessed. "I . . . I mean, thanks for what you've done for me, of course—"

"You've earned it," Rasmussen said. "In fact, I figure you've earned the right to sue the former managers at Sollo Electronics for fraud."

Hiroshi looked at him in astonishment. "Uh, right." He thought about it. "But what would that get me?" He had the money now.

"It would punish a breach of contract and an abuse of your trust. Again, it's a question of fair exchange. My favorite topic, as you will no doubt have noticed. Which is why I've already filed several suits. You're welcome to be listed as a coplaintiff if you care to be." Rasmussen waved his hand dismissively. "Doesn't matter right now. Think it over."

Hiroshi looked at the astonishing piece of paper in his hands: the Bank of America crest, Rasmussen's looping signature. "Most of all I'd like to know why you wanted to meet me. What you expect. I sort of assumed that you would . . . I don't know, ask me to sign a contract or something."

"Where would that get us?" Rasmussen shook his head. "Contracts serve as a written record of obligations. I don't see that we need take on any new mutual obligations right now. I wanted to meet you because I believe in getting to know people face-to-face, in the personal touch—there's nothing else like it. I wanted you to understand that I'm genuinely interested in you, in what you might do next, and I expect you to have a lot more ideas. Even more trailblazing projects. I also want you to know I'm ready to lend an ear for whatever you might be thinking of. Whether you need help getting an idea off the ground, or marketing a product." He took a business card from his jacket pocket and jotted down a cell phone number on the back. "Only a very select few get this number, so please treat it as confidential. Here. You can reach me anytime."

Hiroshi took the card. "Thank you," he said.

"And what I just said will be as true ten years from now as it is next week," Rasmussen continued. "Please don't feel any pressure."

"Okay," said Hiroshi.

And then the investor was gone. Hiroshi could hardly believe someone like Jens Rasmussen had just been there—someone who flew in a private jet, owned a yacht, and donated five million dollars to a forestry campaign every year. But there was the check as proof it hadn't all been a dream. He looked up. A sea mist was rolling in off the water, which was unusual for this time of year. But then it had been an unusual day. Hiroshi put the check inside his old *Masters of the Universe* notebook. Then he sat there and felt something he hadn't felt for a very long time. He didn't know what to do next. He opened his computer, but even as the screen started to glow he realized he couldn't possibly check his e-mail or do anything so mundane. He switched the computer off and put it away. The mist outside was thickening into fog as he watched. The tower of MacGregor

House was merely a silhouette. And Hiroshi's room, so neat and tidy now, suddenly seemed small and empty.

Had he forgotten some appointment he'd made? All of a sudden he felt that must be it. Something was nagging at him, but when he looked at his appointment book, there was nothing there. All the same, he had to get out of there. He threw on a jacket—the only jacket he had now—slipped his shoes on, and left. He met nobody in the corridors. The dorm was emptier than he had ever seen it on a Saturday night. The door squealed shut behind him as he left. The fog was everywhere now. There wasn't much traffic on Memorial Drive, just a few dim headlights glowing through the gray fog. The trees on the center strip were like the looming shadows of ogres, and he couldn't see the river at all.

Hiroshi crossed the street. He knew he could walk along the bicycle path on the banks of the Charles River for hours if he had to. Walk until he was tired out. Maybe that would stop his thoughts from going round and round. He wasn't the only one who was out and about. Someone was standing by one of the trees along the path, a familiar figure. He came slowly closer.

"You?" he said in astonishment.

Eventually everything Brenda would entrust to other hands had been unpacked and put away, and then the pizza arrived, a huge pizza with salad, and Italian red wine. The mood around the table was cheerful as could be, and even Juanita laughed occasionally and talked about something other than books.

In fact, the mood was so cheerful that Charlotte made her excuses early, not wanting to spoil everyone else's fun. "I have somewhere I should be," she claimed. "Don't mind me."

Brenda accompanied her to the door. "Thank you for coming," she said and hugged her.

Charlotte smiled wistfully. "You enjoy your first night in your very own home."

The fog was rolling in as she set out. It thickened astonishingly quickly, and Charlotte missed a turn. Before she knew where she was, she was downtown, driving past Cloud Eight, and for some strange reason her eyes were stinging. Whatever was wrong with her? When she finally got home, she shoved her sweaty clothes into the laundry basket and climbed into the shower to rinse off all the grime, the dust, the sweat. And that nagging sense of unease. Just as she was coming out of the bathroom, toweling her hair dry, the phone rang. She bent over and looked at the display. James. She put out her hand but then stopped before she picked up. She waited. It rang five times and then stopped. At the sixth ring her voice mail would have taken the call.

So James had just wanted to know whether she was there.

All at once the unease she thought she had washed away in the shower was back. As she got dressed, she realized she didn't want to spend the whole evening sitting around wondering whether James would come. She could call back, she told herself as she blow-dried her hair. But she didn't; instead, she put on a jacket and went out into the fog, which by now hung thick in the air. It was no weather for driving. No weather for sightseeing either. All the same, she wasn't staying home, not tonight, not now. *Just drive.* She could drive slowly; she was in no hurry. How could she be in a hurry if she didn't know where she was going? But didn't she? At every intersection she knew without thinking whether to turn or keep on going. There was something telling her exactly where to go. This must be how the birds felt as they migrate, following their instincts.

It was uncanny. She drove along McGrath Highway, an elevated road from which drivers could usually see out over the roofs of the town or look through second-floor windows and spot people watching television. Tonight, however, she saw none of that. She was wrapped in a featureless gray blur. It was as though she and the two or three other cars on the road were floating in empty space, in the nothingness before the universe began.

She shuddered and finally turned off. She was down by the Charles River, by the MIT dormitories. She found a parking spot and left her car there, continuing onward on foot. There was a smell of salt, of seaweed, of fumes. She stopped in front of MacGregor House and looked up at the smears of light spilling out of the windows into the gloomy fog, wondering which one was Hiroshi's room. Back in Tokyo she would have known. How long ago it all was.

She turned away, crossed the street, and walked over to the river. Though she could hear it, she saw nothing at all. There was a thin strip of asphalt, the bicycle path, then the riverbank and beyond that only the lapping of the water. She found herself thinking of the shrine, the altar. Her memory told her she had been lost in a thick fog then as well. . . . She heard footsteps behind her and turned around, startled. It was Hiroshi.

"You?" he said, evidently just as astonished as she was.

"Hello," she said and hugged herself tight. "What a coincidence."

He had stopped. "Do you really still believe that?" he asked, and she could hear him struggling with incredulity. "Do you believe we've just run into each other by chance?"

She looked at him. His face, so foreign to her but so familiar at the same time. The thin curve of his eyebrows, the shine of his dark black hair. She still saw the boy she had known then. The boy who had pulled her back from the bottomless pit of time.

"I don't know why I'm here," she confessed. "I didn't want to stay home tonight. I drove around, going nowhere . . . and now here I am."

He nodded thoughtfully. "It's hardly been an ordinary day. This is the first time I've ever just left the dorm for no reason with no destination in mind."

He didn't say any more. He didn't need to. She knew what he meant. That the two of them should meet one another like this, on an evening when hardly anyone was around, at a spot where neither of them ever normally went, was beyond the realm of coincidence.

The fog seemed to enfold them, cutting them off from the rest of the world. At a moment like this it was easy to believe in fate, in predestination. The unease that had been nagging at her had vanished. For the first time in days, she felt she was where she was supposed to be. On the other hand, she was getting cold.

"Do you collect stamps, or anything like that?" she asked.

Hiroshi looked surprised. "What? No."

"Do you have anything else you could show me?"

He considered the question. It really looked like he didn't get it. "My room?"

"Okay," said Charlotte. "Show me your room."

6

When Hiroshi woke up the next morning, something was different. It took him a while to realize what it was. He was happy.

Charlotte. He turned his head carefully, looking at her in astonishment as she lay there asleep next to him. It was broad daylight. Bright white light flooded the room, and her black hair spilled across the pillow. Sleeping like that, with such a peaceful expression on her face, she was more beautiful than ever—an angel caught here in his bed. How passionate she had been. He remembered the sounds she had made, the whispered nothings in his ear, as though remembering a dream. Yes, he was happy. For the first time in his life, everything was as it should be. He hadn't known it was possible to feel like this. So this was happiness.

His happiness lasted up until the moment Charlotte opened her eyes. First, she was confused, still caught in the web of sleep, but then she looked around, looked at him, and to Hiroshi's horror he saw reappraisal in her eyes. No, worse than that—regret. Everything was by no means as it should be.

"What's the time?" Charlotte asked huskily.

"No idea."

"I have to get dressed."

She sat up and threw the covers back. A musky smell rose up—her smell, their smell, the smell of sex and passion—and Hiroshi was overwhelmed, almost intoxicated. He could only watch helplessly as she bent over, naked, beautiful to look at, a flawless vision, and picked up her clothes from where they lay on the floor. It was probably the cleanest floor in any of the MIT dormitories, he thought miserably.

"Is that all you have to say after last night?" he asked at last.

Charlotte stopped what she was doing and looked at him, visibly annoyed. "What's that supposed to mean? I slept with you. That was what you wanted, wasn't it?"

"What?" Hiroshi couldn't believe his ears. "What makes you think that?"

She slipped her bra on. "Just say it. Did you or didn't you?"

"Well of course I did. But that's not all! It's not enough." Now the words came gushing out of him, pouring out in the desperate hope that if he could only find the right ones, he could set everything right. "I want you, don't you understand? I want . . . listen. There are over six billion people in the world who we could have met, millions of places where either one of us could have ended up, and even if we'd gone to the same place it could have been at different times. There were so many ways we might not have met, and despite all that we did. That can only mean it was fate that we found one another. It can only mean we were meant for one another. It can't mean anything else."

She was holding her panties, absorbed in turning them the right way out, but now she dropped her hand and lifted her head. She looked around the room, at the almost-empty shelves, the bare walls, the computer, the few remaining books.

"It wouldn't work," she said.

"Why not?"

"Because it wouldn't work." She slipped her panties on and stood up impatiently. She picked up her T-shirt and looked at Hiroshi. "I'm going to marry James. Get used to it."

Hiroshi felt his face harden to stone. He had offered her his naked, beating heart, and she had stomped all over it.

"It doesn't matter whether you marry him or not," he explained. It was a pointless, spiteful thing to say—it would change nothing, he knew that—but he had to say it anyway. "Fate is fate. You can't run from it."

She pulled on her pants. She picked up her jacket, which she wouldn't need today. "It's better if I just go," she said, running her fingers through her hair. Then she sat down on the end of the bed to pull her shoes on.

Hiroshi sat up. "Do you love him?" he asked.

"I'd hardly be with him if I didn't," she said, not looking up.

"Why not just say yes?"

She turned her head. Her eyes blazed. "All right then," she said. "Yes. Yes, I love him. Happy now?"

What did she have against him all of a sudden? How could she have flung herself at him so ravenously the day before and this morning treat him more or less as though he had raped her? By now there was nothing left of the extraordinary happiness he had felt when he woke up, nothing but an unreal memory.

"How do you know you love him?" Hiroshi pushed on. "I don't mean like loving—I don't know—your dog or something, but . . ." She tied her laces and stood up. He fumbled for words; he felt he was at the threshold of madness. "Does your heart fill with joy when you see him? Is life better when you're with him? Do you see more beauty, more colors? Is he the one fate chose for you? Is he the man meant for you since the beginning of time, the man you were meant for?"

She just stood there looking at him incredulously. "Don't you think you're being a little sentimental?"

He looked back at her, could have looked into her eyes for a thousand years if need be. "Do you?" he asked.

She snorted. "You don't know the first thing about the beginning of time," she hissed between gritted teeth.

Then she left.

When Charlotte left MacGregor House, she had to take a moment to get her bearings. The street was flooded with bright sunshine and looked utterly unlike the fog-shrouded gloom of the night before. She strode over to her car, climbed in, and slammed the door. She started the engine and swung out into the first gap in traffic. She didn't think twice about whether she was being watched. She should have. Seven pairs of eyes followed her from the windows of MacGregor House, and thirteen from Burton-Conner next door—all of them male. Eight people knew her car had been in the parking lot all night.

That morning the news spread like wildfire that Charlotte Malroux had spent the night in MacGregor House, and some three hundred students racked their brains for the rest of the day, wondering with whom she had spent it. It was only a matter of time before the rumor reached Harvard as well—and James Michael Bennett III, heir to Bennett Enterprises. The news caught up with him on Monday morning, before his first seminar, in a dark-paneled hallway where the air was still redolent of the good old days when the upperclassmen smoked cigars before lectures.

"Where did you hear that?" he asked, his face a mask.

Lawrence Kelly squirmed. "Oh man, you know how it is with these rumors. A guy who knows one of my hall mates heard it from someone in B-C, who heard it from someone in MacGregor ... Pretty well everyone knows by now. The only thing nobody knows is who she spent the night with."

But James knew. He had suspected as much straightaway; he had known there was more to it than what she had told him. A childhood friend? Bullshit.

"I mean," Lawrence went on, "theoretically she could have just spent the night with a girlfriend—"

"It wasn't a girl," James snarled.

Half of Harvard must be laughing at him by now. And he had other reasons to be furious, too. He had spent all of Saturday without Charlotte because of that stupid house move, and on Sunday he hadn't been able to reach her. So he had carried on with Project Terry Miller, but she was turning out to be one hell of a tough nut to crack. He had gone so far as to suggest a trip to Hawaii in his father's jet—which wouldn't be easy to organize—but even that had brought him not one step closer to his goal.

Time to go work off his anger on someone who truly deserved it.

"Come with me," he ordered, putting a heavy hand on Lawrence's shoulder. It was time for him to prove his loyalty. "Someone's about to learn he picked a fight with the wrong guy."

The Infinite Corridor is the main hallway linking all the main buildings of MIT. Thronged with students whenever classes are in session, it is the shortest way to walk from one end of campus to the other. The corridor is dead straight, so that on certain days of the year—at the end of January, and early in November—the setting sun shines along its whole length.

Hiroshi had no idea how many course announcements, club flyers, and other notices were displayed on the bulletin boards along its length—far too many to count, though. Early that morning he had gone to bug Prof. Bowers one more time about his project application. ("You'll know just as soon as I do," the prof had told him. "I'll send you an e-mail straightaway. You really don't need to show up here every Monday morning. That won't make things happen any faster.") Now he was on his way from his systems optimization seminar over to the library in the Rodgers Building when all of a sudden a broad-shouldered figure appeared from nowhere and blocked his path. Hiroshi had to take a step back before he recognized James, the man Charlotte supposedly loved. James was furious. Not hard to guess why.

"We gotta talk." The words came from his mouth like the rumble of a distant volcano.

Hiroshi dropped his shoulders and tried to relax his stance. "What about?" he asked.

"Don't you play dumb with me, you Nip," James spat at him. "You know exactly what about."

He had brought along two buddies, who were doing their best to look as mean as him. Actually, they looked kind of worried, as though they were medical attendants in charge of a patient who might suddenly flip out. Not very reassuring.

"Perhaps you could tell me all the same," Hiroshi suggested. "Sometimes people jump to the wrong conclusions."

James lurched forward alarmingly, his muscle-bound frame filling Hiroshi's field of vision. He clenched his fists.

"Okay then," he spat in Hiroshi's face. "I'll tell you straight out. You keep your hands off my fiancée or I'll bash your face in so hard, you'll be on a liquid diet for the rest of your miserable life."

Hiroshi shifted his right foot a little so that his feet were as wide apart as his shoulders. He had unobtrusively taken up the basic jujitsu stance. He regretted now that he had only ever taken the beginner's class at school.

"As far as I know," he replied, "women get to decide that for themselves these days. Twenty-first century, if that means anything to you."

"If you can't understand what I'm saying, I can tattoo it on your yellow hide," James snarled. "You keep your dirty fingers off my—"

Then without even finishing the sentence, he threw a punch. Hiroshi barely saw it coming, but he saw enough. He had no idea of how to use jujitsu locks or strikes, but he understood dodging. He shifted his weight to the side in an instant, and James found himself flailing at empty air.

"Coward!" James roared.

"Lamer!" Hiroshi shot back.

The students all around them saw what was happening, of course. A fistfight at MIT was almost unheard of, and most of them simply scattered. Many of them had no problem spending their nights rampaging through virtual labyrinths on their computer screens, hewing down virtual enemies in fountains of blood, but physical violence in real life was something else altogether. Those who didn't simply take off kept a wary distance, creating a kind of arena around Hiroshi and James.

James swung again, harder this time, and Hiroshi broke into a sweat. And then it happened—James brushed him on the shoulder and connected on the chin. It was just a glancing blow but the pain shot through Hiroshi like lightning. It gave him a very clear idea of what awaited him if this uneven fight should turn against him.

At that moment a professor arrived, a wiry, gray-haired man a head taller than James Michael Bennett III. Hiroshi had no way of knowing, of course, but the prof also happened to bear a striking resemblance to Bennett's father. "What is going on here, if I may ask?" he said.

James stopped where he was. He and Hiroshi looked at one another, then at the professor. Endgame. No. Stalemate, it seemed.

James took a step back and dropped his fists, shaking his arms loose. "Okay, Kato," he declared. "Today you've got away. But don't think you're safe. I have plenty of other ways of getting at you."

Hiroshi said nothing. He simply stared at his opponent, badly shaken by Bennett's animal rage. Charlotte wanted to marry this guy? What on earth did she see in him?

"You know how it is," James continued with a savage grin. "We'll cross paths again." He turned to go. "I'm looking forward to it."

James Michael Bennett III was wrong. Their paths had crossed before but never would again. That was the last he would see of Hiroshi Kato.

Charlotte had spent all of Sunday at home, curled up in her favorite chair, gazing into space. She had heard the telephone ringing but hadn't reacted. She just sat there, her knees drawn up, her arms around her legs, thinking of anything except last night. How she had forgotten the whole world. How she had lost control completely. How she and Hiroshi had been as one. She had never experienced anything like it, and it scared her. She had had to get away.

Luckily, her stomach had eventually rumbled, urging her into the kitchen to make coffee and a slice of toast. Cup in hand, she stared out of the window at the sunshine. The leaves on the trees danced in the light. Everything looked so peaceful, so full of new life. It was strange that she wasn't worried about James. For some reason, this seemed to have nothing to do with him. What had happened was between her and Hiroshi. Maybe it only had to do with her?

After that she roamed restlessly through her apartment. She looked at her computer as though she had never seen it before in her life, and at her bookshelf as though it were a nest of scorpions. Maybe she could get to work on her assignment. She didn't feel like it one bit but told herself it might take her mind off things. And so it did. She dove into the books, into the assigned reading, and wrote as though in a trance about events hundreds of thousands of years in the past. She didn't react when James drove up and parked in front of the house, didn't open the door when he rang the bell.

She stayed home on Monday as well. She couldn't head over to campus today and act as though nothing had happened, as though everything were just the same as ever. She didn't want to see anybody, didn't want to talk to anybody. The permanent American smile and good cheer would get on her nerves today. Something was bubbling beneath the surface inside her, and if anybody said so much as "Hi!" or told her something was "great," she knew she would burst out screaming.

When she thought of Saturday night, it was as though she were remembering the actions of someone else entirely. What had possessed her to go find Hiroshi, to throw herself at him like that? She had destroyed that friendship irrevocably. She sat back down at her computer but couldn't concentrate. Instead, she found herself watching the clock and wondering where she would be right now, what she would be doing, if nothing had ever happened with Hiroshi.

The telephone rang. It was Brenda asking whether she had gotten home safely and how the rest of her weekend had been. Charlotte dodged the question.

"I wanted to ask you something," Brenda said. "It's about Thomas . . . I mean, Dr. Wickersham."

Charlotte raised her eyebrows. Thomas? "Yes?"

"He called me yesterday. He wants to go out on a date. I wanted to ask you if he's okay."

She didn't ask whether she should accept. Brenda was not the kind of woman who ever asked other people what she should do—she always knew.

Could Charlotte tell her that Wickersham was "okay"? He was decent, conscientious. He was dependable. He was unmarried, true, but paleoanthropology wasn't a career for homebodies, especially with all the fieldwork. He could be entertaining, and he knew how to spread good cheer, but he was serious about teaching. He cared about his subject and about his students. And he was utterly incorruptible. She couldn't imagine anyone even trying to bribe him. He was, Charlotte realized with a sudden pang, everything James was not.

"Yes. Wickersham's okay," she said and had to fight back the tears. "Brenda, he's totally okay."

The trembling only started when he got back to his room. For at least a quarter of an hour, Hiroshi sat at his desk, drenched in sweat. He had never in his life seen such concentrated aggression, such hatred.

Of course, he could tell himself a hundred times over that James was an idiot, a primitive, a moron at the mercy of his basest instincts, that he was nothing but an egomaniac moneybags, but that didn't mean that he wasn't dangerous. James would have really hurt him if he could have. And he would have done so knowing his money would protect him. That nothing would happen to him, because he was rich, because he could afford the best lawyers and pay any fine the court imposed.

Hiroshi stared at his bed and thought for the thousandth time of the night he and Charlotte had spent there together. He wanted to understand—really understand—what she saw in James. What he had, what made her say she loved him. It had to be some mistake. Sooner or later she would recognize she was mistaken, and then he would just have to be there for her. They would be together in the end. The thought calmed him. It was a thought he could hold on to.

The shock was receding. He breathed deeply and considered. Should he be afraid James might take his anger out on Charlotte? He should probably call and warn her. He took out his phone. Of course, he only reached her voice mail. That could mean anything at all, but it probably only meant she didn't want to talk to him. Whatever. He left a message telling her what her beloved had done and spoke until the time was up. What good would that do her if the worst came to the worst? None. He would have liked to drive over to be with her, to defend her, but he feared if the worst truly did come to the worst, that wouldn't do any good either. Maybe he should call the police. But what would they do against the son of one of the richest men in the city? It was a tricky situation. He remembered the name of a friend Charlotte had mentioned the night they had met at Phi Beta Kappa. Brenda something . . . Gilliam, that was it. Brenda Gilliam. They had known one another in Delhi, and Charlotte had run across her again here in Boston—just like she had him. Brenda's father was a professor of medicine at Harvard. It should be easy enough to find the address.

Hiroshi switched on his computer. As it booted up, he realized how thirsty he was. Dry as a bone. He leapt to his feet, went down the hall to the drinks machine, and got an ice-cold can of apple soda. His hands trembled as he opened it. He wasn't quite over the shock yet. It took him less than five minutes to find the address and telephone number of Prof. John Gilliam, in Cambridge. He called and introduced himself as a childhood friend of Charlotte Malroux. Luckily, the woman who took the call, Mrs. Gilliam, recognized the name. He didn't want to compromise Charlotte needlessly, so he made sure he told the story in such a way Mrs. Gilliam would think there was nothing at all to the rumor that had so enraged James. She promised to tell her daughter as soon as possible but added that, alas, she had moved out of the family home just last weekend. Brenda, she assured him, would know what to do.

After the call Hiroshi spent a while staring into space and wishing he had taken all the martial arts courses his school had ever offered. He would have loved to fight James, to beat the daylights out of him, if only he had even the ghost of a chance. His gaze fell on his e-mail inbox. Prof. Bowers had sent him a message. He opened it—and froze. His application had been refused. Not just the proposed additions, but the whole project. Bowers wrote that the academic referees had not seen his experiment as deserving of subsidy. He added that he was sorry. Hiroshi felt the breath knocked out of him. James! What had his parting threat been? "I have plenty of other ways of getting at you." The words rang in his ears.

There was no question that James Bennett was behind this. His father was a major donor to all the universities in Boston. Somebody like that could pull whatever strings he wanted. He could lean on people. Derailing some insignificant foreign student's project proposal was a trivial matter for him. Hiroshi read the message again, not wanting to believe what he saw. The rage swelled inside him, a wild, bloodred rage, anger bordering on madness. Okay. James Michael Bennett III wanted war? He'd have war. Hiroshi Kato was not going to give up easily. He would fight to the last drop of blood. He would—

Hold on! Hiroshi laughed out loud. He'd completely forgotten; he didn't even need a grant. He jumped to his feet, took down his old *Masters of the Universe* notebook, and opened it. There it was, a check for more than three million dollars. He could fund his experiment without the university. And at that moment, as he held Rasmussen's check in his hands, a flash of insight shot through him like a bolt of lightning. He saw what was at work here. For a moment the dark night was dispelled, and every outline was clear and sharp. Now he knew why everything had had to happen the way it did. He understood how destiny worked. And he understood the part he had to play.

Sunday morning had been the moment of truth. If it had all turned out the way he had wanted it to, then he and Charlotte would be together, and he would be so happy that he would have forgotten his dream. He would have made a life inventing this or that handy little gizmo for Rasmussen, he would have become more or less rich, and he would have died happy, with Charlotte at his side. But fate had other plans for him. Charlotte was meant for him—but she would come at a price. All this time he had wondered why Charlotte chose James over him. Now he realized the reason was utterly banal: because he was rich. Charlotte herself was from a wealthy family, and she was so used to the idea that birds of a feather should flock together that she never even thought to question it. James was rich; he was a good match, and that was enough for her. Enough to convince her that whatever she felt for him was love.

He understood now that he would only win Charlotte if he realized all his plans, if he realized his dream and created a world where there was no difference between rich and poor, a world where everyone was rich. He had not been granted this vision so that it could gather dust in a notebook from his childhood days. Fate wanted him to make the vision come true, and if he would not do it of his own free will, then fate would force his hand. The path he must take was clear. The best thing to do was to forge ahead. No half measures. The first draft of his proposed study project had been a tentative first step, but the second proposal was little more. Even if he was to finance this experiment out of his own pocket, it would still be a waste of time. No. If he was going to do this, he had to do it all the way. He picked up the phone and called Jens Rasmussen.

"I have a project," he called him. "Mind you, it's several orders of magnitude above anything we were talking about on Saturday. I'll need help to make it happen."

"Do you have something I can read?" Rasmussen asked.

"Nearly done," Hiroshi lied. No need to tell the guy his project plan currently consisted of a hundred pages of Japanese in a child's careful handwriting.

"Okay. I'm still in Boston, at the Park Plaza. Maybe we could meet tomorrow for breakfast? Seven o'clock, say?"

"Seven o'clock. Okay." Hiroshi happily agreed. That gave him a good eighteen hours to get something down on paper.

This time James wouldn't be turned away. When Charlotte opened the door, he pushed his way through and hustled her back into the apartment. He was furious, yes, but he had his fury under control. Control was his watchword now. Control meant that he set the rules. He insisted on that with his friends, that they all understand that he set the rules, nobody else. And that counted for his wife as well, of course. For her, above all. It was time for Charlotte Malroux to learn that.

"There's a rumor going around that you've been screwing that Jap," he snarled once they were in her room. "Your childhood friend."

"Oh really," she said, unimpressed. "A rumor going around?"

"There is. And I want to hear from you how much truth there is to it."

Charlotte looked at him coolly. "I didn't know that you cared so much about fidelity."

"What?" James couldn't believe his ears. "That goes without saying! What the hell do you think? Shouldn't I care if the woman I'm going to marry jumps into bed with another man?"

"That's not quite what I meant," she said, turning away. "I was thinking rather of your behavior." She walked across to the closet and opened the door on his clothes. "She took out a shirt and felt the material, then passed it to him. "You were wearing this when you screwed little Wynona from the pedagogy seminar. You fucked her in her car because you decided she wasn't worth the price of a hotel room." She threw him the shirt and picked up the next. "You were wearing this last Thursday when you were trying to score with Terry Miller from art history. Hey, she's really got your balls in a vise, hasn't she?"

James stood there and took the shirt from her. He was rooted to the spot. How the devil did she know all that? Had she been watching him? Had she set a detective on him? No. There was no way she could know. On Thursday he had been quite alone in the bushes with Terry. Nobody could have been watching them. Charlotte was guessing. Bluffing.

"I beg your pardon?" He mustn't put a foot wrong now. "What are you talking about? None of that's true."

"James! You know it and I know it. Isn't that your motto? 'You can't fuck every woman in the world . . . but that's no reason not to try.'" She sounded strangely indifferent, as though deep in some other thoughts. She took one of his favorite pairs of pants from the wardrobe. "Two days after you took me to Cloud Eight, you scored with one of the waitresses there. The blond girl who served us, the one with the thin waist. Her name's Kimberley Watts. You . . . let's see now . . . you've screwed nearly every secretary in your father's office, including two who were only hired since you met me." She flung the pants at him. "Do you want me to go on?"

James was flabbergasted. "How do you know all this?"

"I just do."

"Listen . . ." Goddamn it all. All he could do was salvage whatever he could. If that meant telling the truth, then so be it. "Okay, I confess, I've had my moments of weakness. But it doesn't mean anything! It's just . . . you know . . . old habits die hard. Stuff I used to do before I met you. I'll stop for sure once we announce our engagement. I'll give it all up."

Charlotte shook her head briefly, almost absent-mindedly. "No you won't," she said. "There's not going to be any engagement."

There were only a few people in the breakfast room at the Boston Park Plaza at that hour of the morning. Sturdy pillars supported the vaulted ceiling, the light from the chandeliers mixed with the blue-gray of early dawn, and the thick carpet underfoot swallowed up the sound of footsteps. Rasmussen had chosen a corner table by the window, tucked away behind a bank of houseplants. He was breakfasting on a pot of tea and a fruit platter. He asked what he could order for his guest, but Hiroshi simply pulled his project proposal from his bag and passed it over to him.

"Just read it, please," he said.

"You could eat something while I read," Rasmussen urged.

"I wouldn't be able to swallow a bite."

"They make the most amazing pancakes here. You're really missing something."

Hiroshi simply shook his head in exasperation.

Rasmussen shrugged. "Okay. At least I tried." He leaned back in his chair, opened the folder, and began to read.

Hiroshi watched him silently. At first the investor took an occasional sip of tea or speared a slice of apple or melon, but soon he put his fork aside, set down his cup, and became absorbed. The further he read, the deeper his concentration. His brow furrowed in thought.

At last, he looked up, and after glancing left and right to make sure they were still alone, he spoke.

"This is . . . words fail me. It's epoch-making. If what you're proposing here actually works, then it's not just an invention, it will change the course of history. It's the project of the millennium. The only comparison I can think of is when man tamed fire. You'll change the world."

Exactly, thought Hiroshi. *That's exactly my goal.* "I'd like to try," he said. "But I need help. You have a list there of everything I need."

"Yes." Rasmussen put the folder down on the table and picked up his napkin. Still frowning in thought, he wiped his mouth. "I know someone crazy enough to fund something like this," he said after a moment's thought. "You would probably have to see him in person though, and explain your idea face-to-face."

"No problem," Hiroshi declared.

"He lives quite far away."

"Also no problem."

"Okay." Rasmussen took his phone from his jacket. "When could you leave?"

Hiroshi shrugged. "Right away if I have to."

Charlotte scanned the columns of doorbells for Hiroshi's name. It made her think of the time in Tokyo when she had visited him at home and stood in front of the intercom panel there, just as helpless. Ah, here it was. Simple. "H. Kato." She rang. No answer. Well, what had she expected? He must be on campus somewhere, working, just as she should have been doing. She took a pen and paper from her bag to leave him a note. As she leaned the notepad against the wall to write, someone came out the door, a tall, gawky kid with Mexican features. He hurried past, but a moment later she heard him stop behind her.

"Charlotte Malroux?" he asked.

She turned. "Yes?"

His eyes opened wide, as though the sight of her had startled him. "You aren't looking for Hiroshi Kato, are you?"

"I am," she admitted. "Do you know where he is?"

For a moment he said nothing but seemed to deflate. "This can't be happening," he mumbled. Then he sighed and said, "You just missed him. By an hour or so."

Charlotte lifted her notepad. "Yes, I was just writing a note to put in his mailbox. Do you know when he'll be back?"

He shook his head. "He won't be. He moved out, the jerk. Early this morning. My room is next to his. We're friends . . . I thought we were, anyway. He just gave me the key and a check for way too much money and told me to settle everything with the house manager. Said he had to go somewhere, he had a vision to follow, or something like that." He held out his right hand. "I'm Rodney, by the way."

She shook his hand distractedly. "Did he say where he was going?"

Rodney's expression was pained. "Not a word."

After that she sat in the car, unable even to turn the key in the ignition. She saw the events of the night before in her mind's eye replayed like a film. How James had called again and again, pleading, begging, whining, cursing, calling her the most dreadful names by the end. How Brenda had come to the apartment to tell her Hiroshi had called her mother. The story of how James had sought him out at MIT. Hiroshi's fear that James might do something to her. She hadn't wanted to believe it and had asked James about it the next time he called. He admitted it straightaway. Worse still, he seemed proud of it. A man had to fight for the woman he loved, blah, blah, blah. She had hung up without a word and pulled the cable out of the wall.

That night the same thoughts had gone round and round in her head like millstones turning. That perhaps she should give the relationship with Hiroshi another chance. That it wouldn't work. That she was drawn to him and yet scared of the attraction. That this must have something to do with her mother, who had never been happy in her marriage. That she did not want to be alone. And then the same thoughts all over again. By morning she had finally decided to talk to Hiroshi about all of it. Just to talk at first. Since she hadn't been able to reach him by phone, she had gotten in the car and driven over to his place. Where was the hand of fate now, the destiny he had believed would bring them together? Hiroshi had clearly convinced himself of that, he was such a romantic. Fate . . . coincidence—that was all there ever was. For instance, the way she had missed him by an hour. Just bad luck.

Charlotte leaned forward and turned the key. Perhaps it was for the best that it had happened this way. She could never have had a future with Hiroshi, even less so than with James. At least now she had some fond memories.

She put the car into gear and drove away.

At first all he saw were clouds, with a suggestion of some vast continent beneath. Then a coast full of fjords and forest, islands, immense rivers flowing out to sea, and at last an astonishing tangle of skyscrapers, which looked like a strange crystalline structure from up here in the air. And then finally the airport, an island unto itself. Hiroshi peered out of the window. So this was Hong Kong.

Once he was through customs with his two suitcases, he spotted his name on a placard as agreed. The man holding it looked like a wrestler, tall and broad-shouldered, and when Hiroshi introduced himself, he saw the man's face wore a forbidding, even fearsome expression.

"My name is Ku Zhong," the man said in flawless English with just a hint of a Chinese accent. "I am Mr. Gu's personal assistant. I am required to ask you whether you would like to go to your hotel first to rest, or whether you want to speak to Mr. Gu straightaway."

Although Hiroshi had a twenty-five-hour flight under his belt, he was still burning with eagerness to talk to Larry Gu, the mysterious Chinese billionaire Rasmussen had told him about. Gu was eighty-one years old, and his personal physicians had no idea how he was still alive. "If it is convenient for Mr. Gu, I would like to speak to him straightaway."

Ku nodded, his face a mask. "Mr. Gu had very much hoped this might be the case. I will take you straight to his office." He gestured curtly toward what had to be the exit. "If you would be so good as to follow me to the car."

The car was a stretch limo with tinted windows, just like in the movies. Hiroshi had assumed Ku would drive, but in fact there was a chauffeur waiting, who opened the trunk, stowed Hiroshi's luggage, and drove them away. They left the airport across a six-lane bridge, headed into the ranks of Hong Kong's high-rises. Other than them, there was very little traffic; he only saw taxis, delivery trucks, and buses. Ku asked conscientiously how his flight had been, and Hiroshi answered that it had been fine. Then Ku took a call and spent the rest of the journey castigating whoever was on the other end in rapid Cantonese. Hiroshi couldn't understand a word.

At last, the limousine pulled up to one of the countless steel-and-glass skyscrapers and glided down into the most luxurious underground parking garage Hiroshi had ever seen. An elevator was waiting, its doors already open.

"Please," said Ku.

They got out of the car and into the elevator, which shot upward. They emerged into a series of brightly lit rooms divided by black marble screens and chrome pillars. Men and women bowed as they passed, and beyond it all was a double door large enough for an elephant to pass through.

"Mr. Gu's office," Ku declared, holding a swipe card up to a reader. "I will wait for you out here."

Hiroshi stood on the threshold. This wasn't an office, it was a cathedral. The room's ceiling was invisible in the gloom. The wall across from where he stood was made entirely of glass, an enormous window that offered a breathtaking view of central Hong Kong as evening drew in. In front of the window stood a desk, deep black and polished to an unearthly sheen. It was almost bare and about the size of a tennis court. Behind the desk sat a wizened little man in a huge armchair upholstered in red-gold leather. He was completely bald, with a long white beard, ancient, and seemingly unimpressive, but he gave off an energy that filled the entire room.

"Hello, Mr. Kato," he said in a thin but somehow resonant voice. "Please don't be shy. Come closer."

Hiroshi took a deep breath and crossed the threshold. The doors swung shut behind him.

TRAVELS

Boston appeared below her. Seen from up here, the city didn't seem to have changed at all. How long had it been now? Three years. More. The fall colors blanketed New England; these would be the last few days of fine weather.

Suddenly, Charlotte was consumed with impatience. She pressed her forehead against the window and tried to make out Somerville and the house she had once lived in, though she knew it was pointless. That chaotic little student apartment—who might be living there now? Would they be able to cope with the plants on the balcony? Was the hibiscus still alive? She would have liked to know. Since she had fled—from James and his insinuations, from all those memories, from her studies, which had suddenly seemed so pointless—she had been living in Paris in her parents' apartment, crammed with dusty heirloom furniture. It was oppressive, but there would have been no sense in getting a place of her own, not with rents costing what they did in Paris.

They were both waiting for her, Brenda beaming with joy and Thomas smiling and cheerful.

"And the little one?" Charlotte asked as Brenda embraced her.

"My mom's looking after him. She can cast some kind of spell— he cries a whole lot less with her than when I'm around."

Brenda looked good. She had blossomed. She had done something with her hair that made her look all grown-up, and she seemed to have put her taste for bright baggy clothes behind her. Thomas hugged her, shy and awkward as always. He had put on weight. Not that he was fat exactly; there was just a little more flesh on his bones. Probably Brenda's good home cooking. And his hair was beginning to turn gray—what there still was of it—while the bald patch had climbed steadily higher up his forehead. The combined effect made him look older than he was.

"Thanks for the invitation," Charlotte said.

"You were our maid of honor," he said, smiling. "I think it's only fair we ask you to come see what happened next."

They were still living in Brenda's blue clapboard house, where the smell of the Atlantic wafted in some days. As she stepped into the orchard, she felt as though she had left Boston only yesterday. No, wait: the garden had changed a little, the trees had grown, and the lawns and beds were tidier than she remembered. It was a little patch of paradise. And soon she would meet its cherub. . . . Instinctively, Charlotte put her hand on her tummy. Children. So far she had managed to dodge the question of whether she wanted any herself. She had always said that she would think about it later. These days she understood all that talk of the biological clock ticking away, where once she had merely scoffed at the idea. But even now she could hardly imagine becoming pregnant. The thought had always been more frightening than anything else. Pregnancy would mean the end of freedom, she felt. That was how it had been for her mother.

Mrs. Gilliam opened the front door, a happy, grandmotherly smile on her face. "He's asleep," she whispered, as though even saying the words out loud would wake him.

Brenda took Charlotte by the arm and took her through to the bright, airy nursery that had once been her own room. The baby lay in a darling little crib, looking like an angel, a cherub indeed. Charlotte bent over to admire him properly. Her heart melted as the little man pursed his lips in his sleep and waved his little fists, puffing and snorting as though hard at work somewhere in dreamland.

Charlotte looked up. "And why Jason?"

"It had to be," Brenda explained. "We spent weeks looking at baby-name books, making lists, I don't know what else, and then we both had the same idea on the very same day. If that's not fate, then what is it?"

Fate. The word still gave Charlotte a pang. "And what if he'd been a girl?"

"That would have meant trouble." Brenda snorted indignantly. "Do you know what Tom suggested? In all seriousness? Olivia! I mean, puh-lease!"

"Olivia Wickersham?" Charlotte said the name aloud to test it out. "What's wrong with that? I don't think it's so bad."

That earned her a punch on the arm. "Hey! What kind of friend are you?"

Maybe it was because they had been talking, but whatever the reason, Jason woke up, gulped in a few angry breaths, and began to wail. Brenda picked him up out of the crib. "He's hungry, I guess." She looked at him lovingly. "Wasn't that a long time, eh? Did Mommy have to go all that way to the airport?"

Baby talk. Charlotte had to grin. The things a baby could make grown men and women do. As Brenda nestled down with her son in an old basket chair by the window to feed him, Charlotte left the two of them alone and went into the kitchen. Mrs. Gilliam was just making coffee. She asked how the flight had been.

"Good," said Charlotte. On the table was an English fruitcake, a Gilliam family recipe that suited fall like nothing else. "Some bumps and thumps at takeoff, but then it was all calm. The seat next to me was free, which was nice."

"Oh yes," said Mrs. Gilliam, putting a cup in front of her. "There's so little room on the planes these days, isn't there?"

As Charlotte sat down, she spotted a little pile of Spanish textbooks on the windowsill. She asked who was learning Spanish.

"Those are mine," Thomas said as he came through the door, back from loading baby gear into the car. "I've been invited to give a short series of lectures at the University of Buenos Aires. Next year, in May."

"In Spanish?" Charlotte asked.

"Oh no, I'll be lecturing in English. I'm not that crazy. But I want to see a little of the city, understand what people are saying." He shrugged. "It can't do any harm, I don't think."

Charlotte opened one of the books. It was full of notes in the margins and underlinings. He was obviously working hard at it. Well, why not? He spoke Arabic, Turkish, and Farsi; he would probably have no trouble with Spanish.

"What will you be lecturing on?" she asked. "Paleoanthropology?"

He grinned. "Of course not. There wouldn't be much to say about that in South America." The classical theory was that mankind had not reached the continent until about fifteen or twenty thousand years ago. "No, they want to take a closer look at the ancient Indian cultures thereabouts. I'll be lecturing on modern excavation techniques."

"That sounds exciting," Charlotte said, turning her attention to her coffee. She stirred the sugar in carefully.

He looked askance at her. "Would I be wrong to think that you no longer take an interest in such things? Have you given up on prehistory?"

She didn't look up. "For the time being at least."

"And what are you doing instead?"

"Nothing." That was the truth. The fact was she did nothing. She spent her days wandering through museums and antiques shops, ignoring the way men looked at her and rebuffing their advances, getting through the days. Shopping, cooking, eating, and sleeping. She sat around in the parks when the weather was fine, or drove out of town deep into the countryside. And somehow the time passed. Three years seemed like nothing at all. From time to time she considered looking for work. But what? A job? More study? "I'm trying to enjoy life."

"It doesn't really sound like that's working."

"It may still happen."

Brenda came in with Jason on her shoulder, wide awake and beaming. "And?" she asked. "Has Tom picked your brains about Buenos Aires yet? He wants to leave us sitting here without him for six weeks, can you believe it?"

Charlotte gave a strained smile. Was that the truth of it? Was Thomas using this lecture tour as a way to escape from his family, the way her father had escaped into his work? "Buenos Aires . . . that was a long time ago. I don't know whether anything I could tell you might still be true."

At dinner she found herself talking about Buenos Aires all the same. How the melancholy strains of the tango floated through the whole city; how crowds of people often danced in the public squares. How unbearably hot and sticky the summer could be, and how something was always going wrong in their house—the refrigerator or the air conditioning or the boiler or the telephone. How the Argentineans were such friendly people but often couldn't resist playing dirty tricks on foreigners. How her own pocket had been picked three times, once by a boy scarcely any older than herself.

At some point she gave such a huge yawn that Brenda declared, "Okay, we've gotten all we need out of you today. Charley, you're taking your jet lag off to bed. How long were you up in the air? Seven hours? Eight?"

"I have no idea," Charlotte had to admit.

She followed Brenda upstairs to the guest room. This was the first time she had been in this part of the house. The last time she had visited the Wickershams here, the programmer had still been living on the top floor, a taciturn woman who only ever said "Hello" when you met her on the stairs. It was a pretty room, neatly decorated in green and white. A tree standing directly in front of the window scratched at the pane with its branches. Brenda wished her good night. Charlotte pulled her pajamas and toothbrush out of her suitcase, which was already in the room—who had brought it up for her?—and then remembered nothing more until she woke up the next morning.

The window was open and she could hear birdsong. It wasn't quite dawn outside yet. The house was completely quiet. What time was it? She looked for her watch but couldn't find it anywhere. Early, at any rate. That was the jet lag. She was wide awake and knew she wouldn't be able to get back to sleep. She sat up and looked around. Just to try it, she put her hand on the wood panels on the wall behind her bed. The panels looked old and must have been here forever. She shut her eyes and tried to feel the history stored up in them. She had to sit still for a long time before the first images swam to the surface. The memories, the feelings. She felt loneliness, yearning for someone waiting back in Chicago. A boyfriend? A husband? No, another woman Charlotte realized with a shock. The programmer had been in love with another woman. A secret affair? Unrequited love? She couldn't quite tell.

Sighing, she took her hand away. The images vanished. When she was younger, it had been like listening to a concert, but these days she caught only faint strains, tangled snatches of voices and feelings she could hardly make out. When she was a child, she would have been able to read the silent woman's whole life story from these walls, but she would not have understood most of it. Now she knew more about life, her mysterious gift had grown weaker. Perhaps, Charlotte thought as she opened her suitcase and put everything she would need into drawers and onto shelves, it was some kind of defense mechanism she had developed over the course of her life. When she was a child, the flood of strange feelings, memories, and images had often been too much for her. She was open to impressions, too open;

indeed, she had often felt vulnerable. How keen she had always been to visit museums and old monuments. For her, it had been the equivalent of riding a ghost train. But perhaps it hadn't just been about the kicks. It must have been her way of trying instinctively to learn how to deal with her gift.

She sat down on the bed and passed her hand over the quilt, feeling the love Brenda had put into stitching it. Brenda, who had a baby now. Charlotte tried to remember when she had been a baby, a toddler. She had almost no memory of the time. Her mother used to say she had been a strange child, and nobody in the family contradicted that. Charlotte herself could only remember isolated moments, out of context, that seemed strangely timeless. The living and the dead had been around her, all mingled together, and often she had not been able to tell which thoughts were her own and which came from other minds.

That was another reason she had left Boston three years ago: the place held painful memories for her. Such things were harder for her than for most people. She couldn't have coped if she'd stayed. But she couldn't spend her whole life running away every time something unpleasant happened. Eventually, there would be nowhere left on earth to go, and then what? Perhaps it was a blessing that her gift was slowly ebbing away.

The days until Jason's baptism on Sunday passed in a blur. Charlotte helped in the kitchen, helped decorate the dining room, helped do laundry. She enjoyed the bustle and hard work. New guests were constantly stopping by. Some simply said hello, admired the baby, and went back to their hotels, while others spent hours sitting on the porch, talking. The coffee machine never stopped.

It was out on the porch that Charlotte met Adrian Cazar, who had studied with Brenda at Boston University. His major had been climatology, and he and Brenda had met in a web-design class;

together they had developed a website on global warming. She handled the design, and he provided the content.

"Well, it was incredibly cold in Paris last winter," Charlotte said. She felt an overpowering need to tease someone. "We thought the snow would never stop. And then even this past summer, I was freezing all the time. I'm not sure this whole global-warming thing isn't just a myth."

Adrian wouldn't let himself be provoked. "Its effects are rather different over in Europe because of the Gulf Stream. While the rest of the world is baking hot, you'll get an ice age."

He was a good-looking guy, the dark type. He reminded her of the lead actor in one of those pirate movies, the one who had played a crazy captain. She couldn't recall the name.

"Ice age?" She still wanted to provoke him. "I think you're just making excuses."

Adrian grinned and looked at her with his big, dark eyes. "No, really. One cold winter or one hot summer means nothing. There have always been variations in the climate, and there always will be. The problem is that average temperatures are rising. Slowly but surely, and we can't stop it. For the time being it's only really been evident in areas where the climate is already extreme—by the poles, in the deserts, and in regions that are sensitive to drought. Nature is changing irreversibly there." A sudden gust of wind pelted them with yellow-brown leaves as though to prove Adrian's point.

"And we're causing it? With exhaust emissions and all of that?"

"Possibly," Adrian said. "Our emissions of climate-active substances could explain the rise in temperatures. What they can't explain, however, is why there were warm periods in the past as well, long before human civilization. Which is why there is still debate about whether we are really having an influence on global climate, or whether we're just kidding ourselves."

Charlotte remembered the knife on the altar, remembered falling into the abyss of time, remembered the strange certainty she had felt ever since that there had been another human race before now, maybe more than one. Suddenly, she didn't feel like teasing Adrian anymore. She listened carefully, seriously, as he explained he wanted to organize an expedition to an island near one of the poles to study the effects of rising temperatures.

"There have been studies like this before, of course," he said. "But so far the research focus has always been on how existing flora and fauna change when spring comes earlier, or when maximum temperatures are higher—that kind of thing. I'm interested in something else, though. I'd like to go to an island that has been completely covered in ice for hundreds of thousands of years and that is only now losing its ice shield as a result of global warming. What happens next? How does nature reconquer such an environment? What kinds of plants take root first? What kinds of animals will settle there? That sort of thing." He took a sip of coffee and made a face. It had gone cold. "That could give us some very interesting perspectives on what happened at the end of previous ice ages."

"It sounds fascinating," Charlotte said and suddenly felt the urge to take part in an expedition herself. Wasn't that what she had always wanted? Instead, she had spent all her years at Harvard in dusty seminar rooms. "When are you setting off?"

Adrian gave a wry smile. "Oh man! You have no idea the kind of preparation goes into an expedition like this. It's just unbelievable. Talking to sponsors all the time, mountains of paperwork, thousands of telephone calls—most leading nowhere . . . I don't even know yet which islands might be suitable."

"If you want a paleoanthropologist along on the trip—okay, a part-qualified paleo person—just let me know," Charlotte said.

He looked like he was seriously considering it. "You can certainly give me your e-mail address," he said.

The day after the baptism Brenda took Charlotte to the airport—on her own this time. Just the two of them, friends from way back. A light fog hung in the air, but it didn't seem to have affected the flights. It affected Charlotte though. Every time she saw fog in Boston, she thought of Hiroshi.

"You're not worried about Thomas going off to Buenos Aires?" she asked Brenda.

Her friend just laughed. "Not at all. I tease him about it, of course. You know, he was single for so long I think he sometimes still needs to feel he's a free man despite his wife and child."

The airport was busy. An announcement repeatedly came over the loudspeakers that Mr. Schwartzing should kindly report to the information desk.

"Six weeks, though. That's a long time."

"Well, sure it is. It'll give him a chance to see how good he has it at home with me. Anyway, apart from all that . . ." Then Brenda gave a start and suddenly grabbed Charlotte's arm to drag her off in another direction. "Hey! Let's go this way. What do you think?"

But it was too late; Charlotte had already seen the magazine. Five copies of it lined up in a row in the news racks of the kiosk in front of them.

James was on the cover. James being led out of a building by police officers.

"My God," Charlotte murmured. As though in a trance, she stepped up to the newsstand, picked up a copy, and opened it. James in handcuffs. His wife Terry with a black eye, her expression furious and her lawyer at her side.

Brenda sighed. "I was so hoping you wouldn't get to hear about it," she confessed. "I told the whole family to steer clear of the topic. I threw away all the gossip magazines in the house . . ."

"What happened?" Charlotte asked numbly. She leafed through the rest of the magazine. It seemed to be a local rag with listings, ads for restaurants and nightclubs, and a few news features about the Boston jet set.

"Oh, what can I say? When he married that Terry Miller, he got more than he bargained for. They've been married for—what?—two years now? And for a year and a half, they've been at daggers drawn. The whole town is talking about it."

"Goodness." Charlotte took a closer look at the photo. He looked dissolute. Bloated, old before his time. Unhappy.

Brenda put an arm around her. "It's not your fault, Charley. None of it's your fault. It's the money that turned him bad, nothing else. It was all that money."

Surprisingly, it wasn't snowing in Moscow. Instead, it was raining, pouring down torrents.

"That's climate change for you," her mother said as she met Charlotte at the airport, using her diplomatic passport to get her past the lengthy immigration procedures. "Everyone's talking about it these days. Over in Siberia the permafrost is melting for the first time in centuries, and anything built on top of it is sinking down into the mud—pipelines, roads, houses. It's a huge problem." She pulled up the hood of her raincoat as they left the building. "I'm just fed up with all this rain. You would have done better to come in the summer."

"But your birthday's in November," Charlotte reminded her.

"You still could have come in summer."

Charlotte raised her eyebrows. "I'm not that fond of Moscow." She didn't find the rain that bad, though. So far at least. It made for a change.

"By the way, we have another visitor from France at the moment," her mother said as they drove along the M-10 from Sheremetyevo airport into downtown Moscow. "He's your third cousin, André Faucault. His father is Pierre Faucault, son of Marie-Claire Baratte, who is . . . now let me see . . . yes, she's your great-grandfather's sister's daughter. On your father's side, of course."

"André Faucault?" Charlotte pondered this news. It sounded a lot like one of her mother's regular attempts at matchmaking. "Do I know him?"

"Oh, you've met before. It was at Aunt Sophie's wedding."

Charlotte groaned aloud. "Maman! I was five years old at the time!"

"Well, quite. And André must have been seven." She was bubbling over with enthusiasm for this André. "He's studying in Strasbourg, at the school of government there, and he has a very good chance of getting a post on the supreme court. He's the best student in his class. And such a nice young man, I can hardly believe it."

"Oh, I'm sure he is," Charlotte responded dutifully.

"I'm sure the two of you will get along beautifully," her mother said happily.

As it turned out, they would at least never have a single argument—since try as they might, they would never agree on anything to argue about. André was a preppy young man with a prominent Adam's apple and the manners of an aide-de-camp. His favorite topics of conversation were his studies and knotty legal problems. Whenever Charlotte said anything, he would listen attentively and then agree with every word. She could have told him she had very different ideas about conversation, but she got the impression he wouldn't have understood. Other than that, the birthday party passed quite cheerfully. Even her father took the day off, acting as though he had no idea what the words "pressing appointment" or "binding obligation" might mean.

The next day they were invited to the private viewing of an exhibition by several young French artists, supposedly the face of the twenty-first century. Charlotte's father was sponsoring the exhibition, so they all had to go along and listen to him make a speech. Then the Russian secretary of state for cultural cooperation would make a speech. It was all high politics; the artists stood around uncertainly at the edge of the room, looking just as irrelevant as they really were. Charlotte was surprised to see the Russian speaker was none other than Mikhail Yegorov, who had been ambassador back in Tokyo.

"Mikhail Andreievitch!" she said to him once the speeches were over and the buffet had begun. "Do you remember me?"

He did. "Charlotte? But of course! I had been wondering—isn't that my old friend Jean's charming daughter, I asked myself? And indeed it is!" He sketched a bow. "And I can't help but notice that you speak excellent Russian."

"A little bit," Charlotte corrected him. She no longer found it quite as easy to pick up a new language as when she was a child.

"You know each other?" her father asked in surprise as he brought two glasses of champagne.

"From a reception in Tokyo," Charlotte said, switching to French. She looked at Yegorov. "If I recall correctly, you were talking about some place called Devil's Island at the time."

Yegorov frowned, remembering. "Ah yes. C'est vrai." He pointed a finger at Charlotte's father. "I had just been telling you about my grandparents when your daughter joined us. She told us about some island as well, didn't she?"

Charlotte nodded. "The Island of the Saints. A Shinto shrine."

Father laughed awkwardly, obviously not remembering. He pressed one glass of champagne into Yegorov's hand and the other into Charlotte's. "I'll go fetch one for myself." With that, he vanished into the crowd.

Yegorov raised his glass to Charlotte. "My father was stationed on the coast. Amderma base, south of the nuclear test ranges at Novaya Zemlya. In other words, at the end of the world. He flew Tupolev interceptors and was always on the alert for an attack by the NATO aggressors. I was allowed to go and visit him there once—although by then he was no longer an active combat pilot, he was a trainer. What a desolate place! I remember bare cliffs, ice, a churning sea, and nothing growing anywhere. It's the Arctic tundra up there. It was hellishly cold, there were storms all the time, and the residential blocks were barely insulated. The airstrip was just a dirt track, and the soldiers used to scratch lichen from the rocks to dry it and smoke instead of tobacco." He laughed. "The glorious Soviet Army was no place for the fainthearted."

"It sounds dreadful," Charlotte said. She looked at the former ambassador. He had aged. His bushy eyebrows shimmered gray, almost white, and he looked thin.

He nodded, reminiscing. "Oh yes, dreadful is the word. And I was there in the summer. Even now I hardly dare imagine what it was like in winter." He took a sip from his glass. "Sometimes I can hardly believe the places mankind has chosen to live. If we ever get as far as building spaceships to travel to the stars, then I tell you one thing, Charlotte: the universe will have to watch out. We humans get everywhere, and once we're there, we stay."

Charlotte had to smile. "You're a philosopher, Mikhail Andreievitch."

He waved away the compliment, although he was clearly flattered. "My grandfather was a silent sort of man, but you always felt he thought a great deal. He wasn't easily frightened. No matter what the trouble was, he always kept his cool. Except when he came to talk of Saradkov Island. Devil's Island."

"It sounds downright scary."

"He had to land there once, because of engine trouble. It was difficult enough landing a jet plane, but beyond that he must have experienced something that frightened him to death. I don't know what—he never told me much more about it—but he wasn't the only one. A lot of the sailors who ply the Arctic Ocean would swear on the Bible there's something wrong with that island. That it's cursed. They say the devil himself sleeps there, buried under the ice." Yegorov stared thoughtfully into the stream of fine bubbles rising in his glass. "Interestingly, there's also an old Siberian legend about a great war between heaven and mankind that lasted until one of the captains of the heavenly host fell and was swallowed by the ice. A black angel. The legend says that if the ice ever melts, the black angel will awaken once more and the war will break out anew—which is why it is always winter in that part of the world. Because the winter came to save mankind."

He shrugged. "I suppose it's a story to reconcile people with fate and with living in eternal cold. It's such an old story that they carry it with them in their genes, so to speak."

"It's no wonder they're afraid."

Yegorov glanced over his shoulder as though worried they would be overheard. Then he leaned toward her and continued in a low voice, speaking in French. "Shall I tell you something really uncanny, though? A friend who works for our Federal Space Agency showed me some recent satellite images of Saradkov taken by radar, or I don't know what. Anyway, the pictures show there really is something stuck in the ice there. I imagine it's not actually a black angel; more likely, it's an iron meteorite or something along those lines. But there really is something there trapped in eternal ice. And in fact the ice is no longer eternal. It's beginning to melt. Now that's uncanny, isn't it? We may well ask ourselves what the ice will reveal."

Charlotte's father rejoined them just then, and Yegorov was visibly unwilling to discuss the topic any further in his presence. Holding a glass in one hand and a plate full of hors d'oeuvres from the buffet in the other, her father said, "You should hurry. The French artists of the twenty-first century seem to be a hungry lot."

That evening Charlotte opened her laptop and wrote an e-mail to Adrian Cazar, telling him that if he was still looking for an island that would suit his criteria he should take a look at Saradkov, in the Russian Arctic.

The next day André set off home again; he could only get away from his studies for a few days. It was hard to know whether, having met her, he was disappointed; he had been scrupulously polite to Charlotte and continued to act too old for his age.

There was no doubt, however, that her mother was disappointed. "You must understand one thing, Charlotte," she told her daughter on the drive back from the airport, pursing her lips. "We women have a sell-by date, so to speak. Even beauty is not enough to protect us. All beauty fades in time."

"I would rather fade than marry into boredom," Charlotte shot back. She thought of Brenda, who had got it right. Whatever the world might say, she had got it right.

Her mother kept quiet for the rest of the drive. Charlotte knew, however, that her silence did not mean resignation; it only meant Mother was thinking up new arguments. So she made sure to get out of the house. No long speeches, just a wave good-bye and out the door while there was a break in the rain.

And what if it did rain, since she could sit in the metro and ride all day long if she felt like it? The Moscow metro was worth the trip all on its own. Charlotte rode the escalators all the way down and then all the way up again, awestruck by the lavish detail in the stations and on the platforms. She let the stream of passengers carry her with them as they hurried along, stony-faced or laughing, chattering, bored, or thoughtful. Sometimes she had to ask the way, since she still had trouble reading the Cyrillic alphabet. She learned languages by ear, by talking and listening.

From time to time she went up to the surface. She wandered along strange streets, looking at ramshackle old buildings, restored houses, and brand-new ones. She gave a fifty-ruble note to a beggar in a threadbare, gray-and-white overcoat. She admired the work of a street artist who stoically kept working in the pouring rain with only a sheet of plastic to protect him. She dodged a dog that barked furiously at her. She was lost in thought.

On one of these trips up to the surface it suddenly began to rain so heavily that all she could do was take shelter in the nearest shop.

Hanging bells jangled as she opened the door, and she stood there for a moment with her pants soaked through, gasping for breath as the rain drummed against the windowpane and blurred the world beyond. Smears of light passed by from the cars creeping slowly along through the downpour. She looked around. It was an antiques shop. Old furniture, oil paintings in bulky frames, faded lace, cut glass. Books. Solid silver tableware. She felt the breath of history on her cheek. She felt the fear, the grief, the hard necessity that had led to all these different objects being offered up for sale. It took a while before she realized there were voices talking farther back in the shop. She heard someone with an English accent stumbling along in broken Russian.

She followed the voices. The next room was full of musical instruments, and an old man with a sour expression on his face— evidently the owner—was standing there listening to another man who had his back to her. The second man had a wild mane of hair and, Charlotte thought at first glance, the same gray-and-white coat as the beggar she had met earlier.

"Perhaps I can help?" she asked in English.

He turned around. She saw a rosy, round face full of freckles, with cheeks like a cherub and cornflower-blue eyes, a gentle mouth, and Cupid's-bow lips. "I beg your pardon?" he said. "Oh, do you speak Russian?"

"A little." Charlotte noticed the man was holding a pocket dictionary. "What would you like to ask?"

He pointed to the instrument in front of him, which looked something like a piano. "I'm trying to explain that I need a document proving this harpsichord really was built by Christian Zell in 1741. I can only buy it if it's an original." He sighed. "He keeps telling me to listen to the timbre, and saying he can sell me some scores to go with it, but that's not what I'm interested in. And as for the timbre . . . it's hopelessly out of tune. It needs an awful lot of repair work."

Charlotte looked at the harpsichord. It was shaped like a concert piano but was much smaller. It was a very modest-looking piece, built of wood, and varnished dark brown, the only ornamentation a thin stripe of gold paint. She put her hand on it. All at once it was easy.

"He's not telling you the truth," she said. "This instrument was built around 1960."

He goggled at her. "Are you sure?"

"Yes. Even when it was built, it was meant as a forgery."

All of a sudden the antiques dealer understood English perfectly well. He turned red and unleashed a string of inventive curses. Charlotte took a step back. The young man with the wild hair took her arm and said, "Come on, let's get out of here!"

They fled into the pouring rain, running through puddles and gutters as though the shopkeeper were still after them, laughing all the while. Charlotte found herself imagining the antiques dealer waving a musket at them as they ran.

"There's a McDonald's at the corner," the young man said. He looked to be around thirty. "Can I invite you for a cup of bad coffee?"

The restaurant was crammed full, and all they could do was lean up against a counter. The man in the gray-and-white coat was called Gary McGray and came from Scotland, near Aberdeen. He made his living by traveling the world in search of antique keyboard instruments—preferably harpsichords—buying them, restoring them, and then selling them to museums, collectors, and musicians. It was the kind of job you had to put your heart and soul into, and it didn't bring in much of an income, but his biggest problem was forgeries. If someone persuaded him to part with a lot of money for an instrument that turned out to be a copy, it drove Gary to the edge of financial ruin, since he had to sell it for less money than he had paid in the first place.

They spent the rest of the day leaning up against the counter, hardly noticing the hours pass. When Charlotte went back home to her parents that evening, she announced, "I'm in love!"

It always worked this way: whenever a new director took over the agency, the first thing he would do was summon all the divisional directors to give their reports. Which was logical enough. Logical, too, that these meetings couldn't be planned down to the minute—if the new director had questions, then he would take his time hearing the answers. Which is why William Hughes Adamson found himself waiting in the secretary's office for over an hour, with his thick leather briefcase on his lap containing his computer and a stack of documents, and nothing to do but stare at the wall. It may all have been very logical, but that didn't mean he had to like it. And he didn't.

Finally, the intercom on the desk buzzed. "Yes, Mrs. Jacobs," said the secretary, then she released the button and gave him a thin smile. "She's ready for you now, Mr. Adamson."

He cast another glance at the clock. One hour and eleven minutes late.

The director's office at DARPA, the Pentagon's research wing, was impressively big and just as impressively furnished. Adamson knew it well. The office had a great view over Arlington, for those who liked that sort of thing, as well as of the huge brown condo opposite. Someone was standing out on a balcony over there right now, watering plants; the other hundred or so balconies were all empty.

Roberta Jacobs, the first female director of DARPA, looked just as young face-to-face as she did in the photos that accompanied the news of her appointment. All the same, he was still surprised to meet her: she was so young, and such a looker. She really looked good. Adamson would even have said sexy. She wore her mahogany-brown hair in a pageboy cut that made her look even younger than her years, and her bangs swung as she shook his hand. She gestured toward a chair, next to which was a coffee cup and a video hookup for his computer. Her most impressive feature was her lively, searching, light blue eyes, which followed his every move keenly as he plugged in the video cable.

He could have given the presentation in his sleep. The only extra work had been picking out which diagrams, photos, and film clips to use. He gave a very brief overview of the basics of the Future Combat System; he could assume she knew most of it. He showed some classified clips of refinements on the BigDog robot, a four-legged machine that could move like a dog over terrain, and then turned to the Autonomous Combat Robot projects. He gave her an update on the Urban Ops Hopper, a jumping jack of a robot that could clear obstacles greater than its own height. The machine was designed to be able to deliver cargo to specified locations in urban combat zones so that they could, for instance, resupply units with ammunition. Here, he had a neat little film clip to show—a robot jumping comically up and down on one leg in a hangar while men in white coats pelted it with cardboard boxes, lumps of wood, stones, sandbags, and other missiles to try to make it lose its balance. All in vain.

"Looks good," the director said. "So what's the problem?"

Adamson stopped the film. "The positioning system. The computers can compensate for jumps and landing, but they don't yet have the capacity to steer it to a predetermined destination in any even remotely complex environment."

He reported progress on the EATR, the Energetically Autonomous Tactical Robot. This was a machine designed to be able to turn any kind of biomass into fuel—to eat, as the name suggested—so that in principle it could operate indefinitely in the field. He reported his division's work on insect-sized reconnaissance drones. He reported on the concept of chemical robots, still very much at the theoretical stage right now.

"That sounds interesting," Roberta Jacobs said. "What's that exactly?"

Adamson cleared his throat. She had crossed her arms under her bosom, which he found distracting, and fixed him with an attentive gaze. She wore a dark blue suit that could have clashed horribly with her hair but suited her. *She looks good,* he thought again. *Could be a successful hotel manager or something along those lines. Instead of which she's in command of the most secret weapons-research program of the most powerful nation on earth.* The idea took some getting used to.

"We call them ChemBots," Adamson explained. "The idea is to develop a completely new kind of machine—soft, flexible units capable of squeezing through openings narrower than themselves. Then they should be able to reassume their earlier shape, with all systems functioning, and carry out their instructions." He pulled up some diagrams that showed the scope of the program. "The idea is to build a bridge between robotics and materials chemistry," he explained. "At the moment our research is focused on transitions between gel and solid states, on material deformation and flux processes in general, or with specific reference to magnetic or electrical stimuli. We're looking at geometric transitions, reversible chemical or colloidal bonds, and bond-breaking—"

"I'd like to see an up-to-date budget plan and a breakdown of results so far," she interrupted him.

"It'll be on your desk tomorrow morning," Adamson declared. All he needed to do was pull up the data and print it out, but the way he had phrased it sounded more impressive. It was one of the first tricks he had learned after arriving here fresh out of MIT.

"Good. Thank you for what you've shown me today," she said. "I'm sorry you had to wait so long."

"No problem," Adamson replied, switching off his computer. As he unplugged the video cable, he added, "While I'm here, I'd like to recommend someone. Kind of. This isn't exactly a Human Resources matter. It's about a fellow student from my time at MIT. Hiroshi Kato."

Her bright blue eyes grew suddenly cold. "They warned me you would get around to this. They even say it's an obsession of yours. Kind of."

Adamson wound the cable back into his laptop bag, untroubled. "I know they warned you. Did you know Dr. Blackwell?" Simon Blackwell had been the director before last, in office when Adamson first started at DARPA.

She tilted her head, but said nothing.

"We didn't see eye to eye," Adamson confessed. He had been too outspoken, and Blackwell had seen him as a threat. "And Dr. Blackwell knew how to bear a grudge." Which was probably one of the reasons he had died of a heart attack at the age of just sixty, right here in this office.

Roberta Jacobs leaned forward, placed her folded hands on the desk in front of her, and said, "You have five minutes."

"Okay." Adamson took the documents out of his case, chose a sheet of paper, and handed it to her. "That's him. Hiroshi Kato. He must be—what?—around twenty-seven years old by now. Japanese mother, American father; he has Japanese citizenship. He studied with me at MIT, a couple of years behind me, and published a number of very interesting articles while he was there. Not quite five years ago, he simply dropped out from one day to the next and vanished without a trace. He hasn't been seen since."

Jacobs looked at the sheet with its photograph from the MIT yearbook. "Go on."

Adamson sat down. "Mrs. Jacobs," he said, "I wouldn't be here if I didn't know how to judge people for their potential. When it comes to robotics, Hiroshi Kato is a genius. He is also, unfortunately, very much his own man. He takes it to extremes. When I approached him and tried to bring him onboard with the Robot 21 strategy paper— I'm sure you know it . . ."

"Adamson's Laws of Robotics." The director nodded.

He smiled self-deprecatingly. "Well, that's something of an exaggeration. I have no idea how it came to have that name."

He knew perfectly well, of course. He had worked hard to make sure it happened that way. It was a textbook case of successful self-promotion.

"Coming back to Kato," he went on, "nothing worked. I even . . ." And here he hesitated. "Right after Kato turned me down quite brusquely, I was appointed as academic referee for a project he proposed. At the time I thought it tactically useful to recommend that it be refused. Not that there was anything academically wrong with it, but because I had hoped to be able to cut a deal with him, so to speak. I wanted to shake him out of his maverick mode. Do you follow me? Granted, it was morally somewhat dubious, but I thought that the end justified the means. Unfortunately, he vanished almost the same day. And I don't like the thought that he may have been working for a foreign power ever since."

Mrs. Jacobs studied the sheet, which summarized everything he had been able to find out about Hiroshi Kato. "What do you suggest?" she asked.

"We should look for him. And see to it he works for the United States." She regularly had lunch with the director of the CIA. It would only take a few words and a smile from her.

Her face gave nothing away. "I'll think about it," she declared at last and stood up. A clear sign his five minutes was up.

"Thank you," said Bill Adamson. It was five minutes more than her predecessor had ever given him.

Back in his office he took one more look at the Hiroshi Kato file. How many times had he read through it? Perhaps the ones who said he was obsessed were right. And what if they were? Every great man in history had his obsession. It was the only way to achieve anything. Without an obsession, all you had was an ordinary life.

It was all here. Hiroshi's project proposal. And the resubmission, asking for extra funds. When he read the specifications and Hiroshi's arguments, it was as clear as day this was only one piece of a puzzle, and that he had not the first idea what the big picture might look like. But he needed to know. And he was willing to bet any sum that for Hiroshi, this project application had been merely the first step toward something big, something truly breathtaking. The question was, what? Bill Adamson wanted to know the answer more than anything in the world. And he would find out. One day he would see the big picture, whatever the cost.

Gary was romantic, tender, a little mad. The first time he saw her naked, he wept with joy. He promised to cherish her as long as there was breath in his body, and when they had sex he was carried away like no man Charlotte had ever known before. They loved, they laughed, they couldn't get enough of each other. In the blink of an eye, the whole world changed and her life began anew. It was as though everything that had happened up until now had only been in preparation for this moment.

Charlotte's talent was stronger than ever. Sometimes she felt even physical distance was no obstacle, that she could read things from afar. The history of the world was an open book to her. The two of them followed her gift, leaving Moscow for Warsaw, then on to Berlin, where they tracked down a harpsichord built by the legendary Pleyel company, a piece that had belonged to the great Polish harpsichordist Wanda Landowska. Ever since she had fled Europe in 1940, it had been thought lost, and its rediscovery was a sensation that put Gary in the headlines.

They went on to Aberdeen and finally to the little town of Belcairn to the north. Gary's home here was a building in the oldest part of town, with a small apartment, a huge workshop, and a garden that had run wild. The rooms had low ceilings and tiny windows, and the whole house was crooked and ramshackle and hard to heat. Charlotte was enchanted. While Gary spent his days in the workshop, as he always had done, she took charge of the house. When she arrived, it was an unloved bachelor pad; she cleaned it from top to bottom, repainted, put up curtains, chose houseplants, bought new crockery and linen, and replaced all his metal shelving units with proper wardrobes and bookshelves. It became a real home. Once the long winter was over, she got to work on the garden.

And every now and then, they would go hunting together. Gary ran a website about restoring historic keyboard instruments. The website brought him not only commissions but also leads as to where an unusual instrument might be hiding, anywhere in the world. When they set off to follow these leads, it wasn't just a trip, it was an adventure, real detective work. They had to track down clues, ask questions, and listen patiently for the revealing detail—and, above all, play their cards close to their chest. As soon as people found out the old wreck that had been moldering in their attic for generations was a valuable antique musical instrument that might be worth real money once it had been restored, they started asking prohibitive prices.

In a vineyard not far from Venice, they tracked down a genuine dulcitone. Gary would only have had to clean away the encrustations left by years in the pigeon loft, but the owner, a suspicious old farmer, didn't want to part with it. A musical-instruments dealer in Geneva offered them a pianino that had supposedly been built in 1955 but which Charlotte soon discovered dated back to 1840—a bargain. In Rotterdam they found a genuine Alfred Arnold bandoneon.

Gary was beside himself with excitement. "These things are incredibly rare," he explained. "The company was confiscated from the family in 1948 and the original plans for the instruments were lost—even today, nobody has ever managed to build anything that makes the same fabulous sound."

Charlotte was astonished to learn how many different kinds of keyboard instrument there were in the world. Gary explained to her the difference between a spinet and clavicytherium, showed her how the reproducing piano played its melodies automatically, talked at length about the terpodion, and enthused about a gigantic instrument built in 1819 called the Apollonicon. She learned what a square piano and a claviharp and an Orphica were. She learned that the adiaphone and dulcitone produced their ethereal sounds by striking tuning forks rather than strings and therefore never went out of tune. She was amazed by the pyrophone, a kind of organ that ran on gas flame rather than on air. It tended to explode during concerts, and several organists had been injured during the nineteenth century.

And so a year went by. Charlotte felt she was walking on air. Life was wonderful. Everything was so simple; the days were filled with plangent sounds from the workshop, which echoed through the house while she cooked and baked, cleaned and tidied. Sometimes she would cycle along the narrow country roads between the lush, green fields, her only regret that there was no farmhouse nearby that sold milk direct from the cow or some such simple treat. When Gary switched out the lights in the workshop in the evening, they ate, talked, and usually ended up making love. Life was wonderful and simple.

It took some time for the problem to come to light. The harsh truth, however, was that even when he had been living on his own, Gary's business model barely made enough money for one person to get by. Now there were two of them, but his work had not changed. Logically, then, the money he made simply was not enough. The only reason they had not noticed earlier was that the discovery of the Pleyel harpsichord in Berlin had swelled the bottom line for the year considerably. But that money was gone.

Neither Charlotte nor Gary really knew how to handle money, let alone run a household. Charlotte had always been used to money being there when she needed it; when she went shopping, she had only ever asked herself what she wanted, not what she could afford. Certainly, she tried to keep track of prices, to keep within a weekly budget, to save where she could, but she didn't get much beyond trying. Gary hardly needed anything for himself and spent nothing on food and clothes but would pay whatever it took for tools and spare parts.

"We mustn't spend every penny we have," he told Charlotte earnestly the evening they realized just how bad things were. "I always need some money in reserve to buy instruments; otherwise, I might just as well shut up shop."

Charlotte stared aghast at their bank statement and the notepad with their calculations. "And what if you tried to do more work on commission?"

"I've tried that. It doesn't bring in much money, because I have to pay a fee to the dealer who referred me. There aren't many customers around here anyway. I'd have to live in the big city, and then it would cost too much to rent a decent-sized workshop."

There was only one answer: they would have to stop traveling together. When they both went, everything cost twice as much, but they didn't necessarily bring in more income—it simply wasn't worth the extra expense. With a heavy heart, they decided Gary would travel on his own from now on and only call Charlotte to join him if he found an outstanding instrument and had to be quite sure of its provenance.

She was bored on her own. She didn't know anyone here, and it wasn't easy making friends with Lowland Scots. And anyway, was it quite fair, the way they lived? Gary carried on just as before, spending his days doing what he loved best, repairing antique musical instruments. The only difference for him was he had a woman now to keep house and warm his bed. What did she get out of the relationship? Nothing but work.

While Gary was away in Istanbul tracking down a sixteenth-century spinet, Charlotte went to Aberdeen and bought stuff she didn't need out of sheer frustration. She spent too much on costly hours on the telephone with Brenda as well, trying to work out where she had gone wrong. Then Gary called her to come to Istanbul on the cheapest flight she could find. The spinet really was from 1578. By the time it was being packed up for shipping, he had calculated the profit they were likely to make on it and said it would be no problem to spend another day in Istanbul. They visited the Hagia Sophia and Topkapi Palace and watched the sunset from a restaurant under the Galata Bridge. Charlotte shut her eyes and listened to the babble of languages all around. She began to riddle out some of the basic structures of Turkish. Her loneliness was forgotten. Life was wonderful again.

When they got back, however, they had their worst argument yet when Gary found out Charlotte had been accepting money from her parents. His masculine pride was wounded and he simply wouldn't calm down, even though she swore never to do it again.

"You did this behind my back!" he raged at her. "If we're to have a life together, then we have to share our fate as well. But that can't happen if you're always pulling on your parents' purse strings. That tells me you don't really care whether our life works out, because you can just climb in your lifeboat and leave. I can't."

She didn't quite understand what he meant, but she was distraught to see him so angry. The worst of it was that while they were together in Istanbul, a hot tip had landed in his mailbox from a Spanish source he had: a 1770 harpsichord was up for sale in Barcelona that had supposedly belonged to the great Antonio Soler. Gary had to set off again straightaway. Charlotte stayed unhappily at home, trying to calm by cleaning the apartment from top to bottom, waiting for Gary to call. He didn't. Instead, he came back two days later, explaining he had bought the instrument on the basis of the documents the dealer had shown him.

"Solid affidavits from experts in the field," he declared. "It would have just been a waste of money to fly you out to Barcelona."

As it turned out, though, the waste of money had been buying the instrument.

"It's not from 1770," Charlotte said as soon as Gary had unpacked the harpsichord from its shipping crate. She went closer, put her hand on it, and closed her eyes. She could feel the irritation of the man who had built it. Something had not gone according to plan. "It's Italian, built in 1955."

Gary shot her a withering look. "You're only saying that to get back at me. You're upset I bought it on my own."

Charlotte took her hand away and stepped back. "Just take a look. He had to use some screws that weren't the genuine article."

Gary fell silent, shut himself away in his workshop, and didn't emerge for the rest of the day. When he showed his face that evening, he was devastated. "Socket screws on the keyboard frame," he groaned. "Anchored in with screw nuts. That method was only invented in 1911. I only saw them when I took off the front casing."

Charlotte looked at him, heartbroken. The soup steamed on the table between them. She felt as though the house had burned down around her ears. "What does that mean?"

"It means I'm in the red again. It means that the last five years' work has all been for nothing."

"Is it really that bad?"

"I was mad to put all my money into that instrument." He said it accusingly, as though it were her fault he had acted so recklessly.

Gary spent all of the next day making phone calls and finally came up with a solution: he would take a job as a restorer for a big auction house in London that specialized in musical instruments. He would spend two weeks in London and then come home for a week at a time to work on his own instruments. He would save money in London by living in a house in Hackney with six others.

"Does it have to be this way?" Charlotte asked cautiously. "I mean, the harpsichord's still a good instrument, never mind those screws."

"It just isn't worth as much. That's how it is." Gary shook his head, his mind made up. "And I won't do it. I won't claim that an instrument is older than I know it to be."

Left to her own devices in Belcairn, Charlotte spent hours at a time in front of the television. She could feel her brain cells dying away as she sat there but couldn't rouse herself to do anything else. Sometimes she mustered the energy to go for a long walk in the fields, but as winter approached the rains came, long, soaking downpours, and she stopped going out. Once, she went into Gary's workshop. She wandered around among the instruments, looking at the shimmering strings and stroking the deep glow of varnished wood. She picked out a tune on some of the keyboards. She could feel their history. How proud the owners had been to have these instruments. How bored the children had been, practicing. And the long, empty years when they had stood forgotten somewhere, years that felt like death. And then overlaid on all this she could feel Gary, fresh impressions of the love and care he put into his work, his concentration. The satisfaction it gave him.

It made her sad. There was something wrong with the world. Gary was so exceptionally good at what he did, so devoted to it, he knew so many things, and put his heart and soul into his work—why couldn't he make a living from it? She had met so many people who hated their work, who cut corners and generally did a bad job but who still managed to make a living. People who gave nothing to the world even half as valuable as what Gary could give but who were swimming in money. Why was that? Why was money so important? And how could money kill love? Why did people let that happen?

An evening or two later the telephone rang, shattering the dull silence in the house. Charlotte picked up quickly, thinking it must be Gary calling.

"It's me," said a voice she had not heard for an eternity. "Hiroshi." Charlotte had to sit down. "You?"

"I told you once that I knew what to do so that everybody could be rich. Do you remember?" His words came from far away. There was a strange echo on the line.

"Yes," she said. "I remember."

"Are you still interested in how it works?"

Charlotte put her hand to her head. What a time to call and talk about it! It was as though he could read her mind. How did he even have her number?

"Yes," she said. "I'm still interested."

"Good," Hiroshi replied. "I'm ready to show you."

HIROSHI'S ISLAND

1

Normally Charlotte had no trouble sleeping on flights, but on the way to Manila she didn't get a wink of sleep. Too many thoughts were chasing around in her head. What it would be like to see Hiroshi after all this time. Memories of Harvard, of Boston.

And, of course, thoughts of Gary.

They had argued when she left. And she still didn't understand what the argument had really been about. After Hiroshi's offer, she had slept on it; once she had decided she would accept his invitation, she had called Gary. He had sounded very strange on the telephone, so she waited until he got home and explained it all to him again. He had raised his voice, worked himself up into a temper, and hurled all kinds of accusations at her—but why? Envy? She had assured him he had nothing to fear, that he was the one she loved. But she hadn't been able to get through to him for some reason.

"Gary," she had said at last, "I don't see why I shouldn't go. You're constantly flying off without me, so now I'm going without you. All we ever do is argue about nothing these days. I can't even begin to understand why. Maybe we should take a little break from each other."

"A break?" Gary practically spat the word out. "You know how that will end."

"What do you mean?" She didn't understand. She was upset Gary had become so paranoid and possessive lately, showing her a new side of him she didn't like one bit. She didn't know whether she could get used to him like this.

The plane descended into a bright, sunlit afternoon in the Philippines. Her next flight was on a propeller airplane with twelve seats, all occupied. A sturdy-looking woman put a crate of tomatoes in the overhead luggage compartment, and a weather-beaten man with calloused hands who looked like a fisherman spent the whole flight reading an American computer magazine. The Pacific glowed deep blue, but as they flew on the color grew lighter, turning an incredible turquoise.

Just when Charlotte had finally dozed off they landed on an island. It was dusk. At some point she had known what this island was called, but now she couldn't remember. The airport building had a jolly little roof that looked like three blue tents standing in a row. A breathtakingly handsome man in uniform was waiting for her at the foot of the gangway. He had brown skin and a neatly trimmed moustache.

"Miss Malroux?" he asked, checking her passport when she said yes. He led her over to a helicopter at the other end of the airfield. It was painted in blue and silver, with the words GU ENTERPRISES on the side. Below the words was a string of Chinese characters, probably the same name, and above was a stylized dragon's head.

The two pilots hardly spoke. One of them gave her two little balls of wax and pointed to his ears.

"This will get loud," he said.

Earplugs. She obediently pressed them in, climbed aboard, and let the pilot buckle her in while the copilot loaded her luggage.

So this was what a helicopter flight felt like. She could have lived quite happily without ever finding out. It took off, howling and shaking, and tilted forward. The island disappeared behind them as twilight fell. They seemed to be in a hurry. *Good*, Charlotte thought. The sooner it was over, the better.

After about an hour she saw another island below; its shape reminded her of a Y chromosome for some reason. Charlotte bent forward. What was that? Part of the island was covered with what looked like yellow foam. It was too dark to see anything more, but whatever it was, it wasn't any ordinary sort of tropical vegetation. There were bright lights at the end of the longest arm of the island. She saw the large H of their landing pad, and next to it a jetty leading out to sea with two boats alongside it. On the other side of the helipad was a tent village. And somebody standing at the edge of the landing field. She knew straightaway it could only be Hiroshi.

The helicopter dropped, shuddering so much that Charlotte felt a little sick. Finally, it settled down right in the center of the big H. The bone-shaking roar of the turbines died down to a whine. As she unbuckled her seatbelt, she suddenly understood why so many people kissed the tarmac at airports. The pilot who had strapped her in opened the door, but Hiroshi was there before him to help her down.

"At last!" he called.

"We can't all just jet off around the world at the drop of a hat!" she yelled back and ducked reflexively. The rotors were still turning, and a blade passed over her like a headsman's sword in search of its allotted task. "I had to talk to Gary about it first."

Hiroshi looked blank and then laughed out loud. "Oh no! I didn't mean it that way. I was thinking of before, of the first time I told you about my idea, back in the garden."

Charlotte nodded. "We were on the swings. That's to say I was actually swinging, and you were just sitting there talking riddles." She looked around, wondering what had happened to her luggage. Ah, there it was. One of the pilots was loading it onto a cart, along with several cardboard boxes of all shapes and sizes, all labeled in Chinese. "And when I said I didn't believe a word of it, you told me to wait and see."

"How long ago was that? Almost twenty years." Hiroshi's eyes gleamed. "And now I'm ready! That's what I meant just now when I said 'at last.' An extra day or two really makes no difference by now."

They left the landing pad and the cloud of oily exhaust from the helicopter. Electric lanterns hung low along a path that led to the tent village she had seen from the air. On the far side she could just make out the dark silhouettes of bushes, trees, and cliffs. The farther they got from the helicopter, the louder the sound of the Pacific on either side, the lazy, powerful slap of waves against the shoreline. A gentle night breeze blew. The air smelled of salt, of unfamiliar flowers, of tropical island—and every now and again there was a pungent jab of rotten decay. An unpleasant smell that struck Charlotte as strangely familiar.

"So this is where you've been the whole time," she said. "On a hidden South Sea island. Not bad."

"We've actually only been here six weeks, to be precise," Hiroshi corrected her. "I spent the years before that on islands as well, but I wouldn't call them exactly hidden. Well defended, perhaps."

She looked him up and down, baffled by the way they were talking as though no time at all had passed since they'd last seen each other. It had been five years. More than that—almost five and a half. It didn't feel anything like so long. For a mad moment Charlotte doubted her own memory. But Hiroshi had grown older. She could see it. He seemed more serious—even more so than before—and was tanned brown, making the fine lines around his eyes more noticeable. He wore shorts, sandals, and a gray T-shirt with no image or logo. For an MIT graduate, that was practically unheard of. But, of course, he hadn't graduated. He had simply vanished without a trace, just a few days after they had . . . it all came back to her. The memories, the mutual attraction. She knew all she would have to do was hold out her hand for him to take. And that Hiroshi was waiting for her to do just that. But she would have been cheating on Gary, and she wouldn't do that. It was over now, all in the past. She and Hiroshi were just old friends now. Childhood friends.

"How did you get my number?" she asked. It was one of the many questions she had thought of during the journey.

"From your mother," Hiroshi answered, as though it were the most natural thing in the world.

"From my—I beg your pardon?" She stopped walking for a moment until the penny dropped. Obvious, really. It wouldn't have been hard. There weren't that many French ambassadors in the world.

She spent the next few moments trying to imagine how Hiroshi had managed to talk to her mother, who still couldn't speak English well, when a skinny man wearing the thickest pair of glasses she had ever see came scurrying out from among the tents. He peered at Charlotte and mumbled a greeting, then gabbed at Hiroshi about camera angles and some other details she didn't catch. He held a clipboard with diagrams under Hiroshi's nose. Hiroshi looked at it for a while and then nodded and said, "Okay. We'll do it that way. Number fifteen over there, aiming southwest, and number nine up on the cliffs."

"Okay." The man gave Charlotte another shy smile and then turned away, flitting off into the darkness.

"That was Miroslav," Hiroshi explained. "My right-hand man. He's also worth at least two fingers of my left hand."

"You don't give your people any time off, do you?"

"No," Hiroshi remarked dryly. "I only hire people who work till they drop."

They reached the camp. The tents were the very latest high-tech models, snow-white domes that reminded her of a science-fiction film set. They must be easy to put up, she reflected, and they were sure to withstand even tropical storms without any trouble.

Hiroshi steered her toward one of the larger tents and drew aside the flaps at the entrance, bowing her in. "Please. This is where I work, sleep, and live. I haven't really changed my habits since Boston in that respect."

Charlotte hesitated. "I haven't even taken care of my luggage."

"You don't have to. Your tent is over there"—he pointed off to where three smaller tents stood together—"and they'll take your things straight there." He smiled delightedly. "And while they're doing that, I'll tell you the idea Hiroshi Kato had when he was ten years old."

It was as though he had last been in this office only yesterday. That had been two years ago, though. Two years during which he had only spoken to Roberta Jacobs on the periphery of larger meetings or briefly in the hallway, when he hardly had a chance to say anything more than hello. And now here he sat. She was wearing the same necklace as before, a heavy thing with lapis lazuli stones. She seemed not to have aged at all in the meantime. Roberta Jacobs was one of those women who never shows her age.

Bill Adamson leaned back, feeling curiously calm and confused all at once. It seemed only yesterday he had been here to give his status report, but something was different. He just couldn't put his finger on what.

"It's about your friend," the director began, folding her hands over a thick document folder. "Hiroshi Kato."

"Ah." Adamson raised his eyebrows. He hadn't been expecting this. "I see."

"I have to confess I was skeptical at first," she said, looking at him expressionlessly. "I filed away the sheet you gave me, but for some reason my thoughts kept coming back to it. Then I happened to be sitting next to the head of the CIA in a session of the National Security Council, and you know how it is, you have to talk about something during the breaks. So I told him about your friend. He wrote down the name and said he'd have a look."

Adamson nodded slowly. That was probably how these things worked. In all the time he had been at DARPA, he had learned one thing at least: that the US's gigantic military apparatus was by no means as focused and effective and dedicated to the nation's good as Hollywood would have you believe.

Roberta Jacobs tapped the folder in front of her. "Well, this is what came up. James put a few people on the case, and they found your Mr. Kato. In Hong Kong."

Adamson felt triumphant, vindicated. China! The greatest rising challenge to the United States. There must be alarm bells ringing in one or two departments right about now. Under certain circumstances it might even cause a stir at the very top. That was good. Now all he had to do was make sure nobody forgot who had put the security services on this trail. *Note to self: keep my name going round.*

"Hong Kong," the director repeated. She was glancing at a small jotter sheet on top of her folder. "Hiroshi Kato has spent the last few years working for a company called Gu Enterprises. It's a multinational, based in Hong Kong, manufacturing electronics, among other things. It supplies the US market with camping TV sets, cheap MP3 players, that kind of stuff." Another glance at her notes. "The founder is one Larry Gu, born in Hong Kong and old as the hills by now, but that doesn't stop him from taking an active role in running his company. He started out as a smuggler and gray-market entrepreneur but built up his fortune with property deals. When Hong Kong reverted to China, he had the option of emigrating to Australia, but he seems to have come to some sort of arrangement with the regime in Beijing. In any case, he's turned up on the CIA's radar often enough helping the Chinese secret service with industrial espionage."

"I see," Adamson said again. "Hiroshi Kato is working for the People's Republic of China."

"At least for its capitalist wing." The director opened her folder. "Kato has spent the last five years more or less continuously in various well-guarded research laboratories leading working groups of up to one hundred members. The CIA managed to smuggle out a few documents—I have no idea how." She took out a sheaf of blueprints and passed them over to Adamson. "Here. I'd like you to take a look at these and explain to me what your friend Kato is building."

Adamson had to fight the urge to grab the documents from her hands. His fingers trembled as he took the blueprints. "When will you want the analysis?" he asked.

Impatience flared in her light blue eyes. "I don't want you to draft a paper," she said. "I want you to open these plans right now, take a look at them, and tell me what you see there. On the spot."

"Oh." Adamson felt himself break a sweat. This was going to be tough. He hoped it wouldn't prove to be a damp squib. He unfolded the first blueprint tenderly, as though it might break in his hands. It wouldn't; this was just a feeble attempt to buy some time, to gather his thoughts.

He suddenly realized what was different about this office since the last time he had been here: all the plants were gone. The two big pots with the fig trees were missing, as was the row of smaller plants, the thick-leaved specimens that had once stood on the little gray board under the window. Even the little cactus next to the printer was absent. For some reason Adamson felt shaken by this observation. He found it almost more unnerving than being put to the test like this first thing in the morning, on a day when he wasn't feeling at the top of his game anyway. Okay. Come what may, he had to get through this. He unfolded the blueprint, which was stamped with the CIA crest and TOP SECRET, and looked at the tangle of lines. At least the labels were in English as well as Chinese.

And lo and behold, there, in the bottom-right corner of the sheet, was the name Hiroshi Kato.

Hiroshi's tent was big and looked even bigger inside, since it was just as sparsely furnished as his room back in MIT had been once upon a time. A folding bed, a desk, a table with two chairs, and that was it. And he must have had a refrigerator somewhere, since he put a glass in front of her and a can of soda that was so cold that drops had pearled on the outside. It was the same brand he had given her back in Tokyo.

"All right," said Charlotte. "I think it's probably finally safe to tell me."

Hiroshi took the other folding chair and sat down opposite her. He leaned forward and looked intensely at her, as though he were an entomologist and she were some unusual insect he had found and was trying to classify. Usually Charlotte would have felt uncomfortable in such a situation, but to her surprise she found she liked it. It reminded her of the days back in Tokyo when they were both children. Hiroshi had looked at her just the same way even back then. Just as intensely, as though he were determined to get to know every atom of her being. Nobody else had ever looked at her quite so intently. Not her parents, nor any man in her life.

A gust of wind rattled the tent roof above them. The noise broke the spell. Hiroshi looked at the ground and seemed to be trying to find the opening lines of a speech he had been giving over and over again in his thoughts for years now. A speech he had practiced, rewritten, and refined.

"I was ten years old back then," he began. "You'll have to bear that in mind. At that age you think that a lot of things are easier than they really are, and you think that some things are harder. Nevertheless, even then I saw something quite clearly that I still see the same way now: when we talk about rich and poor, we're not talking about money but rather about work. If being rich just meant having a lot of money, it would be simple to make everybody rich: all we would have to do is print more money and hand it out. That doesn't work, though, since money is nothing but printed paper. It's not about money—it's about work. Being rich means being able to get others to work for you."

Now it was her turn to look at him. She could take her time about it. The fine wrinkles around his eyes suited him, even if they made him look tired. He must have spent far too much time over the last few years staring at computer screens, working late into the night, not getting enough sleep. He certainly knew what he was talking about when he talked about work; there was no question about that.

"Yes," she said just to let him know she was listening. At the same time she wondered again why this topic was so important to him. Why he was so obsessed with it.

"Being rich," Hiroshi went on, "means having more than others have—indeed, having so much more that those others have no choice but to take some of what is yours and are prepared to work in order to have it. That's the principle. And following this principle"— he lifted his hand and raised his index finger to make his point—"it is by definition impossible for everybody to be rich, since not everybody can have more than other people have. No more than everybody can be more intelligent than average, or taller than average, and so on."

Charlotte blinked in surprise and felt her eyes grow tired. It felt strange, as though she were not really here but simply dreaming all this. "But you said you could do it, didn't you? You claimed you knew what you would have to do so that everybody could be rich. You even said it was simple."

Hiroshi nodded, smiling. "Yes. My main point is that it's fundamentally impossible for everybody to be rich as long as we stick to the principle that a rich man is one who can make others work for him, because he has more than they do. It's just not possible. But if we turn the problem on its head and simply concentrate on the work—the work that has to be done if anyone at all is to live a rich life, including the gardening and the cooking and making all those luxuries that go with it—well, if we just look at the work and ask how we can arrange for everybody to have this work done for them, then we conclude that it's possible to build machines to do the work.

In other words, robots. The word itself comes from Czech—*robota*, meaning "work." In the ideal case, a robot is a machine that could do anything a person could do. If everybody had enough robots, then everybody could live the life that the rich live today. That's the long and the short of it."

Charlotte took a sip of soda. It tasted unpleasantly sharp, artificial. "But all you've done is change the terms of the problem," she pointed out. "If everybody had these robots, then yes. But I assume it's not easy to build even one such robot. Meaning that even a robot would be expensive. Meaning that not everybody could afford one, so we're back where we were—back in the world of rich and poor."

Hiroshi raised his eyebrows. He grinned. No, he wasn't just grinning; he seemed to be savoring some private joke. "Well you see, that's the basic fallacy. It took me quite a lot of thought to recognize it as such, but perhaps you really need to be ten years old to even be able to see through that kind of faulty thinking. You're quite right that it's not easy building even one such robot. But the thing is—you only need to build one of them!"

Now Charlotte was baffled. Or perhaps she was dreaming all this. Perhaps she was actually still squeezed into an airplane seat with a crick in her neck and cramps in her calves. Perhaps she was asleep and just dreaming she was here. People said funny things in dreams.

"Just one?" she asked. "How's that supposed to work? One single robot can't do all the work for everybody at once, can it?"

Hiroshi was still grinning. The grin seemed to float free of his face and fill the room. "It wouldn't have to. Work for everybody at once, that is. But think about it for a moment: a robot that can do everything a person can must logically be able to build another robot like itself, an identical copy of itself. Then there are two, and these can make copies of themselves in turn, and then there are four. And on and on it goes, faster all the time. By the next generation there are sixteen robots, then thirty-two, sixty-four . . . It's an exponential function. After about sixty cycles there would be enough robots for everyone on Earth to have one. And you can keep on making as many as you like, as many as you need." He sat up straight, leaned back, and ran his hands over his hair. "That was the idea ten-year-old Hiroshi had on the swing."

Charlotte felt disappointed, irritated. If all this wasn't a dream, then she might well ask whether it had been worth flying halfway around the world for it. Okay, it wasn't a bad idea for a ten-year-old, but to hold on to it all the way through to adult life was odd to say the least. She pushed the glass away and moved her head from side to side, trying to get rid of the tension in her neck.

"And is that what you're doing here?" she asked, more harshly than she intended. "Building a robot?" It was downright weird to come to such a remote island for that. Wouldn't a great big factory be better, or a well-equipped laboratory?

"No," Hiroshi said. "That's not what I plan to do. Since, of course, it's not as easy as I imagined when I was ten."

"Go on then."

"As I said, when you're a child you think some things are easier than they are, and some are harder. In this case, my basic fallacy was to believe a man could build a robot. That was a mistake. Nobody can do that."

Charlotte blinked again. Her eyes were stinging. "What? But people do build robots, don't they?"

"Quite. But a single man, all on his own, can't even make a ball-point pen. Never mind a robot of the kind we're talking about. To manufacture something of the sort, you need an awful lot of raw materials and parts that other people have built in turn. In fact, it's our technological civilization as a whole that builds ballpoint pens and cell phones and cars and skyscrapers and planes. And robots. One man on his own is only a part of a function matrix. One man can only perform part of any task, but his work is tied into all the other parts of the task so that in the end, we have products and services."

"So you can't do it. Make everybody rich, I mean."

"Oh, but I can. You just have to take a different approach."

"How's that?"

Hiroshi bowed his head and smiled softly. "You're dead tired, Charlotte. And it takes quite some time to explain. I'll show you tomorrow."

He couldn't do it sitting down, and he couldn't do it here at the desk. Adamson got up and carried the blueprint over to the coffee nook in the corner and spread it out on the low table there. Then he stood and considered the drawing.

"What other documents do we have?" he asked.

"Just more blueprints," Roberta Jacobs said.

Okay. That meant it was up to him to figure it out. Maybe she just wanted to know how he would handle the situation. Adamson took several deep breaths. *Just keep calm. It's not half as bad as it seems.* Basically, he told himself, this was all familiar ground. If he had learned one thing over the last few years, it was that his particular talent was not thinking up genius ideas on his own. His talent was seeing the sparks of genius in what other people invented. That had been the secret of his success at MIT: he had been forced to gather people around himself and build teams, then urge them on to do the very best work they were capable of, so that in the end some of their success rubbed off on him. How often had he done this kind of thing? Looking at designs that others showed him? He knew he could recognize groundbreaking work when he saw it, trailblazing ideas, the stuff of genius. Often he knew it long before the designers themselves realized their ideas were something out of the ordinary. It no longer even bothered him that he had never had such a stroke of genius himself. His role was no less important. Teamwork was the key to it all, meaning the people who could build teams and lead them were just as necessary.

So, what did they have here? A diagram for some device. Adamson leaned forward and looked closely at the dimensions and the design as a whole. "This is pretty small, whatever it is," he said, raising a hand. "The whole machine's no bigger than the palm of my hand."

The director harrumphed in agreement. She was standing next to him now; he could smell her perfume. She was so close that he could have put his arm around her.

Adamson concentrated on the drawing. The list of components was short. "It's a machine made of surprisingly few moving parts. Twenty-six parts, all quite radically innovative . . ."

He forgot the director, forgot how close she was standing, forgot even the smell of her perfume. He became absorbed in the diagram, saw the parts take shape, saw how they fitted together to make one machine. How they moved, interlocked, joined as one. He felt a flood of excitement as he understood how the machine fitted together. It was more elegantly planned and more thoroughly conceived than anything he had seen in his life. This wasn't just a design with some clever refinement or neat innovation, it was genius from start to finish.

"Here," he said, tracing the diagram with his finger. He suddenly realized he had gotten down on his knees in front of it. "This is the chassis. This half-moon shape here is part of a motor with a linear drive, just using a simple magnetic field generated by this element here. And this . . ." An extendable claw. Precision work. Then a sharp blade on the other arm of the claw . . . a knife. This module could cut, take hold of things, or anchor the whole device, depending on its instructions.

Roberta Jacobs bent over him to look. Her necklace brushed Adamson's shoulder. She pointed to a cluster of odd little notches. "What are those for?"

"Yes, what are they for?" Where had he seen that sort of thing before? He couldn't recall. His finger swept across the sheet—the energy supply, something that had to be some sort of relay, but more finely calibrated; maybe better to call it a transistor, though it was the oddest transistor he'd ever seen.

Suddenly, he realized what he had been missing all this time. He really wasn't in top form today. "The device is designed to hook up with others. Do you see this groove along the edge? It makes no sense unless we assume the thing is meant to connect with other machines, either of the same type or something very similar. Which means that . . . wait a moment . . . that these surfaces here are contact fields to transmit electrical impulses. And then these surfaces would be coated with . . . what? Silicon?" Adamson was so excited that the feeling was almost sexual. My God, he had always suspected Hiroshi was a sly old fox, but he had never thought he was this good. He framed the cluster of notches with both hands. "This area here is a processor chip, but turned inside out, so to speak. It's an integrated circuit. I'd have to take a closer look, but I'm willing to bet that it can receive command impulses from the next machine along and then recognize where they are meant for. If they're instructions for this machine, it carries them out, or if they're for another unit, they get passed along." He got up so suddenly that he almost barged into the director. "That's only a part of the puzzle here. It's one function in the whole. In itself it's a simple automaton that can either cut or use its claw to anchor itself, depending on instructions. But the actual function only becomes clear once we can see it at work together with all the other devices."

He hurried back to the desk and picked up the next blueprint, unfolding it and bringing it over to lay on top of the first. There were similarities, but differences, too. This part, for instance, didn't have a cutting blade, but rather . . . aha! It was a unit that could contract and expand to move around, like a mussel or an inchworm.

"It's a puzzle," Adamson repeated excitedly. He pointed at another section that the first plan had not shown. "Here. A hard drive. You give this unit a command, it takes it along to wherever it 'walks' to, and then it can transmit commands to the other units it docks together with."

There was one more plan. Adamson unfolded it with the numb certainty he would only get to see a tiny part of the whole device Hiroshi had created here. Three parts of a puzzle that might have a hundred pieces. They would never be able to riddle out what the whole thing would look like. This part was larger, but it would still fit into his pants pocket. "A pump," Adamson realized at last. "Do you see this? That's the moving part. More or less like a heart muscle. And these are the valves. These connections here allow it to dock into neighboring units . . ." He looked up and into her eyes. "Is this really all we have?"

Roberta Jacobs nodded. "At least it's all the CIA gave me."

"Is there any chance of getting hold of more material?"

She looked back at him appraisingly but seemed uncertain. Did she know something more that she couldn't tell him? That wouldn't be unusual. In this line of work, everybody had more secrets than was really good for them.

"I don't know," she admitted at last. "From what they tell me, the lab our agent had access to only makes these three units. We have no idea what happens in the other labs. The CIA only has limited resources, and to be blunt with you, this isn't a top-priority case."

"Too bad."

She turned away and went back to her desk, where she snapped the folder shut. "Is it? Too bad? What can you see here that I can't?"

"Genius," Adamson declared just as bluntly. "Kato has obviously created a machine that consists of several diverse units, each with a narrowly defined function. We won't know what the machine as a whole does, what it's intended for, and what it can actually achieve, until we see all the units. All the pieces of the puzzle."

"Parts that move from place to place. Others that cut. Others that pump. What kind of machine could that be?"

Adamson shrugged. "I have no idea. But I know genius when I see it at work, and this"—he pointed to the blueprints on the coffee table—"is genius. I'd like someone capable of thinking all that up working for us instead of for the Reds."

"Hmm." Roberta Jacobs gazed pensively into empty space for a moment. "I don't know whether that's really where the front line still runs. Opinions vary on that one."

"What if we simply got in touch with him and made an offer? Hiroshi Kato, I mean."

The director opened her folder and looked at a sheet inside. "Money? I don't know. I see here that Kato invented some device that's been a worldwide sales success for years now—some kind of gizmo they sell in hardware stores and so on. In any case, he doesn't need to worry about how to fund his retirement. According to my reports, whatever his motives are, money isn't one of them."

Adamson looked at the plans in front of him and felt a pang. "There are other ways to motivate people."

Charlotte opened her eyes and stared up into featureless white space. Still dazed with sleep, she wondered whether she was in heaven, but then the moment passed and she realized that it was just the inside of the tent, a milky white expanse of cloth with no seams or other features the eye could linger upon held up by a nest of lightweight poles she could only dimly make out if the sun happened to shine directly on them. So she hadn't dreamed it. She really had flown half-way around the world to a lone island in the middle of the Pacific to see Hiroshi's idea.

Why on earth had she done such a thing? She turned over in bed and propped herself up on one elbow. Though it was remarkably comfortable for a folding camp bed, she still felt the long journey in her bones. What had woken her? She had no idea. A noise. Voices. She could hear voices somewhere off in the distance beyond the tent walls, raised voices, and laughter. Okay. So they were having a good time out here. Good for them. But it still didn't tell her what her part in all this was. Robots building other robots. Really, he could have just put that into a letter. File under "Happy Memories from Childhood Days." Anybody else would have done just that. Anybody but Hiroshi.

She was only here because she had needed to get away from Gary for a while. That was it. Get a change of air. She hadn't really needed to come all the way to the Pacific for that, though of course the air here was excellent. Having said which . . . she sniffed. There it was again, that strange smell of rot, of decay. Every now and again a whiff of something like a garbage dump. So much for the good air here. Maybe she should have just gone off to the Highlands somewhere and holed up in a hotel. She didn't really want to know what Hiroshi had thought up. For some strange reason, she was even afraid to find out more. Odd, when she really thought about it, but there it was.

Charlotte got out of bed and looked around. There was her suitcase, open, everything there. A neat little folding washstand. And hadn't Hiroshi said there was a shower around here somewhere as well? She wrapped the thin bathrobe around herself, picked up her toiletry bag, and slipped her feet into her sandals. She popped her head outside the tent. Broad daylight. A busy hubbub up ahead in one of the bigger tents, strongly suggestive of work and research, and then palms beyond . . . and then behind the palms something shining bright yellow, an intense, artificial yellow. Ah yes, she had spotted that yesterday from the helicopter. There was something back there. Probably part of the current experiment. Or another tent. Well, no doubt she would find out.

The shower was in a tent right next to hers and clearly labeled. After she had washed she felt much better, and when she found a hair dryer ready and waiting for her back in her tent, she began to feel human once more. She'd just regard the whole interlude as some crazy kind of holiday. Maybe there'd be a chance to talk over old times with Hiroshi. About their childhood, for instance. Or if they were both brave, about what had happened between them back at Harvard. When she emerged into the more-or-less-fresh air, her hair dried, dressed for the day, a young Asian woman with henna hair popped up out of nowhere and waved to her.

"Breakfast!" she called, her accent suggesting she might not know very much more English than this. Next thing, Charlotte was in the canteen tent, a big, bright, airy place with seven tables and more than forty seats. The tent walls were rolled up on the side facing the beach, giving a magnificent view of the Pacific. "The others already eaten; they at work," the woman said as she served Charlotte coffee, a fruit basket, and a plate with a couple of croissants. They were as good as anything she could have bought in Paris. Shortly thereafter Hiroshi turned up; the waitress had obviously told him she was awake.

"So?" he asked. "Did you sleep well?"

"I'm gradually shaking off the feeling this is all a dream," Charlotte admitted.

He sat down across from her. "That's odd, I'm just beginning to get that feeling. I can hardly believe you really came."

In other words, he was still in love with her. She looked down at her coffee. What was this connection between them? She felt she would never understand it. No more than she would ever understand Hiroshi. There was not a language spoken anywhere in the world that could help you really understand another human being.

"So you buried yourself away all these years," she pronounced. "In endless work. It shows."

"Did I bury myself? You just didn't know where I was. Nobody knew. It had to be that way. But that doesn't mean I didn't keep up with what was going on in the world."

"You didn't even tell your best friend where you were going. What's his name? Rodney. I think he was really hurt."

"I've visited him since then and explained," Hiroshi said. "He understands. But okay, perhaps he only forgave me because he's happy anyway. Who knows."

"Happy? What's his news?"

"He got his dream job—working for the SETI project. He's married, too. His wife's an astronomer. I imagine the two of them talk night and day about the missing-aliens problem."

Charlotte tore her croissant into little morsels. Married. The word was like a black hole. Why hadn't she married Gary? For some reason, it had felt like the wrong thing to do, and then it felt wrong that it felt wrong.

"And your parents?" she asked. Questions, that was the thing: ask questions and stop him from asking about her. She didn't want to talk about herself, not today, not now. "How are they?"

Hiroshi's face fell. "My mother's fine. She has a job she likes, and she's always arguing with her boss, which she also likes." He sighed. "My father died."

She lifted her head and felt a pang, even though she had never known the man. She had only seen a photo and knew what Hiroshi had told her.

Ah yes. And there was what she knew from the penknife.

"I'm sorry to hear that," she said. "Did the cancer come back?"

Hiroshi shook his head. "Not even. He just went for a routine checkup at the hospital. Like every year. But somehow one thing led to another, there was an infection that needed treating, fever or I don't know what, and in the end he died."

"That's dreadful. He wasn't even that old, was he?"

"Just over fifty." Hiroshi's eyes clouded over with sadness. "That was two years ago. I came out of hiding for the funeral and flew to America. I owed it to him, I think. And that was when I finally met his family." He sighed. "I can't even bring myself to call them *my* family, although I suppose they are. Anyway, it was hatred at first sight. The coffin was hardly in the ground and they were already setting out to make sure I would never get a dime of the Leak family fortune. As if I cared about that. It's enough that I share chromosomes with those people." He laughed bitterly. "It would be an interesting case study in US law. It turns out that when they had my father sign the settlement, they had built some clever little loopholes into the contract so that when he died the money they had given him would revert safely to the family. That was really interesting."

She looked at him. It must have affected him deeply, but he wouldn't let it show. "That's a horrible story."

"And so unnecessary. As if an inheritance meant anything to me. Anyway, I don't want their money."

He let the sentence hang in the air, so Charlotte found herself asking, "What do you want?"

He looked at her. "I don't want their money. I want to destroy their world."

He wouldn't say anything more about it, and when she tried to ask about what had happened, all he said was, "It doesn't matter." He seemed to regret having let the remark slip. That was when Charlotte really became interested in what he might have dreamed up out here.

When she demanded that he finally tell her the secret as he had promised, Hiroshi asked, "Do you remember what I was telling you last night?"

Charlotte nodded. "Robots that build robots."

"Exactly. Except that it's not as easy as you might imagine. Once you get down to brass tacks, you soon realize any kind of machine that makes stuff is much bigger than the stuff it makes, and much more complex, too. To make even a dumb little plastic party hat, you need a machine as big as a bus, and to make a bus, you need a factory the size of a city block. And so on. There's no such thing as a machine that can make a copy of itself."

"With one exception," Charlotte added. She had to speak up. She had thought of it last night as she was falling asleep.

Hiroshi looked at her, suitably impressed. "What would that be?"

"Women," she said. "Women can make copies of themselves. With a bit of software from the man, but there are species where the female doesn't even need that."

He laughed, visibly relieved he hadn't overlooked something. "Well, okay. But those are living beings. That's fundamentally different. The new life-form they make is much smaller to begin with, and then the trick is that it can grow by itself. That works for living creatures, but just try it with a table or a DVD player."

"If you'd come up with women as an example, you'd better believe I would have something to say about it. Comparing women to machines—ugh!"

He shook his head. "Honestly, I never thought of it. Not in all these years. Probably because I don't want other living beings to take over the work that has to be done. We tried that model once—and we know how that turned out."

Charlotte drained the last of her coffee. "Okay, so now it's your turn. Hiroshi tries his model."

He leaned back and folded his hands in front of him. "I approached the problem from the other end. What's simple to build, and what sorts of machines can we build simply? That was my basic question. Look at it that way, and it's really more of a geometrical problem. What's the simplest form a machine can take? What's the very bare minimum? I spent years pondering these questions when I was a kid—"

"When you were a kid?"

"I realized quite early on it wouldn't be all that simple to make a robot that can build robots."

"I imagine you did."

He didn't respond directly but seemed sunken in reminiscence. "It's really very practical to still be a child, to know little or nothing of what they call reality. It means you can sometimes go down paths that a grown-up would refuse to consider. An adult would say, 'Well, that wouldn't work anyway, I know that much.' So he stays on the beaten track, while the child is cheerfully striking out in entirely new directions. At the time I said to myself, 'Well, a robot may not be able to build a whole other robot, but perhaps it can build an arm. And even if it can't build an arm, then it can at least build a finger. Then you can have another robot build a foot, and so on.' Eventually, you'd have enough fingers and arms and feet and heads to be able to put together whole robots after all." He opened his hands out into a fan and then interlaced his fingers. "Of course, it doesn't work that way either, but the basic premise was good and took me other places. My idea was to build not a single robot but an ensemble of several functional parts, each as simple as possible in itself. Then, taken together, these make up an effective whole and can work with one another. Then, depending on how they arrange and align themselves, they can actually build more functional parts. I call the whole thing a 'complex.'"

Charlotte shook her head. "I really can't imagine how that would work. Sorry."

He looked at her thoughtfully. "Okay. Imagine you have a very simple machine composed of, say, just twenty-six parts. On its own it only knows how to make one of these parts. However, you also have twenty-five other machines that also each know how to make one other part. Then in the end you would have enough for one more machine, wouldn't you?"

"Yes." Charlotte considered all this. "But the other machines— what if they are made up of other parts in turn?"

"Then you'll need a few more machines."

"And they in turn are made of other parts. The whole thing gets out of hand."

Hiroshi raised his brows. "That's what I meant when I said it's more of a geometrical problem. You have to construct the parts so that each of them has as many uses as possible."

"And you did that."

"I had an uneventful childhood and not much else to do."

Charlotte thought about it. "I can't really imagine what such a machine would look like. Only twenty-six parts and able to produce one of its own constituent pieces."

"It's just an example. In reality, once again it's a little more complicated than that. You have to be able to make the parts from something, meaning raw materials have to be extracted somehow. Then you have to shape them, drill them, and so on. So what I did was to break down all the processes of machine-tool technology into the most basic possible steps, into their constituent parts, so to speak. And then I developed the simplest possible machines that could perform one or at most two of those functions."

"What kind of functions should I be thinking of here?"

He ticked them off on his fingers. "They have to be able to saw, join, weld, quench, clamp, cut, turn, drill, press—"

Charlotte waved a hand. "Okay, okay, I understand."

"Not all of those functions are equally important. Some of these functions have to be able to interact with the world around. So one such function is to be able to identify raw materials, and that's done by a unit I call the prospector. But then the material is actually extracted by another unit, the miner. Then it's taken away to be processed by the transporter. And so on. Then there are two absolutely central functions on top of all this. The first is power generation and transmission, which is the most fundamental of all, since nothing happens without energy. And the second is programming. There has to be some control system for how all the individual pieces work together. If a unit ends up in the wrong place or starts work at the wrong moment, then the whole thing falls apart."

Charlotte tried to imagine how that would work. She looked down into her cup as she pondered, so that Hiroshi asked whether she wanted more coffee.

"No, thanks. I . . ." She tried to put into words the images that were going through her head. "So what you've done, almost, is build a flock of little robots that are all different but that can make more of themselves by working together. And they build the other robots one by one rather than all at once. Have I got that right?"

"Exactly!" He was enthusiastic now. "You've said it just right. That's exactly it. A flock of robots under central control. And they reproduce by working together to build one part after another until there's another flock. That's the basic idea."

Charlotte picked up her cup. "But once you've got a flock of robots, how does it make me a fresh cup of coffee?" She couldn't imagine that, no matter how hard she tried. Had she argued him into a corner with her question? It certainly didn't look like it.

Hiroshi's eyes lit up. "Excellent question." He was beaming all across his face. "And you're quite right—at the moment they can't. That has to do with the way coffee is produced—you have to plant the bushes, tend to them, water them, harvest the beans, and all of that, then you have to process your harvest until you eventually have roasted coffee beans to grind and brew. All that lies in the future for the time being. There have to be a great many more of our complexes—our flocks, as you say—before some of them can devote themselves full-time to coffee. In every case, a complex is a unit in its own right that can communicate with other complexes at a higher level—in this instance it would be a 'coffee complex,' a flock of flocks, all busy producing coffee. Later on we could have as many of these higher levels as you can imagine—flocks of flocks, and flocks of flocks of flocks. The higher the level, the less central control or programming these complexes would need. Rather, they'd increasingly be able to work together as a sort of swarm. That's the way our brains work, more or less."

"But there would have to be a 'ship complex' to transport the coffee, wouldn't there?"

"Not necessarily. The complexes could do their work in totally different ways from humans. I can quite easily imagine that a sufficiently large number of functional units could make a sort of pipeline on the seabed and then pass the coffee on to its destination one bean at a time."

It was a breathtaking image. "A pipeline on the seabed? You would need an incredible number of units for that."

"So what? They make themselves, on their own, as many as I choose. All I have to do is write the program for it. As soon as it's written, the whole thing just happens by itself. Programs don't wear out."

For a moment her thoughts were a blank. She tried to imagine the world Hiroshi saw in his mind's eye, but she couldn't. All she knew was it would be a very different world from the one she knew.

"Putting all that aside," Hiroshi went on, "it's early days yet. So far we've only been able to implement all the functions we would need for the units to replicate themselves. The first big hurdle is having the first complex create another. The hardest part there is what we call the cell division: creating a second control module that will accept the software from the first. It needs a lot of fine work to build such a module and particular parts. But as soon as it works, then off we go. Evolution can begin."

"Evolution? Didn't you say just now that we're dealing with something very different from a life-form?"

"True enough. It's a widespread fallacy, however, to think evolution applies exclusively to living beings. It doesn't. Evolution has been at work in technological processes, too, from the year dot. If you want to have a chance of understanding industrial civilization today, then you must look at it as something that has evolved. There's really no central control to speak of. We've had a history of centrally planned economies after all, and if we learned anything it's that beyond a certain degree of complexity, central planning doesn't work. Which is why these complexes have to develop on their own, in a quasi-evolutionary manner. New units will have to come along and perform further functions that hadn't been needed before. Initially, that will happen under human guidance, but eventually the highest-level complexes will respond independently to human needs and do what we want them to do."

Charlotte looked at the coffee cup in her hand and studied the pattern. "Maybe. But I still can't imagine how your minirobots would make me a cup of coffee. How it gets onto the table in front of me."

"We can run through that process. Ten years from now there'll be a big multicomplex over in Brazil running the coffee plantations—"

"You can skip that bit. I don't even have any idea how coffee plantations work right now. I only just know how to make coffee. Grind, brew, filter, pour, and so on."

"All right then. The coffee beans come through the pipeline to the crusher units, whose function is—well, you can guess. Then the ground coffee falls into a container made up of form units, whose only function is to hold stuff. Heater units boil the water supplied by the pump units . . ."

"Next you'll tell me that there's a coffee-filter unit as well."

"No, the coffee filter isn't part of our flock; it's another product. Just like the beans, it's manufactured somewhere and brought to where you need it—"

"Through another pipeline? A coffee-filter pipeline?"

"I think it might make more sense to have a general-purpose transport pipeline to every house, bringing whatever is needed."

"And then?"

"The transporter units carry the filter into place, the coffee percolates . . ."

Charlotte moved her cup forward. "Now I'm curious."

Hiroshi raised his hands. "Maybe it's just a perfectly ordinary coffee machine, and you have a humanoid household robot that picks up the coffee and brings it to you. Think about it—the functional units can reproduce as often as we like. Once there are enough of them, they can create whole factories building all sorts of things."

Charlotte shut her eyes for a moment. She had to, even if it wasn't good manners. She was overwhelmed by the world Hiroshi had envisaged. She opened her eyes again and said, "I want to see something now. I suppose you've built a flock of robots?"

"Yes, of course. That's why we're here. To test the first complex."

"Show me," Charlotte demanded.

They went into the tent Charlotte had already noticed that morning. Just as she had thought, it was a lab. Tables full of tools, computers, and precision machinery lined the walls; the middle of the tent was clear save for a gleaming, silver cube about the size of a small refrigerator, its skin shimmering like steel scales.

"We've tested all the subroutines one last time," Hiroshi declared as though he expected Charlotte to know what that meant. "As soon as we give it the go-ahead, there will be constant video surveillance of the complex at work, from all angles. What it does is fairly complicated, so we can expect a few faults. That's what we're working on at the moment—fault tolerance."

"But you do know that it basically works?"

Hiroshi stopped in his tracks. "Let's just say that I'm fairly sure."

"You must have tested something, you and your team."

"As I mentioned, we've tested the individual functions. But now comes the integration test. We haven't been able to test the replication process as a whole, not yet."

Well then. She didn't much care about the details. Charlotte put her hands on her hips and looked around. The lab tables were all cluttered with stuff. The men and women on Hiroshi's team would be bored once their robots started doing all the work for them. They wouldn't know what to do with their time.

"Where is everyone?" she asked.

"Probably swimming," Hiroshi said.

"Swimming? I thought your people were all work and no play."

Hiroshi smiled. "I sent them swimming so that we could have some time to ourselves. The test's all ready; we just have to press the button. But I didn't want to do that until you got here. I wanted you to see it with me."

There it was again, that strange link between them, the mystery of their connection. It had nothing to do with love. They liked one another, no question, and perhaps they had been lovers once, but whatever connected them was something else. Something that gave Charlotte the shivers.

She took a deep breath. "Why? Why do I have to see it as well?"

"Because it has to do with you. Because you were the inspiration for it."

"Am I supposed to be happy about that?" she murmured, and she shrugged as though she wanted to cast a weight from her shoulders. She looked at the gleaming metal block in the middle of the tent. "Is that it? The complex?"

"Yes."

"Can you make it do something? So that I can see what it looks like."

"No problem." Hiroshi hunched over a keyboard, tapped in a command, and then picked up a dark gadget that looked like a pocket flashlight gone wrong. "This is an upgrade of my Wizard's Wand, with integrated laser pointer and Bluetooth connection. Ninety-nine dollars in most DIY stores."

He switched the thing on and pointed its thin red beam at a clear spot on the tent floor, about three meters from the metal block. It was fascinating. The block started to move, then fell apart into hundreds of individual parts. It looked as though thousands of steel-winged insects had clustered together to form a cube and were now going their separate ways. A few seconds later all the various parts were in motion, flowing like a stream of gleaming chrome-plated Lego bricks across the gray-brown floor, rustling and clattering as they threw themselves noisily into the task of moving from one place to another. Less than thirty seconds later the block was standing where Hiroshi had commanded it to go with the laser beam, and after the last unit had settled into place, the silence returned.

"Wow," Charlotte said. "You really are a wizard."

Hiroshi bent over the keyboard again and entered more commands. "We'll do the whole thing again, but slower, so that you can see how it works."

Another laser beam, and the block began to rattle and hum once more, making a scraping, scratchy sound. This time, though, she could see it was not one flowing movement but more like a tiny army striking camp. First, a series of little square units detached themselves from the rest and climbed down the other units' backs like acrobats in a circus. Then they laid themselves down on the floor, unrolling like a long tongue, pointing toward the new position.

"These are the positioner units," Hiroshi commented. "They make the map, so to speak, for all the other units to read."

Now a whole crowd of other units followed. She could see at this speed that they were all different, and that most of them didn't move on their own. They were carried along by units zooming back and forth like little flatbed trucks along the road that the positioners had marked out.

"Transporter units. The name says it all, doesn't it?"

As the block took itself apart, she could see how a scaffold of positioner units gave the whole thing its shape. These, too, gradually left their places and threaded their way through between the transporters to re-create the structure in the new position. Eventually, all the units were there anew, all neatly in place. The last positioner units into the cube were those that had first rolled out onto the floor.

Charlotte hadn't expected to be this excited. "That's amazing! What else can it do? Show me something else."

"I've programmed something in specially," said Hiroshi, clearly pleased she liked his toy. He put down his Wand and typed in a few more commands. With its characteristic scurrying rustle, the block changed into . . . some other shape. A weird-looking machine with a hopper on the top and a tangle of rods and spines on one side.

"What's that?" Charlotte asked.

"One moment."

Hiroshi rooted through a drawer, then another, until finally he had found what he was looking for: a big ball of red wool. He walked over to the transformed machine and threw the wool into the hopper. The machine hummed into life, creaking and clattering, and began to knit.

"That's unbelievable," Charlotte exclaimed.

Inching out of the side of the machine came a knitted scarf, growing longer and longer at incredible speed.

"The truth is I only wrote that as a demonstration program," Hiroshi said. "Just for you, in fact. We won't be using it for the rest of the experiment. It's good, though, isn't it?"

"It's more than that." Charlotte plucked up the nerve to step closer as it rattled away. She peered into the hopper; the wool was almost all gone by now, the ball hopping and rolling around as it shrank. When the scarf was finished, the machine fell quiet again.

Hiroshi picked up the scarf and handed it to her. "A souvenir. I heard that it gets cold in Scotland now and then."

"Yes, you could say that." She felt the scarf. It was soft and fluffy, practically perfect. Good wool, too; she wondered where Hiroshi had got hold of it.

"What I'm proudest of there is the way the program can start knitting on its own," Hiroshi declared. "The hardest part was having it find the beginning of the yarn. Then, to be honest, all the other processes are just copied from commercial knitting machines, adapted to the pincer unit's capabilities."

Charlotte ran her hands over the scarf, feeling suddenly feverish. "What else can it do?"

"This, for instance," Hiroshi said, entering another command.

The machine changed again, became short and squat, and stretched out some kind of arm. Hiroshi fetched a rough-hewn stump of wood and put it in front of the machine. The arm came to life at once. Transporter units scurried along it, bringing other units that attacked the wood and cut it into chunks that were carried away by more transporters. Soon the stump tipped over onto its side, the arm repositioned itself, and the cutters got to work on the other side of the wood. They sawed and sliced for a few minutes until there was nothing left. The transporter units carried the cutters away. Now a new unit with a long antenna scurried along the arm and began to poke around where the stump had stood.

"The prospector unit," Hiroshi explained.

Obviously, it was satisfied there was no more wood left, since it scooted away. Something hummed inside the machine for a while. Then more transporters came flitting out, laying out a staggering number of toothpicks on the ground one by one.

"Incredible," Charlotte breathed.

"If you need toothpicks," Hiroshi said modestly. "This was a fairly early program, which we've expanded since then. Now the complex can do the same thing with metal."

"With metal?" Charlotte asked, surprised. "Don't the blades become blunt?"

"Yes, but the units can sharpen each other up again."

Charlotte didn't answer. All she could do was look from the scarf in her hands to the bizarre machine that had made it and back again. She felt she was standing on the edge of an abyss. What was happening here? What kind of machine was this that could knit scarves, turn tree stumps into toothpicks, and probably make coffee if need be? It was all very entertaining, but even she knew this was not a game, that this machine was not a toy. If ever she had seen a vista of terrifying possibilities, then it was here.

She turned away to catch her breath. He was watching her; she could feel it. She turned and looked at him. "Do you really want to set this thing loose on the world?"

"Just on this island to begin with," Hiroshi said.

"And who will guarantee that it stays on the island?"

"Every unit has an automatic cutout that means it falls to bits in salt water. It's an imposed limitation, of course; we can remove it later. For the time being, though, it's there to set everybody's mind at rest."

"Every unit? Even the ones that the machine produces on its own? The next generations?"

"Those, too." He tilted his head. "Besides, we won't be reaching any higher-echelon complexity here. There's no cause for concern. We'll still be in the domain of centrally controlled programs for a long time yet."

She turned to look at the complex again, which seemed to stand there like a faithful dog awaiting its command. "I don't know. Somehow it's an unsettling thought."

"That's a quite normal reaction," Hiroshi said. "If everything goes according to my plans, then it's the end of the world as we know it. A new world will be born. It would be unnatural not to feel any fear at that prospect."

"And you? Aren't you afraid?"

"No. I believe the new world will be better than the old."

Just then the flap at the tent door rustled. They both turned. It was the young man from the night before—Miroslav, Charlotte recalled. He was wearing nothing but swimming trunks. His hair was wet, and he looked even skinnier than she remembered.

"What is it?" Hiroshi asked brusquely. He obviously didn't welcome the interruption.

Miroslav held up a piece of paper. "Just in from Hong Kong. Marked urgent. The fax sounded the alarm; otherwise, I wouldn't even have heard it out on the beach."

"And? What's the message?" Hiroshi held his hand out.

"We have to postpone the test." Miroslav passed him the fax. "Mr. Gu has informed the board of directors, and they have serious reservations. They're asking that you come to Hong Kong for a conference to decide how to proceed."

Hiroshi took the sheet and read it in silence. His face darkened.

"What's the worst-case scenario?" Miroslav asked. He was shivering slightly. Perhaps because it was relatively cool in the tent. "Will they cancel the project?"

Hiroshi looked up from the fax and gazed into space for a moment. Then he looked at his assistant and smiled. "No. The project won't be cancelled. You see . . . unfortunately, this fax only arrived five minutes after we started. What a shame, eh?"

"Five minutes after . . . ?" Miroslav was visibly startled. "That wouldn't work. The time stamp is right there on the fax. They'll be able to compare it to the video footage and see it arrived before the experiment began."

Hiroshi folded the sheet carefully. "No problem. Just set the system clocks on all the computers back by an hour. And on the video system. We start the experiment in fifty minutes."

2

A flurry of activity erupted all around them.

Miroslav hastily pulled on a shirt and shorts, then squatted down by the computers and started busily fiddling with them. Right after that the others trotted in, young people from all over the world but mostly Asian, their hair wet, their arms sandy, their skin red from the sun. Charlotte hadn't even seen most of them before now, much less learned their names. They greeted her as they passed—some of them absent-minded, some curious, some shy—and got to work, visibly excited to be starting at last.

Hiroshi popped up again. He had gone to the office to organize his trip and send a message to Hong Kong announcing his arrival and little else.

"How does it look?" he asked Miroslav.

"Just the server still to go," his assistant said without looking up. "Then we can get started."

Hiroshi's team swung into action with impressive zest and enthusiasm. She was sure each and every one of them knew what they were doing here could change history. The atmosphere in the control room for the moon landings couldn't have been much different. As for her? Charlotte folded her arms and thought of her own childhood dream. Paleoanthropology. The first human race. What had become of that? Nothing. Unlike Hiroshi, she no longer had a dream, had no vision to follow.

The lab benches formed a U shape in the tent. At the open end, where there were no tables, two of the women began to take down the tent panels. Charlotte watched them carefully roll them to each side and tie them to the tentpoles, then she glanced out over the landscape. What she saw was so unexpected that she had to blink several times before she understood what she was looking at. The island was a garbage dump.

In among the palms lay heaps of rusty household appliances, steel drums, tires. The gentle hillsides were covered with empty cans, plastic bottles, and the Styrofoam shells of TV dinners. Once-green slopes were piled with all sorts of rubbish and trash. What could have been a tropical paradise was instead a nightmare.

Hiroshi came to her side. "Dreadful, isn't it? That's what the industrial countries call recycling. It's actually too much work for them to really sort through all their leftover rubbish once the easily recyclable materials have been taken for reuse. Cheaper just to load everything up in containers and ship it off to the Third World. Most of the time, countries like this have no other way to earn money than to allow them to unload their trash here and forget about it."

"That's revolting," Charlotte said. She looked around, noticed again the wet hair of the people around her. "And you sent your team swimming in there?"

Hiroshi pointed back over his shoulder. "There's a much more hygienic beach up by the jetty. This island's not full up yet either. Otherwise, it would stink even worse than it does." He pointed toward the curious, yellow, billowing mass she had seen from the helicopter. "All that over there comes from Europe. They pack their rubbish neatly into plastic bags."

"It's disgusting." Charlotte suddenly felt dirty. "Couldn't you have found some other island?"

Hiroshi shook his head. "It had to be this way. As soon as I heard about this island, I knew I wanted to carry out the tests here."

"Why in the world would you want to do that?"

"Two reasons. First of all, because it makes it vastly easier for the complex to find new materials to build with. Working this way, I don't need as large a starting configuration as if I had set out to mine for raw materials in the ground. And second, because it shows the potential this technology has to deal with the mess we've made of the world so far. Do you know how many landfills and garbage dumps there are on the planet? The number is beyond belief. The amount of trash is beyond belief. You could easily cover the whole surface of the moon with it. Even if my invention does nothing but clear up all the trash we've made, it would be a blessing for that reason alone."

Why did that make her think of her house in Belcairn, Scotland, at the ends of the earth? Why did it make her think of Gary, of how she only wanted to be happy with him and for some reason was not? Charlotte came to with a start. It seemed like a betrayal to think that way.

Hiroshi was already fiddling around with his Wizard's Wand. He steered the silver cube out of the tent step by step. Outside, they had painted a set of coordinates in green on the bare earth between the tent and the garbage dump; a great big cross marked the spot where the experiment would start.

"How are we for time?" Hiroshi called.

Miroslav looked at the big clock hanging on one of the tentpoles, which he had likewise set back an hour. "Thirty-three minutes still."

"And everything's ready?"

"Everything's ready."

"Okay," Hiroshi said. "We don't have to be quite so literal about the five minutes. We could just as easily have started half an hour before the fax arrived. Last check and starting sequence!"

Miroslav picked up a clipboard with a checklist. "Start video surveillance!" he called out.

"Running," reported a man with a pronounced Asian fold to his eyes.

"Energy?"

"One hundred percent," a woman with dark brown curls called back. She looked about forty and was far and away the oldest person on the team.

"Starting position correct?"

"Right on target," Hiroshi said.

Miroslav got up, walked over to Charlotte, and held out a little black box that looked like some kind of remote control. "If you please," he said, looking at her with eyes made enormous by his thick glasses. "Just press the button."

Charlotte gave a start. "Me?"

"Please!" Hiroshi called out.

Did she have to? It wasn't her job. She had nothing to do with all this. She had had a very different dream . . . But she took the device. What choice did she have? And she put her finger on the button. It was a large button, the only one on the box. The button that would start it all. Someone pointed a video camera at her. They were all smiling. Expectantly, as though Charlotte would make a valuable contribution by pressing this button.

Hiroshi's gaze locked with hers, as though they were two magnetic poles bound together for all eternity. He smiled in invitation, a proud smile—so proud it was painful. As though he had done all this just for her. But why would he do such a thing? It was all so strange. *Don't think about all that now.* Charlotte pressed the button, and outside in front of the tent, the block began to clatter and rattle.

So. It was done. If this was the start of a new world, then let it begin. She handed the remote control back to Miroslav and returned his smile as best she could. Everyone around her was leaving their places, going outside to see what was happening. Charlotte passed both hands over her face, gathered her hair back, and took a deep breath. *Well then,* she thought. *Let's take a look at what we've done.*

When she went to join the others in the ring they had made around the silver block—around what the block had become—she couldn't believe her eyes. Charlotte had already been impressed by what Hiroshi had shown her before, shocked by the speed and elegance with which the units moved. But compared with the spectacle before her, all that had merely been five-finger exercises, tricks the machine could perform with no effort at all. Now the complex was really getting to work. It made Charlotte shiver to look at it. To see this flock of robots, each no bigger than the palm of her hand, flitting about like jet-assisted ants, to watch the whole apparatus turn itself into a scuttling, clattering, rattling, humming form that changed shape every few seconds, creeping toward the garbage dump, putting out feelers, drawing them back, stretching itself out and then contracting, passing a steady flow of stuff through its body. It was breathtaking. The first little heaps of neatly stacked and sorted raw materials were already taking shape behind the machine: metal, plastics, wood, and so on.

Had there really been so many separate units in the cube? A gleaming steel horde was scurrying about in front of her, like Lego bricks gone wild, more than twice as many as she had imagined fit in the block. The units hadn't already replicated themselves, had they? They couldn't possibly have done it that fast. No, now she could see: they were just getting to work. The little claws and blades and all their other tools were sweeping the ground clean and digging and cutting shapes for molding, then other units scurried over and beat the sides smooth, all in fluid movements, like a swarm of insects descending upon the island—a swarm of steel locusts that devoured not the fields but the heaps of rubbish. And now the first molten metal was flowing into the mound. It hissed, and steam and smoke rose up . . .

Charlotte came up to stand next to Hiroshi, who was watching his creation at work, a blissful smile on his face. "The energy," she said. "Where do they get the energy for all this?"

She had been prepared to wait for him to shake himself free of his reverie, but she didn't need to. Rather, he seemed delighted that she was so curious.

"Most people never even ask," he said smiling. "Well, at the moment the energy is simply supplied by a generator." He pointed to a low, dark green tent next to the lab, and Charlotte spotted a thin cable running to one of the larger units. It hadn't been plugged in for the demonstration back in the tent, so clearly the complex was capable of storing a certain amount of energy. "Again, this was a question of the initial configuration. Energy is a central problem, but at the replication stage it doesn't much matter where it initially comes from. We wrote the metaprogram so that it relies on energy from a generator until there are more than twenty complexes. Then they get to work building solar panels, and that supplies all the further stages."

She looked at him and wondered once more what went on in this man's mind. She would probably never understand him. "Twenty complexes," she echoed. "Be honest now—are you ever planning to switch this machine off?"

He smiled enigmatically. "There will come a point when the machine can't even be switched off."

A sound that had nothing to do with the robotic units and their activity made all heads turn. It was the helicopter arriving.

"How long can you stay?" Hiroshi asked.

Charlotte blinked and considered what day it was, how long Gary would still be in London. "One week? Maybe two."

"Okay. Come to Hong Kong with me, then."

He eventually stopped counting how many hands he had shaken. "Rasmussen," he told one and all. "Jens Rasmussen. I represent Mr. Kato's interests."

"Pleased to meet you," they mostly said. "But he'll be coming in person, too?"

"I'm expecting him."

Rasmussen liked coming to Hong Kong—always had. Most people when they heard the name only ever thought of high-rises towering over the canyons of streets and teeming hordes of people all frantically going about their business. But those who got to know the city better were surprised to find they could walk along the island for hours on end. Strolling through forests and across green meadows, they came upon countless enchanting views of the coves and bays along China's coastline, and ancient trees dating back to the days when Hong Kong was a sleepy little backwater.

It was a shame he would not have time to go hiking on this visit. When the board meeting had been announced, it was more like an alarm drill than an invitation. Everything was top of the line, of course—the hotel, the limousine that had picked him up, the tea and canapés served before the meeting. And, of course, Ku Zhong, Gu's omnipresent and omnicompetent assistant, was taking care of everything, a broad-shouldered, stern-faced shadow who was loyal to his lord and master to the point of servility. Sometimes, at least by Western standards, beyond.

As always, the clearing away of the remaining food and drink signaled the meeting was about to start. Larry Gu never ate or drank at the conference table and never allowed anybody else to do so either. Two men from the security staff went around the room one last time with typically Chinese thoroughness. They left not one square inch of the walls or floor unexamined, even though the conference room was doubtless fully equipped with all the latest counterespionage technology. Then the great door at the front of the room opened silently. Rasmussen straightened his tie. It was all very theatrical. Gu loved that. Somebody had told him once that Gu had made a DVD compilation of all the moments in James Bond films that featured conference rooms, doors opening, walls turning around, and other architectural tricks. Apparently, he watched it over and over, especially whenever there was to be some new building work anywhere in his empire. And just like every time he saw Larry Gu, Rasmussen was startled to see that the ancient little man seemed even smaller than he had remembered him from the time before.

He pottered in through that enormous door with tiny little steps. It seemed to take hours for him to cross the five yards to the head of the conference table. Ku, expressionless as always, stayed by his side the whole time. Everyone in the room unconsciously held their breath as Gu clambered up into his seat. The chair was so big he could comfortably have lain down to sleep in it. It was always fascinating to see the white-bearded old man glance around the table and greet them all with a nonchalant "*Huān yíng*" as though he had just dropped by to say hello. The conference room had excellent acoustics despite its cavernous dimensions. Rasmussen had often wondered how this was possible. In any event, it worked, for Larry Gu would not allow microphones at his meetings. He spoke in a quiet, penetrating voice—and everyone in the room heard his every word.

"Now then," he began, "let's keep this short. You all know why we are here today. I think you should have had plenty of time over the last few days to study the documents you all received and to form your own opinions." He looked around the table, twirling his thin white beard.

The first to raise his hand was Piet Timmermans, a wiry Dutchman, the company's director for Europe. "To be quite frank, I cannot imagine how this might work," he said when Gu had gestured for him to speak. "With all due respect for your decisions, Mr. Gu, and for Mr. Kato's technical capabilities, which I am not in a position to judge, all of this is sheer science fiction. And the budget you have assigned to it is money out the window." He peered over the rim of his glasses at the documents. "How much was that? Fifty million? There were many better things you could have spent it on, if you ask me."

Gu smiled, unconcerned. "Well, it was my money. I can't take it with me after all."

Timmermans shrugged. "Just my opinion."

This was something that Rasmussen had liked about Gu from the very first. Larry Gu was absolutely merciless toward disloyalty—persistent rumor had it that in his younger days he had personally cut out the tongue of a treacherous business partner—but nobody in Gu's employ had ever suffered any ill consequences from speaking his mind. Quite the opposite. Rasmussen couldn't always follow Gu's sometimes bizarre appointments and promotions, but he thought he saw a trend in which the old man surrounded himself largely with people who held different opinions from his own—although in recent years Rasmussen had come to suspect ever more strongly that Gu mostly did that for his own amusement.

Jeffrey Coldwell, director for North and South America, a bull-necked Southerner, was said to have an extremely checkered past. He had been growing increasingly restless, visibly irked that Timmermans had raised his hand before him. "I'm worried about quite the opposite," he thundered when at last it was his turn to speak. "Let's assume the damn thing really does work—then what? A universal machine that can manufacture anything at all, including copies of itself? Great God in heaven, if that's not crazy, then I don't know what is. I find it unbelievable that we were not told about this decision earlier. This kind of thing requires discussion. And, most importantly, before it's had five years of investment and who knows how many thousands of hours of research and development. For instance, who actually owns the products the machine manufactures? Has anybody even considered these questions?"

"They belong to whoever owns the machine, I would say," responded Zhou Qiang, one of the directors for Asia.

"Or whoever owns the raw materials," countered Brad Summer, director for Australia. "You could make a case for that."

"It may well be that we are entering uncharted legal territory here," Larry Gu put in with a sly grin. He was clearly tickled to bits that he had caused such an uproar among his directors.

Coldwell slapped his hand down onto the table. "I simply don't understand the business model. What's this machine for? Somebody who buys this need never spend another penny in his life—the thing produces everything he'll ever need. Isn't that the idea? A universal machine that makes everything, produces whatever you want, completely automatically and at no further cost."

"Exactly," Gu confirmed, stroking his beard. "The modern equivalent of Aladdin's lamp."

"And then what? How are we supposed to make money off that?" Coldwell raved. "We'd be sawing off the branch we're sitting on. Sawing off all the branches there even are—chopping down the whole damn forest. Sooner or later a machine like that would wipe out every industry there is. An atom bomb couldn't do as much damage as this thing, if it really works."

"Isn't that somewhat exaggerated?" Brad Summer objected.

Rumor had it Coldwell couldn't stand his Australian colleague. It certainly showed now as he barked, "Have you even read the dossier? Have you thought it through? This machine can duplicate itself. And once it's done that, it can duplicate itself again. And again, and so on. Nuclear explosions work exactly the same way, in case you weren't paying attention in school. All in the blink of an eye. We aren't even guaranteed to sell more than a single one of these machines, if our first customer just gives away the copies for free." He sank back down in his seat and shook his bull head, exhausted. "No. if you ask me, somebody didn't think this through."

Brad Summer raised his eyebrows, making his round face look rather bovine. "I don't know what you're getting so worked up about. It would be a good thing if everybody had what they needed."

"Do you think so?" Coldwell shook his head. "Well, I don't know how you Aussies do business, but the way I learned it, we earn money by finding out what people need but don't have. That's the only way the game works, see? Hey. Take my housekeeper, for example." He waved an arm in what may or may not have been the direction of

America. "Jessica Gomez, forty-two years old, single, two children. She's got a heart of gold, she's an amazing cook, as long as you like Mexican cooking—and you know what? I do. She keeps my house in tip-top condition. Okay. I pay her good money for that. Also okay. That's the way it works. But you give this woman a universal machine that will stock her fridge and make the sneakers and sweatshirts for her boys, and do you think she'll ever do a hand's turn of work for me again in her life? She ain't doing that because she's bored. She's doing it because she needs the money. If she had everything she needed, I'd never see her again."

"And then you might have to iron your own shirts?" Gu put in, his voice dripping with sympathy that could only be meant ironically. He pointed at a cell phone that Ku Zhong was holding out to show him. "I am most unwilling to interrupt this splendid debate, but we have just heard that the jet with Mr. Kato onboard will be landing in less than half an hour. And we have also learned that Mr. Kato will be bringing a guest along, a lady. So if you still wish to fight, I request that you do so now."

Hiroshi awoke to the soft, repeated chiming of a gong, slightly louder each time. The alarm clock. Of course. He put out his hand and switched it off.

Even in the company jet, the flight to Hong Kong took almost eight hours. Since they would head straight into the conference room when they arrived—and he had to be in top form once he got there—and since there was a comfortable bed in the plane, they had lain down to get some sleep. Chastely, fully dressed, but it had been good. And it was wonderful to hold Charlotte in his arms again.

He looked at her, studying her face, quite relaxed in sleep, calm and as beautiful as ever. She would always be beautiful her whole life long; she was that kind of woman. It felt so incredibly right that she was there with him. Hiroshi didn't want to think about the fact she would be leaving him again in a few days to go back to her Scottish craftsman. She must be like a fish out of water with a man like that.

A map displaying the plane's route had appeared on the little screen on the wall above them. He saw they would be landing very soon. In half an hour at most. Hiroshi looked away, buried his face in Charlotte's neck, and wished this moment would never end. The movement woke her, however, and she sat up, dazed with sleep. She looked around and seemed quite startled before she remembered where she was.

"Oof," she said. "Are we already there?"

"Not long now," Hiroshi said sadly.

"The time passed quickly." She felt the mattress. "A real bed in an airplane is something else again, I have to say. I'm used to narrow seats."

Hiroshi sat up reluctantly. "We should freshen up. You can go use the bathroom first if you like."

"What passes for a bathroom on a plane," she said but crawled past him eagerly enough and vanished into the tiny cabin.

Hiroshi used the time to check his mail. Miroslav had sent him video clips showing the first new units being assembled and joining the complex. He showed them to Charlotte when she returned, freshly combed and smelling of something good.

"It's crazy," she said, genuinely impressed. "It really works. Your complex has had its first children."

Hiroshi made a face. He didn't like the comparison, even if everyone used it. "They're not children. They're replicas. Machines." He looked up. "Otherwise, what we're doing there on Paliuk would be considered child labor."

She laughed, not seeming to understand he was serious. "I'm just saying. This construction is somehow so—how can I even put it . . . ? Not one of your machines looks anything like what one would imagine they should. To be honest, I've been asking myself the whole time how you came up with all the ideas for it."

Hiroshi looked at her. How beautiful she was. And how she belonged to him, even if she didn't want to see it. "Do you want to know the truth?" he asked.

She raised her eyebrows. "Of course."

"Most of it I dreamed."

"Dreamed?"

"Yes. Even when I was a kid, I would spend all day racking my brains over some problem and then the answer would come to me at night in my dreams."

He could still remember those dreams vividly. They had been bold, colorful, and somehow quite different from his other dreams, even the erotic ones—which had sometimes been fairly bold and colorful themselves. If he had been even the slightest bit religious, he would have been ready to swear some god had talked to him and revealed the shapes of everything he was to build.

"You dreamed it," Charlotte said again, tucking a strand of hair back from her forehead, lost in thought. "That's really very strange."

A soft chime, different this time, then the pilot's voice. They had permission to land, and regulations required that all passengers strap themselves in for landing. Hiroshi switched off his computer, shut the lid, and put it away.

"Are you worried about what they're going to say?" Charlotte asked once they were sitting alongside each other, their ears popping as the plane rapidly lost height.

"Why should I be worried?"

"Because you ignored clear instructions."

"And what are they going to do, apart from get a little worked up?"

She turned to him and looked at him in that way of hers he liked so much, that made him feel so close to her. "Aren't you afraid that one day you'll go too far?" she asked.

Hiroshi thought for a moment and then shook his head. "No. I'm only afraid that I won't go far enough."

Obviously, she hadn't slept quite enough on the plane. As the car stopped in front of the huge glass tower block and they were supposed to get out, Charlotte was suddenly utterly overcome by exhaustion. She would have liked more than anything to stay in the car, curled up on the soft, warm leather of the backseat, and shut her eyes.

"Will they even let me in?" she asked Hiroshi, hoping she would be escorted to a hotel room somewhere to sleep it off.

Hiroshi, however, seemed fit as a fiddle. "They'll have to," he said, squaring his shoulders. "I've already announced you."

Charlotte struggled to keep her eyelids open as gravity tugged them down again. "Announced me? What as?" *Hopefully, not as his fiancée or something embarrassing like that.*

Hiroshi gave a quick smile. "As my muse."

"Oh my word!"

It was no good, though. The chauffeur shut the car door and wished them a pleasant stay; other staff in smart uniforms rushed up to take charge of their baggage and hold the gleaming doors open for them . . . and in they went. A vast cavern of glass and steel swallowed them up. The elevator was about as large as a student apartment, albeit unfurnished. They went up and up until it seemed they would reach the sky itself. Security guards scanned them with flat, plastic-shrouded wands. "In case of bugs," one of them told her, a shy young man who clearly liked the look of her but was determined not to let her notice.

Then the conference room. A table the size of an airfield, where men in dark suits stood up and shook their hands and said how very glad they were to see them. It was so cool that Charlotte shivered. She would have liked a cup of coffee, but Hiroshi had explained on the way over that would be impossible during the meeting itself.

Hiroshi introduced a bald, wiry man as Jens Rasmussen, his business partner for all his other inventions. Rasmussen seemed a little more relaxed and a whole lot more pleasant than the others around the table. And then finally, the boss of the whole corporation, Larry

Gu, a wizened old man who looked like a white-bearded cicada. He didn't stand up to greet them but simply bowed slightly in his seat.

At last, they got to sit down. Charlotte ducked her head down between her shoulders and told herself the meeting couldn't last forever.

"Welcome," said the old man in a soft voice, almost a whisper. "I am particularly pleased to meet a living, breathing muse, if only once in my life." The muted laughter around the table stopped as soon as Gu lifted his hand—not even lifted; he simply put his hand on the table and raised one finger. He had trained his people well, she had to hand it to him. "We have prepared a few questions before your arrival, Mr. Kato, and we hope you will be able to answer them to everyone's satisfaction. We are all agreed that your experiment is a quite extraordinary feat of research, albeit with no clear result as yet, and that it therefore deserves our fullest attention. Mr. Timmermans, your own objection, please."

A thin man who looked like he could have been a particularly humorless school principal raised his head. "Piet Timmermans, director for Europe. I've studied your proposal, Mr. Kato, and I have to say I am fundamentally not convinced. I don't wish to accuse you of seeking to perpetrate a deliberate swindle here. But I must assume you are simply mistaken. If your proposal had been placed in front of me five years ago, I would have turned it down flat and refused to invest so much as a penny. I simply cannot imagine a machine of the sort that you describe here could function at all."

Hiroshi had been sitting still as a statue, staring straight at the man on the other side of the table. When it was clear he had said all he had to say, Hiroshi came to life. "Well, Mr. Timmermans, I don't wish to rush to judgment on your powers of imagination," he replied politely enough, but with an edge to his voice Charlotte had never heard before, "but you are quite mistaken."

He opened up his computer and unspooled a thin cable from a little hatch in the table Charlotte hadn't noticed before, then plugged it in. The next moment a screen behind them lit up, and the image on Hiroshi's computer appeared.

"I received this video footage from the Pacific shortly before we landed," Hiroshi declared and began to play the series of clips that he and Charlotte had already watched on the plane. The video showed the machines building a new unit from parts they had themselves produced, the new unit quivering and quaking into motion, and then joining the flock of other units as though it had been with them from the start. "You see, the machine works and works exactly as planned."

Timmermans pressed his lips together tightly, his face pale. The other men around the table—all men, Charlotte realized—glanced incredulously at one another.

"Mr. Kato," said a heavyset Chinese man sitting by old Gu's side, probably his bodyguard, "you had instructions not to begin the experiment until after this meeting."

Hiroshi gave a curt nod. "Unfortunately, those instructions only arrived half an hour after we had started our test. To be frank, I had not reckoned with receiving any such instructions, since the original agreement gave me a free hand in everything related to this project."

"You could have stopped the test," the big man insisted.

"That would have invalidated the results," Hiroshi objected. "So I decided not to."

Murmurs rippled along the table like waves on a shore. Larry Gu lifted his finger once more and silence fell. "Well now, we can still stop it if we wish to," he breathed. "Although perhaps we do not even need to. In any case, now that the test is done we are no longer dealing with mere theories and the, ah, limits of our imagination. We now have concrete data. At the moment I can only see that as an advantage."

The next to speak was a stern American with sparse, red-blond hair who clutched the table tightly with both hands as he spoke as though to stop himself from leaping up and grabbing Hiroshi by the throat. "I'm interested to know what you think should happen with the products that your machine is—maybe—going to manufacture one day," he barked. "Seems to me there's a whole lot left unexplained here. For instance, who do those products belong to? And even before we get to that, what about the copy this machine makes of itself—if it does. Who does that belong to?"

Hiroshi unplugged his computer and closed it. The screen behind them winked out, and the room went dark once more even though it was broad daylight outside. The light was low, since the huge window was made of tinted glass, darker toward the top of the pane. It gave a view of Hong Kong, the tower blocks, the coast, and the sea, and though there must have been bustle and life down there, none of that mattered up here. It was as though the sun were setting over the city.

"You're talking about who owns what," Hiroshi stated.

"I am indeed. I'm talking about ownership, property. Property law. These are fundamental matters; perhaps the most fundamental of all in finance."

"They are matters that will very soon be obsolete," Hiroshi countered. There was a new note of steely certainty in his voice. This was getting interesting.

The American's jaw dropped. Clearly, he hadn't expected any such reply.

Hiroshi straightened in his chair. "Ownership is merely a concept that has been put forward as a solution to the problem of scarcity. Possibly not even the best solution, but nevertheless one that has stood the test of time. When there's a shortage of something—or could potentially be a shortage, we've seen that argument as well—then people hurry to claim ownership so that the shortage won't affect them. But if there is no shortage of anything—if there couldn't conceivably be any such thing as a shortage—then it's pointless to want to own anything. Why would you? Let's take water as an example. How much water does each of you own, gentlemen?" he asked, looking round the table.

"I have a whole pool full," someone said.

"That's not water you can drink," Hiroshi replied. "And you have no hesitation about replacing it with new water if it gets dirty. Why is that the case? Because, at least in the industrialized world, water is always readily available. It's enough to know there is no shortage and that in the ordinary course of things, there never will be. Which is why most people don't stockpile water, except for a few bottles of mineral water perhaps." He put his hands on his computer. "I am developing a machine that will do the same thing for every conceivable consumer good and resource. Worldwide, and for everybody. Everything that anyone might need will be on tap. Available, whenever you need it, however much or many you need. What point would there be in property and ownership then? None at all. Two generations from now, nobody will even understand what we meant by it."

The American gasped for air and squirmed in his seat, coughing and spluttering. "That's . . . that's crazy talk. That has got to be the nuttiest idea I have ever heard in all my born days. Property is just going to turn up its toes and die? Are you a goddamned hippie or— what *are* you? Property is important. It's part of who we are. People define themselves by it."

"You're mistaken. The terms people use to define themselves are culturally constructed, and they're changing all the time. Let me ask you one thing: If you could have a car any time you needed one just by snapping your fingers—wherever you were and wherever you needed to get to—and if you could be quite sure this service would be available to you your whole life long, then would you still want to own one? Would you want to shoulder the burden of taking it in to be serviced, washing it, paying for insurance, and all the rest? I wouldn't. I bet you wouldn't either."

"Some people take pride in having a car not everybody can afford."

Hiroshi shrugged. "As I've said, that kind of thinking will no longer apply in future. There will be nothing that anybody cannot afford—cannot have any time he chooses."

The American laughed out loud. "I think I'm going crazy here. What kind of business model is that? How do you intend to earn money this way?"

"I don't," Hiroshi replied nonchalantly. "Money will also cease to exist. When everybody can have whatever they want, what's the point of money?"

The American looked at him, stymied. He opened and shut his mouth a couple of times like a fish out of water, but not a sound came out. The man finally sank back in his chair, slapped his hands down flat on the table in front of him in a gesture of helplessness, and gasped, "I give up. The guy's living in cloud-cuckoo-land."

Now an earnest, gray-haired Asian man leaned forward in his chair. Folding his hands, he said, "I would like to say a word at this juncture, Kato-san. Do I understand you correctly—that you want to create a situation where, thanks to your self-replicating machine, everybody will have as much as they want of whatever they want in abundance?"

"Precisely," Hiroshi said, nodding. "Abundance is just the word. It sums up my whole project."

"Good, then I have indeed understood. Please understand, however, that since this is the case, I must now express my concerns about the amount of raw material at our disposal. Even today we are already experiencing bottlenecks in the world supply of many materials, and we are still very far from being able to provide an abundance of all things to all people. The world population is also increasing, and if you now propose to supply all these people with abundance, are you not concerned that you will use up all the available raw materials in the blink of an eye?"

The men at the table nodded. Obviously, this was a concern shared by many. Charlotte looked up at Hiroshi expectantly. She had never thought about that, but it seemed to her a deeply relevant and disturbing point.

Hiroshi, however, seemed entirely at ease. "No," he said immediately. "I am not concerned. In fact, I expect quite the opposite. Please bear one thing in mind: thanks to my machine, there is as much labor available on tap as we might wish—as much as we need. That not only means that we will be able to exploit the existing resources far more efficiently than the current cost structures allow, it also means recycling itself will be an inexhaustible resource. Under these conditions, I see no reason why we should have a recycling quotient of anything less than one hundred percent—in which case, the materials at hand will last literally forever, since they can always be reused." He folded his hands. "If this seems utopian to you, please consider that nature operates exactly the same way and has done for billions of years. Every atom in your body, gentlemen, is billions of years old and has been in the bodies of the dinosaurs, the algae, and the unicellular organisms. Nothing is ever lost in the world of biological life—everything is simply reused again and again. I see no reason why we should not apply the same principle to lifeless matter, to the world of goods and machines."

For a moment there was stunned silence all around the table. They were impressed, no question. Hiroshi had found the first chink in the armor of their incredulity, and if he kept on like this he would win them all over to his side. All of a sudden Charlotte wasn't in the least bit tired; rather, she was on the edge of her seat. How often did you get a chance like this in life—to sit in the boardroom of a global corporation and watch world-changing decisions being made? Never in her life would she have believed that conference rooms really did look just like Hollywood showed them.

Someone cleared his throat. It was a roly-poly, cheerful-looking man who looked as though he wouldn't hurt a fly. Appearances were deceptive—nobody lacking the killer instinct would ever have become a director.

"What about energy?" he asked. "Everything these machines do requires energy after all. There's no way around that. I might even suppose that your machines use more energy than conventional production technologies. Where are you going to get all this energy? It's common knowledge by now that our fuel sources are running low. Oil, uranium, whatever else we put in our tanks—it's all running out. You can't recycle those. Not even nature can. Everything's headed toward entropy in the end, and the heat death of the universe."

"We've got a while until then." Hiroshi nodded. "In principle, you're quite right; my machine does consume more energy on average. That's logical enough after all, since it's replacing human labor. However, these machines will obtain all the energy they need for themselves. We needn't worry about it."

"Oh yes? And how are they going to do that?"

Hiroshi raised his arm and pointed skyward. "By using a source of energy that, in human terms at least, is inexhaustible. The sun."

"What do you mean? Are you going to fit out your minirobots with solar cells? I hardly think that would be enough."

"You're quite right; it wouldn't be. We'll need full-scale power stations." Hiroshi couldn't stay in his chair. He stood up and walked around the conference table as he spoke. "You've seen one complex at work today, and you've seen a photograph of what this complex looks like when it's at rest. It's not much bigger than a small refrigerator. But please don't let that image fool you into thinking that's how things will look in the end, that every household will have its miracle machine, but everything else will stay the same. No, this complex is just the seed, and when it takes root and bears fruit we'll see a completely new industrial structure where everything is connected to everything else and human labor is only needed now and again as a hand on the tiller. And even that will be needed less and less often as the structure develops its own ever-greater complexity, since we can use well-known computing principles and concepts, such as swarm behavior, intelligent agents, and neuronal networking, to give this new industrial system a considerable degree of autonomy. So, in the new world we not only have an Aladdin's lamp in every kitchen but a complex of complexes that themselves are made up of further complexes right the way down as far as you like, and all these units will be connected to each other, exchanging material, information— and energy, too. There will be complexes that do nothing else but supply energy. And that will be a simple matter, simpler than you can possibly imagine at the moment."

"I look forward to seeing it," the American growled for all to hear.

"Current global energy consumption," Hiroshi continued, "is somewhere in the order of fifteen terawatts. That's fifteen thousand gigawatts, or fifteen million megawatts, and that includes all the energy we use to heat our homes, move goods and people, power our industry—everything. We obtain this energy by burning coal and oil, or by the fission of uranium atoms. There are one or two other methods as well." He was walking along the window wall now, silhouetted against the dim cityscape that could be seen through the darkened glass. "But, gentlemen, compare this amount of energy, this fifteen terawatts, with the energy the sun pours down upon Earth every day and has done for billions of years. That's one hundred eighty thousand terawatts—twelve thousand times what we currently need. Which means we would need to convert just one tiny part of the surface of Earth into a solar power station to make every other source of energy redundant."

"That's still a heck of a large area."

Hiroshi stopped pacing. "On a globe it would be a spot you could barely make out. And again, bear in mind we have unlimited labor at our disposal. We would only have to program this power station; the machines themselves would build it. And maintain it." He moved off again around the table. "Now you may well protest that the most suitable land areas—deserts, for instance—are mostly in politically unstable countries right now, and so on. Quite right. But here, too, my answer is that we will create abundance. Political instability is essentially the result of hunger, endemic disease, shortages at every conceivable level. Once we can give people everything they need, then politically unstable conditions will also be a thing of the past."

"But will your machines be able to do that? End hunger?" Timmermans broke in. "You'll need to grow crops, and crops need land. And land itself is in limited supply."

"True," said Hiroshi. "But we have unlimited labor at our disposal. We can tend gardens intensively where right now we have field upon field of monoculture. We can water every stalk of wheat individually if need be. We can make the deserts bloom."

"And run up against the solar power stations we're building there."

Hiroshi laughed out loud. "Can you imagine a world where the deserts we take for granted today will have all disappeared, save for one tiny scrap of land? We can settle that conflict fairly easily."

Charlotte watched him finish walking around the huge table as if he were completing a ritual. Memories bubbled up inside her, each one rising through her mind and popping to show a picture of the little boy who had seemed so remarkable even then, the boy who was afraid of nothing, who would never turn away from any goal he had set himself. She had known him then, and she saw now that Hiroshi was still that boy, grown now, grown up, but a fully formed version of the seed he had borne within himself even then. Perhaps people never truly changed. Perhaps people were like the planets, following their orbits unswervingly and only looking different because they reflected different light.

A man spoke up who had been silent until now, a serious-looking, brown-skinned man, doubtless Indian.

"Mr. Kato," he said gently, almost imploringly, "what will people actually do in this world that you envisage?"

"They'll do as they like," Hiroshi answered straightaway. He replied almost as a reflex.

"Is that enough? To do as one likes? Only as we like?"

Hiroshi stopped pacing and looked at the man as though seeing him for the first time. "Do you do as you like, Mr. Chandra?" he asked. "Right now, at this very moment, are you doing something that you wouldn't do if you didn't have to?"

Chandra wagged his head in that curious gesture Charlotte remembered so well from her time in Delhi. Indians didn't shake their head to say no, they wagged it.

"Not an easy question to answer," he said. "I am attending this meeting in my capacity as director for India and East Africa. If the meeting had not been called, then doubtless I would be doing something else right now. I am primarily here because it is my duty. On the other hand, the discussion today has been so entirely fascinating that I would very likely have come of my own free will. Broadly, I can say that I hold a post I am very glad to have. If you asked me whether I would hold the same position even in a world where one was no longer forced to work for a living, then I would say yes. Because it's interesting work and I feel I am doing something worthwhile. But that does not mean there are not parts of the job I do not enjoy so much. That's entirely normal."

Hiroshi nodded. "Well then. You've answered your own question. Art collectors will find that painters are still hard at work, but garbage collectors will probably find better things to do than go to work."

"That's fine, but what about waiters? Prison wardens? Lawyers? Nurses? Childcare workers? What about cooks? Are people only ever going to eat meals cooked by robots in the future?"

Hiroshi hesitated. The others may not have noticed, but Charlotte saw it. This was the first objection that actually ruffled him.

"I don't know how the world of work will change in the future," he admitted at last. "Nobody can know. The only thing that's certain is it will change. Some jobs will disappear before others. Some jobs can never be replaced by robots. We'll also have to establish what other kinds of satisfaction people find in their vocations, apart from money, since you can be sure money will no longer exist in its current form."

"I think you are more likely to cause dreadful boredom for large swaths of the population," the Dutchman chided him, pursing his lips. "Your invention will change the world so that most people will spend most of their lives in front of the television, since they will otherwise be bored to death."

Hiroshi started pacing again. "I don't believe that," he said resolutely. "I think boredom is something that must be learned. A little child is never bored, at least not in the way you mean. Children always have plans; they're always up to something. Being bored is something we learn in school and then, for sure, a great many of us learn it in our jobs. And then when we have become used to being bored, it's hard to unlearn the habit, possibly because some fundamental biological mechanism that aims to save energy takes advantage of our shortcomings." He had finished his tour of the table and was back at his seat. "Perhaps there will be a transitional era, a time of readjustment. Maybe. But in the long run, we will not be bored in the world to come," he proclaimed, grasping the back of his seat as though he stood at a lectern. "We will simply stop doing boring things, and instead we will devote ourselves to the interesting things in life. And, gentlemen, no matter how hard I look, I can find nothing wrong with this future and no cause for concern."

They sat there, unmoving, looking at him as though paralyzed. The spell only lifted when Larry Gu began to clap softly and broke the silence.

"Thank you, Mr. Kato," he whispered in a voice that sounded like a dental drill in a neighboring room. "I think I speak for everybody when I say we have no objections to you continuing your work. We will all be pleasantly surprised by the world you are busy creating, and we are most interested—"

Just then, Hiroshi's cell phone beeped. It was the worst possible time for it to happen. Charlotte noticed the gleam of displeasure at this interruption in the old man's eyes. And she noticed how Hiroshi jumped.

"I beg your pardon," he said, picking the phone up from the table. He turned pale when he read the message on the display.

Hiroshi had committed a terrible faux pas. Charlotte didn't need to be told—she saw it in the eyes of everybody around the table and in their reactions. Doubtless, it was obligatory to switch off cell phones before a board meeting, and Hiroshi had simply forgotten— or perhaps he had deliberately neglected to do so.

He looked up. "I beg your pardon once more for this interruption. This is an emergency report from the test grounds that has been sent with priority override; any other message would have been put on hold. I am most dreadfully sorry for the unfortunate timing, but I am afraid we will have to return to Paliuk straightaway."

"Has something happened?" Larry Gu asked.

Hiroshi hesitated, cradling the cell phone in his hand. "Let's just say that an unexpected development in the experiment makes my personal presence there indispensable."

He was getting home later every night, and it was all thanks to those damned blueprints. Even the doorman had noticed. "Good evening, Mr. Adamson. Hardly worth going home these days, is it?" he'd quipped recently.

And despite that, he had gotten nothing done. He just sat there with the blueprints spread out on his desk, staring at them as though waiting for divine inspiration or for his gaze to burn holes in the paper. He'd noticed a few things, of course. That the paper on which the plans were drawn smelled faintly of something that might have been joss sticks. And that the Chinese didn't care about sticking to international conventions for technical drawing. And that Hiroshi Kato didn't seem to care about the conventions for anything.

All useless insights, of course. The truth was he spent his evenings staring at the plans until he felt his eyes would start bleeding, understanding nothing at all. He still had no idea what the big picture was supposed to look like when all these parts combined. Instead of understanding anything, he was developing a growing hatred of Hiroshi Kato in particular and of geniuses in general, of anybody capable of inventing things he would never have thought of in his whole lifetime. Things he only understood when he saw them finished and ready under his nose. Being able to recognize genius was his only useful talent, aside from a knack for business networking, and now it had failed him.

But this evening he had spotted something that might get him a little further. And he had only seen it because the ceiling light had begun to flicker so distractingly that he had to switch it off. Only then did he notice the tiny shadows cast on the paper by his desk lamp, impressions along the upper edge of the blueprint. They were numbers. Someone had put a piece of paper on top of this diagram and jotted something down, probably a telephone number. Adamson opened his desk drawer and took out a soft pencil. Carefully, he rubbed across the dents and grooves until he could see what they were. There was a name underneath the number: Mitch Jensen. The telephone number began with 703-482. That was the CIA's dial code. He shoved the drawings aside, switched his computer on, and pulled up the internal phone directory. There was indeed a Mitch Jensen with the CIA, and that was his telephone number. Bingo. That could only mean he knew something about this whole business.

Adamson thought for two days about whether he dared use the number, and then late one afternoon he called this Mitch Jensen. First came the usual back-and-forth as they made sure they were speaking on a secure line, and then he introduced himself. "William

Adamson. I'm head of robotics at DARPA. I'd like to talk to you about Hiroshi Kato."

Mitch Jensen coughed. It sounded like a smoker's cough, and it also somehow sounded as though Jensen didn't take regulations quite as seriously as the rest. "I heard that you're kind of obsessed with the guy," he drawled, coughing again.

"So they say," Adamson admitted cheerfully. "But that doesn't mean much, does it? Just because you're paranoid, doesn't mean they aren't out to get you."

Laughter. Adamson felt he could work with a man who laughed like that.

"Okay," Jensen said. "Do you ever happen to be in Langley? We could meet, have a beer."

3

"What happened?" Charlotte asked once they were finally back in the limo on their way to the airport.

"Something went wrong," was all Hiroshi would say.

Then he was on the phone to Miroslav. She heard nothing on his end of the conversation to shed any more light on the matter. Hiroshi simply repeated variations on "Hmm" and "I see" and "Ah crap."

As they got in the car, he had told the chauffeur to get them there "as fast as you can," and the man was using every trick in the book. He dodged into every gap in traffic and drove slightly above the speed limit, but would it make any difference in the end? The flight would take eight hours anyway, an eternity longer than the drive to the airport.

Charlotte felt so sorry for Hiroshi. For a moment it had seemed he had won a clear victory, that he had won them all over to his side—and then a single text had been enough to bring the whole thing crashing down like a house of cards. Not because of the interruption itself, though that was certainly a breach of etiquette, but because Hiroshi has been so clearly shaken by the news. They had left the board of directors in uproar. Even Larry Gu, who had been on Hiroshi's side from the start, was visibly rankled. For the first time he had cast doubt on his own decision to support Hiroshi's project.

Charlotte looked out at the cars and trucks flowing along the roads like corpuscles through blood vessels. She tried to imagine what might be going on in the conference room just then. They were probably still sitting there, talking till they were blue in the face. The American would be triumphant about his doubts, and the Dutchman would be saying he had told them so. And the rest of them would be glad the world as they knew it wasn't going to change anytime soon.

As she listened to the engine hum, she reflected that it had been built by human hands rather than by scurrying flocks of minirobots. Despite all the impressive progress he had made, despite all that she had seen, Hiroshi's idea might simply be too ambitious to work. Perhaps he was aiming too high. But even then, was that so bad? She thought about it and realized she could forgive that kind of failure. Failure had a grandeur of its own. At least he had tried. She, on the other hand . . . she had run away from her own vision. There was no grandeur in that.

The limousine crossed the bridge, and the airport appeared in front of them. "I have to hang up," Hiroshi said into the telephone. "Listen, Miro, you'll have to manage everything on your own somehow until I get there. Don't call while I'm in the air, got that? No matter what happens. Your call would be patched through the jet's comms systems, and the company controls all those channels. I want to be the one who decides what information gets out and when. Okay?"

They went through the obligatory checks and controls in record time and were driven onto the runway in a little electric cart. It was windy, and Charlotte had to hold her hair down. The jet was on the tarmac, but at least twenty technicians in gray overalls were still scurrying around and over it. Charlotte felt queasy at the thought of the hurry they were in to get the plane cleared for takeoff.

Hiroshi worked straight through the flight. He sat at the table with his computer open before him, never turning his gaze from the screen. He read, studied, wrote, and pondered his problems without ever even noticing she was there. Charlotte let him be. She could see he was in despair, even if he didn't want anyone to know. She knew all the same. Although she was still tired, she was so amazed by everything that had happened that she couldn't rest. She could have watched a movie but didn't want to disturb Hiroshi. At some point she went to the back of the plane and lay down on the bed, even though she was quite sure she wouldn't sleep. But she fell asleep after all, into dreams of deep chasms, falling without end.

"He saw his life's work in ruins before him." Hiroshi had read that sentence in a book somewhere, and now he remembered it and thought, *So that's what it feels like.*

Miroslav had left everything as it was when things came grinding to a halt. He had kept the video surveillance going to the very end and secured all the footage; they would be able to analyze everything.

The two of them paced out the area where the complex had been at work. It looked like a bomb had hit the site. Yellow poles sprouted from the ground everywhere to mark units that had lost their connection to the main complex at one point or another and never made contact again. It didn't help that the units were scattered around among heaps of scrap and garbage. Nevertheless, the security cutouts had done their job: the central guidance program had correctly assessed the situation as beyond recovery and switched itself off as intended. That data log was also stored and available. Enough data for several years of further analysis. A few units had made it to the shoreline, where the seawater had washed over them. Also as intended, they had fallen to bits as the cutout kicked in.

"Take pictures of that as well," Hiroshi said. "That should calm them down. At least it shows that there was never any danger from the test."

"It's done," Miroslav replied. "I've been photographing absolutely everything. This is the most photographed garbage heap in history."

After that they studied the video footage together. Everybody else had already watched the events unfold so many times that they knew the story by heart. "There. This is the point where that unit first loses contact," someone would say, sucking nervously at a cigarette or drinking straw. "Now the fallback routine kicks in. The main action is abandoned, and it reestablished . . . Yes! Got it!"

It was as though they hoped that the film had changed since last time they had watched it.

The main cause of failure was all too obvious. All the original units had been marked with UV paint so that they could be easily identified simply by switching to the matching spectrum on the video footage. That way they could follow exactly which element was doing what and when. The units that the complex had built on its own had no such markings, making things a little more difficult. But all they needed to do to spot the real cause of the problem was play the footage back in reverse from the moment things finally went off the rails. Seen like this, it was obvious everything had started to go wrong with one of the third-generation units—ones that had themselves been built by units of the preceding generations.

"The complex can't build its own units with the necessary precision," Hiroshi declared, his hand on the video "Stop" button. "That's where the trouble lies, I'm sure of it. The defects accumulate with each step along the replication pathway, and then eventually we get malfunctions."

Everybody nodded. They had all reached the same conclusion already.

"It's like with audio cassettes back in the old days," said Therese, the only one who was old enough to remember life before the digital era. "You would make a tape, and it sounded good. If you copied that tape to another cassette, you got a little white noise. Copy it again and there was more, until you eventually had a tape that was all crackle and hum and no music at all."

It was a vicious circle, as so often the case with technology. If they wanted to make the new parts with greater precision, then the units would have to be more complicated, meaning in turn they would be harder to manufacture and require more parts. And so on, round and round. It felt hideously like an insoluble paradox.

He saw his life's work in ruins before him.

Hiroshi threw himself once more into his diagrams and sketches, drawing, thinking, racking his brain for hours on end. It couldn't be true. It couldn't be true it didn't work. There had to be some way to make it right. He had been so sure that it would work, as sure as he was that the sun would rise every morning. Perhaps he had just overlooked something. Every little detail counted in technical work, every decision led somewhere and had consequences that could not be foreseen when you first stepped down that path. He had to go back to the beginning, back to the roots of the idea, back to the source. Back to the dreams that had started it all. Those dreams—they had been so vivid; he had seen so clearly how everything moved, how everything was connected, like clockwork that would run for eternity. The problem he was grappling with here could not be insoluble. There had to be a way. The principle was right.

At some point Charlotte appeared and put her hand on his arm, rousing him from his thoughts. "You never give up, do you?" she asked.

Hiroshi rubbed his face with both hands and felt stubble. He could smell sweat—his own. He was also very hungry. Dimly, he became aware he had been poring over the documents for several days now, interrupted only by short naps on the bare ground. "I haven't been taking care of you as my guest," he mumbled, embarrassed. "I'm sorry. It's all so . . ." He looked around and spotted the diagrams that were all that was left of his dreams. "I'm doing something wrong. I just don't know what."

"I should get back home. I need to set off soon."

He blinked. Ah yes. She couldn't stay forever. Of course not. She wanted to get back to her Scottish handworker, the man who built musical instruments that actually worked.

"I'll tell them to send the helicopter," he said. "And I'll get them to book your flight back."

"Miroslav has already taken care of all that." She gave a sad smile. "I just wanted to say good-bye."

Now he could hear it. The helicopter was already on its way. He was losing his grip.

He saw his life's work in ruins before him.

"Then at least I'll come with you to the landing pad, if you've got no objection," he said, standing up.

She stood before him, put her arms around his neck, and kissed him. "No objection at all," she whispered. "But after that you should go and clean yourself up. Remember, Archimedes had his best idea in the bath."

She caught her onward flight in Manila without having managed to reach Gary and let him know she was on her way. She tried to tell herself it wasn't her fault if he had his phone switched off the whole time, but nothing helped. She still felt it was somehow her mistake, that she was doing something wrong.

She couldn't sleep. She would probably never be able to sleep again. The stewardess brought magazines and was so solicitous that Charlotte read one after another, hoping that perhaps she would nod off midarticle. Politics! That had always been the surest way to put her to sleep. No wonder, since her father was an ambassador. But this time not even politics helped. Then she chanced upon an article about recent archaeological finds. Researchers from the US and Germany had examined a find from Ethiopia, the bones of animals hunted for their meat more than three million years ago, and discovered clear traces of early human tool use. This didn't quite turn paleoanthropology on its head, but it did cast doubt on what had been fairly fundamental assumptions. The assumption that only *Homo* knew how to make stone tools, for instance. *Homo* hadn't been around three million years ago. Which meant that *Australopithecus* already knew how to make and use tools. That would date the start of the Stone Age further back by almost a million years—a major shift for prehistory's frame of reference.

Charlotte shut the magazine, put her head back, and closed her eyes. It was as though the topic were following her around. She picked the magazine up again and looked at the masthead. It wasn't a specialist journal, of course, but it looked like a reputable news source. She had no idea what to make of it. She had thought that chapter of her life was over. She had had a strange vision, sure, but nothing had come of it. She had found no convincing way to test her idea. And she had attended one of the best universities in the world, thanks to her mother, who would have been satisfied with nothing less. Perhaps she should just have a child.

While she was waiting to board the plane to Aberdeen, the last leg of her trip, she unpacked the red scarf Hiroshi had given her. The scarf his machine had knitted. There was something strange about it. Charlotte held it in both hands, closed her eyes, and tuned out the hubbub of voices and loudspeaker announcements in the boarding area that surrounded her like acoustic fog. She concentrated wholly on the scarf. She felt where the wool had come from. She had a fleeting impression of the shearer who had taken it from the sheep—an Australian, a tough, pious man who was in love with a girl from the wrong religion and felt torn in two. Then she saw a lightning image of the machinist in the woolen mill who had spun it into yarn, felt her worries about a rash she had developed in an intimate area, her fear it might have something to do with a man she had slept with. So far it was all as Charlotte would have expected. But there was nothing at all about how the scarf was actually made. A yawning void. It was as though the wool had simply knitted itself into a scarf on its own. It was the strangest article of clothing she had ever held in her hands.

It was strange to come home and not be met at the airport. She took a taxi, remembering even as she did so that she would have to be careful with money again; she had been happily able to forget all that during her trip. Having to think about such things once more was like running her tongue over her teeth and finding a gap. The taxi driver was friendly and in a chatty mood. He took her for a tourist and gave her a card with his cell-phone number.

"Day or night, just call and I'll be at your doorstep," he said. "There are too many dodgy blokes in this business. You book a cab in advance and then they never even get out of bed. Not what you need when there's a flight to catch, is it?"

Charlotte liked his go-getting attitude. She put the card in her bag. As they pulled up, she saw Gary's car parked in front of the house. She should have been pleased he was home, but for some reason she had a hollow feeling in the pit of her stomach. She still had to catch her breath after everything that had happened. Make sense of all that craziness in the South Pacific.

There was a smell of fresh grass and wood smoke in the air. It seemed to have rained that morning, with drops still glittering on the bushes and the fields. Charlotte took her suitcase and carried it up to the house. She opened the door. Gary was sitting at the kitchen table and looked up, startled. Opposite him sat a girl. Younger than Charlotte and rather plain: thin, with a sharp nose and brown curls all over the place. Charlotte put down her suitcase but couldn't say a word. It was clear what was going on here. Of course. But that wasn't what troubled her so. What troubled her was how relieved she suddenly felt.

Gary leapt to his feet. As he hurried over to where she stood, he seemed to take pains to stay between her and the girl. "Come outside with me for a moment," he said awkwardly. "There's something I have to explain."

Charlotte shook her head. What could possibly need explaining? But she followed him. And so they stood in front of the slumped, crooked house that had been their home. Gary, too, was standing crooked and slumped, nervously picking lichen out of the cracks in the wall, unable to say a word—a pitiful sight. Charlotte looked away. She didn't want to remember him like this.

"Go on then, say it. Who is she?"

Her name was Lilith, he finally confessed. Her father owned the auction house where Gary worked. One day she would inherit it—"And for goodness' sake, Charlotte, don't get the wrong idea, but at least it offers a bit of security. It's better than scraping by with odds and ends of work up here in a Scottish backwater. . . . And besides, I was sure you were never coming back," Gary concluded lamely. "Take a break, you said—you know how that always ends. I could see that someone like you wasn't going to waste her time explaining to someone like me . . ." He trailed off, as though he had run out of words. A last, lonely raindrop dripped from the eaves above and splashed on his head. He blinked but didn't say another word.

"And you just thought, why wait?" Charlotte looked at the man she had lived with for more than two years, the man she had loved, and knew it was over.

He said nothing. She hugged him. Startled, he let it happen, even clumsily tried to return the gesture.

"Look after one another," she said. "I'll let you know where to send my things as soon as I know myself."

Then she went and got her suitcase as the thin girl watched, alarm showing in her eyes. Back on the street, she took out her phone and the driver's card. She reached him as he was still on his way back to Aberdeen.

"That was quick," was all he said.

TRAVELS

Adamson wondered yet again how Rhonda coped with the twins every day. He was drenched in sweat from the mere attempt to comb Mia's hair. At least she wasn't delightedly decorating the bathroom with her mother's expensive shampoo like her sister, Jane, who was well on her way to dirtying the clean dress he had finally managed to put on her. The basic lesson of every management course he had ever taken was to concentrate on one task at a time. In a household with two four-year-old children, that was a joke.

"Stay still a moment," he ordered, lifting the brush in what he hoped look like a convincing threat.

"But it hurts!" Mia protested, looking at him with big eyes.

He put the brush back down. It was no good; these girls could twist him round their little fingers when they wanted to. Of course it hurt. The twins had their mother's hair, and she spent a good deal of time every morning cursing in front of the mirror. She needed more time just to keep her hair in order than he took for his whole morning routine.

"Jane," he scolded, "you leave that alone, that's Mummy's shampoo. She doesn't want you playing with it. Wash your hands now, there's a good girl."

Multitasking. Known and proven to be inefficient—any manager who boasted of using the technique only disqualified himself from any job that really mattered—but when dealing with children, it was the only possible strategy.

Rhonda stuck her head around the bathroom door. "Say, did you go see the doctor yesterday?" she asked. Gray-white spatters of some unappetizing-looking substance clung to her face and apron, doubtless part of the recipe she was trying out.

"Of course I did," he said. "By the way, you have something on your face there."

Rhonda rolled her eyes. "I have something all over. When I'm finished making this pie, we're going to have to rip out the whole kitchen and build a new one. So what did he say?"

"What would he say? Everything's okay. If I wanted to jump aboard a space flight tomorrow or take up deep-sea diving, I would have his full medical blessing."

She groaned piteously. "Is life even remotely fair? We women subject ourselves to sports and gyms and who knows what and try every diet that's going, and we just get more and more out of shape. You spend your whole day sitting on your butt, you eat like a lumberjack, and you're as fit as a fiddle."

"You're not out of shape," he objected. He'd learned in recent years what a husband ought to say at such moments.

"You're lying, Bill Adamson," she shot back, flattered.

He reached out a hand. "Come on, let's get that blob off your nose. It looks like bird crap."

"Bill! Don't use that language in front of the children." The fond smile switched to an angry glare. *Don't even try to understand women.*

"Bird excrement?" he suggested.

"You're impossible," she said. "I have to go blow up the kitchen." And with that she was out the door.

The two girls looked at their father, aghast. They looked lovely in their blue dresses. Lovely, except for the knots and tangles in their hair.

"What's Mummy doing now?" Mia asked. She was always the more nervous of the two.

"She's just trying out a new recipe," Adamson explained. "That's because it's Uncle Mitch's birthday today, and he's coming over to dinner. It just turns out to be a more difficult recipe than Mummy thought." And then inspiration struck. "But I bet if you two girls come here and let me brush your hair nicely, we might be able to stop the kitchen from exploding."

Mitch turned up twenty minutes late as always, nevertheless looking as though he had been in a hell of a hurry. Unlike his sister, who grew rounder with every passing year, the CIA analyst looked hungrier—and more watchful—as the years went by. He looked like a bird of prey, Adamson mused.

"So? What's new?" Adamson asked once they had all given Mitch his presents.

"No talking shop at my dinner table," Rhonda scolded.

So they waited until after dinner. Adamson went out on the deck to join his brother-in-law, who was smoking his after-dinner cigarette.

"You heard that Larry Gu died?" he asked.

Adamson nodded. "It made the news. Google Alerts helps me with stuff like that."

"Okay." Mitch leaned forward, propped his elbows on the balcony, and took a breath of the cool evening air. "So it looks like Beijing has nationalized his company. They don't call it that anymore—those guys ain't dumb. But it comes down to the same thing. State-run enterprise. In other words, it belongs to the party." He gave a humorless laugh. "Did you know that the Communist Party of China is the world's biggest capitalist? Nobody in the world has more money than those guys. All those state-owned corps—Gazprom, Saudi

Aramco . . . they're all huge. It defies belief. If they were actually traded on the exchanges, big bad capitalist giants like Google, Microsoft, Exxon, and so on would be small fry. That's something these goddamned pinkos should wise up to."

Adamson cleared his throat. It wouldn't be wise to get involved in such arguments, or they'd be out here all night. "Do we have any idea why they did that? Or was it just on principle?"

"Not at all. Most of the time they let Hong Kong corporations go their own way. Special Economic Zone—you know the drill. The Chinese are completely pragmatic about these things. No, from what we can tell, they're looking for something they suspect the company has hidden away." Mitch glanced at him mockingly. "A machine our friend developed."

"Well fancy that," Adamson said, unsurprised.

"Though we have no idea where the thing could be hiding either. We don't even know what kind of machine it was. They've made it damn hard for our agents. I've got to hand them that."

"And . . . is there any news of our friend?"

Mitch shook his head and peered out into the darkness of the garden. "It's all just business as usual. He's sitting in that house of his up in the mountains in California, making money hand over fist with nanotech inventions and donating it to wacko groups looking for aliens. Oh yeah, and recently he's been giving money to the Atlantis nuts, too." He took one last drag on his cigarette and then flung it out into the night. "And we still don't have permission to listen in on him. It makes me sick."

It was good to hear Brenda's voice. Even if it was just over the phone, it went a long way toward calming Charlotte's nerves.

"All in all it's great," she answered happily when Brenda asked how things were going in Mexico with her bunch of nuts. "The sun's shining, I get to speak Spanish again . . ."

"Aren't you holding that conference of yours in English?"

"Well yes, English is the official conference language. But I get out of the conference center when I can. As much as I can, in fact."

The conference center looked like a spaceship that had made an emergency landing in the Miguel Hidalgo suburb of Mexico City. Which made it a pretty good venue for a conference on alternative theories on prehistory. Most of the speakers were advancing some variation on the hypothesis that at some time before the dawn of history, mankind had been in touch with beings from the stars— some even posited the human race had been created by aliens.

Charlotte leaned against the balustrade in the gallery and watched the hustle and bustle in the hall below. Chairs and name plaques were being set up on the central stage where the big podium discussions took place in the afternoons. In the evenings the hall hosted concerts by offbeat, avant-garde bands. There was still more than an hour to go before the next scheduled event, but people were already sitting down in the auditorium and making sure they had their video cameras at the ready. Others were reading or deep in excitable conversation.

"How are things here?" Charlotte repeated Brenda's question. "We have a lot of papers on topics like 'Did the Neanderthals make contact with aliens?' or 'The search for Atlantis' and that sort of thing. But there are others as well; it's just those are the ones the journalists grab hold of for their headlines. There are some reputable scientists here as well, serious people." Wasn't she just trying to put a brave face on things, though? The prevailing atmosphere made it awfully difficult to hold on to the idea this was a scientific event—a venue for hypothesis, argument, and verification—rather than just a propaganda forum for half-baked ideas. She also had to admit that the Open Horizon Forum that was hosting the conference was not exactly an organization of intellectual firecrackers.

"Oh, it's fun," she went on doggedly. "And it's certainly thought-provoking. We'll all have a lot to talk about when we go home. Of course, any claims made here will need double-checking, but that's true anywhere these days, isn't it?"

"Charley," Brenda said indulgently, "it's fine if you're just having fun. Or doing something crazy. That's allowed, you know."

Charlotte felt a lump in her throat. Come what may, Brenda would always be on her side, unwaveringly so. She was a rock. A mainstay of Charlotte's life.

She swallowed and did her best not to sniffle as she asked, "And what's up with you? Is everybody doing well? Does Jason still have that cold?"

"He told me yesterday he would feel much better if he didn't have to get up so early every morning," Brenda chuckled. "It's still an ordeal to get him to go to school. But I'm actually calling about something else. Do you happen to remember Adrian? Adrian Cazar? He was at Jason's christening. The two of you chatted out on the deck. Climatologist."

A vague memory of a slim young man who looked a little like Johnny Depp. "Yes," Charlotte said. "I remember him."

"He asked me for your phone number. I thought I'd better check with you before I gave it to him."

Charlotte made a face. "Uh-huh. Why does he want it? You know I've sworn off men. I'm a nun now, chastely devoted to paleoanthropology."

Brenda laughed merrily. "Yeah, yeah. Until the next man comes along. That sounds pretty much like Tom's motto that the best way to stay trim is to eat nothing at all between meals. Anyway, Adrian wanted to talk shop. It's about some scientific project he's planning. He was keeping very quiet about the specifics, said he would have to tell you himself."

"I'm not sure. I have plenty to keep me busy with my own work, unscientific though it might be. I can't do everything."

"Oh come on, Charley. He's a serious guy. You should at least listen to what he has to say. You can always say no after that."

Charlotte sighed. "Well all right then. I'll do as you say. He can call me. But not until this conference is over. I can't concentrate on anything else until I've delivered my lecture."

"You'll do fine," Brenda said with infectious certainty. Oh Brenda. She would have loved to have more children, but that looked unlikely. After three miscarriages, there was little hope of a brother or sister for Jason.

After hanging up, Charlotte roamed around the conference center restlessly, wondering how she could fill the three hours that remained until her lecture. Not that there was any point being nervous. Nobody would come anyway. They had given her the worst possible slot—a time when anybody with any sense would be off looking for a bite to eat—in one of the most remote and least attractive rooms. She would consider herself lucky if she didn't end up standing in front of rows of empty chairs. Though there were moments when she hoped that was precisely what would happen. Like now, for instance.

After going back to Harvard, she had stopped caring about academic convention. She no longer bothered attending the seminars that struck her as nothing more than busywork. Why collect credits for their own sake? Instead, she had gotten transfer credits by taking a course in forensics and general criminology at a police academy. The professor had told her she had a gift for it and asked whether she would be interested in a career in forensics. No, she told him. Then she had set out to review all the material evidence that underlay current thinking on human prehistory. She was determined to take a personal look at the evidence wherever possible. It was an ambitious project but by no means impossible; after all, there were far more paleoanthropologists in the world than actual finds.

The core of her project was to apply forensic standards to the paleoanthropological evidence, to dissect the established arguments the way an attorney might pick them apart in court. For every single find, she planned to work out which of the accepted academic conclusions stood up to scrutiny and which could be blown apart as unfounded conjecture. She would cross-examine every last fragment of skull and hominid tooth, every scrap of bone and skeletal remains that had ever been excavated and cataloged as early human or hominid.

This was no way to make friends, of course. In the academic world a great deal of weight is attached to *who* says what, not just *what* they say. The unproven hypothesis of a renowned scholar carries much more clout than the provable claim of some nobody without a title, degree, or publication record. Many established researchers felt personally aggrieved by Charlotte's project. So far none of the prestigious scientific journals of record had accepted any of her articles.

Nonetheless, she had some startling revelations to make. She had, for instance, been able to examine the Broken Hill skull in the Natural History Museum in London. This was generally accepted to be a well-preserved fossil of *Homo rhodesiensis*, a transitional form between the common ancestor of Neanderthals and modern humans, *Homo heidelbergensis*, and early *Homo sapiens*. The skull was dated to sometime between 125 thousand and 300 thousand years ago and had a cranial capacity of 1,300 cubic centimeters, not far off the volume of the modern human brain.

But the most remarkable feature of the skull was the bullet hole.

The hole was on the right side of the skull, easily visible on most published photos. The classic interpretation was that holes such as these were made by large predators or caused by a fall. But if you examined the bones under a microscope—and if you had recently completed a course in basic forensics at the Boston Police Academy—then it looked a hell of a lot like a bullet entry wound.

From at least 130 thousand years ago.

Charlotte had been able to establish that the hole expanded on the inward side of the skull—typical of bullet entry wounds—and that even in its fossilized state the bone showed the characteristic network of fracture lines radiating out from the hole itself. Furthermore—and this was something the published photographs usually did not show—a large part of the skull was missing on the opposite side. This wasn't unusual for a skull find; since skulls are hollow and are often found buried in stone, it was almost inevitable that the bone would be further crushed at some point after death. But at several points along the edge of this larger hole, Charlotte had spotted marks that would make any criminologist swear on the stand that this skull had been broken open *from the inside*. For instance, by a projectile exiting at high speed, taking a mass of mangled brain tissue along with it. A gunshot wound, in other words.

It was impossible to publish such findings in a reputable academic journal. And this was just one of several dozen finds she had cast doubt upon in the last few years. Of course, she had used her own particular talent to help her examinations, but it had never served as a substitute for proof. At most, she used it to get pointers as to what she should be looking for next. But no matter what she found, no matter how carefully she framed her arguments, she couldn't get a foot in the door in the academic world. Which was why she had ended up at this conference, where she needed no more qualifications than "Charlotte Malroux, student of paleoanthropology at Harvard."

She stopped in front of a bulletin board showing the day's events. Perhaps she should go listen to another lecture. That would keep her mind occupied until her own session. She noticed that a Prof. Diego Fernando Andrade, from Ecuador, was giving a lecture that day. Charlotte had chatted with him briefly at the speakers' reception on the first evening. Prof. Andrade was a prim, fussy old gentleman who taught at the Pontifical Catholic University of Ecuador in Quito and was visibly taken aback by the more colorful side of the conference. He wasn't used to this sort of thing, he told her. He also told her what he would be lecturing on: a set of pre-Columbian ceramic artifacts that were held in the Museum of Quito and which had been a headache for historians for years. They were small figurines, each of which seemed to be wearing a space suit. The trouble was that these figures were at least twelve hundred years old and must have been made well before anyone on Earth had ever seen a space suit. Some of the sculptures were featured on the official program for the conference, and they did indeed look like designs taken from the latest science-fiction movie.

He told her the theory that the figurines were linked to folk legends considerably older than the artifacts themselves. He was most put out by the way his lecture had been announced. The casual reader got the misleading impression he would be advancing claims that mankind had not only been visited by aliens in the dim and distant past but also had been caught up in some kind of galactic war.

He sighed. "I can only hope nobody back home will ever see the program," he said. "My superiors would not approve in the least. We have all taken an oath to teach nothing that contradicts the Catholic faith."

Charlotte was still undecided as she went down the broad staircase to the main hall. What if Prof. Andrade turned out to be such a wonderful speaker that she ended up with an inferiority complex? That couldn't be ruled out; after all, the man had been through seminary, and the Jesuits were well-known for their public-speaking skills. Perhaps she'd do better just to sneak off to the cafeteria and nurse a large latte macchiato. Or maybe she should lock herself in the restroom.

Standing by the door to the lecture hall was a hideous plaster cast that had been in the entrance lobby up until now. Someone had moved it. It was a cast of a stele from Guatemala showing a weird fire-breathing monster that also seemed to be wearing a space suit. The audience was already beginning to stream into the hall, visibly excited about what they might learn. Charlotte had to stop for a moment and take a deep breath. Did she really want to do this? She looked at the label and read the inscription. "El Baúl Stele, copy of the original at Santa Lucía Cozumalhuapa, Guatemala, probably Mayan."

"So what do you think?" asked a voice next to her. "Did fire-breathing beasties wage war against mankind?"

Charlotte spun round. "Hiroshi!"

There he was. Standing there chatting to her as though it hadn't been six years since they'd last seen each other.

"Hello, Charlotte," he said. His eyes lit up. He looked good, really good. Lean, in a simple white linen suit with an achingly cool pair of sunglasses perched on his nose.

Charlotte shook her head in amazement. "That's just . . . I mean really, this is some surprise. What in the world are you doing here?"

He raised an eyebrow and rubbed the side of his nose with his thumb. "Just between you and me, I give this group a little money. So I thought I'd drop by and see what they do with it all."

"You sponsor this event?" She knew he had made money. Brenda had once saved a newspaper article about young inventors for her, part of which had been about Hiroshi Kato and the successful company he had founded in California.

He nodded briefly. "Yes. I do that kind of thing from time to time. I've also given some money to the Science Heritage Foundation, and before that I supported the Explorer Travel Trust."

It took Charlotte a moment to understand what he was saying: he didn't sponsor these organizations, he'd been sponsoring her! The ETT at Harvard had given her a grant for her first trips to examine the finds she wanted to look at. Once someone in the trust had read her reports, however, they declined any further grants on the grounds her work was not compatible with the basic principles of Harvard research. After that the Science Heritage Foundation had financed her research for a while, but then they had raised their own doubts about her academic conduct and cut her support.

Hiroshi smiled. Evidently, he could see that she had understood. "I'm also funding SETI," he added. "For Rodney's sake. I have to do something with all the money."

"You could come and listen to my lecture," Charlotte suggested. "That way at least I'd have one person in the audience."

"If you're okay with that," Hiroshi said. "In fact, it's the other reason I came."

After the lecture—which went much better than she had feared, drawing a bigger crowd than she'd expected, and leading to an interesting discussion—they just had time for a glass of wine in the cafeteria before Hiroshi caught his flight that evening.

"It was a good lecture," he said. "You should write a book on the subject."

"Oh Lord!" she groaned. "Everybody says that."

"I'm not surprised."

Write a book. Easier said than done. She had started to take a few notes and to rework her academic articles, given that the specialist journals hadn't taken much interest in them, but she still wasn't sure. She didn't want to make the same mistake she had had to point out in so many of her fellow researchers: she didn't want to jump to any conclusions without having considered all possible alternatives. She didn't want to follow the obvious implications blindly, and she felt the danger of doing so was much greater when writing a book, putting down her thoughts in black and white for all time. It was different in a lecture or a discussion, when she could tell by people's reactions whether she had made herself clear. It gave her the chance to rephrase things if need be. Even the chance to change her mind.

She looked down into her glass of disappointing white wine. "So you've been following what I've been doing all these years," she stated.

"From time to time," he said evasively.

"And you? What have you been up to?"

"I imagine you can probably guess."

She looked at him. Yes, she could quite easily guess. "You're still working on your project. You never give up."

He glanced around as though worried they might be overheard, then leaned toward her and said in a conspiratorial tone, "I'm just about to crack it. Just about to. It's merely a matter of decades."

"Decades!"

"Well, perhaps centuries."

She couldn't help but laugh. "Is it really as bad as all that?"

"It's like I'm a donkey with a carrot dangling in front of my nose." He lifted his hand and brought his finger and thumb close together, less than a quarter of an inch apart. "So close. Just beyond reach." He sighed and put his hand down. "It gets frustrating sometimes."

She took a sip of her wine and then put it down, determined to leave the rest undrunk. Sour wine they made hereabouts. "Whatever happened to the machine you made back then? The complex?"

He leaned back in his chair. "Well, that's an odd story. We struck camp and shipped everything off, but by the time the ship got back to Hong Kong the crate with the complex in it had vanished."

"Somebody stole it, then."

"That's the official version at least." He smiled ever so slightly. "Although some people claim in all seriousness that the complex still had a program running. Supposedly, it turned the crate into sawdust and then jumped into the sea . . ."

She grinned as well. "The things people say."

"Crazy, isn't it?" Then he turned serious again. "Anyway, it's just as well it went missing. Otherwise, the Chinese military might have found some way to weaponize it. It's always easier to build weapons than to make something constructive. Destruction is fundamentally easier after all."

"Besides," Charlotte added, "you wouldn't want anyone building on your research and possibly beating you to it."

She had clearly struck a nerve with that. "Merely a fortuitous side effect," he spluttered, then hastily changed the subject. "Listen, come visit me if you like. I can show you some of what I'm doing." He took a card from his pocket and passed it across to her. "Here, this is my address. It's outside of town, up in the mountains. Quite remote. But you can ask anyone in the area how to get there; they all know the house. It used to belong to a famous country singer they're still mighty proud of."

"And now you live in the famous house," Charlotte said. "All on your own."

He looked at her without expression. "Not quite. I live with a woman."

That gave her a pang. Of course, he had every right to . . . of course. She had always fended him off. She had done everything in her power to show him that he had no hope with her. Of course. All the same . . .

"Well that's nice," she said brightly, nodding and smiling, though her face had frozen into a mask. "I'm happy for you."

When Adrian Cazar called that evening, she agreed to meet him in Boston and seriously consider his proposal that she join him on an expedition to a Russian island in the Arctic Ocean.

It was true: Hiroshi Kato lived with a woman. Her name was Patricia Steel, she came from Kentucky, she was 53 years old, and she was his housekeeper. She lived in a cozy three-room apartment in an annex and shook her head every morning when she came to work at the estate itself. The house had six bathrooms and twenty-one rooms, some of them the size of ballrooms, all with floors of tropical hardwood polished till it was almost black and enormous windows offering breathtaking views over the Cascade Mountains. And almost all of the rooms were empty. There was a bedroom the size of a small gym hall where the only item of furniture was a futon in the middle of the floor with a snow-white cover over it.

In one of the biggest halls, down a few steps from the rest of the house, a large basket chair stood on its own. Standing there on the dark, polished floor, it looked like an island in a sea of dark water. Patricia Steel's eccentric employer would sometimes spend whole days at a time sitting there, motionless, sunk in strange seas of thought, staring out over the mountain peaks and valleys beyond the windows. She was not permitted to speak to him on those days. All she was allowed to do was bring him food and drink on a tray that she put down beside him on the floor. Often, though, it was still there the next day, untouched.

The study was not quite so empty. Five long conference tables were laid out in a huge U shape with a total of twenty-one computers lined up on them, working day and night. They made a noise like a squadron of helicopters approaching from somewhere over the horizon. Patricia Steel was not even allowed to vacuum in there (that was done instead by a little robot that looked like a large drop of mercury when there was nobody in the room) and never even went into the study anymore. Nor did Patricia Steel know there was a fully equipped laboratory in the basement. The only way in was through a secret door with a high-security dial lock, and the lab had not a single window.

Hiroshi Kato spent several days after his return from Mexico sitting in the chair. He looked out over the valley that had inspired the singer to write love songs people still sang today, but for once he was not pondering some deep problem of nanotechnology. He was pondering his own nature and motives. Why had he said that? Why had he let Charlotte think he had somebody? She was unattached at the moment, he knew that. And she had clearly been pleased to see him. She had been relaxed around him, no question. He thought of how they had strolled through the exhibition of curiosities and anomalies to fill the time until she was due to speak. Charlotte had been worrying over her lecture, so at first they simply reminisced, but she had gradually unwound and become more confident, more self-assured.

She had obviously enjoyed those hours together. It would have been the perfect opportunity to let one thing lead to another, to give them another chance. Instead, he had made a mess of it all. And not even by his own stupidity—he had done it deliberately. Why? Did he still feel she was too good for him? That was nonsense. By now he was richer than her parents had ever been, and he had done it all on his own. And there was nobody around now who could tell them what not to do.

Well, it might not have worked out. Relationships were no simple matter, and he certainly didn't have much of a track record himself. But a chance—it would have been a chance. . . . He hadn't wanted to take it. That was why. He was so close to solving his riddle, so close to building his universal machine for real that he couldn't allow any distractions. And a love affair would have been a distraction, no matter how it worked out—what a distraction. Love was always an adventure leading who knew where; he saw that all around him. He had spent so many years concentrating all his powers to one purpose alone that he was ready to sacrifice everything he had for his fated task, his one and only goal. Even in the best case, a love affair would have irreparably shattered his concentration, scattered his focus, and could easily stop him from making the decisive breakthrough. And he couldn't risk that. Never before had one man been so close to changing the world for the better, so close to rewriting destiny, and never before had the world been in such urgent need of change. All modesty aside, it was the truth. He owed it to himself not to make a mess of this. And if loneliness was the price he had to pay, then he would have to take that burden upon himself.

What he had told her about decades or centuries hadn't been true. Nobody could say how long it would take. All he needed was the right idea, and that could come tomorrow. It could even be that all he needed was a dream.

Besides, Charlotte had rebuffed him so many times. It would do her no harm to learn what it felt like just once.

"You should really think about patenting what you have so far," said Rasmussen.

"I don't have anything. Just a couple of pictures on a computer screen."

"You have working replication algorithms." Rasmussen pointed out the window. "There are an awful lot of clever people out here working on the very same thing. A self-replicating nanomachine is the holy grail of nanotechnology. Do you have any notion how many patents are submitted every single day? Every new theory, every tiny incremental improvement—it all gets patented. You have no idea how they're competing for claims out there; it's a cutthroat business. And if someone manages to make that final breakthrough before you get your application into the patent office, then you'll be left in the dust, Hiroshi. You'll have to pay someone else for the right to use your own invention."

Hiroshi leaned back and put on what Rasmussen privately thought of as his Japanese face. "They're not working on the same thing as I am," he declared. "Not remotely. I admit that I don't know what goes on in the patent office, but I believe I'm more or less up to date on the theoretical work and the projects that are underway. And I don't see anyone who has successfully moved away from the biological metaphor. Everybody's tinkering around trying to build these insanely complicated nanomachines that are supposed to work like living beings. And they're all wondering what keeps going wrong. Or they're just using genetically manipulated bacteria, and all that tells me is they'll never get any further than the compounds of carbon and protein structures."

"Don't underestimate these people. It could be just as you say, but that doesn't mean that nobody will ever have the same idea as you. Quite the opposite, in fact. It could happen any day now. Any one of these researchers might suddenly decide to give up on self-replicating mechanisms and try a self-replicating complex instead."

"So what? What good will it do him? He'll end up stuck down the same dead end that I'm in."

Rasmussen sighed. Hiroshi didn't seem to want to listen. "That doesn't matter. He'll patent the idea, and that means that whatever it may actually lead to belongs to him. On top of which, it'll be published, and it'll get noticed. All the big brains in the business will be all over it—people like Binnig, Drexler, Merkle, the guys who invented nanotechnology. And I don't want to step on your toes here, but when there are a whole lot of smart guys all working intensively on the problem, someone may very well solve your problem with the bonding angles." He clasped his hands together. "You can make all of this work for you if you just patent what you have."

"You don't understand," Hiroshi said. "I'm not interested in patents. Not for this." He leaned forward and put his hand on the screen. "If this actually works, Jens, then I'll create a whole new world. A world in which patents play no part. And if it doesn't work, if I can't do it . . . then I don't need a patent either."

Charlotte sat in the kitchen and listened with half an ear as Brenda and her son argued.

"Homework first," Brenda said for probably the thousandth time since Jason had started school. "That's the rule. You know very well."

"But I said I'd go out with George!" Jason whined.

"Good. Then if I were you, I would hurry up and do the homework."

"I can do it tonight, Mom, just this once. There's not even that much."

This constant bickering about schoolwork. Sometimes it got on Charlotte's nerves. But she was sure she would miss it.

"There's no such thing as 'just this once,'" Brenda said implacably. "Not while your grades are where they are. We talked about all this, remember?"

"But George is gonna be here soon!"

"No problem. I'll give him a slice of cake, and he can make himself comfortable in front of the TV."

"Oh man!" Surrender, followed by angry footsteps storming up the stairs.

Brenda came back, rolling her eyes. "I'm curious as to what will happen next year," she said as she picked up her coffee cup and sat down opposite Charlotte, "when he has to do all his homework in Spanish. Ah well, you never know your luck until you miss it, as they say."

Charlotte was shocked to realize that by the time she came back from her expedition they would have moved. That this was the last time she would sit in this kitchen, the last time she would visit them in this house, which they had turned into such a cozy, friendly home and safe haven for her in the storms of her life. She had thought that it would always be there. She was almost in tears.

"Have you really thought about this?" she asked one more time. "Buenos Aires. It's not going to be easy for either of you. And as for Jason. He's only just got used to going to school at all."

"I just think we're too young to settle down here contentedly for the rest of our natural days," Brenda declared. "And it's Tom's big chance. Not just a teaching post—a whole department! And one that is practically uncharted territory. He would never get that anywhere else. So we're packing our bags. I'm used to moving around, remember?"

"I'll miss this house. I'll miss all of you."

"That's why they invented airplanes, Charley. You make sure you come and see us."

Charlotte nodded glumly. When Brenda was gone, what was there to keep her in Boston? Nothing. She wasn't welcome at Harvard, and she had lost touch with most of her friends here during the years with Gary.

"Anyway, once we're gone my mother will look after your apartment, so don't you worry about that. And by the way, Tom asked me to thank you for that tip about getting in touch with Prof. Andrade. They spoke on the phone, and he seems to be a charming man. Tom said he was so happy to have someone other than the flying-saucer nuts interested in his ceramics that . . . oh, here's George!"

George was a gangly black boy with beautiful, almost grown-up manners—he called Brenda "Miss Wickersham" when he asked politely after Jason. Brenda told him her son was still doing his homework and asked whether George might like a slice of cake.

"Oh yeah!" he said, his eyes lighting up.

"Have you done your homework?" Brenda asked as she took the cake out of the pantry.

"Ages ago," George said, waving his hand dismissively. "It was easy today."

Charlotte snuck a look at the boy as he sat there devouring the cake with every sign of enjoyment, and swapped glances with Brenda, who was smiling broadly. No doubt she would shortly be feeding her English fruitcake to little Argentinean children. Lucky them.

"A machine that will make everybody rich?" James Bennett III tried to blow a smoke ring. He failed miserably. "That's the craziest thing I've ever heard."

Nancy Coldwell snuggled up on his chest and put her leg across his thigh. "I thought so, too, at first. But Jeffrey said it's not so crazy. He said if it works, it'll change the world more than fire, printing, and the Internet all put together." She began to play with his nipples. "And you can say a lot of things about Jeffrey, but you can't say he's easily fooled."

One of those psychologists should do a study on this, James reflected. *Why women always start yammering on about their ex-husbands once you've gotten them into bed.* He must have made one hell of an impression on her, this Jeffrey, what with tangling with the Chinese mafia when he was starting out and being charged with incitement to murder all those times. And how, despite all that, he had become director for the Americas for a worldwide corporation based in Hong Kong.

James stubbed out his cigarette and put the ashtray over on the nightstand. He rolled out from under her to see whether there was another whiskey in the minibar. No such luck. Nothing even remotely acceptable in alcohol content. And he could have damn well used a whiskey right then. Nancy wriggled over to join him, pressing her large breasts against his back, and reaching a hand between his thighs. In other words, she wanted another round. Or, more likely, she was just playing the sex maniac to make him marry her sooner. Not that James Bennett III would ever have dreamed of doing such a thing. The great advantage of his current situation—possibly the only advantage—was he could counter any such suggestions with the argument he was still getting over his divorce. But she could still have another round.

After that he must have fallen asleep, since it was much darker outside when he finally woke up. He had been dreaming about that machine, even if he no longer remembered what his dreams had told him.

"Did your Jeffrey ever explain how this machine is supposed to work, how exactly it will make everybody rich?" he asked Nancy, who was finally beginning to look worn-out.

She looked at him with smoldering bedroom eyes. "Yes, he did."

"And?"

"Imagine a universal machine that can build anything that can be built. Logically, that means it can also build another universal machine. So there's two of them. Then they both build another universal machine and there are four—and so on and so forth. Eventually, you have enough universal machines to build anything that people need. Nobody ever needs to work again."

James frowned in thought. He felt just as tired as she looked. "A universal machine? There's no such thing."

"Oh but there is. The computer is one, for instance. Only works on data, though. This machine is just the next step. That's how Jeff explained it to me."

"Aha." He would have liked to ask her whether *she* was easily fooled. Better not, though. They had run into each other at a private viewing of an exhibition where he had given the opening speech in place of his father, who couldn't make it, and she had practically flung herself at him. Since she had everything a woman should have and some to spare, he had decided, well, why not? The affair had been going on for a few weeks and was still fun—and he didn't want the fun to end.

Nancy stretched and yawned and gazed pensively into space. "If only I could remember the inventor's name. Jeff told me, but it was something Japanese. . . . What were those cities called where we dropped the bombs? Something along those lines."

James felt the hairs on the back of his neck stand up on end. *Hiroshi, as in Nagasaki.* "Was the name Hiroshi Kato, by any chance?"

"That was it!" She looked at him with real admiration. "How do you know that?"

James slumped back into bed, feeling as though he had been sandbagged. Hiroshi Kato. The Jap who had taken Charlotte from him, turned her against him; the man who was to blame for the misery into which his otherwise wonderful life had sunk. For some reason, the name set alarm bells ringing, making him think—no, fear—there might be something to it after all. The name raised his hackles, all right.

What would be the point of having everybody be rich? The whole fun being rich was that some people, just a few, were richer than everybody else—and that he was one of them. If everybody was rich, then nobody would be rich. If everybody was rich, then nobody would wait hand and foot upon him, James Bennett III. Nobody would serve him coffee, make his bed, cook his meals, do his laundry, and all of that. And even if robots were going to do all that work, what woman would ever be interested in him again if he didn't have his wealth to make him interesting?

"I knew someone by that name once," he murmured, since Nancy was lying across him and waiting for an answer. "But that's got to just be a coincidence."

All at once he was in a hurry to wrap up this date. When they were finally standing down in the lobby and he took out his gold MasterCard to pay for the room, for the first time in his life he was afraid that the day would come when he would no longer be able to lord it over everybody else. If such an invention really existed, if there really was a universal machine, then he had to do whatever he could to get his hands on it.

Visibly troubled that the guests were checking out when they had only just checked in that afternoon, the young man at the counter asked whether everything had been all right. They had paid for a night after all.

"Yeah, yeah," James grumbled. "Some business has come up though. Urgent. Always the same."

"When will I see you again?" Nancy Coldwell asked, pouting and looking at him with lovey-dovey eyes as they left the hotel. She was in love with him, all right—him and his money.

"I'll call you," he said and put her in a taxi.

He wondered how he could get his father interested in this business. But he didn't spend long thinking about it; there was no point. Of all the CEOs on the planet, his father was the least likely to grab an invention like that and make it the biggest money spinner in history. All James had to do was remember all those philanthropic, tree-hugging, save-the-planet organizations his dad supported—mostly in ways the general public never even got to hear of—to know his father would much rather release the machine as a "gift to humanity." Dad would probably give him that lecture again about all the inventions Benjamin Franklin had deliberately never patented.

No. He wouldn't breathe a word about it to his father. He would wait patiently until his time had come.

Hiroshi saw her coming. At first, of course, he had no idea it was Charlotte at the wheel of the red SUV that came roaring up the hairpin bends. For some reason, he had felt the urge to go roaming through the empty rooms in the towers at the top of his house, which gave a quite different view of the mountains all around. He had stopped in front of the window that faced out front. That's when he noticed the car and saw the breakneck speed it was doing up the curves.

The roads hereabouts were ancient, never designed for speeds like that. Hiroshi held his breath as the car sped around the bend with the six-hundred-foot drop below and wondered whom he should call if it went off the road. Whether there would even be any point in trying to help. Then the car pulled up in his front driveway, and Charlotte got out. Well how about that? Hiroshi watched her talking to Mrs. Steel, no doubt explaining who she was and what she wanted, and he watched his housekeeper admit the guest. He ran his fingers through his hair and went downstairs. She was happy to see him there, but there was a curious gleam in her eyes as she said hello.

When he took her by the arm to give her a tour of the house, she whispered, "Why didn't you tell me the woman you live with is your housekeeper?"

"I didn't feel like it," Hiroshi confessed. "Up until then you had always been the one who was with somebody whenever we met, and I thought it was about time to turn the tables."

"You're an idiot," she declared.

He said nothing. She was probably right.

"Do you actually have any furniture?" she asked once they had walked through the second empty room.

"That's a closet over there," Hiroshi declared, pointing at a wall that looked no different from the rest of the paneling.

She raised her eyebrows. "How could I possibly have overlooked that?"

"I'm not so keen on furniture."

"Well, it's kind of stylish. But it just looks a little empty. You don't have much stuff, do you?"

"Only what I really need."

"But you didn't need such a big house."

"There are other reasons for that."

He wondered whether he should show her the lab. The main reason he bought the house, apart from its remote location, was the basement rooms. It had once housed a private sound studio that was not just soundproofed but cut off from the outside world in every other way as well. The country singer had spent his life expecting the onset of nuclear war; the first time Hiroshi had toured the house, he had found two years' worth of canned food and army rations in a spare room. The supplies were all still there, though most of them were probably inedible by now.

Hiroshi had ordered several million dollars' worth of equipment for the basement and had imagined he would be able to use it all to gradually realize his project—on his own this time. He hadn't imagined he would run into such fundamental problems, though. Now the lab stood mostly unused; he hadn't been down there for almost a year. He'd show it to Charlotte some other time, he decided.

"No sofa," she remarked as they walked into his thinking room, the one with the basket chair. "You don't seem to have many visitors."

"True. Rodney's been here, but otherwise . . . well. Jens stops in from time to time to see if I have anything he can sell." Noticing the name meant nothing to her, he added, "Jens Rasmussen. You met him back in Hong Kong. The thin, bald guy."

She nodded. "You do have a bedroom, though, don't you? Or do you work around the clock these days?"

It was a moment almost like back in Boston in the fog. Hiroshi looked at her and wondered whether she had come here intending to sleep with him or whether she was just considering the idea now.

"No, I have a bedroom. Do you want to see it?"

"For completeness' sake."

He led her there. Even after all this time, he was very pleased with the room he had chosen. The window gave onto a thick tangle of pines right next to the house, a stand of trees that was almost intimate, where a spring burst out of the rock. When he woke up in the morning, the sunlight sometimes caught the stream and glittered as though a ghost were bathing there. The slender, sunlight-dappled trees were like a living tapestry, never the same from one day to the next.

"You even have a bed. I'm reassured." Charlotte had stopped in the doorway. She looked around, and though she wasn't actually shaking her head, she looked as though she was thinking about it. "You're a strange fellow, Hiroshi Kato."

"I concentrate on the essentials."

"And that's your work. Which is bizarre, really, given that you actually want to abolish work. What will you do with your life once that happens?"

Hiroshi had sometimes wondered that himself. He felt he was exerting all his powers to the utmost, stretching himself to the very limits. And that one day he would have to pay the price. Perhaps he would end up like Moses, who was said to have led his people to the Promised Land, though he never actually set foot there himself. Idle thoughts.

"There's not much chance I'll ever have to worry about that," he answered. "Come on, I'll show you my study. You'll like it—it's crammed full of stuff. And I have two chairs there."

"Hey, two chairs. Big spender."

"Keep your cool when we have lunch in the dining room," Hiroshi said, shutting the bedroom door. "There's even six chairs around the table in there."

"Good thing you warned me."

Why had she actually come? Not to poke fun at him, surely? He asked her.

"I felt like it, if you can believe that," she said.

But that wasn't the real reason, he knew. Just as she knew as well that the answer wasn't enough.

"I've agreed to go on an expedition that will last three months, and . . . well, I thought I'd come and see you before I set out."

She didn't seem to want to talk about this expedition. From the sound of it, it wasn't just another trip to see early hominid fossils in some research lab or museum.

Hiroshi wasn't quite sure what he should say to that. Since they had just then reached the study door, he simply opened it wide and said, "Well. This is it."

She stood in the doorway and heaved a deep sigh. "Aha. It's almost . . . cozy." She had to laugh then, and she passed her hands over her face as though she needed to rub her eyes. "To tell you the truth, it looks a bit like a high-end computer store."

Hiroshi walked in. "These are no ordinary off-the-shelf computers," he explained. "They're high-performance UNIX workstations with parallel processors—what they call supercomputers. If you want more computing power than I have here in this room, you would have to go to NASA or IBM or the labs where they simulate nuclear explosions." That was only a bit of an exaggeration. He was really rather proud of what he had achieved here with relatively modest expenditure. And in a much more appealing setting than those boring computer clusters in their stark, air-conditioned halls.

Charlotte followed him; it seemed she had to make an effort to cross the threshold of this room. The motion detector kicked in, and the computer screens came to life one after another, showing the simulations that were running right now. She stood between the monitors and folded her arms. She looked at the images as though she were in an art gallery.

"What are these pictures?" she asked at last. "They look like molecules or something. Huge molecules."

"That's what they are," said Hiroshi.

She turned around indignantly. "I thought you were working on robots?"

"Those are robots."

"You just said yourself that they're molecules."

He pulled up a chair for her. "Sit down. This will take a while."

She sat down obediently, crossed her arms, and glanced back and forth from him to the screens. He sat down across from her. He wasn't sure he could explain all this in such a way that anyone else could understand. He hadn't expected Charlotte to actually visit, and now she was really here, as beautiful as ever, if not more so. He was at least as irritated as he was pleased. The whole thing was very complicated.

"The problem with those robots back on Paliuk," he began, "was that the replication wasn't exact enough. The first-generation units were copies of the originals, sure, but only to within a certain percentage tolerance. They were just a little bit imprecise. That meant that the second-generation units were even less precise, and all of those small errors added up over time. It was inevitable that at some point they'd make a unit that couldn't dock with the others, that had a groove that was too wide or too narrow, that couldn't clasp hold correctly—whatever it may have been. A unit sufficiently imprecise that the whole complex couldn't work together any longer."

Charlotte nodded. "I remember. We could see that on the video footage at the time."

"Exactly." That was right. She had still been there to see it. He remembered now. "The cause of all that was the manufacturing process. You saw how the units worked. For instance, how they dug molds, cast the parts, and then finished them the way you always have to with casting work. But they could only work with limited precision—for technical reasons. If I had wanted them to work with greater precision, then I would have had to build larger, more complicated units. That in turn would have meant making more new parts for every step of the replication and making them more precisely, and that would have been more complicated in turn . . . well, so on and so forth. We would have been running in place. The geometrical progression could have just stretched onward to infinity."

Charlotte looked skeptical. Perhaps she was regretting she'd even come. "It does sound as though it would fundamentally never work."

"Yes, that was my fear for a while. But then I thought of another way to approach it. A way that doesn't just avoid the whole problem of imprecision from the get-go, but even opens up a whole new array of possibilities."

"And what's that?"

"Building the new units not piece by piece, but atom by atom."

Her eyes widened. "Nanotechnology."

"Yes, that's the popular term, though it's a broad field encompassing very diverse technologies and implementations. What they mostly have in common is they work on the nanometer scale. The laws of nature are different down there; they're not what we're used to in daily life."

Charlotte frowned in thought. He could see she was pondering the matter. Clearly she knew the concept—well, no surprise there. Who didn't these days? Nanotechnology had been hyped up for years now. He had made good money off the trend himself with a couple of inventions spun off from his main research. There was hardly a car manufacturer these days who didn't offer supposedly scratchproof and self-cleaning nano-paints so that you never needed to visit the car wash again. For a while, nano-coated toilet bowls had been the latest thing. They would never need cleaning, or so it was claimed, since nothing—not dirt, not bacteria—could cling to the nanotech surface on the inside. Hiroshi had analyzed the coating and had known straightaway what would actually happen. The coating inexorably broke down over time—through quite normal external influences, such as oxidation and exposure to ultraviolet light—so that the dirt actually clung all the more tightly and could hardly be removed at all. Since that had become public knowledge, everyone had stopped buying nano-coated toilets.

"Isn't that using a sledgehammer to crack a nut?" Charlotte asked. "I mean—hello? Atom by atom? How long does that take? Is that even possible?"

"Perfectly possible. Otherwise, we'd hardly be sitting here. Nature's been doing it for billions of years. There are any number of processes running inside a cell that work by manipulating individual atoms. DNA is a highly efficient data-storage medium. It saves information by arranging individual molecules in a particular order. Protein synthesis is a nanotech process. And so on. There's no question it's possible."

"Okay, but those are cells. Which brings us back to biology, though. You never wanted to go there."

"Nor do I now."

Charlotte was still frowning in thought, her brow furrowed. She looked around the room at the computers on the table.

"All right then, as far as I know the things we use in everyday life are made up of quite a lot of atoms. Is that why you have so little furniture? Because you have to build it all atom by atom, and it takes a hundred thousand years to make a couch?" She laughed. "I'm sorry I keep coming back to the subject, but you should really get a couch."

Hiroshi had to laugh as well. "No, that's not the reason. And it wouldn't take that long if you went about it the right way."

"It takes nine months to make a child. And they're fairly small."

"True. But in living organisms, processes never run as fast as actually possible. Nowhere near. It's rather like the information-processing capacity of the brain: the impulses only travel at about a hundred meters per second, tops. Computers can run much faster, since their impulses travel at the speed of light."

"Nature's in no hurry, then."

"Why would she be? She has literally all the time in the world."

"Okay." Charlotte looked at him appraisingly. "So assuming we went about it the right way and worked as fast as actually possible—how long would it take to build a couch?"

Hiroshi thought for a moment, making a rough estimate of the number of atoms and the steps needed in that sort of replication. "Maybe a second."

"A *second*?"

"Under optimal conditions," Hiroshi put in. "The limiting factor is not the number of atoms we have to move, but the volume we have to work with. If we assume that it would take one half-second to produce a steel cube that measures one centimeter on each side, then it would hardly take any longer to coat the floor of an entire corridor with steel plating one centimeter thick, since the units can work everywhere at once."

"Wow!" Charlotte said. "That's fast."

Hiroshi thought of something. "One moment," he said, jumping to his feet and hurrying to the kitchen. There, he found Mrs. Steel already busy making lunch, dicing zucchini, tomatoes, and onions with rapid strokes of the knife.

"Aren't you going to offer the lady anything?" she scolded him. "I'd have done it myself, but I never go into the study, as you know."

"That's why I'm here. What do we have?"

Hiroshi had long given up thinking about what to eat. Early on he had occasionally asked for a particular dish, for a hamburger or some such thing, whereupon she would launch into an indignant lecture about how unhealthy that sort of food was. Someone like him who spent the whole time buried in his work and took so little exercise couldn't take chances on anything but the healthiest possible diet, she told him. Lots of organically grown vegetables, no sugar or white flour. In the end, Hiroshi had given her a free hand in choosing the food and cooking the meals, and ate whatever she put in front of him without protest. It hadn't done him any harm—so far at least.

Mrs. Steel opened the refrigerator. "I can press you some fresh fruit juice or make tea. Whatever you like."

"How about water?" From what he could remember, Charlotte didn't care for juice and liked tea even less. And there was no point at all in asking Mrs. Steel for soda.

The housekeeper pursed her lips, took a small green bottle from a drawer, and handed it to him. "How about this? Natural spring water from Lavish Valley."

This was crazy, thought Hiroshi. Here they were with their own spring on the estate, and they were buying bottled water that had to be trucked in hundreds of miles.

"Okay," he said.

"Wait." Mrs. Steel took a tray and placed two bottles, two glasses, and a bowl of fruit on it. "Do you want to take that with you, or shall I bring it?"

"I'll take it. You look after lunch." Hiroshi picked up the tray. The fruit bowl was heavy. "What's it going to be?"

"Healthy, that's what it's going to be," Mrs. Steel said. She shrugged. "It doesn't have a name. I'm just using what we have on hand. It has to be enough for one more today, that's all."

"Don't we have enough?"

"I make sure that everything's fresh and that as little as possible goes to waste," she informed him in a tone of voice that said, *And now get out of my kitchen.*

Charlotte started in on the grapes with gusto. "To be honest, I still don't understand what you're doing with your time," she said. She spat out a couple of seeds and then pointed around at the computers. "With all this."

"I'm simulating nanomachines," Hiroshi said.

"Why just simulate them? Why not build them?" She bit into another grape.

Hiroshi's eye twitched and he rubbed at it. "It's something of a chicken-and-egg problem," he admitted, wondering how on earth he could explain it best.

"Chicken and egg?" Charlotte repeated, nibbling. "I don't understand."

"I started with simulations because you can do everything with those—no risk, no trouble, no big investments. I had to write my own programs, of course, but that's not difficult."

"Okay, but where does it get you? What can you do if you can do everything? What do you actually get apart from pretty pictures?"

"Diagrams," Hiroshi said. "Think of it as a drawing board for sketching microscopically small machines." He turned to one of the monitors, where a new unit of some twenty million atoms was just taking shape. Every atom was represented by a tiny sphere, its color indicating which chemical element it was. "What you have to bear in mind is that atoms aren't really little balls like you see here. Atoms are actually incredibly complicated things, almost inconceivably so. The paradox is that although atoms are supposed to be the smallest building blocks of matter, for the most part they actually consist of nothing but empty space and electrical fields. And every kind of atom is different. Every chemical element has properties that none of the others have. They have different valences; they form different bonds with other atoms; they act upon one another at different distances—all of that. You can't just swap them out for one another like swapping a red Lego block for a blue one. An atom of copper behaves quite differently from an atom of iron; a phosphorous atom is different from an oxygen atom. . . . Every atom has its own geometry when you use it in a construction." He smiled. "It would be an interesting question to ask—why are there so many different chemical elements anyway? I sometimes think that perhaps that's how many Lego blocks you need to build a universe."

"And you've written all this into your program? It knows exactly how the various atoms behave?"

"Quite. And I use it to test out variants. I've been using it for years now." He held his hands up in front of him and curved the fingers inward to make a hollow globe. "Imagine that my system is like one of those Russian dolls where one doll fits inside the next. Right in the middle is the program representing the atoms, which calculates how they interact and group themselves if you place them in certain positions. Then, nested around that is a program that constantly shifts these positions and sometimes swaps elements, dropping in an iron for a carbon, or a sodium for a lithium, and so on." He held his hands a little farther apart. "Then, one level further up there's a program working to try out all the various strategies. Which changes are most effective? Is it better to take one small step at a time, or to swap out half of the atoms every now and again, or to shift them all to entirely different positions? Then, the highest level is a control program that looks at each molecule produced and decides what it might be good for. Whether it's a useful building block. Then, it reports down to the lower levels whether there's been an improvement, in which case they carry on with what they've been doing, or not, in which case they go back to the previous version. And on and on it goes. It's a sort of synthetic evolution." He lowered his hands. "Though the basic principle is still the same as it was on Paliuk. I'm basically building the same machines I had back then—positioners, transporters, prospectors, cutters, and so on. Just millions of times smaller."

"But you don't know exactly how to build them."

"Ah but I do," Hiroshi declared. Now they were getting to the heart of the matter. "I know just how to do it."

"Then why not build them?"

"Because I would need one of these machines in the first place in order to build others."

She opened her eyes wide and then laughed out loud. "That's a pretty pickle!"

Hiroshi spun his chair around and reached for the keyboard of the computer he mainly worked at. This was where he fed software to all the other machines. "Pay attention now; I'll explain everything. When we're working at the level of direct manipulation of atoms—which they call nano-assembly, by the way—there are three main problems. You've already spotted the first one: the numbers problem. It's not much use if all we can do is move one atom at a time. We've been able to do that for a while with scanning tunneling microscopes, or with AFM. But to build something that we could even see, we would need to move trillions of atoms, and then it matters enormously whether you can move ten or a thousand or a billion of them at once, since that means it could be one second or one year—or one hundred thousand years—until the thing's ready."

"The couch, for instance," Charlotte teased.

"For instance."

"And the other two problems?"

"The other two problems," Hiroshi declared, "are known as the 'fat-fingers problem' and the 'sticky-fingers problem.'"

"You guys invent fun names for things at least," Charlotte declared and set about finishing all the rest of the grapes. "If nothing else."

"The fat-fingers problem is this—that you have to be able to bring an atom into position somehow. To do that you need a manipulator arm, which obviously has to be made on the atomic scale itself. Then you have to put a second atom next to the first so that the two of them can bond. So you need another manipulator arm—"

"And sooner or later the arms are going to get in each other's way," Charlotte concluded.

"Exactly. Even if you can avoid that with some nifty bits of construction—and I find that I can—there's still the question of why the atom you've been carting around might even want to leave the end of the manipulator arm. It's held in place by atomic bonds, and there is a whole array of those that might be in play at any one time—covalent bonding, ionic bonding, metallic bonding, the Van der Waals forces, dipole interactions, hydrogen bridging, and so on. So, it's not enough to be able to move an atom where you want it; you also have to make the manipulator arm let go of it. That's the sticky-finger problem."

"Which you have also solved," she guessed.

"To an extent," Hiroshi said.

"That doesn't sound too convincing."

He turned to the computer. "I'll show you where it all goes wrong." He pulled up the image he'd studied more often than any of the rest, the image he knew by heart; the one that he had stared at until he felt drops of blood must be bursting from his forehead. "Here it is. I call it the impossible molecule."

He looked at the creation. Consisting of barely more than twenty thousand atoms, it was tiny by nanotech standards. It was shaped vaguely like a lancet, narrowing at one end. It didn't narrow to a tip with only a single atom at the end, though, as one might expect, but rather into a complex intertwining geometry of various different atoms. A tube ran through the whole length of the structure so that atoms could be fed down toward the tip, and halfway down, the whole thing was pinched at the waist like a sandglass by the electric forces at work. It was beautiful. There was no other way to say it. Even if it was his nightmare, his greatest riddle, his unyielding enigma, it was beautiful.

"This is the only structure I've found so far that solves all three problems of nanotechnology," he said. "The only finger that really works. This molecule can position atoms without getting in the way of other manipulator arms, it can pick up and let go, and just to sweeten the deal, it has an astonishing throughput capacity. The only problem is that there's no way to build it with the currently available means. There are a whole bunch of atoms in there that have to be in positions they would never take up on their own, bonding at angles that they couldn't actually form." He spun the image around and pointed at the screen. "Here, for example. This group of aluminum atoms—impossible in that position. Or this area toward the back, the nest of carbon, hydrogen, and silicon atoms—can't be done. But if you leave it out, the finger doesn't work."

"That means either you have to find some totally different concept, or perhaps what you are trying to do can't be done."

"It's even more complicated than that," Hiroshi confessed. "The big joke is that we could build this molecule if we already had it to work with. If we could manage to place all these atoms in what are actually impossible positions, then they would stay there. Look at this," he said and started an animation he had written. A construction unit popped up on-screen and the animation started. Transporters brought atoms, holding them with the fingers and passed them to construction units that took hold of them with manipulator arms that similarly ended in fingers, which brought them to the assembly site and placed them in position. The units rippled and flowed gracefully as they moved, like the legs of a millipede.

"It really looks like your complex from back on the island," Charlotte said after watching for a while and seeing how the fingers built a duplicate of themselves. "By the way, I still have the scarf your machine knitted me."

Hiroshi had to smile. What a thing to think of right now.

When the animation was over and the finished finger was clearly visible, Charlotte leaned back in her chair and said, "Well. You certainly have a problem."

A gong chimed somewhere at the back of the house. Hiroshi shrugged. "Who doesn't? At any rate, it passes the time. That was the signal that lunch is served."

As they ate, Charlotte told him more about the expedition she would be taking part in. "The leader is a man called Adrian Cazar, a climatologist at Boston University. He wants to survey a Russian island in the Arctic where the effects of climate change are particularly obvious. It seems the island has been covered in ice for at least the past hundred thousand years. Now the satellite images show us the ice sheet has collapsed twice recently—once seven years ago, and then again last October. He asked me to join them."

"And what do you expect to find there?" Hiroshi asked, intrigued. "As a paleoanthropologist?"

Charlotte pointed her fork at him. "Good question. I once happened upon a passing remark in a travel report about Siberia that human artifacts dating back at least ten thousand years have supposedly been found on islands in the Siberian Arctic. As I say, it was just mentioned in passing. I expect the author didn't even find it remarkable."

"But you did."

"It set the alarm bells ringing. Ten thousand years ago? There were hardly any humans on the planet at that point. Back then our big problem was survival, not overpopulation. Nobody was suffering from obesity. Why in the world would humans have settled such an inhospitable region? If you have a free choice, then you go and live where life is best, don't you?" She dug her fork into the vegetable gratin. "As far as I could check up on it, it's true. And I've been interested in the topic ever since." She pointed at her plate. "This tastes wonderful by the way. The fresh herbs are fantastic."

"I'll be sure to tell her." Hiroshi thought about all this. "But you don't know whether you'll find anything on this particular island, do you?"

"No," Charlotte sighed. "I'm beginning to think it was a crazy idea. I'll probably find that my main job is interpreter, since none of the others speak Russian. It might have come in handy as well that my father's the French ambassador to Russia. We needed a lot of clearance papers—it's a restricted military zone up there. And perhaps . . ." She stopped. There was one more thing she had wanted to say, but she thought better of it at the last moment.

Hiroshi looked at her. "Perhaps?"

"Oh, nothing." She forced a smile. "I'm being positive about it. Three months on an island where it never gets warmer than ten degrees even in high summer. If nothing else, it will be an unforgettable experience."

CHARLOTTE'S ISLAND

1

At last, they were sitting in the helicopter that would bring them and their equipment to Saradkov Island. It was a big Russian Air Force machine that looked like a flying train wagon on the inside and generally gave the impression of having seen service in the Second World War. The pilot was a man with Mongolian features and an unfriendly kiss-my-ass attitude. He had grunted a few words of greeting and then not said another word since. Despite the bitter cold, the first thing he did was to take off his flight jacket, and now he was sitting at the joystick with his shirt half-open. He wore an Elvis T-shirt beneath it.

The copilot, however, was cheerfulness itself. He was astonishingly young—in fact, Charlotte found herself thinking, he looked like a high-school kid, some happy mother's pride and joy. She found it hard to believe he could fly this helicopter. But he was friendly and interested in the expedition and spoke pretty good English—as one might expect of pilots these days, Charlotte reflected. In fact, all the Russians they had dealt with so far had spoken at least passable English. Most of them were so keen to try out what they knew on the American visitors that Charlotte increasingly felt she had nothing to do. She would have to look at the whole thing as an interesting adventure holiday, she told herself, snuggling deeper into her down jacket. It was as thick as a sleeping bag, but she was still shivering. Three months on an Arctic island. How often did a person get to experience something like that? That said, she was gradually coming to realize why the Arctic islands were not a particularly popular holiday destination.

For a while it had seemed they would spend most of their three months just getting there. The group had met in Amsterdam, where they were joined by Leon van Hoorn, a Dutch photojournalist who worked for various well-known magazines and whom Adrian had somehow persuaded to come along and document their expedition. Leon was at least ten years older than the rest of the group and had already been all over the world; when he began to tell one of his stories, she felt like a timid homebody. He was also a big man in excellent shape who gave off an air of unshakable self-confidence. He made her feel he would be watching out for her, and Charlotte felt much better having the journalist along as part of the group. Even now he looked as though he flew in helicopters the way a Parisian took the metro. He was sitting opposite Charlotte and flirting at the top of his voice with Angela MacMillan, the biologist, who sat next to him with a book on her lap.

A book! Charlotte couldn't imagine how anybody could concentrate on a book in a situation like this—in the belly of a roaring, rattling aircraft that stank of diesel fumes, where the noise threatened to shake every bone in their bodies to powder. But Angela was, if anything, cooler than Leon. A stern-looking woman with a helmet of close-cropped hair—"Washing and brushing your hair is just a waste of time," she had declared—the biologist was admirably tactless and always said exactly what she thought. "I don't know what you're doing here," she had told Charlotte to her face as soon as they shook hands for the first time. And when Leon van Hoorn had been recounting his adventures in Antarctica, she asked him what it was like having sex in such conditions. Leon had laughed and asked why she wanted to know. "Well, I like the look of you," Angela had said without further ado. "Could be I jump your bones." That had left even the worldly Leon speechless.

So far, though, nothing further had come of it that Charlotte could see. From Amsterdam they had flown to Helsinki, since Adrian had gotten it into his head that he had to see as much of Europe as possible while he was there. In the hotel the two women had shared a room, and Angela had declared she still had to take a good look at Leon, then launched into a lecture on the varieties of courtship behavior in the animal world and the function of each. Charlotte understood about half of it. That was the first time she had seriously felt she was in the wrong place. Angela wasn't for the fainthearted, but she was a lot of fun. Charlotte wondered how she would get on with her father, the diplomat, the man who practically never said what he was really thinking.

From Helsinki they rented a car and drove to St. Petersburg, where Adrian wasn't satisfied until he'd taken a city tour. The next day they took the train to Murmansk, which was the first time Morley got sick.

Morley Mann was a climatologist, like Adrian. He specialized in computer climate simulations, and he was Leon's opposite in every way: tousle-haired, rail thin, diffident, and so vulnerable that he awoke protective instincts in even the toughest among them. In St. Petersburg he had insisted on getting something to eat before they boarded the train and chose a fast-food stand that looked so unappetizing that Charlotte wouldn't even have trusted their paper napkins. "I have to keep my blood sugar up," Morley had explained. Shortly after Volkhov, he had rushed to the toilet to throw up for the first time. It was clear Morley would have trouble up in the Arctic.

Adrian had told her Morley had insisted on coming along. For the experience. To prove he was a man, perhaps. She learned that he had read a self-help book telling him to do what he was afraid of and was determined to follow its advice. Which was why he was now hanging slumped in the safety webbing, white-faced and halfway to a coma.

"Don't worry about me," he had croaked. "I'll be fine once we get there."

In Murmansk they had collected the equipment that had been shipped ahead and boarded a Russian Navy icebreaker, which took them to a military base on Novaya Zemlya. Inevitably, Morley had gotten seasick on the way. At the base their equipment was thoroughly examined for something like the seventh time before they were allowed to load everything onto the helicopter. Then they took off. It made no difference that it was already evening; they were north of the Arctic Circle, and the sun would not dip below the horizon until October.

Adrian told the copilot everything there was to tell about the expedition: that they were from Boston University, that the data they collected on Saradkov Island would be fed into a worldwide project researching up to a hundred polar islands over the coming years in order to improve climate models, that Saradkov would be the first Russian island in the database. He had already repeated these details a hundred times to the sponsors and funding bodies, to the press, and even to her, Charlotte. When he was done, the copilot asked whether Adrian had heard that Saradkov was also known as Devil's Island. Charlotte put her head back and shut her eyes, pretending she hadn't heard. She had deliberately said nothing to Adrian about the legends.

"Devil's Island?" Adrian repeated. "Why's that?"

The copilot laughed. "Well, I have my own theory. Do you know what the island looks like? On the map, I mean?"

"Sure," Adrian replied. They had a whole folder of satellite images, radar scans, and so on.

"Okay. The island is a sort of stretched oval, except that it also has two spits of land that run out into the sea, north-northwest.

They're the ends of the two mountain ridges either side of the big glacier—did you see?"

"I know what you mean. Two tongues of land that drop away steeply."

"Exactly. So, those are the devil's horns, I think. The island looks like a devil's head, don't you see? Hence the name."

"Uh-huh," Adrian said. "That makes sense."

Charlotte thought that it made no sense at all. Quite the opposite. As far as she was concerned, it was possibly the least plausible explanation anyone could have come up with for an old folk legend. The only way to see the shape of the island was from the air. Only an airman could come up with an idea like that.

She turned and peered through the porthole by her left shoulder. The view was unchanged: a gray sea, almost black, moving in a curiously sluggish fashion, with more and more ice floes drifting on the surface. A leaden, featureless sky above it all. Desolation as far as the eye could see.

Devil's Island. What had she gotten herself into?

The island eventually appeared below them like the back of a white whale floating, crippled, in the water. The helicopter circled it. Saradkov was about twelve square miles of snow and ice with two parallel lines of bare rock rising out of it. That was all. At the southernmost tip, where the pilot was headed now, scraps of dark brown rock showed through on the shoreline. From up here it looked as though they were about to land on the brim of a rather squashed hat. It couldn't be much less welcoming than this on one of Jupiter's moons, Charlotte thought.

"There's the hut," said Adrian.

Charlotte followed his gaze. A little farther up from the sloping shore stood a tiny, dark, forlorn dot. She blinked in surprise. If that really was the old weather station, then . . . then everything was even huger and more barren than she had thought. Nobody knew what kind of condition the hut was in; nobody had been on Saradkov

Island for decades. They were welcome to use the building if they wanted, but they had been instructed to bring good tents just in case. Which they had of course done.

It was a bumpy landing. The helicopter shuddered and swung left and right, and the pilot had to take it up again for another approach. When they finally landed, it was with all the grace of a hammer dropping on an anvil. The pilot kept the engine idling, obviously worried the ignition wouldn't catch if he switched it off, so they had to unload their equipment with the rotor blades sweeping over their heads with a threatening *wumm-wumm-wumm*. The copilot helped them unload.

When Adrian made some remark about the rough landing and what a shame it was they hadn't had good weather for the approach, the young Russian laughed. "This is good weather. If it had been bad weather, we would have had to turn back."

Charlotte saw Adrian flinch at the news. He seemed genuinely shocked. "That's good to know," he said lugubriously.

"The older pilots say that back in the sixties someone managed to land a jet on the island—during a storm, no less," the copilot went on. "He had some kind of malfunction. But, to be honest, I think that's a myth."

Morley had been stumbling zombie-like through the process of unloading, giving only token assistance, but he seemed to be slowly coming to his senses. The unhealthy pallor of his face gave way now to an unhealthy red flush, doubtless due to the cold wind that scoured their skin. At last, everything was unloaded and the helicopter's cargo bay was empty, though all five of them checked to be sure. It was unsettling. It had looked like so much when they collected it from the shipping company back in Murmansk—when they loaded it onto the helicopter, it had been a mountain of gear—but in this desolate expanse it seemed a miserable little heap. This was supposed to last them three months? Five people? Charlotte felt certain they must have miscalculated.

The pilot made a gesture that looked like telephoning. "Ah yes," the copilot remembered. "You have to test your radio transmitter before we take off again. Regulations."

Adrian fetched the device, which was the size of a briefcase and reassuringly rugged, with thick, solid switches that could be worked even by gloved hands. The antenna was twenty yards of cable, which took two people to string it up like a clothesline.

Charlotte wanted to take one end, but Adrian shook his head and passed her the earphones and mic. "Your job is to do the talking."

At last, she was needed. Charlotte pressed the transmission button. "This is Saradkov research base," she said in Russian. "Calling Rogachevo base. Rogachevo, please copy."

The headphones crackled and hissed, and then she heard a deep voice, tinged with amusement. "Saradkov, this is Novaya Zemlya, Rogachevo base. Receiving you loud and clear. How's the weather up there?"

Charlotte had to smile. "Too cold for swimming, I'm afraid."

"What a pity. Who knows, perhaps you'll have a warm summer." The voice became businesslike. "Test confirmed. I wish you the best of luck. Rogachevo, over and out."

"Thank you. Saradkov, over and out." Charlotte switched off. She was glad to be able to take off the headphones and pull her hood back up.

When she looked up, the copilot caught her eye. "They say you're the daughter of the French ambassador," he said.

"That's right," Charlotte replied in Russian.

"You speak excellent Russian. If anybody told me you were from Moscow, I'd believe it."

Charlotte stood up and smiled. "You're exaggerating."

"Not a bit."

The pilot waved to her, obviously to show that the base had confirmed the radio link with him as well. He even seemed to attempt a smile, though Charlotte wasn't quite so sure about that. She waved back all the same.

The copilot shook her hand and then everybody else's, wished them all the best, and finished by saying, "See you in three months!"

Then he turned and walked back to the helicopter, waving once more as he buckled himself in. The next moment the engine roared back to life and the aircraft took off. It thundered away over the sluggish, gray sea, trailing a dirty plume of dark exhaust. They all watched the helicopter until it was out of sight and out of earshot.

So here we are, thought Charlotte. Five people cut off from the world. No telephone, no Internet, no television. For three months. All alone and left to ourselves. But although the cold was already creeping into her limbs, she was amazed to discover she wanted to whoop for joy.

They all stood there motionless, despite the cold. Each of them seemed to savor the moment when their Arctic adventure began. Then Leon van Hoorn came back to the group, having photographed everything—the handshakes, the helicopter lifting off—from a distance. He had even scurried off to the side again and again during the process of unloading to snap a few shots.

"Brisk weather, isn't it?" he called, packing his camera back into its padded case. "Makes you almost wish that global warming would hurry up and do its stuff."

The two climatologists glared at him as one.

"Not funny, Leon," Adrian said.

He raised his hands apologetically and grinned. "Got you. I shouldn't try cracking jokes. That's what my ex always told me."

Adrian nodded grudgingly and then looked around at the others. "Okay. First item on the agenda: living quarters." He looked dubiously at the ramshackle hut that stood a couple of hundred yards away at the foot of the cliff. "The weather station here on Saradkov was in use from 1949 to 1967. Meaning that place has been standing empty for forty years and change. It's probably just a ruin."

"We should take a look at it all the same," Angela said. "It's the only bit of human history around here."

Adrian raised his eyebrows. "There'll be time for all kinds of sightseeing soon enough. We should start off by finding a spot for the tents. As flat as possible, and sheltered from the wind . . ." He stopped and looked all along the coastline. There was no shelter from the wind here. "Flat anyway."

"I think we should have a look at the hut first," Leon said. He raised his hand to show he meant no criticism. "Just a word of advice from someone who's been around a bit. The great advantage of a hut is that it has solid walls. You very soon learn to appreciate that, especially in a snowstorm."

Charlotte suddenly saw in her mind's eye how a raging storm might tear her tent loose and sweep it away. Nonsense, of course; the tents they had chosen were stormproof. Nevertheless, she looked imploringly at Adrian.

He nodded noncommittally. "Okay. Let's take a look at it. Before this turns into a debate."

They toiled up the slope over bare rock and patches of snow that crunched beneath their boots. Charlotte decided the place could easily serve as a film set for a story about some other planet. Nothing grew here, not even lichen. The brown rocks and the cliffs above were stark and bare.

The hut was not much more to look at from close up than it had been from a distance: a simple blockhouse built of weathered gray wood with a steeply sloping roof and a tin chimney sticking up from it. It had a door made of planks and a single small window in each wall. And it was tiny, meant to house the one or two people posted out here to perform their desolate tour of duty.

"It's not exactly the Hilton," Adrian said once they were standing in front of it.

"But it's still standing," Angela pointed out, clearly in favor of solid walls around herself.

"Huts like this are usually built to last, and the cold preserves everything," Leon declared. "Woodworm and all the rest have no chance. The huts Ernest Shackleton and Robert Scott built down in Antarctica more than a hundred years ago are still standing. You could still live in them today. Comfortably, even."

Angela looked askance at him. "How do you know that? Were you ever there?"

Leon nodded. "I was there, oh, about five years ago doing a photo feature about McMurdo Station, the American research base out on the Ross Ice Shelf. Five weeks in the Antarctic. That's cold! This is a trip to the beach by comparison."

There was no lock on the door. It was fastened by a simple wooden bar that could also be opened from the inside with a handle through a slit cut in the door.

"The wind must whistle in through there," Adrian commented, opening the door.

They stepped into a little lobby, where the Soviet meteorologists had presumably hung up their outer clothing and kept their boots. A door to the right gave onto a storeroom, which still held a stack of firewood and two sacks of coal.

"This is already looking good," Leon said delightedly.

The door on the left opened onto a narrow closet with a seat and a hole. There was no smell at all; the cold must have simply frozen all the excrement.

"Looks like they simply shook quicklime over it," Angela pronounced after peering knowledgeably down the hole.

The door across from the entrance led into the actual living quarters. A heavy cast-iron stove in the middle of the room must have been used for cooking as well as heating. Charlotte had expected the room to smell of old clothes, damp wood, and stale air, but there was no such stench. Instead, it smelled of . . . nothing at all. The obvious reason was that there were no clothes hanging to dry that could have caught the damp—the only textiles in the place were the mattresses on the two beds at a right angle to each other. The wood was dry with cold. And despite the best efforts of whoever had built this place, the wind presumably gusted through strongly enough to keep it well ventilated.

"Cozy," Angela declared. "We girls get the beds."

Adrian also seemed to like what he saw. "I have to confess I had expected worse. Food scraps all over the floor and rats dancing around, that sort of thing." He glanced at a framed portrait of Lenin that hung on the wall. "Okay. Let's get the kit in here."

Morley squatted down in front of the stove and opened a hatch. "Pretty basic technology. I wonder how we'll get on with it."

"Careful," Leon warned. "We'll have to take a good look at the chimney before we fire up that stove. It might be rusted shut or have something blocking it. In which case we'd poison ourselves with the carbon monoxide."

"We'll set up our own stove to begin with," Adrian said. They had brought along a liquid-fuel heating stove. "Otherwise, it's not bad." He turned and looked around. "You get the feeling they only just left."

"Making sure they took their radio set with them." Leon stepped up to the heavy desk that was bolted to one wall and ran his gloved hands over parallel scratches. "Look, that's where it stood." Then he pointed to empty clamps running up the wall. "And that could have been the wire up to their antenna."

"In which case they must have had a generator," Morley said. He looked up at the ceiling where a bare lightbulb still dangled in its socket. "Yup. For sure."

"They took that with them too, then." Leon reached under the desktop and pulled open a drawer. "Hey, look at this." He brought out a thick old ledger. "It's the station logbook, isn't it?" He opened it up at the back cover and leafed through the empty pages until he hit the last entry. "Bingo. Nineteen sixty-seven. Twenty-first of something." He passed the book to Charlotte. "You know Russian."

Charlotte glanced down at the page full of neat Cyrillic handwriting and sighed. "Now we get to see that I couldn't be from Moscow."

Leon stared at her, baffled. "I beg your pardon?"

She looked back at him. Ah yes. He hadn't understood any of what she said to the copilot, since they had been talking in Russian. "I can *speak* Russian, but I have trouble reading it. I don't have much of a memory for other alphabets."

However, if she deciphered the words letter by letter, and spelled them out loud . . . she studied the date on the last entry. An *O*, a *k* . . . well that was easy. "*Oktyabr*. October. Twenty-first October, 1967."

Leon looked at her in amazement. "How on earth do you learn Russian without being able to read it?"

"By ear. Listen and repeat." Charlotte shrugged. "I don't know exactly how it works. Whenever I go to a new country, I simply understand the language."

"Wow. I wish I could say the same."

Adrian came up to Charlotte, took the logbook from her, and began to leaf through it. Clearly a daily journal, it contained all sorts of numbers—temperature, air pressure, wind speed, and direction. He whistled softly. "This is a treasure trove. Even if we don't understand all the text, we can read the numbers. Which are a lot more useful anyway." He stopped at a page where a faded black-and-white photograph was glued into the book. "Have a look at that."

They all huddled together and looked. The picture showed the hut, buried in snow almost to the windows; two men in thick fur coats posed in front of it with fierce smiles on their faces.

Adrian pointed at the date written above it. "Nineteen sixty-two. Can you make out the month, Charlotte?"

That was easy, too. The only month with three letters. He could have done that himself. "May."

"In May?" Morley gasped. "So much snow in May? That's astonishing."

"You see?" Adrian said, turning to Leon. "Global warming is already well advanced. One cold winter or rainy summer in Europe doesn't mean a thing."

"I never said it did," Leon said peaceably.

"Okay." Adrian looked around thoughtfully. "The women get the beds, of course. Do we have enough room on the floor?" He took a good look at the space available to them. "It'll be a bit of a squeeze, but it'll have to do."

Charlotte was suddenly reminded of her first year at Harvard, where she had shared a room in the dorm with a woman called Carrie Walsh. Strange: the layout had been almost exactly the same as here. The way the beds stood, the desk they had constantly squabbled over . . . all just the same. This room had shelves where they had wardrobes. The only extra piece of furniture here was the stove. Strange indeed. Well, it was only three months. They would be over soon enough.

They fetched the equipment and unrolled the sleeping bags. They piled up the crates of food, numbered by week, along with the fuel cans, in the storeroom, where everything would stay cold. The liquid fuel was specially developed for Arctic use and had a freezing point of minus seventy degrees centigrade. They would never have temperatures like that here. In the summer months it would be between minus ten and minus two, and in July they could hope for peak temperatures of around two degrees. They'd probably be strolling around in T-shirts by then, Charlotte thought, and shivered.

They had another look at the earth closet. "We won't use that," Adrian declared. "We'll set up the expedition toilet in here instead." They had brought along a type of toilet that was used on Antarctic expeditions. All the excrement was collected in special plastic bags into which they had to pour a precise dose of chemical fluid. Once the bags were full, they could be burned.

Morley took charge of the stove, partly because he was exhausted from carrying gear and was beginning to turn pale once more, and partly because he was the undisputed technological wizard of the group. So Adrian gave him the task of preparing the lightweight stove and firing it up, which he tackled with gratitude and determination.

Amazing the difference when a room was no longer as cold as an ice locker, but full of cheerful, crackling warmth. When everything had finally been stowed away and Charlotte could take off her boots, hang up her down jacket, and walk around their cozy little parlor in her socks, it was almost better than Christmas.

"I'm dog-tired," Angela declared.

Adrian looked at his watch. "No wonder. It's two o'clock in the morning."

Of course. It was deeply unsettling that the sun never set outside. Charlotte felt ready to drop as well, but she had assumed that had to do with the exertions of the journey and carrying all those crates. It felt like late afternoon to her, but that was only because of the light. The sun simply circled the horizon, a bright spot behind the uniform gray cloud cover that blanketed the sky.

They opened the supply crate labeled WEEK ONE and heated up a goulash, military rations that came with dry crackers so tough that they could probably break a filling. It tasted wonderful. Adrian and Leon went back out to fill a big pot with snow to melt on the stove so that they would have water in the morning for washing and coffee—though nobody would be washing very thoroughly during their stay here. Brushing teeth and the occasional damp washcloth would have to be enough. The next shower they could look forward to would be in September. But Charlotte was so tired she didn't care. She crept into her sleeping bag and fell asleep at once.

Charlotte was woken by the chattering of her own teeth. It was hard work even to move. She felt like a joint of beef in a supermarket deep freeze. She fumbled at the zipper on her sleeping bag with stiff fingers. Tiny crystals of ice rustled down—hoarfrost that had formed on the outside of the bag. She looked around, blinking. The others were still asleep. One of the men was snoring; Morley, she figured. Frost flowers had blossomed on the windows. It had to be a nightmare. Of course it was a nightmare. There was no way she would survive this cold all the way through to September. She would develop pneumonia and die, and the others would have to bring her freeze-dried corpse back home.

She crept farther down into her sleeping bag, pulled the zipper back up, and by some miracle fell asleep again. Then next time she woke up, it was because somebody was shaking her and saying, "Up you get. Coffee's almost ready." And it was warm. Angela was strolling around the room stark-naked. They had gotten the stove going again and hung up a curtain in the corner for a little privacy for washing. Charlotte was still so frozen that all she could do was take a damp cloth to her hands and face. She'd never be as cool as Angela about these things anyway.

"We can't keep the room heated all the time," Adrian explained at breakfast. "We don't have that much fuel. It'll have to be enough that we heat up once a day to keep ourselves warm."

"My toothpaste was frozen solid this morning," Angela said. She seemed amused.

"So was my contact-lens fluid," Morley put in, less happy about it. Which explained why he was blinking and peering around like a mole this morning.

"You have to take stuff like that inside the sleeping bag with you," Leon advised them. "That's what I do with my cameras, because of the batteries. Otherwise, they lose all their charge overnight in the cold."

Charlotte warmed her hands on the metal coffee mug and listened while the others talked. They had spread the dossier out in front of them and were discussing the best way to proceed. Angela insisted the first priority was to document the biota well away from the hut and its surroundings. When Leon asked what exactly that meant, she explained. "Everything around here is contaminated. Whatever lives nearby has been brought in by man. But I'm interested in how life reconquers land in such a cold climate once the ice has gone. The first biota will be the algae washed up on the waves, and then lichens will follow, and so on. It's very exciting."

Adrian had his logbook on his lap. He had told Charlotte on the journey here that even in the age of ubiquitous computing, research scientists preferred to keep handwritten records of everything. He and Morley were bent over a large satellite image of the island and talking about how they would map the glacier. With a little luck, Adrian said, they might even witness how it calved in the summer months. Their eyes lit up at the prospect.

Charlotte didn't find it quite such a tempting thought, but she told herself that if she understood them right the glacier wasn't actually going to crack and send blocks of ice tumbling down directly onto the hut. They were well protected here by the rock ridge above, the higher of the two mountain chains. The most likely place for the glacier to calve would be either north-northwest, in the bay between the devil's horns, or at the opposite end of the island. She plucked one of the satellite pictures from the stack. The satellites that had taken these pictures were equipped with radar as well as cameras, and the images showed the relief down below the ice. Near the center of the island, about two and a half miles from the hut as the crow flies, she made out a tiny, dark point. She pointed at it and asked if anyone knew what that was.

Adrian glanced briefly at the picture in her hands. "That's a radar image. So it's probably iron ore."

Charlotte picked up another image that was time-stamped five years later and held it next to the first. "Does iron ore move about?"

They all looked up. With the two pictures side by side, they could see the dark spot was not in the same place as it had been five years earlier.

Morley waved his hand dismissively. "Then it's a meteorite. That's why the dot's so small; a normal iron deposit wouldn't look like that. The thing's stuck in the ice, and the glacier is carrying it along."

"A meteorite?" Leon pricked up his ears. "That's fascinating. Something like that can get stuck inside a glacier? I can't even imagine how that would happen. Aren't they red-hot when they've passed through the atmosphere and strike the ice? It would melt its way right through, wouldn't it?"

Morley seemed to find the topic anything but fascinating. "Sure, it impacts, smashes a crater in the ice, and then sinks. How deep it sinks is simply a function of the thermal capacity of the meteorite versus that of the ice. After all, water can absorb an awful lot of heat. But even if the meteorite melts its way right through to the bottom of the ice, it'll be pushed along by the glacier as it moves."

"Can't we go and look at the impact crater?" Charlotte asked.

Leon nodded and seemed interested, too.

"Why?" Adrian looked at her, frowning. "We don't know anything about meteorites. Besides, the thing must be stuck several yards down in the ice. We'd never even be able to get at it."

Leon grinned. "But it would make for some great pictures. Research expedition in search of a meteorite in the eternal ice. People love that sort of thing."

Adrian turned up his nose. "Then Hollywood can go make a movie about it." He turned back to the big map and tapped it with his pen. "Okay then, this is what we're going to do. We'll set up our recording instruments first thing. Then we'll unpack the dinghy and explore up and down along the coast, as far as the winds will let us. We're looking for any signs of life and at the condition of the glacier. This is the really urgent stuff we have to prioritize."

They got to work. They found a foxhole the Soviet meteorologists must have used back in the day and installed their own meteorological instruments to measure wind speed, temperature, precipitation, and so on. Morley installed the generator they had brought with them in the storeroom and connected it to the wiring in the hut so that they could switch on the lightbulb and use the sockets that were in place. Unlike Adrian, he wasn't willing to forgo his laptop.

"I'll take it into my sleeping bag," he told Charlotte, who was tidying up, since nobody else would. "They say we geeks sleep with our computers anyway."

Charlotte gave him a thin smile. "Just as long as the sockets work fine."

"No problem," Morley declared. "Soviet sockets are more or less the same as the modern European model, whatever that may mean. And I've got an adapter that fits those."

The wind proved merciless. It blew, strong and unpredictable, whipping the sea into sharp, icy waves, while dark clouds gathered in the light gray sky to the north.

"I'd put off the boat trip," said Leon, who was supposed to steer when they did go out. "It doesn't look good."

Adrian nodded. "The air pressure has plummeted. Better to wait until the weather has calmed down again." He sighed. "Yesterday would have been the time to go."

So they changed their plans for the day. Leon set out to take pictures, while the two climatologists climbed the cliffs to have a look at the ice shield. Angela decided to head south along the coast to have a look at the vegetation. Charlotte offered to help her.

They wouldn't cover any great distance on their outing. Every few steps Angela squatted down to look at something on the ground. When she squealed with joy, Charlotte had to hand her a fresh plastic bag to stow the scraps of gray-brown vegetation or slimy algae she had found. Along the way Angela gave a lecture about polar flora and fauna; among other things, Charlotte learned the characteristic features of cold deserts, that lichens were not actually plants but classified as fungi, and that there were around some twenty-five thousand kinds of lichen. Angela seemed to know them all.

It was bitterly cold as they picked their way along the shoreline, treading gingerly over cracks in the rock and slippery stones underfoot, constantly stopping to squat down and unpack the specimen case. There was no point trying to fumble the bags out with her gloves on, and in no time at all Charlotte felt she would lose her fingers to frostbite. And it was only minus ten—that was nothing.

"It's the wind," Angela said. "Adrian explained it to me. The wind-chill factor makes your skin lose heat more quickly, so that minus ten feels more like minus twenty."

It was good to know the reason, but it didn't keep her any warmer. Charlotte was glad when Angela asked her to take the samples they had collected thus far back to the hut and put them in the store room. Though the hut had cooled down again, there was no wind in there, so it was comparatively pleasant. Charlotte didn't want to go straight back out, so she leafed through the old logbook and painstakingly deciphered a few entries.

"Damage to the generator. We are using batteries for our radio reports," it said on October 2, 1963, and then a week later: "We have managed to repair the generator. Light to read by at last!" How had whoever had written these lines managed until then? Was it already Arctic night in October? Charlotte didn't know. She chose another entry at random. "May 9, 1966. I have started to read Sholokhov's *And Quiet Flows the Don*. Enthralling. Well deserved the Nobel Prize."

Charlotte opened the front cover and looked at the entries there. There was no way this could be the official logbook, which would have contained several data points for every single day. This was more like a diary. When a meteorologist wrote a diary, the state of the weather was just part and parcel of it. Perhaps it would be worth taking the trouble to read it all the way through. Little by little, of course. She had plenty of time after all—more than enough.

When Adrian and Morley returned from their trip up to the glacier, Morley was snow white and completely exhausted. He collapsed onto his sleeping bag, still wearing all his gear, and fell asleep even before the meal was ready. The next day he complained of a headache, a sore throat, and muscle cramps, and said he was a loser and an idiot. They let him sleep on, and sometime around noon he was back on his feet. He came back from the next trip equally tired out but not quite so downcast.

"I'm saving up some of my complaints for later," he declared. "That's the only way to make it work."

One day soon after that the wind died down and the sea calmed. The two climatologists agreed it would stay like this for a while and that they could risk a boat trip. The three men uncrated the inflatable dinghy, blew it up with the electric pump, and carried it to the shore. Leon was the only one who had any experience with such boats, and he mounted the outboard motor. Morley stowed the gear. Adrian asked Charlotte whether she would like to go in his place; the boat could only hold three people, and he would be out on the boat plenty of times, he said. Charlotte shuddered at the thought of having only that thin sheet of plastic to hold her up above the icy water of the Arctic Ocean. If the worst came to the worst, there was no way her life jacket would save her—how could it?

"No," she said decisively. "Thank you, but no."

So the three men set out. They vanished behind the ice-covered cliffs to the north, only to reappear two hours later.

Morley was seasick but excited. "It's a really unusual formation," he chattered enthusiastically, his face pale green. "A kind of ice cap anchored in place by the valley structures of the rock below. That means we would never have seen any basal sliding at all if it wasn't for the general rise in temperature. We absolutely have to make a survey of the escarpment."

"In other words," Adrian translated, "if the temperatures exceed a given value for long enough, we might see the whole ice shield slip off all at once." He snorted with pleasure. "That would be quite a sight!"

Leon's comments were more pragmatic. "I have to get some pictures from onshore while those two sail around the front of the glacier. Those cold colors, white, blue, gray, with the bright red dinghy out front—it'll look fantastic!"

Over the next few days Angela joined them so they could put her ashore at otherwise inaccessible spots to take plant samples.

"That woman's afraid of nothing," Leon said when they came back. It wasn't quite clear from the tone of his voice whether he admired her or was afraid on her behalf.

Every evening they had to release all the air from the boat, which was more work than blowing it up because of the safety valves. Then they would fold it up and stow it in the store room; otherwise, even a moderate wind would carry it away.

Little by little they fell into a daily routine. Although it was more or less light the whole time, they tried to stick to the normal clock. After a week they realized that strictly speaking they were in a different time zone here on Saradkov than the last time they had adjusted their watches in St. Petersburg. They had been on Moscow Time ever since, but Saradkov was three time zones farther east. Since they had gotten used to their rhythm by now, they decided it made no difference.

Eventually, they even got used to the constant cold. They watched wistfully as their breath plumed white in the cold air, sad for the loss of body heat. They crammed in as much food as they could and looked forward to every opportunity to warm themselves, even if it was with just a cup of coffee from the thermos flask. Though everyone told her she couldn't be as cold as she claimed—her sleeping bag was an Arctic model tested to minus twenty degrees—Charlotte slept in two sweat suits layered one over the other, three pairs of socks, and a cap. She let them talk. All that mattered was that she was finally sleeping well.

To her own surprise, she liked Saradkov more and more with every passing day—precisely because the island was so inhospitable, so exhilarating, so elemental. There were no centuries of tradition and convention wrapping around life out here. She no longer lived in the cotton-wool padding she had been used to as a child of the upper classes. Everything here was unfeigned, direct, raw in its reality. The cold broke through the armor of civilization, the wind blew away the masks that people habitually wore, and everyday life was stripped down to the bare essentials, making her realize what was really important and what was mere ballast. Charlotte felt that for the first time in her life she was truly in contact with reality. How bizarre that the Arctic, so hostile to all life, should teach her how to live. She even began her own research work. She dug out her excavation kit, her hammers and brushes and shovels, her own logbook and little digital camera, and set out looking for any trace of early human settlement.

Leon asked if he could come along and take some photos and wanted to know how she had gotten the idea that she would find anything of the sort up here. "If anyone ever made a list of the most forsaken corners of the world, wouldn't this island be up near the top?"

So she told him everything that was known about the pre-Dorset culture. How the ancestors of today's Inuit, or Eskimos, had crossed the Bering Strait no later than three thousand years before Christ and had spread all the way from Alaska to Greenland, and how they had done it without boats by walking across the winter ice, without dogsleds, and without shelters ready and waiting along the way. Genetic analysis of a hank of hair excavated from a pre-Dorset site had shown that these early Inuit must have been related to groups in Eastern Siberia and on the Aleutian Islands—but not to the

American Indians, who had made their own way to America much earlier.

"And that's where the trail goes cold," Charlotte declared, never lifting her eyes from the ground as they made their way across the black-brown rocks. "All we know is that the remote ancestors of this early culture must have come from Africa in the end. And the question I ask myself is, why did they end up here in this inhospitable environment, in this cold?"

Leon was stumped. "Yes, it's strange. I never thought about it."

"We estimate that at the end of the last cold period ten thousand years ago there were between five and ten million people alive on Earth. That's the population of a city like New York spread across the entire surface of the globe. You might think they had enough room."

Leon cocked his head. "I don't know. I've spent a lot of time living with nomads—in Mongolia, in Africa. It's a lifestyle that needs much more land than agrarian or industrial society. It's hard for people like us to understand. A Himba man driving his herds through northern Namibia feels crowded in if he happens to cross paths with more than one other herdsman in a week. And we're talking here about Kunene, a region with a population density of one inhabitant for every five hundred acres, the better part of a square mile—just in raw numbers."

"Okay. But now think of ten million people scattered all across Earth's available land surface; that's almost six square miles per person." Charlotte stopped and looked at the desolate, lifeless expanse all around her. "I see no reason why anybody would settle in a region like this."

"So probably you won't find any traces to indicate that anyone ever did."

"Maybe. But it can't be all that different in Eastern Siberia, and they've found settlement sites there." She shook her head. "There's something wrong with our picture of human history. I just don't know what it is."

He looked good with his thick curls of ash-blond hair bursting out from under his hood and his weather-beaten face. Charlotte wondered for a moment what it would be like to live with a man like this who traveled so far and went on so many interesting adventures. Certainly, in a relationship like that you'd have all the freedom you could wish for, and you might experience things that few others did. . . . Well, she liked the look of him. As did Angela. Only she would never have flat-out said so. However, Angela had still not followed up on her declaration. Unless you counted the way she paraded herself naked before him every morning, but she would doubtless have done that anyway.

Leon was looking thoughtfully at her in turn. "Is that really why you came here? To see whether you could find spearheads or hand axes? Here, on a flyspeck of an island that's only twelve square miles, hardly six hundred miles from the North Pole?" He shook his head. "For some reason, I find that hard to believe."

"You don't have to," Charlotte answered curtly and set off again. "Nobody's asking you to."

But he was right. She wouldn't find anything. Adrian had told her about the sites in Eastern Siberia to lure her in, and she had told herself he needed an interpreter. But both of those reasons were just pretexts. She was really here because Mikhail Andreievitch Yegorov had told her about a dark dot on Saradkov Island. On Devil's Island.

A period of bad weather followed. Sleet fell, and the sky turned almost black. Stormy winds lashed snow all across the island, so that all they could see out the window was a blizzard of white. Gusts of wind hammered the hut like giants demanding entry. So much snow blew in through the narrow slit of the latch that drifts formed on the floor.

They stayed in the hut for days on end, glad not to have pitched their tents. Adrian was the only one who struggled out into the wind, at regular intervals, to read the instruments. Though the foxhole was only a few yards away, he looked like a snowman every time he came back. He seemed uplifted by this kind of weather. Luckily, they had just cleaned the stovepipe. They fired up the stove with wood and coal from the Soviet supply and made themselves comfortable without having to use the fuel they had brought with them.

They used the enforced leisure to go over their notes. Angela sat at the microscope and tried to catalog exactly what she had found. Adrian and Morley discussed climatological theories, of which Charlotte understood not a word. Leon looked through all the photos he had taken on his camera display, transferred them to extra memory cards he had brought with him, and wrote a first draft of his story.

Charlotte didn't want it to be too obvious she was sitting there empty-handed. That all the striding around outside these past few weeks had only been to order her thoughts. That this expedition was becoming increasingly like a Zen retreat for her. She jotted notes in her excavation logbook, but these consisted of nothing more than her arguments and ideas. There were no finds to log. And at some point she stopped writing.

The blizzard didn't let up. They passed the time playing cards. Leon had an inexhaustible repertoire of unusual games and taught them several. Morley was the only one who didn't want to join in; instead, he took the old station logbook and typed up the weather data into his laptop. "It's useful comparative material!" he declared.

Charlotte looked over at him again and again as he sat there at the roughly finished table, carefully going through the book page by page, double-checking every line of figures he entered, utterly absorbed in what he was doing. She felt a twinge of guilt as she watched him, since the sight reminded her she had intended to decipher the entries in the logbook. Even though she really had nothing else to do, she had kept on putting it off.

"Hey, do you think the meteorite could have struck in 1966?" Morley suddenly asked as they were deep in a game of Last Chance.

Adrian looked up from his cards, caught off guard. "What?"

"Here." Morley held the old journal out to them. He had opened it to a page with a crude sketch in the middle that showed the outline of the island and a cross inside with two lines pointing off at a downward slant. "Doesn't it look like that?" He looked at the picture again. "Pity it's such a rough sketch. It would be great if we could use it to determine whether the meteorite really stayed in one place for forty-five years and only started to move in the last five years."

Adrian put his cards aside. "I think Charlotte should translate the text next to it."

Morley passed her the logbook. Charlotte took it, feeling awkward now that all eyes were on her. How could she have overlooked this sketch? The paper smelled old and dusty.

"'Monday, June 13,'" she read haltingly. "'Temperature -2.8 degrees Celsius. Continuous strong wind from NE for days now, 70 to 90 kmh. Clear skies, no precipitation. Air pressure constant at—'"

"I have all that," Morley said impatiently. "All the numbers anyway. Anyone can understand those."

"Okay." Charlotte glanced farther down the page. "'Sudden noise in the afternoon. A jet fighter, very low, as if it wanted to land on the island.'"

She stopped and caught her breath. *Could this even be . . . ?*

"New paragraph," she said. The writing was less neat now, the lines hastily written. "'Visit. Lieutenant Pyotr Yegorov had to make an emergency landing up on the ice. Engine trouble. He is very shaken, talking of devil's fingers that came out of the ice and reached for him and his plane. Old stories of monsters and bogeymen! When will the human race learn to accept reason? Can understand, however, why he is so shaken. He was lucky to have a headwind, or he would have crashed into the sea. He was staggering around with no protective clothing when we found him. Gave him food and vodka and put him to bed, running a fever. Pavlov is trying to raise the authorities, but radio interference much stronger than usual; do not know whether he will manage to connect.'"

"So the cross must show where the jet landed, I suppose," Morley said. "And the arrows were its angle of approach." He sounded disappointed.

"What else does it say?" Leon asked.

"'Tuesday, June 14, 1966,'" Charlotte read out. "'Temperature'—okay, I'll leave all that out. Basically, it's the same as the day before, but the wind dropped." She spelled out the next few words and read them to herself first quietly to be sure she understood. "'Lieutenant Yegorov is better but still feverish. Asked us to go to his plane and fetch some things from the cockpit—a folder with important documents, if I understand him right. Weather stable, so we have decided to set off after lunch.'"

She had to read the next paragraph several times over. She hesitated. Surely she must have misunderstood something? Otherwise, it was impossible . . .

"What happened next?" Adrian asked. "This is getting exciting."

Charlotte cleared her throat. "I don't know . . . Well, there's a dash, and then, 'Back from the ice. Cannot explain what we saw. The plane has vanished.'"

2

Leon whistled softly through his teeth and put his cards aside. "In other words, the black dot on the satellite image isn't a meteorite at all. It's the jet. It sank into the ice." His eyes were glittering feverishly all of a sudden.

Adrian looked at him skeptically. "Well, I don't know. I've never heard of an airplane sinking into a glacier."

For a moment there was a strange tension in the air. This had to be what it felt like when treasure hunters found the long-lost map, the old parchment with the X that marks the spot.

Morley lifted one hand and waved it to get their attention. "Not so fast. Okay, you won't find it in the textbooks. But I once talked to a glaciologist . . . well, we were drinking, and just before the last beer he really got talking. In any case, there are rumors of a phenomenon that might just fit. It's something like a quicksand effect, but with ice. It's a persistent legend, and it would explain a few puzzling accidents, missing polar explorers, that sort of thing. It's just that there have never been any reliable observations that would meet scientific standards."

"I don't pay any attention to stories like that," Adrian declared. "It's just one small step from there to the Loch Ness Monster and the yeti."

Morley nodded. "Sure, but think of the story of freak waves. Seamen had been telling stories about them for centuries but not a single scientist believed them. Then a few years ago we actually caught sight of them on satellite images." Now he had the same treasure-hunting gleam in his eye. "If that's really what happened—if there's a jet plane trapped in a glacier up there—that would be the jackpot for glaciology."

"It would be a sensational story no matter what," Leon added.

Adrian looked at the two of them, still dubious. Then he nodded to Charlotte. "Keep reading. What else is there?"

Charlotte looked back at the old logbook, scanned the Cyrillic scrawl on the rough paper, and tried to concentrate. It wasn't easy. "'Lieutenant Yegorov still has a high fever. We told him his plane is no longer there. He told wild stories about spiders attacking him and is firmly convinced the spiders took his aircraft.'" Fever. That was it. All of a sudden Charlotte felt she, too, had a fever. "Next day." She hurried through the weather report. "'Relatively low wind, sunny, -11 degrees. Finally made contact with command. Received orders to look for any sign indicating where the aircraft may be. Pavlov and I climbed up again this afternoon. Last roll of film unfortunately ruined.'" She cleared her throat. "Dash. Then it goes on: 'Hard to say where plane may have landed. If we assume that a jet fighter needs a very long landing strip on smooth ice, then Lieutenant Yegorov may have landed much farther to the north than he told us. In which case, aircraft fell into the bay. Pavlov has sent our report. Alerted that naval ship is on its way to collect the lieutenant and investigate the matter.'"

She turned the page. "Next day: 'Snowing, light wind. The lieutenant is coughing hard. Pavlov thinks he may have pneumonia. Our stock of medicines does not contain effective treatments. Hope that the ship comes soon.'" She skipped two days with only short entries. "Here: 'June 20. Cloudy. Minus 14 degrees, light snow. The SOKOL is at anchor. Thirty men arrived by boat. They have taken the lieutenant. Doctor seems concerned. Pavlov and I questioned separately. Helicopter has landed soldiers on the plateau to search everywhere. No sign of aircraft, not even in sea.'" The handwriting became a hasty scrawl, as though whoever had written in the diary had done so in secret. "'June 21. An officer asked us directly whether we are working for the imperialists. Ridiculous accusation! Seems they cannot imagine any other explanation for disappearance of the Tupolev. A soldier told me that Lieutenant Yegorov is being questioned on suspicion of espionage.'"

Angela shook her head. "I don't get it. If we can see the plane from space with radar, then wouldn't they have been able to find it back then?"

"No, not at all," Morley said. He even seemed amused by the suggestion. "They would have needed radar interferometry, and that wasn't developed until the nineties."

Charlotte leafed back and forth through the book to make sure no pages had been torn out. "Then he didn't make any entries for about a week," she said. "Here, on June 29, he writes, 'Have the island to ourselves again. Complaints that we were not punctual with weather reports several times. All seems like a bad dream. How can a plane simply vanish?'"

Leon could hardly sit still. "But we know where it is!" He pointed to the folder of satellite images Morley had at his elbow. "Pass those over. If that's really the airplane, then it can't be as far down in the ice as a meteorite. We could find it."

"And do what? Dig it up?" Adrian asked.

"It would be enough if we could dig up the tailfin. Preferably with the Red Star on it."

Charlotte shut the book. "Let's just go take a look." She lifted her head and looked out the window, where gusts of white still tumbled past. "When the weather improves, I mean."

Morley had taken one of the satellite images from the folder and placed it in front of the group. "That wouldn't be a problem." He pointed to the coordinate grid that overlay the picture. "All we would need to do it follow the GPS data, then drill a grid pattern at ten-meter intervals all around and—bingo!"

"Do you think so?" Adrian asked. "That no more than five meters of ice has formed over the past fifty years?" That was all the length of drill bits that they had at hand.

Morley smiled slyly. "Could be that more than five meters has formed. But then again, in the last ten years a lot of ice has vanished again. A whole lot. I wouldn't be the least bit surprised if we got up there and found the plane sticking halfway out."

"I don't know." Adrian sounded deeply unconvinced. "It seems like a waste of time to me."

"Look at it this way," Leon put in. "I'll be documenting everything. 'Climate research expedition finds lost Soviet jet'—that would be the story, with lots of great photos to go with it. Brightly clad research scientists on the eternal ice. Newspaper people love that kind of thing. That's front-page material."

"Eternal ice?" Morley grumbled. "The ice around here is anything but."

"You'll all be famous," Leon went on, taking no notice. "And just think what a difference it would make next time you apply for a funding grant. Are you just the climatologist Dr. Adrian Cazar, or are you the *famous* climatologist Dr. Adrian Cazar?"

Morley spluttered with laughter. "Hey! Great argument!"

Adrian looked skeptically at the photojournalist. "And you'd earn a lot of money with this as well, wouldn't you?"

Leon shrugged. "In your shoes I wouldn't be too bothered about that."

A gust shook the hut for the hundredth time that day. The wind howling through the latch moaned eerily.

"All right. Fine by me," Adrian finally conceded. "If the weather ever improves."

Two days later the storm stopped as though a switch had been thrown. For the first time since they had arrived on the island, the cloud cover broke and they could see blue sky.

"That's ideal," Morley declared as they began to pack.

And Leon said, "Perfect weather for photographs. It's now or never."

Angela was the only one who asked whether she should even come along. "I won't be able to do anything except stand in the way."

"You heard the guy," Adrian answered, nodding toward Leon. "Do you want to stay as the biologist Angela MacMillan, or do you want to be the *famous* biologist Angela MacMillan?"

"I'd rather be famous for discovering a species of plant than a jet plane."

Leon was checking his cameras for the fourth or fifth time. "Just tell me real quick, then," he put in. "When was the last time anyone became famous for discovering a plant species?"

Even Angela couldn't answer that one. "All the same. What am I supposed to do up there? I mean, the climb is hardly a walk in the park, I can see that. That first part of the ascent is practically a sheer wall. Wouldn't it be better for me to wait here and make a hot meal for when you come back?"

"I'd like it if you came along," the photographer said frankly. "If only for compositional reasons. For one thing, an expedition of only three people looks too darn small, and secondly, that lime-green parka of yours will be a welcome burst of color."

That was the kind of language Angela understood: simple and direct. "Okay," she said. "I'll come along, then."

Charlotte checked her gear. Two and a half miles as the crow flies didn't sound like much, but the expedition would take all day. The climb up to the plateau was the real challenge; Morley said it had pretty near killed him on the first day. So they packed their backpacks with thermos flasks full of hot tea, and nuts and fruit bars for an energy boost. And their scientific equipment as well, of course—the bore sampler with its drill bits, a samples case, all kinds of hooks and shovels, marker paint, radio beacons, and the like. On top of which, Morley insisted they bring life jackets.

"Whatever for?" Charlotte protested.

"We don't know what kind of glacial phenomena we may run into."

"My backpack's heavy enough."

"The life jackets aren't heavy. They're bulky." It was true: they were chunky things, stiff as a board and made from a hard, artificial foam material. They had also been designed by someone with a limited grasp of the female anatomy. Although more modern models existed that inflated automatically upon contact with water and were otherwise just thick rolls of material, they had been beyond Adrian's budget.

"Morley's right," Adrian said. "Where a plane can sink, a person can."

Charlotte shook her head reluctantly. "That was almost half a century ago."

"True," said Adrian, shouldering his backpack. "But the glaciers were in a lot better shape back then than they are now."

They compromised by tying the life jackets onto their backpacks when they finally set off. They would only put them on once they reached the plateau.

The first part of the expedition was a trek on foot along a chain of hills around the southern tip of the island, then east toward the glacier. Their path took them between jagged, snow-covered cliffs up a steep track in the ice that looked as though it had been built for a bobsleigh run. Barely ten minutes in, Charlotte was soaked through with sweat. They had to keep their concentration sharp every second; one false step would send them slipping all the way back down the slope they had just so laboriously climbed up. Charlotte preferred not to think about the injuries someone could get from such a fall. Soon there was nothing in her world but the rasping of her own breath and the creaking of crampons digging into the white, cold mass. Up above them silent plumes of snow puffed out from the tall cliffs that fringed the sky, then pattered down onto them as glittering dust. Sometimes the ice squeaked underfoot as though they were walking over gemstones.

They passed bottomless chasms in the glacier that shimmered blue in the depths. On either side of the path were formations that looked like avalanches frozen in place. Snow, rain, ice, and wind had created bizarre sculptures that sparkled like diamonds in the sunlight. It was as though they were climbing upward into a strange world where humans were never meant to tread. Halfway up they took their first rest break.

"This is the easiest ascent we could find," Adrian explained, panting.

Morley, who had been part of that first scouting survey, couldn't even talk; green-faced and gasping, he sat on the ground gulping for air like a stranded fish. The only one who wasn't short of breath was Leon van Hoorn. He had been constantly hurrying ahead to take pictures of them from up above, then dropping back to frame them against the sky as they climbed, then catching up again, with no visible effort, to snap them in profile or in closeup as they hauled themselves onward, panting.

"Wonderful," he never tired of saying. "You're doing brilliantly."

"Hey," Charlotte gasped after a couple of minutes catching her breath. "Does someone like you just get to travel wherever you like? I mean, without even thinking how you'll photograph what you see or who you can sell the picture to?"

"No," Leon answered curtly, lifting his camera again to take a shot of Charlotte as she spoke. "That's the price you pay for this kind of life. Accept it or stay home—that's what my teacher told me."

"Oh great," Charlotte said and found herself thinking of Hiroshi and what he had told her about earning a living—that most jobs twisted people's lives out of shape; that this was why he wanted to free people of the necessity of work. For the first time she began to understand him a little. But she didn't want to think of Hiroshi just then. Not here, not now. At that moment there was only the ice and the cold wind that robbed her face of all feeling, the sun above the horizon, her muscles aching, and her lungs burning, and the next step to be taken. "Come on," she urged. "Let's get going."

Not all was still and frozen. Before they reached the plateau, they passed trickles of meltwater, thin streams gurgling down off the face of the glacier that disappeared into the cracks and crevices in the ice.

"Oh yeah," Morley gasped. "Something's happening there. Not good. Not good at all."

And then at last they were up above, standing at the edge of an immense, unreal white plain of frozen silence. The only sign of a human presence were the remains of the wind-speed tower, rearing up from the highest peak of the mountain chain to their left, a nearly unrecognizable tangle of steel girders, smothered in snow, that had once housed the Soviet meteorological gear that measured the Arctic storms. They revived themselves with long swigs of hot tea, enjoying how the icy pain let go of their lungs, and tried to ignore Leon, who was prowling all around them with his camera to his face.

"Okay," Morley said eventually, taking the GPS reader from his windbreaker, where it hung on a cord around his neck. He had already entered the coordinates they were aiming for. They would simply hike on until they zeroed in on target. "The rest is just a walk in the park."

He had spoken too soon. The ice shield that covered the whole island sloped slowly upward toward the center, so that they were still always climbing, however slightly, as they hiked. It wore them down.

Charlotte dropped back until she was walking alongside Angela, who was marching forward with machinelike regularity. "Hey," she said once she was sure the men were out of earshot. "You and Leon . . . is that still a thing?"

"What about me and Leon?"

"Well, back in Amsterdam you said you liked the look of him," Charlotte said, gazing at her own breath freezing into a cloud. "And then in Helsinki you said you'd have to take a closer look . . ."

Angela laughed. "I've finished taking my look. You can have him. I've noticed that you want him."

It was childish, of course. Girlish dreams. No question. It was wicked even. Yes. But indulging in fantasies of her and Leon made the rest of the trip so much sweeter—irresistibly so. . . . Now Charlotte smiled when he pointed the camera at her. She flirted with the lens, that dark, gleaming eye. She cast it smoldering glances when he focused in on her. Let him wonder what she meant by that. Quite a lot. Perhaps, she told herself, they might find some pretext for a trip up onto the glacier together. Just Leon and her and a tent. Did these sleeping bags zip together? She knew there were some models designed in such a way that two bags could be joined together to make one big one, though she hadn't checked to see whether that was true of the ones they had brought. The grandiose scenery! The endless emptiness! This stark, seemingly unchanging landscape, where even time itself seemed frozen into place. It was sublime. Primeval. It had to be an incredible experience to come here with a man, a real man, to be alone here with him. Alone together.

Charlotte looked at the photographer. How nimble he was. How surefooted as he went for the best angles. How elegantly he wielded the camera. Leon smiled back, seeming to understand her thoughts, to enjoy what was unfolding between them. The pounding of her heart was due to more than just the upward slope of the glacier they were marching across. How strong the sun was up here! It was a good thing she had put on sunblock. And a pity she hadn't asked Leon to help her apply it. Next time perhaps. It was childish. Girlish dreams. Wicked even. But she enjoyed it.

Something glittered on the ground ahead, something unusual enough to get her attention. Charlotte stopped where she was and bent down. It wasn't a smooth bubble of ice, nor a snow sculpture formed by wind and frost; it was something metallic. Something quite ordinary. Some sort of hook, chrome-plated, maybe a door handle or some such thing. She wondered how it had gotten here.

Maybe it was from the missing jet? She put out her hand and was just about to pick it up when Leon called after her. "Charlotte!"

She straightened up and saw him waving his arm.

"Come on! We got it!"

She had fallen behind. The others were all standing around Morley, who was holding his GPS in his hand and pointing down at the ground. Zeroed in. Obviously, they were there at last.

"Come on!" Leon called again. "I want everyone in the picture."

She hurried, almost ran. By the time she joined the others, she was out of breath and coughing, while they were already striking poses as though they had discovered the North Pole. Charlotte joined them and put her hood back, never mind how cold it was, and shook her hair free because she knew it would look good on camera.

And she forgot to mention the metal object she had found.

"It has to be around about here," Morley said again, taking one step to the side, the GPS still in his hand. Then one more step. He was trying to pace out an area corresponding to the zeroes on his screen.

Adrian was already at work organizing the drilling. After they had all taken off their backpacks and put on their life jackets, he collected the pieces of the drill kit and began to assemble it.

"Excellent," Leon called out, shooting like crazy. "The researchers at work. Super!" His camera whirred as he took shot after shot.

The sun was shining, the endless ice gleamed, the sky shone a deep blue.

"This is pointless," Charlotte grumbled as she strapped on her jacket. It was uncomfortable and stiff as a board. "The ground's like concrete here."

"But we don't know what might happen once we start drilling," Adrian responded.

"What could happen? Almost fifty years later?"

"We don't know," he insisted.

"And then? If one of us falls into ice-cold water, what then? He may not drown, but he'll freeze for sure."

Adrian clearly didn't want to think too hard about the worst that might happen. "Best to play it safe," was all he said, and he turned back to the drill.

Leon prowled around them in ever-greater circles, stalking them like a panther and taking photographs the whole time. A panther in a bright-red anorak. "Ladies!" he called. "Maybe you could . . ." Then the rest was lost as he lifted the camera to his face once more.

"What?" Angela hollered back. "Speak up!"

"Could you do something that looks like you're working!" Leon waved his arms. "From over here it looks like Adrian is doing everything, and you two are just standing and watching."

Charlotte and Angela glanced at each other. The biologist chuckled. "Well, that's what's happening, isn't it?"

"Hold on a moment. It'll look better right away," Adrian called back. He turned to Charlotte. "When Morley and I lift the first ice cores, you can be ready with the samples case." He looked at Angela. "And you can—hmm, perhaps you can put up one of the marker poles. As though you're giving us coordinates." He pointed to a spot about five yards away. "Over there, for instance."

Leon stood off to the side, waiting. Even from a distance, they could almost feel his impatience.

"Couldn't drilling like this damage the jet?" Charlotte asked. "If it's really down there."

Adrian shook his head. "This is an ice drill. It wouldn't have a chance against metal."

"Folks! The sun will be disappearing behind the clouds any moment now!" Leon called again. "I'm not asking too much here, am I? Just do something. The main thing is that you aren't just standing around."

"Yeah, yeah!" Adrian looked around for Morley, who was still pacing the ice with his GPS. "Morley, how does it look?"

"I suggest we sink the first drill here"—he coughed and pointed down at his feet—"then in a grid at ten-meter intervals. That should do it."

"Okay, take this then." Adrian passed him the drill bits he hadn't mounted yet.

"Hey, look what I found over here!" Leon called out. "What are these things?"

Charlotte turned her head and saw the photographer bending over, saw him reach out his hand, and she realized he was standing exactly where she had seen that gleam of chrome earlier. At the same time she realized what nonsense it had been to think it might be part of the vanished Tupolev jet: not a scrap from that impact could have lain on the glacier for forty years without being covered over with ice and snow. But before she could say anything, Leon screamed. It was a sound full of surprise and pain.

Adrian turned around. "Leon?"

Leon didn't answer. He was still standing there, stooped over, his hand outstretched, and he wasn't moving.

"Leon!"

For one complacent moment Charlotte was sure Leon was just playing a silly trick. Then Angela broke into a run and the others followed, leaving everything where it was. Leon still wasn't moving. And the closer they got to him, the more clearly they could see why.

He had been impaled.

Angela stopped abruptly and put her hands in front of her mouth. Adrian stopped, too, and gasped, "Jesus Christ!" And Morley stumbled backward as though sandbagged, then turned around and threw up on the virgin white snow.

Right where Leon's hand had touched the ground, three gleaming metal spikes reared up from the ice and speared his body like a fork spearing a canapé. One of the spikes had entered his right hand

and emerged halfway up his forearm, only to pierce his head below the right eye. Another spike had gone into Leon's right knee and come out at his lower back. And the last was lodged in his left thigh just below the hip. It was a vision from the worst of nightmares.

"Oh my God!" Angela exclaimed. "*Oh my God oh my God oh my God!*"

Perhaps the worst thing was Leon was still alive. He wasn't even bleeding. There was not a drop of red on the snow around him.

Charlotte approached him. She did not know what she was doing or why; that moment she knew nothing at all. Her mind was completely blank, as empty as the icy wasteland. Her heart was beating so slowly that it seemed an iron weight lay upon it. Leon looked straight at her.

"This hurts so mu . . ." she heard him whisper, almost below hearing.

It was the last thing Leon van Hoorn would ever say. In the next instant he began to shrivel. His eyes lost their focus. His face slackened, and his features fell away. His skin wrinkled as though the bones, muscles, and fat beneath it were melting away. And then they saw that he was indeed melting: within seconds his head was no larger than a dried apple, his mouth was a tiny hole, his eyes had vanished, and the face was unrecognizable. The whole body dwindled away. His legs buckled, and his feet lifted clear of the ice, dangling like husks. Even his clothing was sucked up. The camera. The sunglasses he had been wearing against snow glare. His shoes shrunk down to little black knots, to clots, then vanished entirely. All that was left were three silver spikes, gleaming like swords, as tall as a man and shimmering all over with a rapid scurrying motion, like a nest of vengeful steel ants.

All of a sudden Charlotte knew that she had seen this motion somewhere before.

"Get out of here!" she screamed, spinning around. "Run!"

3

They only stopped when they thought they were far enough away to be safe. Just as Leon had said, the sun had gone behind the clouds—but not completely: bright rays broke through here and there, one of them falling on the exact spot where Leon had been . . . *absorbed*. The spikes seemed to be getting smaller, withdrawing into the ice they had come from.

"What was that?" Morley gasped, pale as snow himself. "What in God's name was that?"

"Nobody will believe us," Adrian gabbled. "Damn it all. Nobody will believe any of this ever happened."

Angela was trembling. Of the four of them, she was suffering most from shock. Her face was wet, and the tears had frozen to ice around the edge of her hood. Charlotte wished that she could cry, too, but she felt frozen inside. She felt nothing. All she could do was think, and all she could think was: Hiroshi. The thought pounded in her head like the pulsing of her blood. *All of this has something to do with Hiroshi's machine!* But how could she explain that to the others? None of them knew Hiroshi, and Charlotte didn't feel up to the task of explaining what she had seen on Paliuk. The feeling that she had lifted the veil of life, that she was connected to the real world, that she was truly alive here—that feeling was gone. This was a nightmare. Who would want to live in a nightmare? The only thing to do with a nightmare was escape it.

"What a goddamned . . ." Adrian stopped and then gave an inarticulate howl. "They'll say we pushed him off a cliff! I can see us there already, in a Russian jail, accused of murder . . ."

"Even the camera's gone," Morley said hollowly.

"Devil's Island." Adrian waved his arms. "Saradkov is also known as Devil's Island. Did you know that?"

"No." Morley shook his head, his eyes wide.

"The copilot told me. He also had some dumb theory about where the name came from . . . Oh shit! The legends were right!"

"Devil's Island," Morley repeated. "Oh great. So what do we do now?"

As if in answer to his question, another steel blade shot out of the ice less than twenty yards away. And then another, closer.

"Run!" Charlotte screamed. What else could they do?

And so they ran again, ran as fast as they could, back the way they had come, while behind them the blades sprang from the ice like bear traps. But the blades were behind them. It seemed that whatever was after them couldn't manage to cut them off, or lay a trap, or aim straight for them.

"We have to split up!" Adrian yelled as they ran. "One of us has to get back to the radio. Call for help."

There was no trace now of the silence that had made such an impression on them as they climbed. Instead, their own ragged panting thundered in their ears, seeming to boom back from the distant glacier walls, and they heard the *SHIKK! SHIKK! SHIKK!* of the blades chasing after them.

"Call for help?" Charlotte shouted back. "You're dreaming. By the time they're here . . ." She didn't finish her sentence, couldn't bring herself to. There was no need to put it into words.

She looked around. Was she imagining it, or were they putting some distance between themselves and the . . . thing? The spikes seemed to be falling back, unable to keep pace. And they had changed: they no longer shot barely two yards out of the ice but stretched up higher, three yards, five, ten, then crumpled and fell in a fruitless attempt to snatch their prey.

Morley stumbled, screamed, fell down . . . Adrian was at his side straightaway, helping him up. Two blades shot up out of the ice behind them like metal monsters and flung themselves at the men—in vain, however, for Adrian and Morley were well out of reach.

Hiroshi. The thought still hammered in Charlotte's mind. The movement she had seen on the spikes, that shimmering silver swarm: she had seen a rougher version of it on Paliuk. Somebody must have built a copy of Hiroshi's machine, must have developed his creation. But why?

As Charlotte ran—staggering through snowdrifts, slipping over ice, struggling forward—she felt she was caught in a dream of helplessly running and never gaining ground. Hiroshi . . . What had he told her about what had happened to his machine? He had programmed it to break out of the crate it was being transported in and throw itself into the ocean. Where each and every unit was supposed to fall to pieces. But what if it hadn't? What if it had somehow stayed . . . *functional*? What if it had grown? A machine that could build copies of itself; was it conceivable that a machine like that could change over time, could improve, and adapt? Could evolve in some mechanistic, technological way? But then . . . how had it gotten here? Why this island, of all places? Something didn't fit.

Angela screamed. Charlotte spun around, bathed in sweat, at the edge of collapse, and saw an enormous arm rear up out of the ice behind the biologist, flex, and stab straight down toward her like a scorpion's tail. Angela was lost. She knew it. She raised her arms as though surrender would save her, falling backward in shock as the thing shot down . . . and then she glided out from under it as though plucked away by an invisible hand. The spike missed her and crashed into the ice, throwing up splinters.

"The life jackets!" Adrian yelled. "We can use them as sleds!" He threw himself down onto his stomach as he spoke, landing on the ice, and then shot away down the glacier at least twice as fast as if he had been running.

Of course. It was all downhill from here. Nevertheless, Charlotte hesitated to copy the others. She stumbled on in desperation until she heard a cracking, splintering sound behind her, horrifyingly near—so near that she dared not even turn around but flung herself forward, landing on her front so hard the air rushed out of her lungs and she sped away. By the time she recovered her senses, she was thumping and sliding down the hill, out of control. Ice and snow sprayed up into her face, her knees smashed repeatedly over ripples in the ice beneath her, and she was entirely at the mercy of gravity.

At least, she thought, *I can't hear those damned things shooting out of the ice anymore.* All that Charlotte could hear now was the scraping rush of her own movement down the glacier. She squeezed her eyes almost shut, unable to see anything anyway, and felt the constant stream of ice crystals striking her face. Strangely, she didn't feel like she was slithering across an ice shield but, rather, as though she were shooting through a white tunnel.

Somebody shouted. Adrian. She couldn't understand his words. All she heard was that he was repeating them over and over with hideous urgency. All of a sudden the sounds made sense: "Turn around! Legs first! Steer!"

Charlotte opened her eyes wide and lifted her head. Straightaway, she saw what the problem was: she was shooting full tilt down a glacier that would eventually—all too soon—end in the Arctic Ocean. If she didn't manage to brake in time, or at least steer toward the gap in the cliffs they had climbed up, she would shoot out over the edge of the glacier into the icy water below. Brake? She was going far too fast for that. She put out her arms and shoved her gloved fists against the ice . . . pathetic. It made no difference at all. She tried with her feet. There was a scratching, scraping sound, but she did not slow down by any meaningful amount. No point even thinking of steering. By now she could see the black sea surging sluggishly below. She didn't have much time left.

Turn around. Maybe that would help. She tried to struggle into position, shoved a shoe into the ice, and ended up sliding along, full-length sideways, which slowed her down a little. Charlotte flailed helplessly, slid onward, then managed to grab hold of a lump of ice or stone or whatever with one hand and turn herself around. She was still on her stomach, sliding backward. She lifted her head.

There were the shining blades. Dozens of them. Coming for her.

A bump in the ice below flung her upward for a moment and she spun in the air, landing painfully hard—but on her back. Now she could steer. She rammed her boots into the ice, sending it spraying up in splinters all around her, and changed course. Like riding a luge in the Winter Olympics, except that she had no sled, just this miserable scrap of foam, and the prize was not a gold medal but her life.

She shot into the gap between the cliffs through which they had reached the plateau. It seemed a hundred years ago now. Beyond the gap there was no point in even trying to control the ride. Here, the only forces in play were gravity, inertia, and sheer blind luck. Charlotte tucked her head down between her shoulders and was flung up and tossed left and right, bashed and bruised, spun around. She rammed into rocks, and her parka ripped open. She felt snow in her face, felt pain, then stopped feeling pain and was only falling, ever downward, falling. *I'll probably break my neck*, she thought. *But even that would be better than being* absorbed.

But she didn't break her neck. She came to in a huge heap of snow and ice and heard someone shouting, "Charlotte! Hey! Are you okay?"

Adrian. That was Adrian shouting. She managed to crawl to her feet. Her head hurt, and she felt it must be bruised all over. She was dizzy. When she looked down to see whether she was indeed standing on her own two feet, possibly even standing upright, she noticed the life jacket had been reduced to scraps and fragments held together by the webbing that had given it its shape. Charlotte looked up. Adrian was standing there, waving his arms wildly. Morley and Angela, so unsteady on their feet that it was painful to watch, were already staggering toward the hut. As though the devil himself were after them.

Ah yes. That was it. Charlotte turned her head and looked up at the gap in the cliffs, trying not to think about how she had come down there hundreds of yards more or less vertically. The devil. But his gleaming silver claws were nowhere to be seen. They had escaped.

"Charlotte!"

Adrian was clambering toward her . . . why? To drag her along behind him? To help her out of the snowbank? But she was already on her feet. She took a step and felt as though the ground were moving beneath her feet, as though the island were tipping into the sea.

"Come on."

He reached her, took her by the arm, and supported her with exaggerated care. As though she were a china doll. But she was okay. Just a few scratches. She shook his hands off, unbuckled what was left of the life jacket, and let it fall.

"That was close," she said and then realized it had been more than close for Leon. She found herself thinking of his Viking mane of dirty blond hair, his eager blue eyes, his impudent smile. Gone, all gone. Absorbed. Devoured.

"Yes," Adrian said. "Goddamn it all."

Every step hurt. As though someone had taken a hammer to her while she was unconscious.

"No injuries?" she asked. "As we came down, I mean."

"You had the wildest ride. You overtook all of us, just shot past—*whoosh!*" He traced a low flat curve in the air with his hand. "When we got to the bottom, there you were on top of the avalanche."

"That's how I feel. Like an avalanche hit me."

But she could walk. If there was nothing worse waiting for them, she wouldn't complain.

Morley and Angela had already been in the hut for about five minutes when they arrived. Just as Adrian was reaching for the door, it opened and something big and bulky came out toward them: the boat, fully assembled. Morley and Angela were shoving it outside.

Adrian leapt back. "Hey, have you guys gone completely mad?"

"Goddamn all self-help books!" Morley said, sobbing, as he tugged and pushed and shoved. "Do what you're afraid of. Whoever wrote that had no idea what he was talking about."

"Fine, sure, but what are you doing?"

"What am I doing?" Morley snapped back. "I want to get off this island."

"Where to, though?"

"Off the island first, think second!" he yelled like someone who might snap at any moment.

Since there was no way past the looming bulk of rubber and nylon, Adrian and Charlotte helped the two of them to get the dinghy completely out the door and then left them to it.

"Shit," Adrian said as he opened the door to the living quarters. "I knew Morley would snap at some point."

He fetched the radio out from under the bed, opened the box, and switched it on. He plugged in the antenna they had stretched out along the ceiling. Outside, they could hear Morley screaming, "No, goddamn it, don't use the pump! Far too slow. Here, use the compressed-air bottles, this is an emergency."

Adrian turned the dial and passed Charlotte the microphone. She squatted down on the floor in front of the transmitter and talked without pausing to choose her words. "SOS. SOS. Rogachevo base, this is Saradkov. This is an emergency. Can you hear us?"

She let go of the "Transmit" button and listened. Nothing. Just an ear-splitting howl of static, a cacophony of crackling and chirruping as though a swarm of electric locusts were flying toward them.

"They're jamming the wavelength," Adrian said, standing over her. "The damn things are jamming us." He jutted out his jaw in grim determination. "Try again. As many times as you can. Try all the frequencies."

Charlotte switched over to the emergency band and tried in English. "Mayday, mayday, mayday. This is Saradkov Island." She bent imploringly over the microphone. "Can anybody hear us? This is an emergency. Our lives are in danger. This is Saradkov Island calling, coordinates: 80 degrees, 49 minutes north—"

"Oh my God!" Adrian yelled. "Look at that!"

Charlotte stopped. She saw the sheer terror in his face; he was looking out the window in the back wall. She stood up. Something was pouring down the side of the mountain, shimmering silver, slow and inexorable as lava but giving off a cold light.

And whatever it was, it was making straight for the hut.

4

"Let's get out of here," Adrian gasped.

They got moving. They had to take the radio with them, that much was obvious. Charlotte switched it off and took out the jack to the antenna, shut the lid, and snapped the hasps. Meanwhile, Adrian hurried to the corners of the room and tore down the antenna itself, rolling it up in his hand. He shoved it in his jacket pocket. "Move."

A quick glance through the window revealed the shimmering silver monstrosity was already damn close. Charlotte leapt to her feet, and they raced out the door. As they ran, Adrian took the radio case from her.

"The boat wasn't such a stupid idea after all," he said, gasping for breath.

The boat was in the water by now, fully inflated. Morley was coming up the beach toward them and stopped in shock when he saw them running. "We still need petrol," he called.

"Too late," Adrian called back. "Quick, into the boat."

"But the tank's nearly—"

"Forget it!"

Morley was about to say something else, but something must have happened behind them just then that made him shut up. A look of abject terror appeared on his face. Charlotte spun round. The silver flood had reached the hut—which collapsed in upon itself as though built of dust and scattered before the wind.

There was no need to say another word. They ran, jumping over the rocks, stumbling but not quite falling, faster than any of them had ever run before in their lives. Angela had been busy fixing the outboard onto the boat, but now she scrambled to push it down to the water. They climbed in, the women first, then Morley; Adrian shoved the dinghy off from the shore and leapt onboard after it. Morley started the motor, turned the prow out to sea, and took them out several hundred yards from the island.

"That's far enough for now," Adrian said, squatting down by a large bag that was sutured into the dinghy wall. When he opened it, Charlotte saw that it contained various bits of survival gear, including a small telescope. "We've got to be able to see what's happening on the island."

Morley cut the motor. "Tank's almost empty. Shit. We should have filled it first thing, then—"

"Then what? We could have made it to Ushakova Island? Across eighty miles of open sea? I doubt it." Adrian zipped the survival bag closed and raised the telescope. "The hut's gone. Like it had never been there."

He passed the telescope to Angela, who reached for it with shaking hands.

"Let's try it one more time," he told Charlotte. "The emergency call."

Charlotte was fighting back sheer panic. Angela and Morley hadn't had time to fit the folding slats that normally served as a deck into the bottom of the dinghy. There really was nothing between them and the icy water but the fabric of the boat. Her knees were freezing cold, and it terrified her to feel the boat bottom shift beneath her with every wave. She concentrated on the radio. *Open the lid. Throw the main switch. Wait until the green light glows.* Adrian took the antenna from his pocket and plugged in the jack. But it was hopeless, just as before. If anything, the jamming signal had grown stronger.

"What is that monster?" Angela asked, lowering the telescope.

"It's a machine," Charlotte answered. "A kind of machine."

"A machine that *eats people*?"

"Machines do what they were built to do. They don't care what that is."

Adrian was staring at Charlotte. "What makes you think so? That it's a machine?"

I think that this machine, or a previous model, once served me a cup of coffee. Could she even say such a thing—here, now—after everything that had just happened? Impossible. Besides, it wasn't true. It hadn't served her coffee; it had knitted her a scarf. But she could hardly say that either. It would have sounded like the onset of madness.

"It looks like a machine to me," was all Charlotte said.

Morley took the telescope from Angela. "It's got to be enormous, the way it sent those limbs after us," he said. "It must have taken over the whole island . . . But whatever destroyed the hut wasn't just an arm or a pincer or what the hell. It looks like something actually flowed down the mountainside."

"A machine made up of many small parts all working together," Charlotte added. "That's what it looked like to me." Small parts, minuscule. Hiroshi had spent the last six years building machines made of no more than a few atoms. That's what it had looked like. Minuscule. What if somebody had beaten him to it?

Morley put down the telescope. "This is terrifying. There's no way we can go back to that island. We have no idea what might be waiting for us." He looked around and then stared at the dinghy as though seeing it for the first time and gulped. "But what are we going to do? There's no fuel left, we've got no food, no water . . ."

A ghastly silence fell.

"We have to keep trying to make an emergency broadcast," Adrian declared. "They might stop jamming the airwaves at some point." They could hear clearly from the tone of his voice that even he thought it was a long shot.

Angela cleared her throat. "We made our last routine report the day before yesterday," she said, counting on her fingers. "That means that Rogachevo will be expecting our next report in five days. Let's say they start to worry once they haven't heard from us for seven days—that means we have to last a week."

"A week!" Morley yelped. "In this tub?"

"People have lasted longer when shipwrecked."

"But not in the Arctic Ocean." Morley rubbed at his legs. "I'm already freezing."

A week? Charlotte, too, realized that it was insanely optimistic to think the four of them could stay alive that long in this cockleshell of a boat. The simple fact they had nothing to drink meant certain death. She said nothing, though.

"May I?" she asked, putting her hand out to Morley.

He passed her the telescope. "Go on. I get sick if I look through it for too long."

Charlotte had trouble holding the telescope steady. The boat wobbled beneath her and there was nothing to hold on to. The island looked utterly innocuous once more. If she hadn't known there had been a hut standing there only a short while ago, she would never have thought anything out of the ordinary had happened. She would almost rather have seen ominous machines stomping around. To see the island looking so apparently harmless gave her the queasy feeling they had overreacted. Had the threat passed? Were they bobbing up and down on the cold waves for no reason at all? Or—and this thought was far worse—could they see nothing because the threat was brewing somewhere else entirely, somewhere they couldn't see at all? Charlotte saw in her mind's eye a forest of huge blades growing up out of the seabed toward their boat. She lowered the telescope and passed it to Adrian. Morley was lying down on his back, his mouth wide open, breathing frantically in and out and shivering—either from fear, or cold, or both. Charlotte could hardly tell the two feelings apart herself any longer.

She leaned against the inflated side of the boat, her back to the island, and stared up at the sky. The image of Leon dwindling away before her eyes would not leave her head, the way he was sucked dry—shriveling, shrinking smaller and smaller—and there was nothing at all they could have done.

She closed her eyes and wondered whether it would hurt to die.

She came to with a start when somebody shook her shoulder. Adrian.

"Was I asleep?" she asked muzzily, holding her head. It hurt. The fall, of course.

"You even snored," Adrian said. "It's five in the morning. Angela and I shared the watch."

Charlotte looked around. The boat still. So it hadn't been a bad dream. Morley was asleep on the black, shuddering bottom of the rubber dinghy, green-faced and breathing raggedly. Angela was sitting by the rudder, rubbing her arms. And the island . . .

"What's that?" Charlotte gasped when she saw the island more than half a mile away. The sun was slanting down behind it, low on the horizon, casting long shadows across the bare southern shore. Which now looked entirely different.

"We noticed it about an hour ago," Adrian said, passing her the telescope. "It looks like the machines are rebuilding the whole island."

Charlotte clambered up and put the telescope to her eye. What had been a rugged cliff, a mountainside, was now a wall of smooth, massive steel ribs hundreds of feet high. It was no longer a mountain, it was a fortress. The beach was gone. In its place gleamed miles of featureless sheet steel. And everything was moving. She could see bizarre formations growing up on the battlements, changing, looking at first like gun emplacements and then radar antennae and then something she couldn't identify at all. But whatever she could or could not recognize, the air of threat was unmistakable.

She swallowed. Her mouth was dry. She would have given a great deal for a cup of strong, hot coffee. "Somehow I still feel like all this is just a dream."

"It must have been at it for a while now, but we didn't notice before," Adrian said. "The coast was in shadow all night long, and there were dark clouds for a while."

"Why did you let us sleep?" Charlotte rolled her shoulders and felt the tension there, as though she were a block of ice. "I'm cold. Horribly cold."

"We couldn't wake you. Eventually, we gave up trying."

Charlotte remembered nothing at all. "Did you keep trying the radio?"

"Yes. Still hopeless."

For a while nobody said anything. The boat swayed, and the sea slapped lazily against its inflatable sides. The silence was unnerving.

Angela came crawling over to join them. "I was afraid you would both freeze to death," she said, her teeth chattering. "Which would be the more merciful way to go."

"I've been thinking. Someone's bound to pick up the signal," Adrian said. "The jamming signal, I mean. They're scanning every frequency all along the coast. Eventually, someone's going to come. Air-sea rescue. A search party . . ." He touched the bag in the dinghy that held their survival gear. "We have three flares."

An almighty crack sounded from the island. They all turned to look.

"That's the third time," Angela said. "But it's never been this loud before."

Charlotte stared at the island that had become a weird steel nightmare and wished fervently that she were anywhere but here. She was already half-frozen. She wouldn't last much longer. Perhaps, she considered, the best thing would be to pluck up their nerve and go back on land. No matter what might happen next.

"Wha' was tha'?" Morley had struggled to sit up, but they could hardly make out his words. "Shit . . . cold . . . I've . . . man . . . you hear s'mthing?" He stopped and stared at the island. "Fuck!" he yelled at last. "What the hell is going on over there?"

"Those things are converting the island," Adrian said, passing him the telescope.

Morley ignored it. "It looks like the Fortress of Solitude," he said. "And we're all out of Kryptonite!" He sounded close to delirium.

There was another crack, so loud this time that the whole sky echoed with the sound.

"Whoa, that's all we've been waiting for!" Morley groaned. "The ice!"

"Do you think it's the glacier calving?" Adrian asked. "Is that the noise?"

Morley put out both arms and grabbed hold of the rope that was strung through eyelets around the outer rim of the dinghy. "No, man," he answered thickly. "The whole damn ice shield is slipping. Hold on tight!"

5

It began with a rumbling. First it was a distant growl like unusually loud thunder. Then a sound as though an army of madmen were rolling barrels full of rocks down the winding stairs of countless towers somewhere behind the mountain chain. And then there was a movement—tiny, almost insignificant, but nevertheless terrifying. They saw something vanish that up until that point had seemed nothing more than a small patch of snow atop one of the cliffs. In fact, it was part of the ice cap. The glacier had begun to slip. Nothing could stop it now. As it came down, it made a sound like the whole earth and sky shattering together. Everything around thrummed with a deep, gut-shaking vibration, a frequency more felt than heard.

"We're not in the direct zone of collapse," Adrian said at the top of his voice, thinking out loud rapidly. "The part of the ice shields that slips off to the north will collapse into the bay, and then the two cliffs will channel the wave it throws up, and even when the rest of the ice splashes down to the south, we'll only catch the edge of those waves."

"Amen," Morley shouted out, gripping the line tight. He pressed his head down against the side of the dinghy.

Charlotte copied his actions. Adrian shouted something else, but the thunder all around was too loud for her to make out his words.

It's just the edge of the wave, Charlotte told herself again as an invisible hand lifted the boat and flung it into the air. *We're not in the direct zone of collapse,* she thought as it dropped back down like a stone. And then a breaker hammered down on them as though someone had tipped a swimming pool full of ice-cold water on their heads. For a terrible moment Charlotte felt nothing at all, felt that she was floating, and if it hadn't been for the line she would have been carried clean away. Then came a furious blow, and the line twisted wildly in her grasp, wrenching her shoulder—and Charlotte was right back where she had been, in a boat that was now half-full of icy water.

"Goddamn!" somebody yelled. Adrian, right next to her. He moved fast, raging and cursing without a break as he bailed water overboard.

Charlotte had never heard most of his curses before in her life, and she was somehow impressed he had such a stock of hitherto unsuspected profanity. The dinghy bucked and writhed, this way and that, as if they were being flung around on a poorly designed roller coaster. Charlotte had no idea how Adrian could do anything but hold on as tight as possible. The sea raged around them, and the spray flew, a nightmare of waves clashing, roaring, and bursting. But Adrian was bailing. *We're not in the direct zone of collapse. It's just the edge of the wave.* Good to know.

Eventually—hours later, it seemed to her—the sea calmed down. Perhaps it had only been a few minutes, but they were the longest minutes she had ever lived through. Minutes of water that had soaked her all the way through. Despite that, she didn't even feel cold. Rather, she felt numb from the neck down, as though she had been given a full-body anesthetic.

"We're through the worst," somebody said. Adrian. Or Morley. It didn't matter who. They weren't in the direct zone of collapse. It was just the edge of the wave.

Now there was ice floating all around them. Charlotte raised her head and turned it with effort. Ice floes everywhere she looked. The debris of the glacier, jostling and shoving restlessly as though angry at how things had turned out. She shivered against her will. She was freezing for real now; the cold had seized hold of her and was gnawing at her body. *It's over*, she thought as she realized she could barely feel her hands. *We won't last another hour like this, never mind a week.*

"Perhaps . . ." she began, then burst into a fit of coughing. She gathered her strength and started again. "Perhaps we should go back on shore. What do you say? We don't know for sure they're still after us." *And even if they are, at least it'll be quicker*, she thought.

Adrian stopped bailing beside her. He glanced from her to the island and back again, his face a mask of terror. "But there's nothing left on land. The hut's gone, our gear is gone . . ."

And then they heard another rumble.

"Oh no," Angela moaned. "Not again."

Adrian and Morley looked at one another, baffled.

"What else can be happening?" Adrian asked, coughing. He was wet, too.

Morley just shook his head, perplexed. He was as pale as a sheet and said nothing.

The noise became louder, and the louder it grew, the more clearly they heard that it was different from the previous noise. This time it came from far below them, a vibration that rose from the depths of the earth and only became a sound when it reached the surface. They could see fine ripples on the sea all around them, spreading out as though the island were a tuning fork held in the water. And then it was no longer a rumbling but a high, piercing whine that hurt their ears. Something cracked like a whip. A thunderclap rolled out over the Arctic Ocean and echoed back from the sky. And then something huge and slim shot up from behind the metal walls of the mountains, shot into the air like an arrow from an enormous bow, and burst into flame high above them, becoming a glare that hurt their eyes. The whining stopped. Whatever it was went up and up, dazzlingly bright, first in utter silence and then, after a few seconds, with a thunderous roar that echoed down to where they watched.

"A rocket!" Adrian yelled. "It's a rocket!"

Nobody contradicted him. What else could it have been? They watched as the dot of light dwindled away higher and higher into the sky, without vanishing from sight or even growing noticeably less intense. The effect was that of a giant running a welding torch across the sky. There was a peculiar sound behind them. They spun about. It was Morley, croaking and hooting, a crazed cry of triumph.

He gasped. "Saved! We're saved!"

"Morley?" Adrian shook his shoulder. "Are you crazy?"

Morley's grin spread right across his face. "Don't you understand? Now they'll come! Anything that floats or flies will be headed this way at top speed to see what's going on!"

Morley was right. In less than half an hour a formation of three jets came thundering overhead and circled Saradkov at a good distance. Adrian fired a flare. One of the jets peeled off, flew above them, and wagged its wings briefly—was that a sign he had seen them? Then they flew off, and it was quiet once more.

"And now?" Angela asked.

"They'll come," Morley said, his voice so burdened with hope that it was painful to hear.

Charlotte couldn't stop shivering. She felt hot from the shaking that gripped her body. Was someone bending over her, talking to her? Angela? Her hair was wet, she had red eyes and was shivering herself. Charlotte could no longer understand what she was saying, could only hear the strange sounds of a foreign language, yearned for someone to take her in their arms and speak words of comfort in French: "*Ne t'inquiète pas. Je suis là. Je m'occupe de toi. Tout va bien—* Don't worry. I'm here. I'll take care of you. Everything's all right."

Everything was shaking. Everything was cold. Time stood still. The cold was devouring her, sucking the life from her body, and freezing her into stone. Nobody came. Hours passed . . . an eternity.

Then there was noise again. A machine coming down from the sky. A helicopter blasting ice-cold air down onto their ice-cold clothes, wrenching the breath from their lungs. Her heart skipped a beat. Hands grabbed hold of her. Someone hoisted her up and wound a thick rope around her. She was lifted up into the air, higher and higher toward the churning silver blades that were sending down the shivering cold air and the deafening roar. Someone was talking to her, yelling at her through the din, but she couldn't understand a word. She fell backward. Blackness rose up all around her, and she sank down into it.

She woke up once, in a soft bed with white sheets. It was warm, incredibly warm, and everything was all right. Then it went dark again.

Bright light. Something shaking her. Would it never end? She didn't know why the shaking terrified her so, but it did. Charlotte opened her eyes and saw a familiar face. Adrian.

"Thank God," he said. "I thought you'd never wake up."

Charlotte blinked and tried to sit up. Then she noticed the IV in her left arm, hooked up to a drip bag full of some clear fluid above her. "What's happening? Where are we?"

"Onboard a Russian ship whose name I can't remember for the life of me. It seems to be an icebreaker or something like that. It's huge anyway."

It all came back to her. The island. Leon. The machines. Escaping, then the boat and the wave that hit them. "They saved us?"

"Well, they fished us out of the water at least."

Charlotte looked around. She was in a sick bay with ten beds, three showing signs of use. Four, including her own. "Where are the others?"

"Down in the canteen or whatever you call it onboard a ship. They're eating. I stayed here because you were tossing and turning dreadfully and babbling away in every language under the sun. They gave you something because you were the worst hit by the cold. It might have made you feverish." He pointed to her arm. "Should I tell the doctor to unplug you? Then we can join the others. I have to admit, I'm hungry, too."

Food was about the last thing Charlotte wanted just then. She looked again at Adrian. He was wearing dark blue fatigues with Russian tags. She looked down at herself. They had dressed her in the same, but without a jacket. At the moment she was wearing a dark blue T-shirt that was much too large for her, leaving her arms free.

"What else is happening?" she asked. "What's going on with the island?"

Adrian sighed. "No idea. They cross-examined us, but I don't know how much they understood of what we were trying to tell them. At any rate, we have someone keeping an eye on us all the time, and there are a whole lot of ships and subs out there—it's kind of impressive."

"Let's go and look." She swung herself upright and sat on the edge of the bed, then she had to stop, as she felt dizzy.

"Wait, I'll tell them."

Adrian hurried over to the massive steel door with its heavy bars, stuck his head out, and called to someone. Meanwhile, Charlotte impatiently eyed the distance to the closest porthole and tried to compare it to the length of her IV hose. It was close enough. She got up, grabbed hold of the bedframe, and waited for the ship to roll that way. She scurried over to the thick, round glass.

Well, look at that. Outside, in the unreal half-light of the endless Arctic day, was a whole fleet. Charlotte squinted. Those weren't just Russian ships out there. Was she seeing things, or was that—

"Hey, hey!" Adrian was back, taking her by the arm. "The doctor's on his way."

Charlotte pointed out at one of the submarines, its conning tower silhouetted dark and massive against the waves. "Isn't that an American flag?"

"What?" He peered through the pane. "Hey, you're right. That's great!" Like all the Americans Charlotte knew, Adrian Cazar found the proximity of US troops reassuring. He had been on edge every time they had to deal with the Russian military.

The doctor appeared, a young man with prominent jug ears who was as nervous as if he had only just graduated the week before. But once Charlotte was back at her bed, he removed the IV deftly.

"Wait here," he said in guttural English. "Captain is coming. He want to . . . ask you questions."

Adrian made a face, and once the doctor had gone, taking the infusion with him, he said, "Well, I just hope I won't starve before he's done."

It took less than five minutes. The man who introduced himself as Captain First Class Vladimir Korodin had ice-gray hair and ice-gray eyes. He was wearing a plain uniform, his only sign of rank the three men who accompanied him and watched his every movement with awe and devotion, nodding obediently as they hurried to carry out his orders.

"They tell me you speak Russian," he said, turning to Charlotte.

"*Da*—That's right," she said.

The captain stood at the foot of her bed as firm as a rock—except for his fingers, which were tapping out a restless rhythm on the bedframe. "Then I would like to ask you to tell me once more what happened. What your friends have reported is, to put it mildly, so fantastical that I was beginning to doubt whether any of my crew really speaks English."

One of the orderlies ducked his head. Evidently, he had been drafted as an interpreter.

Charlotte nodded. She would have preferred not to have to remember it all, but it was a small price to pay for being rescued. So she told him what had happened and answered all his questions.

"Ask him if that's really an American ship out there," Adrian added once she was finished.

The captain understood that much English. Without waiting for Charlotte to translate, he said, "Yes. That is a submarine of the US Sixth Fleet. Of course the Americans noticed the rocket launch, and since a launch from Russian territory without warning is against the test-ban treaties, we were obliged to allow them access to prove that we had nothing to do with the rocket." A shadow flitted across his face. "Back when I was a young man, something like this would have started the Third World War."

A curly-haired sailor appeared in the doorway, looking like a uniformed cherub. He had been running, and now he said breathlessly, "Captain! They're here."

Korodin gave a brief nod. "Good. Thank you. I'll be there at once." He looked at Adrian and Charlotte. "And I would ask you to join me on the bridge as soon as you can." He glanced at the doctor, who was lurking in the background. "Do what you can for her. This is important." Another glance, this time at the orderly who had looked so shamefaced earlier. "You show them the way."

Then he left, followed by the other two orderlies.

The doctor checked Charlotte over one more time and seemed satisfied with what he saw. "You have come through it very well. You will probably have no frostbite," he told her in Russian. He was visibly relieved not to have to speak English any longer. "Before you leave our ship, I will give you a cream and tell you how to apply it to the wounds on your feet."

Charlotte just nodded. Wounds on her feet? She hadn't even noticed. She realized for the first time that some of her toes were bandaged. She put on the fatigue jacket and a pair of man's shoes because of the bandages. Though they were far too big for her, they still managed to pinch her feet. Then she and Adrian followed the bashful orderly. As they walked, Charlotte noticed he was losing his hair in neat little circular patches at the back of his head.

The bridge was the size of a ballroom. Computer screens gleamed everywhere, and crewmen were sitting at brightly lit consoles. There was an air of calm determination. At the back, Captain Korodin had ordered that a large table be put in place that was clearly not part of the normal equipment. As they arrived on the bridge, two men were just crawling out from underneath it with drills and screwdrivers. The screws fastening the table to the floor gleamed bright and new.

Morley and Angela were already there. They were standing next to a group of men whose uniforms were a pale blue, in contrast to the dark blue uniforms they had seen on the ship so far. The men in dark blue were giving a wide berth to this group and glowering at them mistrustfully. They were American sailors, with yards of gold braid on their sleeves. The competition, so to speak. No wonder she could feel a breath of frost in the air on the bridge.

One of the Americans approached them. "Commander John Penrose, ma'am, US Navy," he barked and put his hand out to Charlotte. "You must be Miss Malroux."

Charlotte nodded. His hand felt warm, dry, and strong. "Pleased to meet you."

"And Dr. Cazar, if I have been informed correctly."

"Adrian," Adrian answered happily.

"I'm afraid," the commander went on, "you'll have to tell us everything you already told Captain Korodin and his people all over again. And please don't be concerned—we're going to be filming you. This isn't to try to catch you out later; we just want to have the most comprehensive documentation of events that we can get. Nobody can explain what's happened here, so that means every scrap of information you can give us is important."

"Sure thing," said Adrian. He seemed immensely cheered to have the commander there as a living link to the mother country.

The captain approached. "Commander Penrose," he said in thickly accented English, "I invite you and your men to take your seats. We are ready."

"Thank you, Captain," Penrose said frostily and gestured to his men. "Are there any new readings from the island?"

Korodin nodded curtly. "The temperature continues to rise. It is now more than fifteen degrees Celsius. Above zero!"

Penrose frowned. "That's—"

"About sixty degrees Fahrenheit, Commander," Adrian put in. "Which is unbelievable in this region. May I ask how you are measuring?"

"They've got an infrared camera." Penrose pointed to a group of Russians standing around a screen at the other end of the console, all of whom had worried looks on their faces. "Okay then. We have a few tricks of our own. Come on, have a seat."

Morley and Angela finally made their way through the knot of people to join them.

"Hi, Charlotte," Angela whispered, putting an arm around her. "How are you doing? You look like you've seen a ghost. More than one, I guess."

"I don't remember anything," Charlotte admitted. "I'm just glad we got off that dinghy."

"Just watch out for the coffee they serve you here," Morley warned her softly. "It's unbelievable stuff. It'll burn your guts out." He looked pale and probably spoke from experience.

They sat down together. The American delegation joined them to their right; the seats to their left stayed empty for the time being. The Russian representatives were still clustered around Korodin, who was holding a telephone to his ear and listening intently, every now and then saying, "*Da.*"

"Not a bad idea, this." A lanky soldier who had just opened his laptop in front of him rapped his knuckles on the table. "Puts us right in the middle of the action. Better than cooling our heels in a conference room, huh?"

"They mostly want to show us that they have nothing to hide," Commander Penrose put in skeptically. "I just hope that's true."

The Russians finally joined them at the table. Korodin now had an interpreter with him, who translated whatever the captain said to him in Russian into barely comprehensible English. This didn't matter: Commander Penrose also had an interpreter beside him, who translated straight from the Russian.

"I have just had a call from Moscow," the captain declared. "The crew of the International Space Station has been able to track the course of the object that took off from Saradkov. The data have been passed to the Russian Academy of Sciences and several other groups and show that it was traveling at fifty-one kilometers per second—and still accelerating." His interpreter was better at mental arithmetic than at English pronunciation; he calculated the speed without skipping a beat as "thirty miles a second."

Commander Penrose rubbed his chin. "That seems pretty darn fast to me."

"It is about fifty times the speed of sound," Korodin replied dryly.

"Given the correct starting trajectory, the object has now reached solar escape velocity," added a Russian officer wearing wire-rimmed glasses. "Meaning that it is now moving fast enough to leave our solar system and enter interstellar space."

The American commander looked at the soldier with the laptop. "Can you confirm, Lieutenant?"

The lanky young man tapped rapidly at the keyboard. "Eh . . . yes, sir. Just in. AFSPC is still tracking. It's beyond the orbit of the moon and flying at . . ." He whistled through his teeth. "Wow. Sixty miles a second. And still firing, looks like."

Korodin nodded once his interpreter had translated. "So you see, this object displays abilities well beyond our current technology. This is not a Russian rocket—and not American either."

"I understand," the commander said, although it didn't entirely sound as though he did. He cleared his throat. "So the question remains what it actually is."

"Aliens," Morley burst out.

Nobody contradicted him. In fact, everyone nodded.

6

Charlotte nearly jumped out of her seat. What? Aliens? What were they talking about? What was happening here? Hiroshi—this all had something to do with Hiroshi's machine. Or was she completely wrong?

Commander Penrose passed a hand over his face. All of a sudden he seemed tired. "Okay, guys," he said, looking around the table. "This is probably one of those moments that's going to end up in the history books. Let's try not to look like idiots." He nodded to the soldier with the laptop. "Jim, show our hosts the satellite image."

The young lieutenant jabbed a few keys and then turned his computer around so that everybody could see the screen. Displayed there was something that looked at first glance like the latest in modern art, and at second glance like a gunshot impact photographed through a microscope.

"We received this image on our way over here," the commander said. "It's an image of Saradkov Island. What we see here is a deep hole in the middle of the island, running down several miles—"

"Pardon me, sir," Adrian interrupted. "Could there be some mistake? We were working with satellite images of the island as well—topographical radar images—and there's no sign of this hole on any of them."

"Well, there is now," Penrose said curtly. "These pictures are three hours old." He leaned forward and pointed at a structure of nested semicircles at the edge of the hole. "Our eggheads say that these are magnetic coils. We can only see part of them, because the satellite wasn't exactly over the mouth of the hole when it took these shots. They tell us the whole thing is a kind of upright linear accelerator that catapulted the object up into space. The barrel of the gun, so to speak. And whatever's racing away from us up there was the bullet."

Korodin had folded his arms and listened to all this without expression. Now he nodded. "Meaning that the engines only needed to ignite when the rocket was in the air, in order not to damage the launch equipment."

"Exactly. And that in turn means there could be other rockets."

Charlotte leaned back in her chair and concentrated entirely on the feeling of the cool plastic against her back. She wasn't dreaming all this, was she? No. She raised her head. The Arctic sea outside the enormous window was gray and sluggish, the ice floes shimmering like teeth torn loose from a gigantic mouth. The steel towers of the submarines swayed ponderously. She no longer felt any urge to contradict them. It seemed to her that in some strange way they both had a part of the truth—that she and the military were both thinking along the right lines.

"We have orders to land troops on the island, inspect the facility there, and take material samples," the Russian captain declared. "Since your president and ours have been on the phone with each other for several hours, you may already know I am authorized to invite you to send some of your own men along."

Penrose nodded. "Thank you, Captain. We will of course accept your offer."

"I don't think that's a good idea," Adrian burst out. "That island is dangerous. More than that: it's deadly. It skewered one of our team and sucked him dry like a spider sucks a fly."

The Russian captain and the American commander turned toward him with almost identical expressions of indignation.

"I understand your concern, young man," Penrose replied, "but dealing with danger is our job. We are trained for that very purpose, so don't worry. We know what we're doing."

He glanced at his Russian colleague, who nodded and said, "Exactly."

The frostiness between the two military groups vanished all of a sudden. They understood one another.

While preparation for the landing party got underway, the military began to take their statements. One American and one Russian soldier each put a video camera on the conference table. The American hooked his up to a computer, while the Russian used a bulky recorder that took cassette tapes. Adrian was first up; the others were asked to wait out of earshot on the other side of the bridge.

"This is all going to go wrong," Morley moaned.

They stood in a group by the window looking down at the deck below, where preparations were in full swing. A helicopter was towed out of a hangar, a row of big black dinghies stood ready, and men in thick thermal parkas were checking their guns. Meanwhile, ever more ships joined the fleet, little gray boats with huge antennae and multibarreled gun placements in the bow.

Angela hugged herself and shivered. "I wish I'd stayed home."

She volunteered to go next once Adrian had rejoined the group. As though she hoped they would get her out of here once she had finished.

Adrian didn't have much confidence in the mission either. "They're watching the island; you can see it up there on one of the monitors," he said, gesturing briefly toward the console. "And they're still picking up movement. No way have the aliens flown off so that we can loot what's left of their base—I don't think so." He was frowning deeply, his brow furrowed with worry. "The Russian guy even told me the directional mics are picking up sound coming from Saradkov. A kind of low buzzing, he said. Like a swarm of insects."

Morley groaned. "This is all going to go wrong, I'm telling you."

Just as Angela finished making her statement, the landing party set out. The boats were put into the water and the crew climbed in, and the helicopter took off. A Russian soldier came and asked them to sit at the conference table for the duration of the mission; just for safety's sake, he said.

Captain Korodin was standing next to the helmsman with an air that suggested this was his customary place. Head held high, he issued curt, sharp commands as he watched events unfold on the radar screen. He never once let go of the phone receiver in his hand as he communicated with Commander Penrose, who was following the action from his submarine. The captain's own English was hardly any worse than his interpreter's. There wasn't much to see, and what they could see was notably unspectacular: five black dinghies headed for the island leaving five trails of gleaming silver wake behind them, and above them a helicopter, a shadow skimming across the featureless sky.

Charlotte would have liked to know what time it was. She had lost all sense of the passing hours. She would have believed it was the middle of the night as readily as anything else. Wasn't there a clock here on the bridge? Here and there she could spot a display that showed minutes and hours, but every one of them showed a different time.

"We're approaching the coast," the loudspeakers crackled. "It's a strange sight. The whole island seems to have been steel-plated. It reminds me of the Death Star . . ."

"What's he saying?" Adrian asked, so Charlotte translated.

The American soldiers who had stayed onboard grinned at the *Star Wars* reference. "Hey, maybe they'll meet Darth Vader," said the one who had worked the video camera.

"The work that has been done here is astonishing," the voice from the loudspeaker resumed. Some of the screens began to display pictures from the cameras onboard the helicopter. As the dinghies reached the shore, the crewmen leaped out and pulled them up on land; they were clearly well trained. "The surface of the steel is corrugated in complex patterns. We can walk on it without any problem. We can see what looks like a large gate up ahead. Lieutenant Miller suggests we head there first."

"Whatever you do, stay together," Korodin replied. "Apart from that, you have a free hand."

Now they could see the gate, rising huge and foreboding from between massive ribs of steel where yesterday—had it only been yesterday?—there had been the bare, rough rock of the southern face of the mountains. Whatever had taken over the island had rebuilt it completely in the space of a few hours.

On the screen showing the helicopter broadcast they could see the terrain from above. The soldiers looked like little dark ants as they marched across the shimmering plain, and they could also see movement up on the battlements. At Korodin's command the cameraman zoomed in: there was nothing standing watch there, nor were there any machines converging to intercept the landing party; rather, the battlements themselves were changing shape, sprouting bizarre metal structures that branched and twisted in the blink of an eye, becoming thicker or thinner or flatter in an instant, changing color . . .

"That's incredible," someone gasped. Charlotte thought she heard a sound here on the bridge—the sound of the hairs standing up on everybody's neck.

For a second there was complete silence. Then a scream rang out that froze the blood in their veins.

"Lieutenant Sinyukhaev!" Korodin barked into the radio. "Report!"

"This is Captain Yuran, Captain," another voice came on, panting and gasping. "The lieutenant has . . . vanished, sir. He simply sank into the ground. I . . . we don't know what happened. It looks as though . . . ah!"

"Captain?"

Nothing. No reply.

Korodin's fist crashed down on the console. "Why don't we have any pictures of what's going on? Helicopter!"

The cameraman onboard the helicopter swung his lens around wildly, looking for the soldiers who had just landed, and pulled back with the zoom until they could see the whole beach. There was nobody there. All the soldiers were gone. So were the boats, the guns, everything.

"Devil take it!" Korodin cursed. "What about the other cameras?"

Hectic activity at the control panels, then someone found some footage that showed at least part of what had happened, a long-distance shot. They saw the men throw up their arms in astonishment and then sink in an instant, and saw the dinghies . . . dissolve. The boats suddenly deflated, collapsed, and then seemed to melt into the ground.

"Helicopter!" Korodin ordered. "Turn back. All ships: increase distance from island."

Just then the picture from the helicopter camera showed something shooting up from the battlements, and then the screen went dark. They watched from the window of the bridge as the helicopter fell. But it wasn't the spiraling crash familiar from the movies; instead, the aircraft burst apart into a cloud of smaller pieces that rained down onto the steel walls of the fortress and melted into them, like drops of mercury falling into a quicksilver sea.

"Get me Moscow," Captain Korodin ordered his radio operator. "I want to talk to Admiral Ulyakov."

For a while nothing happened. The captain had left the bridge, and the helmsman steered left, then right, while the other officers stared into space.

"Holy shit," murmured the American soldier with the video camera. "Patrick Miller has two daughters, five years old and two. Hannah and Lauren. I don't even want to think . . ."

Just then Captain Korodin returned to the bridge, a look of grim determination on his face. Without looking left or right he marched to his place by the helm. "*K-107* and *K-334*, set course for the island," he ordered. "Prepare to fire from optimum barrage distance. Target that gate."

Someone passed him the telephone; obviously, Commander Penrose was calling. Korodin listened for a long while before he answered. "I understand, Commander, but I have clear orders from my commander-in-chief." Another pause. "I am sorry. I understand the scientific interest, but the security of my country takes precedence over any such concerns." Apparently, the commander knew an attack was planned and was against it. "Commander, I hardly need remind you that we are on Russian sovereign territory. Yes. I am sorry, but those are my orders. You would do exactly the same thing if our circumstances were reversed."

"Now there's bad blood between the two of them again," Morley murmured. "What a surprise."

The two ships the captain had ordered into position reported for duty. "Open fire, all barrels," Korodin commanded almost offhandedly.

A moment later they heard the roar of artillery. Searing lines of fire hissed out one after another toward the island, hit the massive steel walls and—almost incredibly—broke through, leaving huge holes. A muffled cheer broke out on the bridge.

"Sustain fire," the captain ordered. "Empty your magazines." There was satisfaction in his voice, too.

The cannon continued to fire. At some point, though, they made no further impression. The holes in the gate and walls around it weren't getting any bigger; rather, they seemed to be shrinking.

"Cease fire! Cameras, close-up!"

The smoke dispersed. Cameras pointed toward the zone that had been at the center of the bombardment just in time to catch the holes in the steel walls and gate close themselves up. There was the sound of indrawn breath.

"That's crazy," Morley murmured. "Alien technology. And here we are, watching live."

"I could do without the experience," Angela said.

Captain Korodin took off his cap, smoothed his ice-gray hair, and put his cap back on again. Then he picked up the microphone. "All ships: the enemy has the capacity to repair damage from a direct hit. We do not know how extensive this capacity is, but we will do our best to push it beyond its limits. All ships in the fleet will coordinate firepower. Submarines are to use sea-to-air missiles; frigates will use artillery and rocketry. Target is the construction that looks like a gate. Until further information is available, we will assume that even for the extraterrestrials a gate is a weak point. It is important that all hits strike the target as close to simultaneously as possible, to maximize the effect. Action to begin immediately. Captain Korodin out." He nodded to an officer who clearly had the task of coordinating all the ships.

The ship on which they stood was also part of this second attack; Charlotte felt it begin to move, felt the floor beneath her feet vibrate as the engines started up. She felt queasy. More than anything else she wanted to stop all this—if only she knew how. She realized that every muscle in her body was tense. She watched Captain Korodin as he stood there, his jaw thrust forward, his head straining on his neck, his eyes fixed upon the island as though he could conquer it with his gaze alone. Had there been somebody close to him among the men lost to the island? Or was this simply the normal rage of a commander whose men depended on him, who was in charge of their safety?

This attack would be futile as well—Charlotte was suddenly certain of that. Morley didn't need to utter his warnings of doom, and indeed he had stopped. He was now sitting there, motionless, staring down at the tabletop. Angela was gnawing at her lower lip. Adrian was watching matters unfold with his usual frowning, skeptical interest. He was the only one who didn't look as though he would rather be anywhere else.

The first reports began coming in from ships that had reached their firing positions. The man at the console passed on each report in a low voice to the captain astonishingly calmly.

"Fire at will," Korodin ordered at last, equally matter-of-fact.

The recoil from the guns on deck shook the whole ship, violent blows that felt as though a gang of enraged giants were beating the stern with huge hammers. Charlotte saw trails of smoke, an immense number of them, converge upon the island from all sides, saw them strike the steel fortifications, then saw the island disappear in a cloud of smoke. Charlotte craned her head. Had it worked? Had the Russians really managed to bomb the island to smithereens, to finish off the grisly technological power that lurked within? She found herself caught up in the mood, wishing for its destruction, unable to imagine any other outcome. Even the recoil had been bone-shakingly powerful.

But then all of a sudden a clamor broke out at the control desks, and the men leapt to their feet. Orders were shouted and hectic activity broke out. The captain, holding a microphone to his mouth, could be heard over it all shouting over and over, "Retreat! Retreat! All ships full speed astern! Immediately!"

"Oh my God," Charlotte heard Adrian whisper next to her. She couldn't stay seated any longer. She hurried to the window and could hardly believe what she saw through the flying spray and the distant clouds of the explosions. Something silver that looked like a huge lizard's tongue detached itself from the fortress and unrolled in a matter of seconds, aiming for one of the ships closest to the island. It stretched and lunged ruthlessly through the air and across the waves until it had reached the ship and made contact. That same instant the Russian ship began to change. It stopped firing. The bridge and conning tower collapsed into themselves, and the stern billowed and bloated, changing color. The whole ship mutated into something that no longer bore any resemblance to a battleship but instead looked like part of some nightmare second fortress, in front of the island. Now she saw that there was already something else inside this armored sea wall: the remnants of the first ship to have been attacked this way. It was this first counterattack that had caused all the commotion and led to the order to retreat. Now their ship was retreating, too. The island vanished out of sight behind them.

Captain Korodin ordered them taken from the bridge and back to the sick bay, evidently the only place he had to put them. After they were given something to eat and drink, the American soldier and the Russian soldier came to take the remaining statements. Both were having obvious trouble focusing on the task.

"What's happening now?" Adrian asked. The Russian soldier, a fresh-faced youth with muscles like steel cables who could hardly take his eyes off Charlotte, simply shook his head; it was impossible to tell whether he knew nothing or simply had orders not to say. The American, a straw-blond Texan with freckles, finally let slip that as far as he knew they were waiting for reinforcements, and waiting above all for two admirals to arrive, one Russian and one American. They would take over command on the spot. The way he said it, he clearly believed everything would be fine and dandy when that happened.

"It takes a little while for a ship to get someplace," he explained. "An aircraft carrier like this has a top speed of thirty knots, as does the escort squadron. And the Arctic Ocean ain't exactly the best operational theater. . . . Anyhow, the first American carrier that can get here is the USS *Harry S. Truman*, and she won't be here before next week. But the Russian president has given us permission to set up a temporary air-support base on the next island—what's it called?

Ushakova, I think—and the first Globemasters are already on their way. They'll land on the ice, build a landing strip, put up a few tents for the men, and set up refueling stations. The jets will be flying in around the same time, refuelling in midair."

Charlotte shuddered. It all sounded so Hollywood. She half expected Bruce Willis to be playing the American admiral.

They managed to sleep for a couple of hours. When they woke up, they learned that the top brass had just arrived and that they were to return to the bridge, please, to tell their story to the new commanders. When they got up there, both admirals were standing in the middle of the bridge, each surrounded by a cluster of staff officers. They were listening to Captain Korodin and his staff explain everything that had happened, with the help of videos and other material.

Rear Admiral Denis J. Whitecomb didn't look the least bit like Bruce Willis. He had a face like a pancake and a doughy handshake, and despite all the gold braid and medals on his uniform, he gave the impression he spent most days working behind a desk. "Well this is a hell of a situation, if the ladies will excuse my language," he said in greeting. The forced brashness of his tone made him seem worryingly incompetent.

His Russian counterpart, Admiral Ulyakov, seemed to consider it a point of honor not to speak a word of English himself. He was broad-shouldered, bull-necked, and bad-tempered; and he stood in the middle of the bridge as though it were his own ship. His pock-marked nose was flushed red, presumably from the unaccustomed Arctic air, but it made him look as though he had spent the previous night drinking with friends and then been dragged out of bed far too early this morning. He listened without expression as his interpreter translated the American admiral's long-winded protestations: that Washington insisted the phenomenon be isolated and scientifically studied, and that the US would supply all the necessary funds, capability, technical equipment, and expert consultants.

"The president is convinced that what we have here is not just a unique opportunity to learn a whole new kind of technology, but duty to history. We owe it to the future to handle this discovery with all due care and attention, and to turn it to the very best advantage we possibly can for all mankind. And let us not forget: since in all probability we are dealing with the remnants of an extraterrestrial incursion, since we are dealing with an alien intelligence that is similar in kind if not in degree to our own, reason demands that we behave in such a manner that if we ever make contact with the beings who created this artifact, we do not prejudice our chances."

After the rough greeting he had given them, Charlotte was astonished at how eloquently the man spoke. In another uniform he could have made a perfectly good priest.

"I am interested in one thing only," Ulyakov declared brusquely. "Namely: Is whatever has seized hold of this island a danger to Russia, or is it not? And if it is a danger, then I will do everything in my power to remove it. That is my strategy."

Whitecomb looked downcast. Evidently he had not counted on such a rough reception. "But . . . our president has reached an under-standing with your president that—"

"Your president is a long way away," Ulyakov interrupted him. "And so is mine. Neither of them can see what we see here. It is easy to consider all angles when you are sitting at a desk, but in the end all that counts is the reality before us. Do you understand me? We are the hands and eyes on the ground. Your president must listen to what you tell him, and my president must listen to me." He waved his hand dismissively. "So, let's get to work."

Whitecomb beamed, displaying a painfully false smile. "Then we agree! That's exactly what we're suggesting: a thorough scientific survey of the situation . . . international experts looking at every pos-sible aspect . . . throw a wide cordon around the island and secure it—"

"Cordon the island? How do you imagine you can do that?" Ulyakov glowered. "An island is a rock that happens to stick up out of the water. Nothing more. You have a submarine of your own here. Have your men actually looked at the island below the waterline?"

The rear admiral blinked in surprise. "Uh . . . to the best of my knowledge . . . I would have to—"

"Well, I sent one of our submarines out," the Russian said. "All the way around the island's coastal shelf. It should be back any moment."

Charlotte and the others glanced at one another unhappily. Why were they here? Nobody seemed to be paying any attention to them. They were just in the way. She also wondered where Admiral Whitecomb had popped up from. He spoke as though he had been in the Oval Office just a few hours ago. But Washington was almost five thousand miles away by the most direct route.

"*K-104* reporting, Admiral," said one of the men at the consoles, presumably the radio operator.

Ulyakov put out his hand to take the telephone receiver, which was on a long spiral cable. Only then did Charlotte realize the admiral was standing on the exact spot Captain Korodin had previously occupied. "Ulyakov," he said. He listened, nodding once or twice. "Good. Transmit the images."

He turned to Whitecomb and gestured to one of the screens. "They have found something."

As it turned out, to say that they had *found something* was rather an understatement. The screen lit up and showed underwater footage of bare, striated rocks patched across with the shadows of ice floes on the surface. It was a monotonous study in white, gray, blue, and black—until the camera caught something that resembled what Charlotte imagined a seabed cable or pipeline might look like. It was neither, though. They saw that as the submarine tracked the object: it was much bigger. It was a steel wall, built along the seabed. And it ran outward from the island. Next came a gap in the rocks and then a ledge, which afforded them a longer view. The massive steel ribs that had formed on the sides of the mountain up on the island simply kept going when they reached the water. Metal arms spread out in all directions like steel roots, running for miles on end. The submarine kept going, its camera trained on the leading end of one of these roots. They could see it inching forward, growing longer and fatter as it went.

"So? What do you have to say now?" Ulyakov asked, turning to his American counterpart. "You want to cordon that? Impossible. You are deluding yourself."

Whitecomb stared at the screen, where the footage was now repeating. He looked utterly crestfallen.

"This is not just a danger to Russia, this is a danger for the whole world." The Russian admiral thrust his head forward. "I will request the president's permission to use atomic weapons. We are going to blast that island sky-high."

7

At these words an electrical frisson ran through the room. Everybody flinched.

"Admiral!" Whitecomb was almost apoplectic. "Please don't be hasty. Some of our president's scientific advisers—serious, well-regarded researchers—think we may be dealing with an alien nano-technological device here. In fact, they think that is the only possible explanation of events. It's a technology that offers almost limitless prospects for the future, possibilities we can't even begin to guess at from where we are today. If we managed to figure it out when it's served up on a plate like this, it would be like . . . it would be as though the ancient Egyptians had suddenly been able to build a nuclear power station. As though the Romans had aircraft. As though the Internet were developed in the Middle Ages."

"Interesting," Admiral Ulyakov said softly. His interpreter left out the undertone with which he said it, but Charlotte could hear that he was wondering—just as she was—why the American was only coming out with this information now. Not that it was hard to guess. The American government's top priority was to get its hands on this technology—and if at all possible to be the only ones who did.

"Aside from that," Whitecomb continued urgently, "it may not even be possible to destroy this thing with atom bombs. Our experts have considered that option as well." He gave a forced laugh. "The things these folks come up with, huh? Makes a guy think. But they've said specifically that even if we blasted the whole island with atom bombs, all that might do is destroy a part of the machinery. Even if ninety-nine percent was destroyed, the shockwave from the explosion would inevitably lift tiny parts up into the stratosphere. And those parts would be seeds that could spread across the whole hemisphere and repeat what they did here on Saradkov wherever they land. Except that this time they would be attacking cities, inhabited areas, our industrial capacity."

"And what do these admirable advisers of yours suggest we do instead?"

"The only way," Whitecomb declared, "is to get the fortress under control."

Ulyakov raised his eyebrows. "I fear that the machinery is more likely to get us under control."

"It's the only way," the American rear admiral insisted.

Ulyakov stared at the floor for a while, his face like thunder, then he raised his head and said, "No. Given the speed at which these roots are spreading, they will have reached the mainland by the time we can set up even temporary research stations. What you say has merely confirmed my decision. We must strike—and we must strike harder and faster than I had thought at first."

"Admiral . . ."

"During the Soviet era, we detonated the most powerful hydrogen bombs ever built. Two hundred megatons. That was on Novaya Zemlya, not five hundred miles from here." He squared his shoulders. "We still have some of those bombs. The time has come to use them."

That was when Charlotte made her move. She didn't stop to think—it was as though her body walked forward on its own initiative, drawing her away from the little group of survivors and over to the two admirals. Nobody stopped her. She was a beautiful woman among men who were barely used to having women around. She was untouchable.

"Excuse me," she said in Russian first to the admiral and then in English for the rear admiral. "There is someone you must consult. Someone who has already built such a machine."

They listened to her. Because she was a beautiful woman and untouchable.

Sometimes Hiroshi got the feeling his mother didn't even want him to come visit. As though all he did was disrupt her comfortable routines.

"You really don't need to make a fuss," he said again as he took another shirt from the wardrobe and put it in his suitcase. "You don't need to take any time off work. I won't get bored all on my own in Tokyo—anything but."

Mrs. Steel had already left that morning. She would spend her time off with her sister in Sacramento and then come back the day before he did. Her main concern on such occasions had always been who would look after the plants, so Hiroshi had finally had the watering system he had designed built and installed: tiny hosepipes buried discreetly in the ground that ran to every individual root cluster. The pipes were hooked up to moisture sensors, and the whole thing was controlled by a computer. The plants couldn't be better cared for even by a human gardener.

"But your machine can't talk to the plants!" Mrs. Steel had protested.

He had to concede that point, though he did add that he was convinced plants preferred the correct dosage of water and nutrients to a conversation, where they wouldn't have much to contribute anyway.

"Remember to pack something for the rain," his mother's voice added over the phone. "The rains have been here for a while now."

Hiroshi rolled his eyes. "I know that!"

"And I can't meet you at the airport. I have stacks of paperwork to get through at the office."

Because Inamoto was too stingy to hire another pair of hands. "You know that you don't have to do that job, don't you?"

"I have to do something with my time." Her usual answer. She hadn't even bothered looking around for another job. Obviously, she enjoyed squabbling with Inamoto.

"Don't worry about the airport. I can manage." He looked at the clock. "I have to get going if I don't want to get stuck in the traffic. See you tomorrow."

"Yes, I'll see you tomorrow." The way she said it made it sound like "Come if you must."

He made all his usual preparations for departure, securing his data and walking through every room in the house, checking whether the windows were all closed, the lights turned off, and so on. One last look at his travel bag, only half-full as always, then he zipped it shut, put it over his shoulder, and left the house.

In recent years he had come to enjoy spending the day before his flights to Tokyo in Mountain View with Rodney and Allison. As always they spent the whole evening debating the couple's favorite topic: If there really is intelligent life out there, why hasn't it gotten in touch?

"How probable is life? That's the real question," Allison summed up at the end of a sumptuous three-course meal. The love of Rodney's life was a short, sturdy woman who was a great cook—which was beginning to show in Rodney's waistline. "And that's where I see a contradiction that I just can't resolve. If we could safely assume that the rise of biological life on Earth was some dizzyingly unlikely event that might not have happened anywhere else in the universe, then of course it's quite clear why we haven't heard from any extraterrestrial intelligence: because there isn't any. But can we really assume that? I don't think we can. I mean, look at it this way—where do we find life on Earth? Answer: absolutely everywhere. In hot regions, cold regions, volcanoes, sulfur lakes, even in the ocean trenches; we find at least bacteria everywhere we look. Even up in space. Did you know that bacteria survived out on the hull of the Apollo moon rockets?"

Hiroshi raised his hands. "It's news to me."

"A bacterium called *Deinococcus radiodurans*. Characteristic feature: extreme radiation resistance. The DNA falls to bits, but after a while it's reassembled—correctly—by self-repairing mechanisms."

"Which raises the question of what kind of evolutionary process could produce a feature like that."

Allison frowned in thought. "Well, yes it does, but in any event, when we look around ourselves we have to conclude that the occurrence of biological life is something quite normal, something that happens wherever certain not particularly rare conditions are in place. And then that raises the much more interesting question of why those conditions shouldn't have been met somewhere out there as well."

"We've found well over two hundred extrasolar planets," Rodney put in, thoughtfully swirling his glass. They were drinking an herbal liqueur as a digestif. "We can say with something approaching certainty that there's nobody within, say, four thousand light years giving any sign of life. And four thousand light years is no small distance."

"Hold on there," Hiroshi said. "You're overestimating your abilities. You're looking for a needle in a haystack here. There are billions of frequencies ETs could be using; you can't listen in on all of them. And perhaps they're not using any of them. Could be that communication via the electromagnetic spectrum is something that technological civilizations give up on sooner or later because there are better options. I mean, no one sends messages in Morse code these days."

His old college buddy smiled wryly. "Just what I've been saying. The aliens are out there, but they're avoiding any contact. Because they are highly developed civilizations and they follow a moral code of leaving the less developed in peace."

"Yeah, yeah," Allison said. "And what makes you think we're not just some kind of reality show for them? Given the amount of stupid crap we get up to, maybe half the galaxy is laughing at us." She picked up the bottle of liqueur. "Hiroshi—another drop?"

Hiroshi put his hand over his glass. "Thanks, but I have to fly all the way across the Pacific tomorrow."

"I would think that's why you'd want some." But she put the bottle down again.

It was always good to visit these two. He'd probably spend a good deal of tomorrow's flight wondering just why that was, as always. Their small apartment was crowded with rickety bookshelves, odd bits of furniture, and exuberant houseplants. Star charts hung on the walls in the living room alongside framed photographs of distant galaxies taken by the Hubble space telescope, and neither of them ever put much effort into tidying the place. But it was good to be here. He wasn't the only one who thought so; the two of them always had friends visiting. Perhaps the mess was part of the charm. The way there had been the same pile of lumber lying in their side driveway for years, and the way Rodney always swore that by the next time Hiroshi came to visit he'd have that garage built. And the way both of them knew it wasn't going to happen.

"If the aliens really are highly developed," Hiroshi mused, "it could be that they're out there, and we simply haven't noticed them." It seemed to him that they'd had exactly this discussion more than once before. It was almost a kind of ritual. And they'd drunk quite a bit of the strong red wine, now that he thought about it. "Imagine you're an ant. And you wonder, is there any other intelligent life out there, or is it just us ants? But when an ant crawls over a parking lot, do you think it notices that someone built that? Can it even recognize cars for what they are?"

"Rebecca says that's an easy question to answer." Allison always wore the same long-suffering expression when she talked about her sister, who found the answers to all life's questions in the Bible. Or, rather, in what her pastor told her the Bible said about any given matter. "If there really were aliens, there'd be something about them in the Bible. At least whether or not they're saved. But there isn't—so they don't exist."

Rodney made a face. "I'd be more likely to believe the government has been in contact with the aliens all this time and is just keeping it quiet," he said. "Area 51, Roswell, and all that—maybe it's even true what they say."

"Don't say that so loud," Allison said with a grin. "You know they come and silence everybody who finds proof."

Just then the doorbell rang. Allison burst into a fit of giggles. "There! Didn't I tell you, Roddy? They're coming for you."

Rodney got up to look out the window. He didn't seem to find it very funny. "Be serious for a moment; there are two men in suits at the door. And a big, black limousine waiting in the street."

"Well of course! It's the Men in Black!" Allison was almost falling off her chair, laughing. It was one of those moments when Hiroshi could understand what Rodney saw in her. "They've come to wipe your memory!"

"Very funny." Not in the least amused, Rodney walked out through the dining room and went down to open the door.

Allison wiped away the tears of laughter. "It's probably just the Jehovah's Witnesses," she said, still grinning. "But that was quite a coincidence, eh?"

Hiroshi looked at his watch. It was long after ten o'clock. "At this time of night?"

It wasn't the Jehovah's Witnesses. When Rodney came back to the living room, he looked even more worried than when he had left. "They're from the Department of Defense. And they want to talk to you, amigo."

"Me?"

"My guest, Mr. Hiroshi Kato," Rodney said, obviously repeating the wording they had used.

Allison was wide-eyed. "You cannot be serious. Are we under surveillance?"

Rodney shrugged helplessly. "No idea. I feel like I'm dreaming."

Hiroshi pushed back his chair. "I'll go talk to them."

The two men waiting at the door weren't dressed in black like Tommy Lee Jones and Will Smith. Rather, they wore light beige suits, which were much more appropriate for the California weather. And they were practically hopping with impatience. As though every minute counted.

"Good evening, Mr. Kato," said the taller of the two, a brown-haired man whose skin was scarred as though by bad acne in his youth. "We're very sorry to have to disturb you at this late hour. We wouldn't do so if it weren't necessary." He held out an ID card. "Neal Hopkins, Department of Defense, Internal Security."

Hiroshi looked at the ID. He had no idea whether it was a genuine card issued by an organization that really existed. It looked real enough, but given a computer, a printer, and half an hour he could have drummed up something that looked just as good himself.

"How did you know where to find me?" he asked.

"We know these things," the other man remarked tersely.

His colleague glanced across at him disapprovingly. Then he told Hiroshi, "A certain Jens Rasmussen . . ." and paused for a moment. "Rasmussen? Yes. He's a business partner of yours, isn't he? He told us that you would probably be here."

That sounded plausible. Of course, he kept Rasmussen up to date on his travel plans, and he had once told him about Rodney and Allison Alvarez. And anybody who searched for Hiroshi Kato's name on the Internet would find Rasmussen Investments on the first page.

"Okay," Hiroshi said, handing back the card. "What's this about?"

The man who was apparently called Hopkins hefted his leather ID briefcase in his hand as though uncertain what to do with it. "We'd like you to watch some video footage. Over in the car," he said, nodding toward the black limousine. "If you can make any sense of what you see there, we'll tell you the rest."

"If I get into this car," Hiroshi asked, "will I be able to get out again when I choose to?"

The man's face pinched into what was probably meant to be a smile. Perhaps his superiors needed to be told he wasn't the best man for the job next time they needed to talk someone into an adventure late at night. "We don't kidnap people, Mr. Kato. We're asking for your help on behalf of the president of the United States."

Wow. Even if that wasn't true, it sounded hugely impressive. "Okay," Hiroshi said. "Let me just go tell my friends."

On the way back to the living room he took his phone from his pocket. He pressed one button to switch it on, then another to dial Rasmussen's number.

"It's me. Did you tell somebody from Defense where I was?"

"Hiroshi!" Rasmussen groaned. Bar music tinkled in the background. "Life would be a whole lot easier if you didn't switch your phone off the whole time. I wanted to give you a heads up, but do you have any idea how many Alvarezes there are in San Francisco? Two pages in the phone book!"

"Fine, sorry. So this is serious?"

"I even called the White House to be sure. Yes. A couple of hours ago the threat level was raised to red alert. There's some sort of crisis at sea, but in Russian sovereign territory, and they want your technical expertise. I don't know anything more than that."

"They're here at the door, and they want me to climb into their big, black car."

"I think in this instance you can do that."

"Okay, thanks." He hung up. Rodney and Allison were looking at him with fear in their eyes. "No need to worry," he said. "This will only take ten minutes."

Rodney took out his own phone. "I'll film you getting into that car. And then I'll call someone, and I'll stay on the line until you get back here," he declared grimly. "Just in case."

The two men accompanied him to the car, opened the back door, and joined him on the seat. The taciturn one took out a laptop and logged on via a fingerprint scanner. It booted up in an instant. He passed it over to Hiroshi's lap. "Here," was all he said.

Hiroshi watched the video footage. It had obviously been taken on an island in the Arctic Ocean; some of the sequences had been filmed underwater.

"Once more, please," he said when the screen went black.

The taciturn man pressed "Return," and the whole thing started again from the beginning. Hiroshi felt a feverish excitement seize hold of him. How was this possible? These were images he had until this moment only seen in his deepest, strangest dreams.

"Where was this footage taken?" he asked. "And what would you like me to do?"

They told him. Hiroshi considered for a moment, then said, "Okay. I just need to call my mother, tell her something's come up." He saw Rodney standing in the living-room window with his telephone to his ear. "And say good-bye to my friends."

"Your luggage," said the man whose badge had identified him as Hopkins. "It's kind of handy you're ready to travel."

"I'll need a computer. And a multiband radio to go with it."

"You'll get them."

They let him out, and he walked back into the house. Allison was waiting for him in the hall, still wide-eyed, and Rodney came to stand next to her, phone in hand. "So?" he asked.

"I have to go. Now. Right away." He reached for his travel bag. "Thanks for everything. I'll be in touch as soon as I can."

"You have to leave? Why? Has something happened?"

Hiroshi looked at him seriously. "Your aliens," he said. "By the look of it, they're here."

In the end they were taken back to the sick bay, where they had no news of whatever might be happening next. But at least it looked as though nobody was preparing a nuclear strike. The ships continued to plow through the Arctic, from time to time an iceberg struck the side, and that was about all the entertainment on offer. At one point a soldier came to the sick bay to have a scrape bandaged. Charlotte overheard him telling the doctor that they were expecting a helicopter with "yet another" American from Amderma air base.

The helicopter arrived shortly after dinner. They couldn't see the landing pad from the sick bay, but the sound was unmistakable. And shortly after that an officer appeared and asked Charlotte in Russian to come up the bridge. "No. Only her," he insisted when Adrian and the others began to get up off their beds as well.

Charlotte was not a little surprised to see another figure standing in the middle of the bridge, deep in conversation with the admirals and other commanding officers. Hiroshi!

"How did you get here so fast?" she asked when he left the group and came over to greet her.

"Ask whoever had them call me," Hiroshi answered with a wry grin. "Just a few hours ago I was with Rodney and Allison. Then all of a sudden some government agents turned up, drove me to an airport, and took me off by helicopter to a military airbase, where they . . . put me in a B-2 bomber. Unbelievable. I mean, I've seen photographs, of course, but when you're actually standing in front of a machine like that you really think you're in a science-fiction movie and the little green men are going to pop out from around the corner. An unladen B-2 without the full complement of weapons can fly halfway around the world at the speed of sound without needing to refuel." He passed his hand through his hair, as though making sure his head was still on his shoulders. "It was interesting. I don't ever want to do anything like that again in my life, but it was interesting."

It struck Charlotte that he was unusually chatty, surprisingly so. He was also still rather green in the face. Maybe that was why.

"So?" she asked. "Can you make anything of all this?"

He puffed out his cheeks. "Well . . . Hrrm. I mean, sure, those are nanites. Nanobots. Nanotechnological machines, whatever else they are. Even if only because there's no other explanation for what I saw in the footage. The only other possible explanation would be CGI. Special effects."

Charlotte thought of Leon and the way he had vanished before her eyes. "This isn't special effects. It all really happened."

"Okay. Then . . ." He paused. "Come over here. I'm just loading one of my programs on the computer. It should be ready in a moment." He smiled briefly. "The secret services of two countries are going to be all over my Internet connection, and then they'll be on my binary code like flies after honey. Well, let them."

They all sat down together at the conference table and gathered around Hiroshi, who had a chunky and somehow military-looking laptop before him. "In the dossier they gave me to read on the flight over there was something about legends surrounding Saradkov Island," he said. "Supposedly more than a thousand years old. One is about a war between heaven and earth, and a black angel who fell down onto Saradkov and was buried in the ice. He was the leader of the heavenly hosts and, as the legend goes, if the ice ever melts, war will begin anew. Which is why it always had to be winter up here."

The Russian admiral nodded. "An old Siberian folktale."

"I can imagine how this story might actually contain memories of a real event—of a probe that shot down from space. A probe that uses nanotech machinery and that has some mission that we know nothing about." Hiroshi folded his hands. "As I see it, this is how events unfolded: the probe struck Earth at some point and sank into the ice. It must have tried to activate itself and carry out its mission.

We should imagine it as something like a seed: the nanites within it had a certain amount of energy and raw material at their disposal already. But when they were surrounded by millions of cubic meters of ice, they had no access either to further energy sources, or to a wide enough selection of elements—all they had were hydrogen and oxygen atoms, and they couldn't carry out their mission with just those. So they did as much as they could and then they waited."

"What for?" Whitecomb asked.

"For conditions to improve," Hiroshi said. "And mostly for carbon."

"Carbon?"

"Carbon is the smallest atom capable of forming four molecular bonds. Which is why it plays a crucial role in nanotechnological constructions." Whatever was happening on the screen in front of him clearly required that he stop for a moment; he paused to think, then rapidly pressed a few keys. "This incident with the Dutch journalist," he said as he worked. "The human body is composed of up to ten point seven percent carbon. For a body mass of seventy-five kilos, that's about eight kilograms of carbon, meaning four by ten to the power of twenty-six atoms."

Whitecomb snorted derisively. "You're not seriously telling us that one human body contains enough carbon to completely steel-plate twelve square miles of island?"

"No, not in the least. But the nanites only needed to develop far enough to get unlimited access to the elements they needed. The ice was unforthcoming, and they had presumably already exploited the adjacent rocks for whatever they could use—I imagine that by the time they could assimilate the carbon in the journalist's body they were just a hair's breadth, so to speak, from rest of the resources they needed. Those eight kilos of carbon were the spark that started the blaze."

Charlotte felt her gorge rise. She remembered Leon van Hoorn as an adventurous, cheerful fellow with a fondness for weak jokes—and now these men were talking of him as nothing but eight kilos of carbon. She heard Admiral Ulyakov saying, "Saradkov Island was surveyed even in Stalin's time for mineral resources. There's nothing there. Just rock."

"Nothing worth exploiting with the power of human labor alone, perhaps," Hiroshi replied. "But at the scale at which nanotechnology sees the world, there are resources almost everywhere. Once the nanites broke through to the ocean—if not before—they had everything they could ever need. Seawater contains every element there is, in solution. Granted, some of them are only there in trace amounts, but when you have as much seawater as you want and as much energy as you need, you can extract whatever you like."

"Energy—now that's a key point," Whitecomb broke in. "One of the people advising the president—Dr. Drechsler or some such—said that the central question is where the nanites are getting their energy from. Nothing can happen without energy, he said."

Hiroshi nodded. "That's right. I suspect their energy is coming from within the earth. The nanites probably put down feelers several kilometers deep and are getting their energy from the temperature differentials."

"From inside the earth? All the way up here?" Whitecomb said skeptically. "Does that give them enough energy for all that?" He pointed toward the island, shimmering darkly on the horizon like the gates of Mordor.

Hiroshi looked at the rear admiral without expression. "It's a little-known fact that the earth's core is almost as hot as the surface of the sun, and that it has not cooled significantly in the billions of years since planetary formation. So yes, I believe that it can supply enough energy for most purposes."

Ulyakov leaned forward. "Doesn't that mean we can just switch off their supply? If we cut off these . . . feelers down into the earth, they're finished. So that's what we must do!"

Hiroshi frowned as he listened to the interpreter. "The question is how we could do that," he replied. "You mustn't imagine there are just one or two thick pipes running down there that we could simply cut off. There are more likely to be millions of them, tubes too fine to see with the naked eye—think of it like a fungus putting down threads."

"An atom bomb will get rid of fungus, too."

"Not this one. The nanites can doubtless store energy, meaning that even after a total disruption, such as a subterranean nuclear explosion, they would still be able to build new connections." Hiroshi glanced appraisingly at his screen. "To be honest, I doubt that an atom bomb would even have a chance to explode. It's entirely possible that the nanites could take it apart faster than it can fall." He cleared his throat and pulled the computer toward himself. "If you'll excuse me. My program is ready to run. I want to try something. "

"May we know what that is?" Rear Admiral Whitecomb asked in a tone that left no doubt that this was not just a question or even a request.

"I want to open communication with the nanites."

"And how do you intend to do that?"

Hiroshi seemed to consider this point. "It would take me several hours to explain that in terms that you could understand. Actually doing it would take a few minutes. And it might not even work. I really think it's best for me to try now and explain later."

The rear admiral traded glances with the other military men around the table, then shrugged. "Okay. Try it."

Hiroshi was already at work. His fingers danced over the keys, his gaze fixed on the bizarre diagrams and rapidly changing columns of figures on the screen. Connected to his computer by a cable was a red-orange box blinking with diodes in every color, which now sprang into hectic life. A multiband radio, somebody had said. Charlotte had no idea what that was, and she had no desire to find out. She just wanted to get out of there.

Outside, dark clouds were gathering, while snow and rain drove against the windows on the bridge. The ship began to pitch from side to side. Charlotte couldn't help but recall the hours they had spent in the dinghy and shuddered at the memory. Though she was still stuck in this nightmare, at least she was no longer so cold. She looked at Hiroshi. What was he really doing? Sending radio signals to the nanites? To machines from outer space? Why did he think they would understand him?

Just then one of the officers watching for activity on the island called out, "Movement!" He leaned over and turned some dials. "The gate's opening!"

In an instant they were all standing behind him, peering at his screen. All but Hiroshi, who carried on working as calmly as if he had heard nothing at all. Indeed, the gate had opened about halfway and showed a dark crack into the mountain. Admiral Ulyakov ordered his crew onto high alert in case artillery or some other weapon appeared from behind it.

"Radio signal has ceased," announced another officer. "No further activity."

Now the island could be seen on all screens, at different resolutions. In some inexplicable way it really did seem as though it had frozen into stillness. Only then did Charlotte realize that up until that moment there had been constant rippling movement all across the massive steel walls—movement she had subconsciously dismissed as being nothing more than reflected light. But now she could see nothing of the sort.

Whitecomb turned to Hiroshi. "Congratulations, Mr. Kato," he said. "It looks like you managed to turn the things off."

Hiroshi snapped his laptop shut. "It that case, could a helicopter take me over to the island?"

"I beg your pardon?"

"To the island," Hiroshi replied patiently. "From this point on I need to be in direct contact with the nanites."

Whitecomb spluttered. "Don't you think you're getting a little ahead of yourself? At the moment we have no idea whether this will last, and—"

"It won't last, not indefinitely." Hiroshi unplugged the multiband device and wound up the cable. "We have no time to lose."

"You did see the videos? What happened to the men in the landing parties?"

"I saw." Hiroshi put the multiband on top of his laptop. "I'll need a warm parka, something like that."

The rear admiral gasped for air. "A parka! You have strong nerves, I'll give you that."

Ulyakov listened to all this through his interpreter and nodded gruffly. "Good. Minimum crew for the helicopter. And they will not land him on the island. Lower him with the winch."

They brought Hiroshi a thick, naval-issue parka with the emblem of the Northern Fleet, pants, and boots to match, and a backpack, where he could stow his laptop and multiband. Hiroshi accepted everything stony-faced. Outside, the helicopter's blades were already spinning. The snow continued to flurry against the windowpanes. It was an extraordinary moment. The officers didn't seem to know whether they should be bidding Hiroshi a solemn farewell or sending him on his way with cheers. Above all, they seemed unhappy that a civilian had taken the job upon himself.

"Good luck," Whitecomb said at last with a forced smile. Somebody opened the door. The ice-cold north wind gusted in.

Hiroshi approached Charlotte, his bundle on his back. "Wish me luck," he said.

"*Ki o tsukete*—Take care," she said.

A shadow flitted across his face. "I don't know what made it stop," he told her quietly in Japanese. "It wasn't me. But for heaven's sake, don't tell anybody that!"

Then he followed a sailor out to the helicopter. The door closed behind him with a dull clang.

8

As the helicopter battled its way through the blizzard, Hiroshi only had eyes for the island. He still couldn't believe that right here in front of him was what he had been dreaming about for years—for his whole lifetime—and in such an unlikely place. Maybe the others only saw steel walls, fortifications, a colossal fortress in the solitude of the polar sea, but he saw the underlying nanite complexes, trillions upon trillions of them, so many that language hardly had any words for the numbers involved, yet all of them integrated, all organized, all awaiting their commands. He saw an infinite number of miniaturized versions of the robots he had built on Paliuk, of that simplest possible machine, and he saw the forms and structures that had until that moment only ever swarmed across his computer screens. There was no other way to see them: either with the mind's eye, or not at all. Nanites were so small that the human eye could not detect them without the help of technology. They would only ever remain pictures on a screen. Yet here they were. They existed. The fact that he couldn't see them meant nothing. Bacteria and viruses were also invisible to the naked eye, yet they existed—albeit on a scale many times larger than nanites.

And down there in the sea, growing ever larger, was the proof of the nano-robots' power: by building themselves anew using the atoms they found all around, they could multiply their number indefinitely, almost infinitely. And since, despite their numbers, they stayed strictly organized, marching in lockstep as it were, working hand in hand to follow a clear plan, one gigantic program, they could build structures on any scale at all: from tiny replicas of themselves right up to such colossal creations as this island. Twelve square miles of rock now clad in shimmering steel. But this was nothing. There were no limits for nanites. They could rebuild a whole planet if they were programmed to, and there was practically nothing anyone could do about it.

Nano-robots did nothing but place atoms next to each other one by one, but that was enough to perform miracles. Fundamentally, the whole history of technology boiled down to this one aspect: how effectively one atom could be placed next to another. It had all begun with flint hand axes, bashing stone against stone until splinters flaked away—splinters made up of so many atoms that early man had no words to begin to describe the numbers involved. Then mankind began to dig for metals, which was nothing more than looking for atoms of particular elements, chosen for their special qualities. Next we learned to organize these atoms—and we called it smelting. Most recently came the highly developed industrial techniques of modern times—for instance, polishing slices of silicon to unprecedented purity, etching them with certain wavelengths of light and then subjecting them to chemical treatment to create computer processors of almost unimaginable capacity.

But all of this was nothing compared with the possibilities that opened up at the zenith of technological development once it became possible to manipulate individual atoms, to pick them up and place them exactly where they were needed; this was the most advanced technology imaginable. The difference between a lump of coal and a diamond was simply a matter of the arrangement of their respective carbon atoms. Nothing more. And what was so special about a diamond? It was a mere toy compared with the materials nanotechnology alone could create.

Hiroshi also couldn't believe that he had just climbed aboard a helicopter that was carrying him to the heart of the most technologically advanced artifact mankind had ever seen. He had spent years working out the fundamental principles of this technology. He had developed a few concepts—but only a few—he believed must be universally applicable. He was a mere beginner compared with the mind that had created this shimmering silver colossus in front of him. A greenhorn. The bizarre structure reared up against a sky of heavy, gray clouds, and the lead-gray waves beat against it.

Nor did he understand why the nanites had ceased their activity. What had he done? All he had been trying to do was take a closer look at what the military had decided were jamming signals. He had wondered what might happen if he treated them as command signals instead and tried to make contact with the central control units that way. That was all. He had put a couple of his pattern-recognition programs to work on them. While the software did its job, he had just sat there thinking banal thoughts about how the Russian and American computer hotshots might decompile his binary code once all this was over. How his pattern-recognition algorithms would find their way into all kinds of software, thanks to the industrial-espionage guys. And how Jens would give him that lecture about patents and squandered profits when he heard about it. All true. In any case, he had identified a couple of patterns that seemed to make sense, and then he had broadcast a complementary sequence of signals just as an experiment. It had been nothing special, and certainly nothing he expected to provoke any reaction from the nanite machinery—perhaps an answering radio signal, but certainly no more than that. And then—standstill. Absolutely astonishing. Absolutely inexplicable.

The island reared up before them, gigantic: a dizzyingly oversized redoubt with shimmering battlements and impregnable fortifications. The sight took his breath away. That, and the knowledge he had no idea what he would actually do now that he was here. He had no plan, nowhere to start, nothing but a computer with a radio transmitter attached. The only thing he knew with absolute certainty was he had to set foot on this island even if it cost him his life. He would never be able to forgive himself if he didn't.

The copilot unclipped his belt and came back to where Hiroshi sat, gesturing that he should do the same. Then he helped him into a kind of padded noose that ran around his back below the arms. At the front, on his chest, was a thick hook into which the soldier clipped the winch cable. Then he shoved the door open with a clang. Snow flurried in. The man shouted something that was lost in the noise of the engines—Hiroshi couldn't even tell whether it was in Russian or English. Not that it made any difference, since he knew what it meant. It was time to entrust himself to the winch. One last check to see that everything was properly in place, that the backpack with the computer was sitting above the noose so that there was no chance of it getting damaged. One last nod, and then he stepped out into empty space.

The air snatched furiously at him as soon as he had dropped a few yards. The searing cold dispelled any feeling that this was all a dream. It was no dream. He was hanging from a thundering helicopter by a vibrating steel cable while the soldiers winched him downward just as fast as they could. Soon he would be the loneliest man on Earth. Nobody would come to save him if anything happened. The footage the agents had showed him in California played out again before his mind's eye. It had included images of men screaming in pain as they died an almost unimaginable death, killed by the very ground beneath their feet. They had literally melted away as billions of nanites took their living cells apart into their constituent atoms of carbon, hydrogen, and oxygen, carrying away the calcium from their bones atom by atom to use elsewhere in nanotech devices.

Hiroshi looked down. The ground was fast approaching. It looked like flawless, freshly polished steel. His feet touched the surface. Nothing happened. He looked closer and saw snowflakes lying intact here and there on the steel, not even melting. He began to breathe again. He quickly took off the backpack and slipped out of harness. He waved upward. The cable with the empty noose whizzed away, and even before it had reached the winch the helicopter had turned and was roaring back to the ship.

He stood there. What now? Hiroshi lifted the backpack to his shoulders and looked up at the gigantic gate. It was standing open, which looked like an invitation. Well, he wasn't going to stay out here. Now that he had made it this far, he wanted to go as deep as possible into the heart of the machine. If for no other reason than that it could only be warmer in there. He marched off, trudging up the shallow slope toward the narrow, dark gap. It was perhaps fifty meters high and five meters across. The closer he came to the gate, the more vividly he recalled the legends about the Bon festival back home and the Japanese legends of the dead. If there really was an entrance to the underworld somewhere, it could only look like this huge gate. He felt somehow uplifted. Even though he had no idea what he would do in there or what he might achieve. Probably nothing.

Hiroshi turned around and looked back at the gray ships lying offshore at what the military men considered—quite mistakenly—a safe distance. He remembered the walkie-talkie they had given him. He took it out of his pocket. It was a chunky thing that looked like a first-generation cell phone, and he had to take his gloves off to switch it on.

"Kato here," he said. "I'm going in."

He didn't wait for an answer. He put the device away, pulled his gloves back on, took a deep breath, and crossed the threshold.

As time went by, Charlotte began to feel cold. The bridge was well heated, but anyone would start to shiver when all there was to do was sit and stare out the window at the unending, gray, storm-tossed monotony of the Arctic day. The snow had stopped, but the wind picked up, lashing the icy waves higher. But there was nothing else to do. Time passed, and the waiting frayed her nerves. The ships cruised up and down in front of the island, and the cameras filmed everything that was going on through their powerful telephoto lenses— meaning nothing at all, ever since Hiroshi had walked through that gate. Everything was being filmed; anyone who watched the footage later would be unspeakably bored.

The tension was palpable as they waited. The officers on the bridge spoke in hushed tones, sipping coffee, turning dials, tapping away at keyboards, bent over maps, but they were all waiting for something to happen. They were like cats lying in wait, ready to spring and pounce upon any movement from the hole. But what movement might there be? Did anybody seriously expect aliens to come out of the gate? Perhaps with Hiroshi in tow? Would they be hostile, dragging him along as a prisoner, or friendly now that all the initial misunderstandings had been cleared up? "Take us to your president," they would say, and then a whole new set of misunderstandings and diplomatic standoffs would ensue.

Charlotte passed her hand through her hair for the hundredth time. She was only doing it so that she had something to do, so that she wouldn't just sit at the abandoned conference table turning slowly to stone. She watched the American admiral, with his gold-encrusted cap and the colorful tags on his dress jacket; he was at the other end of the bridge, speaking into a chunky cell phone. His staff officers were standing all around him, trying to shield him from view; clearly, the Russians weren't supposed to listen in on whatever he was telling the president.

No, Charlotte told herself, the aliens were gone. They'd flown off. They were on their way out of the solar system. If indeed there had ever been any alien life-forms at all. Perhaps it had only ever been a robot mission, nano-robots with some unknown task to perform.

And given how long ago their masters must have sent them, they may well have died out entirely in the meantime.

Hiroshi had sent two updates from inside the installation. He was walking through endless halls, he told them, that looked like huge industrial facilities. There was nobody in sight, not a sign of life anywhere. Nothing was moving. Had the photos he had been sending them arrived, he asked? That had caused something of a stir, since in fact not a single photo had reached them. Charlotte had learned from a Russian officer that Hiroshi's radio was a special military model with boosted transmission and an encrypted channel. And the built-in camera was supposed to be able to send every picture instantaneously at the push of a button. But the last call had come over a very bad connection, full of gaps and distortion. Most importantly, it had been a worryingly long time ago.

Unexpectedly, the others arrived. Unable to endure the uncertainty down in the sick bay, they had pleaded until they were finally allowed to go up to the bridge. Charlotte tried to explain to them who Hiroshi was and what he had said about the nano-robots on the island, but she couldn't really fill in the important details and was met with impatient glances. Then she pricked up her ears as she overheard a scrap of talk. The Russians were doubtful they could really triumph. What if Hiroshi didn't report in again soon? What if he didn't come back at all? He could be dead by now, gone without a trace, taken apart for his constituent elements like the soldiers of the landing party. Nobody even thought of Leon van Hoorn anymore. After all, there was no video footage of his death. These days anything that wasn't captured on video might just as well not have happened.

"I don't like it," Admiral Ulyakov growled ever more often. As he grumbled away, he glared at his officers with a look that made them flinch as though they felt personally responsible for the situation.

"What to do?" she heard from the American group. "How long can we wait?"

It wasn't hard to read their thoughts: even a civilian must have damn well realized they were jumpy as a cat on a hot tin roof back here. If he couldn't get a signal inside the installation, then the fool should retrace his steps to make a report, give them some sign of life, or at the very least let them know how long it might be until he could next make radio contact. If he kept quiet like this, then it could only mean he had been taken prisoner, or that he was dead— or he was such a dumb cluck he deserved everything that happened to him, and more, if they were forced to act. It was just that nobody knew what they could do. Otherwise, they were hardly likely to have waited this long. And now they were no further than they had been before.

"Admiral!" one of the sailors watching at the screen suddenly called out.

Ulyakov jutted his jaw forward. "Speak!"

"K-104 reports that the . . . uh, the pipelines on the seabed are changing." He listened to the voice over his headphones. "They seem to be going away."

"As I recall, all of our submarines are equipped with cameras," the admiral growled. "Is K-104 perhaps different?"

"One moment—I'm getting a visual." He pressed a button, and an underwater shot appeared on several of the screens. It showed one of the long metal structures running out from the island, gleaming in the circle of a floodlight—and dwindling away.

Ulyakov stood in front of a screen, leaning forward as he watched what was going on, his hands folded behind his back, quite motionless. "Good," he said finally. "That's the first good news since I got here."

"He did it." Whitecomb smacked his fist into the palm of his hand. "The goddamned son of a bitch got those things under control."

Another observer raised his head. "Movement on the island itself. Something happening on the fortress walls."

There was a collective gasp. Even the ship seemed to give a start, though it was only the impact of a particularly heavy wave breaking across it at that moment.

"Where are the cameras?" barked Ulyakov, the only one who hadn't grabbed onto a handhold.

The pictures on the screens changed as the cameras zoomed closer in on those areas where movement was visible. The battlements up on the wall that had been coldly gleaming edges of sharp metal now became visibly softer and rounder and seemed to be surrounded by mist. The huge ribs of steel that girded the mountain fortress, which before had shone like newly polished steel, seemed to flow and collapse in upon themselves . . . and then simply blew away.

"Fuck!" Rear Admiral Whitecomb yelled. "The thing's dissolving!"

Which was exactly what it was doing. The fortifications fell to dust and blew away in the wind. And the whole process was happening faster and faster. Soon they could see the bare rocks once more. The outline of the gate was hardly recognizable as such. The two huge quays running out into the sea, which the nanites had created from the two warships and their crew, dissolved into the water and colored it red as blood.

Ulyakov ordered a helicopter into the air and told it to circle the island and shoot footage from above. It all showed the same picture: dust on the wind where mighty walls had stood, pale gray or reddish-pink plumes of dust blowing away in the storm. The launch pit that had run miles down into the earth had been replaced by a deep, dark hole in the rock, collapsed into rubble. The downward wind from the rotor left marks up on the plateau as though an enormous broom were sweeping through sawdust. The whole process lasted less than half an hour. Afterward, all that had seemed so invincibly strong had vanished, and Saradkov looked like the surface of Mars.

"There's somebody there!"

One of the cameras pointed to the spot where the gate had stood and where now there was only a gaping, dark hole in the mountainside like the toothless mouth of an aged giant. A human figure could be seen, staggering and stumbling, with only shapeless rags on his body. It was Hiroshi. In his hand he held part of a keyboard, evidently all that was left of his computer. As the camera zoomed in closer, they could see he was shivering with cold. The clothes he had left on his body were barely enough to keep him clad and were certainly not enough to protect him from the Arctic cold. Hiroshi staggered into the open air—just in time, for the rock face collapsed behind him as the corridors and galleries that the nanites had burrowed into the cliffs fell in upon themselves.

He hadn't expected anything like that. He would have liked to stop and catch his breath, but it was still dangerous by the rock face and the caves. He had to go onward, into the ice-cold wind and the storm. He looked down at his hands. His fingers were frozen blue, clenched unmoving around the miserable remnants of the laptop. At last, he stood still and waved in the direction of the ships. Surely they had to be watching?

There. Behind him. A helicopter appeared over the mountain ridge and came down to land. Hiroshi stumbled toward it. A man jumped out as the machine touched down and came running toward him, then put an arm around him. Then, at last, a door that shut out the wind. A blanket to wrap around him. He couldn't stop shivering, but now it was only a matter of time.

Rear Admiral Denis J. Whitecomb was waiting for him on the helicopter landing deck, surrounded by his staff officers. Some of them, who looked like experienced bruisers, were staring at him with a cool, determined look in their eyes.

"Welcome back, Mr. Kato," said the rear admiral, standing there in his splendid US Navy uniform. "I am afraid there are a great many things you still have to explain to us."

ISLAND IN
THE STARS

1

JOINT INVESTIGATION COMMITTEE
SARADKOV ISLAND EVENT
CHAIR: SENATOR RICHARD COFFEY (US)
DEPUTY CHAIR: MINISTER ANATOLY MIKHAILOV (RUSSIA)
DOCUMENT STATUS: CONFIDENTIAL
EXTRACT FROM THE WITNESS TESTIMONY OF MORLEY MANN (US)

Chair: Can you tell us in one or two sentences what you believe happened on Saradkov?

Witness: An extraterrestrial probe had been frozen in the ice sheet on the island for thousands of years. It was freed when climate change caused some of the ice to melt, and then it became active.

Chair: And did you do anything to influence subsequent events—that is, after the probe became active—in any way?

Witness: No.

JOINT INVESTIGATION COMMITTEE
SARADKOV ISLAND EVENT
CHAIR: SENATOR RICHARD COFFEY (US)
DEPUTY CHAIR: MINISTER ANATOLY MIKHAILOV (RUSSIA)

DOCUMENT STATUS: CONFIDENTIAL
EXTRACT FROM THE WITNESS TESTIMONY OF CHARLOTTE
  MALROUX (FRANCE)

Chair: What is your relationship to Mr. Kato?

Witness: We're friends. We've known one another since we were ten
  years old. That was when we first met, and then later we met up
  occasionally after that.

(. . .)

Deputy chair: What were your motives for joining the expedition to
  Saradkov? You're a paleoanthropologist. What's a paleoanthropologist doing on an Arctic island?

Witness: I was there as interpreter. None of the others speak any
  Russian.

(. . .)

Chair: When it came to how we could stop the unsettling events on
  Saradkov Island, what gave you the idea of calling on Mr. Kato of
  all people?

Witness: I knew what he was working on, and I had the feeling he
  was more likely than anyone else to know what we could do against
  this probe.

Deputy chair: I'd like to have a little more detail here. What was he
  working on? As far as I understand it, his work had nothing to do
  with contacting a possible alien intelligence, did it?

Witness: No, he was working on robots.

Deputy chair: I'm having trouble seeing the connection.

Witness: These were special robots. Large numbers of very small
  robots designed to work together in various configurations. About
  this big.

(The witness indicates the size of the palm of her hand.)

About six years ago Mr. Kato gave me a demonstration of these
  robots in action. It was most impressive, even if in the end they
  didn't actually work as he had intended. When I visited Mr. Kato

shortly before my departure to Saradkov, he showed me computer simulations of even smaller robots that he'd been working on in the meantime. Robots that are designed to be built from single atoms.

Chair: Did he show you any actual examples of such robots?

Witness: No. As I have said, he only showed me computer simulations. He told me there were fundamental technological barriers to actually building them.

Chair: What was the nature of these technological barriers?

Witness: As far as I understand, it's not actually possible to arrange the atoms in the way we would need to.

(...)

Deputy chair: Inasmuch as I understand these things, nanotech constructs are by definition so small that they cannot be seen by the naked eye. There you were on a remote Arctic island, beset by all kinds of weird phenomena—what in the world gave you the idea that you were dealing with nano-robots?

Witness: The way they moved.

(Witness gives a long pause. She is emotionally distraught.)

The blades that impaled Leon . . . Mr. van Hoorn . . . I saw a pattern on them, a kind of movement, a very characteristic way of moving, flowing, like a wave . . .

(Pause.)

I don't know now. But whatever it was, it made me think of Hiroshi's . . . of Mr. Kato's robotics experiment when I saw them moving like that. For a moment I even thought his robots might have achieved autonomy and somehow reached the island. I wasn't thinking of nanites. Mr. Whitecomb was the first one to mention that.

Chair: Rear Admiral Whitecomb.

Witness: Yes. Some experts back in Washington had gotten the idea.

Chair: Can you describe more closely the movement on the blade?

Witness: It was a kind of moving shimmer, flowing along the blade. That's how it looked at least. And when I saw Hiroshi's robots moving six years ago, that's exactly what they looked like. A shimmering, like something flowing along. Like a pail full of little silver balls being tipped out, but they weren't balls, more like disks. And they didn't roll; they moved one another along or crept . . .

(Pause.)

You have to have seen it for yourself. Once you've seen it, you recognize it. Then the pattern on the blade . . .

(Pause.)

It was rather like when you dabble your hand in a basin full of water and see ripples. Then next time you see the ocean, you know the waves are basically the same thing. Water, movement. The same way, the shimmer on the blade made me think of Hiroshi's robots.

(. . .)

Deputy chair: I must return to my question. What gave you the idea to tell the admirals about Mr. Kato?

Witness: The thought just struck me. That's all. If you like, I took a wild guess. To be honest, I was even exaggerating a bit when I told them about Mr. Kato on the boat. I just didn't want anybody using atom bombs.

Charlotte could have wept with relief when she got to Moscow and saw her mother waiting at the airport. Somehow that meant it was really over. She hugged her mother, so happy to see her that she had to fight back the tears. At that moment she would have gladly married any cousin her mother put in front of her—though luckily her mother hadn't thought of that.

"You and your mad adventures," was all she said.

"Yes," Charlotte confessed. "That was the maddest of them all."

"I hope you learned something."

"I did. I really did."

Charlotte felt bad about leaving the others in the lurch. There had been a long tug-of-war between the superpowers over the inquiry: the American government had wanted to hold it in Washington, the Russians in St. Petersburg. At last, they had agreed on Iceland, neutral territory. When the witnesses were called to make their statements in Reykjavík, in a hotel that had been sealed off from the world at enormous expense, the media had gotten wind of it and started rumors about negotiations for a new disarmament treaty.

Though public interest had dropped off, the inquiry still rumbled on. In the end, giving one statement after another and then one more, with no end in sight, had gotten to be too much for Charlotte. She had shamelessly invoked her status as a diplomat's daughter to make her escape. She had signed everything they put in front of her before she left—she agreed to keep everything she had seen secret, not to seek payment for damages or any other reparations, and to a dozen other conditions—and then she had gotten on the next plane out.

So here she was. Home—or not. In fact, it took her only a few days to realize it was dreadful. Her mother seemed cooler and more distant than ever—prickly, even—only concerned with etiquette and the look of things, and quite determined to show no feelings at all. Her father took flight in noncommittal pleasantries and supposedly vital engagements. When he was home at all, he exuded shallow good cheer and batted away every attempt at serious conversation. All he had to say about Charlotte's experience in the Arctic was that the speaker of the Russian parliament had inquired after her health. With every passing day, she sank deeper into lethargy. More than ever before she understood why she had always felt the urge to escape, even as a little girl. But where should she go? She had lost all hope she would be able to find elsewhere what she had spent so long looking for.

She finally made the effort to call Brenda's mother, who assured her all was well with her apartment in Boston and gave her Brenda's new telephone number in Buenos Aires. She also told her the move to Argentina had gone well and that even Jason really liked it.

Brenda squealed with joy when she picked up the phone. "We love it," she hollered when Charlotte asked how they liked their new life. "We have this huge house with palm trees all up the driveway and a crazy overgrown garden. . . . The faculty at the university are just wonderful. . . . Jason spends his whole day moping around, of course, morning till night. I have no idea whether he understands anything at school. I caved in the end and bought him one of those computers they play on, a gamestation or whatever they're called, but I'm insisting he only ever gets the games in Spanish. Maybe that will help."

Brenda was the first one to take any interest in what had happened to Charlotte on Devil's Island. Charlotte remembered the papers she had signed swearing her to secrecy and didn't want to say anything over the telephone. She muttered something about telling Brenda the next time she saw her.

"Well, just come visit," Brenda said cheerfully. "You can be the first to stay in our guest room. Well, *one* of the guest rooms, but who's counting?"

Then she added that as well as the guest apartment, they had set up another room as a second child's room. They were in the process of adopting a nine-year-old girl from Bangladesh named Lamita.

"Older than Jason?" Charlotte asked. "Isn't that going to be rather awkward?"

"It is, but we have to do it." And there was a tone in Brenda's voice that Charlotte had never heard before: pain. "You remember Parimarjan, don't you? The boy who always splashed us with water over at my compound. He works for a bank in Kolkata these days, and he has a lot of business in Bangladesh and . . . well, anyway, Lamita is a bankruptcy asset seized from a textile factory that went bust near Khulna. The poor girl was an asset, can you imagine? The owner of the company bought the girl from her parents when she was five and had her working ten hours a day. It was slavery. Pure and simple. And her parents can't be found, or don't want her back . . ." Even across two continents and an ocean, Charlotte could hear Brenda pause to take a breath to keep herself under control.

"That's a dreadful story," Charlotte said, feeling even as she spoke how inadequate the words were.

"Yes. Which is why we're taking her. Jason will just have to get used to having an older sister."

Earth-shattering though the news was, hearing it saved Charlotte. It reminded her that other people had problems, too, and shook her out of her resignation. She decided to leave Moscow and go back to Boston to look after her apartment and her research project, and then, as soon as she had everything straightened out, to visit Brenda and Tom in Argentina.

JOINT INVESTIGATION COMMITTEE
SARADKOV ISLAND EVENT
CHAIR: SENATOR RICHARD COFFEY (US)
DEPUTY CHAIR: MINISTER ANATOLY MIKHAILOV (RUSSIA)
DOCUMENT STATUS: CONFIDENTIAL
EXTRACT FROM THE WITNESS TESTIMONY OF HIROSHI
KATO (JAPAN)

Chair: When the whole installation fell to pieces—when it turned to dust—that was some kind of self-destruct mechanism, am I right?
Witness: That's right. First the nanites took apart everything they had built, then they took each other apart as well. Until there was nothing left.
Chair: How did you trigger the self-destruct?
Witness: It was easy. Destruction is the easiest option after all.
Chair: That doesn't answer my question.
Witness: The radio signal that the nanites were broadcasting contained a particular sequence that repeated over and over, with a

pause after every repetition. What I did was read this sequence as a question, so to speak, and to interpret the pauses that came afterward as waiting for an answer. Since the nanites had ceased all activity shortly before—without any interference from me, as I've explained—I conjectured that they had somehow noticed they had gotten out of control, which prompted them to send a query as to whether they should self-destruct. More or less the way our rockets self-destruct when they leave their flight paths.

Chair: I don't see it. Why would a mechanism like that do such a thing? Send a query to self-destruct?

Witness: Because it can't judge the necessity in every case. A rocket can tell whether it's deviated from its set trajectory; that's easy. With nano-robots, it's not so simple. Quite the opposite: it's extremely difficult for them to tell whether they're doing the right thing.

Chair: But when you sent this radio sequence, you didn't know it would trigger an order to self-destruct.

Witness: It would be too much to say I knew for sure. But I was pretty certain.

Chair: And how could you be so certain?

Witness: Let's say I was relying a great deal on my intuition.

(. . .)

Chair: Where did this probe come from, in your opinion?

Witness: Wherever it was from, it was sent by intelligent life-forms who are technologically greatly more advanced than we are. Or at least were when they sent the probe on its way.

Chair: Are you phrasing it that way because you think these beings may no longer exist?

Witness: Yes. That's even the more likely scenario.

Chair: Why?

Witness: They sent the probe. It had been traveling for some time, at least several thousands of years. When it reached Earth, it landed in a region where it couldn't, at first, function as planned. Then thousands more years passed. If the civilization that sent out the probe had progressed at all technologically in the intervening time, why didn't they come themselves?

(...)

Deputy chair: The rocket the probe launched—what was its purpose, in your opinion? Might it be, for instance, to take terrestrial soil samples back home?

Witness: I don't think so. Something like soil samples could be analyzed on the spot, and the results could be sent back by radio. That's the quickest and safest way. No, I'm assuming it was a copy of the original probe, now on its way to the nearest star.

Deputy chair: What do you mean, a copy?

Witness: We already have the theoretical concept of what's called a Von Neumann probe. The idea is to launch an automated mechanism toward the nearest solar system, which will touch down in some suitable spot and use the raw materials it finds there to build at least two exact copies of itself. Then it launches these toward the next nearest systems from there before it gets to work on its actual task, exploring the system it's arrived in, for instance. So then you have at least two such probes out there, and they in turn will launch at least four more, then it's eight, sixteen, thirty-two, and so on—an exponential series that reaches huge numbers quite quickly. If you take this concept and then apply even some relatively conservative hypotheticals—so no assuming that we have faster-than-light drives, or anything like that—then you find we can seed an entire galaxy the size of the Milky Way within a mere half million years.

Deputy chair: What did you call that? A Von Neumann probe?

Witness: Named for the mathematician John von Neumann. He did some important theoretical work on self-replicating automata. Though he never actually suggested using them for spaceflight himself.

(The chair and deputy consult briefly with their staff.)

Deputy chair: And you think we encountered such a probe on Saradkov?

Witness: Yes. If you have the ability to build self-replicating nano-constructs, it's the obvious thing to make.

(...)

Chair: So that's what you believe is the background to this whole story. An intelligent species sent out explorer probes to roam the whole galaxy, and then after that they either died out or went into decline.

Witness: Exactly. That's what it looks like.

SARADKOV ISLAND EVENT QUARANTINE REPORT

The survivors of the Saradkov Island Expedition (these being Adrian Cazar, PhD; Charlotte Malroux; Morley Mann, MA; Angela MacMillan, MA) and the technical consultant who joined the group during the course of events and subsequently spent several hours on the island (Hiroshi Kato) were subject to a quarantine of 11 (eleven) days before being discharged. During this time they underwent medical examination for the presence of foreign bodies and substances in their tissue.

Procedures Used

—Whole-body computer tomography (except in reproductive organs)

—Whole-body sonography

—Whole-body MRI

—Spectral analysis of blood, lymph, and urine

—Microscopy on all bodily fluids

—Tests for alterations to antibodies

Results

No anomalies detected

JOINT INVESTIGATION COMMITTEE
SARADKOV ISLAND EVENT
CHAIR: SENATOR RICHARD COFFEY (US)
DEPUTY CHAIR: MINISTER ANATOLY MIKHAILOV (RUSSIA)
DOCUMENT STATUS: CONFIDENTIAL
EXTRACT FROM THE WITNESS TESTIMONY OF HIROSHI
KATO (JAPAN)

Chair: So you were convinced right from the start we were not dealing with extraterrestrial life-forms?

Witness: Yes. As I saw it, this was clearly a technological construct. A
kind of robot, if you like.

Chair: Of extraterrestrial origin?

Witness: That is what we are forced to conclude.

Chair: What I would like to understand is how you could possibly
arrive on this island in the Arctic Ocean and come face-to-face
with extraterrestrial technology, but instead of being utterly overwhelmed like everyone else, you knew immediately what you were
dealing with and how to tackle it. I don't understand it. In my view,
it's extremely hard to believe.

Witness: As I have already explained several times, I did not know
how to tackle it. The construct stopped its expansion of its own
accord. All I did was recognize we were indeed dealing with a
machine operating along nanotechnological principles.

Chair: How were you able to recognize this?

Witness: Because I've been a researcher in the field for many years
now. I recognized some familiar underlying principles. And by
the way, I wasn't the only one—I've since learned that the US
president's team of scientific advisers included experts who also
immediately came to the conclusion we were dealing with nanotechnology.

Chair: Do I understand what you're saying? Your research actually anticipated the fundamental principles of a technology developed by extraterrestrial, nonhuman life-forms?

Witness: That's actually less surprising than it sounds. If I might explain?

Chair: Please do.

Witness: Discussion about how we could communicate with extraterrestrial intelligence has always assumed that this sort of contact would have to begin with an exchange of mathematical propositions. That's because the principles of mathematics are abstract—they're not tied to any particular form of biological life; any sufficiently intelligent life anywhere in the universe will understand them in the same way. Obviously, not using the same symbols, but the principles remain the same. One plus one always makes two, regardless of notation. As soon as intelligent life has developed the concept of number as such, then the whole of mathematics is implied.

If you take it one step further and assume the existence of machines—justifiably, if we're positing communication with extraterrestrial civilizations—then we can suppose that every technological culture will at some point build a data-processing machine. What we call a computer. The most general computer conceivable is the Turing machine, which reduces all executable programs to only three operations—read, write, and move the read/write mechanism along the storage medium. As far as we currently know, this is the most fundamental data-processing machine that can exist, and we therefore think that even a completely alien intelligence would have the same insight. Obviously, it would use other terminology, but the principle would be the same.

So, if we now go beyond data processing, we get to other forms of processing—industrial, for instance. How do we shape objects? How do we mold matter? My research aimed at identifying fundamental principles here in much the same way. I was trying to write a universal grammar for materials processing, so to speak. I was able to show that all production processes can be reduced to fundamental operations such as cut, join, heat, cool, identify, sort, compress, produce or transmit energy, guide and hold still, turn, drill, and so on and so forth.

Chair: That would be the Kato machine, so to speak?

Witness: I beg your pardon?

Chair: You gave us the Turing machine as an example.

Witness: Oh yes. Well then. If you like.

In the breaks between depositions, they took him to the hotel breakfast room, where the blinds were down around the clock so that nobody got the idea of lurking around outside with a telephoto lens. Hiroshi punched a button for coffee, then peered through the slats of the blind as the machine gurgled and groaned. The media circus that had greeted them was long gone, and only a few reporters still shivered at their posts. The demonstrators, too, had gone, leaving only a little knot of dauntless souls waving placards that demanded "Nuclear-free zones—worldwide!" and "Peace in our time." During the first few days there had been some far-from-peaceful clashes with the Icelandic police. Senator Coffey's declaration that these were not disarmament talks but Russian–American round tables on joint scientific projects had been largely ignored.

There was a beep. His drink was ready. Hiroshi took the cardboard cup between his fingertips and carried it over to a chair. He savored the first sip of coffee and then leaned his head back, closing his eyes, just for the sake of it.

"You seem worn-out, Mr. Kato," said the young lawyer the American government had provided him.

Hiroshi opened his eyes and tilted his head forward. "Yes, I'm tired. I can barely sleep. I'm not used to such soft beds."

He was here as a witness, they had told him, not a defendant. The lawyer was there to make sure he said nothing that would incriminate him.

It was all very well organized. They had been kept apart so that they couldn't influence one another's statements. There was at least one pair of watchful eyes on each of them. He hadn't seen Charlotte since the meeting aboard the Russian battleship; he had heard she had already left. He didn't know any of the other expedition members anyway.

"To be honest," the lawyer said, "sometimes you look as though you have something on your mind. Is there perhaps something you're keeping to yourself, which I should know about as your lawyer?"

Hiroshi looked at him. It was an interesting way to put it. "No," he said, "there isn't."

Somebody had thought it would be a good idea to give him a lawyer with a Japanese background. But John Takeishi, born and bred in Seattle, was about as Japanese as the Tokyo burger that one of the big fast-food chains was pushing these days. Granted, he spoke passable Japanese, but he knew nothing about the way of life or culture.

"Is that actually a fun job?" Hiroshi asked. "Lawyering, I mean. I've often wondered. So many people become lawyers in America. Do they just do it for the money?"

Takeishi looked surprised. "I'm no big-money lawyer, if that's what you mean. Guys like that don't work for the government."

"That's not what I mean. I was asking whether it's a fun job."

"Sometimes."

"Now, for example?"

Takeishi grinned. "Now is good. I'm really just sitting around. But later I'll be able to tell people I was in Reykjavík."

"Is it a job you'd do if you didn't need to earn a living? If money were no object?"

The young lawyer laughed. "No."

"What would you do?"

"Music. Jazz." His face shone with pleasure as he spoke. "I play clarinet in a jazz quartet. When everybody can make it, we meet once a week to rehearse, and then once a quarter we play a gig somewhere, usually at a tiny club with maybe twenty people or so. We play Dave Brubeck–style stuff, if that means anything to you."

Hiroshi shook his head. "Nothing at all."

"Hey, come on, you have to know 'In Your Own Sweet Way'—it's a standard." He hummed a couple of bars of a melody Hiroshi had never heard in his life. "We even have some fans. Just way too few that we could make a living from it." The pleasure vanished from his face. "Which is why we all keep our day jobs. But the jobs stop us from being able to rehearse as much as we would need to, to get really good. So it looks like we won't really get anywhere with the music, and the jobs will win out in the long run."

Hiroshi nodded thoughtfully. So few people ever got the chance to do what they really yearned to do with their lives. And the ones who couldn't always couldn't for the same reason: they were poor. Either really, truly poor, or scared by the threat of poverty.

Hiroshi turned back to his coffee. John Takeishi had been quite right to remark that he had something on his mind. But it wasn't what he suspected: more than anything else, it was uncertainty. Uncertainty over whether his grand plan would succeed.

That was what was stopping Hiroshi from sleeping. Not the soft mattresses.

JOINT INVESTIGATION COMMITTEE
SARADKOV ISLAND EVENT
CHAIR: SENATOR RICHARD COFFEY (US)
DEPUTY CHAIR: MINISTER ANATOLY MIKHAILOV (RUSSIA)
DOCUMENT STATUS: CONFIDENTIAL
EXTRACT FROM THE WITNESS TESTIMONY OF ADRIAN CAZAR (US)

Deputy chair: What influenced your decision to make Saradkov the goal of your expedition?

Witness: Its position in the Arctic Ocean. Saradkov is in a class of islands that has had a stable ice sheet for thousands of years. We wanted to find out what effects global climate change was having on this ice sheet.

Deputy chair: Whether it is melting?

Witness: Well, in layman's terms, yes. Although there are a great many other criteria that we also look at.

Deputy chair: You are an American. Why didn't you find an American island for your purposes, or maybe a Canadian one?

Witness: Well, there aren't that many American islands in the Arctic Circle, and they've all been pretty well surveyed. Same for the Canadian ones—almost too well. Since half of the Arctic Circle is in Russia, and the climatic conditions in the far north of the Eurasian landmass are significantly different from those of the North American continent, I thought it would be revealing to study the Russian islands using the same methods that had already been used over on the American side.

Deputy chair: Good, but why Saradkov in particular, an island so far north and so small that many maps don't even show it? Why not one of the Eastern Siberian Islands, for instance?

Witness: Yes, we could have done that. To be honest, I don't even know any longer how I settled on Saradkov. Somebody told me about the island, I suppose.

JOINT INVESTIGATION COMMITTEE
SARADKOV ISLAND EVENT
CHAIR: SENATOR RICHARD COFFEY (US)
DEPUTY CHAIR: MINISTER ANATOLY MIKHAILOV (RUSSIA)
DOCUMENT STATUS: CONFIDENTIAL

EXTRACT FROM THE WITNESS TESTIMONY OF ANGELA
MACMILLAN (UK)

Chair: As a biologist, what was your motivation in taking part in this
expedition?

Witness: We knew from satellite images that the coastline on
Saradkov had been free of ice some of the time for a few years. I
wanted to observe how life reestablished itself on a stretch of land
that had been completely without life until recently. What happened, how quickly. Unfortunately, what we found was more like
the opposite.

Chair: What do you mean by that?

Witness: Well, why am I sitting here? Because that damned machine
came to life. Unlife. The killer machine. If it hadn't stopped, it
would have eaten the whole bloody planet by now, wouldn't it?

It seemed strangely unreal to be heading back home. Hiroshi felt he
was only dreaming the drive up the forest road to his house, dreaming the sunshine and blue skies above. Pulling up in front of his
house, hearing the sound of his steps in the gravel. Seeing the door
open and Mrs. Steel standing there, looking him up and down with
a gaze that was half-reproachful, half-worried.

"So they finally let you go," she said after a while.

"Yes," Hiroshi said.

"And? Is everything all right?"

"Everything's all right. Just as I said it would be, Mrs. Steel."

He had been allowed to call her from quarantine to let her know
he would be back later than planned. A government agent had been
listening in on the call, so he had stuck to the official version, telling
her he had been exposed to the carrier of a serious disease and had to
wait it out until they knew whether he was infected as well. But she
mustn't worry about it, he had added; it was just a formality. He was
quite sure he wasn't ill.

"Shall I make you something to eat?"

"Later," Hiroshi said. "I have something to do first."

Before he went into the computer room, he went into an adjoining room and opened the closet there. Inside stood an old black-and-white television that looked as though it had just been left here and forgotten. But appearances were deceptive. As indeed they were intended to be. In fact, a slim cable ran from the set to a clever little mechanism Hiroshi had installed in the wall himself and then carefully concealed. It consisted of a video camera that watched over the computer room via a long fiber-optic cable no thicker than a hair, the kind of cable used for endoscopy and blood-vessel operations. The end of the cable was no more than a tiny point in the dark wood, nonmetallic and giving off no energy signature, so that nobody sweeping for bugs would detect it. The camera was always on; a computer analyzed the images and automatically recorded any kind of change or motion.

Now Hiroshi watched this footage on the monitor. Just as he had suspected, government agents had dropped by during his absence to take a look at his hard drives. He watched them unscrewing the backs of his computers with the same practiced care they had presumably used to disable the expensive alarm systems all around the house. They took out the hard drives and downloaded them onto their own computers, brought along for the purpose. It was all very well organized.

He watched the footage through to the end in fast-forward. Hiroshi had seen no reason to make a sound recording; they would certainly have detected a microphone after all. He didn't need to know what they had said. It was enough to be able to see where they had put in their own bugs. It took him half an hour to detect all the devices and disable them. Of course, he was giving himself away by doing so, letting them know that he had his own security system that they hadn't detected. But that didn't matter now.

Once he knew he was no longer being observed, he set to work restoring his data. After his discussions with Jens Rasmussen, Hiroshi had written up a top-to-bottom data security routine that he now followed with almost religious devotion every time he left the house for any length of time. It took a little while but was mostly automatic: there was a routine that took all his data apart into numerous packages, none of which was the least bit revealing on its own, and then encrypted these with the most robust protection programs around. Then it deposited them in various data havens, mostly in the Pacific region. A second routine took care of what had stayed behind; all that the intruders had found on the hard drives were files specifically created as decoys, with another program he had written himself that went to considerable lengths to make sure they looked like nothing of the sort. Quite the opposite: all the details—the time stamps and file histories, caches and temporary files, the debug logs, e-mails and not inconsiderable encryption on these files as well—were enough to convince an expert he was looking at the current status of everything Hiroshi was working on. Now Hiroshi wiped all the hard drives, fired up a communications program, and downloaded all his data packets once more. This would take a few hours, but once it was done he would be able to work again, and meanwhile he could go down to the laboratory in the basement, whose existence not even Mrs. Steel suspected.

There was no fooling the government, though. The intruders had been here, too, as he learned from a surveillance system much like the one in his computer room. Hadn't they noticed that he hadn't set foot in the lab for ages? Or didn't they care? Hiroshi felt a first twinge of irritation as he went to fetch his tool kit. The entrance to the lab was behind a snugly fitting teak panel on one wall of his meditation room. Mrs. Steel would never go in there as long as the door was closed, so Hiroshi duly closed it. Then he activated the hidden catch that kept the panel in place and looked closely at the code lock on the steel door behind it. It was unharmed and looked untouched.

Very clever indeed these secret service guys. He tapped in the entry code, pulled the panel closed, and then shut the door behind him as the neon tubes flickered to life all around the lab.

It took him another hour to remove all the bugs and video cameras, and he felt the irritation boiling into anger as he worked. Once all the junk they had left behind was in the trash can where it belonged, he had to stop to collect himself. Stand still and breathe deeply. This was an important moment, perhaps the most important in his whole life. He couldn't afford a single false step now. Once he had found his still point, he got to work. On the way home he had stopped at a huge electronic superstore and paid cash for a multiband broadcaster, doing all that was humanly possible to make sure the purchase could not be tracked. Now he took it out of his travel bag and put it on the drainer by a hand sink and put his laptop next to it. He plugged the multiband into the computer and switched them both on.

As the computer booted up, Hiroshi thought of Saradkov Island. He remembered the cold, remembered how helpless he had felt—and how utterly astonished he had been when he had discovered how easily he could direct the nanites. It was almost as though he had built them himself. They had even obeyed some commands given in the code he had used back on Paliuk to direct the old robotic complex.

He had spent all night pondering the matter in Reykjavík, wondering how such a thing was possible. Had he developed a logical set of commands that was considerably more universal than he had thought without even knowing it himself? He couldn't believe that. There was nothing universal about a sequence like 1-0-0-0-1-1-1-0, no inevitable inherent meaning that would make him and the aliens on some unguessably distant planet both use the same code as the command to prime a nanite complex for further instructions. Or was there? No. Though he no longer remembered why he had assigned the command codes that way and no other, he did recall that it had been almost random, making this coincidence no less astounding than if intelligent life-forms from another planet had sent a probe bearing a plaque engraved with a Shakespeare sonnet. It was completely and utterly improbable. There must be another explanation. He just didn't know what it was yet. Nor did he even need to know for the time being. It worked whether or not he understood why.

Hiroshi took a packet of ultrasterile microscope slides from the cupboard, broke the seal, and put the transparent box next to the computer. It was fully booted by now. Hiroshi started the communication program and typed in the sequence of commands that he would need shortly. Then he put on a pair of thin latex gloves, took a slide from the box, and went to the mirror. He held the thin glass slide up to his forehead with his right hand and pressed the "Return" key with the index finger of his left hand. The first package of instructions went through to the multiband. It was broadcasting at a range of two meters. Nobody beyond the walls of the lab would even notice. Hiroshi felt nothing, but he saw in the mirror how a tiny, dark dot formed on his skin, barely bigger than the mark a soft lead pencil might make if he tapped it against his brow. If he hadn't seen it form, he would never have been able to find it. He held his breath, slowly lifting the slide. Once he had reached the dot, he stopped and pressed the "Return" key once more with his other hand. The dot moved. It left his skin and slid along the glass about half a centimeter.

It was done. Hiroshi carefully put the slide down on a bed of green foam rubber. Only then did he dare to breathe. His hands were trembling. This tiny dot on the wafer-thin piece of glass was made up of around a hundred thousand nanite complexes. They were the last on the planet, if he had done everything else right. On Saradkov he had ordered them to nestle themselves down into the tissues of his forehead and then ignore all further commands for a set period. During that time, he had given the kill order for all the other nanites. It had worked. They had all been medically examined from top to toe during their quarantine to see whether any of them had nanites in their body. But Hiroshi had known before the doctors even started that none of their tests could detect anything of the sort. His only concern had been whether the nanites in the skin on his forehead still existed, or whether perhaps they had somehow received the kill signal despite his precautions and obeyed—which he would never even have felt.

Now he knew. They had not. They still existed, and they were obeying his commands. And once he had unriddled them completely—understood them completely—they would obey him completely. They would be the seed from which a future would grow to surpass mankind's wildest dreams. And he, Hiroshi Kato, would have created this new world. His lifelong dream was within reach. Fate was on his side. Now he knew that for sure.

A small news item a few days later reported a private-jet crash somewhere in the Midwest. Three people had died: James Bennett II, president and majority shareholder of the technology giant Bennett Enterprises; Frank Rizzio, the chief financial officer; and the pilot of the jet, whose name was not mentioned.

Very few people outside of Boston paid any attention to the news.

2

It was the first board meeting at Bennett Enterprises since the funeral. And it was the first time James Michael Bennett III took his seat at the head of the long, night-black boardroom table.

One of the directors, Manuel Estrada, head of the marketing department, rose clumsily to his feet. "Mr. Bennett," he began, evidently uncomfortable this duty had fallen to him, "on behalf of the whole board I would like to extend you our deepest sympathy on the occasion of your father's unfortunate—"

"Thank you," James Bennett III replied tersely. "I appreciate that. I really do. But life goes on. Our competitors aren't asleep on the job—let's get to work." He leaned forward, planted his elbows on the table, and folded his hands, much like his father had used to. "I will settle into the role just as quickly as I can, and then I'll make all the necessary decisions about how we shall proceed. And I expect reports from all of you so that I can reach those decisions. Oral reports here and now, and then written reports in two days' time at the latest, five pages maximum. All the important figures, latest developments, problems." He looked at the marketing director, who was still on his feet. "Perhaps you could start, Manuel."

The board meeting lasted half an hour longer than scheduled. When the members were finally on their feet to leave, the new chairman said, "By the way, Alan, do you have a couple more minutes?"

Alan Crockett was head of Human Resources, a burly man with a hangdog look. He was also in charge of industrial security.

"Close the door," James Bennett III said when they were alone. Crockett did as he was told and came back to the table.

"Does the name Jeffrey Coldwell mean anything to you?" Crockett considered the question. "Should it?"

"He's a manager. Originally from Alabama. Graduated London School of Economics. For several years he was regional director, North and South America, with Gu Enterprises, in Hong Kong." James Bennett III stabbed his finger at Crockett. "Find out where he's hiding. I want to talk to him. And consider this top secret." He dropped his hand and picked up the folder on the table in front of him. "That will be all for now."

Separating each nanite from the others and examining them under his atomic force microscope was a task that stretched Hiroshi to the limits of his endurance and powers of concentration. Though the nanites were large compared with most molecules, it was still impossible to observe them directly; the only way to discover their exact shape was to probe them with a cantilever, atom by atom, and then feed the results into software that would convert them into images. Since some distortion was inevitable on every reading he took, he had to repeat each measurement several times. He also had to be able to recognize systematic errors and compensate for these. It meant hour upon hour working at his instruments and never letting his concentration slip for a second.

It was spooky how often he found his own designs repeated in these nanites. With only a few exceptions, he could relate most of the images his analytical software showed him to the nanite function categories he had arrived at by pure theory. He almost found himself wondering whether he had a twin somewhere on a distant planet, a soul mate in an alien body—or, indeed, whether he had been mentally influenced by extraterrestrials. Had he, Hiroshi Kato, been an unwitting cat's-paw all along? That was the point when he found he always had to stop, shut his eyes, and breathe deeply, to find his still point and get rid of the feeling he'd landed in a Stephen King story.

He told himself quite reasonably that his designs had not come about by burning the midnight oil at his drawing board; rather, they were the product of evolutionary algorithms. In other words, they had almost come about of their own accord—all he had done was make it possible with his simulations programs. And just as the laws of geometry dictated that there were only five Platonic solids—the tetrahedron, cube, octahedron, dodecahedron, and icosahedron—so the characteristics of the individual atoms may well dictate that these nanites were the only possible nano-robots.

Not that this explained the matter of the control codes. Okay. But he didn't have to understand everything all at once.

Being in Buenos Aires again after all these years was like a dream. So much had changed. Yet it seemed to Charlotte that under all that was new, all that was different, the city she had known as a teenager still showed through, shimmering. There was the Plaza de Mayo, where she had only ever been able to go in secret, because there had so often been demonstrations there, and a diplomat's daughter mustn't get involved. There was Calle Florida, with its high-end boutiques, where her mother could spend hours on end. The dizzyingly broad Avenida 9 de Julio, where the French embassy stood. As she strolled the streets, she saw two cities at once: the Buenos Aires of her youth, and the city of today. After a while she noticed she had a headache, probably due to this strange form of double vision as well as the humidity she remembered so well—and the memories it awoke.

She met Brenda at the Obelisk, just as they had agreed. From a distance her old friend looked afflicted by some deep melancholy. Charlotte wondered whether the heart-wrenching strains of the tango were already at work on her, the rhythm that pulsed beneath the surface of the city like a ceaseless heartbeat. But when they hugged, everything felt just as it always had.

"I could have met you at the airport," Brenda said without letting go.

"You've met me at so many airports."

"Never at Ezeiza, though."

"You can take me there when I leave."

"Out of the question. I'm not going to let you leave." She released Charlotte from her embrace and then held her at arm's length to take a good look at her. "At least you didn't lose anything to frostbite up there in the Arctic. Meaning we can go to Persicco for an ice-cream sundae with everything. My treat."

They took a taxi to the ice-cream parlor. "You speak Spanish pretty well already," Charlotte said on the way.

"With a thick American accent," Brenda said, batting away the compliment. "Now Tom, *he* speaks good Spanish by now. Because he has to with the students every day."

As they attacked the elaborately decorated mounds of ice cream with their spoons, they caught up on what had been happening in each other's lives since they had last been together. Charlotte had to tell all about her experiences in Russia. Even though she didn't believe that there might be Russian or American agents shadowing her and sitting among the other guests at the ice-cream parlor, she didn't feel comfortable reporting what had really happened here, in a relatively public space. And the curious thing was she no longer even felt the need to share her secret. In Reykjavík she had almost burst with the urge to tell someone, which was like a burning itch, but now she was back in the rhythm of everyday life, where all was as it had always been, what she had lived through seemed too extreme, too fantastic, for her to want to talk about it. As time went on it had also become harder and harder for her to actually put what had happened into words. Nobody who had not been there could ever really understand it. Sometimes, looking back, she could hardly believe it herself; it was like the memory of a bad dream rather than of a real event.

So instead, she mostly told Brenda about the complicated journey they had taken to get there, about Morley's odd little ways, and about how they had managed in the piercing cold of the Arctic. And finally, without going into details, she explained that Leon had died, and there had been a lengthy inquiry into the incident.

"But why in Reykjavík?" Brenda asked, but when Charlotte simply shrugged, she dropped the question and then confessed she had expected her to have paired up with Adrian by the time they came back. "For some reason, I had the feeling he was keen on you. And you would have made a lovely couple."

Charlotte chased the last stubborn spoonful of vanilla ice cream around the bottom of her glass and found herself thinking of Leon, of how masculine he had looked in his parka. "Adrian? No, he behaved like a big brother, that was all. And I don't think it was because he's shy."

"Maybe he's gay?"

Charlotte considered the possibility. Somehow that didn't seem likely either. "We just didn't click. Maybe climatology is all he lives for."

After that Brenda told her about the move, about all the little differences she still hadn't gotten used to in daily life in Argentina, and about how Lamita's adoption had worked out. "We would have been right up the creek without Pari. He dragged us along to the right offices and told us when to put a banknote inside our passport, and all of that. We had to fly to Dhaka twice before we could bring her back with us. Thank goodness we found a nanny who gets along well with Jason; we've been a bit more flexible since then."

"And how's she coping here?"

Brenda tilted her head, thinking. "Well now. It's only been a few weeks, so I think it'll be hard to say for a while. She only speaks Bengali, so that's a problem, and . . . I hope we'll manage."

"I'm sure you will," Charlotte said with feeling.

At last it was time to set off. "Girls' time is over for today," Brenda declared with a melancholy sigh. They took another taxi. "I don't dare get behind the wheel here. I probably never will. Just look at the way they drive! I mean, they see the highway code as just a set of recommendations really, don't they?"

When they arrived, Jason showed up to say hello but refused to let Charlotte kiss him on the cheek and stormed off in a huff when she greeted him in Spanish. Tom wasn't back yet. Brenda showed her the guest room, the other main rooms, and the garden, and then they sat down in the kitchen for coffee.

At some point the girl made an appearance as well. A dark, thin face peering around the corner, shy but inquisitive, only to vanish again instantly when Charlotte looked that way. Her curiosity finally won out; the little girl scampered into the kitchen, staying close to the wall, and hid behind Brenda, who smiled wryly and put an arm around her. From the safety of this position, she peered again at the visitor, more closely this time.

Charlotte leaned forward. "*Tomar naam ki?*—What's your name?"

The thin little girl blinked in astonishment, then whispered back in Bengali. "Lamita. My name's Lamita."

"How are you, Lamita?"

"I'm fine." The girl leaned in closer to Brenda and glanced up at her, full of gratitude.

Brenda meanwhile was looking wide-eyed at Charlotte. "Since when do you speak Bengali?"

Charlotte tried to remember. "I think some of the gardeners at our house in Delhi were from Bengal. I mean, I seem to remember always hearing the language out in the garden."

"You're a godsend. We've had such trouble trying to talk to the child, you just wouldn't believe it. She understands me, but I can't understand her. If she has an ache or a pain, I can't even get her to tell me where it hurts. It's as if we'd taken in a pet."

Charlotte looked at Lamita. The girl really did seem like a shy forest animal somehow, or like a creature beaten and mistreated for an age, suffering and silent. "I'm here for a while. Maybe I can talk to her a bit."

"You must." Brenda turned to her adoptive daughter and looked at her. "Would you like something to eat? Cake?"

Lamita nodded wordlessly, her eyes huge.

"Yes? Please say yes."

"Yes," the girl whispered with a look of terror in her eyes, as though she had only ever been punished when she dared to speak.

"By now I just feel sick whenever I see cut-price T-shirts," Brenda said as Lamita sat next to her, devouring a slice of cake. "A T-shirt for a dollar—who can make a living from that? I can't stand buying cheap clothing anymore. Behind every shirt and pair of pants, I see a kid like Lamita, sitting in an airless room from morning till night and sewing until her fingers bleed."

"I thought the factory had gone bust?"

"Well that one did. But how many other textiles factories do you think there are out there? And other companies making other stuff, all along the same lines? Hundreds of thousands."

Charlotte found herself thinking of Hiroshi and his plan to end poverty for good and create prosperity for all with the help of robots that built robots. It might have been a completely crazy plan, but at least he meant well. And perhaps the plan wasn't even that crazy. She looked at Lamita and wondered how many children like her were slaving away under unspeakable conditions at that very moment just so people in rich countries had something to buy.

Burntwood Lake lay in the north of the Canadian province of Saskatchewan, thirty miles or more from the nearest marked road, and even that road was not something anyone used to city life would recognize as such. The only way even to find the lake was to have a good off-road vehicle and know the landscape like the back of your hand, meaning that not many people ever did.

So the lake had become the favored retreat for those few souls who could last out the cold winters this far north, enjoying the peace and quiet and the solitude. Some of them had built cabins in the woods around it, which the government knew nothing about. If one or two of them also brewed moonshine in their own stills, who cared? A shot of conversation juice was just what you needed after a day spent fishing on the lake.

Remote though the area was, there was nevertheless a webcam in one of the cabins that gave real-time Internet views of the northeast shore of Burntwood Lake and its little island. The student who had installed it went by the user name NorthernLight in the Internet forums, and he had made sure to include a solar-powered battery pack to keep the webcam computer running, along with an antenna that kept the whole thing connected to the Internet via a relay at the northern edge of Grass River Provincial Park, by Cranberry Portage. His uncle was a park ranger and had helped him mount the relay antenna and patch it discreetly into the park's own telephone system. NorthernLight studied computer science in Winnipeg and loved being able to check in anytime to see what was happening on "his" lake. And he was far too proud of his setup to have secured the website with a password. The whole world should be able to share his labor of love.

Which was precisely what sealed the fate of Burntwood Lake, Saskatchewan.

Hiroshi's computer room was no longer a simulation lab: it had become a control room much like NASA mission control. Except that Hiroshi was all alone in front of his monitors. One of the screens showed Burntwood Lake. He was watching it anonymously via a far-flung network of various servers, most of which were not in the US; nobody would ever be able to find out later that at this particular moment he had been connected to the webcam of the lake-fishing fanatic who went by the name NorthernLight. That was important.

On another screen he was watching a graphic-interface depiction of what the nanites he had dispatched were up to. They were busy. They had reproduced their population by a factor of one hundred billion before they even set out, and now it was all happening rather fast. Watching them at work gave him some idea of what they must have done back on Saradkov Island. Based on all the reports, it had all happened very fast there as well. At first, he had taken that with a grain of salt; his calculations had shown that they would have to have been reproducing and building at positively dizzying speeds. But the reality of what he was watching now exceeded even those figures.

The most fascinating aspect was he didn't even need to leave the house. At first, he had worked out all kinds of complicated plans for how he could travel and cover his tracks. But there was no need for any of that. All he had to do was dose a nanite metacomplex with the right commands, then put them down on the floor of his lab, and send them on their way to carry out his orders. Not that he'd even needed to do that; they could have set out directly from the glass beaker he kept them in. No material actually presented an obstacle to the nanites. These machines could dismantle armor, alarm systems, electric fences, and who knows what else atom by atom with no trouble at all. They could slip through the opening they had made and then put all the atoms right back into place. This was one of the basic routines written directly into the transporter units; there was no need even for a specific, separate command.

The only real problem was guiding them on their way through rock and soil, under rivers and roads, all the way to their goal. These nanites could do a great deal but they couldn't read GPS signals—that would have been asking too much of a robotic complex that had arrived on Earth from the unknown depths of space. So Hiroshi had to steer them. To do this, he had needed to modify their programming somewhat. Which was good practice anyway, since some modification would be needed for the plan he had in mind.

How could he keep in touch with the complex while it was out in the world? He could have used radio, of course. That was the nanites' standard operating procedure, so to speak. But then he would have run the risk of detection—he was sure the government still had him under surveillance. Hiroshi had finally hit upon a simple but astonishingly effective solution: the metacomplex simply built a microscopically thin telephone cable from copper and iron atoms as it went along. The cable was hooked up to a nanoscale transmitter back in Hiroshi's lab. All he had to do was set his multiband to the very lowest signal strength and place it where the nanites had set out from. Then he could communicate with the complex as it went on its way, and nobody was any the wiser.

Hiroshi had tested all this out first, of course. And of course the first few attempts had gone wrong—drastically wrong, even. But he had eventually enjoyed his first success: he had ordered a nanite complex to set out for the farthest edge of his extensive estate and construct a cube of pure iron. Then Hiroshi had taken a stroll through the garden and, lo and behold, there was the cube, nestled at the foot of the fence.

None of what came next had been hard. The nanites may not have had a navigation system for planet Earth, but they were able to record distances and directions they traveled down to the micrometer. All Hiroshi needed to do was measure the distance between his lab and the target—the island in the middle of Burntwood Lake—as precisely as he could and then program the nanites with instructions along the lines of "First go 2,507 kilometers, 318 meters, and 12 centimeters north, then go 1,689 kilometers, 781 meters, and 3 centimeters east." Once they reached their target, they had orders to build a long red pole from the ground up, which he duly spotted on the picture broadcast by the webcam right in the middle of the island. Bull's-eye on his first attempt. It was almost unnerving.

He hadn't pushed the nanites anywhere near their limits in terms of how fast they could get there. There was no need, after all. He didn't quite know how fast they could have gotten there if so instructed— within a couple of hours?—but it was fine by him that they had taken a week. It had given him time to prepare himself for what came next. Because the next order he gave the nanites was to carry out a program that was already stored in their memory, a program they had brought with them when they came to Earth. Hiroshi hadn't altered a line of it; he wanted to see how it played out of its own accord.

He checked one more time that the camera was running, then gave the order to start. It started right away, breathtakingly fast. Rootlets sank down into the earth, probing for energy, just as they had done the whole way over—although never in such vast numbers. The nanites replicated, the metacomplex became a meta-metacomplex and then a metacomplex to the third power, the fourth, soon to the fifth power, and even higher. Positioning elements ran out for miles all around, branching out like the roots of a tree in their search for certain rare minerals. Transporter elements raced along the newly created tracks, carting along the prospector units, the diggers, the cutters, and finally the molecular structures that would capture the cargo atom by atom so that it could then be taken elsewhere and unloaded. They built up a stockpile of all the elements they would need.

Other digger units did nothing but dig a hole down into the ground, deeper and ever deeper. Other nanites collected the earth that had been moved and took it apart into individual molecules, which were either added to the stockpiles for later use or simply thrown away. The first building work began: swarms of nanites ferried a stream of iron and carbon atoms into the hole, where other nanites assembled them into huge steel rings with a very specific internal structure. Other nanites built conduits and cables, huge motors and generators, and curious circuitry.

And the hole that ran straight down into the earth from the middle of the island grew deeper and deeper. A hundred yards. Two hundred. Five hundred. A mile. Two. Three. When it was nearly three and a half miles deep, digging finally stopped and the machine built itself a bottom to the shaft, and then the stockpiles of material all around the site began to stream down to build a rocket atom by atom, which would take a probe full of nanites off to space. Meanwhile, the generator complexes loaded up the energy storage units, filling them to bursting point.

Hiroshi watched, fascinated, as the rocket was built, studying each component as it emerged, marveling at the care and design that had gone into all the details. The recording was still running—good. For this machine had more technological riddles in every cubic inch of its construction than any single human being would be able to unravel in a lifetime of work. The construction of the shaft itself, however, was no great riddle: it was a simple linear motor. The array of magnetic coils would grasp the rocket in their fields one after another in quick succession and hurl it upward at accelerations that no living being would have been able to survive. Since there were no living beings onboard, that was not a problem. The rocket would be traveling at three times the speed of sound by the time it left the mouth of the shaft, after which its own engines would kick in and accelerate it still further, taking it up into space in less than two minutes.

And it looked like it wasn't long now until takeoff.

Just then the third screen blinked. It ran a simple message program connected to a small computer in the kitchen, which Mrs. Steel could use to get in touch if absolutely necessary.

"Mr. Kato, you have a visitor. A Miss Malroux has just arrived and asks whether she can speak to you."

"In fact, I'm not supposed to disturb him at all," said the housekeeper, a sturdy woman whose blond curls lay on her scalp as though cemented into place. "It's only for emergencies, he said. Only if the house is on fire or someone's injured, or if the police turn up, or the president calls. Those were his very words. Because right at this moment he's at work on a very important project where any interruption could mean that the whole undertaking was in vain." She was still leaning over the little white laptop, which lay on a folded tea towel on the kitchen counter next to an array of pepper grinders of various sizes. The cursor was blinking below the message she had just sent. "But you've already been here once. I don't think he'd want me to just send you on your way again."

I hope not, Charlotte thought. She perched herself on a barstool by the kitchen counter with the cup of coffee that Mrs. Steel had set in front of her. She sat down with exaggerated care, as though it might all go wrong if she made any unnecessary noise up here or disturbed the stillness of the house. But probably Hiroshi wouldn't want her sent on her way. She held fast to the thought.

She had considered calling on her way here. Asking if it would be all right for her to come. But she hadn't called out of a sudden fear that he might say no, and then what? So she had arrived unannounced in the hope he would find it more difficult to say no if she were standing right in front of him. In the end, it hadn't helped at all. Now she was even less than a voice on the phone. She was a message sent from the kitchen to his study.

Mrs. Steel was tapping her fingers restlessly on the marble worktop. She was waiting for an answer, but Charlotte suddenly realized she also had no idea what to do now. She had probably just been busy with some housework, and now there was an unexpected visitor in her kitchen, and she couldn't get on with her day.

"What is this very important project he's working on?" Charlotte asked despite knowing perfectly well the housekeeper wouldn't tell her. Not that she even needed to ask: she could imagine it quite well for herself. On Saradkov, Hiroshi had seen the nano-robots in action that only a little while before he had told her couldn't be built. It was only logical he would want to find out how they had been.

"I don't know," Mrs. Steel said. "All I know is he works at it day and night. It's never been as bad as this. Nobody's allowed in to see him. All the shutters are down. I'm not allowed to open the doors or even clean up around the place." She pulled a cloth from her apron and wiped down the counter, quite superfluously. "And then there's the security detail that patrols the grounds these days. Over there, you see them? Those two with their guns and the dog? They're part of the arrangement. Oh of course you must have seen them as you arrived. It's dreadful, isn't it?"

Charlotte shrugged. She had become more or less used to such security arrangements as a child. "They're doing their job."

"Oh they are. But carrying those guns—I tell you, it gives me a funny turn every time I look at them. And they don't just let me through when I come back from doing the shopping. They check my car every time. Supposedly, somebody could have planted a bomb in it or a bug or I don't know what. Ever since he got back, Mr. Kato has been most concerned that he might be being bugged." She sighed. "He turns up at the most impossible times of day and night, and when he does he's hungry as a wolf—well, no wonder! I throw something together for him, he bolts it down—pardon my saying so, but there's really no other way to describe it—and then he's off again. And it's been like that ever since he came back. I mean, I'm happy, of course, that he even remembers to eat, but as for what it's doing to his health . . . this lifestyle can't be good for him."

"He's always had a tendency to go to extremes," Charlotte said, thinking of their childhood in Tokyo, and how she had visited him at home once. His tiny little corner of the room, everything neatly in its place but tools everywhere. And the dorm room in Boston. Almost monastic in its stark simplicity. She had often found herself thinking of that room recently. That and his stubbornness in wooing her. And the extraordinary way he had gone about it. No, Hiroshi was definitely not like other men.

Mrs. Steel trotted back over to the little white laptop that sat there like a toy. Obviously, there was still no answer. "Perhaps he's asleep," she said. "He has to sleep eventually after all."

Charlotte just nodded and took a sip of her coffee. She had never taken him seriously when he had insisted it was fate their paths should always cross. When he had claimed they were meant for one another. She had always supposed words like that were merely talk, the kind of thing men said because they thought it would make it easier to get her into bed. Although in Hiroshi's case she hadn't even thought that. In the end it had been *her* dragging him into bed. And then *him* saying he wanted more than that.

Oh, she didn't know what to think now. For the first time in all these years, she wondered whether Hiroshi might have been right. Whether they really were meant for each other in some way, perhaps not in any very romantic way. Whether they could ever be anything more than childhood friends. She had never seriously considered a relationship with Hiroshi; whenever he had started talking about it, it had always struck her as a crazy idea, not worth thinking about. But now, for the first time, she tried to imagine it. Wondered what such a relationship might look like. How they would live. Whether they would have children . . . children! The fact that children even crossed her mind surprised her most of all. What was it like to live with an inventor? That was the question. That, and whether she wanted that kind of life. Whether she could stand it. She didn't know.

"There," Mrs. Steel exclaimed. "An answer."

It was only two words: "Not now."

Two words that were like a slap in the face. Charlotte felt herself turn red. All at once all her hopes and questions and self-scrutiny seemed utterly ridiculous. How long could you fend a man off before he gave up? How often could you pick someone else before he changed his mind? Suddenly, she was certain the last straw had been in Reykjavík when she had made her escape from Iceland without even trying to talk to Hiroshi before she left. He would never forgive her that.

"Ah well," she said. Her voice sounded strange in her ears. "You have to expect this sort of thing when you just turn up unannounced. Maybe it'll work out next time." She had forced her face into a smile but felt that it must look like a grimace.

"Would you like to leave him a message?" the housekeeper asked, looking terribly flustered. "I'll give you something to write with. I'll find you the back of an envelope—"

"No. Thank you. I think it . . . I don't think there's any need." Charlotte looked at her watch and took her car keys out of her bag. She had a rental car she had picked up in San Francisco. "If I hurry, I should be able to catch the evening flight to Boston."

Boston. Not that she knew what to do with herself there either.

At first, Hiroshi hadn't even noticed there had been a message blinking on the screen. He had clicked it away without even reading it and then written a hasty answer to make sure there were no more disturbances—all in an instant, his fingers flying over the keys—and then he had turned back to watch what was happening deep underground below Burntwood Lake.

This was it! That had to be the start sequence. The last of the fastenings decoupled. In a moment the rocket would be hanging there in the magnetic field. But it wouldn't stay still for long, since the coils could only store a limited amount of energy.

There! Acceleration. He could literally see the storage units unleashing their whole store of energy into the coils in two or three convulsive movements, hurling the rocket out of the shaft and up into the sky. It was incredible how it picked up speed. Mach 1—the sonic boom must have shaken the whole launch site to its foundations. Mach 2, 3, and then it was out. Ignition. Hiroshi held his breath. All at once the seconds stretched out endlessly. But no antiballistic missiles appeared to intercept it, nothing that could stop the rocket's trajectory. One hundred miles . . . two hundred, and still accelerating . . . three hundred. Well, he could safely say it was in outer space by now.

The radio signals the rocket was sending back to base and that base was sending on to him along more than twelve hundred miles of microscopically thin data cable were becoming weaker with every second. Hiroshi followed the rocket's course, stony-faced. Now came the moment when he had rewritten some of the programming. The moment of truth . . . yes. The rocket changed course. It shifted by just a few degrees, but enough to keep it within the plane of the ecliptic and send it toward Jupiter. Just as he had planned.

With a mixture of deep satisfaction and exhaustion, Hiroshi sent the base an instruction to cease radio communication with the rocket. Once that was done, he sent the kill signal, the order that would make the nanites take the whole launch site apart and then the data cable that led back to him and finally each other. Until there was nothing left. He didn't wait for all this to finish but broke the connection straightaway, including the one to the webcam. Then he sank back into his seat and massaged his temples. Only now did he feel the strain he had been under the whole time he had been watching.

And this was only the start. The real challenges all lay ahead.

Unlike the incident in the Russian Arctic, this launch did not pass unnoticed by the wider world. Quite the opposite. Given that it had taken place in one of the remotest regions of the North American continent, an astonishing number of people caught wind of it. There was even a bit of wobbly video footage that somebody had taken with their smartphone showing the rocket climbing into the sky at the head of a column of fire, which looked noticeably different from the usual TV images. The webcam owner had been ordered to hand over the whole contents of his server to the police, of course. The news channels portentously reported that the log files were currently being evaluated, and they all played the same slow-motion clip of the rocket shooting up out of the hole—images that showed nothing at all, really, other than a cylindrical blur popping up and then vanishing.

Footage of Burntwood Lake itself showed the devastation caused by the launch. When the shaft had collapsed in on itself, it had swallowed not only the island but all the water in the lake. The helicopters sent by the big news networks were circling over a waste of mud and dead fish. The Canadian prime minister condemned the incident and repeatedly emphasized his government had nothing to do with it. He declared that no effort would be spared to get to the bottom of the matter and find out the truth. One commentator, however, put forward the question of what laws might be used to prosecute whoever was responsible. After all, it was not actually illegal for private individuals to launch spacecraft in Canada, although this was more because no such law had ever been needed than because legislation had been considered or debated. Meaning that all that was left was a suit of criminal damage, but that would need to be proven first. Since Burntwood Lake wasn't even in a nature reserve, that whole tranche of legislation did not apply.

In a statement, the US president assured his Canadian counterpart of his fullest support in the search for the perpetrators of what he called "this subversive act." He went on to say with firm resolve that they would not tolerate the American continent being used as a base for any actions that might endanger world peace.

Hiroshi wasn't surprised to see them standing at his door the next day. The first was a man called Elmer Garrett, whose long, lantern-jawed face Hiroshi remembered well from Reykjavík—Garrett had questioned him several times, and today he wore a grim expression. There were two other men whose names Hiroshi didn't bother to remember, and John Takeishi, the young lawyer who would rather have been a jazz clarinetist. Garrett said there had been an incident in Canada. Perhaps Hiroshi had heard about it. Very like what had happened on the island in the Russian Arctic. They had a few questions they would like to ask him.

Hiroshi asked them to come in and told them that yes indeed, he had heard something about the incident in Canada.

"What do you know about it?" Garrett asked, having presented a business card that described him as a "special investigator."

"What I saw on TV," Hiroshi replied. "And on the clips going around the Internet."

"What do you make of it?"

Hiroshi shrugged. "By the look of it, I would say that there were more extraterrestrial probes waiting for their moment."

They all nodded. Evidently, they had already thought of this on their own. It was hardly a very original conclusion.

"May I ask where you were at the time?" Garrett asked, pulling out a little notebook that made him look as though he were reenacting a favorite scene from a Humphrey Bogart movie.

"Here," Hiroshi replied truthfully. "I'm not going anywhere these days."

Garrett wrote it all down. "And can anyone confirm that?"

"My housekeeper."

3

"What if we were to assume," Adamson said, "that Hiroshi Kato caused that incident in Saskatchewan?"

It was the wrong thing to say and the wrong time to say it, as he realized as soon as he'd spoken. Nor had it been a good idea to waylay his boss here in the lobby. Roberta Jacobs looked at him in dismay, even in shock, as though he had just molested her.

"Bill!" The way she spat his name out spoke volumes, a whole encyclopedia of disdain. "Do you never get the feeling that this man has become an obsession?"

"Over in Russia he stopped one of those things in its tracks. And if he can do that, then he can start one."

She had recovered her poise. Now she was getting angry. "Hiroshi Kato made a statement," she said, making every word count. "He says he doesn't know what stopped that probe. Our analysis of the radio signals he sent and received supports that statement. Sure, once he was on the island he managed to trigger the self-destruct. But he handed over that code to us and to the Russians in case any other probes became active. As for whatever else Mr. Kato can or cannot do, I would like you to stick to the facts rather than let your imagination run away with you. We've had specialists looking at his research and how far he's gotten."

"What does that mean? Which specialists?"

"CIA specialists who copied every scrap of data on his computers. Established experts in nanotechnology who went through that data. Satisfied now?"

Adamson swallowed. "I'm quite sure that—"

"And everybody else is quite sure that not," Jacobs interrupted him. "If you will excuse me, Mr. Adamson, I have an appointment."

With that she stalked off toward the front door. Adamson watched her go. He could probably thank his lucky stars that he worked for a government agency; in a private company, he'd have been fired by now. However, his behavior was not entirely without consequences. Two days later he learned that he would be transferred to another department. Effective immediately.

"Space-colonization planning!" Even as he sat in the living room with his brother-in-law that evening, Adamson still couldn't quite believe what had happened. "I didn't even know that DARPA had anything to do with loony tunes like that. And now I'm in charge of it."

Mitch Jensen furrowed his brow. "Outer space? Isn't that NASA's bird?"

"You'd kind of think so, wouldn't you?" Adamson took a slug from the can of Bud he was holding. It was too warm to taste like much. "They could have just come straight out and called it make-work. Hell, they could have me carting wheelbarrows of sand up and down the parade square."

CNN was on the television. The sound was turned down, but the pictures spoke for themselves. The only story was the lake that had been destroyed in Northern Saskatchewan.

"I say Kato pulled a fast one," Mitch Jensen declared, nodding toward the TV. "He knows more than he's letting on. All that data on his computers—that was all fake, if you ask me." He emptied his can and then crumpled it in his fist. "It's just that nobody does ask me."

"You guys still watching him?"

Mitch shook his head slowly. "Mr. Hiroshi Kato is now officially off the list of suspects. Circular to all departments concerned. The president has taken him under his wing. They're considering which medal to give him for what he did on Saradkov Island." He weighed the can in his hand, aimed, and then threw it neatly into the cardboard box that stood by the television. "The man's above reproach. Up on a pedestal. He has nothing to fear."

Jeffrey Coldwell still didn't know quite what to make of all this. He didn't even know which way to look.

On the one hand, there was this piece of paper on the table in front of him. An employment contract offering a salary around five times what he was earning right now. Five times! That would mean the end of the dry spell he'd been in ever since Larry Gu had died and he'd been dismissed from Gu Enterprises. Sure, he hadn't actually been fired. Even the Communist Party top brass knew that could look bad. But they also knew how to persuade a guy to quit of his own free will.

They had had to sell the ranch, and of course they got way too little for it, as always when you had to sell in a hurry. Then Nancy had gotten the divorce, which had cost him all the money he still had. The hell with it—she had been way too young for him anyway. But after that he had just had to take whatever jobs came up, and they had been anything but his dream career. He was a textbook example of the failing professional. And it all looked downhill from here. But this contract was his chance to get back to where the grass was greener. To get things back on track. To drag himself up by his bootstraps. Which was why his eyes kept coming back to the salary.

But his eyes also drifted again and again to the man on the other side of the desk—the incredibly ugly, glass-and-steel desk that sat in the middle of the light, wood-paneled office like a turd in the punchbowl. Coldwell had looked up James Bennett III, of course, before catching his flight to Boston. Half an hour on the Internet had turned up more pictures than anyone could ever want of glamorous receptions, elegant parties, and other social events. The young man in the pictures had looked like the American dream: handsome, happy, successful.

Just amazing what image-manipulation software can do these days, he had thought when he shook the hand of the new chair of Bennett Industries. The James Bennett III he met in the flesh looked like the funhouse mirror image of the man in the photographs: puffy with drink, somehow crooked and out of proportion, his hair dull and thinning, his eyes unsteady. Anything but good company. But there was still that salary to think of. He didn't have to work for the guy because he liked him. He wasn't holding down his current job for the fun of it either.

He cleared his throat once Bennett had finished explaining what he wanted. "To be straight with you, Mr. Bennett, I signed a confidentiality agreement. Strictly speaking, I shouldn't even comment on what you've just told me."

Bennett raised his eyebrows, which made him look almost exactly like a cheap movie villain. "Do you really believe the Communist Party of China will send lawyers over and haul you up before an American court if you tell me?"

"Not lawyers. They'll send killers."

"I understand." Bennett toyed with the platinum-plated ballpoint pen he had used to write that incredible salary into the contract himself. "In fact, I'm not really interested in what Mr. Kato did in Hong Kong. I'm interested in what he's doing now. As I understand it, that isn't covered by your confidentiality agreement, am I right?"

"That's exactly how I see it." Coldwell nodded. He had only even mentioned it to show he knew what secrets meant and how to keep them.

In fact, he wasn't worried that the Chinese government would send killers after him. First of all, he was small fry for them, and second, he had seen worse and survived it. The early years in Hong

Kong hadn't exactly been a walk in the park. He had run into trouble with the Triads. At one point, he had thrown himself from a car right before a hail of bullets turned it into a colander. He knew all about solving problems with a fistful of banknotes and a handshake. And he had learned to live with the idea that that often meant the one causing trouble would meet with an untimely death.

"What's my role?" he asked. "What would I do here exactly?"

Bennett seemed to have been waiting for the question. "You'll set up your own department. Outside the rest of the organization and answering only to me. You'd have a sufficiently large budget and the freedom to use it as you see fit. And, of course, I would expect you to be able to keep secrets. But above all, Mr. Coldwell... Jeff... I expect you to bring me whatever Hiroshi Kato's working on. If you can, bring me him, too. I want to control everything he creates. Nothing more, nothing less. And let me put it like this: I would rather he were no longer working at all than that he were working for somebody else. If you understand what I mean."

"I do indeed." Coldwell nodded slowly and thought about what he'd just heard. Back in the old days it would have been on posters—"Dead or Alive." "It may require, shall we say, unconventional methods to achieve that."

Bennett twisted his face into a grin like a shark's. "Officially, I don't know anything about that. But I won't be watching you too closely." The grin widened. "As I understand it, you've built up some experience with unconventional methods over the course of your career."

Coldwell raised his eyebrows. "I'm surprised you know about that."

"I have my sources," Bennett said. The way he said it sounded a little strange. Almost suggestive.

To hell with it. "I see," Coldwell said and took the contract. Bennett passed him the platinum-plated pen to sign with, which he took as a good omen.

It took three weeks to put together a good team, gather all the information it needed, and work out a plan. It took another three weeks to practice and prepare, and then the first group took up position among the pines not far from Hiroshi Kato's mansion and trained its binoculars on it.

"House used to belong to a country singer. Famous guy," one of the men remarked as he swept the glasses over shuttered windows, closed French doors, and an unused pool.

"Really? Who?" asked the man next to him.

"Name escapes me." He put down his binoculars. "Hey, Bob, who was the singer who did 'He's Got the Whole World in His Hands'? That version with the steel-guitar intro?" He started to imitate the sound of a steel guitar but thought better of it. "Huge hit about . . . huh, twenty years ago."

"Johnny . . . Johnny someone. I know who you mean," the man called Bob said. "He lived here?"

"Yep."

"Cool."

They watched the house until they knew the daily routines—when the gardener came, and when he left; when the patrol guards took their break (they had instructions never to take their break at the same time as the day before, but of course they ignored them); and when the shifts changed. They watched as a skinny little Japanese guy came out of the house once and talked to the gardener; he was the man from the photographs they had all studied. When they saw that the housekeeper, an older woman with a head of blond hair that could be seen from miles away, drove off and wasn't coming back, they passed on the information to their backup team, who found out Patricia Steel was visiting her sister Barbara in Sacramento, where her brother-in-law ran a grocery business specializing in organically grown fruit and vegetables.

"Okay, that's one less witness," Coldwell said when they updated him on the situation. "Let's do this thing."

The next morning the night guards were in for an unpleasant surprise when the two vans arrived with the relief shift. Both vehicles had the black paintwork, tinted windows, and logo of J. Irons Security Inc. they had been expecting, and the men who climbed out were dressed in familiar uniforms, but they were also wearing silicone-rubber masks of the presidential candidates in the last election. They shot all the dogs straightaway and then pointed their weapons at the night watch, who less than ten minutes later were handcuffed, blindfolded, and locked in the garden shed. The fake guards marched up to the house. They knew where the alarms were and how to disarm them. While some of them spread out around the perimeter of the house, others broke through the front door with the tools they had brought. It only took a few seconds. Then it was their turn for an unpleasant surprise: the house was empty.

It was unnervingly empty. Most of the countless rooms had no furniture at all. They found one room with a mattress on the floor and a thin cover over it, and another with just a chair. The only rooms furnished anywhere near normally were the kitchen and the dining room next door. At last, in the farthest corner of the house from the front door, they found a big room with a spectacular view of the garden and the valley beyond. It held a few tables arranged in a U shape. In the middle of one tabletop lay a few small pieces of plastic that turned out, upon closer inspection, to be keys snapped off from a computer keyboard. They had been arranged to spell out two words: FUCK YO*.

Rodney Alvarez looked at the clock. It was past midnight. Again. When Allison wasn't there—she was visiting a friend in Phoenix—he never managed to go to bed, no matter how firmly he resolved to do so. Just one more website, he had said to himself what seemed like ten minutes ago, but that had led to one more and then another after that. . . . Tomorrow he'd be yawning his head off again in the office.

Enough, already. He put his computer to sleep with a resolute flourish and stood up. He stretched and then realized with a guilty start that he had forgotten to unload the dishwasher. He wondered whether he could put it off till morning. Not a good idea: he was always rushed for time in the morning, and he would be half-asleep and good for nothing. On the other hand, Allison would be back by the time he came home from the office. *Do it now then, quickly.* He trotted off to the kitchen and opened the machine. There was a clean, cold smell. First step: grab all the spoons from the cutlery basket in one fistful, get them over to the drawer by the stove. Just as he picked up the knives, there was a ring at the door. At ten to one? Rodney tiptoed into the hall and peered through the peephole.

It was Hiroshi.

What was going on now? Rodney opened the door. "Don't you think this is a strange time of night to be calling on honest, hard-working citizens?"

Hiroshi gave a thin smile. "Don't you think that's a strange way to greet an old friend?" He pointed to the knives. Rodney was still clutching them in his hand like a bouquet of flowers.

"One last bit of housework," Rodney said, opening the door wide. "I was just going to bed. Come on in. Long time no see."

Hiroshi came in, stepping inside briskly and neatly in that typical way of his. Rodney always found himself thinking of old samurai movies when he saw Hiroshi walk. He had a small tote bag slung over his shoulder. And somehow, for some reason he looked like . . . like a refugee. Rodney had no other way to describe it, and he also had no idea what made him think so, but there it was.

"Yes," Hiroshi said. "Long time no see. And we were kind of rudely interrupted last time."

"So we were." Rodney felt a pang of guilt. When Hiroshi had sent an e-mail announcing he was back home, he had written a quick reply but had never quite gotten around to making the phone call that he had promised. "Those guys from the government who seemed in such a hurry. Was it something serious?"

Hiroshi nodded. "It was."

"Wow." Rodney looked around. It was a good thing he had tidied the place up a little earlier so that Allison wouldn't turn right around and leave again as soon as she got back. But of course it looked nothing like the home sweet home it was when she was here and in charge. "Come on into the living room. Can I fix you something? Coffee? Tea? Or do you want a beer?"

He switched on the light. All things considered, it didn't look too bad in here.

"Nothing, thanks." Hiroshi sat down on the sofa and put his bag beside him. "I'm not staying long."

"Hey look, it's no problem, I could pull the guest bed out in . . ." Rodney stopped when Hiroshi shook his head. "Okay. Just a suggestion." He sat down opposite Hiroshi and put the knives down on the coffee table. Somehow he couldn't shake the crazy feeling that he was about to hear something he really didn't want to. "Okay. So what was it? If you're allowed to talk about it."

"Actually, I'm not, but that makes no difference," Hiroshi said. "Someone's after me. I have no idea who. I thought it wiser to get away."

"After you?" That didn't sound good, but it also didn't sound like the real reason Hiroshi had turned up. "What have you been up to?"

Hiroshi didn't respond. Instead, he unbuckled his bag and took out a small plastic box. "Rodney. The aliens you're looking for— they're already here. They have been for thousands of years. Here on Earth." He lifted the box and opened the lid. "Look."

"The . . . ?"

Rodney was speechless. He leaned forward and peered into the box. Nothing there. Or almost nothing. A dark spot like a speck of rust.

He looked at his old college buddy, worried. "Is everything okay?"

Hiroshi nodded impatiently. "I mean that little dark fleck. It's not a fleck; it's several million incredibly small, incredibly powerful robots. Robots that came here from outer space thousands of years ago."

Then he went on to tell his story. It was heady stuff at this late hour of the night. It sounded like the digested version of a story already squeezed to bursting, a story of Arctic islands, Russian subs, and a steel fortress that fell to dust. Rodney strongly suspected he had fallen asleep at his computer and was in the middle of a really weird dream. He blinked rapidly. Maybe it would help if he pinched himself.

"Stop," he said. "Wait. Give me the whole thing again from the top. Take it slowly. Some of us are sitting in the cheap seats here. Robots—okay. Incredibly small—I'll swallow that. But what do you mean by powerful?"

"These are nanomachines, Rod. They can manipulate matter at the atomic level. They can take anything apart, and they can build anything you like. They could build the world anew if we ordered them to—or they could destroy it as well, of course." He closed the box lid. "I've had a good look at them, as much as I could. There are about three hundred different types. The control units have a central memory bank, a kind of metals-based DNA, with an unimaginable number of blueprints and schematics all stored and ready to build. I've even managed to analyze some of them—some, out of millions. It's unbelievable. They contain far, far more than even an interstellar probe would need to carry out its mission—it has all the inventions and discoveries of a technological civilization unimaginably more advanced than our own. As though they had deposited all their achievements there."

"And that's what whoever is after you wants."

"That, and the robots themselves."

"The robots that can build whatever you command." Rodney frowned in thought. He still felt as though he was dreaming. "To tell you the truth, I can't really imagine that. How it might work."

Hiroshi nodded. He seemed amused. "Would you like to see?" he asked.

"What?"

"How they build? We could finish that garage of yours."

Rodney had to laugh. Mostly because Hiroshi said that they could *finish* it, which suggested he had ever even started. Good old Japanese politeness. "Yes," he said, grinning. "I'd really like to see that."

Hiroshi took something else from his bag. It was a Wizard's Wand, though he seemed to have modified it heavily. Maybe it was the new model.

"Come on then," he said, getting up.

And he strode off with his Wand in one hand and the plastic box in the other. Rodney clambered to his feet and hurried after him, catching up at the front door. "Wait. What are you going to do?"

"Build your garage."

"Now? In the middle of the night?"

"Don't worry, we'll be quiet." Hiroshi opened the door and walked outside. The moon was near full and shining brightly. Rodney followed him to the spot where he and Allison parked their cars and where he swore he would build a garage every time New Year resolutions came around. So far, all he had managed to do was buy a bit of the lumber that he imagined might serve for the frame. It had been lying on the ground for years now, however, and it probably was no longer in the best condition.

"All right then—where to where?" Hiroshi asked.

What was happening here? Rodney no longer felt like he was dreaming, but this was still an absurd bit of playacting, wasn't it? Perhaps the best thing would be to just play along. He paced out the width of their driveway.

"Back wall should go here," he said, sweeping his hand across. "Then the side wall. Front end over there, with the door."

Hiroshi took the Wizard's Wand and held it in the middle so that the cameras at each end could take their shots. A little green light glowed. Then he lowered the wand and pressed a button that produced a faint, red laser beam. He traced the beam along the ground, following the contours Rodney had given him, a rectangle that surrounded his old Honda and the other spot where Allison usually parked her car. Then he sketched an outline on the wall of the house where the garage would adjoin it. Something about the way he did it made him look like a Jedi knight with his light saber.

"Like this?" Hiroshi asked. He lifted the Wand again and pressed another button, making the laser beam split apart into a fan of light, disco-style, which drew the contours of the long-planned garage on the night air.

A garage made of light. Absurd. "Yes, roughly," Rodney said.

"Okay." Hiroshi switched off the laser and put the plastic box down on the ground, then pressed another button.

And then—nothing happened.

Playacting, then. Or maybe Hiroshi really had gone mad. Which would have been no surprise given the way he worked the whole time, never taking a vacation, never taking a break.

"Isn't it kind of chilly out here?" Rodney said cautiously. "We could go back inside."

"We could," Hiroshi said affably. "But you wanted to watch."

"Watch what?"

"This." He pointed to the edge of the driveway. Only then did Rodney see that a sort of dark stripe had formed there. And not only that, it was getting wider as he watched. And higher. As true as he was standing there, something was growing up out of the ground. Walls, gleaming pale in the moonlight, blooming from the earth in ghostly silence, taking shape as though from thin air. It looked like

CGI—if he'd seen it in a movie theater, he wouldn't have batted an eyelid. But this was no special-effects sequence.

"Nano-robots at work," he heard Hiroshi say. "I told them to analyze building materials—wood, nails, plastic, all the usual stuff. So they have those molecular structures stored already. Now they're just grabbing hold of the atoms they need and putting them together: carbon, hydrogen, oxygen, iron, sulfur, a few more elements you find all over the place. They're not working anywhere near maximum speed, though. I haven't figured out how to optimize that yet."

Rodney simply stared, unable to believe what he was seeing. "This is incredible. Tell me it isn't a dream."

In less than three minutes the walls were standing. Without a pause, the roof took shape—first the frame, then the battens in between, and finally the tiles over them. All neatly in place. Last of all a garage door appeared in front and sank down like a curtain.

"Done," said Hiroshi. "Now you can say that you're the only SETI researcher who's had his garage built by alien robots."

He picked up two little gizmos from the ground and passed them to Rodney, who recognized them as remote controls as soon as he took them. He pressed the "Open" button and the door rose smoothly and quietly. It was like one of those superexpensive high-end installations only millionaires could afford. "Alien robots?"

"It was a probe. Von Neumann probe." Hiroshi squatted down, peered into his plastic box, and waited for something. "Somewhere out there is a civilization of intelligent life-forms who are unbelievably far ahead of us technologically and have been for thousands of years. They sent out rockets that can reach half the speed of light, more even, and once these arrived at their destination they built more rockets to fly off to more solar systems."

"And then what? If they built the rockets, what are they doing now?"

"I don't know yet," Hiroshi said. By now his incredibly small, incredibly powerful robots all seemed to be back home, for he shut the lid, picked up the box, and stood up. "I'm still poking around in the programming there."

"That's the first time I've ever heard you admit to having trouble with other people's code."

"First off, these 'other people' are extraterrestrial, and second, these are no normal procedural programs. They're not object-oriented. They're control programs, agent-based, quasi neuronal, extremely multilayered. With programs like that, you can't just read the code and understand them right away; you have to simulate it if you want to know what they even do." Hiroshi coughed. "And that's been my hobby ever since I got back."

Rodney blinked and gazed at the garage. It looked just like what he had planned. Then he looked at the two remote controls in his hand. *Better leave the door open for now so that Ally can drive straight in tomorrow. Won't she be surprised!*

"I'm beginning to understand why they're after you," he said.

4

Hiroshi found an apartment in Minamata in one of the huge vacation resorts at Yunoko, right by the sea. It was off-season, and most of the windows were shuttered. When he peered through the slats of his own blinds, he felt he had been transported into a postapocalyptic film, one of those stories where a global plague had swept away most of mankind, and he was one of the few survivors. It wasn't especially lovely, but nobody knew him here, and he was left in peace. Which was exactly what he needed. He was also a long way from the part of town where his grandparents lived. There was little danger of bumping into them on the street.

Would his pursuers track him down here? Possibly, but they would have a harder time of it. Here in Japan he was just another face in the crowd, and they were the strangers. To be on the safe side, Hiroshi had not visited anybody he knew when he landed, not even his mother—to keep her out of danger—and he hadn't used his credit card since Tokyo. He had withdrawn a good-sized wad of cash at an ATM, right up to his card limit. Then he had ordered his nanites to analyze the atomic structure of the banknotes, and now he could have them create an exact replica of that cash whenever he needed more money. That should work for a while, at least until somebody noticed there were multiples of the same serial number in circulation.

That was the heart of the problem he was wrestling with right now. Obviously, the nanites would also have been capable of reordering the atoms of the ink in which the serial numbers were printed and creating any other number instead—if only he were able to give them the right commands. But he couldn't. Moreover, he had no idea what such fine-tuned commands might even look like. He couldn't decide where to place every single atom—that was beyond the reach of the human intellect and would take up far too much time. Creating even the smallest object that way would take centuries. No, the whole logic of atomic-scale construction demanded some way of organizing the work in which the command units at the very highest metalevel would trigger sequences of code in the subroutines, which would then trigger further sequences in the sub-subroutines, and so on, down to the level of the nanite, which did no more than take one atom from *here* and put it over *there* across a radius no larger than the wavelength of light.

He had modified one of his Wizard's Wands to control the nanites. It was somewhat more elegant than lugging around a bulky multiband set wherever he went and typing in commands by hand, but even this had its limits. And he was nowhere near exhausting all the possibilities the nanites offered. The garage he had built for Rodney, for example: it had taken a minute or two to build, but actually inputting the individual commands had taken almost a month. After which time he had a program loaded onto the Wizard's Wand, ready and waiting, that was missing only a few variables—the exact dimensions of the garage. Measuring dimensions and plugging them into other programs was exactly what he had built the Wand for in the first place. In other words, he could just as easily have built Rodney a garage that was ten yards across or a hundred; it wouldn't even have taken much longer. But all that program could do was build garages. And only that particular type. And that particular shade of ivory.

He had just finished the program when he noticed the intruders on his surveillance system. He had considered sending his security detail after them, who would doubtless have been able to chase them away—but then what? If somebody was out to get him, they'd be back—and maybe next time he wouldn't spot them first. No, the time had come to drop out of sight. He had sent Mrs. Steel off on a vacation that officially he owed her anyway. She would find some way to live with the discovery he wasn't coming back but her salary continued to be paid. Then Hiroshi had ordered the nanites to take all his computers apart into their constituent molecules, and then he too had left, exiting via a tunnel the nanites dug for him and then sealed up behind them so seamlessly that it was as though it had never been.

That sort of thing was relatively easy once he had found functions ready in the memory that he only needed to call up. Atomic-level analysis of an object, for instance: he had even embedded this routine in a program he had written himself so that all he needed to do was sweep around the edges of the object with the laser on his Wizard's Wand to trigger an analysis. Building a tunnel, taking something apart atom by atom—by now he could do all these things merely by pressing a couple of buttons and gesturing with his Wand. It was as though he really was a wizard.

Despite all that he was lagging far, far behind what was really possible. He hadn't even scratched the surface of the immense library of finished constructions that every base complex carried in its command units the way a cell carries DNA. With one or two exceptions: building a launch site with its own rocket shaft, for instance, was a function anyone looking at the basic programming would stumble upon straightaway—logically enough, since this was the probe's prime directive. Many of the building sequences Hiroshi had analyzed were for huge and technically elaborate machines whose purpose and function he didn't understand. He would have had to build them first and then investigate—and run the risk of having to deal with a bomb.

One last area he had barely looked into was that of the new materials nanotechnology made possible. He had built Rodney's garage from wood whose atomic structure was based on analysis of an oak beam in the ceiling of Hiroshi's study. The garage door itself, with all its mechanisms, was the same as the door on the five-car bay in Hiroshi's house. So far, so good, but this was essentially squandering the possibilities of the nanites. When you could place atoms in precisely defined positions, it became possible to create materials that did not occur in nature but had incredible properties. Hiroshi had spent years following all the latest developments in nanotech research, which, for instance, had developed carbon nanotubes that were light as a feather and stronger than diamond. And nobody in the field doubted this was just the beginning. Hiroshi could have built Rodney a garage with walls thinner than a human hair that would have shrugged off a rocket-propelled grenade. In fact, it would have been simpler, and quicker to build.

Though that would have made for a rather conspicuous garage.

When it wasn't raining too hard, Hiroshi strolled along the beach for hours at a time. The sky was a featureless, pale blur, and the sea was a dull, metallic gray, roughly the shade of cast iron.

After a while he realized he was all alone on the floor where he'd taken an apartment. A huge saltwater aquarium stood in front of the elevator, where one ugly fish swam round and round, looking dreadfully bored. Every time the elevator doors opened, it would swim up to the front of the tank and gape at Hiroshi as though glad of the distraction. Unless it was just the harsh lighting from inside the cabin that fascinated it so.

Hiroshi thought about many things out on his long walks— about himself, his life, why he did the things he did. What it was that drove him. For that was how he felt: like a driven man. For instance, why had he come to Minamata of all places? If all he had wanted to do was drop out of sight, then any other city in Japan would have done just as well, if not better. But no, he had chosen Minamata, the city of his grandparents, who had never particularly liked him and whom he had never particularly liked in return.

He could come up with a whole list of clear, convincing reasons, of course: First of all, Minamata wasn't Tokyo, where he could have bumped into a number of people who knew him and who, unlike his grandparents, were not old and sick and only in the habit of setting foot outside their door to go see the doctor. Second, he more or less knew his way around here, thanks to all those dreary childhood visits. That made it easier to organize matters. For instance, he knew this resort, by sight at least—indeed, back when he was a kid he used to dream of going on vacation here one day. And third, nobody here knew him, seeing him as just another—rather eccentric—guest. But however clear and convincing these reasons sounded, Hiroshi felt very strongly they were only half the truth. Which was why he was sunk in thought as he tramped along the gray sand, one foot in front of the other, beneath a gray sky, while the wind blew salt onto his lips. He was looking for the other half of the truth.

Some days the beach was not enough. Then he would walk onward into the residential neighborhoods, where he tried and failed to lose his way among the unfamiliar, narrow streets. Once he found himself in a vast cemetery, where he strolled around for a long while, feeling curiously at ease as he drank in the silence emanating from the graves, the deep peace of the place. This, he told himself, was the final purpose of human existence: to cease all functions, to surrender all the atoms of our body to the greater whole. Here, too, he understood at last what had brought him to Minamata: it was the memory of Aunt Kumiko, who had frightened him so much as a child and for whom he felt so terribly sorry when he looked back. He thought of her now as a poor, suffering creature—deformed, tormented—who had spent all those long years in the same bed plagued by fears she could not share with others. Aunt Kumiko had started him on his path, had been the reason he had first become interested in atoms. It was only right that he had come here.

He also thought about Rodney and that last evening he had spent at his house. In retrospect, he was worried he might have put him and Allison at risk after all. But he hadn't been able to resist telling him about Saradkov, about the nanites, about the envoys from the depths of space. . . . Rodney Alvarez, who had yearned to write his thesis about Starfleet's Prime Directive, who had spent a lifetime with his eyes lifted longingly to the starry sky above; Rodney, all aflame with the question of where our fellow sentients were, our fellow races from far-off planets. If he didn't have the right to know all that had happened, then who did?

They had sat up into the small hours of the morning. Rodney had a multitude of questions, hardly any of which Hiroshi had been able to answer. Where had the probe come from? No idea. If the nanite complexes had that information in their memory—which could very easily be the case—Hiroshi hadn't been able to find it. And what kind of beings had built and launched the probe? What did they look like? Did they breathe oxygen or something else? Here, too, all Hiroshi knew was that many of the things that the stored blueprint programs could build seemed to be aircraft or other vehicles, and that the cabins and seating would be about the right size for human beings; it was safe to assume the aliens were not unlike us.

"That's almost disappointing," Rodney had said. "Not sea creatures the size of whales? Not an insect race with totally alien and incomprehensible social structures? Not beings of pure energy? You're telling me they're—Vulcans?"

"Maybe Klingons."

"Even more disappointing. Those guys, we even know their language," Rodney had said, and somehow it sounded as though he was only half joking. Who could say? Hiroshi had once read somewhere that ever since a linguistics prof had developed the Klingon language for the *Star Trek III* movie, there had been more academic papers written about it than about the languages of many real cultures.

"Perhaps there are far more restrictions on the evolution of intelligent life than we've ever thought," Hiroshi had conjectured—the kind of thought they could have spent a long time debating, except Rodney had ignored it entirely and instead peppered him with more questions about Saradkov.

"The way you tell it, the probe was setting out to take over the whole planet. That would be technically possible, wouldn't it? Nobody could actually stop these nanites?"

"Nobody who didn't have access to the same technology at least."

"We'd have looked pretty silly then."

"Very silly indeed. But they stopped. Everything up until then may just have been some kind of defense mechanism to make sure they weren't disturbed while they built and launched the rocket."

Rodney had frowned in thought and fumbled about with those darn knives of his on the coffee table, then said, "Illogical. A Von Neumann probe would have to launch at least two probes of its own."

"True," Hiroshi had conceded.

And it was odd: every time he thought back to that moment when all activity on the island had so suddenly ceased, he remembered how it had seemed to him as though it had stopped in shock or surprise—though he knew perfectly well the nanites were capable of a great deal, but not of being surprised. Yes, and then in the same instant those radio signals had begun, more or less offering him the self-destruct code. He still didn't understand that even now.

Then Rodney had started chuckling about how Hiroshi had ordered the nanites to build him a garage. "I mean, based on what you're telling me, you could have built a damn rocket in my garden."

"And what would you have done with that?"

"Hey, maybe a weekend trip to the moon. I know Ally would have liked that . . . or maybe we could drop in on the ISS. . . ."

Hiroshi hadn't wanted to rant about the risks that kind of fun might present for Rodney and Allison. "Strange as it may sound, having them build a garage was more of a challenge for me. Just calling up one of the preset programs wouldn't have taught me anything."

"Okay. On top of which, a garage is a whole lot less suspicious."

"Though your neighbors may scratch their heads when they see it in the morning."

Rodney had just given a hollow laugh. "Neighbors, what neighbors? Around here everyone just minds their own business."

They had talked until around—what?—half past three? Then Rodney had made him coffee after all, good and strong, and he had set off again, headed north. On the way he had slept in the car, until he reached Seattle and booked himself a flight to Japan. He had been pretty woozy at the ticket desk and had simply showed his Japanese passport without stopping to think someone might still be after him or how they could be looking for him. All the same he had the idea of asking the woman at the desk to make sure the name on the ticket read "Gato Hirushi," which she had finally done after he gave her a long and deliberately rambling lecture about Japanese scripts and the problem of Latinizing Japanese names.

And now here he was, with his laptop and all the important programs and files, along with his modified Wizard's Wand and the nanites. And if he were honest with himself, he had no idea what to do next. Money wasn't the problem. If this whole business with the duplicate banknotes ever became too risky, he could simply have the nanites make diamonds; it was one of the simplest exercises he could set for the assemblers, so to speak. And he could find someone to sell them to easily enough. No, the question was what exactly he should do with all the knowledge, all the possibilities the nanites gave him. He was closer than he had ever been to making his lifelong dream come true, but somehow his certainty that he was guided by the hand of fate had left him. He felt abandoned, left to his own devices. And he didn't want to spend the rest of his life on the run.

A few days later he came back from one of his walks along the beach, stepped out of the elevator, and looked into the eyes of the lonely fish in its aquarium, and suddenly knew what he would do.

That was the end of the endless hours on the beach. From then on he stayed in his room and had his meals delivered; all it took was a call through to management, and he was happy to pay their extra charges. His computer worked ceaselessly, and Hiroshi only slept when the machine was running a memory-hungry simulation analysis in parallel. He had set himself the task of searching through the nanites' metallic DNA systems—their "library" as he called it—more systematically to look for usable procedures. Hiroshi had decided to build a methyl mercury collector—nano-robots that would reproduce and spread through the world's oceans in search of molecules of methyl mercury, which they would then collect and bring to a few specified depots. And they would stay on task until the seas were free of the poison that caused Minamata disease.

Not that this was even remotely the most pressing of mankind's problems. Not at all. That was clear. Hiroshi had chosen this project in part because if it worked, it would have an impressive result—a whole planet would be cleansed of one particular poison—and in part because it set him a challenge that would help him learn a great deal about the nanites. And finally, he was doing it in memory of poor Aunt Kumiko.

After a few days he had what looked like a viable design. For the first time, he planned to actually rebuild some of the nanites themselves—using other nanites to do so, of course. He would build a prospector unit that specialized in finding methyl mercury. Methyl mercury has a very high affinity for sulfur, and being a positively charged ion, forms bonds with anions such as hydroxide or chloride—meaning that when the prospector had found the methyl-mercury molecules, an accompanying cutter would have to break their ionic bonds. Then a transporter would have to take the methyl mercury away to a collector—and after that? That was when things got difficult.

His biggest problem was how to get the collector units over to the depots once they were full. He needed a motor that could steer a nanoscale construct through the waters and currents of the seas to a specified destination—a navigation system that could find the depots—and he also had to find the best place to put them. Lastly, he needed nanites waiting in the depots for the collector units to unload them, separate the mercury from the methyl group, and create the space where the gradual accumulation of mercury could be safely stored. Another problem, as so often the case in technologies of this kind, was the energy supply. The nanite complexes would have to sink down to the seabed from time to time to send miles of feelers down toward the earth's core. After loading up on energy, they could get back to their task. All this was hard work. And there were many moments when Hiroshi simply didn't know what to do next, when he despaired at the thought he had the most powerful tools in the planet at his disposal and couldn't use them.

As he searched frantically through the library that had come to him as a legacy of an inconceivably technologically advanced civilization, Hiroshi found himself confronted again and again by a blueprint program that left him utterly baffled. When he fed the construction sequences into his simulator, the result was something that looked like a sponge, or like a network of bizarre blood vessels; what was it supposed to be, or do? He had no idea. Whatever it was, its growth patterns called up all sorts of associations, but none that took him any further forward. At that point, he would ordinarily have just shrugged and gone on to look at the next program, but for some reason this one nagged at him. And somehow it gave him the idea of using his downtime, when there were smaller simulations running, to search the Internet for the latest research on Minamata disease.

He didn't find much. It was partially understood, but only partially, and there was unlikely to be significant further research, since the syndrome hardly occurred anymore, thanks to higher environmental standards. Methyl mercury was absorbed quickly in the stomach and then got into the bloodstream, where it crossed the blood–brain barrier and built up in the central nervous system and the brain itself. Symptoms included muscle weakness, deafness, partial blindness, and motor-system dysfunctions, even paralysis and insanity. And it was incurable.

By early December, Hiroshi was ready. The resort was filling up again with guests for the winter season and Christmas, and the management was beginning to wonder why he was staying quite so long. This was a problem, he knew, but he couldn't be bothered by it just then. He was bone-tired as he walked along the beach one cold morning, just as dawn broke, and put his mercury collectors to work. He didn't have to do much, just chuck the sugar cube he had soaked with nanites into the sea. Then he reached under his coat and pressed the button on his Wand to give them their starting signal. That was all. The nanites would take care of everything else themselves. Of course, there was nothing to see. Nevertheless, Hiroshi stood there for a while as the sun rose in lilac splendor over the mountains behind him and wondered what he should do next. He watched the waves. The tide was coming in, and with every wave that broke the water crept closer to his shoes. How the water shone as it foamed silver between the pebbles and stones. How carefully it washed every grain of sand . . . in that instant Hiroshi understood what that blueprint was. The branching network that had fascinated him so.

Of course, he would have to check, run the requisite simulation, build it virtually first. Of course. But it was one of those hypotheses that he just *knew* would prove true. After all, the human brain was a material structure. Thoughts could be expressed in terms of patterns of neural impulses, and you could even record these if you managed to run a sufficiently fine network of implants alongside each and every neuron. And that was exactly what those branches on the blueprint could do: follow the neural pathways and place sensors at all the junctions. Coupling the nanites to a brain. It was the only conceivable way to have perfect and assured control over the almost-omnipotent tool that they were. The only way to unleash their full power and have absolute power over them.

All at once Hiroshi knew this was the only way he could learn the last secrets of the nano-robots. The only question was whether, once set out on this road, he would ever find his way back.

Coming out of his self-imposed isolation was like liberation. Hiroshi felt he had been frozen and then thawed out. The dining rooms were all full now, and loud, but that didn't trouble him at all; rather, he enjoyed feeling invisible among the crowds. He watched old couples and young families, children shrieking, squabbles, and harmony. Now he was far from the only one out walking on the beach; children raced across the sand in their thick parkas, throwing stones into the water or flying kites while their parents watched, smiling. And it did him good to sit in the bar in the evening over a beer, close to the television so that its noise drowned out the chatter of the other guests, the rattling of the slot machines, and the clack of balls on the pool table in the background.

That was where Hiroshi heard about the catastrophe.

First, he saw a weather-beaten man with a blue watch cap on the screen, waving his arms frantically and shouting, "Everywhere! Everywhere! All the way to the horizon!" By itself, that could have meant anything, so all Hiroshi did was frown in puzzlement. His beer arrived and he took the first swallow. It tasted good. Then the picture changed to a beach covered with white objects, which men in protective clothing and face masks were shoveling into trucks. The white things were dead fish. Hiroshi put his glass down with a lurching feeling of impending disaster.

"A catastrophe for the fishing industry," declared a man in suit and glasses who was a professor at Tokyo University.

The anchorman for this special bulletin explained that scientists assumed they were dealing with a hitherto unknown pandemic, which was supported above all by the distribution patterns. When they plotted the worldwide reports of huge carpets of dead fish floating on the sea, the resulting map clearly showed the epidemic had originated somewhere near the southern coast of Japan. A graphic came up on-screen to support his words. "The United Nations has convened an emergency session," the anchorman added. Scientists were hard at work searching for the pathogen.

Hiroshi sat there, rigid with shock, horrified. He had done something wrong. Horribly wrong.

He paid, leaving the rest of his beer undrunk, and went back to his room, struggling to keep himself from breaking into a run. The corridor was quiet and empty, even though most of the rooms were now occupied. Hiroshi picked up his Wand and another complex of the mercury collectors, and went to the aquarium by the elevator. The fish gaped at him as though it had a dim presentiment of what was about to happen.

"Sorry, old friend," Hiroshi whispered sadly. "But I have to be sure."

He tipped the nanites into the water, activated them, and waited. Nothing. In order not to be quite so conspicuous, Hiroshi sat down on the couch in the corner by the elevator, where nobody ever sat, picked up one of the brochures and pretended to read it. The fish stared at him unwaveringly.

Just as Hiroshi was beginning to wonder whether the nanites could find enough atoms in the aquarium to replicate themselves, it happened: the fish closed its eyes, jerked uncontrollably several times, turned tail, and floated belly-up to the surface. Hiroshi put down the brochure, got up, and went back to his room. He hadn't thought of that. Of course, the fish living in the oceans today had accumulated methyl mercury in their bodies, just like they did all the other pollutants in the sea. The collectors he had sent out were far too small to be able to differentiate between seawater and the body tissues of a fish: they tore the mercury right out of the living bodies, and when they did that too often, they killed the body itself. And in this instance even the self-destruct signal wouldn't help, since the radio waves wouldn't reach the nanites underwater.

It took Hiroshi seven days of uninterrupted work to create another complex that could hunt down and destroy the mercury collectors. During that time the mysterious fish plague spread right around the globe, causing heated public and scientific debate. Experts issued dire warnings for the future of world food security. The populations of several species of fish were already severely threatened, and the search for the pathogen remained fruitless.

The morning after Christmas, Hiroshi put his hunter complexes into the sea and activated them. Then he paid and checked out.

In Tokyo he didn't find his mother at home. She was at the cemetery, he learned from a neighbor who ran into him at the door, a little old woman who recognized him even though he could have sworn he'd never seen her in his life.

"Which cemetery?" Hiroshi asked. "And what's she doing there?"

"Aoyama. You can take the metro from Hiroo to Ebisu. It's number 34."

Aoyama Cemetery was the most prestigious in all of Tokyo. The only people who could afford a grave there were rich, and they had to be lucky with the lottery draw for burial plots as well. What was his mother doing there?

But there she was, tending a grave marked by a narrow, gray marble column and a flowerpot about the size of a salad bowl.

"Oh, it's you," she said, not stopping her work.

Hiroshi came up beside her and read the headstone. It was Mr. Inamoto's.

"Last August. It was his heart. He died during the Bon festival. Strange, isn't it?" His mother put her trowel down and stood up.

"Is that your new job?" Hiroshi asked.

She took off her green, rubber gardening gloves, her gaze still fixed on the headstone. "He asked me to marry him, you know. Three times. At our age! Crazy old man." She looked at Hiroshi. Small tears had gathered in the corners of her eyes, shining like drops of mercury. "I always said no. And now I'm sorry. Now, when it's too late."

Hiroshi said nothing. The two of them stood there for a while in silence.

"Sometimes I think that's all there is to life," he said at last. "Always knowing that you've done something wrong when it's too late to change it."

His mother put her arm around him. He had the feeling she'd gotten smaller.

"It's good that you're here," she said. "A nice surprise."

5

The flight to Buenos Aires tired her out more this time around. It might have had something to do with the bad air in the cabin, which gave her a headache and an unpleasant sensation of pressure behind her eyes. Charlotte was glad to see all four of them waiting at the airport: Brenda, Thomas, Jason, and Lamita.

"You're the Christmas present for the whole family," Brenda said by way of greeting. "So we've all come."

Charlotte hugged each of them in turn. Even Jason didn't resist. She felt she could cry, but she didn't want to let it show. No crying at Christmas! Lamita was wearing a pretty dress and spoke both English and Spanish well by now. If anything, her Spanish was stronger. And Charlotte noted, as they made their way through the airport, that she no longer put up with all her brother's teasing and tricks. When Charlotte told Brenda how much she liked Lamita's dress and the embroidery work on it in particular, her old friends took her elbow and whispered, "She did all that herself, can you believe it. Came to me one day with some rags from the old-clothes chest and asked me if she could have them. 'Of course,' I said. Then she asked me for a needle and thread and sewed them onto her dress."

"But it looks wonderful!" Charlotte said. "Perhaps she'll be a designer someday?"

Brenda shrugged. "It's crazy, isn't it? But I really wouldn't be surprised."

When they came out from the concourse into the open air, the heat was merciless. High summer, which certainly didn't help her headache. And the ride downtown seemed to take forever.

"How's research?" Charlotte asked Thomas to take her mind off it.

He laughed. "Oh man. Now that's no question for the season of peace and goodwill."

"As bad as all that?"

"You know, as soon as we get to the topic of who settled where and when, and who got there first, it all becomes political. So the government gets involved. And let's put it this way: the Ecuadorian government is not exactly full of experts in prehistory."

It was Charlotte's turn to laugh. "I can imagine."

"And what about you? Has Harvard sent a commission yet to rescind your degree?"

"It's bound to happen eventually." By now she had realized the fundamental problem of arguing for a theory that questioned every tenet of established wisdom: the tenured academics demanded proof, and to get that, you had to do research—but you never got any funding, since you were arguing a suspect theory. If you looked long and hard enough, there was always some crackpot willing to finance even the craziest research proposal, but if you took that money you'd never get published in a journal of record, because the editors would suspect you'd allowed the donors to influence your findings. And if it wasn't published in a journal of record, for all intents and purposes it didn't exist—that was the vicious circle.

They finally arrived. Her headache had subsided to a dull, rhythmic throbbing behind her temples, which she was growing used to. Surely it would pass soon. What was new, however, was the curious tingling sensation in her hips, which she chalked up to sitting for so long, first on the airplane and then in the car. How on earth could she relax when everybody was driving like lunatics, even two days before Christmas?

The house looked just as she remembered it. So did the garden, except that everything looked dreadfully dry.

"It takes some getting used to," Brenda said. "Christmas in the middle of summer."

Charlotte peered up at the cloudless sky and the incandescent sun. "I don't know. . . . Was it as hot as this at Christmas when we lived here? I can't remember."

"Everything's better when you're a kid," Brenda said. Then she cast a glance at her adoptive daughter. "When we were kids at least."

The Christmas tree in the hall looked at least as magnificent as the one in the White House—Charlotte had seen a photo of it in a newspaper on the flight down. The presents were already under the tree, wrapped enticingly in glittering paper. Both children almost started hopping up and down with impatience at the sight.

"Let me get my suitcase," Charlotte said to Thomas. "I want to put some things under the tree as well. Just a couple of little . . ."

Throb. Throb. Throb. She was getting used to it. Perhaps she'd ask Brenda for an aspirin later. She squatted down and reached for the luggage strap.

And then suddenly the film snapped.

Then there's light again, light and a smell she recognizes, but she doesn't know where from—a nasty, sharp smell of too much hygiene. And Brenda's there with her round face like the full moon and her curly, brown hair, and she'll never get that hair under control as long as she lives. "Everything's fine," she's saying, and, "Don't worry." However, when she says it she looks as though nothing is fine and she's the one who's worrying. But Charlotte believes her, because she's her best friend and she's never lied to her. "Good," she says and falls back to sleep.

The next time she woke up, she was alone and clearheaded enough to realize she was in a hospital. Clearheaded—something about her head; that reminded her . . . she had no hair left. When she put her hands to her head, she could feel her scalp shaved smooth and new growth breaking through here and there. And at the back of her head there was an enormous bandage.

"What happened to me?" she asked the first nurse who came into the room.

The woman raised her hands uncomprehendingly. "*Lo siento, no hablo inglés.*"

"*Yo quería saber lo que me pasó,*" Charlotte said, asking her the same question in Spanish.

The nurse gave a sad smile. She was a slender woman with dark skin. "I'm sorry. I'll go and fetch the doctor."

The doctor came along a little later, sat down on her bed, and asked how she was feeling. He wore an old-fashioned pair of spectacles. The face behind them was furrowed by hundreds of sharp lines that spoke of a lifetime of concern. He had large bags under his eyes, and the whole effect made him look like a melancholy dog, perhaps a boxer.

"I don't know," Charlotte confessed. "Somehow I don't feel anything at all." She put her hand to the bandage. "You operated on me?"

"We had to." More lines and more melancholy. "You have a tumor on the brain stem that was about this big." He held his hands apart to show something the size of an egg. "It was pressing against the brain itself, which was what made you lose consciousness. We removed what we could, but unfortunately that wasn't even half of it."

Charlotte waited for some sort of feeling to kick in—fear, panic, horror, anything like that—but there was nothing. Only a huge, indifferent emptiness.

"That . . . doesn't sound good," she said at last.

"It's not good at all. By all standards of modern medicine, your tumor is inoperable. It's probably already metastasized. The only thing we can try is a strong dose of chemotherapy."

"What would my chances be?"

"Poor."

At last, she felt something. A soft, quiet sadness. "I'm only thirty-four," Charlotte said quietly.

The doctor looked at her with such pity it was as though she were his own flesh and blood. "Unfortunately, Señora, that is not to your advantage here. With cancer, the prognosis is better the older you are. This is because when you are young, the cells still divide very quickly, do you understand?"

"When do we start?"

"In a few days. As soon as the wound from your operation has healed properly."

The next morning her mother appeared. Her mother! Charlotte found it surreal to see her standing there at the end of the bed.

"We're going to take you to Paris," she said.

Charlotte was aghast. To Paris? Where her mother would care for her? To the apartment that was like a museum of their family history? Not even that. It was like a mausoleum. "I don't want to go to Paris."

"Don't talk nonsense. You must have the best doctors in the world, and right away." Her mother spoke with such finality that it was as though the tumor would have to stay behind in Argentina and find another victim if only they set out fast enough. "Your father is talking to the principal consultant now."

"But I don't want to go," Charlotte said again.

Mother looked at her incredulously. "What do you mean?"

"I want to stay here."

"Here?" The way she said the word spoke volumes. *Here? At the ends of the earth? With these savages?*

Brenda finally appeared a bit later. "What's the trouble with your mother?" she asked. "I just ran into her out on the hallway. She was . . . I don't know. Did you have a fight?"

Charlotte swallowed. "Brenda?" she asked softly, feeling as though she was about to ask something indecent. "I'd like to . . . could I . . . ?"

Brenda looked startled. "What is it?"

"Could I stay with you for a while?"

Brenda burst into tears and hugged her tight. "Stay," she sobbed. "Stay as long as you like."

Direct flights to the mainland US were totally booked so early in the New Year. Hiroshi had to take a flight via Hawaii, where he had a three-hour layover. Three hours to fill somehow. The first thing he did was scan the area for video cameras and for anybody following him. He found plenty of cameras but nobody on his tail, which could either have been because nobody was following him, or because he had no idea how to spot a tail. Once he had satisfied his paranoia, he went to one of the restaurants in the transit lounge. On the flight out he had eaten laughably little, and a hamburger would be better than nothing.

There wasn't much going on at this hour. Two tables down, a woman was sitting with her two children, boys absorbed by their french fries and some kind of crispy nuggets they were dipping into tubs of sauce. The woman looked over at him for just a moment longer than if she were looking at a stranger. Hiroshi had to look twice before he realized he knew her.

"Dorothy?" he asked, astonished.

She smiled. It was a strange smile, a mixture of pain and relief. "Hello, Hiroshi. I have to say, I wasn't quite sure . . ."

He couldn't believe his eyes. "What are you doing here?" He looked at the two boys, the older of whom was six or seven. "Are they yours?"

Dorothy nodded. "Nathan and Matthew."

"You're married, then."

"Yes. Jim had to head back a couple days early or you could have met him, too. He's an IT specialist, and there are always problems around New Year's. We were over here visiting my in-laws for Christmas. The kids love it, you know, the beach more than anything."

"I can imagine." Though in fact he couldn't.

"And you?" She looked at him.

And him? "So-so," Hiroshi said.

"Did you . . ." she began, then bit her lip and asked, "Are you happy?"

Hiroshi looked at her. She was, for sure: happy.

"No," he said. "No, I'm not." Not in the least.

He stopped, thought back on all that had happened, all that he had done. "Dorothy . . . I'm sorry about back then. I couldn't have done anything else. But I could have done it more . . . tactfully."

Dorothy looked at him for a moment, utterly inscrutable, and then told him it was okay, that she didn't hold anything against him. But she had to get going, she said, to catch their flight to Portland.

His flight was on to Los Angeles, and he still had an hour to go, plenty of time for reflection. On the flight he did nothing but think about the past. Could this encounter have been chance, if meeting Charlotte in Boston hadn't been? It would have been intellectually dishonest to buck the question. Hiroshi had a very clear sense that all of this was trying to tell him something, but he had no idea what.

He would also have liked to know how Dorothy felt today about what had happened back then. About the Sunday morning when he had so brutally broken up with her. Whether she was glad now it had turned out like that, since otherwise she wouldn't be happily married to Jim, wouldn't have Nathan and Matthew. Or whether she still regretted it, just a little, in some hidden corner of her heart. He would really have liked to know. But there hadn't been time for all that, and it really hadn't been the right setting for such questions. Sure, he had her telephone number now—she lived in Oregon—but somehow he knew he would never ask her. He didn't want to shatter his illusion that Jim was just second best. Besides, he had no desire to meet the guy. At this moment, as he looked back over his life, over all that had happened, everything seemed self-evident, every event, every decision he had taken seemed inevitable, precisely plotted. Not that this helped him figure anything out. When he landed in Los Angeles, he was no closer to understanding than he had been when he boarded.

He was so lost in thought as he disembarked that he only noticed the men lying in wait for him when it was almost too late.

Bud the Brain, as he liked to be known, raised his walkie-talkie to his lips. "Bingo. He's in line at passport control."

There was no doubt that was the man they were after. Sure, it wasn't exactly easy telling one Japanese from another, but he had studied the photos obsessively; he would have known the guy even in a false beard and sunglasses.

It was pretty clever how Coldwell had gotten wind of it. Not just the way he used his contacts with Homeland Security to get through to the office that collected all the passenger data for arrivals to America—no, there was the whole business with Japanese names, too, and the different ways they could be written. You had to think sideways to come up with that. That was the kind of thing that showed Coldwell had spent quite a while in Asia. He knew all the tricks.

This was going to be so easy it would almost be boring.

He raised the walkie-talkie again. It broadcast on an encrypted channel and was, needless to say, completely illegal. "Bud to all. We'll grab him when he comes out of customs. Blue Group waits in the walkway on the right; Yellow Group waits on the left. And remember: easy does it, quiet as you can."

There was no need even to say it, since they'd gone over all the moves on the way over. But a couple of his boys were more brawn than brain, so it did no harm to remind them of all the details.

Kato was at the desk, passing his passport and green card to the officer, who checked them both, nodded, handed them back, and waved him through.

"He's coming," Bud the Brain announced.

But Kato must have noticed something. Whatever it was, he went neither left nor right but instead ducked lightning-fast under a No Entry tape and scuttled off upstairs to a part of the airport Bud hadn't scouted out.

Shit. This wasn't going to be so boring after all.

"Brain to all. He smelled a rat. He's gone up the stairs behind immigration. Anybody know what's up there?"

A crackling sound. Someone spoke, giggling. "Nothing. There's nothing up there."

"What's that supposed to mean? There has to be something. There are stairs leading up."

It was Sergei. Until just a couple of weeks ago, Sergei had worked here as a pickpocket, and he knew this airport better than the architect who built it. "Customs and Border Protection are supposed to have their offices there when they clear out of Terminal One. October, maybe. Till then there's nothing up there but empty rooms and locked doors."

"Where can he get out?"

"Nowhere," Sergei giggled again. "Dead end. Our friend has run right into a trap."

So it was going to be boring after all. "Okay, let's go get him. Yellow Group to me, Blue Group covers."

He waited on the stairs with his free hand in his pocket near his gun in case the guy came back and wanted a fight. That would cause a bit of a stir, but it would be better than letting the guy get away. Coldwell would straighten it all out if need be. But it didn't come to that. The four men in Yellow Group were there quick as greased lightning. Bud lifted the No ENTRY tape. He was wearing airport overalls and had an ID clipped to his breast, so no one paid any attention. And up they went.

The corridor was empty. Most of the doors were still in plastic wrap, with even the locks sealed shut. They were locked and loaded when they came around the first corner. Another empty corridor.

Sergei grinned. "Nothing doing," he said. "Corridor stops around that next corner."

Bud grinned, too. He cleared his throat and called out, "Mr. Kato? We know that you're there. We don't want to have to do anything to you. We just want to bring you to meet someone who really needs to talk to you."

No answer. He signaled to Sergei, who checked his gun and then peered around the corner. He turned around. "You sure he came up here?"

Shit, thought Bud the Brain when he looked as well. The rest of the corridor was empty. The hallway ended in a wall of ivory-tinted construction slats, and there was no sign of anyone.

"Shit!" Bud shouted. "Come on, get back, go go go. He must have gone through one of the doors."

"How do you figure he did that?" Sergei was beginning to get on his nerves. "Those are deadbolts. Good ones. Customs and Border, you get me? Nothing but the best for those guys."

"He's got to be somewhere."

"You really sure he even came up here?"

"Are you looking for a smack across the chops?"

They raced back to the staircase and then worked their way down all the doors. There was one with a security seal missing, and they broke it open. Nothing there but a huge open space that ran the whole length of the corridor. Still a building site; the dividing walls hadn't even been installed yet. There was no other exit, and no footprints. It was as though Kato had vanished into thin air. All at once

Bud the Brain understood why Coldwell had warned him, "Expect the guy to have a few tricks up his sleeve."

This must have been the kind of thing he meant.

Hiroshi stood motionless behind the wall. He had only just managed to let it down in time, with the help of his Wand and the nanites. He held his breath and listened. He heard them come nearer, talking in animated voices, and then leave again. Right after that he heard a crash; obviously, they had broken open one of the doors he had passed, expecting to find him behind it. He looked down and, peering at the display on his Wand, scrolled noiselessly through the stored command sequences. There was only limited space in the memory. He had moved the tunnel-building program back onto his laptop when he had been working on the hunter complex. Bad mistake. Luckily, the garage-building program was still there. And luckily it had managed to build a very strangely shaped garage—no roof, a garage door that was only four inches across and faced the wall of the corridor, out of sight, and the slatted walls reaching from floor to ceiling.

That had been close. Way too close.

However, he now knew he had been too unsure of himself back in Hawaii when he was worried he couldn't spot a tail; he'd been able to see these guys in time. The question was whether they would be so conspicuous next time. Probably not. There was no question of whether there would be a next time. There would be, without a doubt.

It eventually fell quiet. Hiroshi nevertheless waited another two hours, which was torture in the narrow confines of his hiding place. Once the air became unbreathable, he triggered the program that ordered the nanites to return every atom they had moved right back where it came from. Within minutes the wall was gone without a trace.

The corridor was deserted; no one was waiting for him. When he was ducking back under the tape at the bottom of the stairs, a guard showed up and barked at him, asking what he wanted. Couldn't he see there was no civilian access here?

"I thought I might find the restroom up there," Hiroshi replied.

"Up ahead on the left," the man snarled, waving his hand vaguely. "Just follow the symbols."

Hiroshi thanked him and then vanished into the crowd. He would have to make a decision.

6

Hiroshi sat in the car and watched the quiet suburban street and the house of Rodney and Allison Alvarez. He had been their guest so many times, and he was about to visit the house for the last time.

They were both home. He had seen them arrive, seen them use the garage as though it were the most natural thing in the world and had stood there forever. He liked that.

He glanced over at the newspaper on the seat next to him. "Are Sharks Now Extinct?" read one of the front-page headlines. He didn't like that.

Nobody had made the connection yet, but it was only a matter of time. Hiroshi had read in an article about Minamata disease that sharks were especially prone to accumulating methyl mercury; some of them had so much stored in their body that only five grams of their flesh contained more than the safe daily dose for humans. No wonder they had been the principal victims of his collector nanites.

He sighed and got out of the car. Every step was an effort.

They were surprised to see him, and genuinely happy. Allison feigned outrage. "All I made is spaghetti! If you'd told us you were coming—"

"Spaghetti's great," Hiroshi said to calm her down.

"And what you did with the garage . . . and the news about the alien probe . . . Rod told me everything, but to be honest I wouldn't have believed a word if it hadn't been for the garage standing there all of a sudden . . . A garage! Of all things! I have a million questions for you, just so you know."

Hiroshi had to smile. "Do I have to answer all of them here in the front hall?"

"No, of course not. Oh, I'm not being much of a host. Come right on in, come on. Wait, I'll get another plate and some flatware . . . Rod, can you look after the wine?"

Then they were sitting at the table, and by some miracle there was enough spaghetti for three. "I always cook twice what we need and make the rest into noodle salad for work," Allison explained. "As for the tomato sauce, well, you can stretch that out with something from the can."

"It tastes great," Hiroshi assured her.

"Enjoy your meal," she said, pointing her fork at him. "Because afterward you're going to have to tell us every last detail about the extraterrestrials, about their probe, the works. Listen, I want to persuade you to let us make it all public. I mean, if we can show solid proof that the aliens launched a probe that landed on Earth thousands of years ago, it would be the sensation of the century. And who has more right to make the announcement that we do at SETI? It's right there in the name—searching for extraterrestrial intelligence is what we do. Okay, so you made Rodney promise not to say a word, but why? I mean . . . you're really going to have to explain yourself."

"That's why I came," Hiroshi said.

"Let the man finish his meal, Ally," Rodney said. "Hey, did you buy new dishes?"

Allison was caught off guard and looked mistrustfully at her husband. "Don't try to change the subject. When have I ever bought new dishes without asking you first . . . oh." She looked down at her plate. "That's really weird. I just used our ordinary . . . look at it shine;

it's kind of golden. Is that from the light in here?" She lifted it up. "Hey, this is really heavy!"

"It's gold," Hiroshi said. It was time they knew.

Rodney frowned. "Is this another of your tricks?"

"What kind of trick?" Allison put in.

Hiroshi nodded. "As I sit here there are billions of nanites swarming all around me. They're in my body, in the air around me, in the floor under my feet. On my way over they were gathering atoms of gold from all around, building up a stockpile, bringing them along. Then when I sat down at your table they began to bring these gold atoms in here along a microscopically thin tube that's running through the ground beneath your house and up one of the table legs. There were also nanites at work in the tabletop itself, gradually taking away all the atoms from the porcelain of your plates and replacing them with gold atoms. I told them to work from the inside out so we wouldn't see the gold shine until it was all ready. Which is why you now have three plates of solid gold."

The two of them stared at him open-mouthed.

"Just my way of saying thank you for the meal," Hiroshi said mildly, and thought, *Just saying good-bye. This is the last time we'll see each other.*

Allison blinked, looked down at her plate, and admitted in a flat voice, "I don't even know what porcelain's made of." It was a strangely inappropriate reaction that proved how deeply surprised she was.

"Kaolin, feldspar, and quartz," Hiroshi said. "Whole lot of silicon and oxygen, a little bit of sodium and aluminum."

"And how did the . . . nanites know not to turn the spaghetti to gold as well?"

"Spaghetti's made of starch. Polysaccharides. They're as different as night and day."

Allison put her face in her hands and took a deep breath. "Oh my God!" she said as she lowered her hands. "Plates that turn to pure gold as I eat off them! This is so crazy, I don't even know what to say."

Rodney looked Hiroshi up and down. "And how did you tell them to do all this? I don't see your Wizard's Wand."

"I no longer need my Wand. The nanites are now directly linked to my brain. They read my thoughts, so to speak."

"Linked to your brain?" Rodney was round-eyed with wonder. "You cannot seriously mean that?"

"I do, Rodney. I discovered a function that built me a neural interface—"

"Are you trying to tell me that alien technology is compatible with the human neuronal structure?" A gleam appeared in Rodney's eyes. He was not far from getting angry.

Hiroshi carefully put down his flatware. He knew this was an evening unlike any other. "There's an explanation," he said. "But you're not going to like it."

"Spit it out. And let me worry about whether I like it or not."

"The probe wasn't what we thought. In fact, it's something else entirely."

And he told them.

One week later astronomers performing routine observations of the night sky noticed a bright object in the constellation of Pisces that was moving unusually fast. It didn't take them long to establish it was headed on a course directly for Earth. They pointed the Hubble Space Telescope toward it and got pictures of a long, thin object at least twelve miles long and at least three miles across. It was huge. If this object collided with Earth, it would mean the end of all life.

The heads of state of all the space-capable nations consulted with one another. More-or-less-detailed plans that had been drawn up for deep-impact scenarios were hastily recovered from desk drawers, where they had been gathering dust. It turned out that most of them were hopelessly out of date. Despite their best efforts to keep the matter secret, there was no clamping down entirely. Rumors began circulating on the Internet of a meteorite on a collision course with

Earth. Government spokesmen declined to comment on the rumors. Meanwhile, the military were calculating the range on their nuclear missiles, and surprising alliances formed between formerly hostile powers. Satellites and radar antennae all turned toward the object as it approached.

What they discovered sent a shiver down the spines of all who heard it.

The computer simulations clearly showed that the object was not going to collide with Earth. It was *slowing down* . . .

7

Today was the day. Though his computer reminded him of that fact, there was no need. He wouldn't have forgotten.

Jens Rasmussen went to his office safe, opened it, and took out the padded envelope Hiroshi Kato had pressed into his hands the last time they saw each other. He had named a day and said, "If I don't get in touch by then, open this."

He did so. Inside were a sheet of paper and a rewritable CD. He read the letter, choked for breath, then read it through again. "If everything has worked as I planned, then a very large object will have been moving toward Earth for the last several days," he read in Hiroshi's neat, elegant handwriting. "Maybe this has not become public knowledge yet, but there could be rumors; they're true. I have recorded a short lecture on the accompanying CD that explains the whole story. Please send the file to the press, and put it on the Internet."

What was this all about? Rasmussen took the CD from its jewel case, slotted it into his computer drive, and started the video. Hiroshi Kato appeared on the screen. He was sitting in the chair by the window of his meditation room, the garden visible behind him through the window. He wasn't smiling. He held a neat little stack of index cards in his hands that presumably held the notes for what he was going to say, though he never looked at them once.

"Most of you will remember the mysterious rocket launch in the north of the Canadian province of Saskatchewan," he began. "I did that. I built the launch site, I sent the rocket on its way, and then I dismantled the site, which regrettably caused considerable damage to that region. What most of you don't know is that there was already one such mysterious launch, from a Russian island. At the time it was officially designated a test launch, and it dropped out of the headlines quite quickly. In the next few minutes I will tell you what actually happened and how that relates to the object currently approaching Earth."

He told the whole story of what had happened on Saradkov Island, about the probe that had landed on Earth thousands of years ago and been frozen in the eternal ice ever since, and about what had happened when it became active. He explained how he had saved some of the nanites to research on his own. He sketched out his own studies in self-replicator theory, and how this had helped him to unriddle how these nanites worked.

"The megastructure currently approaching Earth is a space station, a habitat for at least a million people. It was built by the nanites I sent out to the asteroid belt between Jupiter and Mars. It's an area where the remains of a former planet orbit the sun. These asteroids are a rich resource for mining all kinds of materials, which is what the nanites duly did, following my orders. First they replicated until there were enough of them—meaning trillions upon trillions of them, so many that we barely have the words to express such numbers. We have to rely on powers of ten. Next, they set out to build the space station out there in the twilight of the asteroid belt in interplanetary space. Once they were done, the nanites withdrew and gave the station its launch command, which fired the rockets to set it off toward Earth. By my calculations it will take up a stable orbit around Earth within a few weeks, ready for the moment when we decide to settle it.

"I would like to be able to say I built this space station, but that's not actually the case. Rather, the control unit of every nano-complex contains an information-storage function that we might best imagine as equivalent to the DNA within our cells. Our DNA contains something like a history of all human evolution, with genes that— to simplify somewhat—could help us grow limbs and organs that we no longer need, and these genes are switched off. Similarly, these information-storage functions contain the blueprints for objects that were not part of the task the nanites were launched into space to fulfill. There are millions of these blueprints. They're hard to understand, and it will take decades even to find out what each one of these programs can build. And even once we know that, we will still know very little about what these objects are and what they are capable of.

"I'm saying all this to tell you that the blueprint for the space station was supplied by the creators of the nanites. However, they didn't include the instructions. Meaning that anyone who goes near it should do so with all due care and attention. According to my simulations, there should be no danger; there seem to be no weapons aboard or anything like that. But whoever boards the space station is in the same situation as a medieval human trying to make sense of a jumbo jet. We cannot expect to understand all that we see.

"You will ask why I did this. For a very simple reason: I wanted to point the way. The space station is large enough to be seen in the night sky from anywhere in the world, and it is built with technology far, far more advanced than our own. I invite all space-faring nations to send their expeditions to this station and to discover all of its workings. Humanity has the chance to learn an immense amount from such research.

"And that's just the beginning. Once we have learned how to use them, the nanites could change—and improve—our lives in ways we can barely imagine today. The possibilities offered by manipulating matter at the atomic level are limitless. There will never again be any shortage either of energy or of raw materials. We will be able to recycle everything we no longer need, one hundred percent. Nobody will ever have to go hungry again; nobody will ever have to do unpleasant work. We can make a paradise on Earth—and it won't even take any effort on our part."

He stopped and seemed to have finished, then remembered something. "Ah yes, another thing: there won't be just this one space station. The nanites in the asteroid belt are already at work on the next habitat, and they're still self-replicating. In a few years' time, there will be enough habitats available for all of us to move off-world if we so desire."

The video ended there.

Rasmussen shut his eyes for a moment. So that had been the secret. That's what he had been hiding all this time. He had always had the feeling Hiroshi hadn't been telling him everything, but now . . . now all the pieces of the puzzle fell into place. Now it all made sense. But that wasn't what had made him choke for breath when he read the letter. Rather, it had been the closing lines.

Jens—if you're reading this, then chances are we'll never see one another again. I'd like you to know that I'm very grateful for everything you've done for me, and I have always considered you my friend. The business side of things was just a game we played together.

All the best,
Hiroshi

They didn't let him fasten his own seat belt—not on a space shuttle. Bill Adamson watched the man in the Roscosmos overalls check and double-check the straps and wondered once more how things could have gotten this far.

That conversation in the director's office. How long ago had that been? Just a few days before, it seemed to him. Weeks. Months.

In any event, Roberta Jacobs had not been alone; there had been a great many men in there as well when he finally entered the room, summoned from his own office by her secretary's almost-hysterical phone calls. Old men. Men who looked exactly as important as they were. One of them could have been Sidney Poitier's twin brother, in uniform, with yard upon yard of service ribbons across his chest.

"Space colonization is your field now," the director said after a few words of introduction that he missed entirely, he was so surprised.

My field is robots! But he hadn't said so. Instead, he had simply asked, "And what does that mean in concrete terms?"

Whereupon the Sidney Poitier clone had looked at him impatiently and said, "Means you're flying."

Rhonda had almost flipped out when he told her. "You're no astronaut, Bill! They can't ask you to do that!"

"Doc says I'm fit enough."

"They want you to fly off to an alien spaceship?"

"Someone's got to do it," Adamson had said, managing somehow to hide the fact that on the inside he was cheering. Hallelujah! Kato, that arrogant kid, had certainly never dreamed of this twist. *Serves him right for being too darned snooty to join the Robot 21 project.* And now he was helping Bill Adamson take the ride of his life.

On the flight over to Baikonur, it had gradually dawned on him he would be aboard one of the brand-new shuttles, and then he had suddenly had misgivings after all. He had asked someone whether there had even been any test flights.

"Of course," they told him.

"How many?"

"One."

Because they had to be built fast, it had been one of those harebrained international-cooperation projects, and he could only hope they hadn't made any dumbass conversion mistakes between inches and metric. The space shuttle was strapped to a gigantic Russian carrier rocket that the Russian copilot, a shaggy blond guy called Boris, would steer during the climb. Then Jackson, the pilot, would fly the shuttle itself. "Say, boys." Boris's voice came over the headset. He was talking to mission control. "How about you let us get started, huh? We don't want the Chinese getting there before us."

In fact, the countdown had started a while back. The hatches were closed and bolted, checklists ticked off—the whole thing sounded reassuringly routine. There were eight of them onboard, four Americans and four Russians, all scrupulously fair and politically aboveboard. The whole equal-rights arrangement only wobbled a little when you remembered that there was only one woman in the crew, a Russian engineer called Ilena.

Lift-off at last. A fist slammed him back into his seat, just as he had been warned. The soft material of the couch suddenly seemed rock hard. Breathing became difficult, and all he could do was pant and rasp. And yes, everything around him was roaring, though not as loudly as he had imagined it might. It basically felt like an uncommonly long roller-coaster ride. And judging by all the shaking and rattling, the rails had built up some rust.

Then the pressure suddenly let up, and his stomach lurched into his throat. Good thing he'd hardly had anything to eat. There was a crash somewhere that sounded as though some important part had broken.

"Carrier rocket disengaged," Boris announced.

"Taking over controls," Jackson said.

A moment later the shuttle's own engines roared to life. It was louder than before, but not quite so brutal. Adamson took a ragged breath. All things considered, he'd had easier rides. Hiroshi Kato could go to hell. The way he'd shot him down at that party back then. As though the project were mere child's play, not worth taking seriously. There had been good people working on it, good minds, the best of the best. Hiroshi Kato had been an arrogant prick. And he had been right, as everyone now knew. That was the worst of it.

Finally, they were up and away and the engines could cut out. Zero gravity. He had been warned that a great many people experienced nausea and was given a good number of sick bags just in case, but he didn't feel anything of the sort—quite the opposite: he felt euphoric. They had to stay strapped in, of course, as the flight wasn't over yet. But he could set his ballpoint pen floating in the air in front of him, and when he nudged it gently it would rotate, dancing around its own axis. Fascinating.

He found himself thinking of the old TV footage of the space missions and what his father had told him about Apollo 11. "Back then we thought, well, anything's possible," his dad had said more than once, with a visionary gleam in his eye. "We thought that's the first step into space, nothing can stop us now. I was convinced my kids would live on the moon, that my grandkids would live on Mars, that my great-grandkids would set out for distant stars."

Adamson had always thought his father was naive. As far as he was concerned, the moon landings went hand in hand with the summer of '68, hippies, free love, LSD, and flower power. America had thrown one huge, collective, wild party in those days; no wonder people got a little starry-eyed when they looked back. But here and now, sitting in a space shuttle on his way to an absolutely unbelievable object, he understood his father for the first time. The first step into space. Hell, yeah!

"There it is," Jackson suddenly said.

He could see a pale fleck out the window that was too big to be a star. The space station. The habitat orbiting Earth at a height of around eight hundred miles. Their destination. The fleck rapidly grew larger until it was a blurry circle and then bigger than the pockmarked face of the moon, growing ever larger as they approached. The space station was colossal. Six miles long. By comparison, their shuttle was a fly headed for a sixteen-wheeler. Even an aircraft carrier, if they somehow managed to boost it into space, would be small next to this. Hell, even a supertanker would have been dwarfed. What they saw out there was nothing less than a city in flight.

He tried to imagine how this incomprehensibly vast object had been built atom by atom, the way Hiroshi had explained it in his video address, by quadrillions of nano-assemblers. It was unimaginable. Now anything really was possible. *But this is all stolen tech,* Adamson told himself bitterly. *All that Hiroshi Kato did was make use of an alien technology. Nothing more than that.*

They flew across its face. He found himself thinking of *Star Wars,* the sequence where Luke Skywalker and the others attack the Death Star. It was all so huge, so immense, so crowded with curious clusters of equipment, antennae, and machines.

"I keep expecting Darth Vader to show up," Ilena said to him, and the pilot laughed in agreement.

They were all thinking the same thing. He found that oddly touching. He had to blink; there was something in his eye. Well damn it—he admired Kato. He always had but had never been able to admit it to himself. Hiroshi Kato was a genius if ever he had met one, but he hadn't seen it; he had only ever felt threatened . . . how idiotic. Kato had made it; he was writing history here, preparing humanity's way toward a better, brighter future. And he, Bill Adamson, still bore a grudge because that skinny little Japanese kid had an idea that he could have had if only . . . well, if only he had had it.

The space station was rotating slowly. So that was true. The radar readings had indicated as much, and the space-flight experts had been expecting it. It only made sense for a large, cylindrical space station to rotate, since that produced artificial gravity on the inside. However, it also meant that it would be practically impossible to dock on the outer edge.

Jackson took the shuttle around to the front of the station with short bursts from the steering nozzles, which made a noise like hammers pounding on the hull. They were approaching the hub.

"Looks like a docking area," the pilot announced.

It was more than that: it was a lock. The hub was a slightly protruding cylinder that didn't rotate along with the station but turned the other way, so that in effect it stood still. As the shuttle approached, an enormous hatch opened in a weightlessly elegant motion.

"Okay. Houston, did you see that? Looks like we're expected."

"Best of luck," came the voice from mission control.

Adamson held his breath as the shuttle drifted into the lock, which was comfortably big enough for a cruise ship. The hatch glided closed behind them. For a moment nothing happened, and then another hatch opened up in front.

"We have atmosphere out there," their flight engineer announced with astonishment in his voice. "Oxygen-nitrogen mix. Air pressure is just slightly below sea level."

"We've lost radio contact with Earth," the copilot reported.

"Let's go, then," Jackson said.

Another nudge from the nozzles took them through to a gigantic hall beyond the hatch, where something grabbed hold of them ever so gently and guided them in to land on the floor.

"Seems to be some kind of magnetic effect," the pilot said.

Four of them would go out, in extravehicular-activity suits just to be on the safe side. That was the plan, and there was no reason to deviate from it at the moment. And Bill Adamson was only there because a couple of months ago he had been promoted downward into the hitherto insignificant position of head of space-colonization research.

He was glad there were experienced astronauts on hand to help him put on the EVA suit. Sure, he had practiced how to do it, as much as he could in the short time available, but not in zero-G. He was all agog as he passed through the boarding lock—after Ilena, who had insisted on ladies first and thereby made sure she was the first human being to set foot on Earth's new companion.

The magnetic soles of their EVA suits functioned just as intended. It was strange to put one foot in front of the other like this; he felt as though he were hanging head down. Step by step. Doors led to rooms, corridors, hallways. *Take pictures of everything; describe everything; document everything.* They had no trouble with radio contact back to the shuttle. Buttresses, walls, load-bearing structures, sliding doors—they were all astoundingly thin but felt ultrastable when the explorers put their hands on them and applied pressure. Most astonishing of all was the precision of the construction. A staircase, a balcony with rails as fine as spaghetti strands—and he could see at once they were all of exactly the same diameter, that everything onboard this structure was built exactly to specification.

Of course, Adamson thought. *Build at the scale of individual atoms and every single one is accounted for.* Compared with this technology, every production technique in human history was hamhanded: forged metal, turned steel, machine finishing, polished or drilled or whatever you like—it was all just a marginal improvement on the hand ax with which, once upon a time, the march of technology had begun.

An elevator.

"We're going to risk it," Ilena announced to the shuttle.

The control panel was simple; Adamson had stayed in hotels where the elevators gave him more trouble. It went down, and they could feel gravity returning, or at least something that felt a lot like it. The centrifugal force of the rotating spindle. When he turned his head, he noticed the difference: an odd, niggling feeling in his sense of balance. They came out in a room full of windows, huge panes of flawless glass from floor to ceiling. And beyond those . . . Ilena caught her breath, awestruck. She said something that sounded Russian, and very, very impressed.

The space station was hollow. A landscape of metal stretched out before their eyes, covering the whole of the inside surface of the spindle—houses, roads, and lakes sprawled beneath them, climbing the walls in a gentle concave curve that reached above their heads. A rolled-up world of shimmering steel, an alien planet obeying an utterly unfamiliar geometry. Sure, when you went down there, wherever you were walking there was ground "below" your feet; you would always have the feeling you were standing at the lowest point of a valley, but one that closed neatly overhead.

"An ark," Adamson heard himself say. Right as he said it, he knew that this—here, now—was the high point of his life, the moment he would talk about until the day he died. "An ark in space. All we have to do is come aboard."

There was water; there was air to breathe. People would be able to live here; they could inhabit this artificial world, unfamiliar though it was. And because people could get used to anything, they would also get used to being able to see every spot on their world at any time, being able to wave up at their friends in the next village just by raising their eyes.

Ilena sighed. "It will be a problem getting enough soil up here for agriculture and livestock. Or do you think there are machines here that make food?"

Adamson looked at her, downcast. Of course! Suddenly he understood what troubled him about the view before them, what he hadn't been able to put his finger on until that moment. There was nothing alive up here. No animals, no plants, not even soil. Which was only logical, since if there was one thing he had learned about during his time as the utterly unmotivated head of space colonization, it was the soil problem. The stuff that just lay around in the fields back home—brown stuff, black stuff, common clay; the stuff that plants, bushes and trees grew in—was anything but simple. Quite the opposite. Arable soil was a highly complex system of minerals, organic detritus, and microorganisms, the product of life, death, and decay.

And he also understood why there was nothing like that here: because the nano-assemblers couldn't build it. They could make computer chips of unprecedented fineness and precision, and their building materials had the most astonishing properties: they could make paper tissues or diamond rings—all that was child's play. But the nanites could not build a living cell. It was beyond their powers. Highly complex processes were at work all the time in living cells, continuously unfolding at dizzying speeds; proteins were being produced, toxins and waste products removed, and so on. They could not be built up atom by atom. It would be like trying to build a motor running at full throttle.

Granted, life was made up of the same atoms as the nonliving world, but it had to grow into its patterns; that was the only way life could arise. It was a completely different approach from the one the extraterrestrial nanites took, and completely different from the approach Hiroshi Kato had taken for his own research. The nano-assemblers may be a perfect tool in their own way, but they had their limits.

"What he didn't say on the video," the secretary of defense said during a special session of the National Security Council, "is that he could just as easily destroy the world if he wanted to. This technology is a weapon like no other in all of history. Mr. President, ladies and gentlemen, Hiroshi Kato is the most dangerous man who ever lived. We have to detain him, no matter what the cost."

Everyone around the table nodded. Nobody said otherwise.

"Okay," the president said in the end. "Do what you need. And keep me informed."

Nor was he the only head of state who received such advice and who gave such an order. Within a few days of Hiroshi's speech going public, every secret service in the world was after him.

Every secret service, and someone else, too . . .

LONELY ISLAND

1

The chemotherapy was dreadful, the worst experience Charlotte had ever had in her life. They gave her something for the nausea, of course, and of course she felt nauseous all the time anyway, miserable and weak, but that wasn't the worst of it. When she lay in bed with the intravenous drip in her arm, it was as though an enemy were pouring through her veins, a demon from primeval times in liquid form, an ancient enemy from the days when the cells themselves had first taken shape and had to fight against the toxic corrosion of the world around them. Exposed to the poison for hours on end, she felt as though she had been hurled back to the very origins of life, the beginning of time, and that she was betraying her own body. She felt like a fortress that had surrendered to some primordial enemy, opened her doors, and cast down her weapons before it. Brenda came and tried to console her, to offer her support; but then at some point Charlotte couldn't stand to have anyone else around, not even Brenda, and had to send her away so she could be alone with herself and her demon.

The first time the endless hours were finally past, when Thomas came and picked her up, she felt like an angel or a spirit, a creature of light sitting next to him. She raised her hands again and again, astonished each time to find she was not transparent.

"I don't know whether it's the right thing to do," she said while Brenda cooked her a light broth, the only food she could imagine keeping down. "It feels so . . . wrong."

"It's a chance though, Charley," Brenda replied desperately. "Just look at it as your chance."

She thought about this. A chance. How many chances did she need? How many chances had she already had? She seemed to have missed them all. Why would it be any different this time of all times?

The next morning all the hair still left on her body began to fall out. She only had a few patches on her scalp anyway, but when she got out of the shower, even they were gone. Her pubic hair fell out in clumps, and when she dried her face, parts of her eyebrows and eyelashes stayed behind in the towel. Three days later she was as hairless as a baby. She stood in front of the mirror and felt that she was looking at a shopwindow dummy. The doctor was surprised and told her he hadn't expected that to happen until the second dose of treatment. But then again, every patient reacted differently. And the hair would all grow back; she needn't worry about that.

"I'm not worried about my hair," Charlotte said. *I'm worried about myself.* But she didn't say that out loud. One look at the doctor's face, lined by a lifetime of worry for others, and she knew he understood without her having to say it out loud.

Besides, she had her mother to worry about her hair on her behalf. She kept calling and trying to persuade her to come to Paris, where she knew some wonderful wigmakers. Wonderful! The idea that she would be able to take a transatlantic flight in her condition was farfetched enough, but the thought she might do so to buy a wig was absurd. Her mother wouldn't be put off, though. Her calls became a form of torture for Charlotte.

The days passed. She would get up with an effort in the morning, drained by every move she made, exhausted even when she tried to rest, and worn-out before evening came. She still felt wrung out, like an old dishcloth, when the next dose of therapy was due.

"Maybe you'll cope better with this one," said the female doctor who greeted her this time. "It happens in a lot of cases. The patients get used to it."

But not her. The second dose was the same nightmare—only much deeper.

A week later Brenda knocked gently at her door. "Charley?" Charlotte sat up with a start. She had been sitting in her armchair, trying to read, and had nodded off. "Yes, what is it?"

"Sorry. I didn't want to wake you. It looked as though you were—"

"No problem. Really. I . . . it's a dull book." She set it aside.

Brenda hesitated. "Say—listen, you're good at languages. Do you think you could translate something for a friend?"

Charlotte looked at her oldest friend. Only then did she notice Brenda was getting her first gray hairs. Strange how you could go through life and never notice things. Was she good at languages? She got by, that was for sure. But to translate? "I've never done it," she said. "I don't know whether I can."

"Would you give it a try?" Brenda took out a sheet of paper, a letter written in Spanish. "It's a divorce case, I'm afraid. One of Tom's colleagues who married a Frenchman. He's a racing driver, if you can believe that. And now he's causing trouble for her; nobody knows why." She passed her the letter. "Anyway, she needs this in French."

So she tried. Since Charlotte needed to hear things aloud to understand them, she shut herself away in her room to read the letter out loud to herself, to hear the sound of the words and the meaning behind them. The legal details required precise translation that took all her concentration. The world around her faded away, time stood still, and she forgot her own body, her weakness, her fears. There was only the letter and the words. She wrote them out, corrected herself, crossed them out, and wrote some more.

Something changed inside her during those hours. When she eventually looked up, she felt a peace she had never known before.

At first she listened, amazed, since it seemed to her that a machine had been humming away softly in the background this whole time and had only just fallen silent. But then she understood that there had never been any machine. She herself had fallen silent for the first time in her life.

She looked around, gazing at the window, the wooden desk where she sat, the bed, and the hand-embroidered bedspread. They were all simply there. Objects that someone had made once upon a time. They had been there before her, and they would still be there after she was gone. She, Charlotte Malroux, would die. That was how it was. Her journey would be over soon. And all in all she had nothing against ending her journey here, in Buenos Aires. She wouldn't do any more chemo. She would simply live out the days that were left to her.

When Charlotte had finished translating the letter and brought it to Brenda in her room, her friend looked at her in surprise, seeming to see the change she had undergone.

"Could you help me to find a room somewhere in town?" Charlotte asked.

They finally settled on Belgrano. It was a safe part of town for a woman living on her own and not far from Núñez, where Brenda and Tom lived; if she needed any help, one of them could be there in an instant. That was the condition Brenda imposed before she would let Charlotte go.

She took a room in a house that belonged to an old couple who usually rented to students. The old woman was from Germany and was delighted to have the chance to dust off the French she had learned at school. She soon learned, however, it would be easier to stick to Spanish. The house lay on a quiet, treelined street far enough from the Avenida Cabildo to be free of traffic and noise, but close enough for Charlotte to be able to do all her shopping on foot— for the time being at least, and only if she stuck to what she really needed. But that was what she wanted: from now on, she would stick to what she really needed.

The best thing was that her room was on the ground floor and had its own deck, where she could sit and look at the garden as it slowly succumbed to the wilderness. It was a sight full of secrets. She decided this was where she would spend most of the time that was left to her. The room was furnished, and most of the furniture was fine. There were some pieces she didn't like, though—the great big black wardrobe of aged oak that didn't go with the rest of the room; the desk, which was too narrow; the mirror, with its pompous gold frame—and she persuaded the landlords to let her replace them with other pieces at her own expense. She spent a few days going through furniture stores, antique dealerships, and street markets looking at items and considering their merits and was astonished to find that it didn't tire her out at all but instead invigorated her. She arranged for transport and wheedled and flattered the delivery men until they had placed her new white wardrobe exactly where she wanted it, with the bookshelf right next to it. Then she painted one wall in a shade of peach she had fallen in love with. She hung new drapes and bought far too many houseplants in colorful pots. For the first time in her life, she made herself a home.

"It looks wonderful!" Señora Blanco marveled when she saw what Charlotte had done with the room. Charlotte just smiled; now that it was all done, she found she had a terrible headache.

The next day she went to see Dr. Aleandro again, who looked at her with his careworn expression and explained it was the tumor. It was growing again, he said, and pressing harder on her brain. Was she quite sure she didn't want to . . . ?

"No," said Charlotte. "I'd just like something for the headaches."

He prescribed her tablets that came with a list of possible side effects longer than her arm. They helped, though. After that she made sure she never overexerted herself. When she went out for groceries, she always lay down to rest for half an hour afterward. Later she discovered an ice-cream parlor that served excellent espresso; from then on she always made sure she stopped there to rest. This was the last summer she would live through; if she couldn't eat ice cream now, then when?

That stillness, that silence within her, never left her now. When she was out and about, she looked at the people scurrying by and felt she had already departed. Most of them were in a hurry, many of them looked unhappy, hungry for something they felt they didn't have, irritable. None of them seemed to know they were alive or realize what an extraordinary thing that was all by itself. Charlotte watched them indulgently, for she remembered all too well she had been the same way.

At last, she began to write letters, to old friends, to former lovers, to everyone she felt she still owed an explanation or at least a few words. She wrote to Gary at his old address in Belcairn, because she didn't have the one in London. She told him how she was and told him she often found herself thinking of the way they had met in Moscow, and of that evening under the bridge in Istanbul. She told him how his devotion to his work impressed her, how much she admired his integrity when he had bought the fake harpsichord. She told him she had loved him while it lasted, that she was happy to have known him, and that she wished him and Lilith all the best.

She wrote to Adrian to thank him for leading the expedition. He was the only one who wrote straight back, a long, deeply felt letter saying just how sorry he was to hear her news and wishing her the best. She cried when she read it but had to laugh when she read the postscript saying he also sent greetings from Morley, who had unfortunately fallen off a ladder while rearranging his bookshelves and now had a complex fracture in his forearm, meaning his handwriting was even worse than usual at the moment.

She even wrote to James. It was a hard letter to write, and she took several days over it. In the end she let him know she had always suspected he was having affairs on the side—that a woman always feels such things—but that she had turned a blind eye and told herself it was nothing to do with her, that he had to get it out of his system. She also said she realized how stupidly she had behaved, that she knew now she had been indulging him, encouraging him almost, because he always dropped the other girls and came back to her, and that had been a cheap way for her to feel good about herself. She wrote that she was sorry she hadn't set down clear ground rules right from the start, and that since she hadn't, it was her fault, too, that things hadn't worked out between them.

When at last she tried to write a letter to Hiroshi, she found she couldn't. There was so much to say, and nothing at all. Every attempt to put her feelings into words ended up in a tangle of broken sentences she didn't understand herself when she reread them. Why had they never been a couple, as he had once wanted so much? They had always been close, and she would almost have said they were more like brother and sister than lovers, but she knew she had always felt that urge as well, like an itch. She didn't understand it, and so the letter stayed unfinished after countless false starts.

"Yes, that's her." Coldwell nodded and handed the photo back to James. "She was with him in Hong Kong that one time."

James felt his jaw grind—a nervous tick he could do nothing to stop these days. "And why was she there? Did he say anything?"

Coldwell shrugged his massive shoulders. "All I heard was the inventor would be bringing his muse along. No idea what that was supposed to mean."

"His *muse*?"

"Do you know the woman?"

James scratched his chin with the edge of the photo. "Yes. Yes, I do. And I also know where she is at the moment." He put the picture back into the file. "Kato will turn up there to see her at some point, sure as night follows day. Get your people together, and go wait for him."

April was drawing to an end and with it the long summer in Buenos Aires. The weather forecast had promised a few more fine days and then rain and cool temperatures. Since it was to be her last summer, Charlotte spent as long as she could outside every evening. She sat on her deck, wrapped in a blanket, listening to the birdsong and to children's voices in the distance, looking at the leaves on the trees that were already beginning to turn, and thinking. Often she would fall asleep there—the painkillers she was taking now against the pressure in her head made her even more tired than she would have been anyway.

One evening she awoke with a start because there was someone standing in front of her, a short, wiry man who seemed somehow familiar. She wasn't frightened—nothing could scare her now—but she had woken up from the creaking of the boards when he stepped onto the deck. She recognized him then. It was Hiroshi.

"Hello, Charlotte," he said.

She looked at him calmly, without moving. There was a silver tint to his hair. The first fine lines were showing around his eyes. "This is a dream, isn't it?"

He shook his head and smiled. "No."

It was a sad smile. She would often think of that later, that he had known what was going to happen.

2

"He's in Buenos Aires?" The secretary of defense looked up from the report at the head of the CIA. The report was only one page, but he had delivered it in person. "Are you sure?"

"Sure as we can be," the CIA man snapped back. The secretary held his gaze and said nothing. The CIA chief sighed and said, "A little while ago Argentinean customs detained some folks. Americans trying to enter the country with weapons and surveillance gear. The authorities got in touch with our embassy, and our chief of station there looked into it. All routine stuff up to that point. But then he found that one of the men—a certain Bud Miller—was carrying photos of Hiroshi Kato."

"I see. After which he was a little more . . . insistent in his questioning, I would imagine."

The CIA man cocked his head to one side, which made his bald spot more evident. "The men were hired to watch a woman named Charlotte Malroux. They seem to think sooner or later Kato is going to show up for a visit."

"And who hired them?"

"A company based in Boston, Bennett Enterprises." The spy chief waved his hand dismissively. "Obviously the chairman wanted get his hands on Kato and his technology. This means all kinds of unwelcome legal consequences for him, of course, and for the board members who were involved. But the real point is we are now watching the lady instead. She's the daughter of a former French ambassador in Argentina, so we're being very discreet about it. And you know what, Kato really did go visit." He looked at his watch. "About an hour ago."

"Okay." The secretary of defense reached for his desk telephone. "Time to act. All the bells and whistles. You get your people down there moving, I'll talk to the president."

A car horn was honking over and over somewhere in the distance. She could hear the clatter of cooking pans as well. A plane passed overhead, its vapor trail gleaming red and gold. Charlotte got up. She had difficulty pulling herself up from the chair. She felt like an old woman, fragile. "Let's go inside, it's getting cold."

"Sure thing," Hiroshi said. She noticed the way he moved a little closer, ready to catch her should she fall, and how he tried not to let her notice he did so.

"I'm fine," she said. "Would you like something to drink? I can make us some coffee."

"Coffee would be great," he replied.

Inside, he looked around as she busied herself with kettle and coffee grinder in the little kitchen nook. "Nice place you've got here," he said after a while. "It all looks very . . . very you. I always imagined you might live somewhere that looks like this."

"Really?" She was surprised he should say so.

"I notice you don't have a couch either," he added, smiling.

She remembered their conversation from so long ago. A lifetime ago, it seemed to her now. "You could grow me one."

"Would you like me to?" He almost sounded as though he meant it.

"No," Charlotte said. "First of all, I don't have room for it, as you see—"

"You didn't live in Japan long enough," he said.

"And second, I only want things around me that were made by human hand. I like them better, even if they're not quite so perfect. I'd like to own nothing that was machine-made."

"Why's that?"

"Because a machine doesn't care whether it builds a table or kills someone."

Hiroshi raised his eyebrows. "Ah," she heard him say. "Yes, that's right. Machines really don't care." There was a note of pain in his voice.

She put the cups down on her little table and brought over the coffee pot and sugar. "Sit," she said, pointing to the armchair. She took the chair by the desk. "And tell me, what brings you here? Where have you been hiding? The whole world wants to shake your hand ever since that space station showed up."

"That's not all they want," Hiroshi said darkly as she poured the coffee.

He sounded despondent. *Yes,* Charlotte thought, *they probably want to pick his brain as well. Of course.* But it was all so far away; she didn't follow the news these days, didn't read the papers or watch TV.

"It's good to see you," she said. "I wanted to write you a letter but somehow . . . well, anyway. And now here you are. I'm glad." She found she was blinking. Why was it so hard to make these happy moments last, to make time stop? Why did time march so relentlessly forward? "I'm not in the best of health, as you may have noticed."

"I know," Hiroshi said. "That's why I came."

"To see me one last time."

"No," he said. "To cure you."

"Cure me?" She shook her head, feeling a flash of anger. "Nobody can do that."

"I can."

She looked at him closely, studying his eyes, how seriously he looked back at her, and she remembered that, yes, when Hiroshi claimed the impossible, he really meant it. "How did you even know I was ill?" she thought to ask. "Or where I live?"

"I found out from Gary McGray." He sipped his coffee. "I tried all the old numbers I had for you. A man picked up in Scotland who said he knows you, and he gave me this address."

"Ah. Good. Did he have any news of himself?"

"He was a bit stressed-out, I think. There was a baby screaming its head off in the background."

So they had a child. At least one. And they were living in Belcairn. That was odd—what about the auction house in London? Well, perhaps Gary would write to her. While there was still time.

"Not my mother this time, then," she said.

"I'm a bit reluctant to phone up embassies at the moment," was all he said to that. He looked around. "Let's get started. I'd like to pull the bed out a bit so that I can sit by the head. Is that okay with you?"

Charlotte nodded, feeling rather rushed into this. "What do you actually plan to do?"

"To put it simply, I'm going to lay my hands on your head."

"Do you believe in that sort of thing?"

"Don't think too much about it." He pulled the bed out into the room at an angle and put the chair at the head of it. "Just lie down there. On your back."

She hesitated. "That's it?"

"Perhaps you could take off your headscarf."

Ah well. Why not. She undid the knot at the back. Her eyelashes had grown back, but there was still nothing but patchy fluff on her scalp; taking off the scarf felt like stripping naked in front of him. On the other hand, she'd already stripped naked in front of him once before. She folded the scarf carefully—it was a batik cloth she had bought from a woman at a flea market—put it on the table, and lay down on the bed.

"Now just lie there and relax," she heard him say. He put his hands on the back of her head near the scar from the operation. "This will take a while."

"Okay." It felt good to be touched again, but she was unsettled nevertheless. Hiroshi had always been a man of science, a thorough-going rationalist; to see someone like him taking refuge in an old superstition was . . . disappointing.

Just then she felt a curious burning sensation that seemed to be spreading out from his hands, seeping into her skull, and then flowing through her whole body like a hot flush. She shuddered.

"That'll pass in a moment," she heard Hiroshi say. "It only feels like that at the beginning."

Fernández Larreta, chief of police of Buenos Aires, was extremely put out by the turn his evening had taken. He was wearing his best tails, since he had been at the opera with his wife; then the interior minister's men had found him during the intermission and hauled him out of the Teatro Colón. And now, instead of listening to the sublime finale of *Don Giovanni*, he was sitting in an office at the ministry listening to a couple of Americans causing an uproar in a mishmash of broken Spanish and heavily accented English.

Where were they even from? Somebody had told him, but he had been far too indignant at the sudden, shameless interruption to listen closely. He thought he recognized one of the faces—the man with olive skin and the fringe of curly, gray hair around his bald pate worked at the American embassy. Miller, or something like that. Yes. He straightened his lapels and tried to follow what they were saying. It was about some Japanese citizen, currently thought to be in Buenos Aires. Good gracious, these *norteamericanos* stuck their noses in everywhere. Even as he listened, however, he was thinking of his wife and the furious glance she had shot him as he left. Heavens above! There would be more drama when he got home.

Better not to think about that now. He turned all his attention to the matter at hand.

"The pursuit and arrest of criminals and other dangerous persons is an internal matter for Argentina," the minister was just saying. "You would not permit our police"—he nodded toward Larreta—"to pursue a suspect on US territory."

"Yes," Miller said. "But this man is so dangerous that you won't be able to deal with him."

"This is what's happening," Hiroshi explained. "I was carrying the parts for several billion specialized nano-robots in my body, which all together mass almost one gram. Once I laid my hands on you, the transporter units from my permanent colony of nano-complexes carried the parts through my skin and through yours, into your bloodstream. Then the connector units they also delivered assembled the parts and made the robots themselves. The best way to imagine it is that you now have tiny little submarines swimming through your veins, each about the size of a virus. The submarines are now hunting down every cancerous cell in your body."

Charlotte heard herself cough, an involuntary sound. That was too much to hope for; she couldn't let herself . . . but all the same she felt something. Or she thought she did. It was like a wave of pins and needles passing through her body, concentrating at the nape of her neck. She wanted to say something, but she suddenly felt so heavy. On top of which, she'd forgotten what she wanted to say. Had it been important? Was anything important now?

She woke with a start. "How do they know?" she called out.

"What?" she heard Hiroshi say, his hands still cradling her head.

She understood. "I fell asleep, didn't I?"

"Yes, but that's fine. Don't worry."

"What kind of host am I? Just dropping off like that." But then she remembered the question that had woken her up. "Your submarines—how do they know which cells are cancerous and which aren't?"

"Ah yes." Hiroshi was smiling; she could hear it in his voice. "There are a great many characteristic features to cancerous cells. They are, for instance, immortal, unlike most of the other cells in your body."

"Cancer cells are immortal?" It seemed absurd.

"Of course. That's precisely the problem: the way they can divide indefinitely. Most normal tissue cells can't do that; they're worn-out after about fifty replications."

She thought about it. It was somehow logical and paradoxical, too: she was dying of a dose of immortality. "You said most tissue cells. . . . Are some tissue cells immortal, too?"

"Yes. For instance, eggs and sperm. And some stem cells. But both of these classes of cell are also very distinctive. Your eggs, for instance—gamete cells—only have half their set of chromosomes."

There was so much she didn't know about her own body. The thought that there were now tiny machines patrolling her body, inspecting each cell in turn to decide which to remove . . . "What if they make a mistake?"

"They don't make mistakes." His hands were still on her head, warm and calming. "I'm still in contact with them."

"In contact? Through your hands, you mean?"

"Actually, by radio. But skin contact improves reception."

Was she supposed to understand that? She felt very strange. Something was happening in her body, but she had no idea what. "I feel feverish. Does that make sense?"

"That's just a leukocyte reaction," Hiroshi said calmly. "The machines don't simply break down the cancer cells; that would be too dangerous. It would swamp your body with more toxins and waste products than it could cope with. So instead they go into the cells and trigger apoptosis. That's the process of controlled cell self-destruction. Most of the debris gets gobbled up by your leukocytes;

you'll have a high white-blood-cell count for a while. The subs themselves will carry off everything that's left over and deposit it either in your gut or your bladder—that takes a little longer. The total mass of tumorous material in your body is no more than a couple of hundred grams. You won't notice anything, though your urine will change color for a while."

"How do you know all this?" Charlotte asked, surprised.

"Before I came to you, I tried it out twice. Once on an old man, and once on a ten-year-old child. They were both supposed to have only days to live, and they're both quite healthy now."

Charlotte shivered. "You really can cure cancer! Hiroshi! You have to give this to humanity. It's so much more important than your space station. My goodness."

"It's not as simple as you think."

"Why not?"

"Because you have to know what I know, and you have to be ready to merge with the nanite complexes." He sighed. "It's the control system, do you understand? My whole brain is shot through with nanoscale conduits. I'm receiving signals from the nanites directly into my mind, and all it takes is one thought from me to send them off to do whatever I want."

Charlotte sat up, turned around, and looked at him, appalled. "You can't seriously mean that. Those things from the island . . . they're in your head?"

"There's no other way," he replied and patted the bed gently. "Please lie down again. I want to be able to watch what's going on inside you."

She lay back down again reluctantly, trying not to think of Leon. This was all so surreal. Perhaps she was just dreaming . . .

"Hiroshi!" she called when next she woke up. "How does that work? These machines came from the depths of space, from who knows where. How are you able to control them with your brain?"

Hiroshi moved his hands gently around, stroking her temples.
"Because you were right."

"I was? What about?"

"There was another human race before us. They built the nanites."

Fernández Larreta felt the moment had come to speak up. There was no way he could allow these interlopers, these foreigners, to drag the good name of the Argentine police force through the mud without at least giving them a piece of his mind.

"With all due respect, Señor," he pronounced, "I doubt you are truly in a position to judge. To be frank, you have said nothing concrete about this perilous Japanese gentleman; you have merely made a few vague claims. I hear the word 'dangerous' a great deal. Why exactly do you say so? Please give us some solid proof."

That made him sit up and look, this Miller. Ha! He hadn't been expecting anyone to put up a fight.

"Professor?" The American turned to the man who had accompanied him, who had an imposing Roman nose. "Would you perhaps . . . ?"

The professor nodded, looked at his watch, and gazed straight ahead for a moment as though doing sums in his head. Then he smiled softly. He hurried across the room and looked out a window that opened onto the dark courtyard of the ministry building. "If you would be so kind as to join me, Señor Larreta," he said, gesturing in invitation. He spoke Spanish with a Mexican accent.

Fine, then. Fernández Larreta had no idea what this was about, but he would maintain his good manners despite everything. He got up and went to stand next to the professor, who was wearing a bolo tie.

"Look up at the sky."

Fernández Larreta looked up, following the professor's outstretched arm. There was a pale, blurry spot of light in the night sky, which moved very slowly as he watched.

"Do you know what that is?"

Larreta shrugged. "Of course. It's the space station. The habitat."

"Precisely. The man we're looking for built that station."

"So?" The chief of police was surprised to hear this, but of course he didn't let it show. "Good for him. I just don't understand why that makes him so extremely dangerous, as you claim."

"Because Mr. Kato did not build this gigantic object with his own two hands," said the professor. "That would have taken him something like a hundred thousand years. He built it using nano-technological robots of extraterrestrial origin that he has somehow learned to control. Are you up to date with how nano-replicators work?"

Larreta looked at him disdainfully. What was this, a classroom test? "I have read what everybody has in the newspapers. I know that they're supposed to be able to build on the scale of individual atoms."

"That's right. Most importantly, they can build copies of themselves atom by atom. Those copies then make copies, and so on and so forth. The problem is they don't just conjure these atoms out of thin air, they take them from their surroundings." The professor turned around and began pacing the room, one hand on his back, gesticulating with the other. Larreta could vividly imagine him doing that in a lecture hall. "Now imagine that these nano-replicators get out of control. They multiply and multiply, and nobody is able to stop them. Imagine it happening here, in this office. Over there on the minister's desk. What would happen? First, the nano-replicators would attack everything around them, taking it apart into atoms to make copies of themselves—the leather on the desktop, the wood beneath, the lamp that's standing there. Since they're built to be as efficient as possible, that would happen with breathtaking speed. In less time than it takes you to draw breath, the desk would be gone, changed into nano-replicators. And then? Do you believe the machines draw the line at humans? Human beings are made of atoms, too, just like animals, plants, everything in existence. Atoms they can use to build further copies of themselves. And since by now there are not simply a few of these nano-replicators but multitudes—the same as the mass of that desk—it would all happen that much faster. Before you could understand what was going on, the minister himself would be taken apart for his atoms, as would you, Señor, and all of us. The room, this building, the whole city block—it would keep on and on, faster and faster. And," he concluded, looking at each of them in turn, "nobody would be able to stop it."

The minister put his finger inside the collar of his shirt. "All that's just a vague theoretical possibility, though, isn't it?"

The professor shook his head slowly and deliberately. "Unfortunately not." He pointed up to the sky. "As you said, there is the space station. You've all seen the pictures. The nano-replicators exist, and they quite clearly work—and Mr. Kato is the only one they will obey. If he so chose, he could unleash them, and it would take only a few hours for them to blanket the whole Earth with copies of themselves. Copies that could then only attack one another. That would be the end of the world—so utterly and definitively the end that it would make nuclear war look like a mild cold. Up until now all this was just the nightmare of scientists who research nanotechnology—they call it the 'gray-goo' scenario. But ever since Mr. Kato's space station arrived, it's no longer a theory but a hideously real possibility. If he should happen to decide to do it this minute, nobody alive on Earth would see the dawn. And if you ask me, that is more power than any one man should have."

"Quite so." The minister gulped. "Tell me what you plan to do and what you need."

It was a dream. Suddenly she was quite sure. Time had come to a stop, the rest of the world had vanished, and there was only her and Hiroshi's voice.

"Do you remember Seito-Jinjiya, the Island of the Saints? That obsidian knife you wanted to touch, no matter what?"

What a question! "Do I remember? That's what gave me the idea of looking for the first human race. It's what ruined my academic career."

Hiroshi's voice again, speaking as though all that was unimportant. "I held you, do you remember? You screamed when you touched the knife, and you fell into the water."

She had to smile. "It all seems a hundred years ago."

"I can't prove it, but I suspect not only that the knife was created during the era of the first human race, but also that it must have had something to do with someone who was involved in creating the nanites. And then your strange ability to read objects . . ." He stopped. "As I say, I can't prove any of this. Nobody will ever be able to prove it. It's just a suspicion . . . or let's say it's how I explain all of this to myself. How I explain I knew so much about these nanites before I ever saw them for the first time. I already had the basic idea—robots that build robots, remember? When we were on the swings in your garden that day, I was already thinking about it. It would probably just have stayed an idea, the kind of naive idea you have when you're a kid and then you quickly forget. But it must have been the soil upon which some seed fell. Something that reached me through you. From that object, from a past we know nothing about. Most of my inventions weren't my inventions at all—they were rediscoveries, something mankind already knew once before."

"So the probe would have been launched from Earth hundreds of thousands of years ago—and then it came back, during our time?"

"Not that probe as such. Since they were launching nanites, they must have planned for the probes to reproduce."

"I see. So they launched a probe that found an alien planet, landed on it, built more rockets and more probes, which flew off in turn and found other planets . . . and then eventually one of those rockets happened to find its way back to Earth?"

"Exactly."

Charlotte had to think about that for a while. Perhaps she dozed off again as she did so; she couldn't say. All she knew was a long time passed before she thought to ask, "The first human race . . . If they were able to invent something like that . . . these nanites . . . then they must have been very advanced, mustn't they? Technologically, I mean."

"No doubt about it," Hiroshi said.

"But in that case . . ." She stopped. What Hiroshi had told her struck a chord somewhere in her mind. It could only have been as he suspected. "I would somehow expect such an advanced civilization to have left more traces behind. That there would be a . . . I don't know . . . a vast machine buried somewhere. A stretch of freeway. Something like that."

"I remember taking a very long walk through Boston and surroundings, and someone telling me that a hundred thousand years is a long time. Long enough for all sorts of things to fall to dust," Hiroshi said. "But it may simply be that there's no record because of the nanites."

"How's that?"

"The first humans may have been just as warlike and aggressive as we are. I'm sure they were. Perhaps there was a war at some point, fought with nano-weapons. Or an accident and they got out of control. Remember, nanites can't just build anything, they can also take anything apart. The one implies the other."

Charlotte tried to imagine it. "You mean the nanites could have destroyed the whole civilization, so that the survivors were left in the Stone Age?"

"You could build nanomachines that swarm out and turn every scrap of ultrapure silicon they find into dust. In the blink of an eye, no computer could function. You could build nanomachines that destroy everything made of paper—that's the end of books, libraries, all human knowledge. Nanomachines that destroy anything made of metal . . . the possibilities are endless."

"You could also build nanomachines that kill people."

"That, too."

"If that's what happened, then why are there still people at all?"

Hiroshi heaved a deep sigh. "I don't know. I haven't found any history books from back then after all, just blueprints. I'm still piecing it all together. But if there was a conflict, then the other side used nanotechnology as well. And if it was an accident . . . we could imagine all sorts of explanations. A last-minute rescue plan. A clash between nanomachine armies that fought each other. Or simply chance." He hesitated. "It's just a thought, but a lot of viruses look as though they might be remnants of nanomachines."

"Viruses?"

"Yes. Viruses aren't alive. They're basically machines that attack living cells and hijack them into producing copy after copy of the virus until they're burned out. It's hard to imagine an evolutionary pathway that could have produced something like a virus. The idea they may have actually been built seems to me to fit quite well."

That reminded Charlotte of something, of a riddle she had spent a long time trying to solve years ago in another life. "The genetic bottleneck," she said.

"I'm sorry?" Hiroshi asked, caught off-guard.

"We've been researching the human genome ever since the nineties. And we've learned that human beings the world over are far more closely related than we had expected. If you run a statistical analysis of mitochondrial DNA—the part of the genome that comes from the mother—then you find out every human being alive today has just a few thousand common ancestors who lived about seventy thousand years ago."

"And how have they explained that?"

"There's a theory about the explosion of a volcano called Toba on Sumatra about seventy-four thousand years ago. Supposedly, an unusually powerful eruption, strong enough to have influenced the planetary climate. The theory is it led to a long cold period, and that

Homo sapiens almost died out during that time." Charlotte took a deep breath. "But a war like you describe . . . that would explain things as well. It would fit the time frame."

"It would also fit the big picture," Hiroshi said.

"What do you mean?"

He stopped, seemed to be considering something. "On Saradkov the nanites suddenly ceased all replication and expansion, and I always said I didn't know why they did that. Do you remember?"

"As if I could forget."

"Ever since I merged with them and gained access to all their programs, I know what stopped them. They did it themselves. They noticed they were back on Earth, and in that scenario their programming required they cease all activity and send radio signals offering to self-destruct."

"Self-destruct?" Charlotte repeated, astonished.

"A safety mechanism."

She thought about this. It made no sense to her. "Why would an explorer probe that happened to wind up back on Earth self-destruct? It would be enough to power down. Or it could carry out its exploration program here on Earth. That wouldn't be such a tragedy."

"There's one reason that would explain it. A horribly simple reason," Hiroshi said. He exhaled, and it sounded like a sob. "The most horrible reason you could imagine."

Night blanketed Buenos Aires. Traffic had thinned after midnight, so it was no trouble to cordon off the streets where things were about to get underway. It wouldn't be long now. Dawn would break soon. The morning rush hour would start. They would have trouble if things lasted that long.

Commander José Guarneri sat in the passenger seat of his car with a clipboard on his lap and a map of Buenos Aires folded to show Belgrano and the surrounding area. He had a radio to his ear and was drawing in the roadblocks with a thick red pen as they were reported in.

"Group four, Rodríguez," he heard. "Commander, there's a man here who's going crazy about the roadblock. He's a newspaper delivery man. He wants to deliver these newspapers no matter what."

Guarneri pressed the transmission button. "Tell him he should think about whether he wants to feature in tomorrow's edition. Headline: Dead in a Hail of Bullets."

That seemed to do the trick. At least, there were no further reports from that direction.

"Group one?" he asked. "Anything happening?"

"Still light in the window, but otherwise nothing to report. No sign of movement."

"How about the directional mics?"

"Occasional quiet conversation between a man and a woman. Sometimes in English, sometimes in what could be Japanese. Then silence again."

"Are they having sex?"

"No idea. If they are, we can't hear anything." The captain cleared his throat. "We could start the operation while it's quiet. Maybe that's when they're asleep."

"Negative," Guarneri replied. "We're not going in." He thought for a moment and then switched to the general band. "Guarneri to all. A reminder: whatever we do, we're waiting till he comes out. The daughter of a former French ambassador to Argentina lives in that house; you guys are not going to screw this up for me, you hear me?" That was something his men could understand.

It wasn't the whole truth, though. Guarneri had a strong feeling even he didn't know all the ins and out of the story. "I don't want anyone setting foot in that house," the chief of police had told him in person and in no uncertain terms. "And if those *norteamericanos* try anyway, you stop them, understand? By whatever means necessary.

Ambassador Malroux is a good friend of mine; I could never look him in the eye again if anything happened to his daughter."

The business with the American agents was all taken care of. They had staked themselves out in the house opposite. Guarneri had given them four of his trusted men as well, officially as protection. They would make sure that the agents didn't do anything stupid.

"And another thing, which is going to stay our little secret, Commander," the chief had told him. "These Americans want to get their man, and they're telling the craziest stories you ever heard to get him. I'm not impressed, but the minister has allowed them to send along more of their own people." And then the chief's face grew grim. "I would very much appreciate it, Commander Guarneri, if the Buenos Aires police proved to be fully up to the task. Bring me that man, and bring him in alive."

Which was exactly what Guarneri intended to do.

"The truth is," Hiroshi said, "they didn't send those probes out to explore other planets."

"Then why did they do it?"

"To destroy them."

Charlotte felt the cold creeping into her bones. "Destroy them? How . . ." She stopped. She knew how nanites could destroy a planet, of course. She had seen it with her own eyes on Saradkov. If the nanites hadn't stopped, if they had simply kept on and on and on, they would have had no chance. None at all. "What a terrible notion."

"Basically, the probes are much like viruses themselves, but on a planetary scale. The program is as simple as can be: land on a life-bearing planet and convert the whole biosphere into rockets that will then carry copies farther out into space. And keep going until there's nothing left of the world."

"They deliberately target life-bearing planets for destruction?"

"Yes."

"Why would anybody do that?"

Hiroshi took a deep breath. "I don't know. I only know that's the case. I know the basic programming for these probes, and it's unmistakable. That's how it was coded. As for the reasons, I can only speculate."

He took his hands off her head. Her skin felt cool where they had been—all night long, as it seemed to Charlotte. Cool and now forlorn.

"I wondered whether perhaps they were at war with an alien power, with some galactic enemy, and at some point felt they had no other choice but to use this weapon. Or whether they were so desperate they didn't care. Or whether it was an act of revenge by the last humans left alive after a devastating attack from space. Whatever the reason, the probes must have been developed in a hurry. Their designers didn't even take the time to give them a new information matrix that would only contain those programs and blueprints the probes really need. They simply took what they had and slapped the killer program on top. Quick and dirty. The way I was building my own nanomachines, before I merged. When it didn't matter whether it was elegant or efficient, just that it worked."

Charlotte rubbed her temples gently and tried to understand. "They launched their rockets with machines designed to destroy alien planets. . . . Where did they send them?"

"Everywhere. In all directions."

"And then what? One of the rockets eventually reaches a solar system, finds a life-bearing planet, crash-lands, and begins its work of destruction . . ."

"And within a few days all life on that planet is wiped out. Without a trace. The whole planetary crust is converted into new rockets, right up until the moment they run out of some important element. But by then they've built and launched millions of new probes, each looking for another new planet to destroy. And so on forever. Even if it took thousands of years for one probe to reach its target, there must be trillions of killer probes all over the galaxy by now. It's a wave of destruction that has been spreading outward from Earth for the last hundred thousand years. These rockets can reach very high speeds as they travel, half light-speed or even more. No matter how I run the numbers, I'm forced to conclude that half the Milky Way has been wiped clean of life by now. That's why we've never made contact with extraterrestrial intelligence; there's none left. Our ancestors killed them all."

She sat up and turned to face him, fighting the giddiness she felt. "But surely not everywhere. Surely there must have been some form of life, somewhere, on some planet who—which—managed to react in time."

"I don't know whether that's something we should hope for," Hiroshi said darkly. "But the chances are minimal."

He raised his hand and pointed out the window. "Just think of that walk we took. Three million years. Even if a species evolves on some planet that might one day develop a technology that could serve to stop the nanites, when the probe arrives it can arrive at any point in those three million years, and from that point the world's fate will be decided within days. But the probes attack any life-bearing planet, even one where life has only just developed. That means there are actually billions of years during which a planet is defenseless. No, once one of these probes arrives, it inevitably means a living world will be turned into a desert and millions more probes will be launched on their way, onward and ever onward." He added, "And there will be no end to it. We have no chance of being able to catch every one of these probes, and we have no chance of being able to render them harmless. Even if we develop interstellar space flight one day, the universe will be dead wherever we go."

"And in the end only Earth will be left," Charlotte said softly.

"Assuming that there is anything left, given the way we're treating it."

Quite so. And it didn't look as though there would be. She felt as though dark clouds were pressing in on all sides, as though a black mist had swallowed her. "Have you cured me?"

"Yes."

"And what about the submarines? Will they stay inside me?"

"No, they're already dissolving into harmless molecules. You'll excrete them over the next few days."

She sighed. "And what was it all for? So that I can live with this dreadful knowledge?"

"I cured you because I could. And because I could, I had to. And I told you all this so that I'm not the only one who knows." Hiroshi gazed ahead, his eyes full of pain. "I told Rodney and his wife as well, but given the way they reacted I don't know whether they'll suppress it entirely or take the knowledge with them to the grave."

A question occurred to her, one that had shot through her head earlier. "How did the nanites on Saradkov know that they were on Earth? How can they find that out?"

"The rocket they built and launched told them. By looking at the constellations. It took a while, because the stars change over the course of a hundred thousand years, but once the rocket knew, it sent back the predetermined code signal. In fact, there's even a module on all the rockets that determines on the approach to a planet whether or not it's Earth—otherwise, there would probably be far more probes arriving here. I assume the one that landed on Saradkov was defective in some way." Hiroshi raised his head and seemed to be listening to something that only he could hear. Then he got up and said, "I have to go now."

Charlotte was startled. She put out her hands toward him. "But why? You've only just arrived."

"They've found me."

"Found you? Who?" she asked, expecting to hear more monstrous revelations.

But all Hiroshi said was, "The police. They've put up roadblocks and they're lying in wait."

"How do you know that?"

He raised his hand and waggled his fingers, hinting at a shape that might have been a cloud. "Let's just say I have my little spies everywhere." He went to the door that led to the deck. "Sayonara."

She sat there motionless and felt she was dying—here, now. "Farewell? Why not just good-bye?"

He hesitated. Then he came back and stood before her, looking down at her sitting there. With a tenderness she would never forget as long as she lived, he took her face in his hands and studied it as intently as if he wanted to remember her features forever.

"I have become the lord of all things," he said softly. "I always thought I would be able to create a wonderful future, but I was wrong. I have too much knowledge and too much power to stay on in this world." He let her go. "We won't meet again. That's why it's farewell."

3

Dawn was breaking as Hiroshi left the house. They were out there. He knew it, however good they were at hiding. He didn't show he knew it as he walked calmly over to the rental car, unlocked it, and climbed in. He started the motor as though nothing were out of the ordinary.

High up above him, invisible to all those surveillance instruments that were doubtless pointed right at him, floated a swarm of nano-components. They were so small that they didn't need propellers to stay aloft but simply hung in the air like bubbles in honey. Taken together, they formed a vast eye through which Hiroshi could look down on the city. At first, this kind of double vision had taken a little getting used to, but he had learned to live with his eye in the sky. By now he could drive the car and simultaneously watch himself driving down the street. Which is how he had seen the police setting up their roadblock and putting sharpshooters at all the exits. They knew where he was, and they were determined to take him.

Well, they wouldn't succeed. The only question was how to avoid anyone getting hurt in their vain attempts to stop him.

The wide cordon actually worked in Hiroshi's favor. All he needed to do was get out of these narrow side streets and reach the Avenida de los Incas. After that there should be no problem.

"He's coming," the captain said and signaled with his hand. "Go go go!"

The policemen took up position, grim-faced. They were a special-weapons unit, kitted out with bulletproof vests and helmets. There was a general sense of relief that the hours of waiting were over. They could hear the lone car coming toward them from somewhere up the street. Two men drew the spiked chain into place a couple of yards beyond their roadblock. Better safe than sorry. Now they could see the headlights approaching.

"Take aim," the captain ordered. "Fire at my command."

Eight men raised rifles to their shoulders. Eight muzzles pointed at the fragile little car that was heading for the roadblock without slowing down.

"He's got to be able to see us," the captain muttered irritably, batting away a couple of mosquitoes. "Antonio, give him the light."

Antonio raised the heavy flood lamp over his head and waved it from side to side. The men saw countless mosquitoes dancing in the beam.

Mosquitoes? the captain wondered. *At this hour of the morning?* The car still showed no signs of slowing.

"Shoot out the tires," he ordered.

The men swung their muzzles a fraction. There were mosquitoes everywhere now, making straight for the rifles for some reason. What the devil had gotten into them?

"Fire!"

Their fingers tightened upon the triggers, and the triggers crumbled as they squeezed. A moment later the muzzles themselves fell apart in a drift of fine, dark powder.

"*Madre de Dios!*" one of the policemen yelled.

The roadblock dissolved as well, collapsing in the blink of an eye. And then the car was upon them and simply drove on through at speed. The men threw themselves aside in the nick of time and just caught a glimpse of the man at the wheel, who was looking straight ahead as calmly as if he hadn't noticed a thing.

The spiked chain had also dissolved into dust. And the mosquitoes were gone.

Fernández Larreta put down the telephone receiver, shaken, and looked at the minister and the Americans. "They say that their rifles . . . crumbled into dust. The moment they took aim."

The minister's jaw dropped. He had loosened his tie a few hours earlier, then he had taken off his jacket, and after that he had undone a couple of buttons at the top of his shirt. By now he looked thoroughly unministerial. The chief of police, by contrast, had retreated to the restroom several times over the course of the night to check his tie was still neatly in place. He looked away, pained. The *norteamericanos* weren't much better: they also looked distinctly disheveled. And the way they chewed gum the whole time! It was distressing, as though they were determined to prove all the clichés right.

"Did you say . . . dust?" Miller repeated, making sure he had understood.

Larreta repeated what the police commander had told him, in his best English. How the car hadn't even slowed down. How the captain had given the order to shoot out the tires. And how the mosquitoes had swarmed.

"Those were no mosquitoes," the professor broke in. "Your people were seeing nanotechnology at work. What they thought were mosquitoes were tiny flying machines capable of breaking iron atoms free from their crystalline lattice structure." He rubbed the side of his nose, thinking. "Astonishing. I wonder how he's controlling them. I really do."

"The scientist from the States thinks that his control system has to be the weak point," Guarneri heard the chief of police say grimly over the radio. "He has to be able to control both at once—the car and his bugs. However he's doing that, he's only human. So he can't cope with too many opponents at once."

"Understood," the commander said. "That means we'll have to attack him from all sides if we can."

"Exactly. Where is he now?"

José Guarneri looked down at his map, though of course he already knew the answer. "Driving west along Avenida de los Incas." He followed the route. "We could try to head him off where it crosses Combatientes de Malvinas. It's a pretty big intersection. We'd have room to fire."

It also had a number of residential high-rises. But that was the case everywhere in this part of Buenos Aires.

"Good," said the chief. "Do it."

Guarneri switched broadcast bands and rattled out a series of orders, thinking fast. They had to work quickly. "Helicopter! Get on his tail, and don't lose sight of him, but for the moment just observe. Prepare to fire as soon as he's at the intersection." Turn the dial, next band. "Get our man with the bazooka in place. And tell him that if he misses and brings one of the buildings down, I will personally tear him a new one." Next band. "Get the armored cars moving, quick!" Clack. "I need snipers in place everywhere, as many as you can deploy, and over the widest possible area." Clack. "I don't want to see so much as a stray dog for the next twenty minutes at the intersection of los Incas–Malvinas, never mind a citizen. Yes, rush hour, I know. Bus, I know that, too. I don't care. If the president's sick child wants to get through that intersection in an ambulance, you don't let it through until I say so, understand me?"

"He's coming," someone said.

They all listened. A lone car roaring down the broad Avenida de los Incas. By now he was paying no attention at all to speed limits or red lights.

Two hundred yards.

"Ready arms," Commander Guarneri ordered.

The man with the bazooka drew a bead on the car. He was concealed behind an advertising billboard that was endlessly rolling its floodlit panels around and around overhead. The man tapped at his earpiece to make sure he still heard the hum of the radio channel. The captain in charge of the roadblocks looked up as a blind went up in a seventh-floor window in the brown-and-white apartment building right by the intersection. He gestured to one of his men to take up position by the front doors. The armored cars with the squadrons of men rolled slowly down the side streets.

One hundred yards.

The snipers got the car in their sights as it approached. The helicopter had been following their man at a safe height. Now it dropped and picked up speed, closing the gap.

"Ready . . ." the commander said over the general band.

Just then something happened to the car. The dozen men watching through telescopic sights saw it . . . change.

"What the . . . ?"

It took only seconds. The headlights blinked out. The contours of the car melted and shifted. The machine that only moments before had been an ordinary midrange automobile rose into the air and thundered over the intersection at an altitude of about six yards. Nobody had time to react. The man with the bazooka shut his eyes. The snipers took their fingers off the triggers without even knowing they'd done so. The armored cars stopped. The policemen stood there staring at the plane as it climbed rapidly, still following Avenida de Los Incas, and vanished into the cloudless morning sky.

Hiroshi flew low, and the landscape rushed past beneath him. Pasture, fences, old-fashioned windmills, black cattle, and decrepit-looking houses. Gradually even these disappeared. The sparse grasses grew ever sparser, the roads—dirt tracks at best—ever fewer, and the farther he flew, the fewer the signs of agriculture on the land below him. That meant he was headed the right way. La Pampa province lay ahead of him. From then on the landscape would become ever drier and harsher, until he eventually reached the salt lakes.

It was pushing him to the limits to fly this thing and simultaneously keep an eye on his pursuers. In fact, he couldn't fly—not in the sense of ever having taken lessons or qualifying for a license. Up until the very last moment he had hoped he wouldn't have to do this at all. The machine was the smallest flier he had found in the nanite blueprint archive, and his practical experience with it was limited to just a few short border hops when he didn't want to be bothered with immigration.

At the moment he couldn't see anyone following him. Not that he could see a great deal, since the nano-camera could not keep up at the speed he was going. He had been forced to abandon it. Once his eye in the sky lost contact with central control, it would simply scatter in the wind and eventually dissolve into dust. But for all that he knew, they were after him. And he cherished no illusions: he wouldn't be able to stay ahead of them for long.

Nor did he need to. All he needed was a moment to rest. No more than that. In the long run, that's what it all came down to: rest.

An AWAC normally stationed at the US military base in Palanquero, Colombia, had been patrolling the Rio de la Plata estuary since shortly after midnight, observing air traffic over Argentinean territory. Two C-130 Hercules transporters were on their way from Guantanamo Bay naval base with a complement of 120 paratroopers from the US Marine Corps outfitted with a full range of weaponry. They would reach the operational theater in about three hours. The 22nd Marine Expeditionary Unit had also been deployed from Camp Lejeune in North Carolina.

A squadron of F-15 fighters over the Atlantic had just undergone midair refueling when the orders came through. "Sierra Bravo, you are now cleared to enter Argentinean airspace. Target is currently at

35 degrees 47 minutes south, and 61 degrees 53 minutes west, moving west-southwest at a speed of around 500 miles an hour. Over."

The squadron leader repeated the coordinates and confirmed.

"Set course for target and force it to land. Target is not to be destroyed. Repeat, target is not to be destroyed. Over."

"Target is not to be destroyed," the pilot repeated. "Wilco, over and out."

He gave the signal to start. The next moment the first of the fighter jets peeled off from the rest and shot off toward the coast.

They were coming. Jets, very low, and coming at a hell of a speed. Hiroshi held his breath, grabbed the joystick tightly, and instinctively ducked his head.

They weren't firing at him. Not yet at least. Instead, they thundered above him so close it seemed they wanted to clip the plane. The noise was almost deafening, and his tiny aircraft shuddered and bucked in the turbulence the jets left behind, terrifying him. He mustn't crash! Then came the other two. Dark dots on the horizon behind him, growing larger incredibly fast. And silently. Of course, they were flying at supersonic speed. If he had seen right, they were F-15s, which could reach Mach 2.5.

Hiroshi looked at the instruments in front of him. They could hardly have looked stranger if they had been built by aliens rather than by humans of that first civilization, dead and gone for unguessed-at eons now. The first time Hiroshi had ordered the nanites to build him this aircraft, he had inspected it thoroughly to try to work out what all the controls did—a wise precaution if he actually wanted to fly in it. So he knew . . . well, there was a switch, or something like it, that could turbocharge the engines; technically, it would probably be possible to leave even an F-15 hanging in the sky behind him. But Hiroshi didn't dare. He was already breaking a sweat flying this thing at five hundred miles an hour; he knew in his bones he couldn't stay in control at Mach 4 or even more. So he did the opposite: he throttled back and lost altitude.

Once the next two jets had roared away above him, presumably pleased to have forced him to land so soon, Hiroshi ordered the nanites to convert the plane into a large all-terrain vehicle. This didn't work quite so smoothly as it had back in the city—when the nanites began to take the jet engines apart in order to build the new motor, they cut out in the air before he had fully landed. He crashed down, maybe a yard or so, with full force. That must have done some damage. The nanites fixed it in the blink of an eye, and a minute later Hiroshi was racing across the ground at full throttle, raising an enormous cloud of dust behind him.

The soldiers of the Santa Rosa de Toay garrison were still at breakfast, locked in heated debate over the forthcoming Club Atlético game, when their sergeant came storming in. He hammered a metal mess tray onto the table until the chatter died down so that he could make himself heard. Then he read out the orders that had just arrived direct from the Ministry of Defense. At first, that was the most incredible thing about the whole business: the thought that anyone in the ministry even knew they were still there, manning this tiny little fort in the middle of nowhere. There had been precious little evidence of that any time they tried to get spare parts or maintenance funds in the last few years.

A moment later the mess hall echoed with the sound of chairs being pushed back, voices shouting, feet tramping, doors slamming. Within ten minutes a squad was headed to Santa Rosa Airport to prepare for the landing of two Lockheed C-130 transporters, while the rest of the soldiers piled into the fastest jeeps they still had and raced west along Route 14. Once they saw the cloud of dust out on the pampas, the one they had been told about, they slowed down.

"*Caramba!*" the corporal shouted out. "What is that?"

His men were asking themselves exactly the same question. Whatever was throwing up that dust seemed to be racing over the harsh terrain as though it were a freeway. But orders were orders. And their orders were to arrest the driver.

"Half of you go on to the intersection with 143 and then head south to cut him off," the corporal ordered, signaling which jeeps should form that squad.

There were mutters of surprise. It would take three hours' driving even to get to the intersection; perhaps two and a half if they went hell-for-leather. It would be quite a ride.

"The rest of us," the corporal continued, "will follow him over the pampas. Let's go!"

The jeeps roared into action. Some picked up speed and vanished toward the west, while the others lurched and bumped over the dirt verge and finally bounced off across the plains, over bone-dry grass, bare, salt-white earth, and stunted, spiny shrubs. The men glanced at one another apprehensively. Half an hour of this and they would all be ready to puke.

"He can't keep going forever," the corporal declared. "We'll catch him before he can get to the rivers."

They all knew that not even he believed that.

His trick of turning the plane into a land vehicle didn't fool the jet pilots for long. If they were even surprised, they didn't stop to show it. They wheeled, turned, and flew straight for him again.

Hiroshi thought about what they might do to him. As far as he could remember, F-15s were mostly designed for air combat and primarily equipped with air-to-air missiles that locked onto their targets with infrared sensors. Weapons like that could do nothing against a moving ground target.

Meaning that they . . .

He saw the impact lines headed toward him. These jets were also equipped with six-barrel 20 mm auto cannon that could fire up to six thousand rounds a minute. Hiroshi wrenched his vehicle to the side at the last moment as the line of explosions raced toward him in the dust, too damn close. The message was clear: *Halt!*

It was high time he sent them a message in return. Hiroshi steered back to his original course and released a few nanites, which dug themselves into the ground behind him and then activated at top speed. It took a little while. The nanites needed a great many different materials for what they were going to build, some of which were not readily available. The two jets had ended their turn, miles away, and were already coming in to intercept him again when two thin, shimmering metal rods rose out of the ground behind him.

"Come on . . ." Hiroshi muttered, his nerves taut. The pilots would undoubtedly try to hit him on their second pass.

The jets roared toward him, growing larger by the second. It was a fearsome sight. At that moment the metal structure behind him unfurled like a flower in bloom to reveal an artillery piece that could have been designed by Salvador Dali. It began to fire just a fraction of a second before the two jets, shooting rounds that seemed to tear violet rips in the air. An F-15 took a round in one wing and went into a spin, recovered with difficulty, and flew away, trailing a thick cloud of black smoke. The other jet also turned and left.

Hiroshi looked around, searching the sky without taking his foot off the gas. It looked good. All of a sudden there were no more jets in sight. Okay. Time to dismantle his field pieces. He looked into the rearview mirror, trying to judge the distance to the plumes of dust thrown up by the vehicles following him overland. They had no real chance of overtaking him, but while he was at it . . .

Their jeeps jolted across the wasteland as fast as they could go and then a little faster. Astonishingly, only one had succumbed to a broken axle. The soldiers decided this was a good omen.

They watched, awestruck, as the jets wheeled and turned above the pampas. They flew over the dust cloud again and again. The soldiers could hear their auto cannon from here, an ugly rattling sound like a hundred axes biting into hard wood in unison.

"US Air Force," the corporal announced, relaying the information from over his headphones. "Don't ask me why. As if our planes couldn't have done the same thing!"

Then those curious violet plumes of smoke shot up. One of the jets flew off unsteadily, trailing smoke, and all of a sudden the others also took fright.

"Chicken!" a voice called out, and the rest of the soldiers laughed. Yes, these *norteamericanos* were cowards.

Nobody wanted to think too hard about what kind of gun that might have been. Who could think of such things when their brains were being rattled around in their skulls? They couldn't even look dead ahead with any certainty; as they looked from the sky back down to the horizon, they got the strangest impression that it was rising before their eyes.

"Is that the 143 already?" the corporal asked under his breath. "It can't be."

It wasn't. But there was something there. They strained their necks to see, then rubbed their eyes incredulously as the jeeps approached, slowed, and finally came to a halt.

The corporal was the first one who recovered enough to speak. "What the devil . . . ? What is that?"

"A wall?" the driver suggested.

The corporal slapped him upside the head in anger. "I can see that, you jackass! Yes, it's a wall! But how did it get here all of a sudden?"

He opened the door and climbed out onto the hood. Hands on his hips, he looked all around. "Incredible," he murmured. It was a wall, large as life, as tall as a two-story building, running across the dry pampas from one end of the horizon to the other.

The minister of defense was indignant. "Scramble the entire air force? Against one man? Have you all gone crazy?"

"He may be one man, but he is no ordinary opponent." The *norte-americano* put a laptop in front of him with an aerial photo on the screen. "That's La Pampa," he declared.

"I can see that," the minister snarled.

"And that," the man continued calmly, switching to the next picture, "is the same landscape ten minutes ago."

"What?" The minister ducked his head and peered closely at the screen. "What's that?"

"Not quite as long as the Great Wall of China, but just as wide."

"A wall?" There was a look of naked terror in his eyes now. "How is that even possible?"

"As I said: just one man, but no ordinary opponent."

The minister blinked rapidly, visibly shaken. "Good," he said, reaching for the telephone. "The air force, then. What do we have them for after all?"

Half an hour later they were back in force, more dark dots against the pale sky than he could count. More attacks than he could deal with. He couldn't turn back all the planes, or defuse all the bombs; he couldn't ward off attack from every direction at once. The nanites were powerful but only when they were given the instructions they needed. And he had more important things to do than fight to no good end. Hiroshi stopped and looked around. Here then. It would happen here. He took a deep breath, then switched off the motor, and gave the order he had been holding back for so long.

The vehicle dissolved under him, melting, then trickled away into the bitter, bare soil without a trace. Then he stood there all alone on the endless plain, under a sky that seemed higher and farther away than anywhere else on Earth. A sky that would keep silent for all eternity. It was utterly silent all around. The black dots racing toward him could have been just a trick of the light. Hiroshi shut his eyes. He knew it would not stay that way for long.

He gave the next order.

Onboard the AWAC was an expert in aerial photography collecting and collating shots sent over by the high-flying jets and a few unmanned drones that were also at work in the operational theater. And at that moment he couldn't believe his eyes.

"Goddamn!"

He gazed at the screen as though he would never be able to tear his eyes away. The curse had been only a whisper, but his commanding officer had heard it nevertheless.

"Officer," he growled as he approached, "you know perfectly well I will not tolerate such language onboard my . . . oh my God!"

Every head turned. The first crewmen stood up from their places, crowding behind the two of them, gradually forming a group of wondering faces around the screen. The picture showed La Pampa, the harshest and most desolate region in Argentina, and it showed the infamous dry pampas, so bare and dry that not even cattle could graze there. There was a set of crosshairs centered on the spot where a moment ago a lone man had stood.

He had vanished. All around him something unbelievable was springing out of the soil so fast they could see it grow. A vast, baroque construction of domes and buttresses, towers, ramparts and ribs, turrets, chasms, spirals and filigree-fine antennae. It grew ever larger, hundreds of yards across by now, big enough to swallow most sports arenas. And yet it was still growing, bulging upward, looking sometimes like a mutant broccoli and sometimes like a skewed coliseum, sometimes like a coral reef on adrenaline and then, finally, like the head of some eyeless monster with millions upon millions of teeth, waiting for its prey.

"I know what that is," one of the radar operators whispered. He cleared his throat as the rest of them looked at him, aghast, and said,

"It's the Mandelbrot set. I know it. I've got a screen saver at home that builds it like that. The 3-D version."

Hiroshi had always been fascinated by the Mandelbrot set—infinite variety derived from a formula that was not just finite but breathtakingly simple. It took only a few lines in any of the classical programming languages to create the underlying code to draw a set. The command sequence to build this vast structure of arabesques and architectural follies had been one of the shortest he had ever used.

He would have liked to have seen how it looked from the outside. The nanites had mostly built it from silicon and oxygen, two of the most common elements, which could easily be found in vast quantities even in the harsh desolation of La Pampa. Silicon and oxygen together yielded something much like quartz; he could well imagine that his fortress shone in the sunlight like an enormous gemstone.

At any rate, there was enough light coming through to him, sparing him the need to create a light source; it would have seemed like an intrusion here. Hiroshi touched the fine incisions on the inside of his cave, the swellings, wreaths, and garlands all around. They felt cold and were razor-sharp. No surprise there. Mathematically speaking, the Mandelbrot set was infinite; you could focus in on even the smallest part of it and find an infinity of ever-smaller, ever-finer structures, self-similar and yet constantly unpredictable. Mathematically speaking, it could never end. Physically, however, it had to come to an end somewhere. Once the set was expressed at the scale of individual atoms, it had to stop. In other words, the spikes, edges, and ripples all around him were sharper than any scalpel. That ought to stop his pursuers for long enough to give him the time to do what he had to do.

He went over it all in his mind once more, making sure he had missed nothing. The nanites in the asteroid belt: on the way down to Buenos Aires, he had stopped for the night somewhere in Guatemala, in a deserted valley off the Pan-American Highway, to put up a dish antenna and establish radio contact. It had been nerve-rackingly slow—it took a good hour for a radio signal to reach the asteroids from Earth—but the nanites had reported in and confirmed his kill signal. Doubtless, they had then instantly begun to take each other apart impassively, obediently, mechanically. By now he could assume that there was not a single nanite left in the asteroid belt. The second habitat they had been working on would remain unfinished, probably for the rest of time. As for what would become of the first habitat . . . well, that was no longer his problem. The nanites that had been around him all this time had also begun to dismantle each other. What they had built would endure, but nothing new would be created. Never again.

He had deleted all his old programs and files. Including the backups. Including the ones in the data havens. The same was true of all the copies of the archive of blueprints, the nanites' information matrix. And even if he had missed a copy, or the secret services had gotten hold of one without his knowledge, whoever got to work on it would run up against the same problem he had faced before he first encountered the nanites: they wouldn't be able to build new nanites, because they were missing the first one to work with, the first cause. And he had never made any record of how to build one. He would take that with him to the grave.

Hiroshi looked at the earth he stood upon, about ten square feet of untouched grass and soil. The nanites had let it be when they built his refuge around him. So this was the end of his journey and the end of his dream. In a little while the last of the nanites would be destroyed, and with them the future that might have been, the future of unlimited wealth for all. It had been a dream that hid a nightmare at its core.

"In other words, he's dug himself a foxhole," the US president said, summing up the report the secretary of defense had given him. He had just been on the phone to the president of Argentina. She agreed with him that they wished to unite the forces of both nations to take control of the situation.

A foxhole? The secretary wondered whether that was the right term. The word reminded him of the stories his grandfather had told him about the World War, about the trench warfare he had seen. A foxhole was a miserable hole dug into the earth with miserable tools, offering miserable protection from enemy attack. Grandpa had left no doubt in his mind that it was a dirty, dangerous business.

"Well maybe," he said. "After a fashion. The luxury version, so to speak."

"So how do you intend to proceed? Do you want to shell it?" The president rubbed his jaw thoughtfully. "All else being equal, it would be good to keep it in one piece. It's a Mandelbrot set, isn't it? Half a mile across. How often do you get to see a thing like that?"

"To be precise, it's the three-dimensional variant. What the mathematicians call a Mandelbrot bulb." The secretary wondered whether he should correct the president on the size of the thing—in fact, Hiroshi's Fortress of Solitude was about sixteen hundred feet across, not even one third of a mile—but decided not to. "No, we won't bring in the artillery for the moment. Too risky. We're waiting for the marines. They're going to try to get in. And they have orders only to shoot if they encounter defenses."

The nanites that had built his fortress had gone to work one last time. They had made him a tatami with white braid, a pot of ink, a calligraphy brush, and a few sheets of parchment. They had also converted his clothing into a white kimono.

He had seen the originals for all these items in a Japanese store in Los Angeles. On his way south to visit Rodney for the last time, he had scanned them, just in case he needed them. They were probably still there; the store didn't strike him as a place that sold much. Hiroshi felt contact with all the nanites around drop away as the complexes dismantled one another. Then at last there was silence. Now the only remaining nanites were the ones in his body.

Not long now.

Hiroshi sat down on the mat in the *seiza* position prescribed for seppuku: heels turned outward, toes crossed, back straight. His knees were one fist's width apart. Chest and shoulders relaxed, all the weight of his body resting in his lower belly. He thought of his father, who had taught him to sit this way, and he felt sorrow for his father, and for himself.

An honorable death is no bad thing, he chided himself.

He reached for the parchment and the brush. Time for his *jisei no ku,* his death poem. He paused and collected his thoughts. The sum of his whole life in just a few words. Well, that was simple. He dipped the brush in the ink and wrote, first in Japanese, then the translation in English beneath. It felt like freedom. Most surprising. Suddenly, it seemed easy to shrug off the shackles of mere matter.

One more thing. He reached for the second sheet and wrote his instructions—no, his request—to those who would find him. He could do no more than ask, and realistically there was not much hope that anyone would heed his wishes. But at least he had tried. Another phrase that could sum up his life.

Then Hiroshi set this sheet aside, too, put his hands in his lap, relaxed his fingers, and breathed. Time for the last two commands. The very last command to the nanites would be to dismantle themselves down to the very last complex, to fall finally and irretrievably apart into pieces that could never again join together to make another nano-assembler. He almost regretted this. He had loved the aesthetics of these molecular machines, had spent hours on end studying the graphic representations of their structure, admiring them—the inescapable logic of the construction, once he had understood the basic principles. He had felt awe in the face of a universe that had contained these possibilities since the very beginning of time.

Over and done. He must take his leave of that, too. Hiroshi bared his torso to a hand's width below his navel, then placed his hand upon the *tanden*.

Then he gave the command that would end it all.

With his left hand upon the "scarlet field," he stretched out his right hand and watched a dark dot form on his palm, quickly growing larger until a blade took shape . . .

EPILOGUE

He had never been to Buenos Aires and had never expected to go. Particularly not first class. Not to mention with such a curious item in his hand luggage.

At the customs desk a grim-faced man pointed to his bag and gestured unmistakably that he should open it. This was when he got to use his brand-new diplomatic passport. The customs man raised his eyebrows and even managed to summon a smile as he waved him through. "Welcome! Enjoy your stay in Argentina."

He could get used to traveling this way.

He crossed the concourse. Crowds of taxi drivers were waiting at the exit. "Do you speak English?" he asked the first driver.

"Yes, yes," the man assured him cheerfully, hurrying over to open the car door for him.

That was probably all the English the driver knew, but it didn't really matter. He climbed in and handed him the sheet of paper with the address. The ride took about half an hour and was mostly along broad avenues that could have been freeways. He saw a great many trees; Buenos Aires was a very green city. A lot of high-rises, too, but with exuberant palms in between them and luxurious green foliage.

The taxi finally stopped on a street lined with small, old villas, half-hidden by their flourishing gardens.

"There," the driver said, pointing to a house.

The passenger paid what the meter said and then added another banknote. He waited till the taxi drove out of sight, then crossed the road. A doorbell with the name R. + L. BLANCO. Underneath that a brass plate inscribed C. MALROUX, TRADUCTORA, with an arrow pointing to a low garden gate with a flagstone path beyond it.

He followed the path. It took him around the house to the rear, to a dark, overgrown garden. A woman sat on the deck at a little wooden table, writing by hand. She was wearing an airy spring dress. She was slim, almost skinny, and her dark hair was the length of matchsticks. He could see she must have once been beautiful. She looked up calmly. She must have heard him coming.

"*Buenos días*," she said.

He cleared his throat and all of a sudden felt out of place in his suit, carrying his leather briefcase. "Good day, Miss Malroux," he said. "My name is William Adamson. I . . . well, I guess you could say I'm here to execute a bequest from Hiroshi Kato."

Hiroshi. It hurt to hear his name. She still wasn't over it. Of course not. She only managed not to think of him for a little while occasionally.

She looked at the man standing at the foot of the deck, his hand on the wooden rail of the four steps that led up to her. He was a plump man, probably around forty, wearing a stylish pair of glasses that had doubtless cost a lot of money. His Adam's apple bobbed up and down as he talked.

"Adamson," she repeated. "I'm sorry, I don't know the name."

He ran his fingers nervously along the rail. "We studied in Boston around the same time. You were at Harvard; Hiroshi and I were at MIT. I was a doctoral student when he was a senior." His eyes drifted. "To be absolutely honest, Hiroshi and I had very little contact while we were there. We were more—how should I put it?—rivals. He was researching robotics just like I was—though we took very different approaches."

Charlotte wondered where this was all leading. Had he come because he hoped Hiroshi had left some papers with her? "I hardly ever ran into people at MIT," she said. "Anybody, really, apart from Hiroshi."

He nodded as though that were self-evident. "Yes, I understand. I simply mention it because . . . well, because it was the case. As for me, I've worked for the American government ever since I finished my doctorate, which put me in a position to be able to follow Hiroshi's work from time to time. You could say that over the years I've become his greatest admirer. Looking back, I have to say that his ideas, his methods, were absolutely groundbreaking."

"Not that that helped him much."

The man blinked, looking for a moment as though he had gotten lost in the past. "Yes. Yes, you might say so. Eh . . . well, it's inevitable that my visit stirs up painful memories. That being the case, can I ask you straight out how much you know of the circumstances surrounding his death?"

Charlotte shrugged. "I know what was in the newspapers. And then there were all these people here asking me about the last night of his life. So I was able to piece a few things together."

"Have you visited the Bulb?"

She shook her head. "I'm sure I will one day, but over the last few months I've been . . . in rather frail health. I couldn't travel." The doctors had confirmed her tumor was gone and called it a spontaneous remission. Such things occasionally happened, they told her. "All I know is that when the soldiers finally got in and found him, he was dead. And that he was wearing a white kimono. Which indicated ritual suicide; that was in all the reports."

He nodded. "Yes, that was widely reported. What wasn't in the reports was that he left a message."

"A message?" She sat up straight, felt a tingle in her spine. It was electrifying.

"A message for you."

Charlotte put her hands to her head, the habit of a lifetime, and was shaken again to find that her long hair was gone. She drew a deep breath. "Come on up," she invited him, pointing to the chair where her clients usually sat when handing over their documents or collecting their translations.

He sat down gingerly, as though well used to chairs breaking under him. Then he lifted his briefcase to his knees and opened it.

"Our experts have told us that in Japanese culture it's traditional for the person committing seppuku to write a last poem. The death poem." He carefully took out a piece of parchment in a clear protective envelope. "This is what he wrote. And it's clearly addressed to you." He held it out to her.

She took it in her hands, which were suddenly trembling. The top half of the sheet was covered in Japanese characters, beautifully drawn, and underneath, in English:

Charlotte,
What might have been!

She put her hand to her mouth and felt very clearly how her heart stopped for a beat or two. Seeing his handwriting like this, and then the poem . . .

"Thank you," she said once she could breathe again, setting the parchment aside. "Thank you very much."

"That's not all," he said hurriedly and took a flat wooden box from his case. "I have to add here that the secret services insisted on minutely examining every object that Hiroshi left behind. Every object and his corpse as well, to be blunt. There was also heated discussion, of course, about how far we should even carry out his last wishes. I argued strongly that we should, but honesty compels me to admit that in the end. . . well, nobody found anything on either object that was of any strategic interest. That's what tipped the balance."

He opened the lid. Inside lay a long dagger—or short knife; she saw that either description would do—with a slightly curved blade, about thirty centimeters long.

"It's called a *tantō*," Adamson told her. "A Japanese sword of the kind prescribed for seppuku."

Charlotte looked at the weapon with horrified fascination. The hilt was made of ribbed metal, and the blade shone flawlessly. "He killed himself with this?"

"Uh . . . no. He was holding it in his hands when they found him, but he was already dead. Not a scratch on him. In fact he suffocated."

"Suffocated?"

Adamson sighed. "It looks like he ordered the last of the nanites to make this sword from the iron they found in his blood. Without iron, the hemoglobin in the bloodstream no longer functions, the flow of oxygen from the lungs is cut off and, well, the result is suffocation."

She put out her hands. "May I hold it just once?"

"Of course you may. It belongs to you now." He passed her the wooden case. "Be careful how you take it out. It's much lighter than it looks. It only weighs about an eighth of an ounce." He added, "That's barely four grams metric."

She stopped midreach. "Four grams?"

"The amount of iron in a human body. In fact, that should only just be enough to make a small nail, but this knife is an astonishing construction. We've scanned it, measured it, analyzed it. It's made up primarily of hollow cells, but it's still extremely stable. All in all, it's an excellent example of applied nanotech within the limits of our present capabilities. Materials science, that kind of thing. Which is why a lot of people wanted to hang on to it . . . but here it is."

She grasped the hilt carefully and had to shut her eyes in shock as she felt the emotions and memories that saturated the knife. Hiroshi! He was there. She could feel him. Holding this dagger made from his blood was like holding his whole life in her hands. His hopes, his desires, his dreams . . . tears sprang to her eyes when she felt how much he had loved her. Her, and her alone.

She opened her eyes and lifted the knife out carefully. It really was as light as a feather. As though the memories it held weighed more than the iron of which it was made. When she had blinked away the tears, she saw that her visitor was looking at her with concern.

"What will you do now?" he asked.

Charlotte realized he was worried she might plunge the blade into her heart as soon as he had gone. She smiled gently. She wouldn't, of course. Hiroshi had given her life back to her; she would treat that gift, too, with respect.

She put the featherlight knife back into its case. "Perhaps I'll try to write our story," she said. "His and mine. We'll see."

ABOUT THE
AUTHOR

© Olivier Favre

Andreas Eschbach studied aerospace engineering at the University of Stuttgart and later founded his own IT-consulting company before becoming a full-time writer. Several of his novels, including *The Jesus Video* and *One Trillion Dollars*, became nationwide best sellers in Germany. He has been awarded both the Kurd-Laßwitz-Preis, Germany's most prestigious science-fiction award, for best science-fiction novel, and the Deutscher Science Fiction Preis, several times. *The Carpet Makers*, his only other book translated into English so far, was listed as one of the best science-fiction books of 2005 by www.sfsite.com and recommended by *Locus Magazine*. In 2002, his novel *The Jesus Video* was adapted for German television. He lives with his wife in Brittany, France.

About the
Translator

Samuel Willcocks is originally from Brighton, on the south coast of England, but now lives with his family in Transylvania, Romania, in the historic city of Cluj, where he spends as much time in the cafés as he does in the libraries. A keen reader in many genres, including science fiction and historical novels, he studied languages and literature in Britain, Berlin, and Philadelphia, before winning the German Embassy Award (London) for translation in 2010. He has been a full-time literary translator ever since and translates from Czech, German, Romanian, and Slovene. When not overindulging in cakes or dictionaries, he can be found at book festivals, sharing his enthusiasm for Central European books and writers with fellow readers, editors, and literary agents.